Praise for *The Likeness*

Chosen as a Best Novel of the Year by
Salon.com
The Christian Science Monitor
Publishers Weekly

A Crime Fiction Favorite by the *Los Angeles Times*

Runner-up for the Best Thriller of the Year by
New York Magazine

"[Tana French] aces her second novel. *The Likeness* [is a] nearly pitch-perfect follow-up to her 2007 debut thriller, *In the Woods*." —*Entertainment Weekly*

"*The Likeness* [is] a book even better than the first, which was very good indeed. . . . The suspense is gut-grinding, but it may hurt more to know who did it. That's an awful dilemma—and a wonderful book." —*New York Daily News*

"[French's] already signature blend of psychological insight, beautiful writing and wry humor is on display once again in *The Likeness*. Expect *The Likeness* to figure on many awards lists, as it should." —*Newsday*

"Tana French puts a clever twist on every lonely child's fantasy of leading a parallel life when she creates an alternate identity for her detective in *The Likeness*. . . . Cassie is a character—the eternal lost child—you can really care about." —*The New York Times Book Review*

"The writing is glorious, and the characters and drama so compelling." —*The Boston Globe*

"Savor French's turns of phrase and simmering suspense until the prospect of finishing shuts all distractions out." —*The Baltimore Sun*

"The novel's plot and edgy characters will ring true."
—*USA Today*

"The verve of her writing illuminates the uncanny experience of stepping into someone else's life. [*The Likeness* is] a sophisticated thriller." —*The Dallas Morning News*

"The novel is exceptional, and readers with an affinity for whodunits authentically set in Ireland will not be disappointed."
—*Minneapolis Star Tribune*

"French is a fine writer and gives Cassie lots of room to roam through fascinating, complex questions of class, identity and relationships. It's an intriguing trip."
—*The Portland Oregonian*

"This book will leave readers eagerly awaiting the next."
—*Rocky Mountain News*

"[A] stunning sequel to her debut, *In the Woods* . . . French cleverly subverts the conventions of the locked room mystery, ratcheting up the tension at every turn with her multidimensional characters. Readers looking for a new name in psychological suspense need look no further than this powerful new Irish voice." —*Publishers Weekly* (starred review)

"Police procedurals, psychological thrills and gothic romance beautifully woven into one stunning story." —*Kirkus Reviews*

"French has written another winner. . . . *The Likeness* has everything: memorable characters, crisp dialogue, shrewd psychological insight, mounting tension, a palpable sense of place, and wonderfully evocative, painterly prose. *In the Woods* was an Edgar Award finalist; this one just might go one step further." —*Booklist* (starred review)

PENGUIN BOOKS

THE LIKENESS

Tana French is the author of eight books, including *In the Woods*, *The Likeness*, and *The Searcher*. Her novels have sold more than three million copies and won numerous awards including the Edgar, Anthony, Macavity, and Barry awards, the Los Angeles Times Book Prize for Best Mystery/Thriller, and the Irish Book Award for Crime Fiction. She lives in Dublin with her family.

BY TANA FRENCH

The Searcher

The Witch Elm

The Trespasser

The Secret Place

Broken Harbor

Faithful Place

The Likeness

In the Woods

TANA FRENCH

The
Likeness

Penguin Books

PENGUIN BOOKS
An imprint of Penguin Random House LLC
penguinrandomhouse.com

First published in the United States of America by Viking Penguin,
a member of Penguin Group (USA) Inc., 2008
Published in Penguin Books 2009
This edition published 2021

ISBN 9780143136491 (mass market)

THE LIBRARY OF CONGRESS HAS CATALOGED THE
HARDCOVER EDITION AS FOLLOWS:
French, Tana.
The likeness / Tana French.
p.   cm.
ISBN 9780670018864 (hardcover)
1. Women detectives—Ireland—Fiction. 2. Murder—Investigation—Fiction.
I. Title.
PR6106.R457L55   2008
823'.92—dc22   2008003940

Printed in the United States of America
10 9 8 7 6 5 4 3 2 1

Set in Adobe Garamond Pro

For Anthony, for a million reasons

The
Likeness

Prologue

Some nights, if I'm sleeping on my own, I still dream about Whitethorn House. In the dream it's always spring, cool fine light with a late-afternoon haze. I climb the worn stone steps and knock on the door—that great brass knocker, going black with age and heavy enough to startle you every time—and an old woman with an apron and a deft, uncompromising face lets me in. Then she hangs the big rusted key back on her belt and walks away down the drive, under the falling cherry blossom, and I close the door behind her.

The house is always empty. The bedrooms are bare and bright, only my footsteps echoing off the floorboards, circling up through the sun and the dust motes to the high ceilings. Smell of wild hyacinths, drifting through the wide-open windows, and of beeswax polish. Chips of white paint flaking off the window sashes and a tendril of ivy swaying in over the sill. Wood doves, lazy somewhere outside.

In the sitting room the piano is open, wood glowing chestnut and almost too bright to look at in the bars of sun, the breeze stirring the yellowed sheet music like a finger. The table is laid ready for us, five settings—the bone-china plates and the long-stemmed wineglasses, fresh-cut honeysuckle trailing from a crystal bowl—but the silverware has gone dim with tarnish and the heavy damask napkins are frilled with dust. Daniel's cigarette case lies by his place at the head of the table, open and empty except for a burnt-down match.

Somewhere in the house, faint as a fingernail-flick at the

edge of my hearing, there are sounds: a scuffle, whispers. It almost stops my heart. The others aren't gone, I got it all wrong somehow. They're only hiding; they're still here, for ever and ever.

I follow the tiny noises through the house room by room, stopping at every step to listen, but I'm never quick enough: they slide away like mirages, always just behind that door or up those stairs. The tip of a giggle, instantly muffled; a creak of wood. I leave wardrobe doors swinging open, I take the steps three at a time, I swing round the newel post at the top and catch a flash of movement in the corner of my eye: the spotted old mirror at the end of the corridor, my face reflected in it, laughing.

1

This is Lexie Madison's story, not mine. I'd love to tell you one without getting into the other, but it doesn't work that way. I used to think I sewed us together at the edges with my own hands, pulled the stitches tight and I could unpick them any time I wanted. Now I think it always ran deeper than that and farther, underground; out of sight and way beyond my control.

This much is mine, though: everything I did. Frank puts it all down to the others, mainly to Daniel, while as far as I can tell Sam thinks that, in some obscure and slightly bizarro way, it was Lexie's fault. When I say it wasn't like that, they give me careful sideways looks and change the subject—I get the feeling Frank thinks I have some creepy variant of Stockholm syndrome. That does happen to undercovers sometimes, but not this time. I'm not trying to protect anyone; there's no one left to protect. Lexie and the others will never know they're taking the blame and wouldn't care if they did. But give me more credit than that. Someone else may have dealt the hand, but I picked it up off the table, I played every card, and I had my reasons.

This is the main thing you need to know about Alexandra Madison: she never existed. Frank Mackey and I invented her, a long time ago, on a bright summer afternoon in his dusty office on Harcourt Street. He wanted people to infiltrate a drug ring in University College Dublin. I wanted the job, maybe more than I had ever wanted anything in my life.

He was a legend: Frank Mackey, still in his thirties and already running undercover operations; the best Undercover agent Ireland's ever had, people said, reckless and fearless, a tightrope artist with no net, ever. He walked into IRA cells and criminal gangs like he was walking into his local pub. Everyone had told me the story: when the Snake—a career gangster and five-star wacko, who once left one of his own men quadriplegic for not buying his round—got suspicious and threatened to use a nail gun on Frank's hands, Frank looked him in the eye without breaking a sweat and bluffed him down till the Snake slapped him on the back and gave him a fake Rolex by way of apology. Frank still wears it.

I was a shiny green rookie, only a year out of Templemore Training College. A couple of days earlier, when Frank had sent out the call for cops who had a college education and could pass for early twenties, I had been wearing a neon yellow vest that was too big for me and patrolling a small town in Sligo where most of the locals looked disturbingly alike. I should have been nervous of him, but I wasn't, not at all. I wanted the assignment too badly to have room for anything else.

His office door was open and he was sitting on the edge of his desk, wearing jeans and a faded blue T-shirt, flipping through my file. The office was small and had a disheveled look, like he used it mainly for storage. The desk was empty, not even a family photo; on the shelves, paperwork was mixed in with blues CDs, tabloids, a poker set and a woman's pink cardigan with the tags still on. I decided I liked this guy.

"Cassandra Maddox," he said, glancing up.

"Yes, sir," I said. He was average height, stocky but fit, with good shoulders and close-cut brown hair. I'd been expecting someone so nondescript he was practically invisible, maybe the Cancer Man from *The X Files*, but this guy had rough, blunt features and wide blue eyes, and the kind of presence that leaves heat streaks on the air where he's been. He wasn't my type, but I was pretty sure he got a lot of female attention.

"Frank. 'Sir' is for desk jockeys." His accent was old inner-city Dublin, subtle but deliberate, like a challenge. He slid off the desk and held out his hand.

"Cassie," I said, shaking it.

He pointed at a chair and went back to his perch on the desk. "Says here," he said, tapping my file, "you're good under pressure."

It took me a second to figure out what he was talking about. Back when I was a trainee posted to a scuzzy part of Cork city, I had talked down a panicked teenage schizophrenic who was threatening to cut his own throat with his grandfather's straight razor. I had almost forgotten about that. It hadn't occurred to me, till then, that this was probably why I was up for this job.

"I hope so," I said.

"You're, what—twenty-seven?"

"Twenty-six."

The light through the window was on my face and he gave me a long, considering look. "You can do twenty-one, no problem. Says here you've three years of college. Where?"

"Trinity. Psychology."

His eyebrows shot up, mock-impressed. "Ah, a professional. Why didn't you finish?"

"I developed an unknown-to-science allergy to Anglo-Irish accents," I told him.

He liked that. "UCD going to bring you out in a rash?"

"I'll take my antihistamines."

Frank hopped off his desk and went to the window, motioning me to follow. "OK," he said. "See that couple down there?"

A guy and a girl, walking up the street, talking. She found keys and let them into a depressing apartment block. "Tell me about them," Frank said. He leaned back against the window and hooked his thumbs in his belt, watching me.

"They're students," I said. "Book bags. They'd been food shopping—the carrier bags from Dunne's. She's better off than he is; her jacket was expensive, but he had a patch on his jeans, and not in a trendy way."

"They a couple? Friends? Flatmates?"

"A couple. They walked closer than friends, tilted their heads closer."

"They going out long?"

I liked this, the new way my mind was working. "A while, yeah," I said. Frank cocked an eyebrow like a question, and for a moment I wasn't sure how I knew; then it clicked. "They didn't look at each other when they were talking. New couples look at each other all the time; established ones don't need to check in as often."

"Living together?"

"No, or he'd have automatically gone for his keys as well. That's her place. She has at least one flatmate, though. They both looked up at a window: checking to see if the curtains were open."

"How's their relationship?"

"Good. She made him laugh—guys mostly don't laugh at a girl's jokes unless they're still at the chat-up stage. He was carrying both the Dunne's bags, and she held the door open for him before she went in: they look after each other."

Frank gave me a nod. "Nicely done. Undercover's half intuition—and I don't mean psychic shite. I mean noticing things and analyzing them, before you even know you're doing it. The rest is speed and balls. If you're going to say something or do something, you do it fast and you do it with total conviction. If you stop to second-guess yourself, you're fucked, possibly dead. You'll be out of touch a lot, the next year or two. Got family?"

"An aunt and uncle," I said.

"Boyfriend?"

"Yes."

"You'll be able to contact them, but they won't be able to contact you. They going to be OK with that?"

"They'll have to be," I said.

He was still slouching easily against the window frame, but I caught the sharp glint of blue: he was watching me hard. "This isn't some Colombian cartel we're talking about, and you'll be dealing mostly with the lowest ranks—at first, anyway—but you've got to know this job isn't safe. Half these people are binned out of their heads most of the time, and the other half are very serious about what they do, which means none of them would have any problem with the idea of killing you. That make you nervous?"

"No," I said, and I meant it. "Not at all."

"Lovely," said Frank. "Let's get coffee and get to work."

It took me a minute to realize that that was it: I was in. I'd been expecting a three-hour interview and a stack of weird tests with inkblots and questions about my mother, but Frank doesn't work like that. I still don't know where, along the way, he made the decision. For a long time, I waited for the right moment to ask him. Now I'm not sure, any more, whether I want to know what he saw in me; what it was that told him I would be good at this.

We got burnt-tasting coffee and a packet of chocolate biscuits from the canteen, and spent the rest of the day coming up with Alexandra Madison. I picked the name—"You'll remember it better that way," Frank said. Madison, because it sounds enough like my own surname to make me turn around, and Lexie because when I was a kid that was the name of my imaginary sister. Frank found a big sheet of paper and drew a timeline of her life for me. "You were born in Holles Street Hospital on the first of March 1979. Father, Sean Madison, a minor diplomat, posted in Canada—that's so we can pull you out fast if we need to: give you a family emergency, and off you go. It also means you can spend your childhood traveling, to explain why nobody knows you." Ireland is small; everyone's cousin's girlfriend went to school with you. "We could make you foreign, but I don't want you fucking about with an accent. Mother, Caroline Kelly Madison. She got a job?"

"She's a nurse."

"Careful. Think faster; keep an eye out for implications. Nurses need a new license for every country. She trained, but she quit working when you were seven and your family left Ireland. Want brothers and sisters?"

"Sure, why not," I said. "I'll have a brother." There was something intoxicating about this. I kept wanting to laugh, just at the lavish giddy freedom of it: relatives and countries and possibilities spread out in front of me and I could pick whatever I wanted, I could grow up in a palace in Bhutan with seventeen brothers and sisters and a personal chauffeur if I felt like it. I shoved another biscuit into my mouth before Frank could see me smiling and think I wasn't taking this seriously.

"Whatever your heart desires. He's six years younger, so he's in Canada with your parents. What's his name?"

"Stephen." Imaginary brother; I had an active fantasy life as a kid.

"Do you get on with him? What's he like? Faster," Frank said, when I took a breath.

"He's a little smart-arse. Football-mad. He fights with our parents all the time, because he's fifteen, but he still talks to me . . ."

Sun slanting across the scarred wood of the desk. Frank smelled clean, like soap and leather. He was a good teacher, a wonderful teacher; his black Biro scribbled in dates and places and events, and Lexie Madison developed out of nothing like a Polaroid, she curled off the page and hung in the air like incense smoke, a girl with my face and a life from a half-forgotten dream. When did you have your first boyfriend? Where were you living? What was his name? Who dumped who? Why? Frank found an ashtray, flipped a Player's out of his packet for me. When the sun bars slid off the desk and the sky started to dim outside the window, he spun his chair around, took a bottle of whiskey off a shelf and spiked our coffees: "We've earned it," he said. "Cheers."

We made her a restless one, Lexie: bright and educated,

a good girl all her life, but brought up without the habit of settling and never learned the knack. A little naïve maybe, a little unguarded, too ready to tell you anything you asked without thinking twice. "She's bait," Frank said bluntly, "and she has to be the right bait to make the dealers rise. We need her innocent enough that they won't consider her a threat, respectable enough to be useful to them, and rebellious enough that they won't wonder why she wants to play."

By the time we finished, it was dark. "Nice work," Frank said, folding up the timeline and passing it to me. "There's a detective training course starting in ten days; I'll get you into that. Then you'll come back here and I'll work with you for a while. When UCD starts back in October, you'll go in."

He hooked a leather jacket off the corner of the shelves, switched off the light and shut the door on the dark little office. I walked back to the bus station dazzled, wrapped in magic, floating in the middle of a secret and a brand-new world, with the timeline making little crackling sounds in the pocket of my uniform jacket. It was that quick, and it felt that simple.

I'm not going to get into the long, snarled chain of events that took me from Undercover to Domestic Violence. The abridged version: UCD's premier speed freak got paranoid and stabbed me, wounded-in-the-line-of-duty got me a place on the Murder squad, the Murder squad got to be a head-wrecker, I got out. It had been years since I'd thought about Lexie and her short shadowy life. I'm not the type to look back over my shoulder, or at least I try hard not to be. Gone is gone; pretending anything else is a waste of time. But now I think I always knew there would be consequences to Lexie Madison. You can't make a person, a human being with a first kiss and a sense of humor and a favorite sandwich, and then expect her to dissolve back into scribbled notes and whiskeyed coffee when she no longer suits your purposes. I think I always knew she would come back to find me, someday.

It took her four years. She picked her moment carefully. When she came knocking, it was an early morning in April, a few months after the end of my time in Murder, and I was at the firing range.

The range we use is underground in the city center, deep under half the cars in Dublin and a thick layer of smog. I didn't need to be there—I've always been a good shot, and my next qualifying test wasn't for months—but for the last while I had been waking up way too early for work and way too restless for anything else, and target practice was the only thing I had found that worked the jitters out of me. I took my time adjusting the earmuffs and checking my gun, waited till everyone else was concentrating on their own targets, so they wouldn't see me galvanizing like an electro-cuted cartoon character on the first few shots. Being easily freaked out comes with its own special skill set: you develop subtle tricks to work around it, make sure people don't notice. Pretty soon, if you're a fast learner, you can get through the day looking almost exactly like a normal human being.

I never used to be like that. I always figured nerves were for Jane Austen characters and helium-voiced girls who never buy their round; I would no more have turned shaky in a crisis than I would have carried smelling salts around in my reticule. Getting stabbed by the Drug Demon of UCD barely even fazed me. The department shrink spent weeks trying to convince me I was deeply traumatized, but eventually he had to give up, admit I was fine (sort of regret-fully; he doesn't get a lot of stabbed cops to play with, I think he was hoping I would have some kind of fancy com-plex) and let me go back to work.

Embarrassingly, the one that got me wasn't a spectacular mass murder or a hostage crisis gone bad or a nice quiet guy with human organs in his Tupperware. My last case in Murder was such a simple one, so much like dozens of others, nothing to warn us: just a little girl dead on a summer morning, and my partner and me goofing off in the squad room when the call came in. From outside, it even went well. Officially, we got a solve in barely a month, society was saved from the evildoer, it looked all pretty in the media and in the end-of-year stats. There was no dramatic car chase, no shootout, nothing like that; I was the one who came off worst, physically anyway, and all I had was a couple of scratches on my face. They didn't even leave scars. Such a happy ending, all round.

Underneath, though. Operation Vestal: say it to one of the Murder squad, even now, even one of the guys who don't know the whole story, and you'll get that instant look, hands and eyebrows going up meaningfully as he distances himself from the clusterfuck and the collateral damage. In every way that mattered, we lost and we lost big. Some people are little Chernobyls, shimmering with silent, spreading poison: get anywhere near them and every breath you take will wreck you from the inside out. Some cases—ask any cop—are malignant and incurable, devouring everything they touch.

I came out with a variety of symptoms that would have made the shrink bounce up and down in his little leather sandals, except that mercifully it didn't occur to anyone to send me to the shrink for a scratched face. It was your standard-issue trauma stuff—shaking, not eating, sticking to the ceiling every time the doorbell or the phone rang—with a few ornamentations of my own. My coordination went funny; for the first time in my life I was tripping on my own feet, bumping into doorjambs, bonking my head off cupboards. And I stopped dreaming. Before, I had always dreamed in great wild streams of images, pillars of fire spinning across dark mountains, vines exploding through solid brick, deer leaping down Sandymount beach wrapped in ropes of light; afterwards, I got thick black sleep that hit me like a mallet the second my head touched the pillow. Sam—my boyfriend, although that idea still startled me sometimes—said to give it time, it would all wear off. When I told him I wasn't so sure, he nodded peacefully and said that would wear off too. Every now and then Sam got right up my nose.

I considered the traditional cop solution—booze, early and often—but I was scared I would end up phoning inappropriate people at three in the morning to spill my guts, plus I discovered that target practice anaesthetized me almost as well and without any messy side effects. This made almost no sense, given the way I was reacting to loud noises in general, but I was OK with that. After the first few shots a fuse would blow in the back of my brain and the rest of the world vanished somewhere faint and far away, my hands turned rock-steady on the gun and it was just me and the paper target, the hard familiar smell of powder in the air and my back braced solid against the recoil. I came out calm and numb as if I'd been Valiumed. By the time the effect wore off, I had made it through another day at work and I could go whack my head off sharp corners in the comfort of my own home. I'd got to the point where I could make nine head shots out of ten, at forty yards, and the wizened little man who ran the range had started looking at me with a horse trainer's eye and making noises about the department championships.

I finished up around seven, that morning. I was in the locker room, cleaning my gun and trying to shoot the breeze with two guys from Vice without giving them the impression that I wanted to go get breakfast, when my mobile phone rang.

"Jesus," one of the Vice boys said. "You're DV, aren't you? Who has the energy to beat up his missus at this hour?"

"You can always make time for the things that really matter," I said, digging my locker key out of my pocket.

"Maybe it's black ops," said the younger guy, grinning at me. "Looking for sharpshooters." He was big and red-headed, and he thought I was cute. He had his muscles arranged to full advantage, and I had caught him checking out my ring finger.

"Must've heard we weren't available," said his mate.

I fished the phone out of my locker. The screen said SAM O'NEILL, and the missed-call icon was flashing at me in one corner.

"Hi," I said. "What's up?"

"Cassie," Sam said. He sounded terrible: breathless and sick, as if someone had punched the wind out of him. "Are you OK?"

I turned my shoulder to the Vice guys and moved off into a corner. "I'm fine. Why? What's wrong?"

"Jesus Christ," Sam said. He made a hard little noise like his throat was too tight. "I called you *four times.* I was about to send someone over to your place looking for you. Why didn't you answer your bloody phone?"

This was not like Sam. He's the gentlest guy I've ever known. "I'm at the firing range," I said. "It was in my locker. What's happened?"

"Sorry. I didn't mean to . . . sorry." He made that harsh little sound again. "I got called out. On a case."

My heart gave one huge whap against my rib cage. Sam is on the Murder squad. I knew I should probably sit down for this, but I couldn't make my knees bend. I leaned back against the lockers instead.

"Who is it?" I asked.

"What? No—God, no, it's not . . . I mean, it's not anyone we know. Or anyway I don't think—Listen, can you come down here?"

My breath came back. "Sam," I said. "What the hell is going on?"

"Just . . . can you just come? We're in Wicklow, outside Glenskehy. You know it, right? If you follow the signs, go through Glenskehy village and keep going straight south, about three-quarters of a mile on there's a little lane to your right—you'll see the crime-scene tape. We'll meet you there."

The Vice boys were starting to look interested. "My shift starts in an hour," I said. "It'll take me that long just to get out there."

"I'll call it in. I'll tell DV we need you."

"You don't. I'm not in Murder any more, Sam. If this is a murder case, it's nothing to do with me."

A guy's voice in the background: a firm, easy drawl, hard to ignore; familiar, but I couldn't place it. "Hang on," Sam said.

I clamped the phone between my ear and my shoulder and started fitting my gun back together. If it wasn't someone we knew, then it had to be a bad one, to make Sam sound like that; very bad. Irish homicides are still, mostly, simple things: drug fights, burglaries gone wrong, SOS killings (Spouse On Spouse or, depending who you ask, Same Old Shite), this elaborate family feud in Limerick that's been screwing up the figures for decades. We've never had the orgies of nightmare that other countries get: the serial killers, the ornate tortures, the basements lined with bodies thick as autumn leaves. But it's only a matter of time, now. For ten years Dublin's been changing faster than our minds can handle. The economic boom has given us too many people with helicopters and too many crushed into cockroachy flats from hell, way too many loathing their lives in fluorescent cubicles, enduring for the weekend and then starting all over again, and we're fracturing under the weight of it. By the end of my stint in Murder I could feel it coming: felt the high sing of madness in the air, the city hunching and twitching like a rabid dog building towards the rampage. Sooner or later, someone had to pull the first horror case.

We don't have official profilers, but the Murder guys, who mostly didn't go to college and who were more impressed by my psychology semi-degree than they should have been, used to use me. I was OK at it; I read textbooks and statistics a lot, in my spare time, trying to catch up. Sam's cop instincts would have overridden his protective ones and he would have called me in, if he needed to; if he'd got to a scene and found something bad enough.

"Hang on," the redhead said. He had switched out of display mode and was sitting up straight on his bench. "You used to be in Murder?" This right here was exactly why I hadn't wanted to get chummy. I had heard that avid note way too many times, over the past few months.

"Once upon a time," I said, giving him my sweetest smile and my you-do-not-want-to-go-there look.

Redser's curiosity and his libido had a quick duel; apparently he figured out that his libido's chances were slim to none anyway, because the curiosity won. "You're the one who worked that case, right?" he said, sliding a few lockers closer. "The dead kid. What's the real story?"

"All the rumors are true," I told him. On the other end of the phone Sam was having a muffled argument, short frustrated questions cut off by that easy drawl, and I knew that if the redhead would just shut up for a second I could work out who it was.

"I heard your partner went mental and shagged a suspect," Redser informed me, helpfully.

"I wouldn't know," I said, trying to disentangle myself from my bulletproof vest without losing the phone. My first instinct was—still—to tell him to do something creative to himself, but neither my ex-partner's mental status nor his love life was my problem, not any more.

Sam came back on the phone sounding even more tense and rattled. "Can you wear sunglasses, and a hood or a hat or something?"

I stopped with my vest half over my head. "What the hell?"

"Please, Cassie," Sam said, and he sounded strained to breaking point. "Please."

I drive an ancient, bockety Vespa, which is like totally uncool in a town where you are what you spend, but which has its uses. In city traffic it moves about four times as fast as your average SUV, I can actually park it, and it provides a handy social shortcut, in that anyone who gives it a snotty look is probably not going to be my new best friend. Once I got out of the city, it was perfect bike weather. It had rained during the night, furious sleety rain slapping at my window, but that had blown itself out by dawn and the day was sharp and blue, the first of almost-spring. Other years, on mornings like this one, I used to drive out into the countryside and sing at the top of my lungs into the wind at the edge of the speed limit.

Glenskehy is outside Dublin, tucked away in the Wicklow mountains near nothing very much. I'd lived half my life in Wicklow without getting any closer to it than the odd signpost. It turned out to be that kind of place: a scatter of houses getting old around a once-a-month church and a pub and a sell-everything shop, small and isolated enough to have been overlooked even by the desperate generation trawling the countryside for homes they can afford. Eight o'clock on a Thursday morning, and the main street—to use both words loosely—was postcard-perfect and empty, just one old woman pulling a shopping cart past a worn granite monument to something or other, little sugared-almond houses lined up crookedly behind her, and the hills rising green and brown and indifferent over it all. I could imagine someone getting killed there, but a farmer in a generations-old fight over a boundary fence, a woman whose man had turned savage with drink and cabin fever, a man sharing a house with his brother forty years too long: deep-rooted, familiar crimes old as Ireland, nothing to make a detective as experienced as Sam sound like that.

And that other voice on the phone was nagging at me. Sam is the only detective I know who doesn't have a partner. He likes flying solo, working every case with a new team— local uniforms who want a hand from an expert, pairs from the Murder squad who need a third man on a big case. Sam can get along with anyone, he's the perfect backup man, and I wished I knew which of the people I used to work with he was backing up this time.

Outside the village the road narrowed, twisting upwards among bright gorse bushes, and the fields got smaller and rockier. There were two men standing on the crest of the hill. Sam, fair and sturdy and tense, feet planted apart and hands in his jacket pockets; and a few feet from him, some-one else, head up, leaning back against the stiff wind. The sun was still low in the sky and their long shadows turned them giant and portentous, silhouetted almost too bright to look at against skimming clouds, like two messengers walking out of the sun and down the shimmering road. Behind them, crime-scene tape fluttered and whipped.

Sam raised his hand when I waved. The other guy cocked his head sideways, one fast tilt like a wink, and I knew who it was.

"Fuck me briefly," I said, before I was even off the Vespa. "It's Frankie. Where did you come from?"

Frank grabbed me off the ground in a one-armed hug. Four years hadn't managed to change him one bit; I was pretty sure he was even wearing the same banged-up leather jacket. "Cassie Maddox," he said. "World's best fake stu-dent. How've you been? What's all this about DV?"

"I'm saving the world. They gave me a lightsaber and all." I caught Sam's confused frown out of the corner of my eye—I don't talk much about undercover, I'm not sure he'd ever heard me mention Frank's name—but it was only when I turned to him that I realized he looked awful, white around the mouth and his eyes too wide. Something inside me clenched: a bad one.

"How're you doing?" I asked him, pulling off my helmet.

"Grand," Sam said. He tried to smile at me, but it came out lopsided.

"Oo," Frank said, mock-camp, holding me at arm's length and eyeballing me. "Check you out. Is this what the well-dressed detective is wearing these days?" The last time he had seen me, I'd been in combats and a top that said "Miss Kitty's House of Fun Wants YOU."

"Bite me, Frank," I told him. "At least I've changed my gear once or twice in the last few years."

"No, no, no, I'm impressed. Very executive." He tried to spin me round; I batted his hand away. Just for the record, I was not dressed like Hillary Clinton here. I was wearing my work clothes—black trouser suit, white shirt—and I wasn't that crazy about them myself, but when I switched to Domestic Violence my new superintendent kept going on at me about the importance of projecting an appropriate corporate image and building public confidence, which apparently cannot be done in jeans and a T-shirt, and I didn't have the energy to resist. "Bring sunglasses and a hoodie or something?" Frank asked. "They'll go great with this getup."

"You brought me down here to discuss my fashion sense?" I inquired. I found an ancient red beret in my satchel and waved it at him.

"Nah, we'll get back to that some other time. Here, have these." Frank pulled sunglasses out of his pocket, repulsive mirrored things that belonged on Don Johnson in 1985, and passed them to me.

"If I'm going to go around looking like that much of a dork," I said, eyeing them, "there had better be a damn good explanation."

"We'll get to that. If you don't like those, you can always wear your helmet." Frank waited till I shrugged and put on the dork gear. The buzz of seeing him had dissolved and my back was tensing up again. Sam looking sick, Frank on the case and not wanting me spotted at the scene: it read a lot like an undercover had got killed.

"Gorgeous as always," Frank said. He held the crime-scene tape for me to duck under, and it was so familiar, I had made that quick easy movement so many times, that for a split second it felt like coming home. I automatically settled my gun at my belt and glanced over my shoulder for my partner, as if this was my own case I were coming to, before I remembered.

"Here's the story," Sam said. "At about quarter past six this morning, a local fella called Richard Doyle was walking his dog along this lane. He let it off the lead to have a run about in the fields. There's a ruined house not far off the lane, and the dog went in and wouldn't come out; in the end, Doyle had to go after it. He found the dog sniffing around the body of a woman. Doyle grabbed the dog, legged it out of there and rang the uniforms."

I relaxed a little: I didn't know any other women from Undercover. "And I'm here why?" I asked. "Not to mention you, sunshine. Did you transfer into Murder and no one told me?"

"You'll see," Frank said. I was following him down the lane and I could only see the back of his head. "Believe me, you'll see."

I glanced over my shoulder at Sam. "Nothing to worry about," he said quietly. He was getting his color back, in bright uneven splotches. "You'll be grand."

The lane sloped upwards, too narrow for two people to walk abreast, just a muddy track with ragged hawthorn hedges spilling in on both sides. Where they broke, the hillside was crazy-quilted into green fields scattered with sheep—a brand-new lamb was bleating somewhere, far off. The air was cold and rich enough to drink, and the sun sifted long and gold through the hawthorn; I considered just keeping on walking, over the brow of the hill and on, letting Sam and Frank deal with whatever seething dark blotch was waiting for us under the morning. "Here we go," Frank said.

The hedge fell away to a broken-down stone wall bordering a field left to run wild. The house was thirty or forty yards off the lane: one of the Famine cottages that still litter Ireland, emptied in the nineteenth century by death or emigration and never reclaimed. One look added another layer to my feeling that I wanted to be very far away from whatever was going on here. The whole field should have been alive with focused, unhurried movement—uniforms working their way across the grass with their heads bent, Technical Bureau crew in white coveralls busy with cameras and rulers and print dust, morgue guys unloading their stretcher. Instead there were two uniforms, shifting from foot to foot on either side of the cottage door and looking slightly out of their depth, and a pair of pissed-off robins bouncing around the eaves making outraged noises.

"Where is everyone?" I asked.

I was talking to Sam, but Frank said, "Cooper's been and gone"—Cooper is the state pathologist. "I figured he needed to have a look at her as fast as possible, for time of death. The Bureau can wait; forensic evidence isn't going anywhere."

"Jesus," I said. "It is if we walk on it. Sam, ever worked a double homicide before?"

Frank raised an eyebrow. "Got another body?"

"Yours, once the Bureau get here. Six people wandering all over a crime scene before they've cleared it? They're gonna kill you."

"Worth it," Frank said cheerfully, swinging a leg over the wall. "I wanted to keep this under wraps for a little while, and that's hard to do if you've got Bureau guys swarming all over the place. People tend to notice them."

Something was badly wrong here. This was Sam's case, not Frank's; Sam should have been the one deciding how the evidence was handled and who got called in when. Whatever was in that cottage, it had shaken him up enough that he had let Frank sweep in, bulldoze him out of the way and instantly, efficiently start arranging this case to suit whatever agenda he had today. I tried to catch Sam's eye, but he was pulling himself over the wall and not looking at either of us.

"Can you climb walls in that getup," Frank inquired sweetly, "or would you like a hand?" I made a face at him and vaulted into the field, up to my ankles in long wet grass and dandelions.

The cottage had been two rooms, once, a long time ago. One of them still looked more or less intact—it even had most of its roof—but the other was just shards of wall and windows onto open air. Bindweed and moss and little trailing blue flowers had rooted in the cracks. Someone had spray-painted SHAZ beside the doorway, not very artistically, but the house was too inconvenient for a regular hangout: even prowling teenagers had mostly left it alone, to collapse on itself in its own slow time.

"Detective Cassie Maddox," Frank said, "Sergeant Noel Byrne and Garda Joe Doherty, Rathowen station. Glenskehy's on their patch."

"For our sins," said Byrne. He sounded like he meant it. He was somewhere in his fifties, with a slumped back and watery blue eyes, and he smelled of wet uniform and loser.

Doherty was a gangly kid with unfortunate ears, and when I held out my hand to him he did a double take straight out of a cartoon; I could practically hear the *boing* of his eyeballs snapping back into place. God only knew what he'd heard about me—cops have a better rumor mill than any bingo club—but I didn't have time to worry about it right then. I gave him the smile-and-stare number, and he mumbled something and dropped my hand as if it had scorched him.

"We'd like Detective Maddox to take a look at our body," Frank said.

"I'd say you would, all right," said Byrne, eyeing me. I wasn't sure he meant it the way it sounded; he didn't look like he had the energy. Doherty snickered nervously.

"Ready?" Sam asked me quietly.

"The suspense is killing me," I said. It came out a little snottier than I intended. Frank was already ducking into the cottage and pulling aside the long sprays of trailing bramble that curtained the doorway to the inner room.

"Ladies first," he said, with a flourish. I hung the stud-muffin glasses off the front of my shirt by one earpiece, took a breath and went in.

It should have been a peaceful, sad little room. Long bands of sun slanting through holes in the roof and filtering past the net of branches over the windows, shivering like light on water; some family's hearth, cold a hundred years, with piles of bird's-nest fallen down the chimney and the rusty iron hook for the cooking pot still hanging ready. A wood dove murmuring contentedly, somewhere nearby.

But if you've seen a dead body, you know how they change the air: that huge silence, the absence strong as a black hole, time stopped and molecules frozen around the still thing that's learned the final secret, the one he can never tell. Most dead people are the only thing in the room. Murder victims are different; they don't come alone. The silence rises up to a deafening shout and the air is streaked and hand-printed, the body smokes with the brand of that other person grabbing you just as hard: the killer.

The first thing that hit me about this scene, though, was how slight a mark the killer had left. I had been bracing myself against things I didn't want to imagine—naked and spread-eagled, vicious dark wounds too thick to count, body parts scattered in corners—but this girl looked as if she had arranged herself carefully on the floor and let out her last breath in a long even sigh, chosen her own time and place with no need for anyone's help along the way. She was lying on her back among the shadows in front of the fire-place, neatly, with her feet together and her arms at her sides. She was wearing a navy peacoat, falling open; under it were indigo jeans—pulled up and zipped—runners and a blue top with a dark star tie-dyed across the front. The only thing out of the ordinary was her hands, clenched into tight fists. Frank and Sam had moved in beside me, and I shot Frank a puzzled look—*And the big deal is?*—but he just watched me, his face giving away nothing.

She was medium height, built like me, compact and

boyish. Her head was turned away from us, towards the far wall, and all I could see in the dim light was short black curls and a slice of white: high round curve of a cheekbone, the point of a small chin. "Here," Frank said. He flicked on a tiny, powerful torch and caught her face in a sharp little halo.

For a second I was confused—*Sam lied?*—because I knew her from somewhere, I'd seen that face a million times before. Then I took a step forwards, so I could get a proper look and the whole world went silent, frozen, darkness roaring in from the edges and only the girl's face blazing white at the center; because it was me. The tilt of the nose, the wide sweep of the eyebrows, every tiniest curve and angle clear as ice: it was me, blue-lipped and still, with shadows like dark bruises under my eyes. I couldn't feel my hands, my feet, couldn't feel myself breathing. For a second I thought I was floating, sliced off myself and wind currents carrying me away.

"Know her?" Frank asked, somewhere. "Any relation?"

It was like going blind; my eyes couldn't take her in. She was impossible: a high-fever hallucination, a screaming crack straight across all the laws of nature. I realized I was braced rigid on the balls of my feet, one hand halfway to my gun, every muscle ready to fight this dead girl to the death. "No," I said. My voice sounded wrong, somewhere outside me. "Never seen her."

"You adopted?"

Sam whipped his head around, startled, but the bluntness was good, it helped like a pinch. "No," I said. For an awful, rocking instant I actually wondered. But I've seen photos, my mother tired and smiling in a hospital bed, brand-new me at her breast. No.

"Which side do you look like?"

"What?" It took me a second. I couldn't look away from the girl; I had to force myself to blink. No wonder Doherty and his ears had done a double take. "No. My mother's side. It's not that my father was running around, and this is . . . No."

Frank shrugged. "Worth a shot."

"They say everyone's got a double, somewhere," Sam said quietly, beside me. He was too close; it took me a second to realize that he was ready to catch me, just in case.

I am not the fainting type. I bit down, hard and fast, on the inside of my lip; the jolt of pain cleared my head. "Doesn't she have ID?"

I knew, from the tiny pause before either of them answered, that something was up. *Shit*, I thought, with a new thump in my stomach: *identity theft*. I wasn't too clear on how it worked exactly, but one glimpse of me and a creative streak and presumably this girl could have been sharing my passport and buying BMWs on my credit.

"She had a student card on her," Frank said. "Key ring in the left-hand pocket of her coat, Maglite in the right, wallet in the front right pocket of her jeans. Twelve quid and change, an ATM card, a couple of old receipts and this." He fished a clear plastic evidence bag out of a pile by the door and slapped it into my hand.

It was a Trinity College ID, slick and digitized, not like the laminated bits of colored paper we used to have. The girl in the photo looked ten years younger than the white, sunken face in the corner. She was smiling my own smile up at me and wearing a striped baker-boy cap turned sideways, and for a second my mind flailed wildly: *But I never had a striped one of those, did I, when did I*—I pretended to tilt the card to the light, reading the small print, so I could turn my shoulder to the others. *Madison, Alexandra J.*

For a whirling instant, I understood completely: Frank and I had done this. We made Lexie Madison bone by bone and fiber by fiber, we baptized her and for a few months we gave her a face and a body, and when we threw her away she wanted more. She spent four years spinning herself back, out of dark earth and night winds, and then she called us here to see what we had done.

"What the *hell*," I said, when I could breathe.

"When the uniforms called it in and ran her name

through the computer," Frank said, taking back the bag, "she came up flagged: anything happens to this girl, call me ASAP. I never bothered taking her out of the system; I figured we might need her again, sooner or later. You never know."

"Yeah," I said. "No kidding." I stared hard at the body and got a grip: this was no golem, this was a real live dead girl, oxymoron and all. "Sam," I said. "What've we got?"

Sam shot me a quick, searching glance; when he realized I wasn't about to swoon or scream or whatever he'd had in mind, he nodded. He was starting to look a little more like himself. "White female," he said, "mid-twenties to early thirties, single stab wound to the chest. Cooper says she died sometime around midnight, give or take an hour. He can't be more specific: shock, ambient temperature variations, whether there was physical activity around the time of death, all the rest of it."

Unlike most people, I get on well with Cooper, but I was glad I'd missed him. The tiny cottage felt too full, full of clumping feet and people shifting and eyes on me. "Stabbed here?" I asked.

Sam shook his head. "Hard to tell. We'll wait and see what the Bureau says, but all that rain last night got rid of a lot—we won't be finding footprints in the lane, a blood trail, nothing like that. For what it's worth, though, I'd say this isn't our primary crime scene. She was on her feet for at least a while after she got stabbed. See there? Blood's dripped straight down the leg of her jeans." Frank shifted the torch beam, obligingly. "And there's mud on both knees and a rip in one, like she was running and she fell."

"Looking for cover," I said. The image surged up at me like something from every forgotten nightmare: the lane twisting into the dark and her running, feet slipping helplessly on pebbles and her breath wild in her ears. I could feel Frank carefully standing back, saying nothing; watching.

"Could be," Sam said. "Maybe the killer was coming after her, or she thought he was. She could've left a trail straight from his front door, for all we'll ever know; it's long gone."

I wanted to do something with my hands, rub them through my hair, over my mouth, something. I shoved them in my pockets to keep them still. "So she got into shelter and collapsed."

"Not exactly. I'm thinking she died over there." Sam pulled back the brambles and nodded at a corner of the outer room. "We've got what looks like a fair-sized pool of blood. No way to be sure exactly how much—we'll see if the Bureau can help there—but if there's still plenty left after a night like this, I'd say there was a load of it to start with. She was probably sitting up against that wall—most of the blood is on the front of her top and on the lap and seat of her jeans. If she'd been lying down, it'd have seeped down her sides. See this?"

He pointed to the girl's top, and the penny dropped with a bang: not tie-dye. "She twisted up the top and pressed it against the wound, trying to stop the bleeding."

Huddled deep in that corner; rush of rain, blood seeping warm between her fingers. "So how'd she get over here?" I asked.

"Our boy caught up with her in the end," Frank said. "Or someone did, anyway."

He leaned over, lifted one of the girl's feet by the shoelace—it sent a fast twitch down the back of my neck, him touching her—and tilted his torch at the heel of her runner: scuffed and brown, grained deep with dirt. "She was dragged. After death, because there's no pooling under the body: by the time she got over here, she wasn't bleeding any more. The guy who found her swears he didn't touch, and I believe him. He looked like he was about to puke his guts up; no way he got closer than he had to. Anyway, she was moved not too long after she died. Cooper says rigor hadn't set in yet, and there's no secondary lividity—and she didn't spend much time out in that rain. She's barely damp. If she'd been in the open all night, she'd be drenched."

Slowly, as if my eyes were only just adjusting to the dim light, I realized that all the dark patches and stipples that I had taken for shadows and rainwater were actually blood. It was everywhere: streaked across the floor, soaking the girl's jeans, crusting her hands wrist-deep. I didn't want to look at her face, at anyone's face. I kept my eyes on her top and unfocused them so that the dark star swam and blurred. "Got footprints?"

"Zip," Frank said. "Not even hers. You'd think, with all this dirt; but, like Sam here said, the rain. All we've got in the other room is a shitload of mud, with prints matching the guy who called it in and his dog—that's one reason I wasn't too worried about walking you through there. Same thing out in the lane. And in here . . ." He moved the torch beam around the edges of the floor, nosed it into corners: wide, blank sweeps of dirt, way too smooth. "That's what it all looked like, when we got here. Those prints you're seeing around the body, those are us and Cooper and the uniforms. Whoever moved her stuck around to tidy up after himself. There's a broken branch of gorse in the middle of the field, probably came off that big bush by the door; I'm guessing he used it to sweep the floor clean as he left. We'll see if the Bureau pulls blood or prints off it. And to go with no footprints . . ."

He handed me another evidence bag. "See anything wrong?"

It was a wallet, white fake leather, sewn with a butterfly in silver thread and swiped with faint traces of blood. "It's too clean," I said. "You said this was in her front jeans pocket, and she bled out all over her lap. This should be covered with blood."

"Bingo. The pocket's stiff with it, soaked through, but somehow this barely gets stained? The torch and keys are the same: not a drop of blood, just a few smudges. Looks like our boy went through her pockets and then wiped her stuff clean before he put it back. We'll have the Bureau fingerprint everything that'll stay still long enough, but I wouldn't bet on getting anything useful. Someone was being very, very careful."

"Any sign of sexual assault?" I asked. Sam flinched. I was way past that.

"Cooper won't say for sure till the post-mortem, but nothing on the preliminary points that way. We might get lucky and find some foreign blood on her"—a lot of stabbers cut themselves—"but, basically, I'm not holding my breath for DNA."

My first impression—the invisible killer, leaving no trace—hadn't been far off. After a few months in Murder, you can tell One of Those Cases a mile away. With the last clear corner of my mind I reminded myself that, no matter what it looked like, this one was not my problem. "Great," I said. "What *do* you have? Anything on her, other than she's in Trinity and she's running around wearing a fake name?"

"Sergeant Byrne says she's local," Sam said. "Lives at Whitethorn House, maybe half a mile away, with a bunch of other students. That's all he knows about her. I haven't talked to the housemates yet, because . . ." He gestured at Frank.

"Because I begged him to hold off," Frank said smoothly. "I have this little idea I wanted to run by you two, before the investigation gets into full gear." He arched an eyebrow towards the door and the uniforms. "Maybe we should go for a wander."

"Why not," I said. The girl's body was doing something funny to the air in there, fizzing it, like the needle-thin whine the TV makes on mute; it was hard to think straight. "If we stay in the same room for too long, the universe might turn into antimatter." I gave Frank his evidence bag back and wiped my hand on the side of my trousers.

In the moment before I passed through the doorway I turned my head and looked at her, over my shoulder. Frank had switched off his torch, but pulling back the brambles let in a flood of spring sun and for the split second before my shadow blocked it again she rose up blazing out of the darkness, tilted chin and a clenched fist and the wild arch of her throat, bright and bloodied and relentless as my own wrecked ghost.

That was the last time I saw her. It didn't occur to me at the time—I had other stuff on my mind—and it seems impossible now, but those ten minutes, sharp as a crease pressed straight across my life: that was the only time we were ever together.

The uniforms were slumped where we had left them, like beanbags. Byrne was staring off into the middle distance in some kind of catatonic state; Doherty was examining one finger in a way that made me think he had been picking his nose.

"Right," Byrne said, once he surfaced from his trance and registered that we were back. "We'll be off, so. She's all yours."

Sometimes the local uniforms are pure diamond—reeling off details about everyone for miles around, listing half a dozen possible motives, handing you a prime suspect on a plate. Other times, all they want is to pass the hassle to you and get back to their game of Go Fish. This was obviously going to be other times.

"We'll need you to hang on for a while," Sam said, which I took as a good sign—the extent to which Frank had been running this show was making me edgy. "The Technical Bureau might want you to help with the search, and I'll be asking you to give me all the local info you can."

"She's not local, sure," Doherty said, wiping his finger on the side of his trousers. He was staring at me again. "Them up at Whitethorn House, they're blow-ins. They've nothing to do with Glenskehy."

"Lucky bastards," Byrne mumbled, to his chest.

"She lived local, though," Sam said patiently, "and she died local. That means we'll be needing to canvass the area.

You should probably give us a hand, seeing as ye know your way around."

Byrne's head sank farther into his shoulders. "They're all mentallers, round here," he said morosely. "Stone mentallers. That's all you need to know."

"Some of my best friends are mentallers," Frank said cheerfully. "Think of it as a challenge." He gave them a wave and headed off up the field, feet swishing wetly through the grass.

Sam and I followed him. Even without looking I could feel the worried little line between Sam's eyebrows, but I didn't have the energy to reassure him. Now I was out of that cottage, all I could feel was outrage, pure and simple. My face and my old name: it was like coming home one day and finding another girl coolly making dinner in your kitchen, wearing your comfiest jeans and singing along to your favorite CD. I was so furious I could barely breathe. I thought of that photo and I wanted to punch my smile straight off her face.

"Well," I said, when we caught up with Frank at the top of the field, "that was fun. Can I go to work now?"

"DV must be a lot more entertaining than I thought," Frank said, doing impressed, "if you're in this much of a hurry. Sunglasses."

I left the glasses where they were. "Unless this girl was a victim of domestic violence, and I'm not seeing anything that points that way, she's got sweet fuck-all to do with me. So you dragged me out here why, exactly?"

"Hey, I've missed you, babe. Any excuse." Frank grinned at me; I gave him a hairy look. "And you seriously figure she's fuck-all to do with you? Let's see you say that when we're trying to ID her, and everyone you've ever known is freaking out and ringing up to give us your name."

All the anger deflated out of me, leaving a nasty hollow at the bottom of my stomach. Frank, the little bollocks, was right. As soon as this girl's face went into the papers alongside an appeal for her real name, there would be a tidal wave of people who had known me as Lexie, her as Lexie, me as me, all of them wanting to know who was dead and who both of us had been if we weren't in fact Lexie Madison, and general hall-of-mirrors overload. Believe it or not, that was the first time it hit me: there was no way in the world for this to be as easy as *Don't know her, don't want to know her, thanks for wasting my morning, see you around.*

"Sam," I said. "Is there any way you could hold off on putting her picture out for a day or two? Just till I can warn people." I had no idea how I was going to word this one. *See, Aunt Louisa, we found this dead girl and . . .*

"Interestingly," Frank said, "now that you mention it, that fits right in with my little idea." There was a jumble of moss-covered boulders piled in the corner of the field; he pulled himself backwards onto them and sat there, one leg swinging.

I'd seen that gleam in his eyes before. It always meant he was about to come out, spectacularly casually, with something totally outrageous. "What, Frank," I said.

"Well," Frank began, getting comfortable against the rocks and folding his arms behind his head, "we've got a unique opportunity here, haven't we? Shame to waste it."

"We do?" Sam said.

"*We* do?" I said.

"Oh, yeah. Jesus, yeah." That risky grin was starting at the corners of Frank's mouth. "We've got the chance," he said, taking his time, "we've got the chance to investigate a murder case from the inside. We've got the chance to place an experienced undercover officer smack in the middle of a murder victim's life."

We both stared at him.

"When have you ever seen anything like that before? It's beautiful, Cass. It's a work of art."

"Work of arse, more like," I said. "What the hell are you on about, Frankie?"

Frank spread his arms like it was obvious. "Look. You've been Lexie Madison before, right? You can be her again.

You can—no, hang on, hear me out—if she's not dead, just wounded, right? You can walk straight back into her life and pick up where she left off."

"Oh my God," I said. "This is why no Bureau and no morgue guys? *This* is why you made me dress like a dork? So nobody notices you have a spare?" I pulled my hat off and stuffed it back in my bag. Even for Frank, this had taken some fast thinking. Within seconds of arriving at the scene, he must have had this in his head.

"You can get hold of info no cop would ever learn, you can get close to everyone she was close to, you can identify suspects—"

"You want to use her as bait," Sam said, too levelly.

"I want to use her as a detective, mate," Frank said. "Which is what she is, last time I checked."

"You want to put her in there so this fella will come back to finish the job. That's bait."

"So? Undercovers are bait all the time. I'm not asking her to do anything I wouldn't do myself in a heartbeat, if—"

"No," Sam said. "No way."

Frank raised an eyebrow. "What are you, her ma?"

"I'm the lead investigator on this case, and I'm saying no way."

"You might want to think about it for more than ten seconds, pal, before you—"

I might as well not have been there. "Hello?" I said.

They turned and stared at me. "Sorry," Sam said, somewhere between sheepish and defiant.

"Hi," Frank said, grinning at me.

"Frank," I said, "this is officially the looniest idea I've ever heard in my life. You are off your bloody trolley. You are up the wall and tickling the bricks. You are—"

"What's loony about it?" Frank demanded, injured.

"Jesus," I said. I ran my hands through my hair and turned full circle, trying to figure out where to start. Hills, fields, spaced-out uniforms, cottage with dead girl: this wasn't some messed-up dream. "OK, just for starters, it's impossible. I've never even *heard* of anything like this before."

"But that's the beauty of it," Frank explained.

"If you go under as someone who actually exists, it's for like half an hour, Frank, and it's to do something specific. It's to do a drop-off or a pickup or something, from a *stranger*. You're talking about me jumping right into the middle of this girl's life, just because I look a bit like her—"

"A *bit*?"

"Do you even know what color her eyes are? What if they're blue, or—"

"Give me some credit, babe. They're brown."

"Or what if she programs computers, or plays tennis? What if she's left-handed? It can't be done. I'd be burned inside an hour."

Frank pulled a squashed pack of smokes out of his jacket pocket and fished out a cigarette. He had that glint in his eye again; he loves a challenge. "I have every faith in you. Want a smoke?"

"No," I said, even though I did. I couldn't stop moving, up and down and around the patch of long grass between us. *I don't even like her,* I wanted to say, which made no sense at all.

Frank shrugged and lit up. "Let me worry about whether it's possible. It might not be, I'll grant you that, but I'll figure that out as we go along. What's next?"

Sam was looking away, his hands shoved deep in his pockets, leaving me to it. "Next," I said, "it's somewhere out on the other side of unethical. This girl must have family, friends. You're going to tell them she's alive and well and just needs a few stitches, while she's lying on a table in the morgue with Cooper slicing her open? Jesus, Frank."

"She's living under a fake name, Cass," Frank said, reasonably. "You really think she's in touch with her family? By the time we track them down, this will all be over. They'll never know the difference."

"So what about her mates? The uniforms said she lives with a bunch of others. What if she's got a boyfriend?"

"The people who care about her," Frank said, "will want us to catch the guy who did this to her. Whatever it takes. That's what I'd want." He blew smoke up at the sky.

Sam's shoulders shifted. He thought Frank was just being smart-arsed. But Sam's never done undercover, he had no way of knowing: undercovers are different. There is nothing they won't do, to themselves or anyone else, to take their guy down. There was no point in arguing with Frank on this one, because he meant what he had said: if his kid were killed, and someone kept that from him in order to get the guy, he would take it without a murmur. It's one of the most powerful lures of undercover, the ruthlessness, no borderlines; strong stuff, strong enough to take your breath away. It's one of the reasons I left.

"And then what?" I said. "When it's over. You tell them, 'Oops, by the way, we forgot to mention, that's a ringer; your mate died three weeks ago?' Or do I keep being Lexie Madison till I can die of old age?"

Frank squinted into the sun, considering this. "Your wound can get infected," he said, brightening. "You'll go into the ICU and the doctors will try everything modern medicine can offer, but no go."

"Jesus Christ on a bike," I said. I felt like this was all I had said, all morning long. "What on *earth* is making this seem like a good idea to you?"

"What's next?" Frank asked. "Come on, hit me."

"Next," Sam said, still looking away down the lane, "it's bloody dangerous."

Frank raised one eyebrow and tilted his head at Sam, giving me a wicked private grin. For an off-balance second I had to stop myself grinning back.

"Next," I said, "it's too late anyway. Byrne and Doherty

and Whatsisname with the dog all know there's a dead woman in there. You're telling me you can get all three of them to keep their mouths shut, just because it suits you? Whatsisname's probably told half of Wicklow already."

"Whatsisname is Richard Doyle, and I'm not planning on getting him to keep his mouth shut. As soon as we're done here, I'm going to go congratulate him on saving this young woman's life. If he hadn't shown great presence of mind by calling us immediately, the outcome could have been tragic. He's a hero, and he can tell as many people as he likes. And you saw Byrne, babe. That's not a happy little member of our glorious brotherhood. If I hint that there might be a transfer in it for him, not only will he keep his mouth shut, he'll keep Doherty's shut too. Next?"

"Next," I said, "it's pointless. Sam's worked dozens of murders, Frank, and he's solved most of them, without needing to pull any wack-job stunts. This thing you're talking about would take weeks to set up—"

"Days, anyway," Frank amended.

"—and by that time he'll *have* someone. At least, he will if you don't fuck up his investigation by getting everyone to pretend there's no murder to begin with. All this will do is waste your time and mine and everyone else's."

"Would it fuck up your investigation?" Frank asked Sam. "Just hypothetically speaking. If you told the public—just for, say, a couple of days—that this was an assault, not a murder. Would it?"

Eventually Sam sighed. "No," he said. "Not really, no. There's not that much difference in investigating attempted murder and actual murder. And, like Cassie said, we'll have to keep this pretty quiet for a few days anyway, till we find out who the victim is, so things don't get too confused. But that's not the point."

"OK," Frank said. "Then here's what I suggest. Mostly you guys have a suspect within seventy-two hours, right?"

Sam said nothing.

"Right?"

"Right," Sam said. "And there's no reason why this should be different."

"No reason at all," Frank agreed, pleasantly. "Today's Thursday. Just through the weekend, we keep our options open. We don't tell civilians it's a murder. Cassie stays home, so there's no chance of the killer getting a glimpse of her, and we've got our ace up the sleeve if we decide to use it. I find out everything I can about this girl, just in case—that would need doing anyway, am I right? I won't get in your way, you've got my word on that. Like you said, you're bound to have someone in your sights by Sunday night. If you do, then I back off, Cassie goes back to DV, everything goes back to standard procedure, no harm done. If by any chance you don't . . . well, we've still got all our options."

Neither of us answered.

"I'm only asking for three days, guys," Frank said. "No commitment to anything. What damage can that do?"

Sam looked marginally reassured by this, but I wasn't, because I knew how Frank works: a series of little tiny steps, each one looking perfectly safe and innocuous until suddenly, bam, you're smack in the middle of something you really did not want to deal with. "But *why*, Frank?" I asked. "Answer me that and yeah, fine, I'll spend a gorgeous spring weekend sitting in my flat watching crap telly instead of going out with my boyfriend like a normal human being. You're talking about throwing huge amounts of time and manpower at something that could well turn out to be completely pointless. Why?"

Frank whipped a hand up to shade his eyes so he could stare at me. *"Why?"* he repeated. "Jesus, Cassie! Because we *can*. Because nobody in the history of police work has ever had a chance like this. Because it would be bloody *amazing*. What, you're not seeing that? What the fuck is wrong with you? Have you gone desk on me?"

I felt like he had hauled off and punched me in the stomach. I stopped pacing and turned away, looking out over the hillside, away from Frank and Sam and from the uniforms twisting their heads into the cottage to gawp at wet dead me.

After a moment Frank said behind me, softer, "Sorry, Cass. I just wasn't expecting that. From the Murder gang, sure, but not from you, of all people. I didn't think you meant . . . I thought you were just covering all the bases. I didn't realize."

He sounded genuinely stunned. I knew perfectly well he was working me and I could have listed every tool he was using, but it didn't matter; because he was right. Five years earlier, one year earlier, I would have been leaping for this dazzling incomparable adventure right alongside him, I'd have been in there checking whether the dead girl's ears were pierced and how she parted her hair. I looked out at the fields and thought, very distinctly and detachedly, *What the fuck has happened to me?*

"OK," I said, finally. "What you tell the press isn't my problem; you guys fight it out between you. I'll stay out of the way for the weekend. But, Frank, I'm not promising you anything else. No matter who Sam finds or doesn't find. This does not mean I'm doing it. Clear enough?"

"That's my girl," Frank said. I could hear the grin in his voice. "For a moment there I thought the aliens had planted a chip in your brain."

"Fuck off, Frank," I said, turning around. Sam didn't look happy, but I couldn't worry about that just then. I needed to get away on my own and think about this.

"I haven't said yes yet," Sam said.

"It's your call, obviously," Frank said. He didn't seem too worried. I knew he might have more of a fight on his hands than he expected. Sam is an easygoing guy, but every now and then he puts his foot down, and then trying to change his mind is like trying to push a house out of your way. "Just call it fast. If we're going with this, for now anyway, we'll need to get an ambulance out here ASAP."

"Let me know what you decide," I told Sam. "I'm going

home. See you tonight?" Frank's eyebrows shot up. Undercovers have an impressive grapevine all their own, but they mostly stay away from the general gossip, in a slightly pointed way, and Sam and I had been keeping things fairly quiet. Frank gave me an amused look, tongue rolling in his cheek. I ignored him.

"I don't know when I'll finish up," Sam said.

I shrugged. "I'm not going anywhere."

"See you soon, babe," Frank said happily, through another cigarette, and waved good-bye.

Sam walked me back down the field, close enough that his shoulder brushed mine protectively; I got the sense he didn't want me to have to pass the body on my own. Actually, I badly wanted to have another look at it, preferably by myself and for a long silent time, but I could feel Frank's eyes on my back, so I didn't even turn my head as we passed the cottage.

"I wanted to warn you," Sam said abruptly. "Mackey said no. He was pretty insistent about it, and I wasn't thinking straight enough to . . . I should've. I'm sorry."

Obviously Frank, like everyone else in my bloody universe, had heard the Operation Vestal rumors. "He wanted to see how I'd take it," I said. "Checking my nerve. And he's good at getting what he wants. It's OK."

"This Mackey. Is he a good cop?"

I didn't know how to answer that. "Good cop" isn't a phrase we take lightly. It means a vast complex constellation of things, and a different one for every officer. I wasn't at all sure that Frank fit Sam's definition, or even, come to think of it, mine. "He's smart as hell," I said, in the end, "and he gets his man. One way or another. Are you going to give him his three days?"

Sam sighed. "If you're all right with staying in this weekend, then yeah, I'd say I will. It'll do no harm, actually, keeping this case under the radar till we've some idea what we're dealing with—an ID, a suspect, something. It'll keep the confusion down. I'm not mad about giving her friends false hope, but sure, I suppose it could soften the blow—having the few days to get used to the chance that she might not make it . . ."

It was shaping up to be a gorgeous day; the sun was drying the grass and it was so quiet I could hear tiny insects zigzagging in and out among the wildflowers. There was something about the green hillsides that made me edgy, something stubborn and secretive, like a turned back. It took me a second to figure out what it was: they were empty. Out of all Glenskehy, not one person had come to see what was going on.

Out in the lane, screened from the others by trees and hedges, Sam pulled me tight against him.

"I thought it was you," he said into my hair. His voice was low and shaking. "I thought it was you."

2

I didn't actually spend the next three days watching crap telly, the way I'd said to Frank. I'm not good at sitting still to begin with, and when I'm edgy I need to move. So—I'm in this job for the thrills, me—I cleaned. I scrubbed, hoovered and polished every inch of my flat, down to the baseboards and the inside of the cooker. I took down the curtains, washed them in the bath and pegged them to the fire escape to dry. I hung my duvet off the windowsill and whacked it with a spatula to get the dust out. I would have painted the walls, if I'd had paint. I actually considered putting on my dork disguise and finding a DIY shop, but I'd promised Frank, so I cleaned the back of the cistern instead.

And I thought about what Frank had said to me. *You, of all people . . .* After Operation Vestal I transferred out of Murder. DV might not be much of a challenge by comparison, but God it's peaceful, although I know that's a strange word to choose. Either someone hit someone or he didn't; it's as simple as that, and all you have to do is figure out which one it is and how to make them knock it off. DV is straightforward and it's unequivocally useful, and I wanted that, badly. I was so bloody tired of high stakes and ethical dilemmas and complications.

You, of all people; have you gone desk on me? My nice work suit, ironed and hung on the wardrobe door ready for Monday, made me feel queasy. Finally I couldn't look at it any more. I threw it in the wardrobe and slammed the door on it.

And of course I thought, all the time, under everything I did, about the dead girl. I felt like there must have been some clue in her face, some secret message in a code only I could read, if I had just had the wits or the time to spot it. If I'd still been in Murder I would have nicked a crime-scene shot or a copy of her ID, taken it home with me to look at in private. Sam would have brought me one if I'd asked, but I didn't.

Somewhere out there, sometime in these three days, Cooper would be doing the autopsy. The idea bent my brain.

I had never seen anyone who looked anything like me before. Dublin is full of scary girls who I swear to God are actually the same person, or at least come out of the same fake-tan bottle; me, I may not be a five-star babe but I am not generic. My mother's father was French, and somehow the French and the Irish combined into something specific and pretty distinctive. I don't have brothers or sisters; what I mainly have is aunts, uncles and large cheerful gangs of second cousins, and none of them look anything like me.

My parents died when I was five. She was a cabaret singer, he was a journalist, he was driving her home from a gig in Kilkenny one wet December night and they hit a slick patch of road. Their car flipped three times—he was probably speeding—and lay upside down in a field till a farmer saw the lights and went to investigate. He died the next day; she never made it into the ambulance. I tell people this early on, to get it out of the way. Everyone always gets either tongue-tied or gooey ("You must miss them so *much*"), and the better we know each other, the longer they feel the gooey stage needs to last. I never know how to answer, given that I was five and that it was more than twenty-five years ago; I think it's safe to say I'm more or less over it. I wish I remembered them enough to miss them, but all I can miss is the idea, and sometimes the songs my mother used to sing me, and I don't tell people about that.

I was lucky. Thousands of other kids in that situation have slipped through the cracks, fallen into foster care or nightmare industrial schools. But on their way to the gig my parents had dropped me off to spend the night in Wicklow with my father's sister and her husband. I remember phones ringing in the middle of the night, quick footsteps on stairs and urgent murmuring in the corridor, a car starting, people going in and out for what seemed like days, and then Aunt Louisa sitting me down in the dim living room and explaining that I was going to stay there for a while longer, because my mother and father weren't coming back.

She was a lot older than my father, and she and Uncle Gerard don't have kids. He's a historian; they play bridge a lot. I don't think they ever really got used to the idea that I lived there—they gave me the spare room, complete with a high double bed and small breakable ornaments and an inappropriate print of *Venus Rising*, and looked faintly worried when I got old enough that I wanted to put up posters of my own. But for twelve and a half years they fed me, sent me to school and gymnastics classes and music lessons, patted me vaguely but affectionately on the head whenever I was within reach, and left me alone. In exchange, I made sure they didn't find out when I mitched off school, fell off things I shouldn't have been climbing, got detention or started to smoke.

It was—this always seems to shock people all over again—a happy childhood. For the first few months I spent a lot of time at the bottom of the garden, crying till I threw up and yelling rude words at neighborhood kids who tried to make friends. But children are pragmatic, they come alive and kicking out of a whole lot worse than orphanhood, and I could only hold out so long against the fact that nothing would bring my parents back and against the thousand vivid things around me, Emma-next-door hanging over the wall and my new bike glinting red in the sunshine and the half-wild kittens in the garden shed, all fidgeting insistently while they waited for me to wake up again and come out to play. I found out early that you can throw yourself away, missing what you've lost.

I weaned myself on the nostalgia equivalent of methadone (less addictive, less obvious, less likely to make you crazy): missing what I had never had. When my new mates and I bought Curly Wurly bars at the shop, I saved half of mine for my imaginary sister (I kept them at the bottom of my wardrobe, where they turned into sticky puddles and got in my shoes); I left room in the double bed for her, when Emma or someone wasn't sleeping over. When horrible Billy MacIntyre who sat behind me in school wiped snots on my plaits, my imaginary brother beat him up till I learned to do it myself. In my mind adults looked at us, three matching dark heads all in a row, and said, *Ah, God, you'd know they're family, aren't they the spit of each other?*

It wasn't affection I was after, nothing like that. What I wanted was someone I belonged with, beyond any doubt or denial; someone where every glance was a guarantee, solid proof that we were stuck to each other for life. In photographs I can see a resemblance to my mother; nobody else, ever. I don't know if you can imagine this. Every one of my school friends had the family nose or her father's hair or the same eyes as her sisters. Even this girl Jenny Bailey, who was adopted, looked like she was probably the rest of the class's cousin—this was the eighties, everyone in Ireland was related one way or another. When I was a kid looking for things to get angsty about, being without this felt like having no reflection. There was nothing to prove I had a right to be here. I could have come from anywhere, dropped by aliens, swapped by elves, built in a test tube by the CIA, and if they showed up one day to take me back there would be nothing in the world to hold me here.

If this mystery girl had walked into my classroom one morning, back then, it would have made my year. Since she didn't, I grew up, got a grip and stopped thinking about it. Now, all of a sudden, I had the best reflection on the block, and I didn't like it one bit. I had got used to being just me, no links to anyone. This girl was a link like a handcuff, slapped on my wrist out of nowhere and tightened till it bit to the bone.

And I knew how she had picked up the Lexie Madison ID. It was in my head bright and hard as broken glass, clear as if it had happened to me, and I didn't like this either. Somewhere in town, at the bar in a crowded pub or flipping through clothes in a shop, and behind her: *Lexie? Lexie Madison? God, I haven't seen you in ages!* And after that it would have been just a matter of playing it carefully and asking the right casual questions *(It's been so long, I can't even remember, what was I doing last time I saw you?)*, picking her way delicately to everything she needed to know. She had been no dummy, this girl.

Plenty of murder cases turn into knock-down-drag-out battles of wits, but this was different. This was the first time I had felt like my real opponent wasn't the murderer but the victim: defiant, clenching her secrets white-knuckle tight, and evenly, perfectly matched against me in every way, too close to call.

By Saturday lunchtime I had made myself nuts enough that I climbed up on the kitchen counter, took down my Official Stuff shoebox from the top of a cupboard, dumped the documents on the floor and went through them for my birth cert. Maddox, Cassandra Jeanne, female, six pounds ten ounces. Type of birth: single.

"Idiot," I said, out loud, and climbed back up on the counter.

That afternoon, Frank called round. At this stage I was so stir-crazy—my flat is small, I'd run out of stuff to clean— that I was actually glad to hear his voice over the intercom.

"What year is it?" I asked, when he reached the top of the stairs. "Who's the president?"

"Quit bitching," he said, giving me a one-armed hug around the neck. "You've got this whole lovely flat to play in. You could be a sniper stuck in a hide, not moving a muscle for days on end and pissing into a bottle. And I brought you supplies."

He handed me a plastic bag. All the main food groups: chocolate biscuits, smokes, ground coffee and two bottles of wine. "You're a gem, Frank," I said. "You know me too well." He did, too; four years on, and he had remembered I like Lucky Strike Lights. The feeling wasn't a reassuring one, but then he hadn't intended it to be.

Frank raised a noncommittal eyebrow. "Got a corkscrew?"

My antennae went up, but I can hold my booze fairly well, and Frank had to know I wasn't stupid enough to get drunk with him. I threw him a corkscrew and rummaged for glasses.

"Nice place you've got here," he said, going to work on the first bottle. "I was scared I'd find you in some foul yuppie apartment with chrome surfaces."

"On a cop's salary?" Dublin housing prices are a lot like New York ones, except that in New York, you get New York for your money. My flat is one mid-sized room, on the top floor of a tall converted Georgian house. It has the original wrought-iron fireplace, enough room for a futon and a sofa and all my books, a tipsy slant to the floor in one corner, a family of owls living in the roof space, and a view of Sandymount beach. I like it.

"On two cops' salaries. Aren't you going out with our boy Sammy?"

I sat on the futon and held out the glasses for him to pour. "Only for a couple of months. We're not at the living-in-sin stage yet."

"I thought it was longer. He seemed pretty protective on Thursday. Is it true love?"

"None of your business," I said, clinking my glass against his. "Cheers. Now: what are you doing here?"

Frank looked injured. "I thought you could use the company. I got to feeling guilty about leaving you stuck here, all on your own . . ." I gave him a dirty look; he realized it wasn't working and grinned. "You're too smart for your own good, do you know that? I didn't want you getting hungry, or bored, or desperate for a smoke, and heading out to the shop. The odds are a thousand to one against you being spotted by anyone who knows our girl, but why take chances?"

This was plausible enough, but Frank has always had a habit of tossing lures in a few directions at once to distract you from the hook in the middle. "I've still got no intention of doing this, Frankie," I said.

"Fair enough," Frank said, unperturbed. He took a big swig of his wine and settled himself more comfortably on the sofa. "I had a chat with the brass, by the way, and this is now officially a joint investigation: Murder and Undercover. But your boyfriend probably already told you that."

He hadn't. Sam had stayed at his own place the last couple of nights ("I'll be up at six, sure, no reason you should be as well. Unless you need me to come over? Will you be OK on your own?"); I hadn't seen him since the murder scene. "I'm sure everyone's delighted," I said. Joint investigations are a pain in the hole. They always end up getting spectacularly bogged down in endless, pointless testosterone competitions.

Frank shrugged. "They'll survive. Want to hear what we've got on this girl so far?"

Of course I did. I wanted it the way an alcoholic must want booze: badly enough to shove aside the hard knowledge that this was a truly lousy idea. "You might as well tell me," I said. "Since you're here."

"Beautiful," Frank said, rummaging through the plastic bag for the cigarettes. "OK: she first shows up in February 2002, when she pulls Alexandra Madison's birth cert and uses it to open a bank account. She uses the birth cert, an account statement and her face to pull your old records from UCD, and she uses those to get into Trinity, to do a PhD in English."

"Organized," I said.

"Oh yeah. Organized, creative and persuasive. She was a natural at this; I couldn't have done it better myself. She never tried to sign on the dole, which was smart; just got herself a job in a café in town, worked there full-time for the summer, then started at Trinity come October. Her thesis title is—you'll like this—'Other Voices: Identity, Conceal-ment and Truth.' It's about women who wrote under other identities."

"Cute," I said. "So she had a sense of humor."

Frank gave me a quizzical look. "We don't have to like her, babe," he said, after a moment. "We just have to find out who killed her."

"You do. I don't. Got anything else?"

He flipped a smoke between his lips and found his lighter. "OK, so she's in Trinity. She makes friends with four other English postgrads, hangs out almost exclusively with them. Last September, one of them inherits a house from his great-uncle, and they all move into it. Whitethorn House, it's called. It's outside Glenskehy, just over half a mile from where she was found. On Wednesday night, she goes for a walk and never comes home. The other four alibi each other."

"Which you could have told me over the phone," I said.

"Ah," Frank said, rummaging in his jacket pocket, "but I couldn't have shown you these. Here we go: the Fantastic Four. Her housemates." He pulled out a handful of photos and spread them on the table.

One of them was a snapshot, taken on a winter day, thin gray sky and a sprinkle of snow on the ground: five people in front of a big Georgian house, heads tilted together and hair blown sideways in a swirl of wind. Lexie was in the middle, bundled in that same peacoat and laughing, and my mind did that wild lurch and swerve again: *When was I . . . ?* Frank was watching me like a hunting dog. I put the photo down.

The other shots were stills pulled off some kind of home video—they had that look, blurry edges where people were moving—and printed out in the Murder squad room: the printer always leaves a streak across the top right corner.

Four full-length shots, four blown-up head shots, all taken in the same room against the same ratty wallpaper striped with tiny flowers. There was a huge fir tree, no decorations, caught in the corner of two of the shots: just before Christmas.

"Daniel March," Frank said, pointing. "Not Dan, not God forbid Danny: Daniel. He's the one who inherited the house. Only child, orphaned, from an old Anglo-Irish family. Grandfather lost most of their money in dodgy deals in the fifties, but there's enough left to give Danny Boy a small income. He's on a scholarship, so he doesn't have fees to pay. Doing a PhD on, I kid you not, the inanimate object as narrator in early medieval epic poetry."

"No idiot, then," I said. Daniel was a big guy, well over six foot and built to match, with glossy dark hair and a square jaw. He was sitting in a wingbacked chair, delicately lifting a glass bauble out of its box and glancing up at the camera. His clothes—white shirt, black trousers, soft gray sweater—looked expensive. In the close-up his eyes, behind steel-rimmed glasses, were gray and cool as stone.

"Definitely no idiot. None of them are, but especially not him. You'll need to watch your step around that one."

I ignored that. "Justin Mannering," Frank said, moving on. Justin had got himself wound up in a snarl of white Christmas lights and was giving them a helpless look. He was tall, too, but in a narrow, prematurely professorial way: short mousy hair already starting to recede, little rimless glasses, long gentle face. "From Belfast. Doing his PhD on sacred and profane love in Renaissance literature, whatever profane love may be; sounds to me like it would cost a couple of quid a minute. Mother died when he was seven, father remarried, two half brothers, Justin doesn't go home much. But Daddy—Daddy's a lawyer—still pays his fees and sends money every month. Nice for some, eh?"

"They can't help it if their parents have money," I said absently.

"They could get a bloody job, couldn't they? Lexie gave

tutorials, marked papers, invigilated exams—she worked in a café, till they moved out to Glenskehy and the commute got too complicated. Didn't you work in college?"

"I waited tables in a pub, and it sucked. No way would I have done it if I'd had any choice. Getting your arse pinched by drunk accountants doesn't necessarily make you a better person."

Frank shrugged. "I don't like people who get everything for free. Speaking of whom: Raphael Hyland, goes by Rafe. Sarky little fucker. Daddy's a merchant banker, originally from Dublin, moved to London in the seventies; Mummy's a socialite. They divorced when he was six, dumped him straight into boarding school, moved him every couple of years when Daddy got another raise and could afford to trade up. *Rafe* lives off his trust fund. Doing his PhD on the malcontent in Jacobean drama."

Rafe was stretched out on a sofa with a glass of wine and a Santa hat, being purely ornamental and doing it well. He was ridiculously beautiful, in that way that makes a lot of guys feel a panicky urge to come out with snide comments in their deepest voices. He was the same general height and build as Justin, but his face was all bones and dangerous curves, and he was gold all over: heavy dark-blond hair, that skin that always looks faintly tanned, long iced-tea eyes hooded like a hawk's. He was like a mask from some Egyptian prince's tomb.

"Wow," I said. "All of a sudden this gig looks more tempting."

"If you're good, I won't tell your fella you said that. The guy's probably a bender anyway," Frank said, with crashing predictability. "Last but not least: Abigail Stone. Goes by Abby."

Abby wasn't pretty, exactly—small, with shoulder-length brown hair and a snub nose—but there was something about her face: the quirk of her eyebrows and the twist of her mouth gave her a quizzical air that made you want to look twice. She was sitting in front of a turf fire, threading popcorn for garlands, but she was giving the cameraperson—Lexie, presumably—a wry look, and the blur of her free hand made me think she had just whipped a piece of popcorn at the camera.

"She's a very different story," Frank said. "From Dublin, father was never on the scene, mother dumped her in foster care when she was ten. Abby aced her Leaving Cert, got into Trinity, worked her arse off and came out with a first. PhD on social class in Victorian literature. Used to pay her way by cleaning offices and tutoring schoolkids in English; now that she doesn't have rent to pay—Daniel doesn't charge them—she picks up a few bob giving tutorials in college and helping her professor with research. You'll get on."

Even caught off guard like that, the four of them made you want to keep looking. Partly it was the sheer luminous perfection of it all—I could practically smell gingerbread baking and hear carolers in the background, they were about one robin redbreast away from a greeting card. Partly it was the way they dressed, austere, almost Puritan: the guys' shirts dazzling white, knife creases in their trousers, Abby's long woolen skirt tucked demurely round her knees, not a logo or a slogan in sight. Back when I was a student, all our clothes always looked as if they had been washed once too often in a dodgy laundrette with off-brand detergent, which they had. These guys were so pristine it was almost eerie. Separately they might have looked subdued, even boring, in the middle of Dublin's orgy of designer-label self-expression, but together: they had a cool, challenging quadruple gaze that made them not just eccentric but alien, something from another century, remote and formidable. Like most detectives—and Frank knew this, of course he did—I've never been able to look away from anything that I can't figure out.

"They're quite a bunch," I said.

"They're a weird bunch, is what they are, according to the rest of the English department. The four of them met when they started college, almost seven years ago now. Been inseparable ever since; no time for anyone else. They're not particularly popular in the department—the other students think they're up themselves, amazingly enough. But somehow our girl got in with them, almost as soon as she started at Trinity. Other people tried to make friends with her, but she wasn't interested. She'd set her sights on this lot."

I could see why, and I warmed towards her, just a little. Whatever else about this girl, she hadn't had cheap taste. "What have you told them?"

Frank grinned. "Once she got to the cottage and passed out, the shock and the cold sent her into a hypothermic coma. That slowed down her heartbeat—so anyone who found her could easily have thought she was dead, right?—stopped the blood loss and prevented organ damage. Cooper says it's 'clinically ludicrous, but quite possibly plausible to those with no medical knowledge,' which is fine by me. So far no one seems to have a problem with it."

He lit up and blew smoke rings at the ceiling. "She's still unconscious and it's touch and go, but she might well pull through. You never know."

I wasn't about to rise to that. "They'll want to see her," I said.

"They already asked. Unfortunately, due to security concerns, we are unable to disclose her location at this time."

He was enjoying this. "How'd they take it?" I asked.

Frank thought about that for a while, head leaned back on the sofa, smoking slowly. "Shaken up," he said at last, "naturally enough. But there's no way of knowing whether they're all four shaky because she got stabbed, or whether one of them's shaky because she might come round and tell us what happened. They're very helpful, answer all our questions, no reluctance, nothing like that; it's only afterwards that you realize they haven't actually told you very much at all. They're an odd bunch, Cass; hard to read. I'd love to see what you make of them."

I swept the photos into a pile and passed them back to

Frank. "OK," I said. "Why did you need to come over and show me these, again?"

He shrugged, all wide innocent blue eyes. "To see if you recognized any of them. That could give a whole different angle—"

"I don't. Come clean, Frankie. What do you want?"

Frank sighed. He tapped the photos methodically on the table, aligning the edges, and tucked them back into his jacket pocket.

"I want to know," he said quietly, "if I'm wasting my time here. I need to know if you're one hundred percent sure that what you want is to go back into work on Monday morning, to DV, and forget this ever happened."

All the laughter and façade had gone out of his voice, and I knew Frank well enough to know that this was when he was most dangerous. "I'm not sure I have the option of forgetting about it," I said, carefully. "This thing's thrown me for a loop. I don't like it, and I don't want to get involved."

"You're sure about that? Because I've been working my arse off these last two days, pumping everyone in sight for every detail of Lexie Madison's life—"

"Which would've needed doing anyway. Quit guilt-tripping me."

"—and if you're absolutely positive, then there's no point in you wasting any more of your time and mine by humoring me."

"You wanted me to humor you," I pointed out. "Just for three days, no commitment, blah blah blah."

He nodded, thoughtfully. "And that's all you've been doing here: humoring me. You're happy in DV. You're sure."

The truth is that Frank had—it's a talent—hit a nerve. Maybe it was seeing him again, his grin and the fast rhythms of his voice snapping me straight back to when this job looked so shiny and fine I just wanted to take a running leap and dive in. Maybe it was the fizz of spring in the air, tugging at me; maybe it was just that I've never been any good at staying miserable for any length of time. But whatever the reason, I felt like I was awake for the first time in months, and suddenly the thought of going into DV on Monday—though I had no intention of telling Frank this—made me itch all over. I was working with this Kerryman called Maher who wore golf sweaters and thought any non-Irish accent was a source of endless amusement and breathed through his mouth when he typed, and all of a sudden I wasn't sure I could make it through another hour of his company without throwing my stapler at his head.

"What's that got to do with this case?" I asked.

Frank shrugged, stubbed out his cigarette. "Just curious. The Cassie Maddox I knew wouldn't have been happy on some nice safe nine-to-five she could do in her sleep. That's all."

Suddenly and fiercely, I wanted Frank out of my flat. He made it feel too small, crowded and dangerous. "Yeah, well," I said, picking up the wineglasses and taking them over to the sink. "Long time no see."

"Cassie," Frank said behind me, in his gentlest voice. "What happened to you?"

"I found Jesus Christ as my Personal Savior," I said, slamming the glasses into the sink, "and he doesn't approve of fucking with people's heads. I got a brain transplant, I got mad cow disease, I got stabbed and I got older and I got sense, you can call it whatever you like, I don't *know* what happened, Frank. All I know is I want some bloody peace and quiet in my life for a change, and this fucked-up case and this fucked-up idea of yours are unlikely to give me it. OK?"

"Hey, fair enough," Frank said, in an equable voice that made me feel like an idiot. "It's your call. But if I promise not to go on about the case, can I get another glass of wine?"

My hands were shaking. I turned on the tap hard and didn't answer.

"We can catch up. Like you said, long time no see. We'll bitch about the weather, I'll show you photos of my kid and you can tell me all about your new fella. What happened to Whatsisname who you were seeing before, the barrister? I always thought he was a little square for you."

Undercover happened to Aidan. He dumped me when I kept breaking appointments, wouldn't tell him why and wouldn't tell him what I did all day. He said I cared more about the job than about him. I rinsed out the glasses and shoved them onto the draining rack.

"Unless you need time on your own, to think this over," Frank added, solicitously. "I can understand that. It's a big decision."

I couldn't help it: after a second, I laughed. Frank can be a little bollocks when he feels like it. If I threw him out now, it would be as good as saying I was considering his wacko idea. "OK," I said. "Fine. Have all the wine you want. But if you mention this case once more, I'm going to give you a dead arm. Fair enough?"

"Beautiful," Frank said happily. "Usually I have to pay for that kind of thing."

"For you, I'll do freebies any time." I threw the glasses back to him, one by one. He dried them on his shirt and reached for the wine bottle.

"So," he said. "What's our Sammy like in the scratcher?"

We finished off the first bottle and got started on the second. Frank gave me the Undercover gossip, the stuff that other squads never hear. I knew exactly what he was doing, but it still felt good, hearing the names again, the jargon, the dangerous in-jokes and the fast, truncated professional rhythms. We played do-you-remember: the time I was at a party and Frank needed to get me some piece of info, so he sent another agent to play the rejected suitor and do a Stanley Kowalski under the window (*"Lexiiiiiie!"*) until I came out; the time we were having an update session on a bench in Merrion Square and I saw someone from college heading our way, so I called Frank an old pervert at the top of my lungs and flounced off. I realized that, whether I wanted to or not, I was enjoying having Frank there. I used to have people over all the time—friends, my old partner, sprawled on the sofa and staying up too late, music in the background and everyone a little tipsy—but it had been a long time since anyone but Sam had been to my flat, a longer time since I had laughed like this, and it felt good.

"You know," Frank said meditatively, a lot later, squinting into his glass, "you still haven't said no."

I didn't have the energy to get annoyed. "Have I said anything that sounds remotely like a yes?" I inquired.

He snapped his fingers. "Here, I've got an idea. There's a case meeting tomorrow evening. Why don't you come along? That might help you decide whether you want in."

And bingo, there it was: the hook in the middle of the lures, the real agenda behind all the chocolate biscuits and updates and concern for my emotional health. "Jesus, Frank," I said. "Do you realize how obvious you are?"

Frank grinned, not the least bit shamefaced. "You can't blame a guy for trying. Seriously, you should come. The floaters don't start till Monday morning, so it'll basically be just me and Sam, having a chat about what we've got. Aren't you curious?"

Of course I was. All Frank's info hadn't told me the one thing I wanted to know: what this girl had been like. I leaned my head back on the futon and lit another smoke. "Do you seriously think we could pull this off?" I asked.

Frank considered this. He poured himself another glass of wine and waved the bottle at me; I shook my head. "Under normal circumstances," he said at last, settling back into the sofa, "I'd say probably not. But these aren't normal circumstances, and we've got a couple of things in our favor, besides the obvious. For one thing, to all intents and purposes, this girl only existed for three years. It's not like you'd have to deal with a lifetime's worth of history here. You don't have to get by parents or siblings, you're not going to run into some childhood friend, nobody's going to ask you if you remember your first school dance. For another thing, during those three years, her life seems to have been pretty tightly circumscribed: she ran with one small crowd, studied in one small department, held down one job. You don't need to get the hang of wide circles of family and friends and colleagues."

"She was doing a PhD in English literature," I pointed out. "I know zip about English literature, Frank. I got an A in my Leaving Cert, but that's it. I don't speak the jargon."

Frank shrugged. "Neither did Lexie, as far as we know, and she managed to pull it off. If she can do it, so can you. Again, we're in luck there: she could've been doing pharmacy, or engineering. And if you get sweet fuck-all done on her thesis, well, hey, what do they expect? Ironically enough, that stab wound's going to come in useful: we can give you post-traumatic stress, amnesia, whatever we fancy."

"Any boyfriend?" There is a limit to what I'm prepared to do for the job.

"No, so your virtue is safe. And the other thing working for us: you know those photos? Our girl had a video phone, and it looks like the five of them used it as the group camcorder. The image quality's not brilliant, but she had a whacking great memory card and it's packed with clips— her and her mates on nights out, on picnics, moving into their new gaff, doing it up, everything. So you've got a ready-made guide to her voice, her body language, mannerisms, the tone of the relationships—everything a girl could ask for. And you're good, Cassie. You're a damn fine undercover. Put it all together, and I'd say we're in with a pretty good chance of pulling this off."

He tipped up the glass to get the last drops and reached for his jacket. "Been fun catching up, babe. You have my mobile number. Let me know what you decide about tomorrow night."

And he let himself out. It was only as the door shut behind him that I realized what I had slipped into asking:

What about college, any boyfriend? as if I were checking the plan for holes; as if I were thinking about doing it.

Frank's always had a knack for knowing exactly when to leave it. After he'd gone, I sat on the windowsill for a long time, staring out over the rooftops without seeing them. It was only when I got up for another glass of wine that I realized he had left something on my coffee table.

It was the photo of Lexie and her mates in front of Whitethorn House. I stood there, with the wine bottle in one hand and my glass in the other, and thought about turning it face down and leaving it there till Frank gave up and came back for it; thought, for a minute, about sticking it in an ashtray and burning it. Then I picked it up and brought it back to the windowsill with me.

She could have been any age. She had been passing for twenty-six, but I would have believed nineteen, or thirty. There wasn't a mark on her face, not a line or a scar or a chicken-pox blemish. Whatever life had thrown at her before Lexie Madison fell into her lap, it had rolled over her and burned off like mist, left her untouched and pristine, sealed without a crack. I looked older than her: Operation Vestal gave me my first lines around my eyes, and shadows that don't go away with a good night's sleep. I could practically hear Frank: *You lost a shitload of blood and you've been in a coma for days, the eye bags are perfect, don't go using night cream.*

At her shoulders the housemates watched me, poised and smiling, long dark coats billowing and Rafe's scarf a flash of crimson. The angle of the shot was a little off-kilter; they had propped the camera on something, used a timer. There was no photographer on the other side telling them to say cheese. Those smiles were private things, just for one another, for their someday selves looking back, for me.

And behind them, almost filling the shot, Whitethorn

House. It was a simple house: a wide gray Georgian, three stories, with the sash windows getting smaller as they went up, to give the illusion of even more height. The door was deep blue, paint peeling away in big patches; a flight of stone steps led up to it on either side. Three neat rows of chimney pots, thick drifts of ivy sweeping up the walls almost to the roof. The door had fluted columns and a peacock's-tail fanlight, but apart from that there was no decoration; just the house.

This country's passion for property is built into the blood, a current as huge and primal as desire. Centuries of being turned out on the roadside at a landlord's whim, help-less, teach your bones that everything in life hangs on own-ing your home. This is why house prices are what they are: property developers know they can charge half a million for a one-bedroom dive; if they band together and make sure there's no other choice the Irish will sell a kidney, work hundred-hour weeks and pay it. Somehow—maybe it's the French blood—that gene missed me. The thought of a mortgage round my neck makes me edgy. I like the fact that my flat is rented, four weeks' notice and a couple of bin lin-ers and I could be gone any time I choose.

If I had ever wanted a house, though, it would have been a lot like this one. This had nothing in common with the characterless pseudohouses all my friends were buying, shrunken middle-of-nowhere shoeboxes that come with great spurts of sticky euphemisms ("architect-designed bijou residence in brand-new luxury community") and sell for twenty times your income and are built to last just till the developer can get them off his hands. This was the real thing, one serious do-not-fuck-with-me house with the strength and pride and grace to outlast everyone who saw it. Tiny swirling flecks of snow blurred the ivy and hung in the dark windows, and the silence of it was so huge that I felt like I could put my hand straight through the glossy surface of the photo and down into its cool depths.

I could find out who this girl was and what had happened

to her without ever going in there. Sam would tell me when they got an ID or a suspect; probably he would even let me watch the interrogation. But right at the bottom of me I knew that was all he would ever get, her name and her killer, and I would be left to wonder about everything else for the rest of my life. That house shimmered in my mind like some fairy fort that appeared for one day in a lifetime, tantalizing and charged, with those four cool figures for guardians and inside secrets too hazy to be named. My face was the one pass that would unbar the door. Whitethorn House was ready and waiting to whisk itself away to nothing, the instant I said no.

I realized the photo was about three inches from my nose; I had been sitting there long enough that it was getting dark, the owls doing their warm-up exercises above the ceiling. I finished off the wine and watched the sea turn thunder-colored, the blink of the lighthouse far off on the horizon. When I figured I was drunk enough not to care if he gloated, I texted Frank: *What time is that meeting?*

My phone beeped about ten seconds later: *7 sharp, see you there.* He had had his mobile ready to hand, waiting for me to say yes.

That evening Sam and I had our first fight. This was probably overdue, given that we had been going out for three months without even a mild disagreement, but the timing sucked all round.

Sam and I got together a few months after I left Murder. I'm not sure exactly how that happened. I don't remember a whole lot about that period; I appear to have bought a couple of truly depressing sweaters, the kind you only wear when all you really want is to curl up under the bed for several years, which occasionally made me wonder about the wisdom of any relationship I had acquired around the same time. Sam and I had got close on Operation Vestal, stayed that way after the walls came tumbling down—the nightmare cases do that to you, that or the opposite—and long before the case ended I had decided he was pure gold, but a relationship, with anyone, was the last thing I had in mind.

He got to my place around nine. "Hi, you," he said, giving me a kiss and a full-on hug. His cheek was cold from the wind outside. "Something smells good."

The flat smelled of tomatoes and garlic and herbs. I had a complicated sauce simmering and water boiling and a huge packet of ravioli at the ready, going by the same principle women have followed since the dawn of time: if you have something to tell him that he doesn't want to hear, make sure there is food. "I'm being domesticated," I told him. "I cleaned and everything. Hi, honey, how was your day?"

"Ah, sure," Sam said vaguely. "We'll get there in the end." As he pulled off his coat, his eyes went to the coffee table: wine bottles, corks, glasses. "Have you been seeing fancy men behind my back?"

"Frank," I said. "Not very fancy."

The laughter went out of Sam's face. "Oh," he said. "What did he want?"

I had been hoping to save this for after dinner. For a detective, my crime-scene cleanup skills suck. "He wanted me to come to your case meeting tomorrow night," I said, as casually as I could, heading over to the kitchenette to check the garlic bread. "He went at it sideways, but that's what he was after."

Slowly Sam folded his coat, draped it over the back of the sofa. "What did you say?"

"I thought about it a lot," I said. "I want to go."

"He'd no right," Sam said, quietly. A red flush was starting high on his cheekbones. "Coming here behind my back, putting pressure on you when I wasn't there to—"

"I would've decided exactly the same way if you'd been standing right here," I said. "I'm a big girl, Sam. I don't need protecting."

"I don't like that fella," Sam said sharply. "I don't like the way he thinks and I don't like the way he works."

I slammed the oven door. "He's trying to solve this case. Maybe you don't agree with the way he's doing it—"

Sam shoved hair out of his eyes, hard, with his forearm. "No," he said. "No, he's not. It's not about solving the case. That fella Mackey—this case has bugger-all to do with him, no more than any other murder I've worked, and I didn't see him showing up on those ones pulling strings right and left to get in on the action. He's here for the crack, so he is. He thinks it'll be a great laugh—throwing you into the middle of a bunch of murder suspects, just because he can, and then waiting to see what happens. The man's bloody *mad*."

I pulled plates out of the cupboard. "So what if he is? All I'm doing is going to a meeting. What's the huge big deal?"

"That mentaller's using you, is the big deal. You've not been yourself since that business last year—"

The words sent something straight through me, a swift vicious jolt like the shock from an electric fence. I whipped round on him, forgetting all about dinner; all I wanted to do with the plates was throw them at Sam's head. "Oh, no. Don't, Sam. Don't bring that into this."

"It's already in it. Your man Mackey took one look at you and he knew something was up, figured he'd have no problem pushing you into going along with his mad idea—"

The possessiveness of him, standing in the middle of my floor with his feet planted and his fists jammed furiously in his pockets: *my* case, *my* woman. I banged the plates down on the counter. "I don't give a flying fuck what he figured, he's not pushing me into anything. This has nothing to do with what Frank wants—it's got nothing to do with Frank, full stop. Sure, he tried to bulldoze me. I told him to fuck off."

"You're doing exactly what he asks you to. How the hell is that telling him to fuck off?"

For a crazy second I wondered if he could actually be jealous of Frank and, if he was, what the hell I was supposed to do about it. "And if I don't go to the meeting, I'll be doing exactly what you ask me to. Would that mean I'm letting you push me around? *I* decided I wanted to go tomorrow. You think I'm not able to do that all by myself? Jesus Christ, Sam, last year didn't *lobotomize* me!"

"That's not what I said. I'm just saying you haven't been yourself since—"

"This is myself, Sam. Take a good look: this is my fucking self. I did undercover *years* before Operation Vestal ever came along. So leave that out of it."

We stared at each other. After a moment Sam said, quietly, "Yeah. Yeah, I suppose you did."

He dropped down on the sofa and ran his hands over his face. All of a sudden he looked wrecked, and the thought of what his day had been like sent a pang through me. "Sorry," he said. "For bringing that up."

"I'm not trying to get into an argument," I said. My knees were shaking and I had no idea how we had ended up fighting about this, when we were basically on the same side. "Just . . . leave it, OK? Please, Sam. I'm asking you."

"Cassie," Sam said. His round, pleasant face had a look of anguish that didn't belong there. "I can't *do* this. What if . . . God. What if something happens to you? On my case, that had nothing to do with you. Because I couldn't bloody well get my man. I can't live with that. I can't."

He sounded breathless, winded. I didn't know whether to hold him tight or kick him. "What makes you think this has nothing to do with me?" I demanded. "This girl is my double, Sam. This girl was going around wearing my fucking face. How do you know your guy got the right one? Think about it. A postgrad who spends her time reading Charlotte bloody Brontë, or a detective who's put dozens of people away: who's more likely to have someone out to kill her?"

There was a silence. Sam had worked on Operation Vestal, too. Both of us knew at least one person who would happily have had me killed without a second thought, and who was well able to get the job done. I could feel my heart banging, hard and high under my ribs.

Sam said, "Are you thinking—"

"Specific cases aren't the point," I said, too curtly. "The point is, for all we know I could be involved up to my tits already. And I don't want to be looking over my shoulder for the rest of my life. *I* can't live with *that*."

He flinched. "It wouldn't be for the rest of your life," he said, quietly. "I hope I can promise you that much, at least. I do plan to get this fella, you know."

I leaned back against the counter and took a breath. "I know, Sam," I said. "I'm sorry. I didn't mean it that way."

"If, God forbid, he was after you, then all the more reason to stay out of the way and let me find him."

The cheerful cooking smell had grown an acrid, dangerous edge: something was starting to burn. I switched off the cooker, shoved the pans to the back—neither of us was going to feel like eating for a while—and sat down cross-legged on the sofa, facing Sam.

"You're treating me like your girlfriend, Sam," I said. "I'm not your girlfriend, not when it comes to this kind of thing. I'm just another detective."

He gave me a sad, sideways little smile. "Could you not be both?"

"I hope so," I said. I wished I hadn't finished the wine; this man needed a drink. "I really do. But not like this."

After a while Sam let out a long breath, let his head fall back against the sofa. "So you want to do it," he said. "Mackey's plan."

"*No,*" I said. "I just want to know about this girl. That's why I said I'd go to the meeting. It's got nothing to do with Frank and his wacko idea. I just want to hear about her."

"*Why?*" Sam demanded. He sat up and caught both my hands, making me look at him. There was a ragged edge to his voice, something frustrated and almost pleading. "What's she got to do with you? She's no relation to you, no friend of yours, nothing. She's *happenstance,* is all, Cassie: some girl who was looking for a new life and ran into the perfect chance."

"I know," I said. "I know, Sam. She doesn't even sound like a particularly nice person; if we'd met, I probably wouldn't have liked her. That's the whole point. I don't want her in my head. I don't want to be wondering about her. I'm hoping that if I find out enough about her, I can drop the whole thing and forget she ever existed."

"I've a double," Sam said. "He lives in Wexford, he's an engineer, and that's all I know about the man. About once a year, someone comes up to me and tells me I'm the spit of him—half the time they actually call me Brendan. We have a laugh about it, sometimes they take a photo of me on their phones to show him, and that's the end of that."

I shook my head. "That's different."

"How?"

"For one thing, he hasn't been murdered."

"No harm to the man," Sam said, "but I wouldn't give a damn if he were. Unless I caught the case, it'd be no problem of mine."

"This girl's my problem," I said. Sam's hands were big and warm and solid around mine, and his hair was falling across his forehead like it always does when he's worried. It was a spring Saturday night; we should have been walking on some beach down the country, surrounded by dark and waves and curlews, or making something experimental for dinner and playing music too loud, or settled in a corner of one of those rare out-of-the-way pubs where people still sing ballads when it gets past closing time. "I wish she wasn't, but she is."

"There's something here," Sam said, "that I'm not getting." He had let our hands drop onto my knees and was frowning down at them, running his thumb around one of my knuckles in a steady, automatic rhythm. "All I'm seeing is a bog-standard murder case, with a coincidence that could happen to anyone. Sure, I got a shock when I saw her, but that's only because I thought it was you. Once that was sorted, I figured everything would go back to normal. But you and Mackey, you're both acting like this girl was something to you; like it's personal. What am I missing?"

"In a way," I said, "it is personal, yeah. For Frank, partly it's exactly what you said—he thinks this would all be a big brilliant adventure. But it's more than that. Lexie Madison started out as his responsibility, she was his responsibility for eight months while I was under, she's his responsibility now."

"But this girl *isn't* Lexie Madison. She's an identity thief; I could go down to Fraud in the morning and find you hundreds more just like her. There is no Lexie Madison. You and Mackey made her *up*."

His hands had tightened on mine. "I know," I said. "That's sort of the point."

The corner of Sam's mouth twisted. "Like I said. The man's mad."

I didn't exactly disagree with him. I've always thought one of the reasons for Frank's legendary fearlessness is that, way deep down, he's never quite managed to connect with reality. To him every operation is one of those war games the Pentagon plays, only even cooler, because the stakes are higher and the results are tangible and long-lasting. The fracture is small enough and he's smart enough that it never shows in obvious ways; but, while he's keeping every angle covered and every situation beautifully, icily under control, some part of him truly believes he's being played by Sean Connery.

I spotted this because I recognize it. My own border fence between real and not-real has never been all that great. My friend Emma, who likes things to add up neatly, claims that this is because my parents died when I was too young to take it in: they were there one day and gone the next, crashing through that fence so hard and fast they left it splintered for good. When I was Lexie Madison for eight months she turned into a real person to me, a sister I lost or left behind on the way; a shadow somewhere inside me, like the shadows of vanishing twins that show up on people's X-rays once in a blue moon. Even before she came back to find me I knew I owed her something, for being the one who lived.

This was presumably not what Sam wanted to hear; he had enough on his plate without adding several new flavors of weird into the mix. Instead—it was the closest I could get—I tried to tell him about undercover. I told him how your senses are never quite the same again, how colors turn fierce enough to brand you and the air tastes bright and jagged as that clear liqueur filled with tiny flakes of gold; how the way you walk changes, your balance turns fine and taut as a surfer's, when you spend every second on the shifting edge of a fast risky wave. I told him how afterwards I never shared a spliff with my mates or took E in a club again, because no high could ever compare. I told him how damn good at it I was, a natural, better than I'll be at DV in a million years.

When I finished, Sam was looking at me with a worried little furrow between his eyebrows. "What are you saying?" he asked. "Are you saying you want to transfer back into Undercover?"

He had taken his hands off mine. I looked at him, sitting across the sofa with his hair rucked up on one side, frowning at me. "No," I said, "that's not it," and watched his face clear in relief. "That's not it at all."

This is the part I didn't tell Sam: bad stuff happens to undercovers. A few of them get killed. Most lose friends, marriages, relationships. A couple turn feral, cross over to the other side so gradually that they never see it happening till it's too late, and end up with discreet, complicated early-retirement plans. Some, and never the ones you'd think, lose their nerve—no warning, they just wake up one morning and all at once it hits them what they're doing, and they freeze like tightrope walkers who've looked down. This guy

McCall: he'd infiltrated an IRA splinter group and nobody thought he even knew what fear was, till one evening he phoned in from an alleyway outside a pub. He couldn't go back in there, he said, and he couldn't walk away because his legs wouldn't stop shaking. He was crying. *Come get me,* he said; *I want to go home.* When I met him, he was working in Records. And some go the other way, the most lethal way of all: when the pressure gets to be too much, it's not their nerve that breaks, it's their fear. They lose the capacity to be afraid, even when they should be. These can't ever go home again. They're like those First World War airmen, the finest ones, shining in their recklessness and invincible, who got home and found that home had no place for what they were. Some people are undercovers all the way to the bone; the job has taken them whole.

I was never afraid of getting killed and I was never afraid of losing my nerve. My kind of courage holds up best under fire; it's different dangers, more refined and insidious ones, that shake me. But the other things: I worried about those. Frank told me once—and I don't know whether he's right or not, and I didn't tell Sam this either—that all the best undercovers have a dark thread woven into them, some-where.

3

So, on Sunday evening, Sam and I went to Dublin Castle for Frank's council of war. Dublin Castle is where the Murder squad works. I had cleared out my desk there on another long cool evening, in autumn: stacked my paperwork in neat piles and labeled each pile with a Post-it, thrown away the cartoons stuck to my computer and the chewed pens and old Christmas cards and stale M&Ms in my desk drawers, turned off the light and closed the door behind me.

Sam picked me up. He was very quiet. He had been up and out early that morning, so early that the flat was still dark when he leaned over to kiss me good-bye. I didn't ask him about the case. If he had found anything good, even the slimmest lead, he would have told me.

"Don't let your man pressure you," he said, in the car. "Into doing anything you don't want to."

"Come on," I said. "When have I ever let anyone pressure me into anything?"

Sam adjusted his rearview mirror, carefully. "Yeah," he said. "I know."

When he unlocked the door, the smell of the building came at me like a shout: an old, elusive smell, damp and smoke and lemon, nothing like the antiseptic tang of DV in the new building up in Phoenix Park. I hate nostalgia, it's laziness with prettier accessories, but every step hit me straight in the gut with something: me running down those stairs with a bunch of files in each hand and an apple caught between my teeth, my partner and me high-fiving each other outside that door after getting our first confession in that interview room; the two of us double-teaming the superintendent down that hallway, one in each ear, trying to hassle him into giving us more overtime. It seemed like the corridors had an Escher look, the walls all tilting in subtle, seasick ways, but I couldn't focus my eyes enough to figure out exactly how.

"How're you doing?" Sam asked quietly.

"Starving," I said. "Whose idea was it to do this at dinnertime?"

Sam smiled, relieved, and gave my hand a quick squeeze. "We don't have an incident room yet," he said. "Till we decide . . . well, how we're doing this; where we're working out of." Then he opened the door of the Murder squad room.

Frank was straddling a backwards chair at the head of the room, in front of the big whiteboard, and all his reassurances about a casual chat between him and me and Sam had been bollocks. Cooper, the state pathologist, and O'Kelly, the superintendent of the Murder squad, were sitting at desks on opposite sides of the room with their arms folded, wearing identical narky looks. This should have been funny—Cooper looks like a heron and O'Kelly looks like a bulldog with a comb-over—but actually it gave me a very bad feeling. Cooper and O'Kelly hate each other; getting them in the same room for any length of time takes a lot of skilled persuasion and a couple of bottles of pretty serious wine. For some cryptic reason of his own, Frank had pulled out all the stops to get them both there. Sam shot me a wary, warning glance. He hadn't been expecting this either.

"Maddox," O'Kelly said, managing to make it sound injured. O'Kelly never had any use for me when I was on Murder, but the second I applied for a transfer, I somehow morphed into the serpent's-tooth protégée who snubbed years of devoted mentoring and buggered off to DV. "How's life in the minor leagues?"

"All sunshine and flowers, sir," I said. When I'm tense, I get flippant. "Evening, Dr. Cooper."

"Always a pleasure, Detective Maddox," said Cooper. He ignored Sam. Cooper hates Sam, too, and more or less everyone else. I'd stayed in his good books so far, but if he discovered I was going out with Sam, I would shoot down his Christmas-card list at the speed of light.

"At least in Murder," O'Kelly said, giving my ripped jeans a fishy look—for some reason I hadn't been able to bring myself to wear my nice new appropriate-image clothes, not for this—"most of us can afford decent gear. How's Ryan getting on?"

I wasn't sure whether the question was bitchy or not. Rob Ryan used to be my partner, back in Murder. I hadn't seen him in a while. I hadn't seen O'Kelly, either, or Cooper; not since I'd transferred out. This was all happening too fast and out of control. "Sends love and kisses," I said.

"Can't say I didn't suspect," O'Kelly said, and sniggered at Sam, who looked away.

The squad room holds twenty, but it was Sunday-evening empty: computers off, desks scattered with paperwork and fast-food wrappers—the cleaners don't come in till Monday morning. In the back corner by the window, the desks where Rob and I used to sit were still at right angles, the way we liked them, so we could be shoulder to shoulder. Some other team, maybe the newbies brought in to replace us, had taken them over. Whoever was at my desk had a kid—silver-framed photo of a grinning little boy with his front teeth missing—and a pile of statement sheets, sun falling across them. It always used to get in my eyes, this time of day.

I was having a hard time breathing; the air felt too thick, almost solid. One of the fluorescents was on the fritz and it gave the room a shimmery, epileptic look, something out of a fever dream. A couple of the big binders lined up on the filing cabinets still had my handwriting down the spines. Sam pulled up his chair to his desk and glanced at me with a faint furrow between his eyebrows, but he didn't say anything, and I was grateful for that. I concentrated on Frank's face. There were bags under his eyes and he had cut himself shaving, but he looked wide awake, alert and energized. He was looking forward to this.

He caught me watching him. "Glad to be back?"

"Ecstatic," I said. I wondered, suddenly, if he had got me into this room deliberately, knowing it might throw me. I dropped my satchel on a desk—Costello's; I knew the handwriting on the paperwork—leaned back against the wall and stuck my hands in my jacket pockets.

"Companionable though this may be," Cooper said, edging a little farther from O'Kelly, "I, for one, would be delighted to come to the point of this little gathering."

"Fair enough," Frank said. "The Madison case—well, the Jane Doe alias Madison case. What's the official name?"

"Operation Mirror," Sam said. Obviously the word about the victim's looks had spread as far as headquarters. Beautiful. I wondered whether it was too late to change my mind, go home and order pizza.

Frank nodded. "Operation Mirror it is. It's been three days, and we've got no suspects, no leads and no ID. As you all know, I think it might be time to try a different tack—"

"Hold your horses there," O'Kelly said. "We'll get to your 'different tack' in a moment, don't you worry about that. But first, I've a question."

"Off you go," Frank said magnanimously, with an expansive gesture to match.

O'Kelly gave him a dirty look. There was an awful lot of testosterone circulating in this room. "Unless I'm missing something," he said, "this girl was murdered. Correct me if I'm wrong here, Mackey, but I'm not seeing any indication of domestic violence, and I'm not seeing anything that says she was undercover. Why did you people"—he jerked his chin at me and Frank—"want in on this one to begin with?"

"I didn't," I told him. "I don't."

"The victim was using an identity I created for one of my

officers," Frank said, "and I take that pretty personally. So you're stuck with me. You may or may not be stuck with Detective Maddox; that's what we're here to find out."

"I can tell you that right now," I said.

"Humor me," Frank said. "Don't tell me till I've finished. Once you've heard me out, you can tell me to fuck off all you like, and I won't say a word. Doesn't that sound like fun?"

I gave up. This is another of Frank's skills: the ability to sound like he's making a vast concession, so that you come across as an unreasonable cow if you won't meet him halfway. "Sounds like a dream date," I said.

"Fair enough?" Frank asked everyone. "At the end of this evening, you tell me to climb back in my box, and I'll never mention my little idea again. Just hear me out first. That OK with everyone?"

O'Kelly grunted noncommittally; Cooper gave a not-my-problem shrug; Sam, after a moment, nodded. I was getting that specific feeling of Frank-related impending doom.

"And before we all get too carried away," Frank said, "let's make sure the resemblance stands up to a closer look. If it doesn't, then there's no point fighting about it, is there?"

Nobody answered. He swung himself off the chair, pulled a handful of photos out of his file and started Blu-Tacking them to the whiteboard. The shot from the Trinity ID, blown up to eight by ten; the dead girl's face in profile, eye closed and bruised-looking; a full-length shot of her on the autopsy table—still dressed, thank Jesus—with her fists clenched on top of that dark star of blood; a close-up of her hands, unfurled and stippled with brownish-black, streaks of silver nail polish showing through the blood. "Cassie, could you do me a favor? Stand over here for a minute?"

You fucker, I thought. I peeled myself off the wall, went to the whiteboard and stood against it like I was having a mug shot taken. I would have bet good money that Frank had already pulled my photo from Records and compared it to these with a magnifying glass. He prefers to ask questions to which he already knows the answers.

"We should really be using the actual body for this," Frank told us cheerfully, biting a piece of Blu-Tack in half, "but I figured that might be a little weird."

"God forbid," said O'Kelly.

I wanted Rob, dammit. I had never let myself think that before, not one time in all the months since we stopped talking, no matter how tired I got or how late at night it was. At first I wanted to kick his ass so badly it was doing my head in, I was throwing things at my wall on a regular basis. So I stopped thinking about him altogether. But the squad room all round me, and the four of them peering intently as if I were some exotic forensic exhibit, and those photos so close to my cheek I could feel them; the acid-trip feeling I'd had all week was swelling into a wild, dizzying wave and I hurt, somewhere under my breastbone. I would have sold a limb to have Rob there for just one instant, raising a sardonic eyebrow at me behind O'Kelly's back, pointing out blandly that the swap would never work because the dead girl had been pretty. For a vicious second I could have sworn I smelled his aftershave.

"Eyebrows," Frank said, tapping the ID shot—I had to stop myself from jumping—"eyebrows are good. Eyes are good. Lexie's fringe is shorter, you'll need a trim; apart from that, the hair's good. Ears—turn to the side for a second?—ears are good. Yours pierced?"

"Three times," I said.

"She only had two. Let's have a look . . ." Frank leaned in. "Shouldn't be a problem. I can't even see 'em unless I'm looking for them. Nose is good. Mouth is good. Chin's good. Jawline's good." Sam blinked, a rapid flick like a wince, on every one.

"Your cheekbones and clavicles appear to be more pronounced than the victim's," Cooper said, studying me with vaguely creepy professional interest. "May I ask how much you weigh?"

I never weigh myself. "A hundred and something. Sixteen? seventeen?"

"You're a little thinner than she was," Frank said. "No
problem; a week or two of hospital food'll do that. Her
clothes are size six, jeans waist twenty-nine inches, bra size
34B, shoe size seven. All of that sound like it'll fit?"

"Near enough," I said. I wondered how the fuck my life
had ended up here. I thought about finding some magic
button that would rewind me, at lightning speed, till I was
lounging happily in the back corner kicking Rob in the leg
every time O'Kelly came out with a cliché, instead of standing here like a Muppet showing people my ears and trying
to stop my voice shaking while we discussed whether I
would fit into a dead girl's bra.

"A brand-new wardrobe," Frank told me, grinning.
"Who says this job doesn't have perks?"

"She could do with it," O'Kelly said bitchily.

Frank moved on to the full-length shot, drew a finger
down it from shoulders to feet, glancing back and forth at
me. "Build is all good, give or take the few pounds." His
finger on the photo made a long dragging squeak; Sam
shifted, sharply, in his chair. "Shoulder width looks good,
waist-to-hip ratio looks good—we can measure, just to be
sure, but the weight difference gives us a little leeway there.
Leg length looks good."

He tapped the close-up. "These are important; people
notice hands. Give us a look, Cassie?"

I held out my hands like he was going to cuff me. I
couldn't make myself look at the photo; I could barely
breathe. This was one question to which Frank couldn't
already know the answer. This could be it: the difference
that would slice me away from this girl, sever the link with
one hard final snap and let me go home.

"Those right there," Frank said appreciatively, after a
long look, "may be the loveliest hands I've ever seen."

"Extraordinary," Cooper said with relish, leaning forwards to peer at me and AnonyGirl over his glasses. "The odds must be one in millions."

"Anyone seeing any discrepancies?" Frank asked the room.

No one said anything. Sam's jaw was tight.

"Gentlemen," Frank said, with a flourish of his arm, "we have a match."

"Which doesn't necessarily mean we need to do anything with it," said Sam.

O'Kelly was doing a sarcastic slow clap. "Congratulations, Mackey. Makes a great party trick. Now that we all know what Maddox looks like, can we get back to the case?"

"And can I stop standing here?" I asked. My legs were trembling like I'd been running and I was furiously pissed off with everyone in sight, including myself. "Unless you need me for inspiration."

"You can, of course," Frank said, finding a marker for the whiteboard. "So here's what we've got. Alexandra Janet Madison, aka Lexie, registered as born in Dublin on the first of March 1979—and I should know, I registered her myself. In October 2000"—he started sketching a timeline, fast straight strokes—"she entered UCD as a psychology postgrad. In May of 2001, she dropped out of college due to stress-related illness and went to her parents in Canada to recover, and that should've been the end of her—"

"Hang on. You gave me a nervous *breakdown*?" I demanded.

"Your thesis was getting on top of you," Frank told me, grinning. "It's a tough old world, academia; you couldn't take the heat, so you got out of the kitchen. I had to get rid of you somehow."

I rearranged myself against my wall and made a face at him; he winked at me. He had played straight into this girl's hands, years before she ever came on the scene. Any slip she made when she ran into that old acquaintance and started trawling for info, any off-kilter pause, any reluctance to meet up again: *Well, you know she did have that nervous breakdown . . .*

"In February 2002, though," Frank said, switching from blue marker to red, "Alexandra Madison shows up again. She pulls her UCD records and uses them to wangle her way into Trinity to do a PhD in English. We don't have a clue who this girl actually is, what she was doing before then, or how she hit on the Lexie Madison ID. We ran her prints: she's not in the system."

"You might want to widen the net," I said. "There's a decent chance she's not Irish."

Frank glanced at me sharply. "Why's that?"

"When Irish people want to hide, they don't hang around here. They go abroad. If she was Irish, she'd have run into someone from her mammy's bingo club inside a week."

"Not necessarily. She was living a pretty isolated life."

"As well as that," I said, keeping my voice level, "I take after the French side. Nobody thinks I'm Irish, till I open my mouth. If I didn't get my looks here, odds are neither did she."

"Great," O'Kelly said, heavily. "Undercover, DV, Immigration, the Brits, Interpol, the FBI. Anyone else who might want to join the party? The Irish Countrywomen's Association? The Vincent de Paul?"

"Any chance of getting an ID off her teeth?" Sam asked. "Or a country, even? Can't you tell where dental work was done?"

"The young woman in question had excellent teeth," Cooper said. "I am not, of course, a specialist in the field, but she had no fillings, crowns, extractions or other readily identifiable work."

Frank arched an inquiring eyebrow at me. I gave him my best puzzled look.

"The two bottom front teeth overlap slightly," Cooper said, "and one top molar is significantly misaligned, imply-ing that she had no orthodontic work done as a child. I would hazard that the possibility of dental identification is practically nonexistent." Sam shook his head, frustrated, and went back to his notebook.

Frank was still eyeballing me, and it was getting on my nerves. I shoved myself off the wall, opened my mouth wide at him and pointed at my teeth. Cooper and O'Kelly gave me identical horrified looks.

"*No,* I don't have fillings," I told Frank. "See? Not that it matters anyway."

"Good girl," Frank said approvingly. "Keep flossing."

"That's lovely, Maddox," O'Kelly said. "Thanks for sharing. So in autumn of 2002 Alexandra Madison goes into Trinity, and in April 2005 she turns up murdered outside Glenskehy. Do we know what she was doing in between?"

Sam stirred and looked up, put down his pen. "Her PhD, mostly," he said. "Something to do with women writers and pseudonyms; I didn't understand the whole of it. She was doing grand, her supervisor says—a bit behind schedule, but what she came up with was good. Up until September she was living in a bedsit off the South Circular Road. She paid her way with student loans, grants, and by working in the English department and in Caffeine, in town. She had no known criminal activity, no debts except the loan for her college fees, no dodgy activity on her bank account, no addictions, no boyfriend or ex-boyfriend"— Cooper raised an eyebrow—"no enemies and no recent arguments."

"So no motive," Frank said musingly, to the whiteboard, "and no suspects."

"Her main associates," Sam said evenly, "were a bunch of other postgrads: Daniel March, Abigail Stone, Justin Mannering and Raphael Hyland."

"Bloody silly name," said O'Kelly. "He a poof, or a Brit?" Cooper closed his eyes briefly in distaste, like a cat.

"He's half English," Sam said; O'Kelly gave a smug little grunt. "Daniel has two speeding tickets, Justin has one, apart from that they're all clean as a whistle. They don't know Lexie was using an alias—or if they do, they've said nothing. According to them, she was estranged from her family and didn't like talking about her past. They don't even know where she was from; Abby thinks maybe Galway, Justin thinks Dublin, Daniel gave me a snotty look and told me that 'wasn't really of interest' to him. They're the same about her family. Justin thinks her parents were dead, Rafe says divorced, Abby says she was illegitimate . . ."

"Or maybe none of the above," Frank said. "We already know our girl wasn't above telling a few little white ones."

Sam nodded. "In September, Daniel inherited Whitethorn House near Glenskehy from his great-uncle, Simon March, and they all moved in. Last Wednesday night, the five of them were home, playing poker. Lexie got knocked out first and went for a walk around half past eleven—late-night walks were a regular part of her routine, the area's safe, the rain hadn't started in yet, the others didn't think twice. They finished up a little after midnight and went to bed. They all describe the card game the same way, who won how much on what hand—little differences here and there, but that's only natural. We've interviewed all of them several times, and they haven't budged an inch. Either they're innocent or they're dead organized."

"And the next morning," Frank said, finishing off the timeline with a flourish, "she shows up dead."

Sam pulled a handful of papers out of the pile on his desk, went to the whiteboard and stuck something in one corner: a surveyor's map of a patch of countryside, detailed down to the last house and boundary fence, marked with neat Xs and squiggles in colored highlighter. "Here's Glenskehy village. Whitethorn House is just under a mile to the south. Here, about halfway in between and a little to the east, that's the derelict cottage where we found our girl. I've marked all the obvious routes she might have taken to get there. The Bureau and the uniforms are still searching them: nothing yet. According to her mates, she always went out the back gate for her walk, wandered around the little lanes for an hour or so—it's a maze of them, all around there—and came home either by the front or by the back, depending on what route took her fancy."

"In the middle of the night?" O'Kelly wanted to know. "Was she mental, or what?"

"She always took the torch we found on her," Sam said, "unless the night was bright enough to see without. She was mad for the old walks, went out almost every night; even if it was lashing rain, she mostly just bundled up warm and went anyway. I wouldn't say it's exercise she was after, more privacy—living that close with the other four, it's the only time she got to herself. They don't know whether she ever went to the cottage, but they did say she liked it. Just after they first moved in, the five of them spent a day wandering all round Glenskehy, getting the lie of the land. When they spotted the cottage, Lexie wouldn't move on till she'd gone in and had a look around, even though the others told her the farmer would probably be out with his shotgun any minute. She liked that it had been left there, even though no one was using it—Daniel said she 'likes inefficiency,' whatever that means. So we can't rule out the possibility that it was a regular stop on her walks."

Definitely not Irish, then, or at least not brought up here. Famine cottages are all over the countryside, we barely even see them any more. It's only tourists—and mostly tourists from newer countries, America, Australia—who look at them long enough to feel their weight.

Sam found another piece of paper to add to the white-board: a floor plan of the cottage, with a neat, tiny scale at the bottom. "However she ended up there," he said, pressing the last corner into place, "that's where she died— against this wall, in what we're calling the outer room. Sometime after death and before rigor set in, she was moved to the inner room. That's where she was found, early Thursday morning."

He gestured to Cooper.

Cooper had been gazing into space, in a lofty trance. He

took his time: cleared his throat primly, glanced around to make sure he had everyone's full attention. "The victim," he said, "was a healthy white female, five feet five inches in height, a hundred and twenty pounds. No scars, tattoos or other identifying marks. She had a blood alcohol content of .03, consistent with drinking two to three glasses of wine a few hours previously. The toxicology screen was otherwise clear—at the time of death she had consumed no drugs, toxins or medications. All organs were within normal limits; I found no defects or signs of disease. The epiphyses of the long bones are completely fused and the inner sutures of the skull bones show early signs of fusion, placing her age around the late twenties. It is clear from the pelvis that she has never delivered a child." He reached for his water glass and took a judicious sip, but I knew he wasn't finished; the pause was for effect. Cooper had something up his sleeve.

He put down the glass, aligning it neatly in the corner of the desk. "She was, however," he said, "in the early stages of pregnancy." He sat back and watched the impact.

"Ah, Jesus," Sam said softly. Frank leaned back against the wall and whistled, one long low note. O'Kelly rolled his eyes.

That was all this case needed. I wished I had had the sense to sit down. "Any of her mates mention this?" I asked.

"Not a one," Frank said, and Sam shook his head. "Our girl kept her friends close and her secrets closer."

"She might not even have known," I said. "If her cycle wasn't regular—"

"Ah, Jaysus, Maddox," said O'Kelly, horrified. "We don't want to hear about that carry-on. Put it in a report or something."

"Any chance of IDing the father through DNA?" Sam asked.

"I see no reason why not," Cooper said, "given a sample from the putative father. The embryo was approximately four weeks old and just under half a centimeter long, and was—"

"*Christ,*" said O'Kelly; Cooper smirked. "Skip the bloody details and get on with it. How'd she die?"

Cooper left a loud pause, to show everyone that he wasn't taking orders from O'Kelly. "At some point on Wednesday night," he said, when he figured his point was made, "she suffered a single stab wound to the right chest. The probability is that the attack came from the front: the angle and point of entry would be difficult to achieve from behind the victim. I found slight abrasions to both palms and one knee, consistent with a fall on hard ground, but no defensive wounds. The weapon was a blade at least three inches long, with a single edge, a sharp point and no distinctive features—it could have been any large pocketknife, even a sharp kitchen knife. This blade entered on the mid-clavicular line at the level of the eighth rib, at an upward angle, and nicked the lung, leading to a tension pneumothorax. To put it as simply as possible"—he threw O'Kelly a snide sidelong glance—"the blade created a flap valve in the lung. Each time she inhaled, air escaped from the lung into the pleural space; when she exhaled, the flap closed, leaving the air trapped. Prompt medical attention could almost certainly have saved her. In the absence of such attention, however, the air gradually accumulated, compressing the other thoracic organs within the chest cavity. Eventually the heart was no longer able to fill with blood, and she died."

There was a tiny silence, only the soft hum of the fluorescents. I thought of her in that cold ruined house, with night birds keening above her and rain gentle all around, dying of breathing.

"How long would that have taken?" Frank asked.

"The progression would depend on a variety of factors," Cooper said. "If, for example, the victim ran for any distance after being stabbed, her breathing would have accelerated and deepened, hastening the development of the tension pneumothorax. The blade also left a minute nick in one of the major veins of the chest; with activity, this nick grew into a tear, and she would gradually have begun to bleed quite heavily. To give a tentative estimate, I would guess that she became unconscious approximately twenty to thirty minutes after receiving the injury, and died perhaps ten or fifteen minutes later."

"In that half hour," Sam asked, "how far could she have got?"

"I am not a medium, Detective," Cooper said sweetly. "Adrenaline can have fascinating effects on the human body, and there is evidence that the victim was in fact in a state of considerable emotion. The presence of cadaveric spasm—in this case, the hands contracting into fists at the moment of death and remaining clenched through rigor mortis—is generally associated with extreme emotional stress. If she was sufficiently motivated, which under the circumstances I would imagine she was, a mile or so would not be out of the question. Alternatively, of course, she could have collapsed within yards."

"OK," Sam said. He found a highlighter pen on someone's desk and drew a wide circle around the cottage on the map, taking in the village and Whitethorn House and acres of empty hillside. "So our primary crime scene could be anywhere in here."

"Wouldn't she have been in too much pain to get far?" I asked. I felt Frank's eyes flick to me. We don't ask whether victims suffered. Unless they were actually tortured, we don't need to know: getting emotionally involved does nothing except wreck your objectivity and give you nightmares, and we're going to tell the family it was painless anyway.

"Restrain your imagination, Detective Maddox," Cooper told me. "A tension pneumothorax is often relatively painless. She would have been aware of mounting shortness of breath and an increased heart rate; as shock set in, her skin would have become cold and clammy and she would have felt light-headed, but there is no reason to suppose that she was in excruciating agony."

"How much force went into the stabbing?" Sam asked. "Could anyone have done it, or would it take a big strong fella?"

Cooper sighed. We always ask: could a scrawny guy have done it? What about a woman? A kid? How big a kid? "The shape of the wound on cross section," he said, "combined with the lack of splitting in the skin at the entry point, implies a blade with a fairly sharp tip. It did not encounter bone or cartilage at any point. Assuming a fairly swift lunge, I would say that this injury could have been inflicted by a large man, a small man, a large woman, a small woman, or a strong pubescent child. Does that answer your question?"

Sam shut up. "Time of death?" O'Kelly demanded.

"Between eleven and one o'clock," said Cooper, examining a cuticle. "As I believe my preliminary report stated."

"We can narrow it down a bit," Sam said. He found a marker and started a new timeline under Frank's. "Rainfall in that area started about ten past midnight, and the Bureau's guessing she was out in it for fifteen or twenty minutes max, from the degree of dampness, so she was moved into shelter by around half past twelve. And she was dead by then. Going by what Dr. Cooper says, that puts the actual stabbing no later than midnight, probably earlier— I'd say she was well on the way to unconscious before the rain started in, or she'd have gone into shelter. If the house-mates are telling the truth about her leaving the house unharmed at half past eleven, then that gives us a half-hour window for the stabbing. If they're lying or mistaken, it could've been anywhere between ten and twelve."

"And that," Frank said, swinging a leg over his chair, "is all we've got. No footprints and no blood trail—the rain got rid of all that. No fingerprints: someone went through her pockets and then wiped down all her stuff. Nothing good under her fingernails, according to the Bureau; looks like she didn't get a go at the killer. They're going through the trace, but on preliminary there's nothing that stands out.

All the hairs and fibers look like matching either her, her housemates or various stuff from the house, which means they don't cut either way. We're still searching the area, but so far we've got no sign of the murder weapon and no sign of an ambush site or a struggle. Basically, what we have is one dead girl and that's it."

"Wonderful," O'Kelly said heavily. "One of those. What do you do, Maddox, carry a crap-case magnet in your bra?"

"This one isn't mine, sir," I reminded him.

"And yet here you are. Lines of investigation?"

Sam put the marker back and held up his thumb. "One: a random attack." In Murder you get into the habit of numbering things; it makes O'Kelly happy. "She was out walking and someone jumped her—for money, as part of a sexual assault, or just looking for trouble."

"If there had been any sign of sexual assault," Cooper said wearily, to his fingernails, "I would, I think, have mentioned it by this point. In fact, I found nothing to indicate recent sexual contact of any kind."

Sam nodded. "No sign of robbery, either—she still had her wallet, with cash in it, she didn't own a credit card and she'd left her mobile at home. But that doesn't prove it wasn't the motive. Maybe she fights, he stabs her, she runs, he goes after her and then panics when he realizes what he's done . . ." He shot me a quick, inquiring look.

O'Kelly has definite opinions on psychology, and he likes to pretend he doesn't know about the profiling thing. I needed to do this delicately. "You think?" I said. "I don't know, I sort of figured . . . I mean, she was moved *after* she died, right? If it took her half an hour to die, then either this guy spent all that time looking for her—and why would a mugger or a rapist do that?—or someone else found her later, moved her, and didn't bother ringing us. They're both possible, I guess, but I don't think either one's likely."

"Fortunately, Maddox," O'Kelly said nastily, "your opinion is no longer our problem. As you pointed out, you're not on this case."

"Yet," Frank said, to the air.

"There's other problems with the stranger scenario, too," said Sam. "That area's pretty well deserted during the daytime, never mind at night. If someone was looking for trouble, why would he hang around a laneway in the middle of nowhere, just on the off chance that a victim might wander past? Why not head into Wicklow town, or Rathowen, or at least Glenskehy village?"

"Any similars in the area?" O'Kelly asked.

"No knifepoint muggings or stranger sexual assaults," Sam said. "Glenskehy's a small village, sure; the two main crimes are drinking after hours and then driving home. The only stabbing in the last year was a group of lads getting drunk and stupid. Unless something similar turns up, I'd say we put the stranger on the back burner for now."

"Suits me," Frank said, grinning at me. A random attack would mean no info within the victim's life, no evidence or motive waiting to be discovered, no reason to send me under. "Suits me down to the ground."

"Might as well," said O'Kelly. "If it's random, we're bolloxed anyway: it's luck or nothing."

"Grand, so. Two"—Sam ticked off a finger—"a recent enemy; I mean, someone who knew her as Lexie Madison. She moved in a pretty limited circle, so it shouldn't be too hard to find out whether anyone had any problems with her. We're starting with the housemates and working our way outwards—staff at Trinity, students—"

"With no luck so far," Frank said, to no one in particular.

"It's early days," Sam said firmly. "We're only at the preliminary interviews. And now we know she was pregnant, we've a whole other line of inquiry. We need to find the father."

O'Kelly snorted. "Good luck with that. Girls these days, he's probably some young fella she met at a disco and shagged down a laneway."

I felt a sudden, confused spurt of fury: *Lexie wasn't like that.* I reminded myself that my info was out of date, for all

I knew this edition had been a five-star slapper. "Discos went out with the slide rule, sir," I said sweetly.

"Even if he's some fella from a nightclub," Sam said, "he'll have to be found and eliminated. It might take time, but we'll get it done." He was looking at Frank, who nodded gravely. "I'll ask the lads from the house to give us DNA samples, to start with."

"We might want to leave that for a while," Frank said smoothly, "all depending, of course. If by any chance her acquaintances should end up under the impression that she's alive and well, we don't want to rattle their cages. We want them relaxed, off their guard, thinking the investigation's wound down. The DNA'll still be there in a few weeks' time."

Sam shrugged. He was starting to tense up again. "We'll work that out as we go. Three: an enemy from her previous life, someone who had a grudge and tracked her down."

"Now that's the one I fancy," Frank said, straightening up. "We've got no indication of any problems in her Lexie Madison life, right? But wherever she was before, something obviously went wrong. She wasn't going around under a fake name just for the laugh. Either she was on the run from the cops, or she was on the run from someone else. My money's on someone else."

"I'm not sure I buy it," I said. Screw O'Kelly's feelings; I could see exactly where Frank was going with this, and I don't like being railroaded. "The killing's completely disorganized: one stab wound that didn't even need to be fatal, and then—instead of finishing her off, or at least holding her so she can't go for help and give him up—he lets her get away, to the point where it takes him half an hour to find her again. To me, that says no premeditation, maybe even no intent to kill."

O'Kelly gave me a disgusted grimace. "Someone stuck a knife in this girl's chest, Maddox. I'd say he knew there was a fair chance she could die."

I have years of practice in letting O'Kelly wash over me.

"A chance, sure. But if someone had spent years thinking about killing her, he'd have it planned down to the last detail. He'd have every base covered, he'd have a script, and he'd stick to it."

"So maybe he did have a script," Frank said, "but it didn't involve anything like violence. Say it's not a grudge that has him chasing her, it's unrequited love. He's got it in his head that they're soul mates, he's planning a lovey-dovey reunion and happy ever after, and instead she tells him to fuck off. She's the one who breaks away from the script, and he can't handle it."

"Stalkers snap," I said, "yeah. But they do it a whole lot more thoroughly than this. You'd expect a frenzy of violence: multiple blows, facial disfigurement, serious overkill. Instead, we've got *one* stab, barely even deep enough to kill her. It doesn't fit."

"Maybe he didn't get the chance for overkill," Sam said. "He stabs her, she runs, by the time he catches up with her she's already dead."

"Still," I said. "You're talking about someone obsessed enough to wait years and follow her God knows how far. That level of emotion, when it finally gets an outlet it's not going to vanish just because the target's dead. If anything, the fact that she'd escaped him again would have made him even angrier. I'd expect at least a few more stab wounds, a couple of kicks in the face, something like that."

It felt good, getting stuck into the case like this, like I was just a Murder detective again and she was just another victim; it spread through me strong and sweet and soothing as hot whiskey after a long day in wind and rain. Frank was sprawled casually in his chair, but I could feel him watching me, and I knew I was starting to sound too interested. I shrugged, leaned my head back against the wall and gazed up at the ceiling.

"The real point is," Frank said, inevitably, "if she's foreign and he followed her over here, for whatever reason, then the minute he knows he's got the job done, he'll be out of the country like a hot snot off a slate. The only way he'll stick around long enough for us to catch up with him is if he thinks she's still alive."

A brief, heavy silence.

"We can run checks on everyone leaving the country," Sam said.

"Checks for what?" Frank inquired. "We haven't a clue who we're looking for, where he or she might be heading, nothing. Before we can get anywhere, we need an ID."

"We're working on that. Like I said. If this woman could pass herself off as Irish, then odds are English was her first language. We'll start with England, the U.S., Canada—"

Frank shook his head. "That's going to take time. We need to keep our boy—or girl—here until we find out who the hell we're looking for. And I can think of exactly one way to do that."

"Four," Sam said, firmly. He ticked off another finger, and his eyes went to me for a split second, then slid away. "Mistaken identity."

There was another small silence. Cooper came out of his trance and started looking distinctly intrigued. My face had started to feel like it was scorching me, like overdone eye shadow or a top cut too low, something I should have known better than to wear.

"Piss anyone off lately?" O'Kelly asked me. "More than usual."

"About a hundred abusive men and a couple of dozen abusive women," I said. "No one's jumping out at me, but I'll send over the case files, flag the ones who got most obnoxious."

"What about when you were undercover?" Sam asked. "Could anyone have held a grudge against Lexie Madison?"

"Apart from the idiot who stabbed me?" I said. "Not that I recall."

"He's been inside for a year now," Frank said. "Possession with intent. I meant to tell you. Anyway, his brain's so fried he probably couldn't pick you out of a lineup. And I've gone through all our intelligence from that period: not a single red flag anywhere. Detective Maddox didn't piss anyone off, there's no sign that anyone ever suspected her of being a cop, and when she was wounded we pulled her out and sent someone else in to start over. No one was arrested as a direct result of her work, and she never had to testify. Basically, no one had any reason to want her dead."

"Does the idiot not have friends?" Sam wanted to know.

Frank shrugged. "Presumably, but again, I don't see why he'd sic them on Detective Maddox. It's not like he was charged with the assault. We pulled him in, he gave us some bullshit story about self-defense, we acted like we believed him and cut him loose. He was a lot more useful outside than in."

Sam's head snapped up and he started to say something, but then he bit his lip and focused on rubbing a smudge off the whiteboard. No matter what he thought of someone who would let an attempted cop killer off the hook, he and Frank were stuck with each other. It was going to be a long investigation.

"What about in Murder?" Frank asked me. "Make any enemies?" O'Kelly gave a sour little laugh.

"All my solves are still inside," I said, "but I guess they could have friends, family, accomplices. And there are suspects we never managed to convict." The sun had slid off my old desk; our corner had gone dark. The squad room felt suddenly colder and emptier, blown through by long sad winds.

"I'll do that," Sam said. "I'll check those out."

"If someone's after Cassie," Frank said helpfully, "she'll be a lot safer in Whitethorn House than she would be all by herself in that flat."

"I can stay with her," Sam said, without looking at him. We weren't about to point out that he spent half his time at my place anyway, and Frank knew it.

Frank raised an amused eyebrow. "Twenty-four seven? If she goes under, she'll be miked up, she can have someone listening to the mike feed day and night—"

"Not on my budget she can't," O'Kelly told him.

"No problem: it'll go on our budget. We'll work out of Rathowen station; anyone comes after her, we'll have guys on the scene in minutes. Will she get that at home?"

"If we think someone's out to kill a police officer," Sam said, "then she bloody well should get that at home." His voice was starting to tauten.

"Fair enough. How's your budget for round-the-clock protection?" Frank asked O'Kelly.

"Fuck that for a game of soldiers," O'Kelly said. "She's DV's detective, she's DV's problem." Frank spread his hands and grinned at Sam.

Cooper was enjoying this way too much. "I don't *need* round-the-clock protection," I said. "If this guy was obsessed with me, he wouldn't have stopped at one blow, any more than he would've if he was obsessed with Lexie. Everybody relax."

"Right," Sam said, after a moment. He didn't sound happy. "I think that's the lot." He sat down, hard, and pulled his chair up to his desk.

"She wasn't killed for her money, anyway," Frank said. "The five of them pool most of their funds—a hundred quid a week each into a kitty, to pay for food, petrol, bills, doing up the house, all the rest of it. On her income, that didn't leave much. She had eighty-eight quid in her bank account."

"What do you think?" Sam asked me.

He meant from a profiling angle. Profiling is nowhere near foolproof and I don't actually have much of a clue what I'm doing anyway, but as far as I could see, everything said she had been killed by someone she knew, someone with a hair-trigger temper rather than a well-nursed grudge. The obvious answer was either the kid's father or one of the housemates, or both.

But if I said that, then this meeting was over, at least as far as I was concerned; Sam would blow every gasket at the thought of me sharing a house with the odds-on favorites. And I didn't want that. I tried to tell myself it was because

I wanted to make the decision, not have Sam make it for me, but I knew: this was working on me, this room and this company and this conversation, pressing subtly just like Frank had known they would. Nothing in this world takes over your blood like a murder case, nothing demands you, mind and body, with such a huge and blazing and irresistible voice. It had been months since I had worked like this, concentrated like this on fitting together evidence and patterns and theories, and all of a sudden it felt like years.

"I'd go with door number two," I said, finally. "Someone who knew her as Lexie Madison."

"If that's where we're focusing," Sam said, "her housemates were the last ones to see her alive, and they're the ones were closest to her. That puts them front and center."

Frank shook his head. "I'm not so sure. She was wearing her coat, and it wasn't put on her after she died—there's a slit in the front right side, perfect match to the wound. To me, that says she was out of the house, away from the housemates, when she got stabbed."

"I'm not eliminating them yet," Sam said. "I don't know why any of them would want to stab her, I don't know why they'd do it outside the house, all I know is that on this job the obvious answer is mostly the one you're after—and any way you look at it, they're the obvious answers. Unless we find a witness who saw her alive and well after she left that house, I'm keeping them in."

Frank shrugged. "Fair enough. Say it's one of the housemates: they're sticking together like glue, they've been interviewed for hours without batting an eyelid, the chances of us breaking their story are virtually nil. Or say it's an outsider: we don't have the foggiest clue who he is, how he knew Lexie or where to start looking for him. There are some cases that just plain can't be broken from the outside. That's why Undercover exists. Which brings me back nicely to my alternative tack."

"Throwing a detective into the middle of a bunch of murder suspects," Sam said.

"Just as a rule," Frank told him, with an amused little lift of one eyebrow, "we don't send undercovers to investigate holy innocents. Being surrounded by criminals is what we tend to *do*."

"And we're talking IRA, gangsters, dealers," O'Kelly said. "This is a bunch of fucking *students*. Even Maddox can probably handle them."

"Exactly," Sam said. "Exactly. Undercover investigates organized crime: drugs, gangs. They don't go in on your run-of-the-mill murder. Why do we need them on this one?"

"From a murder detective," Frank said, concerned, "that amazes me. Are you saying that this girl's life is worth less than a K of heroin?"

"No," Sam said, evenly. "I'm saying there are other ways to investigate a murder."

"Like what?" Frank demanded, going in for the kill. "In the case of this particular murder, what other ways have you got? You don't have an ID on the victim"—he was leaning in towards Sam, ticking off fingers fast—"a suspect, a motive, a weapon, a primary scene, a print, a witness, trace evidence or a single good lead. Am I right?"

"It's *three days* into the investigation," Sam said. "Who knows what we'll—"

"Now let's look at what you *have* got." Frank held up one finger. "A first-rate, trained, experienced undercover who's the spitting image of the victim. That's it. Any reason why you don't want to use that?"

Sam laughed, an angry little sound, swinging his chair onto its back legs. "Why I don't want to throw her in there for shark bait?"

"She's a detective," Frank said, very gently.

"Yeah," Sam said, after a long moment. He let the front legs of his chair down again, carefully. "She is." His eyes skated away from Frank, across the squad room: empty desks in dimming corners, the explosion of scribbles and maps and Lexie on the whiteboard, me.

"Don't look at me," O'Kelly said. "Your case, your call."

If this thing went splat, and he obviously thought it would, he wanted to be well out of range.

All three of them were starting to get right up my nose. "Remember me?" I inquired. "You might want to start trying to convince me, too, Frank, because I'd say this was at least partly my call."

"You'll go where you're sent," said O'Kelly.

"It is, of course," Frank told me reproachfully. "I'm getting to you. I felt it would be polite to start by discussing matters with Detective O'Neill, what with this being a joint investigation and all. Am I wrong?"

This is why joint investigations are from hell: nobody is ever quite sure who the big boss is, and nobody wants to find out. Officially, Sam and Frank were supposed to agree on any major decisions, but if it came to the crunch, anything to do with undercover was Frank's call. Sam could probably override him, since this had started out as his investigation, but not without an awful lot of string-pulling and a damn good reason. Frank was making sure—*I felt it would be polite*—that Sam remembered that. "You're dead right," I said. "Just remember, you need to discuss matters with me, too. So far, I haven't heard anything very convincing."

"How long are we talking about?" Sam asked. He was asking Frank, but his eyes were on me, and the look in them startled me: they were intent and very grave, almost sad. That was the second when I realized Sam was going to say yes.

Frank saw it too; his voice didn't change, but his back had straightened and there was a new spark in his face, something alert and predatory. "Not long. A month, max. It's not like we're investigating organized crime and we could need someone on the inside for years. If this doesn't pay off inside a few weeks, then it's not going to."

"She'd have backup."

"Twenty-four-hour."

"If there's any indication of danger—"

"We'll pull Detective Maddox out straightaway, or go in and get her if we need to. Same if you develop information that means she's no longer necessary to the investigation: we'll have her out that same day."

"So I'd better get cracking," Sam said quietly, on a long breath. "OK: if Detective Maddox wants to do it, then we'll do it. On condition that I'm kept fully informed of all developments. No exceptions."

"Beautiful," Frank said, sliding off his chair fast, before Sam could change his mind. "You won't regret it. Hang on, Cassie—before you say anything, I want to show you this. I promised you videos, and I'm a man of my word."

O'Kelly let out a snort and said something predictable about amateur porn, but I barely heard him. Frank fished around in his big black knapsack, waved a DVD labeled in marker scrawl at me and shoved it into the squad room's cheapo DVD player.

"Date stamp says the twelfth of September last," he said, turning on the monitor. "Daniel got the keys to the house on the tenth. He and Justin drove down that afternoon to make sure the roof hadn't fallen in or anything, the five of them spent the eleventh packing up their stuff, and on the twelfth they all handed in the keys to their flats and moved out to Whitethorn House, lock, stock and barrel. They don't hang about, this lot." He hoisted himself onto Costello's desk, beside me, and hit Play on the remote.

Darkness; a click and rattle, like an old key turning; feet thumping on wood. "Sweet Jesus," someone said. A finely modulated voice with a Belfast tinge: Justin. "The *smell*."

"What are you being shocked about?" demanded a deeper voice, cool and almost accentless. ("That's Daniel," Frank said, next to me.) "You knew what to expect."

"I blanked it out of my mind."

"Is this thing working?" a girl asked. "Rafe, can you tell?"

"That's our girl," Frank said softly, but I already knew. Her voice was lighter than mine, alto and very clear, and the first syllable had hit me straight in the back of the neck, at the top of my spine.

"My God," said a guy with an English accent, amused: Rafe. "You're *recording* this?"

"Course I am. Our new home. Only I can't tell if it's doing anything, because I'm only recording black anyway. Does the electricity work?"

Another clatter of feet; a door creaked. "This should be the kitchen," Daniel said. "As far as I remember."

"Where's the switch?"

"I've got a lighter," said another girl's voice. Abigail; Abby.

"Brace yourselves," said Justin.

A tiny flame, wavering in the center of the screen. All I could see was one side of Abby's face, eyebrow raised, mouth a little open.

"Jesus H. Christ, Daniel," said Rafe.

"I did warn you," said Justin.

"In fairness, he did," said Abby. "If I remember, he said it was a cross between an archaeological site and the nastier bits of Stephen King."

"I know, but I thought he was exaggerating as usual. I didn't expect him to be *understating*."

Someone—Daniel—took the lighter off Abby and cupped his hand around a cigarette; there was a draft coming from somewhere. His face on the wobbly screen was calm, unperturbed. He glanced up over the flame and gave Lexie a solemn wink. Maybe because I had spent so long staring at that photo, there was something astonishing about seeing them all in action. It was like being one of those kids in books who find a magic spyglass that lets them into the secret life of some old painting, enthralling and risky.

"Don't," said Justin, taking the lighter and poking gingerly at something on a rickety shelf. "If you want to smoke, go outside."

"Why?" asked Daniel. "So I don't smudge the wallpaper, or so I don't stink up the curtains?"

"He's got a point," said Abby.

"What a bunch of wusses," said Lexie. "I think this place is terrifantastic. I feel like one of the Famous Five."

"Five Find a Prehistoric Ruin," Daniel said.

"Five Find the Mold Planet," said Rafe. "Simply spiffing."

"We should have ginger cake and potted meat," Lexie said.

"Together?" asked Rafe.

"And sardines," said Lexie. "What *is* potted meat?"

"Spam," Abby told her.

"Ew."

Justin went over to the sink, held the lighter close and turned on the taps. One of them sputtered, popped and eventually let out a thin stream of water.

"Mmm," said Abby. "Typhoid tea, anyone?"

"I want to be George," said Lexie. "She was cool."

"I don't care as long as I'm not Anne," Abby said. "She always got stuck doing the washing up, just because she was a girl."

"What's wrong with that?" asked Rafe.

"You can be Timmy the dog," Lexie told him.

The rhythms of their conversation were faster than I had expected, smart and sharp as a jitterbug, and I could see why the rest of the English department thought this lot were up themselves. They had to be impossible to talk to; those tight, polished syncopations didn't leave room for anyone else. Somehow, though, Lexie had managed to slot herself in there, tailored herself or rearranged them inch by inch till she made a place for herself and became part of them, seamless. Whatever this girl's game was, she had been good at it.

A small clear voice at the back of my head said: *Just like I'm good at mine.*

Miraculously, the screen lit up, more or less, as a forty-watt bulb came on overhead: Abby had found the light switch, in an unlikely corner by a grease-draped cooker. "Well done, Abby," said Lexie, panning.

"I'm not sure," said Abby. "It looks even worse now that I can see it."

She was right. The walls had obviously been papered at some stage, but a greenish mold had staged a coup, creeping in from every corner and almost meeting in the middle. Spectacular Halloween-decoration cobwebs trailed from the ceiling, swaying gently in the draft. The linoleum was gray-ish and curling, with sinister dark streaks; on the table was a glass vase holding a bunch of very dead flowers, stalks broken and sagging at odd angles. Everything was about three inches thick with dust. Abby looked deeply skeptical; Rafe looked amused, in a horrified kind of way; Daniel looked mildly intrigued; Justin looked like he might throw up.

"You want me to *live* there?" I said to Frank.

"It doesn't look like that *now*," he told me, reproach-fully. "They've really done a lot with it."

"Have they bulldozed it and started over?"

"It's lovely. You'll love it. Shh."

"Here," Lexie said; the camera jerked and swung wildly, caught cobwebby curtains in a horrible seventies orange swirl. "You mind that. I want to explore."

"I hope you've had your shots," Rafe said. "What do you want me to do with this?"

"Don't tempt me," Lexie told him, and bounced into shot, heading over towards the cupboards.

She moved lighter than me, small steps tipped up on the balls of her feet, and girlier: her curves were no more impres-sive than mine, obviously, but she had a dancing little swing that made you notice them. Her hair had been longer then, just long enough to pull into two curly bunches over her ears, and she was wearing jeans and a tight cream-colored sweater a lot like one I used to have. I still had no idea whether we would have liked each other, if we had had the chance to meet—probably not—but that was beside the point, so irrelevant that I didn't even know how to think about it.

"Wow," Lexie said, peering into one of the cupboards. "What *is* it? Is it alive?"

"It may well have been," Daniel said, leaning over her shoulder. "A very long time ago."

"I think it's the other way around," said Abby. "It didn't use to be alive, but it is now. Has it evolved opposable thumbs yet?"

"I miss my flat," said Justin lugubriously, from a safe distance.

"You do not," Lexie told him. "Your flat was three foot square and made from reconstituted cardboard and you hated it."

"My flat didn't have unidentified *life-forms*."

"Whatsisname upstairs with the sound system who thought he was Ali G."

"I think it's some kind of fungus," Daniel said, inspecting the cupboard with interest.

"That does it," said Rafe. "I am not recording this. When we're old and gray and wallowing in nostalgia, our first memories of our home should not be defined by *fungus*. How do I turn this thing off?"

A second of linoleum; then the screen went black.

"We've got forty-two clips like that," Frank told me, hitting buttons, "all between about one minute and five minutes long. Add in, say, another week's worth of intensive interviews with her associates, and I'm pretty sure we'll have enough information to put together our very own DIY Lexie Madison. Assuming, that is, that you want to."

He froze the frame on Lexie, head turned over her shoulder to say something, eyes bright and mouth half open in a smile. I looked at her, soft-edged and flickering like she might fly off the screen at any second, and I thought: *I used to be like that. Sure-footed and invulnerable, up for anything that came along. Just a few months ago, I used to be like that.*

"Cassie," Frank said softly. "Your call."

For what seemed like a long time, I thought about saying no. Back to DV: the standard Monday crop of the weekend's aftermath, too many bruises and high-necked sweaters and sunglasses indoors, the regulars filing charges on their boyfriends and withdrawing them by Tuesday night, Maher sitting beside me like a big pink ham in a sweater and sniggering predictably every time we pulled a case with foreign names.

If I went back in there the next morning I would never leave. I knew it solid as a fist in my stomach. This girl was like a dare, flung hard and deadly accurate straight at me: a once-off chance, and catch it if you can.

O'Kelly stretched out his legs and sighed ostentatiously; Cooper examined the cracks in the ceiling. I could tell from the stillness of Sam's shoulders that he wasn't breathing. Only Frank was looking at me, his eyes steady and unblinking. The air of the squad room hurt everywhere it touched me. Lexie in dim gold light on the screen was a dark lake I could high-dive into, she was a thin-ice river I could skate away on, she was a long-distance flight leaving now.

"Tell me this woman smoked," I said.

My ribs opened up like windows, I'd forgotten you could breathe that deeply. "Jesus, you took your time," said O'Kelly, heaving himself out of his chair and pulling his trousers up over his belly. "I think you're bloody certifiable, but nothing new there. When you get yourself killed, don't come crying to me."

"Fascinating," Cooper said, eyeing me speculatively; a part of him was obviously working out the odds that I would end up on his table. "Do keep me posted."

Sam ran a hand over his mouth, hard, and I saw his neck sag. "Marlboro Lights," Frank said, and hit Eject, a big grin slowly breaking across his face. "That's my girl."

I used to believe, bless my naive little heart, that I had something to offer the robbed dead. Not revenge—there's no revenge in the world that could return the tiniest fraction of what they've lost—and not justice, whatever that means, but the one thing left to give them: the truth. I was good at it. I had one, at least, of the things that make a great detective: the instinct for truth, the inner magnet whose pull tells you beyond any doubt what's dross, what's alloy and what's the pure, uncut metal. I dug out the nuggets without caring when they cut my fingers and brought them in my cupped hands to lay on graves, until I found out—Operation Vestal again—how slippery they were, how easily they crumbled, how deep they sliced and, in the end, how very little they were worth.

In Domestic Violence, if you can get one bruised girl to press charges or go to a shelter, then there's at least one night when her boyfriend is not going to hit her. Safety is a small debased currency, copper-plated pennies to the gold I had been chasing in Murder, but what value it has it holds. I had learned, by that time, not to take that lightly. A few safe hours and a sheet of phone numbers to call: I had never been able to offer a single murder victim that much.

I had no clue what currency I had to offer Lexie Madison—not safety, obviously, and truth didn't appear to have been one of her main priorities—but she had come looking for me, alive and dead she had padded closer on soft feet till she arrived with a spectacular bang on my doorstep: she wanted something. What I wanted from her in exchange—I really believed this, at the time—was simple: I wanted her the fuck out of my life. I knew she would drive a hard bargain, but I was good with that; I had done it before.

I don't tell people this, it's nobody's business, but the job is the nearest thing I've got to a religion. The detective's god is the truth, and you don't get much higher or much more ruthless than that. The sacrifice, at least in Murder and Undercover—and those were always the ones I wanted, why go chasing diluted versions when you could have the breath-taking full-on thing?—is anything or everything you've got, your time, your dreams, your marriage, your sanity, your life. Those are the coldest and most capricious gods of the lot, and if they accept you into their service they take not what you want to offer but what they choose.

Undercover picked my honesty. I should have seen this coming, but somehow I had been so caught by the dazzling absoluteness of the job that I had managed to miss the most obvious thing about it: you spend your day lying. I don't like lying, don't like doing it, don't like people who do it, and to me it seemed deeply fucked-up to go after the truth by turning yourself into a liar. I spent months picking my way along a fine double-talk line, cozying up to this small-fish dealer and spinning jokes or sarcasm to mislead him with literal truths. Then one day he fried both his brain cells on speed, pulled a knife on me and asked me if I was just using him to get to know his supplier. I skated the fine line for what felt like hours—*Chill out, what's your problem, what have I ever done to make you think I'm trying to screw you over?*—stalling and hoping to God that Frank was listening to the mike feed. Dealer Boy put the knife in between my ribs and shrieked in my face, *Are you? Are you? No bullshit. Yes or no. Are you?* When I hesitated—because of course I was, even if it wasn't for the reason he had in mind, and this seemed like too crucial a moment for lies—he stabbed me. Then he burst into tears, and sometime in there Frank arrived and carted me discreetly off to the hospital. But I knew. The sacrifice had been demanded and I had withheld it. I had thirty stitches for warning: *Don't do that again.*

I was a good Murder detective. Rob once told me that all through his first case he had elaborate visions of fucking up, sneezing on DNA evidence, waving a cheerful good-bye to someone who had just let slip the giveaway piece of with-held info, bumbling vacantly past every clue and red flag. I never had that. My first Murder case was about as banal and depressing as you get—a young junkie knifed in the stair-well of a nightmare block of flats, great blood smears down grimy flights of stairs and eyes watching behind chained doors and the smell of piss everywhere. I stood on the landing with my hands in my pockets so I wouldn't touch anything by mistake, looking up at the victim sprawled on the steps with his tracksuit bottoms half pulled down by the fall or the fight, and I thought: *So this is it. This is where I was coming to, all along.*

I still remember that junkie's face: too thin, a faint fuzz of pale stubble, his mouth a little open as if all this had startled him silly. He had a crooked front tooth. Against all the odds and O'Kelly's nonstop depressing predictions, we got a solve.

On Operation Vestal the Murder god chose my best friend and my honesty, and gave me nothing in exchange. I transferred out knowing there would be a price to pay for the desertion. At the back of my mind I expected my solve rate to plummet, expected every vicious guy to beat the living daylights out of me, every raging woman to scratch my eyes out. I wasn't scared; I was looking forward to it being over. But when nothing happened I realized, like a slow cold tide, that this was the punishment: to be turned loose, allowed to go on my way. To be left empty by my guardian god.

And then Sam phoned and Frank was waiting at the top of the hill, and strong implacable hands were reeling me back in. You can put all of this down to a superstitious streak if that's easiest, or to the kind of intense secret life that a lot of orphans and onlies have; I don't mind. But maybe it goes some way towards explaining why I said yes to Operation Mirror, and why, when I signed on, I figured there was a decent chance I was going to get killed.

4

Frank and I spent the next week developing Lexie Madison Version 3.0. During the day he pumped people for information about her, her routine, her moods, her relationships; then he came over to my flat and spent the night hammering the day's crop into my head. I'd forgotten how good at this he was, how systematic and thorough, and how fast he expected me to keep up. Sunday evening, before we left the squad room, he handed me Lexie's weekly schedule and a sheaf of photocopies of her thesis material. On Monday he had a thick file of her KAs—known associates—complete with photos and voice recordings and background info and smart-arsed commentary, for me to memorize. On Tuesday he brought an aerial map of the Glenskehy area, made me go over every detail till I could draw it from memory, gradually worked his way inwards till we got to floor plans and photos of Whitethorn House. This stuff had taken time to get together. Frank, the fucker, had known long before Sunday night that I was going to say yes.

We watched the phone videos again and again, Frank hitting Pause every few seconds to snap his fingers at some detail: "See that? How her head tilts to the right when she laughs? Show me that angle . . . See the way she looks at Rafe, and there, at Justin? She's flirting with them. Daniel and Abby, she looks at straight on; the two lads, it's sideways and up. Remember that . . . See her with the cigarette? She doesn't tuck it into the right-hand side of her mouth, the way you do. Her hand crosses over, and the smoke goes in on the left. Let's see you do it . . . See that? Justin starts getting all worked up about the mildew, and straightaway there's that little glance between Abby and Lexie, and they start talking about the pretty tiles to take his mind off it. There's an understanding there . . ." I watched those clips so many times that when I finally went to sleep—five in the morning, mostly, Frank sprawled on the sofa in all his clothes—they slid through my dreams, a constant under-current, tugging: the brusque cut of Daniel's voice against Justin's light obbligato, the patterns of the wallpaper, the rich tumble of Abby's laugh.

They lived with a kind of ceremony that startled me. My student life was spur-of-the-moment house parties, frantic bursts of all-night study and nonmeals involving crisp sandwiches at weird hours. But this lot: the girls made breakfast at half past seven every morning, they were in col-lege around ten—Daniel and Justin had cars, so they drove the others—whether they had tutorials to give or not, home around half past six and the guys made dinner. On week-ends they worked on the house; occasionally, if the weather was good, they took a picnic somewhere. Even their free time involved stuff like Rafe playing piano and Daniel read-ing Dante out loud and Abby restoring an eighteenth-century embroidered footstool. They didn't own a TV, never mind a computer—Daniel and Justin shared a man-ual typewriter, the other three were in enough contact with the twenty-first century to use the computers in college. They were like spies from another planet who had got their research wrong and wound up reading Edith Wharton and watching reruns of *Little House on the Prairie*. Frank had to look up piquet on the internet and teach me to play.

All this stuff, of course, got right up Frank's nose and inspired him to more and more creative flights of bitchery ("I'm thinking this is some weird cult that believes technol-ogy is the work of Satan and chants to house plants at the full moon. Don't worry, if they start gearing up for an orgy, I'll get you out; by the looks of them, it's not like you'd enjoy it. Who the hell doesn't have a *television*?"). I didn't tell him this, but the more I thought about it, the less bizarre their lives seemed and the more they enchanted me. Dublin goes fast, these days, fast and jam-packed and jostling, everyone terrified of being left behind and forcing themselves louder and louder to make sure they don't disappear. I had spent my time since Operation Vestal going fast too, headlong and gritted, anything not to stop, and at first the unabashed, graceful leisure of these four—*embroidery,* for Christ's sake—was as shocking as a slap. I had forgotten even how to want something slow, something soft, something with wide spaces and its own sure-footed swaying rhythms. That house and that life hung in my mind cool as well water, cool as the shadow under an oak tree on a hot afternoon.

During the day I practiced: Lexie's handwriting, her walk, her accent—which luckily for me was a light old-fashioned County Dublin, probably picked up from some TV or radio talk-show host, and not all that different from my own—her inflections, her laugh. The first time I got that right—a delighted, helpless bubble of a laugh, running up the scale like a tickled kid's—it scared the shit out of me.

Her version of Lexie Madison had been, comfortingly, a little different from mine. Way back in UCD, I played Lexie as cheerful, easygoing, sociable, happiest at the center of the action; nothing unpredictable about her, no dark edges, nothing that could make dealers or buyers see her as a risk. At the beginning, at least, Frank and I thought of her as a custom-made precision tool, built to suit our needs and do our bidding, with a very specific goal in mind. The mystery girl's Lexie had been more mercurial, more volatile, more willful and capricious. She had come up with a Siamese kitten of a girl, all bounce and chatter and little explosions of mischief with her friends, aloof and ice cool with outsiders, and it bothered me that I couldn't trace that thread backwards and work out what her goal had been, what job she had precision-made this new self to do.

I did consider the possibility that I was making things more complicated than they needed to be, and she had never had a goal at all; that when it came to personality, at least, she was just plain being herself. It isn't easy, after all, wearing someone else against your skin for months on end; I should know. But the thought of taking her at face value, no pun intended, made me edgy. Something told me that underestimating this girl would be a big, big mistake.

On Tuesday evening Frank and I were sitting on my floor, eating Chinese takeaway off the banged-up wooden chest I use for a coffee table, across a sprawl of maps and photos. It was a wild night, wind slamming at the window in great irregular bursts like some mindless attacker, and we were both in a jittery mood. I had spent the day memorizing KA info and building up enough excess energy that by the time Frank arrived I was doing handstands to keep myself from shooting straight through the ceiling; Frank had come in moving fast, sweeping stuff off the table and talking non-stop while he dealt out maps and food cartons, and I was wondering—there was no point in asking—what was going on, somewhere in the hidden levels of that X box game he calls a brain, that he wasn't telling me.

The combination of geography and food calmed us down a little—this was probably why Frank had gone for Chinese; it's hard to be edgy when you're full of lemon chicken. "And here," Frank said, maneuvering the last of his rice onto his fork with one hand and pointing with the other, "that's the petrol station on the Rathowen road. Open from seven in the morning till three at night, mainly to sell smokes and petrol to locals who're in no condition to be buying either one. You sometimes do cigarette runs there. Want more food?"

"God, no," I said. I had startled myself by being starving—normally I eat like a horse, Rob used to be constantly fascinated by how much food I could put away, but Operation Vestal had sort of sidelined my appetite. "Coffee?" I had a pot already going on the cooker; Frank's eye bags were reaching the point where they would scare small children.

"And lots of it. We've got work to do. Gonna be another long night, babe."

"Surprise, surprise," I said. "What's Olivia think of you sleeping over at my place?"

I was fishing, and I knew from the fraction of a pause as Frank pushed his plate away that I had guessed right: undercover strikes again. "Sorry," I said. "I didn't mean to—"

"Yeah, you did. Olivia got smart and dumped me last year. I get Holly one weekend a month and two weeks in summer. What's your Sammy think of me sleeping over at your place?"

His eyes were cool and unblinking and he didn't sound annoyed, just firm, but the message was clear: *Back off.* "He's fine with it," I said, getting up to check the coffee. "Anything for the job."

"You think? The job didn't seem to be his main priority on Sunday."

I changed my mind: he was pissed off with me about the Olivia thing. Apologizing would only make it worse. Before I could think of anything useful to say, my buzzer rang. I managed to keep the jump down to a minimum, had a graceful Inspector Clouseau moment where I whacked myself neatly across the shin with the sofa corner on my way to the door, and caught Frank's sharp, curious up-glance.

It was Sam. "And there's your answer," Frank said, grinning and hoisting himself up off the floor. "You, he'd trust anywhere, but me he's keeping an eye on. I'll take care of the coffee; you go canoodle."

Sam was exhausted; I could feel it in the weight of his body when he kissed me, the way he let out his breath in something like a sigh of relief. "God, it's good to see you," he said; then, as he spotted Frank waving from the kitchen, "Oh."

"Welcome to the Lexie Lab," Frank said cheerfully. "Coffee? Sweet and sour pork? Prawn cracker?"

"Yeah," Sam said, blinking. "I mean, no; just coffee, thanks. I won't stay, if you're working; I just wanted to . . . Are you busy?"

"You're fine," I told him. "We were having dinner. What've you eaten today?"

"I'm grand," Sam said vaguely, dumping his holdall on the floor and struggling out of his coat. "Could I borrow you for a few minutes? If you're not in the middle of something."

He was asking me, but Frank said expansively, "Why not? Have a seat, have a seat," and waved him to the futon. "Milk? Sugar?"

"No milk, two sugars," Sam said, collapsing onto the futon. "Thanks." I was pretty sure that he was starving, that he wasn't going to touch anything Frank had bought, that the holdall contained all the ingredients for something a lot more evolved than lemon chicken, and that if I could just get my hands on his shoulders I could rub that tension away in five minutes flat. Going undercover was starting to seem like the easy part here.

I sat next to Sam, as close as I could get without touching. "How's it going?" I asked.

He gave my hand a quick squeeze and reached round to his coat, draped over the back of the futon, to find his notebook. "Ah, sure, all right, I suppose. Just eliminating, mostly. Richard Doyle, your man who found the body, his alibi's solid. We've ruled out all the DV files you flagged; we're working on the rest and on your murder cases, but nothing yet." The thought of the Murder squad combing through my files, with the rumors sizzling in their heads and my face for victim, sent a nasty little twitch down between my shoulder blades. "It doesn't look like she used the internet at all—no internet activity under her log-in on the college computers, no MySpace page or anything like that, the e-mail address Trinity assigned her hasn't even been used—so no leads there. And not even a sniff of any arguments in college—and the English department is mad for the old rumors. If she'd had problems with anyone, we'd have heard."

"I hate to say I told you so," Frank said sweetly, gathering up mugs, "but sometimes, in life, we have to do things we hate."

"Yeah," Sam said absently. Frank bent to hand him his coffee with a servile little flourish, and winked at me behind Sam's back. I ignored him. One of Sam's rules is that he doesn't fight with anyone working the same case, but there are always people like Frank who figure he's just too thick to notice when he's being messed with. "So I wondered, Cassie . . . The thing is, eliminating could take forever, but as long as I've no motive and no leads, I've no other choice; there's nothing to tell me where to start. I thought, if I just had some idea what I was looking for . . . Could you profile this for me?"

For a second I felt like the air in the room had gone dark with pure sadness, bitter and ineradicable as smoke. Every murder case I ever pulled, I had done my best to profile right here in my flat: late nights, whiskey, Rob stretched out on the sofa cat's-cradling an elastic band and testing everything I came up with for holes. On Operation Vestal we'd brought Sam along, Sam smiling shyly at me while music and moths swirled at the windowpane, and all I could think was how happy the three of us had been, in spite of everything, and how fatally, devastatingly innocent. This prickly, crowded place—greasy smell of cold Chinese, my shin hurting like hell, Frank watching with those sidelong amused eyes—this wasn't the same thing, it was like a mocking reflection in some creepy distorting mirror, and all I could think was, ludicrously, *I want to go home*.

Sam moved a sheaf of maps to one side—gingerly, glancing up at us to make sure he wasn't messing anything up—and put down his mug. Frank scooted his arse to the very edge of the sofa, leaned his chin on his interlaced fingers and did enthralled. I kept my eyes down so they wouldn't see the look on my face. There was a photo of

Lexie on the table, half hidden under a carton of rice; Lexie up a ladder in the kitchen of Whitethorn House, wearing dungarees and a man's shirt and an awful lot of white paint. For the first time ever, the sight of her felt good: that handcuff bite on my wrist jerking me down to earth, that coldwater slap in the face slamming everything else out of my mind. I almost reached out and pressed my hand onto the picture.

"Yeah, sure, I'll profile," I said. "You know I can't give you a lot, though, right? Not on one crime." Most of profiling is built on patterns. With a stand-alone crime, you have no way of knowing what's pure chance and what's a clue, stenciled in by the boundaries of your guy's life or by the secret jagged outlines of his mind. One murder on a Wednesday evening tells you nothing very much; three more matching ones say that your guy has a window that night, and you might want to look twice when you find a suspect whose wife plays Bingo on Wednesdays. A phrase used in one rape could mean nothing; used in four, it becomes a signature that some girlfriend or wife or ex, somewhere, is going to recognize.

"Anything," Sam said. He flipped his notebook open, pulled out his pen and leaned forwards, eyes fixed on me, ready. "Anything at all."

"OK," I said. I didn't even need the file. I had spent more than enough time thinking about this, while Frank snored like a water buffalo on the sofa and my window went from black to gray to gold. "The first thing is that it's probably a man. We can't rule out a woman for definite—if you get a good female suspect, don't ignore her—but statistically, stabbing's usually a male crime. For now, we'll go with a guy."

Sam nodded. "That's what I figured, too. Any ideas on what age he is?"

"This isn't a teenager; he's too organized and too controlled. We're not talking about an old man, either, though. This didn't take an athlete, but it did take a basic level of fitness—running around lanes, climbing over walls, dragging a body. I'd go with twenty-five to forty, give or take."

"And I'm thinking," Sam said, scribbling, "there's local knowledge there."

"Oh yeah," I said. "Either he's local or he's spent an awful lot of time around Glenskehy, one way or another. He's very comfortable in the area. He hung around for ages after the stabbing; killers who're off their turf tend to get uneasy and split as fast as they can. And going by the maps, the place is a maze, but he managed to find her—in the dead of night, with no street lamps—after she got away from him."

For some reason this was harder than usual. I had analyzed the living bejasus out of every fact we had, gone back over every textbook, but I couldn't make the killer materialize. Every time I reached out for him, he streamed between my fingers like smoke and slid away over the horizon, left me staring at no silhouette except Lexie's. I tried to tell myself profiling is like any other skill, doing a backflip, riding a bike: get out of practice and your instinct goes rusty; that doesn't have to mean it's gone for good.

I found my cigarettes—I think better if I have something to do with my hands. "He knows Glenskehy, all right, and he almost definitely knew our girl. For one thing, we've got the positioning of the body: her face was turned away, towards the wall. Any kind of focus on the victim's face—covering it, disfiguring it, turning it away—usually means it's personal; the killer and the victim knew each other."

"Or," Frank said, swinging his legs up onto the sofa and balancing his mug on his stomach, "it's pure coincidence: that's just the way she landed when he put her down."

"Maybe," I said. "But we've also got the fact that he found her. That cottage is well off the lane; in the dark, you wouldn't even know it was there unless you were looking for it specifically. The time lag says he wasn't exactly hot on her trail, so I doubt he actually saw her go in there, and once she was sitting down the wall would hide her from the road.

Unless she had her torch on and our guy spotted the light—and why would you switch on a torch if you were trying to hide from a homicidal maniac?—then he had to have a reason for checking there. I think he knew she liked the cottage."

"None of that says she knew him," Frank said. "Just that he knew her. If he'd been stalking her for a while, say, he could feel like there was a personal connection, and he'd have a good handle on her habits."

I shook my head. "I'm not completely ruling out a stalker, but if that's what we're dealing with, he was at least an acquaintance of hers. She was stabbed from the front, remember. She wasn't running away, and she wasn't jumped from behind; they were face to face, she knew he was there, they could well have been talking for a while. And she didn't have any defensive wounds. To me, that says she wasn't on guard. This guy was up close and she was at ease with him, right up until the second he stabbed her. Me, I wouldn't be all that relaxed with a complete stranger who showed up at that hour in the middle of nowhere."

"All of which will be a lot more use," Frank said, "just as soon as we have a clue who this girl knew, exactly."

"Anything else I can look for?" Sam asked, ignoring him—I could see the effort. "Would you say he's got a record?"

"He probably has some kind of criminal experience," I said. "He did a damn good job of cleaning up after himself. There's a good chance he's never got caught, if he's this careful, but maybe he learned the hard way. If you're going through files, you could try looking for stuff like car theft, burglary, arson—something that would take cleanup skills but wouldn't involve any direct contact with victims. No assault, including sexual assault. Judging by how crap he is at killing people, he'd had no practice being violent, or practically none."

"He's not that crap," Sam said quietly. "He got the job done."

"Barely," I said. "Through dumb luck, more than any-thing. And I don't think that's the job he went there to do. There are elements of this crime that just don't match up. Like I said on Sunday, the stabbing reads as unplanned, spontaneous; but everything around that moment is a whole lot more organized. Your guy knew where to find her—I don't buy the idea that he just happened to wander into her, at midnight on some back lane in the middle of nowhere. Either he knew her routine, or they'd arranged to meet. And after the stabbing, he kept his head and he took his time: tracked her down, searched her, erased his foot-prints and wiped her stuff clean—and that says he wasn't wearing gloves. Again, he wasn't planning on a murder."

"He was carrying a *knife*," Frank pointed out. "What was he planning on, whittling?"

I shrugged. "Threatening her, maybe; scaring her, impressing her, I don't know. But someone this thorough, if he'd gone out there intending to kill her, he wouldn't have made such a bollocks of it. The attack came out of the blue, there had to be a moment when she was stunned by what had just happened; if he was aiming to finish her off, he could have done it. Instead, she's the one who reacts first—she takes off running, and gets a good head start, before he can do anything about it. That makes me think he was almost as stunned as she was. I think the meeting was planned for a completely different purpose, and then some-thing went badly wrong."

"Why follow her?" Sam asked. "After the stabbing. Why not leg it out of there?"

"When he caught up with her," I said, "he found out she was dead, moved her and went through her pockets. So I'm betting one of those things was his reason for going after her. He didn't hide or display the body, and you wouldn't spend half an hour looking for someone just to drag her a few yards for the hell of it, so moving her seems more like a side effect: he got her into shelter in order to conceal the light from a torch, or to be out of the rain, while he achieved his real goal—either to find out for sure whether she was dead, or else to search her."

"If you're right about him knowing her," Sam said, "and about him not meaning to kill her, then couldn't he have moved her because he cared about her? He felt guilty enough already, didn't want to leave her out in the rain . . ."

"I thought about that. But this guy's smart, he thinks ahead, and he was very serious about not getting caught. Moving her meant getting blood on himself, leaving more footprints, taking more time, maybe leaving hairs or fibers on her . . . I can't see him taking that kind of extra risk just out of sentimentality. He had to have a solid reason. Checking whether she was dead wouldn't take long—less time than moving her, anyway—so my best guess is that he followed her, and moved her, because he needed to search her."

"What for?" Sam asked. "We know he wasn't after cash."

"I can only think of three reasons," I said. "One is that he was checking for anything on her that might identify him—making sure she hadn't written down the appointment in a diary, trying to delete his number off her mobile, that kind of thing."

"She didn't keep a diary," Frank said, to the ceiling. "I asked the Fantastic Four."

"And she'd left her mobile at home, on the kitchen table," Sam said. "The housemates say that was normal; she always meant to bring it on her walks, but she mostly forgot it. We're going through it: nothing dodgy so far."

"He didn't necessarily know that, though," I said. "Or he could have been looking for something more specific. Maybe she was supposed to give him something, and that's what went wrong: she changed her mind . . . Either he took it off the body, or she didn't have it on her in the first place."

"The map to the hidden treasure?" Frank inquired, helpfully. "The Crown Jewels?"

"That house is full of old bits and bobs," Sam said. "If there was something valuable in there . . . Was there an inventory done, when your man inherited?"

"Ha," Frank said. "You've seen it. How would anyone inventory that? Simon March's will lists the good stuff—mostly antique furniture, a couple of paintings—but that's all gone. The death duties were massive, anything worth more than a few quid had to go to pay them off. From what I've seen, all that's left is your basic attic tat."

"The other possibility," I said, "is that he was looking for ID. God knows there's enough confusion around this girl's identity. Say he thought he was talking to me and then had doubts, or say she dropped a hint that Lexie Madison wasn't her real name: your guy might have gone looking for ID, trying to figure out who he'd just stabbed."

"Here's what your scenarios have in common," Frank said. He was lying back with his arms folded behind his head, watching us, and that glint in his eye had got cockier. "Our guy planned to meet her once, which means he might very well want to meet her again, given the chance. He didn't plan to kill her, which means it's highly unlikely that there's any further danger. And he came from outside Whitethorn House."

"Not necessarily," Sam said. "If one of the housemates did it, he—or she—might have taken Lexie's mobile off her body, to make sure she hadn't called 999 or recorded anything. We know she used the video camera all the time; they could well have been worried that she'd put the attacker's name on there."

"Prints from the phone back yet?" I asked.

"This afternoon," Frank said. "Lexie and Abby. Both Abby and Daniel say that Abby passed Lexie her mobile that morning, on their way out to college, and the prints back that up. Lexie's are overlaid on Abby's in at least two places: she touched the phone after Abby did. Nobody took that phone off Lexie's body. It was at home on the kitchen table when she died, and any of the housemates could have found that out without needing to chase after her."

"Or they could've taken her diary," said Sam. "We've only their word for it that she didn't keep one."

Frank rolled his eyes. "If you want to play that game, we've only got their word for it that she even *lived* there. For all we know, she could have had a row with them a month ago and moved into the penthouse of the Shelbourne as the mistress of a Saudi prince, except there's not one speck of evidence that points that way. All four of their stories match up perfectly, we haven't caught any of them in a lie, she got stabbed *outside* the house—"

"What do you think?" Sam asked me, cutting Frank off. "Do they fit the profile?"

"Yeah, Cassie," Frank said sweetly. "What do *you* think?"

Sam so badly wanted it to be one of them. For a moment I actually wished I could say it was, and never mind what that would do to the investigation, just to see the drained look evaporate off his face, a spark come into his eyes. "Statistically," I said, "sure, close enough. They're the right age, they're local, they're smart, they knew her—not just that: they're the ones who knew her best, and that's where you mostly find your killer. None of them has a record, but like I said, one of them could have done stuff we don't know about, somewhere along the way. At first, yeah, I liked them for it. The more I hear, though . . ." I ran my hands through my hair and tried to figure out how to say this. "Here's the one thing I don't like taking their word for. Do we have any kind of independent confirmation that she normally went for these walks on her own? That none of the housemates went with her?"

"Actually," Frank said, feeling on the floor for his smokes, "we do. There's an English postgrad called Brenda Grealey, had the same supervisor as Lexie." Brenda Grealey was on the KA list: large, with sticking-out gooseberry eyes, plump cheeks already beginning to droop and a lot of ginger curls. "She's the nosy type. After the five of them moved in together, she asked Lexie if she ever got any privacy, living with all those guys. I get the feeling Brenda meant it as a double entendre, she was hoping for some kind of wild sex gossip, but apparently Lexie just gave her a blank look and said she went for solo walks every evening and that was all the privacy she needed, thanks, she didn't hang out with people unless she liked their company. Then she walked off. I'm not sure our Brenda realized she'd been bitchslapped."

"OK," I said. "In that case, I really can't see a way to make any of the housemates work. Look at how it would've had to play out. One of them needs to talk to Lexie in private, about something big. So, instead of going about it the inconspicuous way, bringing her for coffee in college or whatever, he goes on her walk with her, or follows her out. Either way, he's breaking the routine—and those five are all about the routine—and telling everyone including Lexie, loud and clear, that something's up. And then he brings along a *knife.* These are nice middle-class intellectuals we've got here—"

"She means they're a bunch of nancy boys," Frank informed Sam, over the click of his lighter.

"Ah, here," Sam said, putting his pen down. "Hang on. You can't rule them out just because they're middle-class. How many cases have we worked where some lovely, respectable—"

"I'm not, Sam," I said. "The killing's not the problem. If she'd been choked to death, or had her head smashed off a wall, I'd be fine with one of them as the doer. I don't even have a problem with the idea of one of them stabbing her, if he happened to be there with the knife in his hand. What I'm saying is that he wouldn't *have* the knife on him to begin with—not unless he was actually planning to kill her, and like I said before, that doesn't fit. I'm willing to bet serious money that those four don't make a habit of carrying knives around; and if they just wanted to threaten someone, or convince someone, it wouldn't even *occur* to them to use a knife to do it. That's not the world they live in. When they gear up for a big fight, they prepare by thinking out debate points, not picking out knives."

"Yeah," Sam said, after a moment. He took a deep breath and picked up his pen again, left it hanging above the page as if he'd forgotten what he meant to write. "I suppose they do, sure."

"Even if we go with the idea that one of them followed her," I said, "and brought along a knife to scare her with for some reason, what did he think was going to happen next? Did he seriously expect to get away with it? They're part of the same social circle. It's tiny, and it's intimate. There's no reason why she shouldn't agree to anything he wanted, then head straight home and tell the other three exactly what had happened. Cue shock, horror, and quite possibly—unless it's Daniel—our knife-wielder getting thrown out of Whitethorn House. These are smart people, Sam. They couldn't overlook something that obvious."

"In fairness," Frank said helpfully, switching sides— apparently he was getting bored—"smart people do stupid things all the time."

"Not like that," Sam said. He left his pen lying across his notebook and pressed two fingers into the corners of his eyes. "Stupid things, yeah, sure. Not things that make no sense at all."

I had put that look on his face, and I felt like crap. "Do they do drugs?" I asked. "People on coke, say, don't always think straight."

Frank snorted smoke. "I doubt it," said Sam, without looking up. "They're straight arrows, this lot. They take a drink, all right, but from the looks of them I wouldn't say they'd even be into the odd bit of hash, never mind the hard stuff. Our girl's tox screen came back clean as a whistle, remember?"

The wind hurled itself up against the window with a bang and a rattle, fell away again. "Then, unless we're missing something huge," I said, "they just don't add up."

After a moment Sam said, "Yeah." He closed his notebook carefully, clipped the pen onto it. "I'd better start looking for something huge, then."

"Can I ask you a question?" Frank inquired. "Why do you have such a hard-on for these four?"

Sam rubbed his hands down his face and blinked hard, like he was trying to focus. "Because they're there," he said, after a moment. "And no one else is, at least not so's you'd notice. Because if it's not them, what've we got?"

"You've got that lovely profile," Frank reminded him.

"I know," Sam said, heavily. "And I appreciate it, Cassie; I do, honest. But right now I've got no one that matches it. I've plenty of local fellas—women as well—in the right age group, some of them have records and I'd say there's a good few are smart and organized, but there's no sign that any of them ever met our girl. I've plenty of acquaintances from college, and a few of them tick just about all the boxes, except as far as I can find out they've never so much as been to Glenskehy, never mind knowing their way around the place. There's no one who matches right across the board."

Frank arched an eyebrow. "Not to labor the point," he said, "but that's what Detective Maddox and I are going after."

"Yeah," Sam said, without looking at him. "And if I find him fast enough, you won't need to."

"Better get a move on," Frank said. He was still lying back on the sofa, watching Sam through lazy, narrowed eyes across the curls of smoke. "I'm aiming to go in Sunday."

There was a second of absolute silence; even the wind outside seemed to have skidded to a stop. Frank had never mentioned a definite date before. In the corner of my eye the maps and photos on the table twitched and crystallized, unfurling into sun-glossed leaves, rippled glass, smooth-worn stone; turning real.

"This Sunday?" I said.

"Don't give me that gobsmacked look," Frank told me. "You'll be fine, babe. And think of it this way: you won't have to look at my ugly mug any more." Right at that moment, this actually did feel like a pretty big plus.

"Right," Sam said. He drained his coffee in long gulps and winced. "I'd better head." He stood up and patted vaguely at his pockets.

Sam lives on one of those creepy housing estates out in the middle of nowhere, he was dropping with fatigue and the wind was picking up again, ripping at the roof tiles. "Don't drive all that way, Sam," I said. "Not in this weather. Stay here. We'll be working pretty late, but—"

"Yeah, stick around," Frank said, spreading his arms and grinning up at him. "We can make it a pajama party. Toast marshmallows. Play Truth or Dare."

Sam took his coat off the back of the futon and stared at it as if he wasn't sure what to do with it. "Ah, no; I'm not going home, sure. I'll head into the squad for a bit, pull a few records. I'll be grand."

"Fair enough," Frank said cheerfully, waving good-bye. "Have fun. Be sure and ring us if you find a prime suspect."

I walked Sam downstairs and kissed him good night at the front door and he headed doggedly off towards his car, hands in his pockets and head bent hard against the wind. Maybe it was just the blast that funneled back up the stairwell with me, but without him my flat felt colder, barer somehow, a thin sharp edge in the air. "He was leaving anyway, Frank," I said. "You didn't have to be such a wankstain about it."

"Possibly not," Frank said, swinging himself vertical and starting to stack up the Chinese cartons. "But, as far as I can tell from the phone videos, Lexie didn't use the term 'wankstain.' In the relevant circumstances, she used 'git'—occasionally 'big smelly git'—or 'prat' or 'dickhead.' Just something to bear in mind. I'll do the washing up if you can tell me, without peeking, how to get from the house to the cottage."

Sam didn't try to make me dinner again, after that. He came in and out at weird hours, slept at his own place and said nothing when he found Frank on my sofa. Mostly he stayed just long enough to give me a kiss, a bag of supplies and a fast update. There wasn't a lot to tell. The Bureau and the floaters had combed every inch of the lanes where Lexie took her late-night walks: no blood trail, no identifiable footprints, no sign of a struggle or a hiding place—they were blaming the rain—and no weapon. Sam and Frank had called in a couple of favors to keep the media from jumping all over this one; they gave the press a carefully generic statement about an assault in Glenskehy, dropped vague hints that the victim had been taken to Wicklow Hospital, and set up discreet surveillance, but no one came looking for her, not even the housemates. The phone company came back with nothing good on Lexie's mobile. The door-to-door turned up blank shrugs, unprovable alibis (". . . and then when *Winning Streak* was over the wife and I went to bed"), a few snotty comments about the rich kids up at Whitethorn House, an awful lot of snotty comments about Byrne and Doherty and their sudden burst of interest in Glenskehy, and no useful info at all.

Given their relationship with the locals and their general enthusiasm level, Doherty and Byrne had been assigned to go through a bazillion hours of closed-circuit TV footage, looking for regular unexplained visitors to Glenskehy, but the cameras hadn't been positioned with this in mind and the best they could come up with was that they were fairly sure no one had driven into or out of Glenskehy by a direct route between ten and two on the night of the murder. This made Sam start talking about the housemates again, which made Frank point out the multiple ways someone could have got to Glenskehy without being picked up on CCTV, which made Byrne get snippy about suits who swanned down from Dublin and wasted everyone's time with point-less busywork. I got the sense that the incident room was blanketed by a dense, electric cloud of dead ends and turf wars and that nasty sinking feeling.

Frank had told the housemates that Lexie was coming home. They had sent her things: a get-well card and half a dozen Caramilk bars, pale-blue pajamas, clothes to wear home, moisturizer—that had to be Abby—two Barbara

Kingsolver books, a Walkman and a pile of mix tapes. Even aside from the fact that I hadn't seen a mix tape since I was about twenty, these were kind of hard to put your finger on—there was Tom Waits and Bruce Springsteen, music for late-night jukeboxes on long strange highways, in with Edith Piaf and the Guillemots and some woman called Amalia singing in throaty Portuguese. At least they were all good stuff; if there had been any Eminem on there, I would have had to pull the plug. The card said "Love" and the four names, nothing else; the briefness made it feel secretive, fizzing with messages I couldn't read. Frank ate the Caramilks.

The official story was that the coma had knocked out Lexie's short-term memory: she remembered nothing about the attack, very little about the days before. "Which has side benefits," Frank pointed out. "If you fuck up some detail, you can just look upset and murmur something helpless about the coma, and everyone'll be too embarrassed to push you." Meanwhile, back at the ranch, I had told my aunt and uncle and my friends that I was going off to do a training course—I kept it vague—and wouldn't be around for a few weeks. Sam had smoothed over my exit from work by having a chat with Quigley, the Murder squad's resident mistake, and telling him in confidence that I was taking a career break to finish my degree, which meant I would be covered if anyone spotted me hanging around town looking studenty. Quigley basically consists of a large arse and a large mouth, and he never liked me much. Within twenty-four hours it would be all over the grapevine that I was taking time out, probably with a few flourishes (pregnancy, psychosis, crack addiction) thrown in for good measure.

By Thursday Frank was firing questions at me: where do you sit for breakfast? where do you keep the salt? who gives you a lift into college on Wednesday mornings? what room is your supervisor's office? If I missed one, he zeroed in on that area, worked around it from every angle he had—photos, anecdotes, phone video, audio footage of interviews—till it felt like my own set of memories and the answer rolled off my tongue automatically. Then he went back to the question barrage: where did you spend the Christmas before last? what day of the week is your turn to buy food? It was like having a human tennis-ball machine on my sofa.

I didn't tell Sam this—it made me feel guilty, somehow—but I enjoyed that week. I like a challenge. It did occasionally occur to me that I was in a deeply weird situation and that it was only likely to get weirder. This case had a level of Möbius strip that made it hard to keep things straight: Lexies everywhere, sliding into each other at the edges till you started to lose track of which one you were talking about. Every now and then I had to catch myself back from asking Frank how she was doing.

Frank's sister Jackie was a hairdresser, so on Friday evening he brought her over to the flat, to cut my hair. Jackie was skinny, bleached blonde and totally unimpressed by her big brother. I liked her.

"Ah, yeah, you could do with a trim all right," she told me, giving my fringe a professional riffle with long purple nails. "How do you want it?"

"Here," Frank said, fishing out a crime-scene shot and passing it to her. "Can you do it to match this?"

Jackie held the photo between thumb and fingertip and gave it a suspicious look. "Here," she said. "Is your woman *dead*?"

"That's confidential," Frank said.

"Confidential, me arse. Is that your sister, love?"

"Don't look at me," I said. "This is Frank's gig. I'm only getting dragged along for the ride."

"You wouldn't want to mind him. Here—" She took another look at the photo and held it out to Frank at arm's length. "That's bleeding disgusting, so it is. Would you not think of doing something decent, Francis? Sorting out the traffic, something useful like that. Took me two hours to get into town from—"

"Would you ever just *cut*, Jackie?" Frank demanded, raking his hair exasperatedly so that it stood up in tufts. "And stop wrecking my head?" Jackie's eyes slid sideways to mine and we shared a tiny, mischievous, female grin.

"And remember," Frank said belligerently, noticing, "keep your mouth shut about this. Clear? It's crucial."

"Ah, yeah," Jackie said, pulling a comb and scissors out of her bag. "Crucial. Go and make us a cup of tea, will you? That's if you don't mind, love," she added, to me.

Frank shook his head and stamped off to the sink. Jackie combed my hair down over my eyes and winked at me.

When she was finished I looked different. I had never had my fringe cropped that short before; it was a subtle thing, but it made my face younger and barer, gave it the big-eyed, deceptive innocence of a model's. The longer I stared in the bathroom mirror, that night while I got ready for bed, the less it looked like me. When I hit the point where I couldn't remember what I had looked like to begin with, I gave up, gave the mirror the finger and went to bed.

On Saturday afternoon Frank said, "I think we're just about good to go."

I was lying back on the sofa with my knees hooked over the arm, going through the photos of Lexie's tutorial groups one last time and trying to look blasé about this whole thing. Frank was pacing: the closer you get to the start of an operation, the less he sits down.

"Tomorrow," I said. The word burned in my mouth, a wild clean burn like snow, taking my breath away.

"Tomorrow afternoon—we'll start you off with a half day, ease you into it. I'll let the housemates know this evening, make sure they're all there to give you a nice warm welcome. Think you're ready?"

I couldn't imagine what, on an operation like this, could possibly constitute "ready." "Ready as I'll ever be," I said.

"Let's hear it once more: what's your goal for Week One?"

"Not to get caught, mainly," I said. "And not to get killed."

"Not mainly; *only*." Frank snapped his fingers in front of my eyes on his way past. "Hey. Concentrate. This is important."

I put the photos down on my stomach. "I'm concentrating. What?"

"If someone's going to suss you, it'll be in the first few days, while you're still finding your feet and everyone's looking at you. So for Week One, all you do is ease your way in. This is hard work, it'll be tiring at first, and if you overdo it you'll start slipping—and all it takes is one slip. So go easy. Take time out if you can: go to bed early, read a book while the others play cards. If you make it to next weekend, you'll be into the swing of things, everyone else will have got used to having you back, they'll barely be looking at you any more, and you'll have a lot more leeway. Until then, though, you keep your head down: no risks, no sleuthing, nothing that could raise a single eyebrow. Don't even think about the case. I don't care if this time next week you don't have one single piece of useful info for me, as long as you're still in that house. If you are, we'll reassess and take it from there."

"But you don't really think I will be," I said. "Do you?"

Frank stopped pacing and gave me a long steady look. "Would I send you in there," he asked, "if I didn't think it could be done?"

"Sure you would," I said. "As long as you thought the results would be interesting either way, you wouldn't think twice."

He leaned back against the window frame, apparently considering that; the light was behind him and I couldn't see his expression. "Possible," he said, "but irrelevant. Yeah, sure, it's dicey as all hell. You've known that since Day One. But it can be done, as long as you're careful, you don't get spooked and you don't get impatient. Remember what I said last time, about asking questions?"

"Yep," I said. "Play innocent and ask as many of them as you can get away with."

"This time is different. You need to do the opposite: don't ask anything unless you're absolutely sure you're not meant to know the answer already. Which means, basically, don't ask anyone anything at all."

"So what am I supposed to do, if I can't ask questions?" I had been wondering about this.

Frank crossed the room fast, shoved paper off the coffee table and sat down, leaning in to me, blue eyes intent. "You keep your eyes and ears wide open. The main problem with this investigation is that we don't have a suspect. Your job is to identify one. Remember, nothing you get will be admissible anyway, since you can't exactly caution the suspects, so we're not gunning for a confession or anything like that. Leave that part to me and our Sammy. We'll make the case, if you just point us in the right direction. Find out if there's someone out there who's managed to stay off our radar—either someone left over from this girl's past, or someone she took up with more recently and kept a secret. If anyone who isn't on the KA list approaches you—by phone, in person, whatever—you play them along, find out what they're after and what the relationship was, and get a phone number and full name if you can."

"Right," I said. "Your mystery man." It sounded plausible enough, but then Frank always does. I was still pretty sure that Sam was right and his main reason for doing this wasn't because he thought it had a snowball's chance in hell but because it was such a dazzling, reckless, ridiculous once-off. I decided I didn't care.

"Exactly. To go with our mystery girl. Meanwhile, keep an eye on the housemates and keep them talking. I don't rate them as suspects—I know your Sammy has a bee in his bonnet about them, but I'm with you, they don't add up—but I'm pretty sure there's something they're not telling us. You'll see what I mean when you meet them. It might be something completely irrelevant, maybe they just cheat on their exams or make moonshine in the back garden or know who's the daddy, but I'd like to decide for myself what's relevant here and what's not. They're never going to talk to cops, but if you go at it right, there's a good chance they'll talk to you. Don't worry too much about her other KAs—we've got nothing that points to any of them, and Sammy and I will be on them anyway—but if anyone's acting even slightly dodgy, obviously, report back to me. Got it?"

"Got it," I said.

"One last thing," said Frank. He unfolded himself from the table, found our coffee mugs and took them over to the kitchen. We had got to the point where there was always, every hour of the day or night, a large pot of strong coffee keeping warm on the cooker; another week and we would probably have been eating the grounds straight from the bag with a spoon. "I've been meaning to have a little chat with you for a while now."

I had felt this one coming for days. I flipped through the photos like flash cards and tried to concentrate on running the names in my head: Cillian Wall, Chloe Nelligan, Martina Lawlor . . . "Hit me," I said.

Frank put the mugs down and started playing with my saltcellar, turning it carefully between his fingers. "I hate to bring this up," he said, "but what can you do, sometimes life sucks. You're aware that you've been—how shall I put this—a little jumpy lately, yeah?"

"Yeah," I said, keeping my eyes on the photos. Isabella Smythe, Brian Ryan—someone's parents either hadn't been thinking too clearly, or had a weird sense of humor—Mark O'Leary . . . "I'm aware."

"I don't know if it's because of this case or if it was going on already or what, and I don't need to know. If it's just stage fright, it might well vanish as soon as you're inside that door. But here's what I wanted to say to you: if it doesn't, *don't panic*. Don't start second-guessing yourself, or you'll talk yourself into losing your nerve, and don't try to hide it. Use it. There's no reason why Lexie shouldn't be a little shaky right now, and there's no reason why you shouldn't make that work for you. Use what you've got, even if it's not necessarily what you'd have chosen. Everything's a weapon, Cass. Everything."

"I'll keep that in mind," I said. The thought of Operation Vestal actually coming in useful did something complicated inside my chest, made it hard to breathe. I knew if I blinked Frank would notice.

"Think you can do that?"

Lexie, I thought, *Lexie wouldn't tell him to mind his own business and let her mind hers,* which was my main instinct here, *and she sure as hell wouldn't answer. Lexie would yawn in his face, or tell him to quit nagging and lecturing like someone's granny, or demand ice cream.* "We're out of biscuits," I said, stretching—the photos slid off my stomach, all over the floor. "Go get some. Lemon creams," and then I laughed out loud at the look on Frank's face.

Frank graciously gave me Saturday night off—heart of gold, our Frankie—so Sam and I could say our good-byes. Sam made chicken tikka for dinner; for dessert I tried an incongruous tiramisu, which turned out looking ridiculous but tasting OK. We talked about small stuff, unimportant stuff, touching hands across the table and swapping the little things that new couples pass back and forth and save like beach finds: stories from when we were kids, the dumbest things we'd done as teenagers. Lexie's clothes, hanging on the wardrobe door, shimmered in the corner like hard sun on sand, but we didn't mention them, not once.

After dinner we curled up on the sofa. I had lit a fire, Sam had put music on the CD player; it could have been any evening, it could have been all ours, except for those clothes and for the fast ready beat of my pulse, waiting.

"How're you doing?" Sam asked.

I had been starting to hope we could make it through

the night without talking about tomorrow, but realistically this was probably too much to ask. "OK," I said.

"Are you nervous?"

I thought this over. This situation was totally bananas on about a dozen different levels. I probably should have been petrified. "No," I said. "Excited."

I felt Sam nod, against the top of my head. He was running one hand over my hair in a slow, soothing rhythm, but his chest felt rigid as a board against mine, like he was holding his breath.

"You hate this idea, don't you?" I said.

"Yeah," Sam said quietly. "I do."

"Why didn't you stop it? It's your investigation. You could have put your foot down, any time you felt like it."

Sam's hand stopped still. "Do you want me to?"

"No," I said. That, at least, I knew for sure. "No way."

"It wouldn't be easy, at this stage. Now that the undercover operation's up and running, it's Mackey's baby; I've no authority there. But if you've changed your mind, I'll find a way to—"

"I haven't, Sam. Seriously. I just wondered why you gave the OK to start with."

He shrugged. "Mackey has a point, sure: we've nothing else on the case. This could be the only way to solve it."

Sam has unsolveds with his name on them, every detective has, and I was pretty sure he could survive another one, as long as he was sure the guy hadn't been after me. "You didn't have anything last Saturday, either," I said, "and you were dead against it then."

His hand started moving again, absently. "That first day," he said, after a while. "When you came down to the scene. You were messing with Mackey, do you remember? He was slagging you about your clothes and you were slagging back, almost like the way you used to with . . . when you were on Murder."

He meant with Rob. Rob was probably the closest friend

I've ever had, but then we had this huge complicated vicious fight and that was the end of that. I twisted round and propped myself on Sam's chest so I could see him, but he was looking up at the ceiling. "I hadn't seen you like that in a while," he said. "That much bounce to you."

"I've probably been pretty crap company, these last few months," I said.

He smiled, just a little. "I'm not complaining."

I tried to remember ever hearing Sam complain about anything. "No," I said. "I know."

"Then Saturday," he said. "I know we were fighting and all"—he gave me a quick squeeze, dropped a kiss on my forehead—"but still. I realized afterwards: that was because we were both really into it, this case. Because you cared. It felt . . ." He shook his head, looking for the words. "DV's not the same," he said, "is it?"

I had mostly kept my mouth shut about DV. It hadn't occurred to me, till then, that all that silence could have been plenty revealing, in its own way. "It needs doing," I said. "Nothing's the same as Murder, but DV's fine."

Sam nodded, and for a second his arms tightened around me. "And that meeting," he said. "Right up until then, I'd been wondering should I pull rank and tell Mackey to bugger off for himself. This started off as a murder case, I'm down as lead detective, if I said no . . . But the way you were talking, all interested, thinking it out . . . I just thought, why would I wreck that?"

I had not seen this coming. Sam has one of those faces that fool you even when you know better: a countryman's face, all ruddy cheeks and clear gray eyes and crow's-feet starting, so simple and open that there couldn't possibly be anything hidden behind it. "Thanks, Sam," I said. "Thank you."

I felt his chest lift and fall as he sighed. "It might turn out to be a good thing, this case. You never know."

"But you still wish this girl had picked just about anywhere else to get herself killed," I said.

Sam thought about that for a minute, twisting a finger delicately through one of my curls. "Yeah," he said, "I do, of course. But there's no point in wishing. Once you're stuck with something, all you can do is make the best of it."

He looked down at me. He was still smiling, but there was something else, something almost sad, around his eyes. "You've looked happy, this week," he said simply. "It's nice to see you looking happy again."

I wondered how the hell this man put up with me. "Plus you knew I would kick your arse if you started making decisions for me," I said.

Sam grinned and flicked the end of my nose with his finger. "That too," he said, "my little vixen," but there was still that shadow behind his eyes.

Sunday moved fast, after those long ten days, fast as a tidal wave built to bursting point and finally crashing down. Frank was coming over at three, to wire me up and get me to Whitethorn House by half past four. All the time Sam and I were going through our Sunday-morning routine— the newspapers and leisurely cups of tea in bed, the shower, the toast and eggs and bacon—that was hanging over our heads, a huge alarm clock ticking, waiting for its moment to explode into life. Somewhere out there, the housemates were getting ready to welcome Lexie home.

After brunch, I put on the clothes. I got dressed in the bathroom; Sam was still there, and I wanted to do this in private. The clothes felt like something more: fine chain-mail armor handmade to fit me, or robes laid out ready for some fiercely secret ceremony. They made my palms tingle when I touched them.

Plain white cotton underwear with the Penney's tags still on; faded jeans, worn soft and fraying at the hems; brown socks, brown ankle boots; a long-sleeved white T-shirt; a pale-blue suede jacket, scuffed but clean. The collar of it smelled of lilies of the valley and something else, a warm note almost too faint to catch: Lexie's skin. In one of the pockets there was a Dunne's Stores receipt from a few weeks back, for chicken fillets, shampoo, butter and a bottle of ginger ale.

When I was dressed I checked myself out, in the full-length mirror on the back of the door. For a second I didn't know what I was seeing. Then, ridiculously, all I wanted was to laugh. It was the irony of it: I had spent months dressing up as Executive Barbie, and now that I was being someone else, I finally got to go to work dressed a lot like me. "You look nice," Sam said, with a faint smile, when I came out. "Comfortable."

My stuff was packed and waiting by the door, as if I were off on some voyage; I felt like I should be checking my passport and tickets. Frank had bought me a nice new traveling case, the hard kind, with discreet reinforcement and a solid combination lock; it would take a safecracker to get in there. Inside were Lexie's things—wallet, keys, phone, all dead ringers for the real things; the stuff from the housemates; a plastic tub of vitamin C tablets with a pharmacist's label that said AMOXICILLIN TABS TAKE ONE THREE TIMES DAILY, to go somewhere prominent. My gear was in a separate compartment: latex gloves, my mobile, spare battery packs for the mike, a supply of artistically stained bandages to go in the bathroom bin every morning and evening, my notebook, my ID and my new gun—Frank had got me a .38 snub-nose that felt good in my hand and was a lot easier to hide than my regulation Smith & Wesson. There was also—seriously—a girdle, the industrial-strength elastic kind that's supposed to give you a smooth silhouette in your Little Black Dress. It's a lot of undercovers' version of a holster. It's not comfortable—after an hour or two you feel like there's a gun-shaped dent in your liver—but it does a good job of hiding the outline. Just the thought of Frank going into the Marks & Sparks lingerie department and picking it out made this whole thing worthwhile.

"You look like shite," he said, examining me approvingly,

when he arrived at the door of my flat. He was carrying a double armful of Bond-looking black electronics, cables and speakers and God knows what: the setup for the wire. "The eye bags are to die for."

"She's had three hours' sleep a night," Sam said tightly, behind me. "Same as yourself and myself. And we're not exactly looking the best either."

"Hey, I'm not giving her hassle," Frank told him, heading past us and dumping the armful on the coffee table. "I'm delighted with her. She looks like she's been in intensive care for ten days. Hi, babe."

The mike was tiny, the size of a shirt button. It clipped onto the front of my bra, between my breasts: "Lucky our girl didn't go in for low-cut tops," Frank said, glancing at his watch. "Go lean over in front of the mirror, check the view." The battery pack went where the knife wound should have been, surgical-taped to my side under a thick pad of white gauze, just an inch or two below the scar Dealer Boy had left on Lexie Madison the First. The sound quality, once Frank had done small complicated things to the equipment, was crystal clear: "Only the best for you, babe. Transmission radius is seven miles, depending on conditions. We've got receivers set up at Rathowen station and at the Murder squad, so you'll be covered at home and in Trinity. The only time you'll go out of coverage is on the drive to and from town, and I don't anticipate anyone shoving you out of a moving car. You won't have visual surveillance, so any visuals that we should know about, tell us. If the shit hits the fan and you need a subtle way to yell for help, say 'My throat hurts' and you'll have big-time backup on the scene inside a few minutes—don't go getting a sore throat for real, or if you do, don't complain about it. You need to check in with me as often as possible, ideally every day."

"And with me," Sam said, not turning around from the sink. Frank, squatting on the floor and squinting at some dial on his receiver, didn't even bother to throw me a mocking look.

Sam finished the washing up and started drying things too thoroughly. I sorted the Lexie material into some kind of order—that high-wire final-exam feeling, taking your hands off your notes at last, *If I don't know it now*—stacked it in bundles and packed it into plastic bags, to leave in Frank's car. "And that," Frank said, unplugging the speakers with a flourish, "should do it. Are we good to go?"

"Ready when you are," I said, picking up the plastic bags. Frank swept up his equipment one-armed, grabbed my case and headed for the door.

"I'll take that," Sam said brusquely. "You've enough to carry," and he took the case from Frank's hand and headed down the stairs, the wheels hitting each step with a hard dull thump.

On the landing Frank turned and looked back over his shoulder, waiting for me. My hand was on the door handle when for a split second out of nowhere I was terrified, blue-blazing terrified, fear dropping straight through me like a jagged black stone falling fast. I'd felt this before, in the limbo instants before I moved out of my aunt's house, lost my virginity, took my oath as a police officer: those instants when the irrevocable thing you wanted so much suddenly turns real and solid, inches away and speeding at you, a bottomless river rising and no way back once it's crossed. I had to catch myself back from crying out like a little kid drowning in terror, *I don't want to do this any more.*

All you can do with that moment is bite down and wait for it to be over. The thought of what Frank would have to say, if I actually pulled out now, helped a lot. I took one more look around my flat—lights off, water heater off, bins emptied, window locked; the room was already closing in on itself, silence seeping into the spaces where we had been, drifting up like dust in the corners. Then I shut the door.

5

The drive down to Glenskehy took almost an hour, even with no traffic and Frank driving, and it should have been excruciating. Sam slumped miserably in the back seat, next to the gadgetry; Frank helped the atmosphere by turning up 98FM nice and loud and bopping along, whistling and nodding his head and beating time on the steering wheel. I barely even noticed either of them. It was a gorgeous afternoon, sunny and crisp, I was out of my flat for the first time in a full week, and I had the window rolled all the way down and wind streaking through my hair. That hard black stone of fear had dissolved the second Frank started the car, turned into something sweet and lemon-colored and wildly intoxicating.

"Right," Frank said, when we hit Glenskehy, "let's see how well you've learned your geography. Give me directions."

"Straight on through the village, fourth lane to your right, way too narrow, no wonder Daniel and Justin's cars look like they've been drag racing, give me good old dirty Dublin any day," I told him, doing his accent. "Home, James." I was on a giddy one. The jacket had been freaking me out all afternoon—it was that lily-of-the-valley smell, right up close, I kept whipping round to see who had come up beside me—and the fact that I was being given the heebie-jeebies by a jacket, like something out of Dr. Seuss, was making me want to giggle. Even passing the turnoff to the cottage, where I had met Frank and Sam that first day, didn't sober me up.

The lane was unpaved and potholey. Trees gone shapeless with years of ivy, hedge branches rattling along the sides of the car and flicking in at my window; and then huge wrought-iron gates, flaking with rust and hanging drunkenly off their hinges. The stone pillars were half drowned in hawthorn grown wild. "Here," I said.

Frank nodded and turned, and we were looking down an endless, graceful sweep of avenue, between cherry trees crowded with exploded balls of flowers. "Fuck me," I said. "Why did I have doubts about this, again? Can I sneak Sam in with me in my suitcase, and we can just live here forever?"

"Get it out of your system," Frank said. "By the time we reach that door, you need to be blasé about all this. Anyway, the house is still shitty, so you can calm down."

"You told me they'd redone it. I expect cashmere curtains and white roses in my dressing room, or I'm calling my agent."

"I said they were doing it up. I didn't say they were *magic*."

Then the drive gave a little twist and opened up into a great semicircular carriage sweep, white pebbles speckled through with weeds and daisies, and I saw Whitethorn House for the first time. The photos hadn't done it justice. You see Georgian houses all over Dublin, mostly turned into offices and undermined by the depressing fluorescents you can see through the windows, but this one was special. Every proportion was balanced so perfectly that the house looked like it had grown there, nested in with its back to the mountains and all Wicklow dropping away rich and gentle in front of it, poised between the pale arc of the carriage sweep and the blurred dark-and-green curves of the hills like a treasure held out in a cupped palm.

I heard Sam take a fast hard breath. "Home sweet home," said Frank, turning the radio off.

They were waiting for me outside the door, ranged at the top of the steps. In my mind I still see them like that, lacquered gold by the evening sun and glowing vivid as a vision, every fold of their clothes and curve of their faces pristine and achingly clear. Rafe leaning against the railing with his hands in his jeans pockets; Abby in the middle, swayed forwards on her toes, one arm crooked to shade her eyes; Justin, his feet precisely together and his hands clasped behind his back. And behind them, Daniel, framed between the columns of the door, his head up and the light splintering off his glasses.

None of them moved as Frank pulled up and braked, pebbles scattering. They were like figures on a medieval frieze, self-contained, mysterious, spelling out a message in some lost and arcane code. Only Abby's skirt fluttered, fitfully, in the breeze.

Frank glanced at me over his shoulder. "Ready?"

"Yeah."

"Good girl," he said. "Good luck. And we're go." He got out of the car and went round to the boot to get my case.

"Mind yourself," Sam said. He didn't look at me. "I love you."

"I'll be home soon," I said. There was no way even to touch his arm, under all those unblinking eyes. "I'll try to ring you tomorrow."

He nodded. Frank slammed the boot—the sound was wild, enormous, bouncing off the house front and setting crows scattering from the trees—and opened the car door for me.

I got out, putting my hand to my side for a second as I straightened up. "Thanks, Detective," I said to Frank. "Thanks for everything."

We shook hands. "My pleasure," Frank said. "And don't worry, Miss Madison: we'll get this guy."

He pulled out the handle of the case with a neat snap and passed it to me, and I dragged it across the carriage sweep towards the steps and the others.

Still none of them moved. As I got closer I realized, with a shift of focus like a shock. Those straight backs, the lifted heads: there was some tension stretched between the four of them, so tight it hummed high in the silence. The wheels of my case, grating across the pebbles, sounded loud as machine-gun fire.

"Hi," I said at the bottom of the steps, looking up at them.

For a second I thought they weren't going to answer, they had made me already, and I wondered wildly what the hell I was supposed to do now. Then Daniel took a step forwards, and the picture wavered and broke. A smile started across Justin's face, Rafe straightened up and raised one arm in a wave, and Abby came running down the steps and hugged me hard.

"Hey, you," she said, laughing, "welcome home." Her hair smelled like chamomile. I dropped the case and hugged her back; it was a strange feeling, as if I were touching someone out of an old painting, amazed to find her shoulder blades warm and solid as my own. Daniel nodded gravely at me over her head and ruffled my hair, Rafe grabbed my case and started bumping it up the steps to the door, Justin patted my back over and over and I was laughing too, and I didn't even hear Frank start the car and drive away.

This is the first thing I thought when I stepped into Whitethorn House: *I've been here before.* It zinged straight through me, straightened my spine like a crash of cymbals. The place bloody well should have looked familiar, all the hours I'd spent staring at photos and video, but it was more than that. It was the smell, old wood and tea leaves and a faint whiff of dried lavender; it was the way the light lay along the scarred floorboards; it was the little taps our footsteps sent flying up the stairwell, echoing softly along the upstairs corridors. It felt—and you'd think I would like this but I didn't, it flashed danger-sign red right across my mind—it felt like coming home.

From there on, most of that evening is a merry-go-round blur, colors and images and voices whirled together into a burst almost too bright to look at. A ceiling rose and a cracked china vase, a piano stool and a bowl of oranges, running feet on stairs and a rising laugh. Abby's fingers small and strong on my wrist, leading me out to the flagstoned patio behind the house, curlicued metal chairs, ancient wicker swing seat swaying in the light sweet breeze; great sweep of grass falling away to high stone walls half hidden in trees and ivy, blink of a bird's shadow across the paving stones. Daniel lighting my cigarette, his hand cupped round the match and his bent head inches from mine. The full ring of their voices hit me like a shock, after the flattened-out video sound, and their eyes were so clear they burned on my skin. Sometimes, still, I wake up with one of their voices strong and close by my ear, fallen straight out of that day: *Come here,* Justin calls, *come outside, the evening's so lovely;* or Abby says, *We have to decide what to do with the herb garden, but we were waiting for you, what do you*—and I'm awake, and they're gone.

I must have talked too, somewhere in there, but I can't remember most of what I said. All I remember is trying to keep my weight forwards on my toes like Lexie did, my voice up in her register, my eyes and my shoulders and my smoke at the right angles, trying not to look around too much and not to move too fast without wincing and not to say anything idiotic and not to whack into the furniture. And God the taste of undercover on my tongue again, the brush of it down the little hairs on my arms. I'd thought I remembered what it was like, every detail, but I'd been wrong: memories are nothing, soft as gauze against the ruthless razor-fineness of that edge, beautiful and lethal, one tiny slip and it'll slice to the bone.

It took my breath away, that evening. If you've ever dreamed that you walked into your best-loved book or film or TV program, then maybe you've got some idea how it felt: things coming alive around you, strange and new and utterly familiar at the same time; the catch in your heartbeat as you move through the rooms that had such a vivid untouchable life in your mind, as your feet actually touch the carpet, as you breathe the air; the odd, secret glow of warmth as these people you've been watching for so long, from so far away, open their circle and sweep you into it. Abby and I rocked the swing seat lazily; the guys moved in and out through the small-paned French windows between the patio and the kitchen, making dinner—smell of roasting potatoes, sizzle of meat, suddenly I was starving—and calling to us. Rafe came outside to lean on the back of the seat between us and take a drag of Abby's cigarette. Rose-gold sky deepening and great puffs of cloud streaming like the smoke of some faraway wildfire, cool air rich with grass and earth and growing things. "Dinner!" Justin yelled, against a clatter of plates.

That long, laden table, immaculate in its heavy red damask cloth, its snow-white napkins; the candlesticks twined with strands of ivy, flames glittering miniature in the curves of the glasses, catching in the silver, beckoning in the dimming windows like will-o'-the-wisps. And the four of them, pulling up high-backed chairs, smooth-skinned and shadow-eyed in the confusing golden light: Daniel at the head of the table and Abby at the foot, Rafe beside me and Justin opposite. In the flesh, that ceremonial feel I had caught off the videos and Frank's notes was powerful as incense. It was like sitting down to a banquet, a war council, a game of Russian roulette high in some lonely tower.

They were so beautiful. Rafe was the only one who could have been called good-looking; but still, when I remember them, that beauty is all I can think of.

Justin loaded up plates with Steak Diane and passed them around—"Specially for you," he told me, with a faint smile; Rafe scooped roast potatoes onto them as they passed him. Daniel poured red wine into mismatched wineglasses.

This evening was taking every brain cell I had; the last thing I needed was to get drunk. "I'm not supposed to have booze," I said. "The antibiotics."

It was the first time any of us had brought up the stabbing, even indirectly. For a fraction of a second—or maybe it was just my imagination—the room seemed to stop motionless, the bottle suspended in midtilt, hands arrested halfway through gestures. Then Daniel went back to pouring, with a deft twist of the wrist that left less than an inch in the glass. "There," he said, unruffled. "A sip won't do you any harm. Just for a toast."

He passed me my glass and filled his own. "To homecomings," he said.

In the moment when that glass passed from his hand to mine, something sent up a high wild warning cry in the back of my mind. Persephone's irrevocable pomegranate seeds, *Never take food from strangers;* old stories where one sip or bite seals the spellbound walls forever, dissolves the road home into mist and blows it away on the wind. And then, sharper: *If it was them, after all, and it's poisoned; Jesus, what a way to go.* And I realized, with a thrill like an electric shock, that they would be well able for it. That poised quartet waiting for me at the door, with their straight backs and their cool, watchful eyes: they were more than capable of playing the game all evening, waiting with immaculate control and without a single slip for their chosen moment.

But they were all smiling at me, glasses raised, and I didn't have a choice. "Homecomings," I said, and leaned over the table to clink their glasses among the ivy and the candle flames: Justin, Rafe, Abby, Daniel. I took a sip of the wine—it was warm and rich and smooth, honey and summer berries, and I felt it right down to the tips of my fingers—and then I picked up my knife and fork and sliced into my steak.

Maybe it was just that I needed food—the steak was delicious and my appetite had resurfaced like it was trying to make up for lost time, but unfortunately no one had mentioned anything about Lexie eating like a horse, so I wasn't going to be asking for seconds—but that was when they came into focus for me, that dinner; that's when the memories start to fall into sequence, like glass beads caught on a string, and the evening changes from a bright blur into something real and manageable. "Abby got a poppet," Rafe said, dumping potatoes on his plate. "We were going to burn her as a witch, but we decided to wait till you got back, so we could put it to a democratic vote."

"Burn Abby, or the poppet?" I asked.

"Both."

"It is not a poppet," Abby said, flicking Rafe in the arm. "It's a late-Victorian doll, and Lexie will appreciate it, because she's not a Philistine."

"I'd appreciate it from a distance, if I were you," Justin told me. "I think it's possessed. Its eyes keep following me."

"So lie her down. Her eyes close."

"I'm not touching it. What if it bites me? I'll have to wander the outer darkness for all eternity, searching for my soul—"

"God, I've missed you," Abby told me. "I've been stuck with no one to talk to except this bunch of wusses. It's just an itsy-bitsy dolly, Justin."

"Poppet," Rafe said, through potatoes. "Seriously. It's made from a sacrificed goat."

"Mouth full, you," Abby told him. To me: "It's kidskin. With a bisque head. I found her in a hatbox in the room opposite me. Her clothes are in bits, and I finished the footstool, so I figured I might as well make her a new wardrobe. There are all these old scraps of material—"

"And then there's its hair," Justin said, pushing the vegetables across to me. "Don't forget the hair. It's horrible."

"It's wearing a dead person's hair," Rafe informed me. "If you stick a pin in the doll, you can hear screaming coming from the graveyard. Try it."

"See what I mean?" Abby said, to me. "Wusses. It's got real hair. Why he thinks it's from a dead person—"

"Because your poppet was made in about 1890 and I can do subtraction."

"And what graveyard? There's no graveyard."

"There is somewhere. Somewhere out there, every time you touch that doll, someone twitches in her grave."

"Until you get rid of the Head," Abby said with dignity, "you don't get to slag my doll for being creepy."

"That's not the same thing at all. The Head is a valuable scientific tool."

"I like the Head," said Daniel, glancing up, surprised. "What's wrong with it?"

"It looks like something Aleister Crowley would carry around, is what's wrong with it. Back me up here, Lex."

Frank and Sam hadn't told me, maybe they'd never seen, the most important thing about these four: just how close they were. The phone videos hadn't been able to catch the power of it, any more than they'd caught the house. It was like a shimmer in the air between them, like glittering web-fine threads tossed back and forth and in and out until every movement or word reverberated through the whole group: Rafe passing Abby her smokes almost before she glanced around for them, Daniel turning with his hands out ready to take the steak dish in the same second that Justin brought it through the door, sentences flicked onto each other like playing cards with never a fraction of a pause. Rob and I used to be like that: seamless.

My main feeling was that I was fucked. These four had harmonies close as the most polished a cappella group on the planet, and I had to pick up my line and join in the jam session without missing a single beat. I had a little leeway for weakness and medication and general trauma—right now they were just happy I was home and talking, what I actually said was beside the point—but that would only carry me so far, and nobody had told me anything about a Head. No matter how upbeat Frank had been, I was pretty positive that the incident room had a sweepstakes going—behind Sam's back; not necessarily behind Frank's—on how long it would be before I went down in a spectacular fireball, and that most of the spread was clustered under three days. I didn't blame them. I should have got in on the action: a tenner on twenty-four hours.

"I want to hear the news," I said. "What's been happening? Was anyone asking after me? Do I have get-well cards?"

"You got hideous flowers," Rafe said, "from the English

department. Those huge mutant daisy things, dyed lurid colors. They wilted, thank God."

"Four-Boobs Brenda tried to comfort Rafe," Abby said, with a one-sided grin. "In his time of need."

"Oh God," Rafe said in horror, dropping his knife and fork and putting his hands over his face. Justin started to snicker. "She did. She and her bosomage cornered me in the photocopy room and asked me how I was *feeling*."

That had to be Brenda Grealey. I couldn't see her being Rafe's type. I laughed too—they were working hard to keep the mood up, and Brenda was starting to sound like a gee-bag anyway. "I think he quite enjoyed it, deep down," Justin said demurely. "He came out reeking of cheap perfume."

"I almost asphyxiated. She pinned me up against the photocopier—"

"Was there wucka-wucka music playing in the background?" I asked. It was feeble but I was doing my best, and I caught Abby's quick sideways smile, the flick of relief across Justin's face. "What on earth have you been watching in that hospital?" Daniel wanted to know.

"—and she *breathed* all over me," Rafe said. "Moistly. It was like being molested by a walrus soaked in air freshener."

"The inside of your head is a horrible place," Justin told him.

"She wanted to buy me a drink so we could *talk*. She said I needed to open up. What does that even *mean*?"

"Sounds like she's the one who wanted to open up," Abby said. "So to speak." Rafe made a fake gagging noise.

"You're disgusting too," Justin said.

"Thank God for me," I said. Talking still felt like poking black ice with a stick. "I'm the civilized one."

"Well," Justin said, giving me a small, tucked-in smile. "Hardly. But we love you anyway. Have more steak; you're eating like a wee bird. Don't you like it?"

Hallelujah: apparently Lexie and I shared the same metabolism, as well as everything else. "It's gorgeous, silly," I said. "I'm still getting my appetite back."

"Yes, well." Justin leaned across the table to spoon steak onto my plate. "You need to build up your strength."

"Justin," I said, "you've always been my favorite."

He flushed right up to his hairline, and before he could hide behind his glass I saw something painful—what, I couldn't tell—flick across his face. "Don't be absurd," he said. "We missed you."

"I missed you, too," I said, and gave him a wicked grin. "Mostly because of hospital food."

"Typical," said Rafe.

For a moment I was sure Justin was going to say something else, but then Daniel reached over to refill his glass and Justin blinked, the flush subsiding, and picked up his knife and fork again. There was one of those content, absorbed silences that go with good food. Something rippled round the table: a loosening, a settling, a long sigh too low to hear. *Un ange passe,* my French grandfather would have said: an angel is passing. Somewhere upstairs I heard the faint, dreamy note of a clock striking.

Daniel cut his eyes sideways at Abby, so subtly I barely caught it. He was the one who had done the least talking, all evening. He was quiet on the phone videos, too, but this seemed to have a different flavor to it, a concentrated intensity, and I wasn't sure whether this just didn't translate well onto camera or whether it was new. "So," Abby said. "How're you feeling, Lex?"

They had all stopped eating. "Fine," I said. "I'm not supposed to lift anything heavy for a few weeks."

"Are you in any pain?" Daniel inquired.

I shrugged. "They gave me supercool painkillers, but most of the time I don't need them. I'm not even gonna have much of a scar. They had to sew up all my insides, but I only got six stitches on the outside."

"Let's see them," Rafe said.

"God," said Justin, putting his fork down. He looked like he was seconds from leaving the table. "You're a ghoul. I have no desire to see them, thanks very much."

"I definitely don't want to see them at the dinner table," Abby said. "No offense."

"Nobody's seeing them anywhere," I said, narrowing my eyes at Rafe—I was ready for this one. "I've been getting poked and prodded all week, and the next person who goes anywhere near my stitches gets his finger bitten off."

Daniel was still inspecting me thoughtfully. "You tell 'em," said Abby.

"Are you sure it doesn't hurt?" There was a pinched, white look around Justin's mouth and nose, as if even the thought had him in pain. "It must have hurt, at first. Was it bad?"

"She's fine," said Abby. "She just said so."

"I'm only *asking*. The police kept saying—"

"Don't *poke* at it."

"What?" I asked. "What did the police keep saying?"

"I think," Daniel said, calmly but finally, turning in his chair to look at Justin, "that we should leave it at that."

Another silence, less comfortable this time. Rafe's knife screeched on his plate; Justin winced; Abby reached for the pepper shaker, gave it a hard tap on the table and shook it briskly.

"The police asked," Daniel said suddenly, glancing up at me over his glass, "whether you kept a diary or a date book, anything along those lines. I thought it was best for us to say no."

Diary?

"Dead right," I said. "I don't want them looking through my stuff."

"They already did," Abby said. "Sorry. They searched your room."

"Ah, for fuck's *sake*," I said, indignant. "Why didn't you stop them?"

"We didn't get the sense it was optional," Rafe said dryly.

"What if I'd had love letters, or—or stud-muffin porn, or something *private*?"

"Presumably that's exactly what they were looking for."

"They were fascinating, actually," Daniel said. "The police. Most of them seemed utterly uninterested: all routine. I would have loved to watch them do the search, but I don't think it would have been a good idea to ask."

"They didn't get what they were after, anyway," I said with satisfaction. "Where is it, Daniel?"

"I have no idea," Daniel said, mildly surprised. "Wherever you keep it, I assume," and he went back to his steak.

The guys cleared the plates away; Abby and I sat at the table, smoking, in a silence that was starting to feel companionable. I heard someone doing something in the sitting room, hidden behind wide sliding double doors, and the smell of wood smoke seeped out to us. "Peaceful one tonight?" Abby asked, watching me over her cigarette. "Just read?"

After dinner was their free time: cards, music, reading, talking, slowly knocking the house into shape. Reading sounded like the easiest option by about a mile. "Perfect," I said. "I've got loads of thesis catching-up to do."

"Relax," Abby said—that small one-sided smile again. "You're only just home. You've got all the time in the world." She stubbed out her smoke and threw open the sliding doors.

The sitting room was huge and, unexpectedly, wonderful. The photos had caught only the shabbiness, missed the atmosphere altogether. High ceiling, with moldings along the edges; wide floorboards, unvarnished and lumpy; horrible flowered wallpaper, peeling in patches to show the old layers underneath—rose and gold stripes, a dull cream-colored sheen like silk. The furniture was mismatched and ancient: a scuffed card table in inlaid rosewood, faded brocade armchairs, a long uncomfortable-looking sofa, bookshelves jammed with tattered leather covers and bright paperbacks. There was no overhead light, just standing lamps and a wood fire crackling in a massive wrought-iron

fireplace, throwing wild shadows scudding among the cobwebs in the high corners. The room was a mess, and I fell in
love with it before I was through the doorway.

The armchairs looked cozy and I was right on the edge
of heading for one of them when my mind slammed on the
brakes, hard. I could hear my heart. I had no idea where I
was supposed to sit; my head had gone blank. The food, the
easy slagging, the comfortable silence with Abby: I had
relaxed.

"Back in a sec," I said, and hid in the bathroom to let the
others narrow things down by taking their places, and to let
my knees stop shaking. By the time I could breathe right,
my brain had come out of neutral and I knew where my seat
was: a low Victorian nursing chair to one side of the fireplace. Frank had shown me photos by the handful. I had
known that.

It would have been that easy: sitting down in the wrong
chair. Barely four hours.

Justin glanced up, with a faint worried furrow between
his eyebrows, when I went back into the sitting room, but
nobody said anything. My books were spread out on a low
table by my chair: thick historical references, a dog-eared
copy of *Jane Eyre* open face-down across a lined notepad, a
yellowing pulp novel called *She Dressed to Kill* by Rip
Corelli—presumably non-thesis-related, although who
knew—with a cover picture of a pneumatic lady wearing a
slit skirt and a gun in her garter ("She drew men like honey
draws flies . . . and then she swatted them!"). My pen—a
blue Biro, the end covered with toothmarks—was still where
I had put it down midsentence, that Wednesday night.

I watched the others over my book for any signs of edginess, but they had all settled to reading with an instant,
trained concentration that was almost intimidating. Abby,
in an armchair with her feet up on a little embroidered
footstool—her restoration project, probably—flipped pages
briskly and twisted a lock of hair round her finger. Rafe sat

across the fire from me in the other armchair; every now and then he put his book down and leaned forwards to poke the fire or add another chunk of wood. Justin lay on the sofa with his notepad propped on his chest, scribbling, occasionally murmuring something or huffing to himself or clicking his tongue disapprovingly. There was a frayed tapestry of a hunting scene on the wall behind him; he should have looked incongruous beneath it, with his corduroys and his little rimless glasses, but somehow he didn't, not at all. Daniel sat at the card table, his dark head bent under the glow of a tall lamp, only moving to deliberately, unhurriedly turn a page. The heavy green velvet curtains were open and I imagined how we would look, to a watcher in the dark garden beyond; how securely wrapped in our firelight and concentration; how bright and tranquil, like something from a dream. For a sharp, dizzying second I envied Lexie Madison.

Daniel felt me watching; he lifted his head and smiled at me, across the table. It was the first time I'd seen him smile, and it had an immense, grave sweetness to it. Then he bent his head over his book again.

I went to bed early, around ten, partly as a character choice and partly because Frank had been right, I was wrecked. My brain felt like it had just done a triathlon. I shut Lexie's bedroom door (smell of lily of the valley, a subtle little eddy swirling up my shoulder and round the neck of my T-shirt, curious and watchful) and leaned back against it. For a second I thought I wasn't going to make it as far as the bed, I'd just slide down the door and be asleep before I hit the carpet. This was harder than I remembered, and I didn't think it was because I was getting old or losing my touch or any of the other appealing possibilities O'Kelly would have suggested. Last time I had been the one calling the shots, deciding who I needed to hang out with, for how long, how close I needed to get. This time Lexie had called them all for me and I didn't have a choice: I had to follow her rules to the letter, listen hard and nonstop like she was on a faint crackly earpiece and let her run me.

I had had this feeling before, on some of my least favorite investigations: *Someone else is running this show.* Most of them hadn't ended well. But then it had always been the killer, a smug three steps ahead of us all the way. I had never had a case where that someone else was the victim.

One thing, though, felt easier. Last time, in UCD, every word out of my mouth had left a nasty taste behind, something tainted and wrong, like bread gone moldy. Like I said, I don't like lying. This time, though, everything I'd said left nothing except the clean-cotton taste of true. The only possible reasons I could come up with were that I was fooling the living bejasus out of myself—rationalization is a major part of the undercover's skill set—or that, in some tangled way that ran deeper and surer than cold hard fact, I wasn't lying. As long as I did this right, almost everything I said was the truth, just Lexie's rather than mine. I decided it would probably be a wise move to peel myself off the door and go to bed before I started thinking too hard about either of those possibilities.

Her room was on the top floor, at the back of the house, across from Daniel and above Justin. It was midsized, low-ceilinged, with plain white curtains and a rickety wrought-iron single bed that screeched like an ancient mangle when I sat down on it—if Lexie had managed to get pregnant in that thing, respect to her. The duvet cover was blue and freshly ironed; someone had changed my sheets. She didn't have a lot of furniture: a bookshelf, a narrow wooden wardrobe with helpful strips of tin on the shelves to tell you what went where (HATS, STOCKINGS), a crap plastic lamp on a crap bedside table, and a wooden dressing table with dusty scrollwork and a three-way mirror, which reflected my face at confusing angles and gave me the creeps in all the predictable ways. I considered covering it up with a sheet or something, but that would have taken some explaining, and anyway I couldn't shake the feeling that the reflection would keep doing its own thing behind there, just the same.

I unlocked my bag, keeping a sharp ear out for any noise on the stairs, and dug out my new gun and the roll of surgical tape for my bandages. Even at home, I don't sleep without my gun handy—old habit, and not one I felt like breaking right at that moment. I taped the gun to the back of the bedside table, out of sight but in easy reach. No cobwebs, not even a film of dust on the back of the table: the Bureau had been there before me.

Before I put on Lexie's blue pajamas, I peeled off the fake bandage, unclipped the mike and stashed the whole shebang at the bottom of my bag. Somewhere Frank was going into a full-blown conniption about this, but I didn't care; I had reasons.

Going to sleep on your first night undercover is something you never forget. All day you've been pure concentrated control, watching yourself as sharply and ruthlessly as you watch everyone and everything around you; but come night, alone on a strange mattress in a room where the air smells different, you've got no choice but to open your hands and let go, fall into sleep and into someone else's life like a pebble falling through cool green water. Even your first time, you know that in that second something irreversible will start happening, that in the morning you'll wake up changed. I needed to go into that bare, with nothing from my own life on my body, the way woodcutters' children in fairy tales have to leave their protections behind to enter the enchanted castle; the way votaries in old religions used to go naked to their initiation rites.

I found a beautiful, illustrated, fragile old edition of the Brothers Grimm in the bookshelf and took it to bed with me. The others had given it to Lexie on her birthday, last year: the flyleaf said, in slanted, flowing fountain pen— Justin's writing, I was almost sure—"3/1/04. Happy Birthday YOUNG girl (when are you going to grow up??). Love," and their four names.

I sat in bed with the book on my knees, but I couldn't read. Every now and then the quick muffled rhythms of conversation seeped up from the sitting room, and outside my window the garden was alive: wind in leaves, a fox barking and an owl on the hunt, rustles and calls and scuffles everywhere. I sat there and looked around Lexie Madison's strange little room, and listened.

A little before midnight, the stairs creaked and there was a discreet tap on my door. I leaped halfway to the ceiling, grabbed at my bag to make sure it was zipped up all the way and called, "Come in."

"It's me," said Daniel or Rafe or Justin, close behind the door, too soft for me to tell which one it was. "Just saying good night. We're going to bed."

My heart was pounding. "Night," I called. "Sleep tight."

Voices tossed up and down the long flights of stairs, sourceless and intertwining like crickets' chorus, gentle as fingers on my hair. *Night,* they said, *good night, sleep well. Welcome back, Lexie. Yes, welcome back. Good night. Sweet dreams.*

I sleep lightly and I have good ears. Sometime in the night I woke up, instantly and completely. Across the hall, in Daniel's room, someone was whispering.

I held my breath, but the doors were thick and all I could make out was the flicker of sibilants in the dark; no words, no voices. I reached out my arm from under the covers, carefully, and found Lexie's phone on the bedside table. 3:17 a.m.

I followed the faint double trail of whispers, weaving between the bat shrills and the rolls of wind, for a long time. It was two minutes to four when I heard the slow grate of a doorknob turning, and then the soft click as Daniel's door closed. A breath of sound across the landing, almost imperceptible, like a shadow moving against blackness; then nothing.

6

Footsteps woke me, thumping downstairs. I had been dreaming, something dark and messy, and it took me a wild second to disentangle my mind and figure out where I was. My gun wasn't beside my bed and I was grabbing for it, starting to panic, when I remembered.

I sat up in bed. Apparently nothing had been poisoned, after all; I felt fine. The smell of a fry-up was creeping under the door, and I could hear the brisk morning rhythm of voices, somewhere far below. Shit: I had missed cooking breakfast. It had been so long since I'd managed to sleep past six, I hadn't bothered to set Lexie's alarm. I stuck the mike-bandage back on, pulled on jeans and a T-shirt and a mammoth sweater that looked like it had belonged to one of the lads—the air was freezing—and went downstairs.

The kitchen was at the back of the house, and it had improved a lot since Lexie's scary movie. They'd got rid of the mold and the cobwebs and the scummy linoleum; instead there was a flagstoned floor, a scrubbed wooden table, a pot of ragged geraniums on the windowsill behind the sink. Abby, in a red-flannel dressing gown with the hood pulled up, was flipping bacon and sausages. Daniel was at the table, fully dressed, reading a book pinned under the edge of his plate and eating fried eggs with methodical enjoyment. Justin was slicing his toast into triangles and complaining.

"Honestly, I've never seen anything like it. Last week only *two* of them had done the reading; the rest just sat there staring and chewing gum, like a pack of cows. Are you sure you don't want to swap, just for today? Maybe you could get more out of them—"

"No," Daniel said, without looking up.

"But yours are doing the sonnets. I *know* the sonnets. I'm *good* at the sonnets."

"No."

"Morning," I said, in the doorway.

Daniel nodded at me gravely and went back to his book. Abby waved the spatula. "Morning, you."

"Sweetie," Justin said. "Come here. Let me look at you. How are you feeling?"

"Fine," I said. "Sorry, Abby; I slept it out. Here, give me that—"

I reached for the spatula, but she whipped it away. "No, you're grand; you still count as walking wounded. Tomorrow I'll come up and haul you out of bed. Sit."

That split second again—*wounded*: Daniel and Justin seemed to pause, suspended midbite. Then I sat down at the table and Justin reached for another slice of toast, and Daniel turned a page and shoved a red enamel teapot across to me.

Abby flipped three rashers and two eggs onto a plate, without asking, and came over to put it in front of me. "Oh, brrr," she said, hurrying back to the cooker. "Jesus. Daniel, I know about you and double-glazing, but seriously, we should at least *think* about windows that would—"

"Double-glazing is the spawn of Satan. It's hideous."

"Yes, but it's *warm*. If we're not getting carpets—"

Justin was nibbling toast, chin on hand, gazing at me closely enough to make me nervous. I concentrated on my food. "Are you sure you're all right?" he asked anxiously. "You look pale. You're not going in today, are you?"

"I don't think so," I said. I wasn't sure I was ready for a full day of this, not yet. And, also, I wanted a chance to check out the house in private; I wanted that diary, or date book, or whatever it was. "I'm supposed to take it easy for another few days. That reminds me, though: what's been happening with my tutorials?" Tutorials officially end at the Easter holidays, but there are always a few that, for whatever reason, drag on into the summer term. I had two groups left, one on Tuesdays and one on Thursdays. I wasn't looking forward to them.

"We covered them," Abby said, loading a plate for herself and joining us at the table, "in a manner of speaking. Daniel did *Beowulf* with your Thursday bunch. In the original."

"Beautiful," I said. "How'd they take it?"

"Not too badly, really," Daniel said. "At first they were aghast, but eventually one or two of them came up with some intelligent comments. It was quite interesting."

Rafe stumbled in with his hair sticking up in clumps, wearing a T-shirt and striped pajama bottoms and apparently navigating by radar. He waved at the room in general, fumbled for a mug, poured himself a lot of black coffee, snagged a triangle of Justin's toast and wandered out again.

"Twenty minutes!" Justin yelled after him. "I'm not waiting for you!" Rafe flipped a hand backwards, over his shoulder, and kept going.

"I don't know why you bother," Abby said, slicing sausage. "In five minutes he won't even remember seeing you. *After* the coffee. With Rafe, always *after* the coffee."

"Yes, but then he moans that I haven't given him enough time to get ready. I mean it, this time I'm leaving him behind, and if he's late then that's his problem. He can get a car of his own or he can *walk* to town, I don't care—"

"Every morning," Abby said to me, across Justin, who was making outraged gestures with his butter knife.

I rolled my eyes. Outside the French windows behind her head, a rabbit was nibbling the lawn, leaving little dark scatters of paw prints in the white dew.

Half an hour later, Rafe and Justin left—Justin pulled up his car in front of the house and sat there, beeping the horn and shouting inaudible threats out the window, until Rafe finally bounded into the kitchen with his coat half on and his knapsack swinging wildly from one hand, grabbed another slice of toast, shoved it between his teeth and dashed out again, slamming the front door hard enough to shake the house. Abby washed up, singing to herself in a rich contralto undertone: "The water is wide, I cannot get o'er . . ." Daniel smoked an unfiltered cigarette, thin plumes curling up through the pale rays of sun from the window. They'd relaxed around me; I was in.

I should have felt a lot better about this than I did. It hadn't occurred to me that I might like these people. Daniel and Rafe, I wasn't sure about yet, but Justin had a warmth to him that was even more endearing because it was so fussy and unpracticed, and Frank had been right about Abby: if things had been different, I would have wanted her for a friend.

They had just lost one of their own and they didn't even know it, and there was still a chance it had been due to me; and I was sitting in their kitchen, eating their fry-up and messing with their heads. Last night's suspicions—hemlock steak, Jesus—seemed so ridiculous and Gothic that I wanted to cringe.

"Daniel, we should start moving," Abby said eventually, checking the clock and wiping her hands on the dish towel. "Want anything from the outside world, Lex?"

"Smokes," I said. "I'm almost out."

She fished a pack of Marlboro Lights out of her dressing-gown pocket and tossed it to me. "Have these. I'll pick up more on the way in. What are you going to do all day?"

"Be a sloth on the sofa and read and eat. Are there biscuits?"

"Those vanilla cream ones you like, in the biscuit tin, and chocolate chip in the freezer." She flipped the dish towel into a neat fold and slung it over the bar of the cooker. "You're sure you don't want someone to stay home with you?"

Justin had already asked me about six times. I raised my eyes to the ceiling. "Positive."

I caught Abby's quick glance across my head to Daniel, but he was turning a page and paying no attention to us. "Fair enough," she said. "Don't faint down the stairs or anything. Five minutes, Daniel?"

Daniel nodded, without looking up. Abby ran upstairs, light in her sock feet; I heard her opening and closing drawers and, after a minute, starting to sing to herself again. "I leaned my back up against an oak, I thought it was a trusty tree . . ."

Lexie smoked more than I did, a pack a day, and she started after breakfast. I took Daniel's matches and lit up.

Daniel checked the page of his book, closed it and put it aside. "Should you really be smoking?" he asked. "Under the circumstances."

"No," I said pertly, and blew a stream of smoke across the table at him. "Should you?"

That made him smile. "You're looking better this morning," he said. "Last night you seemed very tired; a little lost, somehow. Which I suppose is only to be expected, but it's nice to see your energy starting to come back."

I made a mental note to up the boing level, gradually, over the next few days. "In the hospital they kept saying it would take a while and not to rush myself," I said, "but they can stick it in their ear. I'm bored of being sick."

The smile deepened. "Well, so I imagine. I'm sure you were a dream patient." He leaned over to the cooker, tilted the coffeepot to see if there was anything left. "How much of the incident itself do you actually remember?"

He was pouring himself the last of the coffee and watching me; his face was serene, interested, untroubled. "Bugger-all," I said. "That whole day's gone, and bits from before. I thought the cops told you."

"They did," Daniel said, "but that didn't mean it was necessarily the case. You could have had your own reasons for telling them that."

I looked blank. "Like what?"

"I have no idea," Daniel said, replacing the coffeepot carefully on the stove. "I hope, though, that if you do remember anything and you're unsure whether to take it to the police, you won't feel you have to deal with it alone; you'll come and talk to me, or to Abby. Would you do that?"

He sipped his coffee, one ankle crossed neatly over the opposite knee, watching me calmly. I was starting to see what Frank meant about these four giving away very little. This guy's expression would have worked equally well whether he had just come from choir practice or from ax-murdering a dozen orphans. "Well, yeah, sure," I said. "But all I remember is coming home from college on the Tuesday evening and then getting really, really sick in a bedpan, and I already told the police all that."

"Hmm," said Daniel. He pushed the ashtray over to my side of the table. "Memory is an odd thing. Let me ask you this: if you were to—" But just then Abby came clattering back down the stairs, still singing, and he shook his head and stood up and started patting at his pockets.

I waved from the top of the steps while Daniel pulled out of the driveway in a fast expert arc, and the car disappeared among the cherry trees. When I was sure they were gone, I shut the door and stood still in the hallway, listening to the empty house. I could feel it settling, a long whisper like shifting sand, to see what I would do now.

I sat down at the bottom of the stairs. The stair carpet had been taken off, but they hadn't got around to doing anything instead; there was a wide unvarnished band across each step, dusty and worn down in the middle by genera-tions of feet. I leaned against the newel post, wriggled till I got my back comfortable, and thought about that diary.

If it had been in Lexie's room, the Bureau gang would have found it. That left the rest of the house, the whole gar-den, and the question of what was in there that she had wanted to hide even from her best friends. For a second I heard Frank's voice, in the squad room: *her friends close and her secrets closer.*

The other possibility was that Lexie had kept it on her, that she had had it in a pocket when she died and the killer had nicked it. That would explain why he had taken the time and the risk to go after her (pulling her into cover, black darkness and his hands moving fast over her limp body, patting down pockets, glazed with rain and blood): if he needed that diary.

That fit with what I knew about Lexie—keep secrets close—but, on a more practical level, it would have had to be pretty small to go into a pocket, and she would have had to swap it over every time she changed clothes. Finding a hiding place would have been simpler and safer. Somewhere it would be safe from rain and from accidental discovery; somewhere she could be sure of privacy, even living with four people; somewhere she could go whenever she wanted, without catching anyone's attention; not her room.

There was a toilet on the ground floor and a full bathroom on the first. I checked the jacks first, but the room was the size of a coat closet, and once I'd looked in the cistern I had basically exhausted the possibilities. The main bathroom was big: 1930s tiles with a black-and-white checked border, chipped bath, unfrosted windows with tattered net curtains. The door bolted.

Nothing in the cistern, or behind it. I sat down on the floor and pulled out the wooden panel from the side of the bath. It came easily; a scraping sound, but nothing that running water or a flush wouldn't cover. Underneath there were cobwebs, mouse droppings, sweeps of finger marks in the dust; and, tucked in a corner, a tiny red notebook.

My breath felt like I'd been running. I didn't like this; didn't like how, with acres to choose from, I had come homing straight to Lexie's hiding place as if I had no choice. Around me the house seemed to have tightened and drawn closer, leaning in over my shoulder; watching; focused.

I went up to my room—Lexie's room—and found my gloves and a nail file. Then I sat back down on the bathroom floor and carefully, holding it by the edges, pulled out the notebook. I used the file to turn the pages. Sooner or later, the Bureau would need to fingerprint this.

I had been hoping for a pour-your-heart-out diary, but I should have known better. This was just a date book, red fake-leather cover, a page for each day. The first few months were covered with appointments and reminders in that quick, rounded writing: *Lettuce, Brie, garlic salt; 11 tut Rm 3017; elec bill; ask D Ovid book??* Homey, innocuous stuff, and reading it made me edgier than anything yet. When you're a detective you get used to invading people's privacy in every way you can think of, I had slept in Lexie's bed and I was wearing her clothes, but this; this was the small day-to-day debris of her life, it had been only for herself, and I had no right to it.

In the last few days of March, though, something changed. The shopping lists and tutorial timetables vanished and the pages went bare. There were only three notes, in a hard, dashed-off scribble. The last of March: *10.30 N.* The fifth of April: *11.30 N.* And the eleventh, two days before she died: *11 N.*

No N in January or February; no mention till that appointment on the last of March. The list of Lexie's KAs wasn't a long one, and as far as I could remember, no one on it began with N. A nickname? A place? A café? Someone from her old life, just like Frank had said, resurfacing from nowhere and wiping the rest of her world blank?

Across the last two days of April was a list of letters and numbers, in that same furious scrawl. *AMS 79, LHR 34, EDI 49, CDG 59, ALC 104.* Scores from some game, sums of money she'd lent or borrowed? Abby's initials were AMS—Abigail Marie Stone—but the others didn't match anyone on the KA list. I stared at them for a long time, but the only thing they reminded me of was the plate numbers on classic cars, and I couldn't for the life of me think of a reason why Lexie would be car spotting or why, if she was, it would be a state secret.

Nobody had said one word about her acting tense or odd, her last few weeks. She seemed fine, every single interviewee had told Frank and Sam; she seemed happy; she seemed just like always. The last video clip was from three days before she died and it showed her clambering down a ladder from the attic, a red bandanna tied round her hair and every inch of her powdered gray with dust, sneezing and laughing and holding out something in her free hand: "No, look, Rafe, look! It's"—explosive sneeze—"it's opera glasses, I think they're mother-of-pearl, aren't they *brilliant*?" Whatever had been going on, she had hidden it well; too well.

The rest of the book was empty, except for the twenty-second of August: *Dad's bday.*

Not a changeling or a collective hallucination, after all. She had a father, somewhere out there, and she hadn't wanted to forget his birthday. She had kept at least one slender tie to the life where she had started out.

I went through the pages again, slower this time, looking for anything I'd missed. Towards the beginning, a few dates here and there were circled: 2 January, 29 January, 25 February. The first page had a tiny calendar for December 2004, and sure enough, there was a circle around the sixth.

Twenty-seven days apart. Lexie had been clockwork and she had kept track. By the end of March, with no circle around the twenty-fourth, she had to have suspected she was pregnant. Somewhere—not at home; at Trinity or in some café, where nobody would see the packet in the bin and wonder—she had taken a pregnancy test, and something had changed. Her date book had turned to a fierce secret, N had moved in and everything else had been stripped away.

N. An obstetrician? A clinic? The baby's father?

"What the hell were you at, girl?" I said softly, into the empty room. There was a whisper behind me and I jumped about a mile, but it was only the breeze riffling the net curtains.

I thought about taking the date book back to my room, but in the end I figured Lexie had probably had reasons of her own for not leaving it there, and her hiding place had apparently worked fine so far. I copied the good bits into my own notebook, put hers back under the bath and slid the panel into place. Then I went over the house, getting to know the details and doing a quick, not-too-thorough search as I went. Frank would expect to hear that I'd done something useful with my day, and I already knew I wasn't going to tell him about the date book, at least not yet.

I started at the bottom and worked my way up. If I found anything good, we were going to have a major admissibility battle on our hands. I was a resident of the house, which meant I could look in the common spaces all I wanted but the others' rooms were basically out of bounds, and I was there under false pretenses to begin with; this is the kind of tangle that buys lawyers new Porsches. Once you know what you're chasing, though, you can almost always find a legit way to get to it.

The house had the effortlessly off-kilter feel of something out of a storybook—I kept expecting to fall down a secret staircase, or come out of a room into a completely new corridor that only existed on alternate Mondays. I worked fast: I couldn't make myself slow down, couldn't shake the feeling that somewhere in the attic a huge clock was counting down, great handfuls of seconds tumbling away.

On the ground floor were the double sitting room, the kitchen, the toilet and Rafe's room. Rafe's room was a mess—clothes piled in cardboard boxes, sticky glasses and snowdrifts of paper everywhere—but in an assured way; you could tell he usually knew where everything was, even if no one else could work it out. He had been goofing off on one wall with charcoal, dashing off quick, fairly impressive sketches for some kind of mural involving a beech tree, a red setter and a guy in a top hat. On the mantelpiece was— eureka—the Head: a porcelain phrenology bust, staring loftily out over Lexie's red bandanna. I was starting to like Rafe.

The first floor had Abby's room and the bathroom at the front, Justin's and a spare room to the back—either it had been too complicated to clear out, or Rafe liked being on his own downstairs. I started with the spare. The thought of going into either of the others put a small, ridiculous nasty taste in my mouth.

Great-uncle Simon had obviously never, ever thrown anything away. The room had a schizophrenic, dreamlike look, some lost store-cupboard of the mind: three copper kettles with holes in them, a moldy top hat, a broken stick-horse giving me a *Godfather* leer, what appeared to be half of an accordion. I know nothing about antiques, but none of it looked valuable, definitely not valuable enough to kill for. It looked more like stuff you would leave outside the gate in the hope that drunk students on a kitsch kick would take it home.

Abby and Justin were both neat, in very different ways. Abby went in for knickknacks—a tiny alabaster vase holding a handful of violets, a lead-crystal candlestick, an old sweet tin with a picture of a red-lipped girl in improbable Egyptian getup on the lid, all shiny clean and lined up carefully on just about every flat surface—and color; the curtains were made of strips of old fabric sewn together, red damask, bluebell-sprigged cotton, frail lace, and she had glued patches of fabric over the bald spots in the faded wallpaper. The room felt cozy and quirky and a little unreal, like the den of some kids'-book woodland creature that would wear a frilly bonnet and make jam tarts.

Justin, sort of unexpectedly, turned out to have minimalist tastes. There was a small nest of books and photocopies and scribbled pages beside his bedside table, and he had covered the back of his door with photos of the gang—arranged symmetrically, in what looked like chronological order, and covered with some kind of clear sealant—but everything else was spare and clean and functional: white bedclothes, white curtains blowing, dark wood furniture polished to a shine, neat rows of balled-up socks in the drawers and glossy shoes at the bottom of the wardrobe. The room smelled, very faintly, of something cypressy and masculine.

There was nothing dodgy in any of the bedrooms, as far as I could see, but something about all three of them kept catching at me. It took me a while to put my finger on it. I was kneeling on Justin's floor, checking under his bed like a burglar (nothing, not even dust bunnies), when it hit me: they felt permanent. I had never lived in a place where I could mess with the wallpaper or glue things down—my aunt and uncle wouldn't have objected, exactly, but their house had a tiptoe atmosphere that prevented anything along those lines from even occurring to me, and all my landlords apparently had this idea that they were renting me Frank Lloyd Wright's finest; it had taken me months to convince my current guy that property values would not plummet if I painted the walls white instead of banana-barf yellow and stuck the LSD-based carpet in the garden shed. None of this had bothered me at the time, but all of a sudden, surrounded by this houseful of happy, cavalier possessiveness—I would have loved a mural; Sam can draw—it seemed like a very strange way to live, on some stranger's sufferance, asking permission like a little kid before I left any mark.

The top floor: my room, Daniel's, two more spares. The one beside Daniel was full of old furniture, tumbled in splayed heaps as if an earthquake had hit: those grayish undersized chairs that never actually get used, a display cabinet that looked like the Rococo movement had thrown up on it, and just about everything in between. Bits and pieces had obviously been taken out—drag marks, bare patches—presumably to furnish the rooms when the five of them moved in. What was left was inches deep in trailing, sticky dust. The room next to mine had more wild debris (a cracked stone hot-water bottle, mud-crusted green wellies, a mouse-shredded tapestry cushion involving deer and flowers) and teetering stacks of cardboard boxes and old leather suitcases. Someone had made a start on going through this stuff, not too long ago: layers of bright finger marks on some of the suitcase lids, one even wiped semi-clean, mysterious outlines in corners and on boxes where things had been taken away. There were tangles of faint shoe prints on the dusty floorboards.

If you were going to hide something—a murder weapon, or some kind of evidence, or some small priceless antique—this wouldn't be a bad place. I went through all the cases that had been opened, staying well clear of the finger marks, just in case, but they were stuffed to the lids with pages and pages of crabby fountain-pen scribble. As far as I could tell, someone, presumably Great-uncle Simon, had been writing a history of the March family through the ages. The Marches had been around for a while—the dates went back to 1734, when the house had been built—but had apparently never done anything more interesting than getting married, buying the odd horse and gradually losing most of their estate.

Daniel's room was locked. The life skills I learned from Frank do include lock picking, and this one looked pretty simple, but I was already antsy from the diary, and that door wound me a notch tighter. I had no way of knowing whether Daniel always locked his room or whether this was specially for me. I was suddenly positive that he had left some trap—a hair across the frame, a glass of water just inside the door—that would give me away if I went in there.

I finished off with Lexie's room—it had been searched already, but I wanted to do it myself. Unlike Uncle Simon,

Lexie had kept sweet fuck-all. The room wasn't tidy, exactly—the books were tossed onto the shelves rather than lined up, the clothes were mostly in piles on the wardrobe floor; under the bed were three empty smoke packets, half a Caramilk and a crumpled page of notes on *Villette*—but it was too sparse to be messy. No knickknacks, no old ticket stubs or birthday cards or dried flowers, no photographs; the only mementos she had wanted were the phone videos. I thumbed through every book and turned every pocket inside out, but the room gave me nothing.

It had that same taste of permanence, though. She had been trying out paint colors on the wall beside her bed, in broad fast sweeps: ochre, old rose, china blue. That flick of envy went through me again. *Screw you,* I told Lexie inside my head; *you may have lived here for longer, but I'm getting paid for it.*

I sat down on the floor, dug my mobile out of my bag and rang Frank. "Hey, babe," he said, on the second ring. "Burned already, yeah?"

He was in a good mood. "Yep," I said. "Sorry about that. Come get me."

Frank laughed. "How's it going?"

I stuck him on speakerphone, put the phone on the floor beside me and stuffed my gloves and notebook back into the bag. "OK, I guess. I don't think any of them suspect anything's up."

"Why would they? Nobody in their right mind would think of something this unlikely. Got anything good for me?"

"They're all at college, so I had a quick look around the house. No bloody knife, no bloody clothes, no Renoirs, no signed confessions. Not even a stash of spliff or a porn mag. They're awfully pure, for students." My bandages were in carefully numbered packets, so that the stains would get lighter as the wound supposedly healed, just in case someone with a very weird mind was checking the bin—in this job, you leave room for a fair amount of weirdness. I found the bandage marked "2" and peeled off the wrapper. Whoever had done the staining lived life with enthusiasm.

"Any sign of that diary?" Frank asked. "The famous diary that Daniel saw fit to mention to you, but not to us."

I leaned back against the bookshelf, hiked up my top and pulled off the old bandage. "If it's in the house," I said, "someone's done a good job of hiding it."

A noncommittal noise from Frank. "Or else you were right and the killer took it off her body. Either way, though, it's interesting that Daniel and company felt the need to lie about it. Anyone acting dodgy?"

"No. They were a little awkward around me to start with, but they would be. Basically, the main thing I'm getting is they're glad to have Lexie back."

"That's what I got from the mike feed. Which," Frank said, "reminds me. What happened last night, after you went up to your room? I heard you talking, but somehow I had trouble catching the exact words."

There was a different note in his voice, and not a good one. I stopped smoothing down the edges of the new bandage. "Nothing. Everyone said good night."

"How sweet," Frank said. "Very Waltons. I'm sorry I missed it. Where was your mike?"

"In my bag. The battery pack sticks into me when I sleep."

"So sleep on your back. Your door doesn't lock."

"I put a chair in front of it."

"Oh, well, then. That's all the backup you need. Jesus, Cassie!" I could practically see him raking his free hand furiously through his hair, pacing.

"What's the big deal, Frank? Last time I never even used the mike unless I was actually doing something interesting. Whether I talk in my sleep isn't going to make or break this case."

"Last time you weren't living with suspects. These four may not be top of our list, but we haven't eliminated them yet. Unless you're in the shower, that mike stays on your body. You want to talk about last time? If your mike had been *in your bag* where we couldn't hear you, you'd be dead. You'd have bled out before we could get to you."

"Yeah, yeah, yeah," I said. "Point taken."

"Got it? On your body at all times. No fucking about."

"Got it."

"OK, then," Frank said, settling down. "I've got a little pressie for you." There was the edge of a grin in there: he'd saved up something good for after the lecture. "I've been tracking down all your KAs from our first Lexie Madison Extravaganza. Remember a girl called Victoria Harding?"

I bit off a piece of surgical tape. "Should I?"

"Tallish, slim, long blond hair? Talks a hundred an hour? Doesn't blink?"

"Oh God," I said, taping the bandage down. "Sticky Vicky. There's a blast from the past." Sticky Vicky was in UCD with me, studying something nonspecific. She had glassy blue eyes, a lot of matching accessories and a frantic, limitless ability to octopus herself onto anyone who might be useful, mainly rich boys and party girls. For some reason she had decided I was cool enough to be worth it, or maybe she was just hoping for free drugs.

"The very one. When did you last talk to her?"

I locked my bag and shoved it under the bed, trying to think back; Vicky wasn't the type that leaves a lasting impression. "Maybe a few days before I got pulled out? I've seen her around town once or twice since, but I always dodged."

"That's funny," Frank said, with that wolfish grin spreading through his voice, "because she's talked to you a lot more recently than that. In fact, you and she had a nice long chat in early January of 2002—she knows the date because she'd just been to the winter sales and bought some kind of fancy designer coat, which she showed to you. Apparently it involved, and I quote, 'the absolute ultimate taupe suede,' whatever class of animal a taupe may be. Ringing any bells?"

"No," I said. My heart was going slow and hard; I could feel it right down to the soles of my feet. "That wasn't me."

"I figured it might not be. Vicky remembers the conversation vividly, though, almost word for word—the girl's got a memory like a steel trap, she'll make a dream witness if it ever comes to that. Want to hear what you talked about?"

Vicky always did have that kind of mind: since there was basically no activity going on inside her head, conversations went in there and came back out virtually untouched. It was one of the main reasons I'd spent any time with her. "Refresh my memory," I said.

"You ran into each other on Grafton Street. According to her, you were 'totally spacey,' didn't remember her at first, weren't sure when you'd last seen each other. You claimed to have a foul hangover, but she put it down to that awful nervous breakdown she'd heard about." Frank was enjoying this: his voice had a fast, focused, predator-on-the-move rhythm. I was having a lot less fun than he was. I had known all this already, only the specifics had been missing, and being right wasn't as satisfying as you might think. "Once you managed to place her, though, you were very friendly. You even suggested going for a coffee, to catch up. Whoever our girl was, she had some nerve."

"Yeah," I said. I realized I was crouched like a sprinter, ready to leap. Lexie's bedroom felt mocking and tricky around me, humming with secret drawers and fake floorboards and spring traps. "She had that, all right."

"You went to the café in Brown Thomas, she showed you her fashion finds and you both played Do You Remember for a while. You, amazingly enough, were pretty quiet. But get this: at one point Vicky asked you whether you were in Trinity these days. Apparently, not long before you had your nervous breakdown, you'd told her you were sick of UCD. You were thinking of transferring somewhere else, maybe Trinity, maybe abroad. Sound familiar?"

"Yeah," I said. I sat down, carefully, on Lexie's bed. "Yeah, it does."

It had been getting towards the end of term, and Frank hadn't told me whether the operation was going to continue after the summer; I was setting up an exit, in case I needed one. The other point of Vicky: you could always rely on her to get gossip all round college in no time flat.

My head was spinning, strange-shaped things rearranging themselves and falling into new places with soft little clicks. The coincidence of Trinity—this girl heading straight for my old college, picking up where I had left off— had given me the creeps all along, but this was almost worse. The only coincidence was two girls running into each other, in a small city, and Sticky Vicky spends most of her time hanging around town looking for useful people to run into anyway. Lexie hadn't ended up in Trinity by chance, or by some dark magnetic pull that had her shadowing me, elbowing her way into my corners. I had suggested it to her. We had worked together seamlessly, she and I. I had drawn her to this house, this life, every bit as neatly and surely as she had drawn me.

Frank was still going. "Our girl said no, she wasn't in college at the moment, she'd been traveling. She was vague about where—Vicky assumed she'd been in the funny farm. But here's the good part: Vicky figured it was a funny farm in America, or maybe Canada. Partly that's because she remembers your imaginary family was living in Canada, but mostly it's because, somewhere between your time in UCD and that day on Grafton Street, you'd picked up a fairly serious tinge of American accent. So not only do we know how this girl got hold of the Lexie Madison ID, and when, but we've got a pretty good idea of where to start looking for her. I think we may owe Sticky Vicky a cocktail or two."

"Sooner you than me," I said. I knew my voice sounded weird, but Frank was too hyped-up to notice.

"I've put in a call to the FBI boys, and I'm about to e-mail them over prints and photos. There's a good chance our girl was on the run in one way or another, so they might turn up something."

Lexie's face watched me warily, in triplicate, from the dressing-table mirror. "Keep me updated, OK?" I said. "Anything you get."

"Will do. Want to talk to your fella? He's here."

Sam and Frank sharing an incident room. Jesus. "I'll call him later," I said.

The deep murmur of Sam's voice in the background, and for a split second out of nowhere I wanted to talk to him so badly it almost doubled me over. "He says he's got through your last six months in Murder," Frank told me, "and all the people you might've pissed off are out, one way or another. He'll keep working backwards and keep you up to speed."

In other words, this had nothing to do with Operation Vestal. God; Sam. Secondhand and at a distance, he was trying to reassure me: he was quietly, doggedly going after the only threat that he understood. I wondered how much he'd slept, the night before. "Thanks," I said. "Tell him thanks, Frank. Tell him I'll talk to him soon."

I needed to get outdoors—partly because of eyeball over-load, all those strange dusty objects, and partly because the house was starting to do things to the back of my neck; it made the air around me feel too intimate and too knowing, like an eyebrow flick from someone you never could fool. I hit the fridge, made myself a turkey sandwich—this gang believed in good mustard—and a jam sandwich and a ther-mos of coffee, and took them on a long walk. Sometime very soon, I was going to be navigating Glenskehy in the dark, quite possibly with input from a killer who knew the area like the back of his hand. I figured it might be a good idea to get my bearings.

The place was a maze, dozens of single-file lanes twisting their way among hedges and fields and woods from nowhere much to nowhere much else, but it turned out I knew my way around better than I'd expected; I only got lost twice.

I was starting to appreciate Frank on a whole new level. When I got hungry I sat on a wall and had my coffee and sandwiches, looking out over the mountainsides and giving the mental finger to the DV squad room and Maher and his halitosis problem. It was a sunny, snappy day, hazy clouds high in a cool blue sky, but I hadn't seen a single human being, anywhere along the way. Somewhere far off a dog was barking and someone was whistling to him, but that was it. I was developing a theory that Glenskehy had been wiped out by a millennium death ray and no one had noticed.

On my way back I spent a while checking out the Whitethorn House grounds. The Marches might have lost most of their estate, but what was left was still pretty impressive. Stone walls higher than my head, lined with trees—mostly the hawthorns that had given the house its name, but I spotted oak, ash, an apple just going into bloom. A broken-down stable, discreetly out of smelling range of the house, where Daniel and Justin kept their cars. It would have held six horses, way back when; now it was all piles of dusty tools and tarps, but they didn't look like they'd been touched in a very long time, so I didn't poke around.

To the back of the house was that great sweep of grass, maybe a hundred yards long, bordered by a thick rim of trees and stone wall and ivy. At the bottom was a rusty iron gate—the gate Lexie had gone through, that night, when she walked out onto the last edge of her life—and, tucked away in a corner, a wide, semi-organized patch of shrubs. I recognized rosemary and bay: the herb garden Abby had mentioned, the evening before. That already seemed like months ago.

From that distance the house looked delicate and remote, something out of an old watercolor. Then a fast little wind rippled down the grass, lifting the long trails of ivy, and the lawn tilted under my feet. By one of the side walls, only twenty or thirty yards from me, there was someone behind the ivy; someone slight and dark as a shadow, sitting on a throne. The hair on the back of my neck rose, a slow wave.

My gun was still taped to the back of Lexie's bedside table. I bit down hard on my lip and grabbed a heavy fallen branch out of the herb garden without taking my eyes off the ivy, which had dropped innocently back into place— the breeze was gone, the garden was still and sunny as a dream. I walked along the wall, casually but fast, flattened myself against it, got a good grip on my branch and whipped back the ivy in one sharp move.

There was no one there. The tree trunks and overgrown branches and ivy made an alcove against the wall, a little sun-splashed bubble. In it were two stone benches and, between them, a thread of water trickling through a hole in the wall and down shallow steps to a tiny, murky pond; nothing else. Shadows tangled together and for a second I caught the illusion again, the benches turning high-backed and sweeping, that slim figure sitting upright. Then I let the ivy fall and it was gone.

Apparently it wasn't just the house that had a personality all its own. I got my breath back and checked out the alcove. The seats had traces of moss in the cracks, but most of it had been scrubbed away: someone knew about this place. I considered its potential as a rendezvous point, one way or another, but it was awfully close to the house to be inviting outsiders around, and the mat of leaves and twigs around the pond looked like it hadn't been disturbed in a while. I brushed at it with the side of my shoe and got wide smooth flagstones. Metal glinted in the dirt and my heart bounced—*knife*—but it was too small. A button: lion and unicorn, battered and dented. Someone, long ago, had been in the British army.

The hole letting the water in through the garden wall was choked with muck. I stuck the button in my pocket, knelt down on the flagstones and used the branch and my hands to clear it out. It took a long time; the wall was thick.

When I was finished there was a miniwaterfall, murmuring happily to itself, and my hands smelled of earth and decaying leaves.

I rinsed them off and sat on one of the benches for a while, having a smoke and listening to the water. It was nice in there; warm and still and secret, like an animal's den or a kid's hideout. The pond filled up, tiny insects hovering above the surface. The extra water drained away through a tiny gutter into the ground, I picked out floating leaves, and after a while the pond was clear enough that I could see my reflection, rippling.

Lexie's watch said half-past four. I had made it through twenty-four hours, and probably knocked a good handful of people out of the incident-room sweepstakes. I put my cigarette butt back in the pack, ducked out through the ivy, and went inside to catch up on thesis notes. The front door opened smoothly to my key, the air inside stirred as I came in and it didn't feel overintimate any more; it felt like a slight smile and a cool brief touch on the cheek, like a welcome.

7

That night I went for my walk. I needed to phone Sam, and anyway, Frank and I had decided that I was better off getting Lexie back into her normal routine as fast as possible, not playing the trauma card too hard, at least not yet. There were bound to be little differences anyway, and with any luck people would use the stabbing to explain those away; the more I pushed it, the more likely it was that someone would think, *Gee, Lexie's a completely different person now.*

We were in the sitting room, after dinner. Daniel and Justin and I were reading; Rafe was playing piano, a lazy Mozart fantasia, breaking off now and then to repeat a phrase he liked or had messed up the first time; Abby was making her doll a new petticoat out of old *broderie anglaise*, head bent over stitches so tiny they were almost invisible. I didn't think the doll was creepy, exactly—she wasn't one of the ones that look like puffy, deformed adults; she had a long dark plait and a wistful, dreamy face, with a tip-tilted nose and tranquil brown eyes—but I could see the guys' point, all the same. Those big sad eyes, staring at me from an undignified position on Abby's lap, made me feel guilty in a nonspecific way, and there was something disturbing about the fresh, springy curl of her hair.

Around eleven I went out to the coat closet for my runners—I had wriggled into my supersexy girdle and tucked my phone in there before dinner, so I wouldn't have to break routine by going up to my room; Frank would be proud of me. I did a wince and a little under-my-breath "Ow" as I sat down on the hearth rug, and Justin's head snapped up. "Are you all right? Do you need your painkillers?"

"Nah," I said, disentangling my shoelace. "I just sat down funny."

"Walk?" Abby asked, glancing up from the doll.

"Yep," I said, pulling on one of the runners. It had the shape of Lexie's foot, a fraction narrower than mine, printed on the insole.

That tiny suspension all through the room again, like a caught breath. Rafe's hands left a chord hanging in the air. "Is that wise?" Daniel inquired, putting a finger in his book to mark his page.

"I feel fine," I said. "The stitches don't hurt unless I twist sideways; walking isn't going to burst them or anything."

"That's hardly what I had in mind," Daniel said. "You're not concerned?"

They were all looking at me, that unreadable quadruple gaze with the force of a tractor beam. I shrugged, pulling at a shoelace. "No."

"Why not? If I may ask."

Rafe moved, threw a taut little trill somewhere in the piano's upper octaves. Justin flinched.

"'Cause," I said. "I'm not."

"Shouldn't you be? After all, if you have no idea—"

"Daniel," Rafe said, almost under his breath. "Leave her alone."

"I wish you wouldn't go out there," Justin said. He looked like his stomach hurt. "I really do."

"We're worried, Lex," Abby said quietly. "Even if you're not."

The trill was still going, on and on like an alarm bell. *Rafe,* " Justin said, pressing a hand to his ear. "Stop."

Rafe ignored him. "Like she's not enough of a drama queen without you three encouraging her—"

Daniel didn't seem to notice. "Do you blame us?" he asked me.

"So you'll just have to worry," I said, shoving my other

foot into its shoe. "I don't care. If I get all jumpy now, I'll be jumpy forever, and I'm not doing that."

"Well, congratulations," Rafe said, ending the trill with a neat chord. "Take your torch. See you later." He turned back to the piano and started flipping pages.

"And your phone," Justin said. "In case you feel faint, or . . ." His voice trailed off.

"It doesn't seem to be raining any more," Daniel said, peering at the window, "but it might be chilly. Are you going to wear the jacket?"

I had no idea what he was talking about. This walk seemed to be turning into something at the organization level of Operation Desert Storm. "I'll be fine," I said.

"Hmm," Daniel said, considering me. "Maybe I should go with you."

"No," Rafe said, abruptly. "I'll go. You're working." He banged the piano lid down and stood up.

"Bloody hell!" I snapped, throwing my hands up and giving the four of them an outraged glare. "It's a *walk*. I do it all the *time*. I'm not taking protective clothing, I'm not taking emergency flares and I'm definitely not taking a bodyguard. Is that OK with everyone?" The thought of a private chat with Rafe or Daniel was interesting, but I could get those some other time. If someone was waiting for me out in the lanes, the last thing I wanted was to scare him off.

"That's my girl," said Justin, giving me a faint smile. "You'll be fine, won't you?"

"At the very least," Daniel said, unperturbed, "you should take a different route from the one you took the other night. Will you do that?"

He was watching me blandly, one finger still caught between the pages of his book. There was nothing in his face except mild concern. "I'd love to," I said, "if I *remembered* which way I went. Since I don't have the first clue, I'll just have to take my chances, won't I?"

"Ah," Daniel said. "Of course. I'm sorry. Ring if you want one of us to come meet you." He went back to his book. Rafe thumped down onto the piano stool and crashed into the Rondo alla Turca.

It was a bright night, the moon high in a clear cold sky, flicking chips of white off the dark hawthorn leaves; I buttoned Lexie's suede jacket up to my neck. The torch beam lit up a narrow bar of dirt path and the invisible fields felt suddenly huge around me. The torch made me feel very vulnerable and not very smart, but I kept it on. If anyone was lurking out there, he needed to know where to find me.

No one came. Something shifted off to one side, something heavy, but when I whipped the torch around it was a cow, staring back at me with wide, sorrowful eyes. I kept walking, nice and slow like a good little target, and thought about that exchange back in the sitting room. I wondered what Frank had made of it. Daniel could have been simply trying to jog my memory loose, or he could have had very good reasons for wanting to check whether the amnesia was real, and I had no idea which it was.

I didn't realize I was heading for the ruined cottage until it rose up in front of me, a smudge of thicker dark against the sky, stars flickering like altar lights in the windows. I switched off the torch: I could find my way across the field without it, and a light in the cottage was likely to make the neighbors very antsy, possibly even antsy enough to come investigating. The long grass swished, a soft steady sound, around my ankles. I reached up and touched the stone lintel, like a salute, before I went through the doorway.

The quality of the silence was different inside: deeper, and so thick I could feel it pressing softly around me. A slip of moonlight caught the crooked stone of the hearth in the inner room.

One wall sloped jaggedly down from the corner where Lexie had curled up to die, and I pulled myself up onto it and settled my back against the gable end. The place should probably have freaked me out—I was so close to her dying,

I could have leaned down across ten days and touched her hair—but it didn't. The cottage had a century and a half of its own stillness stored up, she had taken only an eyeblink; it had already absorbed her and closed over the place where she had been.

I thought about her differently, that night. Before, she had been an invader or a dare, always something that set my back stiffening and my adrenaline racing. But I was the one who had flashed into her life out of nowhere, with Sticky Vicky for a pawn and a wild why-not chance dangling from my fingertips; I was the dare she had taken, years before the flip side of the coin landed in front of me. The moon spun slowly across the sky and I thought of my face blue-gray and empty on steel in the morgue, the long rush and clang of the drawer shutting her into the dark, alone. I imagined her sitting on this same bit of wall on other, lost nights, and I felt so warm and so solid, firm moving flesh overlaid on her faint silvery imprint, it almost broke my heart. I wanted to tell her things she should have known, how her tutorial group had coped with *Beowulf* and what the guys had made for dinner, what the sky looked like tonight; things I was keeping for her.

In the first few months after Operation Vestal I thought a lot about leaving. It seemed, paradoxically, like the only way I could ever feel like me again: pack my passport and a change of clothes, scribble a note ("Dear everyone, I'm off. Love, Cassie") and catch the next flight to anywhere, leave behind everything that had changed me into someone I didn't recognize. Somewhere in there, I never knew the exact moment, my life had slipped through my hands and smashed to smithereens. Everything I had—my job, my friends, my flat, my clothes, my reflection in the mirror— felt like it belonged to someone else, some clear-eyed straight-backed girl I could never find again. I was a wrecked thing smeared over with dark finger marks and stuck with shards of nightmare, and I had no right there any more. I moved through my lost life like a ghost, trying not to touch anything with my bleeding hands, and dreamed of learning to sail in a warm place, Bermuda or Bondi, and telling people sweet soft lies about my past.

I don't know why I stayed. Probably Sam would have called it courage—he always goes for the best angle—and Rob would have called it pure stubbornness, but I don't flatter myself that it was either one. You can't take credit for what you do when your back is against the wall. That's nothing more than instinct, falling back on what you know best. I think I stayed because running seemed too strange and too complicated. All I knew was how to fall back, find a patch of solid ground, and then dig my heels in and fight to start over.

Lexie had run. When exile somehow hit her out of a clear blue sky, she didn't fight it the way I did: she reached out for it with both hands, swallowed it whole and made it her own. She had had the sense and the guts to let go of her ruined old self and walk away so simply, start over again, start fresh and clean as morning.

And then, after all that, someone had strutted up to her and whipped that hard-won new life away, casually as plucking a daisy. I felt a sudden zip of outrage—not at her but, for the first time, for her.

"Whatever it is you want," I said softly, into the dark cottage, "I'm here. You've got me."

There was a tiny shift in the air around me, subtler than a breath; secretive; pleased.

It was dark, big patches of cloud covering the moon, but I already knew the lane well enough that I barely needed the torch, and my hand went straight to the latch of the back gate, no fumbling. Undercover time works differently; it was hard to remember that I'd only been living there a day and a half.

The house was black on black, only a faint crooked line of stars where the roof ended and the sky began. It seemed

The Likeness · 181

bigger and intangible, edges blurring, ready to dissolve into nothing if you came too close. The lit windows looked too warm and gold to be real, tiny pictures beckoning like old peep shows: bright copper frying pans hanging in the kitchen, Daniel and Abby side by side on the sofa with their heads bent over some huge old book.

Then a cloud skated off the moon and I saw Rafe, sitting on the edge of the patio, one arm around his knees and a long glass in the other hand. My adrenaline leaped. There was no way he could have followed me without me seeing him, and I hadn't done anything dodgy anyway, but still, the look of him made me edgy. The way he was sitting, head up and ready, at the edge of that great spread of grass: he was waiting for me.

I stood under the hawthorn tree by the gate and watched him. Something that had been taking shape in the back of my mind had just made it to the surface. It was the drama-queen comment that had done it: the snide edge to his voice, the irritable eye roll. Now that I thought about it, Rafe had barely said a word to me since I arrived, apart from "pass the sauce" and "good night;" he talked around me, at me, in my general direction, never to me. The day before, he was the only one who hadn't touched me to welcome me home, just taken my suitcase and gone. He was being subtle about it, nothing overt; but, for some reason, Rafe was pissed off with me.

He saw me as soon as I stepped out from under the hawthorn. He raised his arm—the light from the windows sent long, confusing shadows flying down the grass towards me—and watched, unmoving, as I crossed the lawn and sat down next to him.

It seemed like the simplest thing to go at this head-on. "Are you mad at me?" I asked.

Rafe turned his head away with a disgusted flick, looked out over the grass. "'Mad at me,'" he said. "For God's sake, Lexie, you're not a child."

"OK," I said. "Are you angry with me?"

He stretched out his legs in front of him and examined the toes of his runners. "Has it even occurred to you," he asked, "to wonder what last week was like for us?"

I considered this for a moment. It sounded a lot like he was in a snot with Lexie for getting stabbed. As far as I could see, this was either deeply suspicious or deeply bizarre. With this gang, it got hard to tell the difference. "I wasn't exactly having fun either, you know," I said.

He laughed. "You haven't even thought about it, have you?"

I stared at him. "That's why you're pissed off with me? Because I got hurt? Or because I didn't ask how you're *feeling* about it?" He shot me an oblique look that could have meant anything. "Well, Jesus, Rafe. I didn't ask for any of this to happen. Why are you being such a dickhead about it?"

Rafe took a long, jerky swallow of his drink—gin and tonic; I could smell it. "Forget it," he said. "Never mind. Just go inside."

"Rafe," I said, hurt. I was only mostly faking it: there was an icy cut to his voice that made me flinch. "Don't."

He ignored me. I put a hand on his arm—it was more muscular than I had expected, and warm right through his shirt, almost fever hot. His mouth set in a long hard line, but he didn't move.

"Tell me what it was like," I said. "Please. I want to know; honestly, I do. I just didn't know how to ask."

Rafe shifted his arm away. "All right," he said. "Fine. It was horrible beyond belief. Does that answer your question?"

I waited. "We were all hysterical," he said harshly, after a moment. "We were wrecks. Not Daniel, obviously, he would never do anything as undignified as get *upset,* he just stuck his head in a book and occasionally came out with some fucking Old Norse quote about arms that remain strong in times of trial, or something. But I'm pretty sure he didn't sleep all week; no matter what time I got up, his light was still on. And the rest of us . . . Just to start with, we weren't sleeping either. We were all having nightmares—it was like some awful farce, every time you managed to get to sleep someone would wake up screaming, and of course that would wake everyone *else* up . . . Our sense of time completely disintegrated; half the time I didn't know what day it was. I couldn't eat, even the smell of food made me gag. And Abby kept *baking*—she said she needed to do something, but, God, piles of gooey chocolate things and bloody meat pies all over the house . . . We had a blazing row about it, Abby and I. She threw a fork at me. I was drinking all the time so the smell wouldn't make me sick, and then of course Daniel started giving me flak about *that* . . . We ended up giving away the chocolate things in the tutorial groups. The meat pies are in the freezer, if you're interested. None of the rest of us are going to touch them."

Shaken up, Frank had said, but no one had mentioned this level of hysteria. Now that Rafe had started talking, he didn't know how to stop. The words were tumbling out hard and involuntary as vomiting. "And Justin," he said. "Jesus. He was the worst by a long shot. He couldn't stop shaking, I mean really shaking—some little smart-arse first-year asked him if he had Parkinson's. It doesn't sound like a big deal, but it was incredibly unnerving; every time you looked at him, even for a second, it set your teeth on edge. And he kept dropping things, and every time he did it the rest of us nearly had heart attacks. Abby and I would yell at him, and then he would start *crying,* like that was going to help anything. Abby wanted him to go to Student Health and get Valium or something, but Daniel said that was ridiculous, Justin had to learn to cope like the rest of us—which was obviously completely insane, because we *weren't* coping. The biggest optimist in the *world* couldn't have said we were coping. Abby was sleepwalking—one night she ran herself a bath at four in the morning and got into it in her pajamas, fast asleep. If Daniel hadn't found her, she could have *drowned.*"

"I'm sorry," I said. My voice sounded strange, high and shaky. Every word he said had hit me straight in the stomach with a kick like a horse's. I had argued this with Frank and talked it through with Sam, I'd thought I had my head around it, but it had never been real to me till that moment: what I was doing to these people. "Oh, God, Rafe, I'm so sorry."

Rafe gave me a long, dark, unreadable look. "And the police," he said. He took another swig of his drink, made a face as if it tasted bitter. "Have you ever had to deal with cops?"

"Not like that," I said. I still sounded wrong, breathless, but he didn't seem to notice.

"They're bloody scary. These weren't uniformed cops fresh out of the bog; these were *detectives*. They have the best poker faces I've ever seen, you don't have a clue what they're thinking or what they want from you, and they were all over us. They questioned us for *hours,* almost every single day. And they make even the most innocent question— what time do you normally go to bed?—sound like a trap, like they're just waiting to whip out the handcuffs if you give the wrong answer. You feel like you have to be on your guard, every second, it's fucking exhausting—and we were exhausted already. That guy who dropped you off, Mackey, he was the worst. All smiles and sympathy, but he obviously hated our guts right from the word go."

"He was nice to me," I said. "He brought me chocolate biscuits."

"Well, isn't that charming," Rafe said. "I'm sure that won your heart. Meanwhile, he was showing up here at all hours of the day and night, giving us the third degree about every single detail of your entire life and making bitchy little comments about how the other half live, which is complete bollocks anyway. Just because we've got the house and we go to college . . . The man's got a chip on his shoulder the size of Bolivia. He would have *loved* a reason to lock us all up. And of course that got Justin even more hysterical, he was positive we were all going to be arrested any minute. Daniel told him that was crap and to pull himself together, but actually Daniel wasn't all that much help, seeing as he thought . . ."

He broke off and stared away down the garden, his eyes hooded. "If you hadn't pulled through when you did," he said, "I think we would have killed each other."

I reached out one finger and touched the back of his hand, just for a second. "I'm sorry," I said. "I am, Rafe. I don't know how else to say it. I'm so sorry."

"Yeah," Rafe said, but the anger had drained out of his voice and he just sounded very, very tired. "Well."

"What did Daniel think?" I asked, after a moment.

"Don't ask me," Rafe said. He threw back most of his drink with a neat flick of his wrist. "I've come to the conclusion that we're mostly better off not knowing."

"No, you said Daniel told Justin to chill out, but he wasn't much help because he thought something. What did he think?"

Rafe jiggled his glass and watched the ice cubes clink off the sides. He obviously wasn't planning to answer, but silence is the oldest cop-trick in the book, and I'm even better at it than most. I leaned my chin on my arms, watched him and waited. In the sitting-room window behind his head, Abby pointed to something in the book and both she and Daniel burst out laughing, faint and clear through the glass.

"One night," Rafe said at last. He still wasn't looking at me. The moonlight silvered his profile and lay along his cheekbone, turned him into something off a worn coin. "A couple of days after . . . It might have been Saturday, I'm not sure. I came out here and sat on the swing seat and listened to the rain. I thought that might help me sleep, for some reason, but it didn't. I heard an owl kill something—a mouse, probably. It was horrible; it screamed. You could hear the second when it died."

He went silent. I wondered if this was somehow the end of the story. "Owls have to eat too," I offered.

Rafe shot me a quick, oblique glance. "Then," he said. "I don't know what time, it was just starting to get light. I heard your voice, under the rain. It sounded like you were right there, leaning out."

He turned and pointed up, at my dark window above us. "You said, 'Rafe, I'm on my way home. Wait up for me.' You didn't sound eerie or anything, just matter-of-fact; in a hurry, sort of. Like that time you rang me because you'd forgotten your keys. Do you remember that?"

"Yeah," I said. "I remember." A light cool breeze drifted across my hair and I shivered, a fast, uncontrollable jerk. I don't know if I believe in ghosts, but this story was something different, pressing like a cold knife blade against my skin. It was way too late, more than a week too late, to worry about whatever damage I was doing to these four.

" 'I'm on my way home,' " Rafe said. " 'Wait up for me.' " He stared into the bottom of his glass. I realized that he was probably fairly drunk.

"What did you do?" I asked.

He shook his head. " 'Echo, I will not talk with thee,' " he said, with a faint wry smile, " 'for thou art a dead thing.' "

The breeze had moved off down the garden, sifting the leaves and fingering delicately through the ivy. In the moonlight the grass looked soft and white as mist, like you could put your hand right through it. That shiver went over me again.

"Why?" I asked. "Didn't that tell you I was going to be OK?"

"No," Rafe said. "Actually, no, it didn't. I was sure you had just died, that second. Laugh if you want, but I've told you what kind of state we were all in. I spent the whole next day waiting for Mackey to appear at the door being grave and sympathetic and tell us the doctors had done everything they could but blah blah blah. When he turned up on Monday, all smiley, and told us you'd regained consciousness, at first I didn't believe him."

"That's what Daniel thought, isn't it?" I said. I wasn't

sure how I knew this, but there wasn't a doubt in my mind. "He thought I was dead."

After a moment Rafe sighed. "Yeah," he said. "Yeah, he did. Right from the start. He thought you'd never made it to hospital."

Watch your step around that one, Frank had said. Either Daniel was a lot smarter than I wanted to tangle with—that little exchange, before I went out, was starting to worry me again—or he had had reasons of his own for thinking Lexie wasn't coming back. "Why?" I demanded, doing offended. "I'm not a *wimp.* It'd take more than one little cut to get rid of me."

I felt Rafe flinch, a tiny half-hidden twitch. "God only knows," he said. "He had some bizarro convoluted theory about the cops claiming you were alive to mess with people's heads—I can't remember the details, I didn't want to hear it and he was being cryptic about it anyway." He shrugged. "Daniel."

For several reasons, I figured it was time to change the tone of this conversation. "Mmm . . . conspiracy theories," I said. "Let's make him a tinfoil hat, in case the cops start trying to scramble his brain waves."

I had caught Rafe off guard: before he could help it, he gave a startled snort of laughter. "He does get paranoid, doesn't he," he said. "Remember when we found the gas mask? Him giving it that thoughtful look and saying, 'I wonder if this would be effective against the avian flu?'"

I had started giggling as well. "It'll look gorgeous with the tinfoil hat. He can wear them both into college—"

"We'll get him a biohazard suit—"

"Abby can needlepoint pretty patterns on it—"

It wasn't all that funny, but we were both helpless with laughter, like a pair of giddy teenagers. "Oh, God," Rafe said, wiping his eyes. "You know, the whole thing would probably have been hysterical, if it hadn't been so God-awful. It was like one of those terrible sub-Ionesco plays that third-years always write: great piles of meat pies popping out of the woodwork and Justin dropping them everywhere, me gagging in the corner, Abby asleep in the bath in her pajamas like some post-modern Ophelia, Daniel surfacing to tell us what Chaucer thought of us all and then disappearing again, your friend Officer Krupke showing up at the door every ten minutes to ask what color M&Ms you like best . . ."

He let out a long, shaky breath, somewhere between a laugh and a sob. Without looking at me, he stretched an arm over and rumpled my hair. "We missed you, silly thing," he said, almost roughly. "We don't want to lose you."

"Well, I'm right here," I said. "I'm going nowhere."

I meant it lightly, but in that wide dark garden the words seemed to flutter with a life of their own, skim down the grass and disappear in among the trees. Slowly Rafe's face turned towards me; the glow from the sitting room was behind him and I couldn't see his expression, only a faint white glitter of moonlight in his eyes.

"No?" he asked.

"No," I said. "I like it here."

Rafe's silhouette moved, briefly, as he nodded. "Good," he said.

To my utter surprise, he reached out and ran the backs of his fingers, lightly and deliberately, down my cheek. The moonlight caught the tip of a smile.

One of the sitting-room windows shot up and Justin's head popped out. "What are you two laughing about?"

Rafe's hand dropped away. "Nothing," we called back, in unison.

"If you sit out there in the cold you'll both get earaches. Come look at this."

They had found an old photo album somewhere: the March family, Daniel's ancestors, starting in about 1860 with vein-popping corsets and top hats and unamused expressions. I squeezed onto the sofa next to Daniel—close, touching; for a second I almost flinched, till I realized the mike and the phone were on my other side. Rafe sat on the arm beside me, and Justin disappeared into the kitchen and brought out tall glasses of hot port, neatly wrapped in thick soft napkins so we wouldn't burn our hands. "So you won't catch your death," he told me. "You need to take care of yourself. Running around in the freezing cold . . ."

"Check out the clothes," Abby said. The album was bound in cracked brown leather and big enough that it took up both her lap and Daniel's. The photos, tucked into little paper corners, were spotted and browning at the edges. "I want this hat. I think I'm in love with this hat."

It was an architectural fringed thing, topping off a large lady with a monobosom and a fishy stare. "Isn't that the lampshade in the dining room?" I said. "I'll get it down for you if you promise to wear it to college tomorrow."

"Good Lord," Justin said, perching on the other arm of the sofa and peering over Abby's shoulder, "they all seem terribly depressed, don't they? You don't look a thing like any of them, Daniel."

"Thank God for small mercies," Rafe said. He was blowing on his hot port, with his free arm draped across my back; he had apparently forgiven me for whatever it was that I, or Lexie, had done. "I've never seen such a goggle-eyed bunch. Maybe they all have thyroid problems, and that's why they're depressed."

"Actually," Daniel said, "both the protruding eyes and the sombre expressions are characteristic of photographs from that period. I wonder if it had anything to do with the long exposure time. The Victorian camera—" Rafe pretended to have a narcoleptic attack on my shoulder, Justin produced a huge yawn, and Abby and I—I was only a second behind her—stuck our free hands over our ears and started singing.

"All right, all right," Daniel said, smiling. I had never been this close to him before. He smelled good, cedar and clean wool. "I'm just defending my ancestors. In any case, I think I do look like one of them—where is he? This one here."

Going by the clothes, the photo had been taken somewhere around a hundred years ago. The guy was younger than Daniel, twenty at most, and standing on the front steps of a younger, brighter Whitethorn House—no ivy on the walls, glossy new paint on the door and the railings, the stone steps sharper-edged and scrubbed pale. There was a resemblance there, all right—he had Daniel's square jaw and broad forehead, although his looked even broader because the dark hair was slicked back fiercely, and the same straight-cut mouth. But this guy was leaning against the railing with a lazy, dangerous ease that was nothing like Daniel's tidy, symmetrical poise, and his wide-set eyes had a different look to them, something restless and haunted.

"Wow," I said. The resemblance, that face passed across a century, was doing strange things to me; I would have envied Daniel, in some unreasonable way, if it hadn't been for Lexie. "You do look like him."

"Only less messed up," Abby said. "That's not a happy man."

"But look at the *house*," Justin said softly. "Isn't it beautiful?"

"It is, yes," Daniel said, smiling down at it. "It really is. We'll get there."

Abby slipped a fingernail under the photo, flicked it out of its corners and turned it over. On the back it said, in watery fountain pen, "William, May 1914."

"The First World War was coming up," I said quietly. "Maybe he died in it."

"Actually," Daniel said, taking the photo from Abby and examining it more closely, "I don't think he did. Good heavens. If this is the same William—and it may not be, of course, my family has always been singularly unimaginative when it comes to names—then I've heard about him. My father and my aunts mentioned him every now and then, when I was a child. He's my grandfather's uncle, I think, although I may have that wrong. William was—well, not a black sheep, exactly; more like a skeleton in the cupboard."

"Definitely a resemblance," Rafe said; then, "Ow!" as Abby reached across and swatted his arm.

"He did fight in the war, in fact," Daniel said, "but he came back, with some kind of infirmity. Nobody ever mentioned what, exactly, which makes me think it may have been psychological rather than physical. There was some scandal—I'm hazy on the details, it was all kept very hush-hush, but he spent a while in some kind of sanatorium, which at the time might well have been a delicate way of saying a lunatic asylum."

"Maybe he had a passionate affair with Wilfred Owen," Justin suggested, "in the trenches." Rafe sighed noisily.

"I got the impression it was more along the lines of a suicide attempt," said Daniel. "When he got out he emigrated, I think. He lived to a ripe old age—he only died when I was a child—but still, not necessarily the ancestor one would choose to resemble. You're right, Abby: not a happy man." He tucked the photo back into place and touched it gently, with one long square fingertip, before he turned the page.

The hot port was rich and sweet, with quarters of lemon stuck full of cloves, and Daniel's arm was warm and solid against mine. He flipped pages slowly: mustaches the size of house pets, lacy Edwardians walking in the flowering herb garden ("My God," Abby said on a long breath, "*that's* what it's supposed to look like"), flappers with carefully droopy shoulders. A few people were built along the same lines as Daniel and William—tall and solid, with jawlines that worked better on the men than on the women—but most of them were small and upright and made up mainly of sharp angles, jutting chins and elbows and noses. "This thing is brilliant," I said. "Where did you find it?"

A sudden, startled silence. *Oh God*, I thought, *oh, God, not now, not just when I was starting to feel like—*"But *you* found it," Justin said, his glass going down on his knee. "In the top spare room. Don't you . . ." He let the sentence drop. No one picked it up.

Never, Frank had told me, *no matter what, never back-pedal. If you fuck up, blame it on the coma, PMS, the full moon, anything you want; just hold your ground.* "No," I said. "I'd remember if I'd seen this before."

They were all looking at me; Daniel's eyes, only inches away, were intent and curious and huge behind his glasses. I knew I had gone white, he couldn't miss it. *He thought you'd never made it, he had some bizarro convoluted theory*—"You did, Lexie," Abby said softly, leaning forwards so she could see me. "You and Justin were rummaging around, after dinner, and you came up with this. It was the same night that . . ." She made a small, formless gesture, glanced fast at Daniel.

"It was just a few hours before the incident," said Daniel. I thought I felt something move through his body, something like a tiny suppressed shudder, but I couldn't be sure; I was too busy trying to hide my own rush of pure relief. "No wonder you don't remember."

"Well," Rafe said, one notch too loudly and too heartily, "there you go."

"But that *sucks,*" I said. "Now I feel like an idiot. I didn't mind losing the sore bits, but I don't *want* to go around wondering what else is missing. What if I bought the winning Lotto ticket and hid it somewhere?"

"Shhh," Daniel said. He was smiling at me, that extraordinary smile. "Don't worry. We forgot all about the album as well, until tonight. We never even looked at it." He took my hand, opened my fingers gently—I hadn't even realized my fists were clenched—and drew it through the crook of his elbow. "I'm glad you found it. This house has enough history for a whole village; it shouldn't be lost. Look at this one: the cherry trees, just planted."

"And check him out," said Abby, pointing to a guy

wearing full hunting gear and sitting on a rangy chestnut horse, beside the front gate. "He'd have a mickey fit if he knew we were keeping motoring cars in his stables." Her voice sounded fine—easy, cheerful, not even a sliver of a pause—but her eyes, flicking to me across Daniel, were anxious.

"If I'm not mistaken," Daniel said, "that's our benefactor." He flipped out the photo and checked the back. "Yes: 'Simon on Highwayman, November 1949.' He would have been twenty-one or so."

Uncle Simon was from the main branch of the family tree: short and wiry, with an arrogant nose and a fierce look. "Another unhappy man," Daniel said. "His wife died young, and apparently he never really recovered. That's when he began drinking. As Justin said, not a cheerful bunch."

He started to fit the photo back into its corners, but Abby said, "No," and took it out of his hand. She passed her glass to Daniel, went to the fireplace and propped the picture in the middle of the mantelpiece. "There."

"Why?" Rafe inquired.

"Because," Abby said. "We owe him. He could have left this place to the Equine Society, and I'd still be living in a scary basement bedsit with no windows and hoping that the nutbar upstairs wouldn't decide to break in some night. As far as I'm concerned, this guy deserves a place of honor."

"Oh, Abby, sweetie," Justin said, holding out an arm. "Come here."

Abby adjusted a candlestick to hold the photo in place. "There," she said, and went to Justin. He fitted his arm around her and pulled her against him, her back leaning against his chest. She took back her glass from Daniel. "Here's to Uncle Simon," she said.

Uncle Simon gave us all a baleful, unimpressed glare. "Why not," Rafe said, raising his glass high. "Uncle Simon."

The port glowing deep and strong as blood, Daniel's

194 · Tana French

arm and Rafe's holding me snug in place between them, a gust of wind rattling the windows and swaying the cobwebs in the high corners. "To Uncle Simon," we said, all of us.

Later, in my room, I sat on the windowsill and went through my various new bits of information. All four of the house-mates had deliberately hidden how upset they were, and hidden it well. Abby threw kitchen utensils when she got angry enough; Rafe, at least, somehow blamed Lexie for getting stabbed; Justin had been sure they were going to be arrested; Daniel hadn't fallen for the coma story. And Rafe had heard Lexie telling him she was coming home, the day before I said yes.

Here's one of the more disturbing things about working Murder: how little you think about the person who's been killed. There are some who move into your mind—children, battered pensioners, girls who went clubbing in their spar-kly hopeful best and ended the night in bog drains—but mostly the victim is only your starting point; the gold at the end of the rainbow is the killer. It's scarily easy to slip to the point where the victim becomes incidental, half forgotten for days on end, just a prop wheeled out for the prologue so that the real show can start. Rob and I used to stick a photo smack in the middle of the whiteboard, on every case—not a crime-scene shot or a posed portrait; a snapshot, the can-didest candid we could find, a bright snippet from the time when this person was something more than a murder victim—to keep us reminded.

This isn't just callousness, or self-preservation. The cold fact is that every murder I've worked was about the killer. The victim—and imagine explaining this to families who have nothing left but the hope of a reason—the victim was just the person who happened to wander into the sights when the gun was loaded and cocked. The control freak was always going to kill his wife the first time she refused to fol-low orders; your daughter happened to be the one who married him. The mugger was hanging around the alleyway with a knife, and your husband happened to be the next person who walked by. We go through victims' lives with a fine-tooth comb, but we're doing it to learn more not about them but about the murderer: if we can figure out the exact point where someone walked into those crosshairs, we can go to work with our dark, stained geometries and draw a line straight back to the barrel of the gun. The victim can tell us how, but almost never why. The only reason, the beginning and the end, the closed circle, is the killer.

This case had been different from the first moment. I had never been in any danger of forgetting about Lexie; and not just because I carried the reminder photo around with me, there every time I brushed my teeth or washed my hands. From the second I walked into that cottage, before I ever saw her face, this had been about her. For the first time ever, the murderer was the one I kept forgetting.

The possibility hit me like a wrecking ball: suicide. I felt like I had fallen off the windowsill, straight through the glass and down into cold air. If this killer had never been anything but invisible, if Lexie had been the core of the case all along, maybe it was because there had never been a killer at all: she was all there was. In that split second I saw it as clearly as if it were unfolding on the dark lawn below me, in all its slow sickening horror. The others putting away the cards and stretching, *Where's Lexie got to?* And then the worry winding tighter and tighter, till finally they put on coats and went out into the night to look for her, torches, rain gusting hard, *Lexie! Lex!* The four of them crammed in the wrecked cottage, gasping for breath. Shaking hands feeling for a pulse, pressing harder; moving her into shelter and laying her out so gently, reaching for the knife, fumbling in her pockets for some note, some explanation, some word. Maybe—Jesus—maybe they had even found one.

A moment later, of course, my head cleared, my breath came back and I knew that was rubbish. It would explain a lot—Rafe's snit fit, Daniel's suspicions, Justin's nerves, the moved body, the searched pockets—and we've all heard about cases where people staged everything from improbable accidents through murders, rather than let their loved ones be branded as suicides. But I couldn't think of a single reason why they would have left her there all night for someone else to find, and anyway women generally don't commit suicide by knifing themselves in the chest. And, above all that, there was the immovable fact that Lexie—even if whatever went down in March had somehow wrecked all this for her, this house, these friends, this life—was about the last person in the world who would have killed herself. Suicides are people who can't see any other way out. From what we had learned, Lexie had had no trouble finding escape routes when she wanted them.

Downstairs Abby was humming to herself; Justin sneezed, a chain of small fastidious yelps; someone slammed a drawer. I was in bed and halfway asleep when I realized: I had forgotten all about ringing Sam.

8

God, that first week. Even thinking about it I want to bite into it like the world's brightest red apple. In the middle of an all-out murder investigation, while Sam worked his way painstakingly through various shades of scumbag and Frank tried to explain our situation to the FBI without coming across like a lunatic, there was nothing I was supposed to be doing except living Lexie's life. It gave me a gleeful, lazy, daring feeling right down to my toes, like mitching off school when it's the best day of spring and you know your class has to dissect frogs.

On Tuesday I went back to college. In spite of the vast number of new opportunities to fuck up, I was looking forward to it. I loved Trinity, the first time round. It still has its centuries of graceful gray stone, red brick, cobblestones; you can feel the layers on layers of lost students streaming through Front Square beside you, feel the print of you being added to the air, archived, saved. If someone hadn't decided to drive me out of college, I might have turned into an eternal student like these four. Instead—and probably because of that same person—I turned into a cop. I liked the thought that this had brought me full circle, back to reclaim the place I'd lost. It felt like a strange, delayed victory, something salvaged against ridiculous odds.

"You should probably know," Abby said, in the car, "the rumor mill's been going mental. Apparently it was a major coke deal gone wrong, also an illegal immigrant—you married him for money and then started blackmailing him—also an abusive ex-boyfriend who just got out of jail for beating you up. Brace yourself."

"Also, I assume," Daniel said, maneuvering past an Explorer that was blocking two lanes, "all of us, singly or in various combinations and for various motives. No one's said so to our faces, of course, but the inference is inevitable." He swung into the entrance of the Trinity car park and held up his ID for the security guard. "If people ask questions, what are you going to tell them?"

"I haven't decided yet," I said. "I was thinking about saying I'm the lost heir to some throne and a rival faction came after me, but I couldn't decide which throne. Do I look like a Romanov?"

"Definitely," said Rafe. "They were a bunch of chinless weirdos. Go for that."

"Be nice to me or I'll tell everyone you came after me with a cleaver in a drug-fueled rage."

"It's not funny," said Justin. He hadn't brought his car—I got the sense they all wanted to stick close together, just now—so he was in the back with me and Rafe, rubbing flecks of dirt off the windowpane and wiping his fingers on his handkerchief.

"Well," said Abby, "it wasn't funny last week, no. But now that you're back . . ." She turned to grin at me, over her shoulder. "Four-Boobs Brenda asked me—you know that horrible confidential whisper?—if it was 'one of those games gone wrong.' I just froze her out, but now I'm thinking I could have made her day."

"What amazes me about her," Daniel said, opening his door, "is that she's so determined to believe we're wildly interesting. If only she knew."

When we got out of the car I got my first real look at what Frank had meant about these four, how they came across to outsiders. As we walked down the long avenue between the sports fields something happened, a change as subtle and definite as water turning to ice: they moved closer, shoulder to shoulder and in step, backs straightening, heads lifting, expressions falling away from their faces.

By the time we reached the Arts block the façade was in place, a barricade so impenetrable you could almost see it, cool and glinting like diamond. All that week in college, every time someone started angling for a good stare at me—edging down the library shelves towards the corner where we had our carrels, rubbernecking round a newspaper in the tea queue—that barricade swung around like a Roman shield formation, confronting the intruder with four pairs of impassive, unblinking eyes, till he or she backed off. Collecting gossip was going to be a major problem; even Four-Boobs Brenda stopped midbreath, hovering over my desk, and then asked if she could borrow a pen.

Lexie's thesis turned out to be a lot more fun than I'd thought. The bits Frank had given me were mainly stuff about the Brontës, Currer Bell as the madwoman in the attic bursting free from demure Charlotte, truth in alias; not exactly comfortable reading, in the circumstances, but more or less what you'd expect. What she'd been working on just before she died was a lot snazzier: Rip Corelli, of *She Dressed to Kill* fame, turned out to be Bernice Matlock, a librarian from Ohio who had led a blameless life and written lurid pulp masterpieces in her spare time. I was starting to like the way Lexie's mind had worked.

I'd been worried that her supervisor would want me to come up with something that made academic sense—Lexie had been no idiot, her stuff was smart and original and well thought out, and I was years out of practice. I'd been worried about her supervisor all round, actually. Her tutorial students weren't going to spot the difference—when you're eighteen, most people over twenty-five are just generic adult white noise—but someone who'd spent one-on-one time with her was a whole different story. One meeting with him reassured me. He was a bony, gentle, disconnected guy who was so paralyzed by the whole "unfortunate incident" that he could barely look me in the eye, and he told me to take all the recovery time I needed and not to worry about deadlines. I figured I could handle a few weeks curled up in the library reading about hard-boiled PIs and dames who were nothing but trouble.

And in the evenings there was the house. We put some work into it almost every day, maybe for an hour or two, maybe just for twenty minutes: sand down the stairs, sort through a box from Uncle Simon's stash, take turns climbing the stepladder to change the ancient brittle fittings on the lightbulbs. The crappiest jobs—scrubbing stains off the toilets—got the same time and care as the interesting ones; the four of them treated the house like some marvelous musical instrument, a Stradivarius or a Bösendorfer, that they had found in a long-lost treasure trove and were restoring with patient, enchanted, absolute love. I think the most relaxed I ever saw Daniel was flat on his stomach on the kitchen floor, wearing battered old trousers and a plaid shirt, painting baseboards and laughing at some story Rafe was telling, while Abby leaned over him to dip her brush, her ponytail whisking paint across his cheek.

They were very tactile, all of them. We never touched in college, but at home, someone was always touching someone: Daniel's hand on Abby's head as he passed behind her chair, Rafe's arm on Justin's shoulder as they examined some spare-room discovery together, Abby lying back in the swing seat across my lap and Justin's, Rafe's ankles crossed over mine as we read by the fire. Frank made predictable snide noises about homosexuality and orgies, but I was on full alert for any kind of sexual vibe—the baby—and that wasn't what I was picking up. It was stranger and more powerful than that: they didn't have boundaries, not among themselves, not the way most people do. Your average house share involves a pretty high level of territorial dispute—tense negotiations over the remote control, house meetings about whether bread counts as personal or shared, Rob's flatmate used to have a three-day snit fit if he used her butter. But these people: as far as I could tell, everything, except thank God underwear, belonged to all of them. The guys pulled clothes out of the airing cupboard at random, anything that would fit; I never did figure out which tops were officially Lexie's and which ones were Abby's. They ripped sheets of paper out of each other's notepads, ate toast off the nearest plate, took sips out of whatever glass was handy.

I didn't mention this to Frank—he would only have switched from orgy comments to dark warnings about communism, and I liked the blurred boundaries. They reminded me of something warm and solid that I couldn't quite pinpoint. There was a big green wax jacket, hanging in the coat closet left over from Uncle Simon, that belonged to anyone who was going out in the rain; the first time I put it on for my walk it gave me a strange, intoxicating little thrill, like holding hands with a boy for the very first time.

It was Thursday when I managed to put my finger on the feeling. The days were starting to lengthen towards summer and it was a clear, warm, graceful evening; after dinner we took a bottle of wine and a plate of sponge cake out onto the lawn. I had made a daisy chain and was trying to fasten it around my wrist. By this time I had given up on the not-drinking thing—it felt out of character, it made the others think about the stabbing and tense up, and besides, whatever antibiotics and booze do together could get me out of there when I needed it—so I was mildly, happily tipsy.

"More cake," Rafe demanded, nudging me with his foot.

"Get it yourself. I'm busy." I had given up on fastening the daisy chain one-handed and was putting it on Justin instead.

"You're a lazy object, do you know that?"

"Look who's talking." I pulled one of my ankles round the back of my head—all the gymnastics as a kid, I'm flexible—and stuck my tongue out at Rafe from under my knee. "I'm active and healthy, look."

Rafe raised one eyebrow lazily. "I'm aroused."

"You're a pervert," I told him, with as much dignity as I could from that position.

"Knock it off," Abby said. "You'll burst your stitches, and we're all too drunk to drive you to the emergency room."

I'd forgotten all about my imaginary stitches. For a second I considered getting wound up about this, but I decided against it. The long evening sunshine and being barefoot and the tickle of grass, and presumably the booze, were making me light-headed and silly. It had been a long time since I'd felt like this, and I liked it. I maneuvered my head round to peer sideways at Abby. "They're fine. They're not even sore any more."

"That's because up until now you haven't been tying yourself in knots," Daniel said. "Behave."

Normally I'm allergic to bossy, but somehow this felt nice; cozy. "Yes, Dad," I said, and disentangled my leg, which sent me off balance so I fell over onto Justin.

"Ow, get off me," he said, flapping a hand at me without much energy. "God, how much do you *weigh*?" I wriggled myself comfortable and stayed put with my head in his lap, squinting up into the sunset. He tickled my nose with a grass stem.

I looked relaxed, at least I hoped I did, but my mind was going fast. I had just realized—*Yes, Dad*—what this whole setup reminded me of: a family. Maybe not a real-life family, although what would I know, but a family out of a million children's-book series and old TV shows, the comforting kind that go on for years without anyone getting any older, to the point where you start to wonder about the actors' hormone levels. These five had it all: Daniel the distant but affectionate father, Justin and Abby taking turns to be the protective Mammy and the lofty eldest, Rafe the moody teenage middle kid; and Lexie, the late arrival, the capricious little sister to be alternately spoiled and teased.

They probably had no more clue about real-life families than I did. I should have spotted from the beginning that this was one of the things they had in common—Daniel orphaned, Abby fostered out, Justin and Rafe exiled, Lexie

Godknowswhat but not exactly close to her parents. I'd skimmed over it because it was my default mode too. Consciously or subconsciously, they had collected every paper-thin scrap they could find and built their own patchwork, makeshift image of what a family was, and then they had made themselves into that.

The four of them had been only eighteen or so when they had met. I looked at them under my lashes—Daniel holding a bottle up to the light to see if there was any wine left, Abby flicking ants off the cake plate—and wondered what they would have been if they had missed each other, along the way.

This gave me a whole bunch of ideas, but they were hazy and fast-moving and I decided I was too comfortable to try and put any shape on them. They could wait a few hours, till my walk. "Me too," I said to Daniel, and held out my glass for more wine.

"Are you drunk?" Frank demanded, when I rang him. "You sounded langered, earlier."

"Relax, Frankie," I said. "I had a couple of glasses of wine with dinner. That doesn't make me drunk."

"It better not. This may feel like a holiday, but I don't want you treating it like one. You stay alert."

I was loitering along a potholey lane, uphill from the ruined cottage. I had been thinking, a lot, about how Lexie had ended up in that cottage. We had all taken it for granted that she was running for cover and couldn't make Whitethorn House or the village, either because the killer was blocking her way or because she was fading fast, so she made for the nearest hiding place she knew. N changed that. Assuming N was a person, as opposed to a pub or a radio program or a poker game, they had had to meet somewhere, and the fact that no places were marked in the diary said they had used the same meeting point every time. And if those times were nights rather than mornings, then the cottage made total sense: privacy, convenience, shelter from wind and rain and no way for anyone to sneak up on you. She could have been heading there anyway that night, long before someone jumped her, and just kept going—maybe on autopilot, after N ambushed her on her way; maybe because she hoped N would be there to help her.

It wasn't the kind of lead detectives dream of, but it was about the best I'd got, so I was spending a lot of my walk lurking in the general area of the cottage and hoping N would help me out by showing up some night. I had found myself a convenient stretch of lane: it had a clear enough view that I could keep an eye on the cottage while I talked to Frank or Sam, enough trees to hide me if I needed it, and enough isolation that no farmer was likely to hear me on the phone and come after me with his trusty shotgun. "I'm alert," I said. "And I've got something to ask you. Remind me: Daniel's great-uncle died in September?"

I heard Frank moving stuff around, flipping pages; either he had brought the file home with him, or he was still at work. "February third. Daniel got the keys to the house on September tenth. Probate must've taken a while. Why?"

"Can you find out how the great-uncle died, and where these five were that day? Also, why probate took so long? When my granny left me a grand, I got it six weeks later."

Frank whistled. "You're thinking they bumped off Great-uncle Simon for the house? And then Lexie lost her nerve?"

I sighed and ran a hand through my hair, trying to work out how to explain. "Not exactly. Actually, not at all. But they're weird about that house, Frank. All four of them. They all talk about it like they own it, not just Daniel—'We should get double-glazing, we need to decide about the herb garden, we . . .' And they all act like this is a permanent arrangement, like they can spend years doing it up because they're all going to live here forever."

"Ah, they're just young," Frank said tolerantly. "At that age, everyone thinks college mates and house shares are forever. Give them a few years and it'll be all semi-ds in the suburbs and Sunday afternoons buying decking at the home-and-garden shop."

"They're not that young. And you've heard them: they're way too wrapped up in this house and each other. There's nothing else in their lives. I don't really think they knocked off the great-uncle, but I'm shooting in the dark here. We've always thought they were hiding something. Anything weird is worth checking out."

"True," Frank said. "Will do. Don't you want to hear what I've been doing with my day?"

That undercurrent of excitement in his voice: very few things get Frank that worked up. "Damn straight," I said.

The undercurrent broke through into a grin so wide I could hear it. "FBI got a hit on our girl's prints."

"Shit! Already?" The FBI guys are good about helping us when we need it, but they always have a spectacular backlog.

"I've got friends in low places."

"OK," I said. "Who is she?" For some reason my knees felt shaky. I got my back up against a tree.

"May-Ruth Thibodeaux, born in North Carolina in 1975, reported missing in October 2000 and wanted for car theft. Prints and photo both match."

My breath went out with a little rush. "Cassie?" Frank said, after a moment. I heard him draw on a cigarette. "You still there?"

"Yeah. May-Ruth Thibodeaux." Saying it made my back prickle. "What do we know about her?"

"Not a lot. No info till 1997, when she moved to Raleigh from someplace in the arsehole of nowhere, rented a fleabag apartment in a crap neighborhood and got a job waiting tables in an all-night diner. She had an education somewhere along the way if she was able to jump straight into a postgrad at Trinity, but it's looking like self-taught or home-schooled; she doesn't show up on the register at any local college or high school. No criminal record."

Frank blew out smoke. "On the evening of October tenth 2000, she borrowed her fiancé's car to get to work, but she never showed up. He filed a missing-person report a couple of days later. The cops didn't take it too seriously; they figured she'd just taken off. They gave the fiancé a little hassle, just in case he'd killed her and dumped her somewhere, but his alibi was good. The car turned up in New York in December 2000, at long-term parking at Kennedy Airport."

He was very pleased with himself. "Nice one, Frank," I said automatically. "Fair play to you."

"We aim to please," Frank said, trying to sound modest.

She was only a year younger than me, after all. I was playing marbles in soft rain in a Wicklow garden and she was running wild in some hot small town, barefoot at the soda fountain and jolting down dirt roads in the back of a pickup truck, till one day she got in a car and she just kept driving.

"Cassie?"

"Yeah."

"My contact's going to do some more digging, see if she made any serious enemies along the way—anyone who might've tracked her here."

"Sounds good," I said, trying to pull my head together. "That sounds like the kind of thing I might want to know. What was the fiancé's name?"

"Brad, Chad, Chet, one of those American yokes . . ." Papers rustling. "My boy made a couple of phone calls, and the guy hasn't missed a day of work in months. No way he hopped across the pond to kill off the ex. Chad Andrew Mitchell. Why?"

No N. "I just wondered."

Frank waited, but I'm good at that game. "Fair enough," he said finally. "I'll keep you posted. The ID might take us nowhere, but still, it's nice to have some kind of handle on this girl. Makes it easier to get your head round the idea of her, no?"

"Oh, yeah," I said. "Definitely."

It wasn't true. After Frank hung up I spent a long time leaning against that tree, watching the broken outline of the cottage slowly fade and reappear as clouds moved across the moon, thinking about May-Ruth Thibodeaux. Somehow, giving her back her own name, her own hometown, her own story, brought it home to me: she had been real, not just a shadow cast by my mind and Frank's; she had been alive. There had been thirty years in which we could have come face to face.

It seemed to me suddenly that I should have known; an ocean away, but it seemed like I should have felt her there all along, like every now and then I should have looked up from my marbles or my textbook or my case report as if someone had called my name. She came all those thousands of miles, close enough to slip on my old name like a sister's hand-me-down coat, she came pulled like a compass needle and she almost made it. She was only an hour's drive away, and I should have known; I should have known, in time, to take that last step and find her.

The only shadows over that week came from outside. We were playing poker, Friday evening—they played cards a lot, late into the nights; mostly Texas Hold-'em or 110, sometimes piquet if only two people felt like playing. The stakes were just tarnished ten-pence pieces from a huge jar someone had found in the attic, but they took it seriously all the same: everyone started with the same number of coins and when you were out you were out, no borrowing from the stash. Lexie, like me, had been a pretty decent card player; her calls hadn't always made a lot of sense, but apparently she had learned to make the unpredictability work for her, especially on big hands. The winner got to choose the next day's dinner menu.

That night we had Louis Armstrong on the record player and Daniel had bought a huge bag of Doritos, along with three different dips to keep everyone happy. We were maneuvering around the various chipped bowls and using the food to try and distract each other—it worked best on Justin, who lost his concentration completely if he thought you were about to get salsa on the mahogany. I had just wiped out Rafe head-to-head—on weak hands he messed around with the dips, if he had something good he shoveled Doritos straight into his mouth by the handful; never play poker with a detective—and I was busy gloating, when his phone rang. He tilted his chair backwards and grabbed the phone off one of the bookshelves.

"Hello," he said, giving me the finger. Then his chair came down and his face changed; it froze over, into that haughty, unreadable mask he wore in college and around outsiders. "Dad," he said.

Without an eyeblink, the others drew closer around him; you could feel it in the air, a tightening, a solidifying as they ranged themselves at his shoulders. I was next to him, and I got the full benefit of the bellow coming out of the phone: ". . . Job opened up . . . foot on the ladder . . . changed your mind . . . ?"

Rafe's nostrils twitched as if he had smelled something foul. "Not interested," he said.

The volume of the tirade made his eyes snap shut. I caught enough of it to gather that reading plays all day was for pansies and that someone called Bradbury had a son who had just made his first million and that Rafe was generally a waste of oxygen. He held the phone between thumb and finger, inches from his ear.

"For God's sake, hang up," Justin whispered. His face was pulled into an unconscious, agonized grimace. "Just hang up on him."

"He can't," Daniel said softly. "He should, obviously, but . . . Someday."

Abby shrugged. "Well, then . . ." she said. She sent the cards arcing from hand to hand with a fast, sassy flourish and dealt, five hands. Daniel smiled across at her and pulled his chair up, ready.

The phone was still going strong; the word "arse" came up regularly, in what sounded like a wide variety of contexts. Rafe's chin was tucked in like he was braced against gale-force wind. Justin touched his arm; his eyes flew open and he stared at us, reddening right up to his hairline.

The rest of us had already thrown in our stakes. I had a hand like a foot—a seven and a nine, not even suited—but I knew exactly what the others were doing. They were pulling Rafe back, and the thought of being part of that sent something intoxicating through me, something so fine it hurt. For a split second I thought of Rob hooking one foot around my ankle, under our desks, when O'Kelly was giving me a bollocking. I waved my cards at Rafe and mouthed, "Ante up."

He blinked. I cocked one eyebrow, gave him my best cheeky Lexie grin and whispered, "Unless you're scared I'll kick your ass again."

The frozen look dissolved, just a little. He checked his cards; then he put the phone down on the bookshelf beside him, carefully, and tossed ten pence into the middle. "Because I'm happy where I am," he told the phone. His voice sounded almost normal, but that angry red flush was still covering his face.

Abby gave him a tiny smile, fanned three cards deftly on the table and flipped them over. "Lexie's drawing to a straight," said Justin, narrowing his eyes at me. "I know that look."

The phone had apparently spent a lot of money on Rafe and wasn't planning to see it flushed down the bog. "She's not," Daniel said. "She may have something, but not the makings of a straight. I call."

I was nowhere near a straight, but that wasn't the point; none of us were folding, not till Rafe hung up. The phone made a big statement about a Real Job. "In other words, a job in an office," Rafe informed us. The rigidity was starting to go out of his spine. "Maybe even, someday, if I'm a team player and I think outside the box and work smarter not harder, an office with a window. Or am I aiming a little high?" he asked the phone. "What do you think?" He mimed *See your one and raise you two,* at Justin.

The phone—it obviously knew it was being insulted, even if it wasn't sure exactly how—said something belligerent about ambition and how it was about bloody time Rafe grew up and started living in the real world.

"Ah," Daniel said, glancing up from his stack. "Now that's a concept that's always fascinated me: the real world. Only a very specific subset of people use the term, have you noticed? To me, it seems self-evident that everyone lives in the real world—we all breathe real oxygen, eat real food, the earth under our feet feels equally solid to all of us. But clearly these people have a far more tightly circumscribed definition of reality, one that I find deeply mysterious, and an almost pathologically intense need to bring others into line with that definition."

"It's all jealousy," Justin said, considering his cards and flipping two more coins into the middle. "Sour grapes."

"Nobody," Rafe told the phone, flapping a hand at us to keep our voices down. "The television. I spend my days watching soap operas, eating bonbons and plotting society's downfall."

The last card came up a nine, which at least gave me a pair. "Well, certainly in some cases jealousy is a factor," Daniel said, "but Rafe's father, if half what he says is true, could afford to live any life he wanted, including ours. What does he have to be jealous of? No, I think the mentality has its origins in the Puritan moral framework: the emphasis on fitting into a strict hierarchical structure, the element of self-loathing, the horror of anything pleasurable or artistic or unregimented . . . But I've always wondered how that paradigm made the transition to become the boundary, not just of virtue, but of reality itself. Could you put it on speakerphone, Rafe? I'm interested to hear what he has to say."

Rafe gave him a wide-eyed, are-you-insane stare and

shook his head; Daniel looked vaguely puzzled. The rest of us were starting to get the giggles.

"Of course," Daniel said politely, "if you'd prefer . . . What's so funny, Lexie?"

"Lunatics," Rafe told the ceiling in a fervent undertone, spreading his arms to take in the phone and Daniel and the rest of us, who by now had our hands over our mouths. "I'm surrounded by wall-to-wall lunatics. What have I done to deserve this? Did I pick on the afflicted in a previous life?"

The phone, which was obviously working up to a big finish, informed Rafe that he could have a Lifestyle. "Guzzling champagne in the City," Rafe translated, for us, "and shagging my secretary."

"What the fuck is wrong with that?" the phone shouted, loud enough that Daniel, startled, reared back in his chair with a look of sheer astounded disapproval. Justin exploded with a noise somewhere between a snort and a yelp; Abby was hanging over the back of her chair with her knuckles stuffed in her mouth, and I was laughing so hard I had to stick my head under the table.

The phone, with a magnificent disregard for basic anatomy, called us all a bunch of limp-dicked hippies. By the time I pulled myself together and came up for air, Rafe had flipped over a pair of jacks and was scooping in the pot, pumping one fist in the air and grinning. I realized something. Rafe's mobile had gone off about two feet from my ear, and I hadn't even flinched.

"You know what it is?" Abby said out of nowhere, a few hands later. "It's the contentment."

"Who said which to the what now?" inquired Rafe, narrowing his eyes to examine Daniel's stack. He had switched his phone off.

"The real-world thing." She leaned sideways across me to pull the ashtray closer. Justin had put on Debussy, blending with the faint rush of rain on the grass outside. "Our entire society's based on discontent: people wanting more and more and more, being constantly dissatisfied with their homes, their bodies, their decor, their clothes, everything. Taking it for granted that that's the whole point of life, never to be satisfied. If you're perfectly happy with what you've got—specially if what you've got isn't even all that spectacular—then you're *dangerous*. You're breaking all the rules, you're undermining the sacred economy, you're challenging every assumption that society's built on. That's why Rafe's dad throws a mickey fit whenever Rafe says he's happy where he is. The way he sees it, we're all subversives. We're *traitors*."

"I think you've got something there," said Daniel. "Not jealousy, after all: fear. It's a fascinating state of affairs. Throughout history—even a hundred years ago, even fifty—it was discontent that was considered the threat to society, the defiance of natural law, the danger that had to be exterminated at all costs. Now it's contentment. What a strange reversal."

"We're revolutionaries," Justin said happily, poking a Dorito around in the salsa jar and looking phenomenally unrevolutionary. "I never realized it was this easy."

"We're stealth guerrillas," I said with relish.

"You're a stealth chimpanzee," Rafe told me, flipping three coins into the middle.

"Yes, but a contented one," said Daniel, smiling across at me. "Aren't you?"

"If Rafe would just quit hogging the garlic dip, I'd be the most contented stealth chimpanzee in the whole of Ireland."

"Good," Daniel said, giving me a little nod. "That's what I like to hear."

Sam never asked. "How's it going?" he would say, in our late-night phone calls, and when I said, "Fine," he would move on to something else. At first he told me bits about his side of the investigation—carefully checking out my old cases, the local uniforms' list of troublemakers, Lexie's students and professors. The more he got nowhere, though, the less he talked about it. Instead he told me about other things, small homey things. He had been over at my flat a couple of times, to air it out and make sure it didn't look too obviously empty; the next-door cat had had kittens at the bottom of the garden, he said, and awful Mrs. Moloney downstairs had left a snotty note on his car informing him that Parking was for Residents Only. I didn't tell him this, but it all seemed a million miles away, off in some long-ago world so chaotic that even thinking about it made me tired. Sometimes it took me a moment to remember who he was talking about.

Only once, on the Saturday night, he asked about the others. I was hanging out in my lurk lane, leaning back into a hawthorn hedge and keeping one eye on the cottage. I had a kneesock of Lexie's bundled around the mike, which gave me an attractive three-boobed look but meant that Frank and his gang would only pick up about 10 percent of the conversation.

I was keeping my voice down anyway. Almost since I went out the back gate, I'd had the feeling that someone was following me. Nothing concrete, nothing that couldn't be explained away by the wind and moon shadows and countryside night noises; just that low-level electrical current at the back of your neck, where your skull meets your spine, that only comes from someone's eyes. It took a lot of willpower not to whip around, but if by any chance there really was someone out there, I didn't want him knowing he'd been sussed, not till I decided what I was going to do about it.

"Do ye never go to the pub?" Sam asked.

I wasn't sure what he was asking. Sam knew exactly what I did with my time. According to Frank, he got into work at six every morning to go through the tapes. This made me itch, in small unreasonable ways, but the thought of bringing it up itched even worse. "Rafe and Justin and I went to the Buttery on Tuesday, after tutorials," I said. "Remember?"

"I meant your local—what's it called, Regan's, down in the village. Do they never go there?"

We passed Regan's in the car, on our way to and from college: a dilapidated little country pub, sandwiched between the butcher's and the newsagent's, with bikes leaning unlocked against the wall in the evenings. Nobody had ever suggested going in there.

"It's simpler to have a few drinks at home, if we want them," I said. "It's a walk to the village, and everyone but Justin smokes." Pubs have always been the heart of Irish social life, but when the smoking ban came in, a lot of people moved to drinking at home. The ban doesn't bother me, although I'm confused by the idea that you shouldn't go into a pub and do anything that might be bad for you, but the level of obedience does. To the Irish, rules always used to count as challenges—see who can come up with the best way round this one—and this sudden switch to sheep mode makes me worry that we're turning into someone else, possibly Switzerland.

Sam laughed. "You've been up in the big city too long. I'll guarantee you Regan's doesn't stop anyone smoking. And it's less than a mile by the back roads. Do you not think it's odd, them never going in there?"

I shrugged. "They are odd. They're not all that sociable, in case you haven't noticed. And maybe Regan's sucks."

"Maybe," Sam said, but he didn't sound convinced. "You went to Dunne's in the Stephen's Green Centre when it was your turn to buy food, am I right? Where do the others go?"

"How would I know? Justin went to Marks and Sparks yesterday; I haven't a clue about the others. Frank said Lexie shopped at Dunne's, so I shop at Dunne's."

"What about the newsagent's in the village? Anyone been there?"

I thought about that. Rafe had done a cigarette run one evening, but he had gone out the back gate, towards the late-night petrol station on the Rathowen road, not towards Glenskehy. "Not since I got here. What are you thinking?"

"I was just wondering," Sam said, slowly. "About the village. You're up at the Big House, you know. Daniel's from the Big House family. In most places nobody cares about that, any more; but every now and then, depending on history . . . I was just wondering if there's any bad feeling there."

Right up into living memory, the British ran Ireland on the feudal system: handed out villages to Anglo-Irish families like party favors, then left them to use the land and the locals however they saw fit, which varied just as much as you'd expect. After independence the system collapsed in on itself; a few faded, obsolete eccentrics are still hanging in there, mostly living out of four rooms and opening the rest of the estate to the public to pay the roofing bills, but a lot of the Big Houses have been bought by corporations and turned into hotels or spas or whatever, and everyone's half forgotten what they used to be. Here and there, though, where history scarred a place deeper than most: people remember.

And this was Wicklow. For hundreds of years, rebellions had been planned within a day's walk of where I was sitting. These hills had fought on the guerrillas' side, hidden them from stumbling soldiers through dark tangled nights; cottages like Lexie's had been left hollow and bloody when the British shot everyone in sight till they found their one cached rebel. Every family has stories.

Sam was right, I had been up in the big city way too long. Dublin is modern to the point of hysteria, anything before broadband has become a quaint, embarrassing little joke; I had forgotten even what it was like to live in a place that had memory. Sam is from the country, from Galway; he knows. The cottage's last windows were lit up with moonlight and it looked like a ghost house, secretive and wary.

"There could be," I said. "I don't see what it could have to do with our case, though. It's one thing to give the Big House kids hairy looks till they quit coming into the newsagent's; it's a whole other thing to stab one of them because the landlord was mean to your great-granny in 1846."

"Probably. I'll look into it, though, on the off chance. Anything's worth checking."

I thumped back against the hedge, felt a quick vibration through the branches as something scurried away. "Come on. How crazy do you think these people are?"

A brief silence. "I'm not saying they're crazy," Sam said eventually.

"You're saying one of them might have killed Lexie for something that a completely unrelated family did a hundred years ago. And I'm saying that's someone who at the very least needs to get out a whole lot more, and find himself a girlfriend who doesn't get sheared every summer." I wasn't sure why the idea got up my nose so badly, or for that matter why I was being such a snippy little bitch. Something to do with the house, I think. I had put a lot of work into that house—we had spent half the evening stripping the moldy wallpaper in the sitting room—and I was getting attached to it. The idea of it as the target of that kind of focused hatred made something hot flare up in my stomach.

"There's a family round where I grew up," Sam said. "The Purcells. Their great-granda or whatever was a rent agent, back in the day. One of the bad ones—used to lend the rent money to families who didn't have it, then take the interest out of the wives and daughters, then throw them all out onto the roads once he got bored. Kevin Purcell grew up with the rest of us, not a bother, no grudge; but when we all got a bit older and he started going out with one of the local girls, a bunch of lads got together and beat the shite out of him. They weren't crazy, Cassie. They'd nothing against Kevin; he was a grand young fella, never did that girl any harm. Just . . . some things aren't OK, no matter how long you leave them. Some things don't go away."

The leaves of the hedge prickled and twisted against my back, like something was moving in there, but when I whipped around it was still as a picture. "That's different, Sam. This Kevin guy made the first move: he started going out with that girl. These five didn't do a thing. They're just *living* here."

Another pause. "And that could be enough, all depending. I'm only saying."

There was a bewildered note in his voice. "Fair enough," I said, more calmly. "You're right, it's worth a look—we did say our guy was probably local. Sorry for being a snotty cow."

"I wish you were here," Sam said suddenly, softly. "On the phone, it's too easy to get mixed up. Get things wrong."

"I know, Sam," I said. "I miss you too." It was true. I tried not to—that kind of thing just distracts you, and getting distracted can do anything from wreck your case to get you killed—but when I was on my own and tired, trying to read in bed after a long day, it got difficult. "Only a few weeks left."

Sam sighed. "Less, if I find something. I'll talk to Doherty and Byrne, see what they can tell me. Meanwhile . . . just look after yourself, OK? Just in case."

"I will," I said. "You can update me tomorrow. Sleep tight."

"Sleep tight. I love you."

That feeling of being watched was still pinching at the back of my neck, stronger now, closer. Maybe it was just the conversation with Sam getting to me, but all of a sudden I wanted to know for sure. This electric ripple from somewhere in the dark, Sam's stories, Rafe's father, all these things pressing in on us from every side, looking for weak spots, for their moment to attack: for a second I forgot I was one of the invaders, I just wanted to yell *Leave us alone*. I unwound my mike sock and tucked it into my girdle, along with my phone. Then I switched on my torch for maximum visibility and started walking, a casual, jaunty stroll, heading for home.

I know a variety of ways to shake off a tail, catch him in the act or turn the tables; most of them were designed for city streets, not for the middle of nowhere, but they're adaptable. I kept my eyes front and picked up the pace, till there was no way for anyone to stay too close without breaking cover or making an awful lot of noise in the underbrush. Then I did a sudden swerve onto a cross-lane, switched off the torch, ran fifteen or twenty yards and squished myself, as quietly as I could, through a hedge into a field left to run wild. I stayed still, crouching down close against the bushes, and waited.

Twenty minutes of nothing, not a pebble crunching, not a leaf rustling. If there was actually someone following me, he or she was smart and patient: not a nice thought. Finally I eased myself back through the hedge. There was no one on the lane in either direction, as far as I could see. I picked most of the leaves and twigs out of my clothes and headed home, fast. Lexie's walks had averaged an hour; I didn't have long before the others started worrying. Over the tops of the hedges I could see a glow against the sky: the light from Whitethorn House, faint and golden and shot through with whirls of wood smoke like mist.

That night, when I was reading in bed, Abby knocked on my door. She was in red-and-white-checked flannel pajamas, her face scrubbed shiny and her hair loose on her shoulders; she looked about twelve. She closed the door behind her and sat down cross-legged on the end of my bed, tucking her bare feet into the crooks of her knees for warmth. "Can I ask you a question?" she said.

"Sure," I said, hoping to God I knew the answer.

"OK." Abby tucked her hair behind her ears, glanced back at the door. "I don't know how to put this, so I'm just going to come straight out and ask, and you can tell me to mind my own business if you want. Is the baby OK?"

I must have looked gobsmacked. One corner of her mouth twisted upwards in a wry little smile. "Sorry. I didn't mean to startle you. I guessed. We're always in sync, but last month you never bought the chocolate . . . and then when you threw up that day, I just figured."

My mind was racing. "Do the guys know?"

Abby shrugged, a little flip of one shoulder. "I doubt it. They haven't said anything, anyway."

This didn't rule out the chance that one of them did know, that Lexie had told the father—either that she was having a baby or that she was having an abortion—and he had flipped out, but it went some way towards it: Abby didn't miss much. She waited, watching me. "The baby didn't make it," I said; which was, after all, true.

Abby nodded. "I'm sorry," she said. "I'm really sorry, Lexie. Or . . . ?" She raised one eyebrow discreetly.

"It's OK," I said. "I wasn't sure what I was going to do about it, anyway. This sort of makes things simpler."

She nodded again, and I realized I had called it right: she wasn't surprised. "Are you going to tell the guys? Because I can do it, if you want me to."

"No," I said. "I don't want them knowing." Info is ammo, Frank always said. That pregnancy could come in useful sometime; I wasn't about to throw it away. I think it was only in that moment, the moment when I realized I was saving up a dead baby like a hand grenade, that I understood what I had got myself into.

"Fair enough." Abby stood up and hitched at her pajama bottoms. "If you ever want to talk about it or anything, you know where I am."

"Aren't you going to ask me who the father was?" I said. If it was common knowledge who Lexie was sleeping with, then I was in big trouble, but somehow I didn't think it was; Lexie appeared to have lived most of her life on a need-to-know basis. Abby, though; if anyone had guessed, it would be her.

She turned, at the door, and gave that one-shouldered shrug. "I figure," she said, her voice carefully neutral, "if you want to tell me, you probably will."

When she was gone—quick arpeggio of bare feet, almost soundless, down the stairs—I left my book where it was and sat there listening to the others getting ready for bed: someone running water in the bathroom, Justin singing tunelessly to himself below me ("Goooooldfinger . . ."), the creak of floorboards as Daniel moved quietly around his room. Gradually the noises wound down, grew softer and intermittent, faded to silence. I turned off my bedside lamp: Daniel would see it under his door if I kept it on, and I had had enough private little chats for one evening. Even after my eyes adjusted, all I could see was the looming mass of the wardrobe, the hunch of the dressing table, the barely there flicker in the mirror when I moved.

I had been putting a fair amount of energy into not thinking about the baby; Lexie's baby. Four weeks, Cooper had said, not quite a quarter of an inch: a tiny gemstone, a single spark of color slipping between your fingers and through the cracks and gone. A heart the size of a fleck of glitter and vibrating like a hummingbird, seeded with a billion things that would never happen now.

When you threw up that day . . . A strong-willed baby, wide awake and not to be ignored, already reaching out filament fingers to tug at her. For some reason it wasn't a silky newborn I pictured: it was a toddler, compact and naked, with a head of dark curls; faceless, running away from me down the lawn on a summer day, trailing a yell of laughter. Maybe she had sat in this bed just a couple of weeks ago, picturing the same thing.

Or maybe not. I was starting to get a sense that Lexie's will had been denser than mine and obsidian hard, built for resistance, not combat. If she hadn't wanted to imagine the baby, that tiny jewel-colored comet would never for a second have flashed across her mind.

I wanted, as intensely as if this were somehow the key that would unlock the whole story, to know whether she had been going to keep it. Our abortion ban doesn't change anything: a long silent litany of women every year take the ferry or the plane to England, home again before anyone even notices they're gone. There was no one in the world who could tell me what Lexie had been planning; probably even she hadn't been sure. I almost got out of bed and sneaked downstairs to have another look at the diary, just in case I had missed something—a tiny pen dot hidden in a corner of December, on the due date—but that would have been a dumb thing to do, and anyway I already knew there was nothing there. I sat in bed in the dark with my arms around my knees, listening to the rain and feeling the battery pack dig into me where the stab wound should have been, for a very long time.

There was this one evening; Sunday, I think it was. The guys had pushed back the furniture in the sitting room and were attacking the floor with a sander and a polisher and a certain amount of machismo, so Abby and I had left them to it and headed up to the top spare room, the one next to me, to pick at the edges of Uncle Simon's hoard. I was sitting on the floor, half covered in ancient scraps of material, sorting out the ones that weren't mainly moth holes; Abby was flipping through a huge pile of fugly curtains, murmuring, "Bin, bin, bin—these might be worth washing—bin, bin, oh God bin, who *bought* this crap?" The sander was humming noisily downstairs and the house had a busy, settled feel that reminded me of the Murder squad room on a quiet day.

"Whoa," Abby said suddenly, sitting back on her heels. "Check this out."

She was holding up a dress: robin's-egg blue with white

polka dots and a white collar and sash, little cap sleeves and a full skirt made to fly up when you twirled, pure lindy hop. "Wow," I said, disentangling myself from my puddle of fabric and going over to check it out. "Think it was Uncle Simon's?"

"I don't think he had the figure for it, but we'll check the photo album." Abby held the dress at arm's length and examined it. "Want to try it on? I don't think it has moths."

"Go for it. You found it."

"It'd never fit me. Look—" Abby got to her feet and held the dress against herself. "It's for someone taller. The waist would be down around my arse."

Abby was maybe five foot two, but I kept forgetting; it was hard to think of her as small. "And it's for someone skinnier than me," I said, trying the waist against mine, "or wearing a serious corset. I'd burst it."

"Maybe not. You lost weight when you were sick." Abby threw the dress over my shoulder. "Try it."

She gave me a quizzical look when I headed for my bedroom to change: it was obviously out of character, but I couldn't do much about that, except hope she would put it down to self-consciousness about the bandage or something. The dress actually did fit, more or less—it was tight enough that the bandage left a bulge, but there was nothing dodgy about that. I did a quick check to make sure the wire didn't show. In the mirror I looked breathless and mischievous and daring, ready for anything.

"Told you," Abby said, when I came out. She spun me round, retied the sash in a bigger bow. "Let's go wow the boys."

We ran downstairs calling, "Look what we found!" and by the time we got down to the sitting room the sander was off and the guys were waiting for us. "Oh, *look* at you!" Justin cried. "Our little jazz baby!"

"Perfect," Daniel said, smiling at me. "It's perfect."

Rafe swung one leg over the piano stool and swept a finger up the keys in a great, expert flourish. Then he started to play, something lazy and tempting with a sideways swing to it. Abby laughed. She gave the bow of my sash another tug, tightening it; then she went to the piano and started to sing.

"Of all the boys I've known and I've known some, until I first met you I was lonesome . . ."

I had heard Abby sing before, but only to herself when she thought no one was listening, never like this. That voice: it was the kind you don't hear these days, a magnificent, full-blown contralto straight out of old war films, a voice for smoky nightclubs and marcel-waved hair, red lipstick and a blue saxophone. Justin put the sander down, clicked his heels together neatly and bowed. "May I have the honor of this dance?" he asked, and held out his hand to me.

For a second I wasn't sure. What if Lexie had had two left feet, what if she *hadn't* had two left feet and my new clumsiness gave me away, what if he held me too close and felt the battery pack hard under the bandage . . . But I always loved dancing and it seemed like forever since I had danced or wanted to, so long ago I couldn't remember the last time. Abby winked at me without missing a note and Rafe threw in an extra little riff, and I caught Justin's hand and let him pull me out of the doorway.

He knew what he was doing: smooth steps and his hand steady in mine as he spun me in slow circles around the room, floorboards soft and warm and dusty under my feet. And I hadn't lost the knack, after all, I wasn't stepping on Justin's feet or tripping over my own; my body swayed with his sure and agile as if I had never walked into a chair in my life, I couldn't have put a foot wrong if I had tried. Ribs of sunlight flashing across my eyes, Daniel leaning against the wall and smiling with a crumple of sandpaper forgotten in his hand, my skirt whirling up like a bell as Justin swung me away from him and then in again. "And so I rack my brain trying to explain all the things that you do to me . . ." Smell of polish, and the sawdust spinning lazy curls through the long columns of light. Abby with one palm lifting and her head thrown back, throat exposed and the song tossed up through the empty rooms and battered ceilings to the whole blazing sunset sky.

For a second it came back to me, when I had last danced like this: me and Rob, on the roof of the extension below my flat, the night before everything went horribly wrong. Somehow it didn't even hurt. It was so far away; I was buttoned tight and untouchable in my blue dress and that was a sweet sad thing that had happened to some other girl, a long time ago. Rafe was picking up the rhythm and Abby was swaying faster, snapping her fingers: "I could say *bella, bella,* even say *wunderbar,* each language only helps me tell you how grand you are . . ." Justin caught me by the waist and spun me off the floor in a great flying circle, his face flushed and laughing close to mine. The wide bare room tossed Abby's voice back and forth as if there were someone harmonizing in every corner and our footsteps rang and echoed till it sounded like the room was full of dancers, the house calling up all the people who had danced here across centuries of spring evenings, gallant girls seeing gallant boys off to war, old men and women straight-backed while outside their world disintegrated and the new one battered at their doors, all of them bruised and all of them laughing, welcoming us into their long lineage.

9

"Well well well," Frank said, that night. "You know what today is, right?" I had no idea. Half my mind was still back at Whitethorn House. After dinner Rafe had dug out a tattered, yellowish songbook from inside the piano stool and kept going with the inter-war theme, Abby was singing along from the spare room—"Oh, Johnny, how you can love"—while she went back to rummaging and Daniel and Justin did the washing up, and the rhythm of it had bounced in my heels, sweet and saucy and tempting, all the way down the lawn and out the back gate. For a second I had actually considered just staying home, leaving Frank and Sam and the mystery pair of eyes to their own devices for one evening. It wasn't like I was getting anything useful done out here. The night had turned cloudy, needle-fine drizzle was spattering onto the communal jacket, and I didn't like having the torch on while I was on the phone; I couldn't see six inches in front of my face. A whole coven of knife-happy stalkers could have been doing the Macarena around the cottage and I would never have known.

"If it's your birthday," I said, "you might have to wait for your present."

"Very funny. It's Sunday, babe. And unless I'm much mistaken, you're still in Whitethorn House, snug as a bug in a rug. Which means we've won our first battle: you made it through the week without getting caught. Congratulations, Detective. You're in."

"I guess I am," I said. I had stopped counting the days, somewhere along the way. I decided this was a good sign.

"So," Frank said. I could hear him arranging himself

more comfortably, turning down the outraged talk-radio caller in the background: he was at home, wherever home was since Olivia had kicked him out. "Let's have a summary of Week One."

I pulled myself up onto a wall and took a second to get my head clear before I answered. Under all the easy messing around, Frank is pure business: he wants reports like any other boss, and he likes them clear, thorough and succinct.

"Week One," I said. "I've inserted myself into Alexandra Madison's home and her place of study, apparently with success: no one's shown any sign of suspicion. I've searched as much of Whitethorn House as is feasible, but I haven't found anything to point us in a specific direction." This was basically true; the diary presumably pointed somewhere, but so far I had no idea where. "I've made myself available as much as possible—to known associates, by attempting to be alone on regular occasions during the day and evening, and to unknown ones by ensuring that I'm visible on these walks. I haven't been approached by anyone who wasn't already on our radar, but at this stage that doesn't rule out an unknown assailant; he could be biding his time. I've been approached at various times by all the housemates and a number of students and professors, but all of them seemed concerned primarily with how I was feeling, that kind of thing—Brenda Grealey was a little more interested in the details than you'd expect, but I think that's just ghoulishness. None of the reactions to Lexie's stabbing or to her return have raised any red flags. The housemates appear to have concealed the full extent of their distress from the investigating officers, but coming from them, I don't consider that suspicious behavior. They're very reserved with outsiders."

"You're telling me," Frank said. "What's your gut say?"

I shifted, trying to find a bit of wall where nothing stuck into my arse. This was a little more complicated than it should have been, since I wasn't about to tell him, or Sam, about the diary or about my feeling that I was being followed. "I think there's something we're missing," I said, in the end.

"Something important. Maybe your mystery guy, maybe a motive, maybe . . . I don't know. I just get this very strong sense that there's something here that hasn't surfaced yet. I keep feeling like I'm about to put my finger on it, but . . ."

"Something to do with the housemates? College? The baby? The May-Ruth thing?"

"I don't know," I said. "I honestly don't know."

Sofa springs creaking as Frank reached for something—a drink; I heard him swallow. "I can tell you this much: it's not the great-uncle. You were way off base there. He died of cirrhosis; spent thirty or forty years locked up in that house drinking, then six months in a hospice dying. None of the five of them visited him. As a matter of fact, he and Daniel hadn't seen each other since Daniel was a kid, as far as I can find out."

I had seldom been so glad to be wrong, but this left me with that same grabbing-at-mirages feeling I'd had all week. "Why'd he leave Daniel the place, then?"

"Not many options. That family dies young; the only two living relatives were Daniel and his cousin, Edward Hanrahan, old Simon's daughter's kid. Eddie's a good little yuppie, works for an estate agent. Apparently Simon figured Danny Boy was the lesser of two evils. Maybe he liked academic types better than yuppies, or maybe he wanted the house to stay with the family name."

Good for Simon. "That must've got up Eddie's nose."

"Oh, yeah. He wasn't any closer to Granddad than Daniel was, but he tried to fight the will, claimed the drink had sent Simon off his trolley. That's why probate took so long. It was a stupid thing to do, but then, our Eddie's not the brightest pixie in the forest. Simon's doctor confirmed that he was an alcoholic and a horrible old man, but sane as you or me, and that was the end of that. Nothing dodgy there."

I slumped down on the wall. I shouldn't have been frustrated, I had never actually thought that the gang had slipped nightshade into Uncle Simon's denture adhesive; but I couldn't shake the feeling that there was something crucial going on around Whitethorn House, something I should be able to put my finger on. "Yeah, well," I said. "It was just a thought. Sorry for wasting your time."

Frank sighed. "You didn't. Anything's worth checking." If I heard that sentence one more time, I was going to kill someone myself. "If you think they're dodgy, then they probably are. Just not that particular way."

"I never said I thought they were dodgy."

"A few days ago you thought they'd put a pillow over Uncle Simon's head."

I pulled my hood farther over my face—the rain was picking up, fine little stinging needles of it, and I wanted to go home. It was a toss-up which one was more pointless, this stakeout or this conversation. "I didn't *think* it. I just asked you to check it out, on the off chance. I can't see them as a bunch of killers."

"Hmm," Frank said. "And you're positive that's not just because they're such lovely people."

I couldn't tell from his voice whether he was winding me up or testing me—Frank being Frank, probably a little of both. "Come on, Frankie, you know me better than that. You asked me about my instinct; that's what it says. I've spent basically every waking second with these four for a week now, and there's been no sign of a motive, no indications of guilty consciences—and like we said before, if one of them did it, the other three have to know. By now *someone* would have cracked, even for a second. I think you're dead right that they're hiding something, but I can't see it being that."

"Fair enough," Frank said, noncommittally. "So you've got two jobs for Week Two. The first one is to pinpoint whatever it is that's tingling your spidey sense. The second one is to start pushing the housemates a little, find out what it is they're not sharing. They've been getting an easy ride so far—which is fine, that's what we planned, but now it's time to start tightening the screws. And while you're doing that, here's something to bear in mind. Remember your girlie chat with Abby, the other night?"

"Yeah," I said. A flicker of something very strange went through me, at the thought of Frank hearing that conversation; something almost like outrage. I wanted to snap at him, *That was private.*

"Pajama parties rule. I told you she was a smart kid. What do you think: does she know who the daddy is?"

I hadn't been able to make up my mind on that. "She could probably make a good guess, but I don't think she's sure. And she's not about to tell me what her guess is."

"Watch her," Frank said, taking another swig of his drink. "She's a little too observant for my taste. You think she'll tell the guys?"

"No," I said. I didn't have to think about this one. "I get the sense that Abby's very good at minding her own business and letting other people sort out their dramas all by themselves. She brought up the baby so I wouldn't have to deal with it alone if I didn't want to, but once she'd made that clear, she was straight out of there—no hints, no probing. She won't say anything. And, Frank—are you going to be interviewing the guys again?"

"Not sure yet," Frank said. There was a wary note in his voice; he doesn't like being pinned down. "Why?"

"If you do, don't mention the baby. OK? I want to spring that one on them myself. Around you, they're on their guard; you'll only get half their reaction. I can get the whole thing."

"All right," Frank said, after a moment. He was trying to sound like he was doing me a favor, but I heard the undercurrent of satisfaction: he liked the way I was thinking. It was nice to know someone did. "But make sure you time it right. Get 'em when they're drunk or something."

"They don't get drunk, exactly, just tipsy. I'll know my moment when I see it."

"Fair enough. Here's my point, though: that's one thing Abby was keeping under wraps, and not just where we're concerned—she was hiding it from Lexie, too, and she's still hiding it from the boys. We've been talking about them like they're one big entity with one big secret, but it's not that simple. There are cracks there. They could all be keeping the same secret, or they could each have secrets of their own, or both. Look for the cracks. And keep me posted."

He was about to hang up. "Anything new on our girl?" I asked. May-Ruth. Somehow I couldn't say it out loud; even bringing her up felt strange now, electric. But if he had found out anything more about her, I wanted it.

Frank snorted. "Ever tried rushing the FBI? They've got a whole plateful of mother-stabbers and father-rapers of their own; someone else's little murder case isn't at the top of their list. Forget about them. They'll get back to us when they get back to us. You just concentrate on getting me a few answers."

Frank was right, at first I think I had seen the four of them as a single unit: The Housemates, shoulder to shoulder, graceful and inseparable as a group in a painting and all with the same fine bloom of light on them, like the luster on old beeswaxed wood. It was only over that first week that they had turned real to me, come into focus as separate individuals with their own little quirks and weaknesses. I knew the cracks had to be there. That kind of friendship doesn't just materialize at the end of the rainbow one morning in a soft-focus Hollywood haze. For it to last this long, and at such close quarters, some serious work had gone into it. Ask any ice-skater or ballet dancer or show jumper, anyone who lives by beautiful moving things: nothing takes as much work as effortlessness.

Small cracks, at first: slippery as mist, nothing you could put your finger on. We were in the kitchen Monday morning, eating breakfast. Rafe had done his Mongo-want-coffee routine and disappeared to finish waking up. Justin was slicing his fried eggs into neat strips, Daniel was eating sausages one-handed and making notes in the margins of what looked like an Old Norse photocopy, Abby was flipping through a week-old newspaper she had found in the Arts block and I was chattering to no one in particular about nothing very much. I had been ratcheting up the energy level, little by little. This was more complicated than it sounds. The more I talked, the more likely I was to shove my foot in my mouth; but the only way I was going to get anything useful out of these four was if they relaxed around me, and that would only happen once everything went back to normal, which, for Lexie, had not involved a lot of silence. I was telling the kitchen about these four awful girls in my Thursday tutorial, which I figured was safe enough.

"As far as I can tell they're actually all the same person. They're all called Orla or Fiona or Aoife or something, and they all have that accent like they've had their sinuses surgically removed, and they've all got that fake-straight fake-blond hair, and none of them ever, ever do the reading. I don't know why they're bothering with college."

"To meet rich boys," Abby said, without looking up.

"At least one of them's found one. Some rugby-looking guy. He was waiting for her after the tutorial last week and I swear, when the four of them came out the door he got this terrified look and then he held out his hand to *the wrong girl* for a second, before the right one dived on him. He can't tell them apart either."

"Look who's feeling better," Daniel said, smiling across at me.

"Chatterbox," said Justin, putting another slice of toast on my plate. "Just out of curiosity, have you ever stayed quiet for more than five minutes at a stretch?"

"I have so. I had laryngitis once, when I was nine, and I couldn't say a single word for five days. It was awful. Everyone kept bringing me chicken soup and comic books and boring stuff, and I kept trying to explain that I felt totally fine and I wanted to get up, but they just told me to be quiet and rest my throat. When you were little, did you ever—"

"Dammit," Abby said suddenly, looking up from her paper. "Those cherries. The best-by date was yesterday. Is anyone still hungry? We could put them in pancakes or something."

"I've never heard of cherry pancakes," Justin said. "It sounds disgusting."

"I don't see why. If you can have blueberry pancakes—"

"And cherry scones," I pointed out, through toast.

"That's a different principle entirely," Daniel said. "Candied cherries. The acidity and moisture levels—"

"We could try it. They cost about a million quid; I'm not just leaving them to rot."

"I'll try anything," I said helpfully. "I'd have some cherry pancakes."

"Oh God, let's not," said Justin, with a little shudder of distaste. "Let's just take the cherries into college and have them with lunch."

"Rafe's not getting any," Abby said, folding the paper away and heading for the fridge. "You know that weird smell off his bag? Half a banana he stuck in the inside pocket and forgot about. From now on we don't feed him anything we can't actually watch him eat. Lex, give me a hand wrapping them up?"

It was so smooth, I didn't even notice anything had happened. Abby and I split the cherries into four bundles and put them in with that day's sandwiches, Rafe ended up eating most of them, and I forgot the whole thing, until the next evening.

We had washed a few of the less fugly curtains and were putting them up in the spare rooms, to keep the heat in rather than as an aesthetic choice—we had one electric storage heater and the fireplace to heat that whole house, in winter it must have been Arctic. Justin and Daniel were doing the first-floor room, while the rest of us did the top ones. Abby and I were threading curtain hooks for Rafe to hang when we heard a tumble of heavy things falling below us, a thud, a yelp from Justin; then Daniel calling, "It's all right, I'm fine."

"What now?" said Rafe. He was balanced precariously on the windowsill, hanging onto the curtain rail with one hand.

"Someone fell off something," Abby said, through a

mouthful of curtain hooks, "or over something. I think they'll live."

There was a sudden low exclamation, through the floorboards, and Justin called, "Lexie, Abby, Rafe, come here! Come look!"

We ran downstairs. Daniel and Justin were kneeling on the spare-room floor, surrounded by an explosion of weird old objects, and for a second I thought one of them was hurt after all. Then I saw what they were looking at. There was a stiff, stained leather pouch on the floor between them, and Daniel was holding a revolver.

"Daniel came off the stepladder," Justin said, "and knocked over all this stuff, and this just fell out, right at his feet. I can't even work out where it was, in all this mess. God knows what else is in there."

It was a Webley, a beauty, glowing with patina between the crusted patches of dirt. "My God," Rafe said, dropping down beside Daniel and reaching out to touch the barrel. "That's a Webley Mark Six; an old one, too. They were standard issue during the First World War. Your crazy greatuncle or whoever he was, Daniel, the one you look like: this could have been his."

Daniel nodded. He inspected the gun for a moment, then broke it open: unloaded. "William," he said. "It could have been his, yes." He closed the cylinder, fitted his hand carefully, gently, around the grip.

"It's a mess," Rafe said, "but it could be cleaned up. All it needs is a couple of days' soak in a good solvent, and then some work with a brush. I suppose ammo would be too much to ask for."

Daniel smiled at him, a quick, unexpected flash of a grin. He tipped the leather pouch upside down and a faded cardboard packet of cartridges fell out, onto the floor.

"Oh, beautiful," Rafe said, picking up the box and giving it a shake. I could tell from the rattle that it was almost full; there had to be nine or ten cartridges in there. "We'll have this up and running in no time. I'll buy the solvent."

234 · Tana French

"Don't mess around with that thing unless you know what you're doing," said Abby. She was the only one who hadn't sat down on the floor to have a look, and she didn't sound all that pleased with this whole idea. I wasn't sure how I felt about it, either. The Webley was a sweetheart and I would have loved a chance to try it out, but an undercover job grows a whole new level when there's a gun bouncing around. Sam wasn't going to like this one little bit.

Rafe rolled his eyes. "What makes you think I don't? My father took me shooting every single year, starting when I was *seven*. I can hit a pheasant in midair, three shots out of five. One year we went up to Scotland—"

"Is that thing even legal?" Abby wanted to know. "Don't we need a license, or something?"

"But it's a family heirloom," said Justin. "We didn't buy it, we inherited it."

Again with that *we*. "Licenses aren't for buying a gun, silly," I said. "They're for owning it." I had already decided to let Frank explain to Sam why, even though the gun had probably never been licensed in its existence, we weren't about to confiscate it.

Rafe raised his eyebrows. "Don't you want to hear this? I'm telling you a tender tale of father-son bonding, and all you can talk about is red tape. Once my father found out I could shoot, he used to pull me out of school for a whole week, every time the season came around. Those are the only times in my life when he's treated me like something other than a living ad for contraception. For my sixteenth birthday he got me—"

"I'm fairly sure we do need a license, officially," Daniel said, "but I think we should leave it, at least for now. I've had enough of the police for a while. When do you think you could get the solvent, Rafe?"

His eyes were on Rafe, ice gray and steady and unblinking. For a second Rafe stared back, but then he shrugged and took the gun out of Daniel's hands. "Sometime this week, probably. Whenever I find a place that carries it." He broke the gun open, a lot more expertly than Daniel had, and started peering into the barrel.

That was when I remembered the cherries, me chattering, Abby cutting in. It was the note in Daniel's voice that reminded me: that same calm, inflexible firmness, like a door closing. It took me a second to remember what I had been talking about, before the others had deftly, expertly diverted the conversation. Something about having laryngitis, being stuck in bed, when I was a kid.

I tested my new theory later that evening, when Daniel had put the revolver away and we had hung the curtains and were curled up in the sitting room. Abby had finished her doll's petticoat and was starting on a dress; her lap was covered with the scraps of material I'd been sorting on Sunday.

"I used to have dolls, when I was little," I said. If my theory was right, then this wasn't risky; the others wouldn't have heard all that much about Lexie's childhood. "I had a collection—"

"You?" Justin said, giving me a quirk of a smile. "The only thing you collect is chocolate."

"Actually," Abby asked me, "have you got any? Something with nuts?"

Straight in with the diversion. "I did too have a collection," I said. "I had all four sisters out of *Little Women*. You could get the mother, too, but she was such a horrible sanctimonious cow that I didn't want her anywhere near me. I didn't even want the others, but I had this aunt—"

"Why don't you get *Little Women* dolls?" Justin asked Abby, plaintively. "And get rid of that awful poppet?"

"If you keep bitching about her, I swear, one of these mornings you're going to wake up and find her on your pillow, staring at you."

Rafe was watching me, hooded golden eyes across his solitaire game. "I kept trying to tell her I didn't even like dolls," I said, over Justin's horrified noises, "but she never got the hint. She—"

Daniel glanced up from his book. "No pasts," he said.

The fall of it, the finality, told me it was something he had said before.

There was a long, not-quite-comfortable silence. The fire spat sparks up the chimney. Abby had gone back to trying bits of fabric against her doll's dress. Rafe was still watching me; I had my head down over my book (Rip Corelli, *She Liked Them Married*), but I could feel his eyes.

For some reason, the past—any of our pasts—was solidly off-limits. They were like the creepy rabbits in *Watership Down* who won't answer questions beginning with "Where."

And another thing: Rafe had to know that. He had been nudging at the boundary on purpose. I wasn't sure whose buttons he had been trying to push, exactly, or why— maybe everyone's, maybe he was just in that kind of mood—but it was a tiny crack, in that perfect surface.

Frank's FBI buddy got back to him on Wednesday. I knew the second Frank picked up the phone that something had happened, something big.

"Where are you?" he demanded.

"Some lane, I don't know. Why?"

An owl hooted, close behind me; I whipped round in time to see it drifting into the trees only a few feet away, wings spread, light as ash. "What was that?" Frank asked sharply.

"Just an owl. Breathe, Frank."

"Got your gun?"

I hadn't. I'd been so wrapped up in Lexie and the Fantastic Four; I'd completely forgotten that what I was supposed to be after was outside Whitethorn House, not inside, and was very likely also after me. That slip, even more than the note in Frank's voice, sent a sharp warning twist through my stomach: *Stay focused.*

Frank caught the second I hesitated, and pounced. "Go home. Now."

"I've only been out for ten minutes. The others will wonder—"

"Let 'em wonder all they like. You don't go wandering around unarmed."

I turned around and headed back up the lane, under the owl swaying on a branch, silhouetted sharp-eared against the sky. I cut round towards the front of the house—the lanes that way were wider, less cover for an ambush. "What's happened?"

"You heading home?"

"Yeah. What's happened?"

Frank blew out a breath. "Brace yourself for this one, babe. My mate in the U.S. tracked down May-Ruth Thibodeaux's parents—they live somewhere in the mountains in Arsefuck, North Carolina, don't even have a phone. He sent a guy out there to break the news and see what else he could pick up. And guess what he found out."

In the instant before I told him to quit playing games and get to the point, I knew. "It's not her."

"Bingo. May-Ruth Thibodeaux died of meningitis when she was four. Your man showed the parents the ID shot; they'd never seen our girl before."

It hit me like a huge breath of pure wild oxygen; I wanted to laugh so badly I was almost dizzy with it, like a teenager in love. She had fooled the hell out of me—pickup trucks and soda fountains, my arse—and all I could think was *Fair play to you, girl.* Here I had thought I lived light; all of a sudden that felt like an adolescent game, like some rich kid playing at poor while the trust fund piled up, because this girl had been the real thing. She had held her whole life, everything she was, as lightly as a wildflower tucked in her hair, to be tossed away at any second as she took off burning streaks down the highway. What I hadn't managed to do even once, she had done easily as brushing her teeth. No one, not my friends, not my relatives, not Sam or any guy, had ever hit me like this. I wanted to feel that fire rip through my bones, I wanted that gale sanding my skin clean, I wanted to know if that kind of freedom smelled like ozone or thunderstorms or gunpowder.

"Holy shit," I said. "How many times did she *do* this?"

"What I want to know is *why*. This is all backing up my theory: someone was after her, and he wasn't giving up. She picks up the May-Ruth ID from somewhere—a graveyard, maybe, or an obituary in an old newspaper—and starts over. He tracks her down and she takes off again, out of the country this time. You don't do that unless you're running scared. But he got to her in the end."

I reached the front gates, got my back against one of the gateposts and took a deep breath. In the moonlight the drive looked very strange, cherry blossom and shadow scattering black and white so thick that the ground blended into the trees without a seam, one great patterned tunnel. "Yeah," I said. "He got to her in the end."

"And I don't want him getting to you." Frank sighed. "I hate to admit it, but our Sammy may have been right about this one, Cass. If you want out of there, you can start playing sick tonight and I'll have you out tomorrow morning."

It was a still night, not even a breeze in the cherry trees. A thread of sound came drifting down the drive, very faint and very sweet: a girl's voice, singing. *The steed my true love rides on* . . . A tingle ran up my arms. I wondered then and I wonder now whether Frank was bluffing; whether he was actually ready to pull me out, or whether he knew, before he offered, that by this time there was only one answer I could give.

"No," I said. "I'll be OK. I'm staying."

With silver he is shod before . . .

"Fair enough," Frank said, and he didn't sound one bit surprised. "Keep that gun on you and keep your eyes open. Anything turns up, anything at all, I'll let you know."

"Thanks, Frank. I'll check in tomorrow. Same time, same place."

It was Abby who was singing. Her bedroom window glowed soft with lamplight and she was brushing out her hair, slow, absent strokes. *In yon green hill do dwell . . .* In the dining room the guys were cleaning the table, Daniel's sleeves rolled neatly to his elbows, Rafe waving a fork to make some point, Justin shaking his head. I leaned against the broad back of a cherry tree and listened to Abby's voice, unfurling out under the window sash and up to the huge black sky.

God only knew how many lives this girl had left behind to find her way here, home. *I can go in there,* I thought. *Any time I want, I can run up those steps and open that door and walk in.*

Small cracks. On Thursday evening we were out in the garden again, after dinner—huge mounds of roast pork and roast potatoes and vegetables and then apple pie, no wonder Lexie had weighed more than me. We were drinking wine and trying to work up the energy to do something useful. The strap had come off my watch, so I was sitting on the grass, trying to reattach it with Lexie's nail file, the same one I had used to turn the pages of her date book. The rivet kept flying out.

"Dammit to hell and blast and *buggeration*," I said.

"That's a highly illogical thing to say," said Justin lazily, from the swing seat. "What's wrong with buggeration?"

My antennae went up. I had been wondering if Justin might be gay, but Frank's research hadn't turned up anything one way or the other—no boyfriends, no girlfriends— and he could just as easily have been a nice sensitive straight guy with a domestic streak. If he was gay, then there was at least one guy I could cross off the Baby-Daddy list.

"Oh, for God's sake, Justin, stop flaunting," Rafe said. He was lying on his back on the grass, with his eyes shut and his arms folded behind his head.

"You're such a homophobe," said Justin. "If I said 'Dammit to fuck' and Lexie said 'What's wrong with fucking?' you wouldn't accuse her of flaunting."

"I would," said Abby, from beside Rafe. "I'd accuse her of flaunting her love life when the rest of us don't have one."

"Speak for yourself," Rafe said.

"Oh, you," said Abby. "You don't count. You never tell us anything. You could be having a torrid affair with the entire Trinity women's hockey team and none of us would ever know a thing about it."

"I have never had an affair with anyone on the women's hockey team, actually," Rafe said primly.

"*Is* there a women's hockey team?" Daniel wanted to know.

"Don't go getting ideas," Abby told him.

"I think that's Rafe's secret," I said. "See, because he keeps up this mysterious silence, we all have this image of him getting up to unspeakable things behind our backs, seducing hockey teams and shagging like a bunny rabbit. I think actually he never tells us anything because he never has anything to tell: he has even less of a love life than the rest of us." Rafe's eyes slid sideways and he gave me a tiny, enigmatic grin.

"That wouldn't be easy," said Abby.

"Isn't anyone going to ask me about my torrid affair with the men's hockey team?" asked Justin.

"No," said Rafe. "Nobody is going to ask about any of your torrid affairs, because for one thing we know we're going to hear all about them anyway, and for another they're always boring as shit."

"*Well,*" said Justin, after a moment. "That certainly put me in my place. Although coming from you . . ."

"What?" Rafe demanded, propping himself up on his elbows and giving Justin a cold stare. "Coming from me, *what?*"

Nobody said anything. Justin took off his glasses and started cleaning them, too thoroughly, on the hem of his shirt; Rafe lit a cigarette.

Abby cut her eyes at me, like a cue. I remembered those videos: *There's an understanding there,* Frank had said. This was Lexie's job, breaking tension, coming in with some cheeky comment so everyone could roll their eyes and laugh and move on. "Ah, dammit to hell and blast and nonspecific fornication," I said, when the rivet went shooting off into the grass again. "Is everyone OK with that?"

"What's wrong with nonspecific fornication?" Abby demanded. "I don't like my fornication specific."

Even Justin laughed, and Rafe snapped out of his cold sulk and balanced his smoke on the edge of the patio and helped me find the rivet. A shot of happiness went through me: I had got it right.

"That detective showed up outside my tutorial," Abby said Friday evening, in the car. Justin had gone home early—he had been complaining about a headache all day, but to me it looked more like a sulk, and I got the sense it was aimed at Rafe—so the rest of us were in Daniel's car, going nowhere on the highway, gridlocked in with thousands of suicidal-looking office workers and underendowed prats in SUVs. I was breathing on my window and playing tic-tac-toe with myself in the steam.

"Which one?" Daniel asked.

"O'Neill."

"Hmm," Daniel said. "What did he want this time?"

Abby took his cigarette from between his fingers and used it to light her own. "He was asking why we don't go into the village," she said.

"Because they're all a bunch of six-toed halfwits down there," Rafe said, to the window. He was next to me, slouching deep in his seat and jiggling one knee in Abby's back. Traffic always drove Rafe nuts, but this level of bad mood strengthened my feeling that something was up between him and Justin.

"And what did you tell him?" Daniel asked, craning his neck and starting to edge into the next lane; the traffic had moved an inch or two.

Abby shrugged. "I told him. We tried the pub once, they froze us out, we didn't bother trying again."

"Interesting," Daniel said. "I think we may have been underrating Detective O'Neill. Lex, did you discuss the village with him at any stage?"

"Never thought of it." I won my tic-tac-toe game, so I put my fists in the air and did a little victory bop. Rafe gave me a sour look.

"Well," Daniel said, "there we are. I have to admit I'd more or less dismissed O'Neill, but if he picked up on that without any help, he's more perceptive than he looks. I wonder if . . . hmm."

"He's more *annoying* than he looks," Rafe said. "At least Mackey's backed off. When are they going to leave us alone?"

"I got *stabbed*, for fuck's sake," I said, injured. "I could've *died*. They want to know who did it. And so do I, by the way. Don't you?" Rafe shrugged and went back to giving the traffic the evil eye.

"Did you tell him about the graffiti?" Daniel asked Abby. "Or the break-ins?"

Abby shook her head. "He didn't ask, I didn't volunteer. You think . . . ? I could phone him and tell him."

Nobody had mentioned anything about graffiti or break-ins. "You think someone from the village stabbed me?" I said, abandoning my tic-tac-toe and leaning forwards between the seats. "Seriously?"

"I'm not sure," Daniel said. I couldn't tell whether he was answering me or Abby. "I need to think through the possibilities. For now, on the whole, I think the best plan is to leave it. If Detective O'Neill picked up on the tension, he'll find out about the rest on his own, as well; there's no need to nudge him."

"*Ow*, Rafe," said Abby, reaching an arm around the back of her seat and smacking Rafe's knee. "Knock it off." Rafe sighed noisily and swung his legs over against the door. The traffic had opened up; Daniel pulled into the turn lane, swung us off the highway in a smooth fast arc and hit the accelerator.

By the time I phoned Sam from the lane, that night, he already knew all about the graffiti and the break-ins. He had spent the last few days in Rathowen station, working his way backwards through their files, looking for Whitethorn House.

"There's something going on there, all right. The files are *full* of that house." Sam's voice had the busy, absorbed note that it gets when he's on a good trail—Rob used to say you could practically see his tail wagging. For the first time since Lexie Madison had appeared with a bang in the middle of our lives, he sounded cheerful. "There's bugger-all crime in Glenskehy, but over the past three years, there've been four burglaries on Whitethorn House—one back in 2002, another in 2003, two while old Simon was in the hospice."

"Did they take anything? Toss the place?" I had more or less dismissed Sam's idea about Lexie getting killed over some small precious antique, after seeing the quality of the stuff Uncle Simon had on offer, but if something in that house had been worth four break-ins . . .

"Nothing like that. Not a thing taken any of the times, as far as Simon March could tell—although Byrne says the place was a pigsty, he might well not have noticed if something was missing—and no sign that they were looking for anything. They just broke a couple of panes in the back door, walked in and made a mess of the place: slashed some curtains and pissed on the sofa the first time, smashed a load of crockery the second, that kind of thing. That's not a robbery. That's a grudge."

The house—The thought of some little scumbucket knuckle-dragging through the rooms, wrecking what he pleased and whipping out his three inches to piss on the sofa, jolted me with fury so high voltage it startled me; I wanted to punch something. "Charming," I said. "Sure it wasn't just kids messing? There's not much to do in Glenskehy on a Saturday night."

"Hang on," Sam said. "There's more. For about four years before Lexie's lot moved in, that house was getting vandalized almost every month. Bricks through the windows, bottles thrown at the walls, a dead rat through the letterbox—and graffiti. Some of it said"—flip of notebook pages—"'WEST BRITS OUT,' 'KILL THE LANDLORDS,' 'UP THE IRA'—"

"You think the IRA stabbed Lexie Madison?" Granted, this case was weird enough that anything was possible, but this was the least likely theory I'd heard yet.

Sam laughed, an open, happy sound. "Ah, God, no. Hardly their style. But someone around Glenskehy still thought of the March family as Brits, landlords, and wasn't exactly mad about them. And listen to this: two separate bits of graffiti, one back in 2001 and one in 2003, said 'BABY KILLERS OUT.'"

"*Baby* killers?" I said, completely taken aback—for a wild second the timeline tangled in my mind and I thought of Lexie's brief, hidden child. "What the hell? Where is there a baby in this?"

"I don't know, but I'm going to find out. Someone's got a very specific grudge—not against Lexie's lot, it's been going on way too long for that, and not against old Simon either. 'Brits,' 'baby killers,' plural—they're not talking about one old fella. It's the whole family they've a problem with: Whitethorn House and all who sail in her."

The lane looked secretive and hostile, too many layers of shadows, remembering too many old things that had happened somewhere along its twists. I moved into the shadow of a tree trunk and got my back up against it. "Why didn't we hear about any of this before?"

"We didn't ask. We were focusing on Lexie, or whoever she is, as the target; we never thought she might have been—what's that they call it?—collateral damage. It's not Byrne and Doherty's fault. They've never worked a murder before, sure; they don't know how to go about it. It never even occurred to them we might want to know."

"What do they say about all this?"

Sam blew out a breath. "Not a lot. They've no suspects for any of it, and not a clue about any dead baby, and they told me good luck finding out more. They both say they know no more about Glenskehy than they did the day they arrived. Glenskehy people keep to themselves, don't like cops, don't like outsiders; whenever there's a crime, nobody saw anything, nobody heard anything and they sort it out their own way, in private. According to Byrne and Doherty, even the other villages round about think Glenskehy folk are stone mentallers."

"So they just ignored the vandalism?" I said. I could hear the edge in my voice. "Took the reports and said, 'Ah, sure, nothing we can do,' and let whoever it was keep fucking up Whitethorn House?"

"They did their best," Sam said, instantly and firmly—all cops, even cops like Doherty and Byrne, count as family to Sam. "After the first break-in, they told Simon March he should get a dog, or an alarm system. He said he hated dogs, alarms were for nancy boys and he was well able to look after himself, thanks very much. Byrne and Doherty got the feeling he had a gun—that'll be the one ye found. They didn't think that was such a great idea, specially with him being drunk most of the time, but there wasn't much they could do about it; when they asked him straight out, he denied it. They could hardly force him to get an alarm if he didn't want one."

"What about once he went into the hospice? They knew the house was empty, everyone around must've known, they knew it would be a target—"

"They checked it every night on their rounds, sure," Sam said. "What else could they do?"

He sounded startled, and I realized my voice had gone

up. "You said, 'Until this lot moved in,'" I said, softer. "Then what?"

"The vandalism didn't stop, but it settled a lot. Byrne called in and had a chat with Daniel, let him know what had been going on, Daniel didn't seem too worried about it. There's been only two incidents since: a rock through the window in October, and graffiti again, in December— FOREIGNERS FUCK OFF. That's the other reason Byrne and Doherty said nothing to us. As far as they were concerned it was all over, old news."

"So maybe it was just a vendetta against Uncle Simon, after all."

"Could be, but I don't think so. I'm betting it's more what you might call a scheduling conflict." There was a grin in Sam's voice: having something solid to go on had changed everything. "Sixteen of the reports give the time when the incident happened, and it's always somewhere between half past eleven and one at night. That's not coincidence. Whoever's after Whitethorn House, that's their window."

"Pub closing time," I said.

He laughed. "Great minds. I figure a lad or two out drinking, every now and then they're on a bad buzz and the old Dutch courage is up, and when the pub throws them out it's off to Whitethorn House with a couple of bricks or a can of spray paint or whatever they've got handy. Old Simon's schedule suited them down to the ground: by half past eleven he was mostly either unconscious—those are the ones where the report doesn't give the time of the incident, because he didn't call it in till he sobered up the next morning—or at least too drunk to go after them. The first two times they broke in, he was *home,* slept through the whole thing. Lucky he'd a good lock on his bedroom door, or God knows what might have happened."

"But then we moved in," I said. A second too late, I heard myself—*they* had moved in, not *we*—but Sam didn't seem to notice. "These days, between half past eleven and one, there's five people wide awake and moving around the house. Wrecking the gaff doesn't seem like so much fun when three big strong lads could catch you at it and beat the crap out of you."

"And two big strong girls," Sam said, and I caught the grin again. "I bet you and Abby would get a couple of punches in. That's what almost happened with the rock through the window. They were all in the sitting room, just before midnight, when the rock came flying into the kitchen; as soon as they realized what had happened, the five of them legged it out the back door to go after your man. Because they weren't in the room, though, it took them a minute to figure out what was going on, and by that time the guy was well gone. Lucky for him, Byrne said. It was forty-five minutes before they called the cops—they went through all the lanes first, looking for the guy—and even then, they were *raging*. Your man Rafe told Byrne that, if he ever caught this fella, his own mammy wouldn't recognize him; Lexie said she was planning to, and I'm quoting, 'kick him in the bollocks so hard he'd have to stick his hand down his throat if he wanted a wank.'"

"Good for her," I said.

Sam laughed. "Yeah, I thought you'd enjoy that one. The others had better sense than to come out with anything like that in front of a cop, but Byrne says they were thinking it, all right. He gave them a lecture about not taking the law into their own hands, but he's not sure how much of it went in."

"I don't blame them," I said. "It's not like the cops had been all that useful. What about the graffiti?"

"Lexie's lot weren't home. It was a Sunday night, and they'd gone to dinner and the pictures in town. They got home a little after midnight and there it was, across the front of the house. It was the first time they'd been out that late since they moved in. That could be coincidence, but I don't think so. The thing with the rock put some respect on our vandal—or vandals—but either he was keeping an eye on the house, or he saw the car go through the village and not come back. He saw his chance, and he took it."

"So you're thinking it's not a village-versus-Big-House thing, after all?" I said. "Just some guy with a grudge?"

Sam made a noncommittal sound. "Not exactly. Have you heard what happened when Lexie's lot tried going into Regan's?"

"Yeah, Abby said you'd talked to her about that. She mentioned something about them getting frozen out, but she didn't go into details."

"It was a couple of days after they moved in. The whole bunch of them go into the pub one evening, they find a table, Daniel goes up to the bar, and the barman doesn't see him. For ten minutes, from four feet away, with only a handful of people in the pub and Daniel going, 'Excuse me, can I have two pints of Guinness and . . .' The barman just stands there, polishing a glass and watching the telly. Finally Daniel gives up, goes back to the others, they have a quiet chat and decide maybe old Simon got thrown out of here too many times and the Marches aren't popular. So they send Abby up instead—they figure she's a better bet than the English guy or the Northern boy. Same thing happens. Meanwhile, Lexie starts talking to the old fellas at the next table, trying to find out what the hell's going on. Nobody answers her, nobody even looks at her; they all turn their backs and keep on with their own conversation."

"Jesus," I said. It's not as easy as it sounds to ignore five people right there in front of you, looking for your attention. It takes a lot of concentration to override all your instincts like that; you need a reason, something hard and cold as bedrock. I tried to keep an eye on the lane in both directions at once.

"Justin's getting upset and wants to leave, Rafe's getting angry and wants to stay, Lexie's getting more and more hyper trying to make these old fellas talk to her—offering them chocolate, telling them lightbulb jokes—and a bunch of younger guys in a corner are starting to throw over dirty looks. Abby wasn't too keen on backing down herself, but she and Daniel both figured this situation could get out of hand any second. They grabbed the others and left, and they didn't go back."

A light rustle of wind swept through the leaves, moving up the lane towards me. "So the bad feeling goes right through Glenskehy," I said, "but only one or two people are taking it that step further."

"That's what I'm thinking. And it's going to be a right laugh finding out who they are. There's about four hundred people in Glenskehy, counting the outlying farms, and none of them are about to give me a hand narrowing it down."

"There," I said, "I might be able to help out. See, this I can profile. Sort of, anyway: nobody collects psychological data on vandals like they do on serial killers, so it'll be mostly guesswork, but at least there's enough of a pattern that I can give you something."

"I'll take guesswork," Sam said cheerfully. I heard pages rustling, a shift of the phone as he got ready to write. "I'll take anything, sure. Go on."

"OK," I said. "You're looking for someone local, obviously—Glenskehy born and bred. Almost definitely male. I think it's one person rather than a gang: spontaneous vandalism mostly involves groups, but planned hate campaigns like this one tend to be more private."

"Anything you can tell me about him?" Sam's voice had gone blurry: he had the phone caught under his jaw, writing.

"If this started about four years ago, then he's probably in his midtwenties to early thirties—vandalism's usually a young man's crime, but this guy's too methodical for a teenager. Not much education—Leaving Cert, maybe, but no college. He lives with someone, either his parents or a wife or girlfriend: no attacks in the middle of the night, someone's expecting him home by a certain time. He's employed, in a job that keeps him busy all through weekdays, or there would have been incidents during the day, when we're all out and the coast is clear. The job's local, too, he doesn't commute to Dublin or anything; this level of obsession says Glenskehy's his whole world. And it doesn't satisfy him.

He's working well below his intellectual or educational level, or he thinks he is, anyway. And he'll probably have had ongoing problems with other people before, neighbors, ex-girlfriends, maybe employers; this guy won't play well with authority. It might be worth checking with Byrne and Doherty for any local feuds or harassment complaints."

"If my fella hassled someone from Glenskehy," Sam said grimly, "there's no way they'd go to the cops. They'd just get their mates together and give him a beating some night, sure. And he wouldn't bring that to the cops, either."

"No," I said, "probably not." A flicker of movement, off in the field across the lane, a dark streak turning the grass. It was way too small for a person, but I moved deeper into the shadow of the tree all the same. "Here's the other thing. The campaign against Whitethorn House could have been triggered by some run-in with Simon March—he sounds like a narky old git, he could well have pissed someone off—but, in your boy's mind, it goes way deeper than that. To him, it's about a dead baby. And Byrne and Doherty don't have a clue about that, right? How long have they been here?"

"Doherty only two years, but Byrne's been stuck out here since 1997. He says there was a cot death in the village last spring and a wee girl fell into a slurry pit on one of the farms, a few years back—God rest them—but that's the lot. Nothing suspicious about either death, and no links to Whitethorn House. And the computer didn't come up with anything in the area."

"Then we're looking for something further back," I said, "just like you thought. God knows how far. Remember what you told me, about the Purcells round your way?"

A pause. "We'll never find it, so. The records, sure."

Most of Ireland's public records went up in a fire in 1921, in the Civil War. "You don't need records. People round here know about this, I guarantee you. Whenever that baby died, this guy didn't get the story out of some old newspaper. He's way too obsessed with it. To him, that's not ancient history; it's a real, fresh, crucial grudge that needs to be avenged."

"Are you saying he's mad?"

"No," I said. "Not the way you mean. He's way too careful—waiting for safe moments, backing off after he got chased . . . If he were schizophrenic, say, or bipolar, he wouldn't have that much control. He doesn't have a mental illness. But he's obsessed to the point where, yeah, I think you could probably call him a little unbalanced."

"Could he get violent? Against people, I mean, not just property." Sam's voice had sharpened; he was sitting up straighter.

"I'm not sure," I said, carefully. "It doesn't seem like his style—I mean, he could have broken down old Simon's bedroom door and whacked him with a poker any time he wanted to, but he didn't. But the fact that he only seems to do this stuff when he's drunk makes me think he's got an unhealthy relationship with alcohol—one of those guys who grow a whole new personality after four or five pints, and not a nice one. Once you throw booze into the equation, everything gets less predictable. And, like I said, this is an obsession with him. If he got the impression that the enemy was escalating the conflict—by going after him when he threw that rock through the window, for example—he could well have upped his game to match."

"You know what this sounds exactly like," Sam said, after a pause, "don't you. Same age, local, smart, controlled, criminal experience but no violence . . ."

The profile I had given him, back in my flat; the profile of the killer. "Yeah," I said. "I know."

"What you're telling me is that he could be our boy. The murderer."

That streak of shadow again, quick and silent through the grass and the moonlight: a fox, maybe, after a field mouse. "He could be," I said. "We can't rule him out."

"If this is a family feud," Sam said, "then Lexie wasn't the specific target, her life's nothing to do with anything and there's no need for you to be there. You can come home."

The hope in his voice made me flinch. "Yeah," I said, "maybe. But I don't think we're at that stage. We've got no concrete link between the vandalism and the stabbing; they could be completely unrelated. And once we pull the plug, we can't go back."

A fraction of a pause. Then: "Fair enough," Sam said. "I'll get to work on finding that link. And, Cassie . . ."

His voice had gone sober, tense. "I'll be careful," I said. "I am being careful."

"Half past eleven to one o'clock. That fits the time of the stabbing."

"I know. I haven't seen anyone dodgy hanging around."

"Do you have your gun?"

"Whenever I go out. Frank already lectured me about that."

"Frank," Sam said, and I heard that remoteness come into his voice. "Right."

After we hung up I waited in the shadow of the tree for a long time. I heard the crash of long grass and the thin scream as whatever predator was out there finally pounced. When the rustles had faded into the dark and only small things moved, I slipped out into the lane and went home.

I stopped at the back gate and swung on it for a while, listening to the slow creak of the hinge and looking up the long garden at the house. It looked different, that night. The gray stone of the back was flat and defensive as a castle wall, and the golden glow from the windows didn't feel cozy any more; it had turned defiant, warning, like a small campfire in a savage forest. The moonlight whitened the lawn into a wide fitful sea, with the house tall and still in the middle, exposed on every side; besieged.

10

When you find a crack, you push on it and you see if something breaks. It had taken me about an hour and a half to work out that, if there was something the housemates weren't telling me, Justin was my best bet. Any detective with a couple of years under his belt can tell you who's going to break first; back in Murder I once saw Costello, who was installed in the eighties along with the decor, pick the weak link just from watching the gang of suspects get booked in. It's our version of *Name That Tune*.

Daniel and Abby were both useless: too controlled and too focused, almost impossible to distract or wrong-foot—I had tried a couple of times to nudge Abby into telling me who she thought the daddy was, got nothing but cool blank looks. Rafe was more suggestible and I knew I could probably get somewhere with him if I had to, but it would be tricky; he was too volatile and contrary, just as likely to storm out in a strop as to tell you what you wanted to know. Justin—gentle, imaginative, easily worried, wanting everyone to be happy—was pretty near to being an interviewer's dream.

The only thing was that I was never alone with him. In the first week I hadn't really noticed it, but now that I was looking for a chance, it stood out. Daniel and I drove into college together a couple of times a week, and I saw a lot of Abby—breakfasts, after dinner when the guys were washing up, sometimes she knocked on my door at night with a packet of biscuits and we sat on the bed and talked till we got sleepy—but if I was ever on my own with Rafe or Justin for more than five minutes, one of the others would drift over or call out to us, and we would be effortlessly, invisibly enveloped by the group again. It could have been natural; all five of them did spend an awful lot of time together, and every group has subtle subdivisions, people who never pair off because they only work as part of the whole. But I had to wonder if someone, probably Daniel, had considered all four of them with an interrogator's assessing eye and come to the same conclusion I had.

It was Monday morning before I got my chance. We were in college; Daniel was giving a tutorial and Abby had a meeting with her supervisor, so it was just Rafe and Justin and me in our corner of the library. When Rafe got up and headed off somewhere, presumably to the bathroom, I counted to twenty and then stuck my head over the barrier into Justin's carrel.

"Hello, you," he said, looking up from a page of tiny, fastidious handwriting. Every inch of his desk was heaped with books and looseleaf and photocopies striped with highlighter pen; Justin couldn't work unless he was snugly nested in the middle of everything he might possibly need.

"I'm bored and it's sunny," I said. "Come for lunch."

He checked his watch. "It's only twenty to one."

"Live dangerously," I said.

Justin looked uncertain. "What about Rafe?"

"He's big and ugly enough to look after himself. He can wait for Abby and Daniel." Justin was still looking way too unsure for a decision of this magnitude, and I figured I had about a minute to get him out of there before Rafe came back. "Ah, Justin, come on. I'll do this till you do." I drummed "shave and a haircut, two bits" on the barrier with my fingernails.

"Argh," Justin said, putting his pen down. "Chinese noise torture. You win."

The obvious place to go was the edge of New Square, but you can see it through the library windows, so I dragged Justin over to the cricket pitch, where it would take Rafe longer to find us. It was a bright, cold day, high blue sky and

the air like ice water. Down by the Pavilion a bunch of cricketers were doing earnest stylized things at each other, and up
at our end four guys were playing Frisbee and trying to act
like they weren't doing it for the benefit of three industrially
groomed girls on a bench, who were trying to look like they
weren't watching. Mating rituals: it was spring.

"So," Justin said, when we were settled on the grass.
"How's the chapter going?"

"Crap," I said, rummaging through my book bag for my
sandwich. "I've written bugger-all since I got back. I can't
concentrate."

"Well," Justin said, after a moment. "That's only to be
expected, isn't it? For a little while."

I shrugged, not looking at him.

"It'll wear off. Really, it will. Now that you're home and
everything's back to normal."

"Yeah. Maybe." I found my sandwich, made a face at it
and dumped it on the grass: few things worried Justin as
much as people not eating. "It just sucks, not knowing what
happened. It sucks *enormously*. I keep wondering . . . The cops
kept hinting that they had all these leads and stuff, but they
wouldn't tell me anything. For fuck's sake, I'm the one who
got stabbed here. If anyone has a right to know why, it's me."

"But I thought you were feeling better. You said you
were fine."

"I guess. Never mind."

"We thought . . . I mean, I didn't expect you to be this
bothered. To keep thinking about it. It's not like you."

I glanced over at him, but he didn't look suspicious, just
worried. "Yeah, well," I said. "I never got stabbed before."

"No," said Justin. "I suppose not." He arranged his lunch
on the grass: bottle of orange juice on one side, banana on
the other, sandwich in the middle. He was biting the edge
of his lip.

"You know what I keep thinking about?" I said abruptly.
"My parents." Saying the words gave me a sharp, giddy little
thrill.

Justin's head snapped up and he stared at me. "What about them?"

"That maybe I should get in touch with them. Tell them what happened."

"No pasts," Justin said, instantly, like a quick sign against bad luck. "We agreed."

I shrugged. "Whatever. Easy for you to say."

"It isn't, actually." Then, when I didn't answer: "Lexie? Are you serious?"

I did another edgy little shrug. "Not sure yet."

"But I thought you hated them. You said you never wanted to speak to them again."

"That's not the point." I twisted the strap of my book bag around my finger, pulled it away in a long spiral. "I just keep thinking . . . I could have *died* there. Actually died. And my parents would never even have known."

"If something happens to me," Justin said, "I don't want my parents called. I don't want them there. I don't want them to know."

"Why not?" He was picking the seal off his bottle of juice, head down. "Justin?"

"Never mind. I didn't mean to interrupt."

"No. Tell me, Justin. Why not?"

After a moment Justin said, "I went back to Belfast for Christmas, our first year of postgrad. Not long after you came. Do you remember?"

"Yeah," I said. He wasn't looking at me; he was blinking at the cricketers, white and formal as ghosts against the green, the thwack of the bat reaching us late and faraway.

"I told my father and my stepmother that I'm gay. On Christmas Eve." A small, humorless snort of a laugh. "God love me, I suppose I thought the holiday spirit—peace and good will to all men . . . And the four of you had taken it so completely in your stride. Do you know what Daniel said, when I told him? He thought it over for a few minutes and then informed me that straight and gay are modern constructs, the concept of sexuality was much more fluid right up through the Renaissance. And Abby rolled her eyes and asked me if I wanted her to act surprised. Rafe was the one I was most worried about—I'm not sure why—but he just grinned and said, 'Less competition for me.' Which was sweet of him, actually; it's not like I was ever much competition to him anyway . . . It was very comforting, you know. I suppose it made me think that telling my family might not be such a huge big deal, after all."

"I didn't realize," I said. "That you'd told them. You never said."

"Yes, well," Justin said. He picked the cling-film away from his sandwich delicately, being careful not to get relish on his fingers. "My stepmother's a dreadful woman, you know. Really dreadful. Her father's a carpenter, but she tells people he's an *artisan,* whatever she thinks that means, and she never invites him to parties. Everything about her is pure faultless middle-class—the accent, the clothes, the hair, the china patterns, it's as if she ordered herself from a catalogue—but you can see the incredible *effort* that goes into every second of it. Marrying her boss must have been like attaining the Holy Grail. I'm not saying my father would have been OK with me if it hadn't been for her—he looked like he was going to be sick—but she made it so, so much worse. She was *hysterical.* She told my father she wanted me out of the house, right away. For good."

"Jesus, Justin."

"She watches a lot of soap operas," Justin said. "Erring sons get banished all the time. She kept shrieking, actually shrieking, 'Think of the boys!'—she meant my half brothers. I don't know if she thought I was going to convert them or molest them or what, but I said—which was nasty of me, but you can see why I was feeling vicious—I said she had nothing to worry about, no self-respecting gay man would touch either of those hideous little Cabbage Patch Kids with a barge pole. It went downhill from there. She threw things, I said things, the Cabbage Patch Kids actually put down their Play-Stations to come see what was happening, she tried to drag them out of the room—presumably so I wouldn't jump them on the spot—*they* started shrieking . . . Finally my father told me it would be better if I wasn't in the house—'for the moment,' as he put it, but we both knew what he meant. He drove me to the station and gave me a hundred pounds. For Christmas." He pulled the cling-film straight and laid it on the grass, the sandwich neatly in the middle.

"What did you do?" I asked quietly.

"Over Christmas? Stayed in my flat, mostly. Bought a hundred-quid bottle of whiskey. Felt sorry for myself." He gave me a wry half smile. "I know: I should have told you I was back in town. But . . . well, pride, I suppose. It was one of the most humiliating experiences of my life. I know none of you would have asked, but you couldn't have helped wondering, and you're all too sharp for your own good. Someone would have guessed."

The way he was sitting—knees pulled up, feet neatly together—rucked up his trousers; he was wearing gray socks worn thin by too much washing, and his ankles were delicate and bony as a boy's. I reached over and covered one of them with my hand. It was warm and solid and my fingers almost circled it.

"No, it's all right," Justin said, and when I looked up I saw that he was smiling at me, properly this time. "Really and truly, it is. At first it did upset me a lot; I felt like I was orphaned, homeless—honestly, if you could have seen the level of melodrama going on in my head . . . But I don't think about it any more, not since the house. I don't even know why I brought it up."

"My fault," I said. "Sorry."

"Don't be." He gave my hand a little fingertip pat. "If you really want to get in touch with your parents, then . . . well, it's none of my business, is it? All I'm saying is, don't forget: we've all got reasons why we decided no pasts. It's not just me. Rafe . . . Well, you've heard his father."

I nodded. "He's a git."

"Rafe's been getting that exact same phone call for as

long as I've known him: you're pathetic, you're useless, I'm ashamed to mention you to my friends. I'm pretty sure his whole childhood was like that. His father disliked him almost from the moment he was born—it happens sometimes, you know. He wanted a big oaf of a son who would play rugby and grope his secretary and throw up outside chi-chi nightclubs, and instead he got Rafe. He made his life a *misery*. You didn't see Rafe when we first started college: this skinny prickly creature, so defensive that if you teased him the tiniest bit he would absolutely take your head off. I wasn't even sure I liked him, at first. I just hung around with him because I liked Abby and Daniel, and they obviously thought he was all right."

"He's still skinny," I said. "And he's still prickly, too. He's a little bollocks when he feels like it."

Justin shook his head. "He's a million times better than he was. And it's because he doesn't have to think about those awful parents of his any more, at least not often. And Daniel . . . Have you ever, once, heard him mention his childhood?"

I shook my head.

"Neither have I. I know his parents are dead, but I don't know when or how, or what happened to him afterwards— where he lived, with who, nothing. Abby and I got awfully drunk together one night and started being silly about that, making up childhoods for Daniel: he was one of those feral children raised by hamsters, he grew up in a brothel in Istanbul, his parents were CIA sleepers who got taken out by the KGB and he escaped by hiding in the washing machine . . . It was funny at the time, but the fact is, his childhood can't have been too pleasant, can it, for him to be so secretive about it? You're bad enough . . ." Justin shot me a quick glance. "But at least I know you had chicken pox, and you learned to ride horses. I don't know anything like that about Daniel. Not a thing."

I hoped to God we wouldn't run into a situation where I needed to show off my equestrian skills. "And then there's

Abby," Justin said. "Has Abby ever talked to you about her mother?"

"Bits," I said. "I got the idea."

"It's worse than she makes it sound. I actually met the woman—you weren't here yet, it was back in about third year. We were all over at Abby's flat one evening, and her mother showed up, banging on the door. She was . . . God. The way she was dressed—I don't know if she's actually a prostitute, or just . . . well. She was obviously out of it; she kept shouting at Abby, but I barely understood a word she said. Abby shoved something into her hand—money, I'm sure, and you know how broke Abby's always been—and practically *hauled* her out of the door. She was white as a ghost, Abby was; I thought she was going to faint." Justin looked up at me anxiously, pushing his glasses up his nose. "Don't tell her I told you that."

"I won't."

"She's never mentioned it since; I doubt she wants to talk about it now. Which is sort of my point. I'm sure you've got reasons, too, why you thought the no-pasts thing was a good idea. Maybe what happened changed all that, I don't know, but . . . just remember you're still fragile, right now. Just give it a little while before you do anything irrevocable. And if you do decide to get in touch with your parents, maybe the best thing would be not to tell the others. It would . . . Well. It would hurt them."

I gave him a puzzled look. "You think?"

"Well, of course. We're . . ." He was still messing with the cling-film; there was a faint pink flush creeping up his cheeks. "We love you, you know. As far as we're concerned, we're your family now. All of one another's family—I mean, that's not right, but you know what I mean . . ."

I leaned over and gave him a quick kiss on the cheek. "Course I do," I said. "I know exactly what you mean."

Justin's phone beeped. "That'll be Rafe," he said, fishing it out of his pocket. "Yes: wanting to know where we are."

He started texting Rafe back, peering nearsightedly at the phone, and reached over to squeeze my shoulder with his free hand. "Just have a think about it," he said. "And eat your lunch."

"I see you've been playing Who's the Daddy," Frank said, that night. He was eating something—a burger, maybe, I could hear paper rustling. "And Justin's out, in more ways than one. Place your bets: Danny Boy or Pretty Boy?"

"Or neither," I said. I was on my way to my lurk spot— I was ringing Frank almost as soon as I got out the back gate, these days, rather than wait even a few extra minutes to hear if he had anything new on Lexie. "Our killer knew her, remember; no way to be sure just how well. That's not what I was after, anyway. I was chasing down the no-pasts thing, trying to work out what these four aren't sharing."

"And all you got was a nice collection of sob stories. I grant you the no-pasts thing is fucked up, but we already knew they were a bunch of weirdos. No news there."

"Mmm," I said. I wasn't so sure that afternoon had been useless, even if I didn't know how it fit in yet. "I'll keep poking around."

"It's been one of those days all round," Frank said, through a mouthful. "I've been chasing our girl and getting zip. You've probably noticed: we've got a gap a year and a half long in her story. She ditches the May-Ruth ID in late 2000, but she doesn't show up as Lexie until early 2002. I'm trying to track down where and who she was in between. I doubt she went home, wherever that is, but it's always a possibility; and even if she didn't, she might have left us a clue or two along the way."

"I'd focus on European countries," I said. "After September 2001, airport security tightened up a lot; she wouldn't have made it out of the U.S. and into Ireland on a fake passport. She had to be this side of the Atlantic before then."

"Yeah, but I don't know what name to chase. There's no record of May-Ruth Thibodeaux ever applying for a passport. I'm thinking she went back to her own identity or bought herself a new one in New York, flew out of JFK on that, switched identity again once she got wherever she was going—"

JFK—Frank was still talking but I'd stopped dead in the middle of the lane, just forgotten to keep walking, because that mysterious page in Lexie's date book had gone off in my head with a flash-bang like a firecracker. *CDG 59* . . . I'd flown into Charles de Gaulle a dozen times, going to spend summers with my French cousins, and fifty-nine quid sounded just about right for a one-way. AMS: not Abigail Marie Stone; Amsterdam. LHR: London Heathrow. I couldn't remember the others but I knew, sure as steel, that they would turn out to be airport codes. Lexie had been pricing flights.

If all she wanted was an abortion she would have headed to England, no need to mess about with Amsterdam and Paris. And those were one-way prices, not returns. She had been getting ready to run again, right off the edge of her life and out into the wide blue world.

Why?

Three things had changed, in her last few weeks. She had found out she was pregnant; N had materialized; and she had started making plans to take off. I don't believe in coincidences. There was no way to be sure of the order in which those three things had happened, but by whatever round-about path, one of them had led to the other two. There was a pattern there, somewhere: tantalizingly close, popping in and out of view like one of those pictures you have to cross your eyes to see, there and gone too quick to catch.

Up until that night, I hadn't had much time for Frank's mystery stalker. Very few people are willing to ditch their whole lives and spend years bouncing around the world after some girl who pissed them off. Frank has this tendency to go for the more interesting theory rather than the more likely one, and I'd filed this one somewhere between Outside Chance and Pure Hollywood Melodrama. But this made three times, at least, that something had smashed broadside into her life, left it totaled, irreclaimable. My heart twisted for her.

"Hello? Ground control to Cassie?"

"Yeah," I said. "Frank, can you do something for me? I want to know anything out of the ordinary that happened in her May-Ruth life in the month or so before she went missing—make it two months, to be on the safe side."

Running away from N? Running away *with* N, to start a whole new life somewhere, him and her and their baby?

"You underestimate me, babe. Already done. No strange visitors or phone calls, no arguments with anyone, no odd behavior, nothing."

"I didn't mean stuff like that. I want anything that happened, anything at all: if she switched job, switched boyfriend, moved house, got sick, took a course in something. Not ominous stuff, just your basic life events."

Frank thought about this for a while, chewing his burger or whatever. "Why?" he asked, in the end. "If I'm going to call in more favors from my friendly Fed, I need to give him a reason."

"Make something up. I don't have a good reason. Intuition, remember?"

"OK," Frank said. He sounded disturbingly like he was picking bits out of his teeth. "I'll do it. If you do something for me in exchange."

I had started walking again, automatically, towards the cottage. "Hit me."

"Don't relax. You've started to sound way too much like you're enjoying yourself in there."

I sighed. "Me woman, Frank. Woman multitask. I can do my job *and* have a laugh or two, all at the same time."

"Good for you. All I know is, undercover relax, undercover in big trouble. There's a killer out there, probably within a mile or so of wherever you're standing right now.

You're supposed to be tracking him down, not playing Happy Families with the Fantastic Four."

Happy Families. I had been taking it for granted that she'd hidden the diary to make sure no one found out about her N appointments, whoever or whatever N was. But this: she had had a whole other secret to keep. If the others had found out that Lexie was about to slash herself straight out of their interlaced world, shed it like a dragonfly shrugging out of its skin and leaving behind nothing but the perfect shape of its absence, they would have been devastated. I was suddenly, almost dizzily glad I hadn't told Frank about that diary.

"I'm on it, Frank," I said.

"Good. Stay on it." Paper crumpling—he had finished his burger—and the beep of him hanging up.

I was almost at my surveillance spot. Snippets of hedge and grass and earth sprang alive in the pale circle of the torch beam, vanished the next moment. I thought of her running hard down this same lane, this same faint circle of light ricocheting wild, the strong door to safety lost forever in the dark behind her and nothing up ahead but that cold cottage. Those streaks of paint on her bedroom wall: she had had a future planned here, in this house, with these people, right up until the moment the bomb dropped. *We're your family,* Justin had said, *all of one another's family,* and I had been in Whitethorn House long enough to start understanding how much he meant it and how much it meant. *What the hell,* I thought, *what the hell could have been strong enough to blow all that away?*

Now that I was looking, the cracks kept coming. I couldn't tell whether they had been there all along, or whether they were deepening under my eyes. That night I was reading in bed when I heard voices outside, below my window.

Rafe had gone to bed before I had, and I could hear Justin going through his nighttime ritual downstairs—humming, puttering, the odd mysterious thump. That left Daniel and Abby. I knelt up by the window, held my breath and listened, but they were three stories down and all I could hear through Justin's cheerful obbligato was a low, fast-paced murmur.

"*No*," Abby said, louder and frustrated. "Daniel, that's not the point . . ." Her voice dropped again. "*Moooon river*," Justin sang to himself, hamming it up happily.

I did what nosy kids have done since the dawn of time: I decided I needed a very quiet drink of water. Justin didn't even pause in his humming as I moved across the landing; on the ground floor, there was no light under Rafe's door. I felt my way along the walls and slipped into the kitchen. The French window was open, just a thumb's width. I went to the sink—slowly, not even a rustle from my pajamas—and held a glass under the tap, ready to turn the water on if anyone caught me.

They were on the swing seat. The patio was bright with moonlight; they would never see me, behind glass in the dark kitchen. Abby was sitting sideways, her back against the arm of the seat and her feet on Daniel's lap; he had a glass in one hand and was covering her ankles casually with the other. The moonlight poured down Abby's hair, whitened the curve of her cheek and pooled in the folds of Daniel's shirt. Something fast and needle-fine darted through me, a shot of pure distilled pain. Rob and I used to sit like that on my sofa, through long late nights. The floor bit cold at my bare feet and the kitchen was so silent, it hurt my ears.

"For good," Abby said. There was a high note of disbelief in her voice. "Just keep on going, like this, for good. Pretend nothing ever happened."

"I don't see," Daniel said, "that we have any other option. Do you?"

"Jesus, Daniel!" Abby ran her hands through her hair, head going back, flash of white throat. "How is *this* an option? This is *insane*. Is this seriously what you want? You want to do this for the rest of our lives?"

Daniel turned to look at her; I could only see the back

of his head. "In an ideal world," he said gently, "no. I'd like things to be different; several things."

"Oh, God," Abby said, rubbing at her eyebrows as if she had a headache starting. "Let's not even go there."

"One can't have everything, you know," Daniel said. "We knew, when we first decided to live here, that there would be sacrifices involved. We expected that."

"Sacrifices," Abby said, "yes. This, no. This I did not see coming, Daniel, no. None of it."

"Didn't you?" Daniel asked, surprised. "I did."

Abby's head jerked up and she stared at him. "*This?* Come *on*. You saw *this* coming? Lexie, and—"

"Well, not Lexie," Daniel said. "Hardly. Although perhaps . . ." He checked himself, sighed. "But the rest: yes, I thought it was a distinct possibility. Human nature being what it is. I assumed you'd considered it too."

Nobody had told me there was a rest of this, never mind sacrifices. I realized I had been holding my breath for so long that my head was starting to spin; I let it out, carefully.

"Nope," Abby said wearily, to the sky. "Call me stupid."

"I would never do that," Daniel said, smiling a little sadly out over the lawn. "Heaven knows, I'm the last person in the world who has any right to judge you for missing the obvious." He took a sip of his drink—glitter of pale amber as the glass tilted—and in that moment, in the fall of his shoulders and the way his eyes closed as he swallowed, it hit me. I had seen these four as safe in their own enchanted fort, with everything they wanted within arm's reach. I had liked that thought, a lot. But something had blindsided Abby, and for some reason Daniel was getting used to being terribly, constantly unhappy.

"How does Lexie seem to you?" he asked.

Abby took one of Daniel's cigarettes and snapped the lighter hard. "She seems fine. A little quiet, and she's lost some weight, but that's the least we could expect."

"Do you think she's all right?"

"She's eating. She's taking her antibiotics."

"That's not what I meant."

"I don't think you need to worry about Lexie," Abby said. "She seems pretty settled to me. As far as I can tell, she's basically forgotten about the whole thing."

"In a way," Daniel said, "that's what's been bothering me. I worry that she may be bottling everything up and one of these days she's going to explode. And then what?"

Abby watched him, smoke curling up slowly through the moonlight. "In some ways," she said carefully, "it might not be the end of the world if Lexie did explode."

Daniel considered this, swirling his glass meditatively and looking out over the grass. "That would depend very much," he said, "on the form the explosion took. I think it would be as well to be prepared."

"Lexie," Abby said, "is the least of our problems here. Justin—I mean, it was obvious, I knew Justin was going to have trouble, but he's just so much worse than I expected. He never saw this coming, any more than I did. And Rafe's not helping. If he doesn't stop being such a little bollocks, I don't know what . . ." I saw her lips tighten as she swallowed. "And then there's this. I am not having an easy time here either, Daniel, and it doesn't make me feel any better that you don't seem to give a damn."

"I do give a damn," Daniel said. "I care very much, in fact. I thought you knew that. I just don't see what either of us can do about it."

"I could leave," Abby said. She was watching Daniel intently, her eyes round and very grave. "We could leave."

I fought down the impulse to slap a hand over the mike. I wasn't at all sure what was going on here, but if Frank heard this, he would be positive that the four of them were planning some dramatic getaway and I was about to find myself bound and gagged in the coat closet while they hopped a plane to Mexico. I wished I had had the sense to test out the mike's exact range.

Daniel didn't look at Abby, but his hand tightened around her ankles. "You could, yes," he said, eventually.

"There would be nothing I could do to stop you. But this is my home, you know. As I hope . . ." He took a breath. "As I hope it's yours. I can't leave it."

Abby let her head fall back against the bar of the swing seat. "Yeah," she said. "I know. Me neither. I just . . . God, Daniel. What do we *do*?"

"We wait," Daniel said quietly. "We trust that things will eventually fall into place, in their own time. We trust one another. We do our best."

A draft swept across my shoulders and I whipped round, already opening my mouth on my drink-of-water story. The glass clanged against the tap and I dropped it in the sink; the clatter sounded enormous enough to wake up all of Glenskehy. There was no one there.

Daniel and Abby had frozen, faces turned sharply towards the house. "Hey," I said, pushing the door open and going out onto the patio. My heart was pounding. "I changed my mind: I'm not sleepy. Are you guys staying up?"

"No," Abby said. "I'm going to bed." She swung her feet off Daniel's lap and brushed past me, into the house. A moment later I heard her running up the stairs, not bothering to skip the creaky one.

I went over to Daniel and sat down on the patio beside his legs, with my back up against the swing seat. Somehow I didn't want to sit next to him; it would have felt crude, too much like demanding confidences. After a moment he reached out one hand and set it, lightly, on top of my head. His hand was so big that it cupped my skull like a child's. "Well," he said quietly, almost to himself.

His glass was on the ground beside him, and I took a sip: whiskey on the rocks, the ice almost melted. "Were you and Abby fighting?" I asked.

"No," Daniel said. His thumb moved, just a little, across my hair. "Everything's fine."

We sat like that for a while. It was a still night, barely a breeze rippling the grass, the moon like an old silver token floating high in the sky. The cool stone of the patio through

my pajamas and the toasty smell of Daniel's unfiltered cigarette felt comforting, safe. I rocked my back just a little
against the swing seat, swaying it in a gentle, regular rhythm.

"Smell," Daniel said softly. "Do you smell that?"

A first faint scent of rosemary drifting over from the
herb garden, barely a tint in the air. "Rosemary; that's for
remembrance," he said. "Soon we'll have thyme and lemon
balm, and mint and tansy, and something that I think must
be hyssop—it's hard to tell from the book, during winter.
It'll be a mess this year, of course, but we'll trim everything
back into shape, replant where we need to. Those old photos
will be a great help; they'll give us some idea of the original
design, what belongs where. They're hardy plants, these,
chosen for their endurance as well as for their virtue. By
next year . . ."

He told me about old herb gardens: how carefully they
were arranged to make sure that each plant had everything
it needed to flourish, how perfectly they balanced sight and
scent and use, practicality and beauty, without ever allowing one to be compromised for another's sake. Hyssop to
loosen chest colds or cure toothaches, he said, chamomile
in a poultice to reduce inflammation or in a tea to prevent
nightmares; lavender and lemon balm for strewing to make
the house smell sweet, rue and burnet in salads. "We'll have
to try that sometime," he said, "a Shakespearean salad.
Tansy tastes like pepper, did you know that? I thought it
had died off long ago, it was all brown and brittle, but when
I cut right back to the roots, there it was: just a tinge of
green. It'll be all right now. It's amazing, how stubbornly
things survive against incredible odds; how irresistibly
strong it is, the drive to live and grow . . ."

The rhythms of his voice washed over me, even and
soothing as waves; I barely heard the words. "Time," I think
he said somewhere behind me, or maybe it was "thyme,"
I've never been sure. "Time works so hard for us, if only we
can let it."

11

What people tend to forget about Sam is that he has one of the highest solve rates on the Murder squad. Sometimes I wonder if this is for a very simple reason: he doesn't waste energy. Other detectives, me included, take it personally when things go wrong, they get impatient and frustrated and irritated with themselves and the dead-end leads and the whole fucking case. Sam gives it his best shot, then shrugs and says, "Ah, sure," and tries something else.

He had been saying, "Ah, sure," a lot that week, when I asked him how things were going, but not in his usual vague, abstracted way. This time he sounded tense and harassed, wound a notch tighter every day. He had gone door-to-door through most of Glenskehy, asking about Whitethorn House, but he got a smooth slippery wall of tea and biscuits and blank looks: *Lovely young people up at the House, keep themselves to themselves, never any trouble out of them, sure why would there be any bad feeling, Detective? Terrible, what happened to that poor girl, I said a rosary for her, must have been someone she met up in Dublin* . . . I know that small-town silence, I'd run into it before, intangible as smoke and solid as stone. We honed it on the British for centuries and it's ingrained, the instinct for a place to close up like a fist when the police come knocking. Sometimes it means nothing more than that; but it's a powerful thing, that silence, dark and tricky and lawless. It still hides bones buried somewhere in the hills, arsenals cached in pigsties. The British underestimated it, fell for the practiced half-witted looks, but I knew and Sam knew: it's dangerous.

It was Tuesday night before the absorbed note came back into Sam's voice. "I should've known better to start with," he said cheerfully. "If they won't talk to the local cops, why would they talk to me?" He had backed off, thought it over and then taken a taxi down to Rathowen for an evening in the pub: "Byrne said the people round there weren't mad about Glenskehy folk, and I figured everyone likes a chance to gossip about the neighbors, so . . ."

He had been right. Rathowen people were a very different story from the Glenskehy bunch: they made him as a cop inside thirty seconds ("Come here, young fella, are you here about that girl got stabbed down the road?"), and he had spent the rest of the evening surrounded by fascinated farmers buying him pints and happily trying to trick him into giving away something about the investigation.

"Byrne was right: they think Glenskehy's a lunatic asylum. Part of it's just what you get between small towns—Rathowen's that bit bigger, they've got a school and a police station and a few shops, so they call Glenskehy a mad backwater. It's more than just your average rivalry, though. They really do think Glenskehy folk aren't right. One fella said he wouldn't go into Regan's for all the tea in China."

I was up a tree, wearing my mike sock and having a smoke. Since I had heard about that graffiti, the lanes had started to make me feel edgy, exposed; I didn't like being down there when I was on the phone, with half my attention somewhere else. I had found a nook high up in a big beech tree, just at the start of the branches, where the trunk split in two. My arse fit perfectly into the fork, I had a clear view of the lane in both directions and of the cottage downhill, and if I tucked my legs up I vanished into the leaves. "Did they say anything about Whitethorn House?"

A small silence. "Yeah," Sam said. "The house doesn't have a great name, in Rathowen or in Glenskehy. Partly that's to do with Simon March—he was a mad old bastard, by all accounts; two of the fellas remembered him firing his gun at them, when they were kids and they went nosing around the Whitethorn House grounds. But it goes back further than that."

"The dead baby," I said. The words sent something smooth and cold through the middle of me. "Did they know anything about that?"

"A bit. I'm not sure they have all the details right—you'll see what I mean in a minute—but if they're anywhere near the mark, it's not a good story. Not good for the Whitethorn House people, I mean."

He left a pause. "So?" I said. "These people aren't my *family*, Sam. And unless this story happened sometime in the last six months, which I'm assuming it didn't or we'd have heard about it by now, it's got nothing to do with anyone I've even *met*. I'm not going to be deeply hurt by something Daniel's great-granddad did a hundred years ago. Cross my heart."

"Grand, so," Sam said. "The Rathowen version—there's some variation, but this is the gist of it—is that, a while back, a young fella from Whitethorn House had an affair with a Glenskehy girl, and she was going to have a baby for him. It used to happen often enough, sure. The problem was, this girl wasn't about to disappear into a convent or marry some poor local fella in a mad hurry before anyone noticed she was pregnant."

"A woman after my own heart," I said. There was no way this story was going to end well.

"Shame your man March didn't feel the same way. He was furious; he was meant to be getting married to some nice rich Anglo-Irish girl, and this could have banjaxed all his plans. He told the girl he didn't want anything more to do with her or the child. She was already pretty unpopular in the village: not just pregnant outside marriage—that was a big deal, back then—but pregnant for one of the Marches . . . Not long after, she was found dead. She'd hanged herself."

There are stories like this scattered all over our history. Most of them are buried deep and quiet as last year's leaves, long transmuted into old ballads and winter-night stories. I thought of this one lying latent for a century or more, germinating and growing like some slow dark seed, blooming at last with broken glass and knives and poison berries of blood all among the hawthorn hedges. My back prickled against my tree trunk.

I put out my smoke on the sole of my shoe and tucked the butt back into the packet. "Got anything to say this actually happened?" I asked. "Apart from some story they tell in Rathowen to keep kids away from Whitethorn House."

Sam blew out a breath. "Nothing. I put a couple of floaters onto the records, but they've turned up bugger-all. And there's not a chance anyone in Glenskehy is going to tell me their version. They'd rather everyone forgot it ever happened."

"Someone's not forgetting," I said.

"I should have a better idea who that is, in the next few days—I'm pulling all the info I can get on the people in Glenskehy, to cross-check against your profile. I'd love a clearer idea of what my fella's problem is, though, before I get talking to him. The thing is, I've no clue where to start. One of the Rathowen fellas says all this happened in his great-granny's time—which isn't much help, sure: the woman lived to be eighty. Another one swore it was way back in the nineteenth century, 'sometime after the Famine,' but . . . I don't know. I think he wants it as far away as possible; he'd say it was in Brian Boru's time if he thought I'd believe him. So I've a window from 1847 to about 1950, and no one's about to help me narrow it down."

"Actually," I said, "maybe I can." It made me feel sticky all over, traitorous. "Give me a couple of days and I'll see if I can get something more specific."

A small pause, like a question, till Sam realized I wasn't going to go into detail. "That's grand. Anything you can find would be great." Then, on a different note, almost shyly: "Listen, I was meaning to ask you something, before all this happened. I was thinking . . . I've never been on holiday, except to Youghal once when I was a little fella. How about you?"

"France, for summers."

"That was to visit family, sure. I meant a proper holiday, like on the telly, with a beach and snorkeling and mad cocktails in a bar with a cheesy lounge singer doing 'I Will Survive.'"

I knew where this was going. "What the hell have you been watching?"

Sam laughed. "*Ibiza Uncovered*. See what happens to my taste when you're not here?"

"You're just looking for topless chicks," I said. "Emma and Susanna and I have been meaning to go away since we were in school, only we haven't got round to it yet. Maybe this summer."

"But now they've both got kids, haven't they? That makes it harder to go off on a girlie break. I was thinking . . ." That shy note again. "I got a couple of brochures from the travel agencies. Italy, mostly; I know you like the old archaeology. Could I bring you on holiday, when this finishes up?"

I had no idea what I thought about this, and no room to figure it out. "That sounds gorgeous," I said, "and you're wonderful to think of it. Can we decide when I get home? The thing is, I'm not sure how long this is going to take."

There was a tiny silence that made me grimace. I hate hurting Sam; it's like kicking a dog too gentle to ever bite back. "It's been more than two weeks already. I thought Mackey said a month max."

Frank says whatever comes in useful at the time. Undercover investigations can last for years, and although I couldn't see that happening here—the long operations are aimed at ongoing criminal activity, not once-off crimes—I was pretty sure that a month was something he had made up at random to get Sam off his back. For a second I almost hoped so. The thought of leaving all this, back to DV and Dublin crowds and corporate clothes, was vastly depressing.

"In theory, yeah," I said, "but you can't put an exact time on something like this. It could be less than a month—I could be home any time, if one of us gets something solid. But if I pick up a good lead and it needs following through, I might be here a week or two extra."

Sam made a furious, frustrated sound. "If I ever talk about doing a joint investigation again, lock me in a closet till I get sense. I need a *deadline* here. I've been holding off on all kinds of stuff—getting DNA off the lads to test against the baby . . . Till you're done in there, sure, I can't even tell anyone we're dealing with a murder. A few weeks is one thing—"

I had stopped listening to him. Somewhere, down the lane or deep in the trees, there was a sound. Not one of the usual noises, night birds and leaves and small hunting animals, I knew those by now; something else.

"Hang on," I said, softly, through Sam's sentence.

I took the phone away from my ear and listened, holding my breath. It was coming from down the lane, towards the main road, faint but getting closer: a slow, rhythmic crunching noise. Footsteps on pebbles.

"Gotta go," I said into the phone, just above a whisper. "Ring you back later if I can." I switched the phone off, shoved it into my pocket, tucked up my legs among the branches and sat still.

The footsteps were steady and coming nearer; someone big, from the weight of them. There was nothing up this lane except Whitethorn House. I pulled my sweater up, slowly, to cover the bottom half of my face. In the dark, it's the flash of white that gives you away.

Night changes your sense of distance, makes things sound closer than they are, and it seemed like forever before someone came into view: just a flick of movement at first, a dappled shadow passing slowly under the leaves. Flash of fair hair, silver as a ghost's in the pale light. I had to fight the instinct to turn my head away. This was a bad place to wait for something to step out of the dark. There were too many unknown things around me, moving intently along their secret routes on their own private business, and some of them had to be the kind that isn't safe for us to see.

Then he stepped into a patch of moonlight and I saw that it was just a guy, tall, with a rugby build and a designer-looking leather jacket. He moved like he was unsure, hesitating, glancing off into the trees on either side. When he was only a few yards away he turned his head and looked straight at my tree, and in the instant before I shut my eyes—that's the other thing that can give you away, that glint, we're all programmed to spot watching eyes—I saw his face. He was my age, maybe a little younger, good-looking in a forgettable clean-cut way, with a hazy, perplexed frown, and he wasn't on the KA list. I had never seen him before.

He passed under me, so close I could have dropped a leaf on his head, and vanished up the lane. I stayed put. If he was someone's friend come to visit, I was going to be up there a long time, but I didn't think he was. The hesitancy, the confused glances around; he wasn't looking for the house. He was looking for something, or someone, else.

Three times, in her last weeks, Lexie had met N—or at least planned to meet N—somewhere. And on the night she died, if the other four were telling the truth, she had gone out for that walk and met her killer.

My adrenaline was pumping hard and I was itching to go after the guy, or at least intercept him on his way back, but I knew that was a bad idea. I wasn't scared—I had a gun, after all, and in spite of his size he didn't look very formidable—but I only had one shot at this, metaphorically, and I couldn't afford to fire it while I was completely in the dark. There was probably no way to find out whether or how he was linked to Lexie, I would have to play that one by ear, but it would be nice to at least know his name before we got into conversation.

I slid down from the tree in slow motion—the scrape of the bark pulled up my top and nearly dragged the mike off me, Frank would think I was being run over by a tank—and got behind it to wait. It felt like hours before the guy came wandering back down the lane, rubbing the back of his head and still looking bewildered. Whatever he was after, he hadn't found it. When he had passed me, I counted thirty footsteps and then followed him, keeping on the grass verge and putting my feet down carefully, staying behind tree trunks.

He had a wankermobile parked on the main road, a hunormous black SUV with depressingly inevitable tinted windows. It was about fifty yards from the turnoff, and the road was bordered by wide open stretches—long grass, ragged nettles, an old milestone sticking up off-kilter—so there was no cover; I couldn't risk getting close enough to read the plate. My guy whacked the hood affectionately, got in, slammed the door too loudly—sudden cold silence, in the trees all round me—and sat there for a while, contemplating whatever guys like that contemplate, probably his haircut. Then he revved the engine and bulldozed off down the road, towards Dublin.

When I was sure he was gone, I climbed back up my tree and thought this over. There was always a chance that this guy had been stalking me for a while now, that the electric feeling at the back of my neck had been coming from him, but I doubted it. Whatever he was after, he hadn't been particularly covert about it that night, and I didn't get the sense that slinking through the wilderness was a major part of his skill set. Whatever had been lurking in the corner of my eye, it wasn't coming into view this easily.

I was clear on one thing: neither Sam nor Frank needed to know about the SUV Prince, not until I had something a whole lot more concrete to tell them. Sam would go ballistic if he found out I was dodging strange men on the same late-night walk where Lexie had failed to dodge her killer. That wouldn't bother Frank one bit—he always figured I was well able to take care of myself—but if I told him then he would take over, he would find this guy and pull him in and interrogate the bejasus out of him, and I didn't want that. Something in me said that wasn't the way to go at this case. And something else, deeper, said that this wasn't Frank's business, not really. He had stumbled into it by accident. This was between me and Lexie.

I phoned him anyway. We had already talked that night and it was late, but he answered fast. "Yeah? You OK?"

"I'm fine," I said. "Sorry, didn't mean to freak you out. I just wanted to ask you something, before I forget again. Has the investigation turned up a guy about six foot tall, solid build, late twenties, good-looking, fair hair with that trendy quiff thing going on, fancy brown leather jacket?"

Frank yawned, which made me feel guilty but also slightly relieved: it was nice to know he actually slept sometimes. "Why?"

"I passed a guy in Trinity a couple of days ago, and he smiled at me and nodded, like he knew me. He's not on the KA list. It's not a big deal—he didn't act like we were supposed to be bosom buddies or anything—but I thought I'd check. I don't want to get blindsided if we run into each other again." This was true, by the way, although the guy in question had been small and skinny and redheaded. It had taken me about ten minutes of racking my brains to figure out how he knew me. His carrel was in our corner of the library.

Frank thought about this; I heard the rustle of sheets as he turned over in bed. "Doesn't ring any bells," he said. "The only person I can think of is Slow Eddie—Daniel's cousin. He's twenty-nine and blond and wears a brown leather jacket, and I guess he could be good-looking, if you go for big and dumb."

"Not your type?" Still no N. Why the hell would Slow Eddie be wandering around Glenskehy at midnight?

"I like them with more cleavage. Eddie says he never met Lexie, though. There's no reason why he would have. He and Daniel don't get on; it's not like Eddie's popping over to the house for tea or joining the gang on nights out. And he lives in Bray, works in Killiney; I can't see any reason why he'd be in Trinity."

"Don't worry about it," I said. "It's probably just someone who knows her from around college. Go back to sleep. Sorry for waking you."

"It's grand," Frank said, through another yawn. "Better safe than sorry. Put a report on tape, with a full description— and if you see him again, let me know." He was already about half asleep.

"Will do. Night."

I stayed still in my tree for a few minutes, listening for out-of-place noises. Nothing; just the undergrowth below me tossing like ocean in the wind, and that prickle, faint and unignorable, scratching at the top of my spine. I told myself that if anything was going to send my imagination into overdrive, it would be the story Sam had told: the girl stripped of her lover, her family, her future, knotting a rope to one of these dark branches for everything she had left, herself and her baby. I phoned Sam back before I could think too hard about that.

He was still wide awake. "What was that all about? Are you OK?"

"I'm fine," I said. "I'm really sorry about that. I thought I heard someone coming. I was picturing Frank's mystery stalker with a hockey mask and a chain saw, but no such luck." This was also true, obviously, but twisting facts for Sam wasn't like twisting them for Frank, and doing it made my stomach curl up.

A second of silence. "I worry about you," Sam said quietly.

"I know, Sam," I said. "I know you do. I'm grand. I'll be home soon."

I thought I heard him sigh, a small resigned breath, too soft for me to be sure. "Yeah," he said. "We can talk about that holiday then."

I walked back home thinking about Sam's vandal, about that prickling feeling, and about Slow Eddie. All I knew about him was that he worked for an estate agent, he and

Daniel didn't get on, Frank didn't think much of his brainpower, and he had wanted Whitethorn House badly enough to call his grandfather a lunatic. I bounced a few scenarios around in my head—Homicidal Maniac Eddie picking off the occupants of Whitethorn House one by one, Casanova Eddie having a dangerous liaison with Lexie and then flipping out when he found out about the baby—but all of them seemed pretty far-fetched, and anyway I liked to think that Lexie had had better taste than to boink some dumb yuppie in the back of an SUV.

If he'd wandered around the house once and not found what he was looking for, the chances were that he would come back—unless he'd just been taking a last look at the place he had loved and lost, and he didn't strike me as the sentimental type. I filed him under Things to Worry About Some Other Time. Right then, he wasn't at the top of my list.

The part I wasn't telling Sam, the new dark thing unfurling and fluttering in a corner of my mind: someone was holding a high-octane grudge against Whitethorn House; someone had been meeting Lexie in these lanes, someone faceless who began with an N; and someone had helped her make that baby. If all three of those had been the same person . . . Sam's vandal wasn't too tightly wrapped, but he could well be smart enough—sober, anyway—to hide that; he could be gorgeous, charming, all kinds of good stuff, and we already knew that Lexie's decision-making process had worked a little differently from most people's. Maybe she had gone for the angst boys. I thought of a chance meeting somewhere in the lanes, long walks together under a high winter moon and branches filigreed with frost; of that smile slanting up under her lashes; of the ruined cottage, and shelter behind the curtain of brambles.

If the guy I was picturing had found himself with a chance at getting a Whitethorn House girl pregnant, it would have seemed to him like a God-given thing, a perfect, blinding symmetry: a golden ball dropped into his hands by angels, not to be refused. And he would have killed her.

The next morning someone spat on our car. We were on our way to college, Justin and Abby up front, me and Rafe in the back—Daniel had left early, no explanation, while the rest of us were halfway through breakfast. It was a cool gray morning, dawn hush left in the air and soft drizzle misting the windows; Abby was flipping through notes and humming along to Mahler on the CD player, switching octaves dramatically in midphrase, and Rafe was in his sock feet, trying to disentangle a massive knot in his shoelace. As we went through Glenskehy Justin braked, outside the newsagent's, to let someone cross the road: an old guy, hunched and wiry, in a farmer's tired tweed suit and flat cap. He raised his walking stick in a kind of salute as he shuffled past, and Justin waved back.

Then the man caught Justin's eye. He stopped in the middle of the road and stared through the windscreen at us. For a split second his face contorted into a tight mask of pure fury and disgust; then he brought down his stick on the hood, with a flat clang that split the morning wide open. We all shot upright, but before any of us could do anything sensible the old man hawked, spat on the windscreen— straight at Justin's face—and hobbled on across the road, at the same deliberate pace.

"What the—" Justin said, breathless. "What the *hell*? What was that?"

"They don't like us," Abby said evenly, reaching over to switch on the windscreen wipers. The street was long and deserted, little pastel houses closed down tight against the rain, dark blur of hills rising behind them. Nothing moved anywhere, only the old man's slow mechanical shuffle and the flick of a lace curtain down the street. "Drive, hon."

"That little *fuck*," Rafe said. He was clutching his shoe like a weapon, knuckles white. "You should have floored it,

Justin. You should have splattered whatever he's got instead of a brain across this wretched street." He started to roll down his window.

"Rafe," Abby said sharply. "Roll that up. Now."

"Why? Why should we let him get away with—"

"Because," I said, in a small voice. "I want to go for my walk tonight."

That stopped Rafe in his tracks, just like I had known it would; he stared at me, one hand still on the window handle. Justin stalled the car with a horrible grinding sound, managed to jam it into gear and hit the accelerator hard. "Charming," he said. There was a brittle edge to his voice: any kind of nastiness always upset him. "That was really charming. I mean, I realize they don't like us, but that was completely unnecessary. I didn't do anything to that man. I *braked* to let him *cross*. What did he do that for?"

I was pretty sure I knew the answer to that one. Sam had been busy in Glenskehy, the last few days. A detective swanning down from Dublin in his city-boy suit, walking into their sitting rooms asking questions, patiently digging for their buried stories; and all because a girl from the Big House had got herself stabbed. Sam would have done his job gently and deftly, he always does; it wasn't him they would hate.

"Nothing," said Rafe. He and I were twisted around in our seats to watch the old man, who was standing on the pavement outside the newsagent's, leaning on his stick and staring after us. "He did it because he's a knuckle-dragging bog monster and he loathes anyone who isn't actually his wife or his sister or both. It's like living in the middle of bloody *Deliverance*."

"You know something?" Abby said coldly, without turning around. "I'm getting really, really sick of your colonial attitude. Just because he didn't go to some fancy English prep school, that doesn't necessarily make him your inferior. And if Glenskehy isn't good enough for you, you're free to find somewhere that is."

Rafe opened his mouth, then shrugged disgustedly and closed it again. He gave his shoelace a vicious jerk; it broke, and he swore under his breath.

If the man had been thirty or forty years younger, I would have been memorizing his description to pass on to Sam. The fact that he wasn't a viable suspect—this guy had not outrun five students out for blood—sent a nasty little ripple across my shoulders. Abby turned up the volume; Rafe tossed his shoe on the floor and shoved up two fingers at the back windscreen. *This,* I thought, *is going to be trouble.*

"OK," Frank said, that night. "I got my FBI friend to have his boys do some more digging. I told him we have reason to believe that our girl took off because she had a nervous breakdown, so we're looking for signs and possible causes. *Is* that what we think, just out of interest?"

"I have no idea what you think, Frankie boy. Don't ask me to climb into that black hole." I was up my tree. I wriggled my back up against one half of the trunk and braced my feet against the other, so I could lean my notebook on my thigh. There was just enough moonlight, between the branches, that I could see the page. "Hang on a sec." I clamped the phone under my jaw and hunted for my pen.

"You sound cheerful," Frank said, suspiciously.

"I just had a gorgeous dinner and a laugh. What's not to be cheerful about?" I managed to extract the pen from my jacket pocket without falling out of the tree. "OK, shoot."

Frank made an exasperated noise. "Lovely for some. Just don't get too chummy. There's always a chance you may have to arrest one of these people."

"I thought you were gunning for the mysterious stranger in the black cape."

"I'm keeping an open mind. And the cape's optional. OK, here's everything we've got—you did say you wanted ordinary stuff, so don't blame me. On the sixteenth of August 2000, Lexie-May-Ruth switched mobile-phone providers to get cheaper local minutes. On the twenty-second, she got a raise at the diner, seventy-five cents extra an hour. On the twenty-eighth, Chad proposed to her, and she said yes. The first weekend of September, the two of them drove to Virginia so she could meet Chad's parents, who said she was a very sweet girl and brought them a potted plant."

"The engagement ring," I said, keeping my voice easy. This was setting ideas exploding in my head like popcorn, but I didn't want Frank to know that. "Did she take it with her when she split?"

"No. The cops asked Chad at the time. She left it on her bedside table, but that was normal. She always left it there when she went to work, in case it got lost or fell in the hash browns or whatever. It wasn't a big fancy rock or anything. Chad's the bassist in a grunge band called Man From Nantucket, and they have yet to get their big break, so he makes a living as a carpenter. He's skint."

My notes were scrawly and went at a funny angle, on account of the light and the tree, but I could just about read them. "Then what?"

"On the twelfth of September she and Chad bought a PlayStation on their joint credit, which I suppose is as good a statement of commitment as any, these days. On the eighteenth, she sold her car, an '86 Ford, for six hundred bucks—she told Chad she wanted to get something a little less beat-up, now that she had the extra money from the raise. On the twenty-seventh, she went to her doctor with an ear infection, probably contracted from swimming; he gave her antibiotics and it cleared up. And on the tenth of October, she's gone. Is that what you were looking for?"

"Yeah," I said. "That's exactly the kind of stuff I had in mind. Thanks, Frank. You're a gem."

"I'm thinking," he said, "something happened between the twelfth and the eighteenth of September. Up through the twelfth, everything says she's planning on staying put: she's getting engaged, she's meeting the parents, she and

Chad are buying stuff as a couple. But on the eighteenth she sells her car, which tells me she's getting together the money to split. That the way you're thinking?"

"Makes sense," I said, but I knew Frank was wrong. That shifting pattern had slid into focus with a soft, final click, and I knew why Lexie had taken off running from North Carolina; knew it as clear as if she were sitting weightless on a branch beside me, swinging her legs in the moonlight and whispering in my ear. And I knew why she had been about to take off running from Whitethorn House. Someone had tried to hold her.

"I'll try and find out more about that week, maybe get someone to re-interview poor old Chad. If we can figure out what changed her plans, we should be able to put our finger on the mystery man."

"Sounds good. Thanks, Frank. Let me know how you get on."

"Don't do anyone I wouldn't do," he said, and hung up.

I angled the screen of my mobile towards the page, so I could read over my notes. The PlayStation meant nothing; it's easy to buy on credit with no plans to pay it off, no plans to be anywhere within reach. The last solid thing that said she intended to stay put was the phone-provider switch, back in August. You don't care about cheaper minutes unless you're going to be around to use them. On August 16, she had been tucked snugly into her May-Ruth life and going nowhere.

And then, less than two weeks later, poor grunge Chad had proposed. After that, not one thing said Lexie was staying. She had said yes, smiled and bided her time till she got the money together, and then run as far and as fast as she could and never once looked behind. It hadn't been Frank's mystery stalker after all, it hadn't been some masked menace slinking out of the shadows with a glinting blade. It had been as simple as a cheap ring.

And this time, there had been the baby: a lifelong tie to some man, somewhere. She could have got rid of it, just like she could have turned Chad down, but that had been beside the point. Just the thought of that tie had sent her slamming off the walls, frantic as a trapped bird.

The missed period and the flight prices; and, somewhere in there, N. N was either the trap trying to hold her here or, in some way I needed to find, her way out.

The others were sprawled on the sitting-room floor in front of the fire, like kids, rummaging through a wrecked traveling case that Justin had found somewhere. Rafe had his legs flung companionably across Abby's—they had apparently made up their fight from that morning. The rug was strewn with mugs and a plate of ginger biscuits and a medley of small battered things: pockmarked marbles, tin soldiers, half of a clay pipe. "Cool," I said, dropping my jacket on the sofa and flopping down between Daniel and Justin. "What've we got?"

"Odd oddments," Rafe said. "Here. For you." He wound up a moth-eaten clockwork mouse and sent it ticking along the floor towards me. It ground to a halt halfway, with a depressed scraping sound.

"Have one of these instead," Justin said, stretching to pull the biscuits across to us. "Tastier."

I got a biscuit in one hand, dipped the other into the traveling case and found something hard and heavy. I came up holding what looked like a beaten-up wooden box; the lid had said "EM" once upon a time, in mother-of-pearl inlay, but there were only a few bits left. "Ah, excellent," I said, opening the lid. "This is like the world's best lucky dip."

It was a music box, tarnished cylinder and splitting blue silk lining, and after a whirring second it plucked out a tune: "Greensleeves," rusty and sweet. Rafe put a hand over the clockwork mouse, which was still fizzing halfheartedly. There was a long silence, just the crackle of the fire, while we listened.

"Beautiful," Daniel said softly, closing the box, when the tune ended. "That's beautiful. Next Christmas . . ."

"Can I have this in my room, to send me to sleep?" I asked. "Till Christmas?"

"Now you need lullabies?" Abby asked, but she was grinning at me. "Course you can."

"I'm glad we didn't find it before," Justin said. "This must be valuable; they'd only have made us sell it, towards the taxes."

"Not that valuable," Rafe said, taking the box from me and examining it. "Basic ones like this go for about a hundred quid—a lot less in this condition. My grandmother used to collect them. Dozens of them, on every surface, just waiting to fall off and smash and send her into a fit if you walked too hard."

"Knock it off," Abby said, kicking his ankle—no pasts—but she didn't sound seriously upset. For some reason, maybe just the mysterious alchemy you get among friends, all the tension of the last few days seemed to have vanished; we were happy together again, shoulders touching, Justin tugging down Abby's sweater where it had slid up her back. "Sooner or later, though, we could find something valuable, in all this mess."

"What would you do with the money?" Rafe asked, reaching for the biscuits. "A few grand, say." In that second I heard Sam's voice, close against my ear: *That house is full of old bits and bobs, if there was something valuable in there . . .*

"Get an Aga stove," Abby said promptly. "The ones that heat the whole house. Warmth *and* a cooker that doesn't crumble into lumps of rust if you look at it funny. Two birds, one stone."

"You wild woman," Justin said. "What about designer dresses and weekends in Monte Carlo?"

"I'd settle for no more frozen toes."

Maybe she was supposed to give him something, I had said, *and that's what went wrong: she changed her mind . . .* I realized I had my hand pressed down on the music box as if someone was trying to take it away. "I'd get the roof redone, I think," Daniel said. "It shouldn't disintegrate for another few years, but it would be nice not to wait that long."

"You?" Rafe asked, giving him a sideways grin and winding the clockwork mouse again. "I'd have thought you'd never sell the thing, whatever it was; just frame it and hang it on the wall. Family history over filthy lucre."

Daniel shook his head and held out a hand to me for his coffee mug—I had been dipping my biscuit in it. "What matters is the house," he said, taking a sip and passing the mug back to me. "All the other things are just icing, really; I'm fond of them, but I'd sell them all in a heartbeat if we needed the money for roofing bills or something like that. The house carries enough history all by itself; and after all, we're making our own, every day."

"What would you do with it, Lex?" Abby asked.

That right there was, of course, the sixty-four-thousand-dollar question, the one that was banging at the inside of my head like a tiny vicious hammer. Sam and Frank hadn't followed up on the antique-deal-gone-wrong idea because, basically, nothing pointed that way. Death duties had cleared the good stuff out of the house, Lexie hadn't been linked to any antique dealers or fences, and nothing had said she needed money; until now.

She had had eighty-eight quid in her bank account— barely enough to get her out of Ireland, never mind get her started anywhere else—and only a couple of months before the baby started showing, the father started noticing and it was too late. Last time she had sold her car; this time, she had had nothing to sell.

It's amazing how cheaply you can ditch your life and get a new one, if you don't ask for much and you're willing to do any work that's going. After Operation Vestal I spent a lot of predawn time online, checking hostel prices and job ads in various languages and doing the maths. There are plenty of cities where you can get a crap flat for three hundred quid a month, or a hostel bed for a tenner a night; figure in your flight, and enough cash to feed you for a few weeks while you answer ads for bar staff or sandwich makers or tour guides, and you're talking a brand-new life for the price of a secondhand car. I had two grand saved up: more than enough.

And Lexie knew all that better than I did; she had done it before. She wouldn't have needed to find a lost Rembrandt in the back of her wardrobe. All she would have needed was the right little trinket—a good bit of jewelry, a rare piece of porcelain, I've heard of teddy bears going for hundreds—and the right buyer; and the willingness to sell bits of this house, out from under the others.

She had run off in Chad's car, but I would have been willing to swear on just about anything that that was different. This had been her home.

"I'd get us all new bed frames," I said. "The springs in mine stick into me straight through the mattress, like the princess and the pea, and I can hear every time Justin turns over," and I flipped the music box open again, to end this conversation.

Abby sang along, softly, turning the clay pipe in her hands: "Greensleeves is all my joy, Greensleeves is my delight . . ." Rafe turned the clockwork mouse over and started examining the gears. Justin flicked one of the marbles expertly into another, which rolled across the floor and clicked neatly against Daniel's mug; he glanced up from a tin soldier, smiling, his hair falling across his forehead. I watched them and ran my fingers over the old silk and hoped to God I had been telling the truth.

12

The next evening, after dinner, I went fishing in Uncle Simon's epic masterpiece for information about a dead Glenskehy girl. It would have been a lot simpler to do this on my own, but that would have meant throwing a sickie from college, and I didn't want to worry the others unless I really needed to; so Rafe and Daniel and I were sitting on the spare-room floor, with the Marches' family tree spread out between us. Abby and Justin were downstairs, playing piquet.

The family tree was a huge sheet of thick, tattered paper covered with a wild variety of handwritings, from delicate, browning ink at the top—James March, born ca. 1598, m. Elizabeth Kempe 1619—to Uncle Simon's spider scrawl at the bottom: Edward Thomas Hanrahan, born 1975, and last of all Daniel James March, born 1979. "This is the only thing in this room that's intelligible," Daniel said, picking a bit of cobweb off the corner, "presumably because Simon didn't write it himself. The rest . . . we can try having a look, Lexie, if you're really that interested, but as far as I can tell he wrote most of it when he was very, very drunk."

"Hey," I said, leaning over to point. "There's your William. The black sheep."

"William Edward March," Daniel said, putting a finger gently on the name. "Born 1894, died 1983. Yes; that's him. I wonder where he ended up." William was one of only a handful that had made it past forty. Sam had been right, the Marches died young.

"Let's see if we can find him in here," I said, pulling a box towards me. "I'm getting curious about this guy. I want to know what the big scandal was."

"Girls," Rafe said loftily, "always sniffing for gossip," but he reached for another box.

Daniel was right, most of the saga was almost illegible—Uncle Simon went in for lots of underlining and no space between lines, Victorian-style. I didn't need to read it; I was only scanning for the tall curves of a capital W and M. I'm not sure what I was hoping we'd find. Nothing, maybe; or something that whacked the Rathowen story right out of court, proved that the girl had moved to London with her baby and set up a successful dressmaking business and lived happily ever after.

Downstairs I could hear Justin saying something and Abby laughing, faint and faraway. The three of us didn't talk; the only sound was the soft, steady rustle of paper. The room was cool and dim, a blurred moon hanging outside the window, and the pages left a dry film of dust on my fingers.

"Oh, here we go," Rafe said suddenly. " 'William March was the subject of much unjust and—sensational?—something, which finally cost him both his health and . . .' Jesus, Daniel. Your uncle must have been trolleyed. Is this even in *English*?"

"Let me see," Daniel said, leaning across to look. " 'Both his health and his rightful place in society,' I think." He took the sheaf of pages from Rafe and pushed his glasses up his nose. " 'The facts,' " he read slowly, running a finger under the line, " 'stripped of rumormongering, are as follows: from 1914 through 1915 William March served in the Great War, where he'—that has to be 'acquitted'—'himself well, later being awarded the Military Cross for his acts of bravery. This alone should—something—all low gossip. In 1915 William March was discharged, suffering from a shrapnel wound to the shoulder and from severe shell-shock—' "

"Post-traumatic stress," Rafe said. He was leaning back against the wall, hands behind his head, to listen. "Poor bastard."

"I can't read this bit," Daniel said. "Something about what he had seen—in battle, I assume; that word's 'cruel.' Then it says: 'He dissolved his engagement to Miss Alice West and took no part in the amusements of his set, preferring to spend his time among the common people of Glenskehy village, much to the anxiety of all parties. All concerned realized that this'—unnatural, I think—'connection could not have a happy result.'"

"Snobs," said Rafe.

"Look who's talking," I said, scooting across the floor to rest my chin on Daniel's shoulder and try to make out the words. So far, no surprises, but I knew—*could not have a happy result*—this was it.

"'About this time,'" Daniel read, tilting the page so I could see, "'a young girl of the village found herself in an unfortunate situation, and named William March as the father of her unborn child. Whatever the truth may have been, the people of Glenskehy, who were then well trained in morals unlike these present times'"—"morals" was underlined twice—"'were shocked at her loose conduct. It was the strong—belief?—of all the village that the girl should remove her shame from their midst by entering a Magdalen convent, and till this should come about they made her an outcast among themselves.'"

No happy ending, no little dress shop in London. Some girls never escaped the Magdalen laundries. They stayed slaves—for getting pregnant, getting raped, being orphaned, being too pretty—till they went to nameless graves.

Daniel kept reading, quiet and even. I could feel the vibration of his voice against my shoulder. "'The girl, however, either despairing of her soul or unwilling to perform the prescribed penance, took her life. William March—whether because he had in fact been her partner in sin, or because he had already witnessed too much bloodshed—was greatly affected by this. His health failed him, and when he recovered he abandoned family, friends and home to begin anew elsewhere. Little is known of his later life. These events may be taken as a lesson in the dangers of lust, or of mixing outside the boundaries of one's natural level in society, or of . . .'" Daniel broke off. "I can't read the rest. That's all there is about William, anyway; the next paragraph is about a racehorse."

"Jesus," I said softly. The room felt cold all of a sudden, cold and too airy, as if the window had slammed open behind us.

"They treated her like a leper till she cracked," Rafe said. There was a taut little twist to one corner of his mouth. "And till William had a breakdown and left town. So it's not just a recent development, then, Glenskehy being Lunatic Central."

I felt a slight shudder run down Daniel's back. "That's a nasty little story," he said. "It really is. Sometimes I wonder if the best thing would be for 'no pasts' to apply to the house, as well. Although . . ." He glanced around, at the room full of dusty battered things, the ragged-papered walls; the dark-spotted mirror, down the corridor, reflecting the three of us in blues and shadows through the open door. "I'm not sure," he said, almost to himself, "that that's an option."

He tapped the edges of the pages straight and put them carefully back in their case, closed the lid. "I don't know about you two," he said, "but I think I've had enough for tonight. Let's go back to the others."

"I think I've seen every piece of paperwork in the country that has the word 'Glenskehy' on it," Sam said, when I phoned him later. He sounded wrecked and blurry—paper fatigue; I knew the note well—but satisfied. "I know a lot more about it than anyone needs to, and I've got three guys that fit your profile."

I was in my tree, with my feet tucked up tight into the branches. The feeling of being watched had intensified to the point where I was actually hoping that whatever it was would jump me, just so I could get some kind of fix on it. I hadn't mentioned this to Frank or, God forbid, Sam. As far as I could see, the main possibilities were my imagination, the ghost of Lexie Madison and a homicidal stalker with procrastination issues, and none of those was something I felt like sharing. During the day I figured it was imagination, maybe with some help from the resident wildlife, but at night it was harder to be sure. "Only three? Out of four hundred people?"

"Glenskehy's dying," Sam said flatly. "Almost half the population is over sixty-five. As soon as the kids are old enough, they pack up and move to Dublin, Cork, Wicklow town, anywhere that has a bit of life to it. The only ones who stay put are the ones who have a family farm or a family business to take over. There's less than thirty fellas between twenty-five and thirty-five. I cut out the ones who commute for work, the unemployed ones, the ones who live alone and the ones who could get away during the day if they wanted to—night-shifters, fellas who work alone. That left me with three."

"Jesus," I said. I thought of the old man hobbling across an empty street, the tired houses where only one lace curtain had twitched.

"I suppose that's progress for you. At least there's jobs for them to go to." Flick of paper: "Right, here's my three lads. Declan Bannon, thirty-one, runs a small farm just outside Glenskehy with his wife and two young kids. John Naylor, twenty-nine, lives in the village with his parents and works on another man's farm. And Michael McArdle, twenty-six, lives with his parents and does the day shift in the petrol station up on the Rathowen road. No known links to Whitethorn House anywhere. Any of the names ring a bell?"

"Not offhand," I said, "sorry," and then I almost fell out of my tree. "Ah, sure," Sam was saying philosophically, "that would've been too much to expect," but I barely heard him. John Naylor: finally, and about bloody time, I had someone who began with an N.

"Which one do you like?" I asked. I made sure I didn't skip a beat. Of all the detectives I know, Sam is the best at pretending he's missed things. It comes in useful more often than you might expect.

"It's early days, but for now Bannon's my favorite. He's the only one with any kind of history. Five years ago, a couple of American tourists parked their car blocking one of Bannon's gates while they went for a walk in the lanes. When Bannon turned up and couldn't move his sheep, he kicked a pretty serious dent in the side of the car. Criminal damage and not playing nicely with outsiders; this vandalism could be right up his street."

"The others are clean?"

"Byrne says he's seen both of them a little the worse for wear, at one time or another, but not enough that he could be bothered pulling them in for public drunkenness or anything like that. Any of them could have criminal activity we don't know about, Glenskehy being what it is, but to look at, yeah, they're clean."

"Have you talked to them yet?" Somehow, I had to get a look at this John Naylor. Going down to the pub was out, obviously, and wandering innocently onto the farm where he worked was probably a bad idea, but if I could find a way to sit in on an interview—

Sam laughed. "Give me time. I'm only after narrowing it down this afternoon. I'm aiming to have chats with all of them tomorrow morning. I wanted to ask you—would you be able to come in for that? Just to give them the once-over, see if you pick up anything?"

I could have kissed him. "God, yeah. Where? When?"

"Yeah, I thought you might want a look." He was smiling. "I'm thinking Rathowen station. Their homes would be best, not to spook them, but I couldn't exactly bring you along there."

"Sounds good," I said. "Sounds great, actually."

The smile in Sam's voice deepened. "To me, too. Will you be able to get away from the others?"

"I'll tell them I've got a hospital appointment, to get my stitches checked. I should be doing that anyway." The thought of the others gave me a strange little pang. If Sam got anything solid on one of these guys—it wouldn't even have to be enough for an arrest—then it was over; I was out, back to Dublin and DV.

"Will they not want to come in with you?"

"Probably, but I won't let them. I'll get Justin or Daniel to drop me off at Wicklow Hospital. Can you pick me up there, or will I get a taxi to Rathowen?"

He laughed. "You think I'd miss the chance? Say half past ten?"

"Perfect," I said. "And, Sam—I don't know how much depth you're planning to go into with these three guys, but before you start chatting to them, I've got a bit more info for you. About that girl with the baby." That sticky traitorous feeling clamped round me again, but I reminded myself that Sam wasn't Frank, it wasn't like he would show up at Whitethorn House with a search warrant and a bunch of deliberately obnoxious questions. "It looks like the whole thing happened sometime in 1915. No name on the girl, but her lover was William March, born 1894."

An instant of amazed silence; then: "Ah, you *gem*," Sam said, delighted. "How'd you do that?"

So he wasn't listening in on the mike feed—not all the time, anyway. It startled me, how much of a relief that was. "Uncle Simon was writing a family history. This girl got a mention. The details don't exactly match up, but it's the same story, all right."

"Hang on," Sam said; I heard him finding a blank page in his notebook. "Now. Off you go."

"According to Simon, William went off to the First World War in 1914, came back a year later deeply messed up. He broke off his engagement to some nice suitable girl, cut off contact with all his old friends and started hanging around the village. Reading between the lines, the Glenskehy people weren't too pleased about that."

"Not a lot they could do," Sam said dryly. "One of the landlord's family . . . He could do whatever he liked, sure."

"Then this girl got pregnant," I said. "She claimed William was the father—Simon sounded a little skeptical about that, but either way, Glenskehy was horrified. They treated her like dirt; the general opinion was that she belonged in a Magdalen laundry. Before anyone could send her off, she hanged herself."

Brush of wind through the trees, small raindrops flicking leaves.

"So," Sam said, after a moment, "Simon's version takes the responsibility right off the Marches and puts it on those mad peasants down the village."

The flare of anger caught me off guard; I almost bit his head off. "William March didn't get off scot-free either," I said, hearing the edge in my voice. "He had some kind of nervous breakdown—I don't have specifics, but he ended up in what sounds like a mental institution. And it might not even have been his kid to start with."

Another silence, longer this time. "Right," Sam said. "True enough. I'm not about to argue over anything tonight, anyway. I'm too happy about seeing you again."

I swear it took me a second to catch up. I had been so focused on the chance of seeing the mysterious N, it hadn't even hit me that I would be seeing Sam. "Less than twelve hours," I said. "I'll be the one looking like Lexie Madison and wearing nothing but white lace underwear."

"Ah, don't be doing that to me," Sam said. "This is business, woman," but I could still hear the grin in his voice when we hung up.

Daniel was in one of the armchairs by the fire, reading T. S. Eliot; the other three were playing poker. "Oof," I said, flopping down on the hearth rug. The butt of my gun jammed itself neatly under my ribs; I didn't try to hide the wince. "What are you doing out? You never get knocked out first."

"I kicked his arse," Abby called across, raising her wineglass.

"Don't *gloat*," Justin said. He sounded like he was losing. "It's so unattractive."

"She did, actually," Daniel said. "She's getting very good at bluffing. Are your stitches hurting again?"

A fraction of a pause, from the table, in the sound of Rafe flipping his stack of coins through his fingers. "It's just 'cause I'm thinking about them," I said. "I've got this followup appointment tomorrow, so the doctors can poke me some more and tell me I'm fine, which I already knew anyway. Give me a lift?"

"Of course," Daniel said, putting his book down on his lap. "What time?"

"Wicklow Hospital, ten o'clock. I'll get the train into college afterwards."

"But you can't go in there *alone*," Justin said. He was twisted around in his seat, the card game forgotten. "Let me take you. I've got nothing else to do tomorrow. I'll come in with you, and then we'll go into college together."

He sounded really worried. If I couldn't get him to back off, I was in serious trouble. "I don't *want* anyone to come with me," I said. "I want to go on my own."

"But hospitals are awful. And they always make you wait for hours, like cattle, jammed into those hideous waiting rooms—"

I kept my head down and rummaged in my jacket pocket for my smokes. "So I'll bring a book. I don't even want to be there to begin with; the last thing I need is someone breathing down my neck the whole time. I just want to get this over with and forget the whole thing, OK? Can I do that?"

"It's her choice," Daniel said. "Let us know if you change your mind, Lexie."

"*Thank* you," I said. "I'm a grown-up, you know. I can show the doctor my stitches all by myself."

Justin shrugged and went back to his cards. I knew I had hurt his feelings, but there was nothing I could do about that. I lit a cigarette; Daniel passed me the ashtray that had been balancing on the arm of his chair. "Are you smoking more these days?" he inquired.

My face must have been totally blank, but my mind was going like crazy. If anything, I'd been smoking less than I should have—I'd been keeping it at fifteen or sixteen a day, halfway between my normal ten and Lexie's twenty, and hoping the drop would be put down to me still feeling weak. It had never occurred to me that Frank had only the others' word for that twenty. Daniel hadn't fallen for the coma story; God only knew how much more he had suspected. It would have been so easy, terrifyingly easy, for him to slip just one or two bits of disinformation into his interviews with Frank, sit back—those calm gray eyes, watching me without any trace of impatience—and wait to see if they found their way home.

"Not sure," I said, puzzled. "I haven't thought about it. Am I?"

"You didn't usually take your cigarettes on your walk," Daniel said. "Before the incident. Now you do."

The relief almost punched the breath out of me. I should have caught that—no smokes on the body—but a research glitch was a whole lot easier to deal with than the thought of Daniel playing, blank-faced, a hand full of wild cards held close against his chest. "I always meant to," I said. "I just kept forgetting them. Now that you guys make me remember my mobile, I remember my smokes too. Anyway"—I sat up and gave Daniel an offended look—"why are you giving me hassle? Rafe smokes like two packs a day and you never say anything to him."

"I'm not giving you hassle," Daniel said. He was smiling across at me, over his book. "I just believe that vices should be enjoyed; otherwise what's the point in having them? If you're smoking because of tension, then you're not enjoying it."

"I'm not tense," I told him. I collapsed back on my elbows, to prove it, and propped the ashtray on my stomach. "I'm *fine*."

"There's nothing wrong with being tense just now," Daniel said. "It's very understandable. But you should find another way of releasing stress, rather than wasting a perfectly good vice." That hint of a smile again. "If you should feel the need to talk to someone . . ."

"You mean like a therapist?" I asked. "Ewww. They said that in hospital, but I told them to fuck off."

"Well, yes," Daniel said. "So I imagine. I think that was a good choice. I've never understood the logic behind paying a stranger of undetermined intelligence to listen to your troubles; surely that's why one has friends. If you do want to talk about it, all of us are—"

"Holy Jesus Christ *almighty*," Rafe said, his voice rising. He slapped his cards down on the table, hard, and shoved them away. "Someone pass me a sick bag. Oh, I validate your *feelings*, let's all *talk* about this—Did I miss something? Did we move to fucking California and no one told me?"

"What the hell is your problem?" Justin demanded, in a vicious undertone.

"I don't like touchy-feely bollocks. Lexie's fine. She said so. Is there any particular reason why we can't all just bloody leave it alone?"

I was sitting up by now; Daniel had put his book down. "That's hardly your decision," Justin said.

"If I'm going to have to listen to this crap, then yes, it bloody well is my decision. I fold. Justin, it's all yours. Deal, Abby." Rafe reached across Justin for the wine bottle.

"Speaking of using vices to release tension," Abby said coolly, "don't you think you've had enough to drink for one night?"

"Actually," Rafe told her, "I don't think so, no." He filled his glass, so high that a drop sloshed over the edge onto the table. "And I don't recall asking for your advice. Deal the fucking cards."

"You're drunk," Daniel said coldly. "And you're becoming obnoxious."

Rafe whipped round on him; his hand was gripping the top of the glass and for a second I thought he was going to throw it. "Yes," he said, low and dangerous, "I am in fact drunk. And I intend to get a whole lot drunker. Do you want to *talk* about it, Daniel? Is that what you want? Would you like us all to have a *talk*?"

There was something in his voice, something precarious as the smell of petrol, ready and waiting to ignite at the first spark. "I don't see any point in discussing anything with someone in your condition," Daniel said. "Pull yourself together, have some coffee and stop acting like a spoiled toddler." He picked up his book again and turned away from the others. I was the only one who could see his face. It was perfectly calm, but his eyes weren't moving: he wasn't reading a word.

Even I could tell that he was handling this all wrong. Once Rafe had worked himself into one of his moods, he didn't know how to snap back out of it. What he wanted was someone to do it for him, change the note in the room to silliness or peace or practicality so he could follow. Trying to bully him was only going to make him worse, and the fact that Daniel had made such an uncharacteristic mistake sent a jab through the back of my mind: amazement and something else, something like fear or excitement. I could have settled Rafe down in seconds (*Oo, do you think I have PTSD? Like Vietnam vets? Someone yell "Grenade" and see if I dive . . .*) and I almost did, it took an effort of will to stop myself; but I needed to see how this played out.

Rafe caught his breath as if he was about to say something, but then he changed his mind, gave a disgusted head-shake and shoved his chair back hard. He grabbed his glass in one hand and the bottle in the other and stalked out. A moment later his door slammed.

"What the hell?" I said, after a moment. "I'm gonna go see that shrink after all and tell him I'm living with total *loopers*."

"Don't you start," Justin said. "Just don't." His voice was shaking.

Abby put the cards down, stood up, pushed her chair in carefully and left the room. Daniel didn't move. I heard Justin knock something over and swear viciously under his breath, but I didn't look up.

Breakfast was quiet, the next morning, and not in a good way. Justin was pointedly not speaking to me. Abby moved around the kitchen with a tiny worried furrow between her eyebrows, till we finished washing up and she prised Rafe out of his room and the three of them left for college.

Daniel sat at the table and gazed out of the window, wrapped in some private haze, while I dried the dishes and put them away. Finally he stirred, caught a deep breath: "Right," he said, blinking bemusedly at the cigarette burned away between his fingers. "We'd better get moving."

He didn't say a word on the drive to the hospital, either. "Thanks," I said, as I got out of the car.

"Of course," he said absently. "Do ring me if there's anything wrong, not that I think there will be, or if you change your mind about having someone with you." He waved, over his shoulder, as he drove away.

When I was sure he was gone, I got a Styrofoam cup of approximate coffee from the hospital café and leaned against the wall outside to wait for Sam. I saw him, pulling into a parking space and getting out of his car to scan the car park, before he saw me. For a fraction of a second I didn't recognize him. He looked tired and pudgy and old, ridiculously old, and for that instant all I could think was: *Who is this guy?* Then he saw me and smiled and my mind snapped back into focus, and he looked like himself again. I told myself Sam always puts on a couple of pounds during a big case—junk food on the run—and I had been spending all my time with twenty-somethings, a thirty-five-year-old was naturally going to look geriatric. I tossed my cup in the bin and headed over.

"Ah, God," Sam said, wrapping me in a massive hug, "it's good to see you." His kiss was warm and strong and unfamiliar; even the smell of him, soap and fresh-ironed cotton, seemed strange. It took a second before I figured out what this felt like: that first evening in Whitethorn House, when I was supposed to know everything around me inside out.

"Hi," I said, smiling up at him.

He pulled my head against his shoulder. "God," he said, on a sigh. "Let's forget all about this bloody case and run away for the day, will we?"

"Business," I reminded him. "Remember? You're the one who wouldn't let me wear the white lace undies."

"I've changed my mind." He ran his hands down my arms. "You look great, do you know that? All relaxed and wide awake, and not half as thin. It's doing you good, this case."

"Country air," I said. "Plus Justin always cooks for about twelve. What's the plan?"

Sam sighed again and let go of my hands, leaned back against the car. "My three lads are coming into Rathowen station, half an hour apart. I figure that's plenty of time; for now, all I want to do is feel them out, not put their backs up. There's no observation room, but from reception you can hear everything that goes on in the interview room. You can just wait in back while I bring them in, then slip out to reception and have a listen."

"I'd like a look, too," I said. "Why don't I just hang out in reception? It might do no harm to let them see me, accidentally on purpose. If one of them's our guy—for the murder, or even just the vandalism—then he's going to have a pretty strong reaction to me."

Sam shook his head. "That's what I'm worried about, sure. Remember the other night, when we were on the phone? You thought you heard someone? If my boy's been following you around, and then he thinks you're talking to us . . . We already know he's got a temper."

"Sam," I said gently, linking my fingers through his, "that's what I'm there for. To get us closer to our guy. If you don't let me do that, I'm just a lazy wagon getting paid to eat good food and read pulp fiction."

After a moment Sam laughed, a small reluctant breath. "Right," he said. "Fair enough. Have a look at the lads when I bring them out."

He squeezed my fingers, gently, and let go. "Before I forget"—he fished inside his coat—"Mackey sent you these." It was a bottle of tablets like the one I'd brought to Whitethorn House, with the same pharmacist's label announcing loudly that they were amoxicillin. "He said to tell you your wound isn't all the way healed yet and the doctor's worried you could still get an infection, so you've to take another course of these."

"At least I'm getting my vitamin C," I said, pocketing the bottle. It felt too heavy, dragging at the side of my jacket. *The doctor's worried* . . . Frank was starting to think about my exit.

Rathowen station was craptacular. I'd seen plenty like it, dotted around back corners of the country: small stations caught in a vicious circle, getting dissed by the people who hand out funds and by the people who hand out posts and by anyone who can get any other assignment in the universe. Reception was one cracked chair, a poster about bike helmets and a hatch to let Byrne stare vacantly out the door, rhythmically chewing gum. The interview room was apparently also the storeroom: it had a table, two chairs, a filing cabinet—no lock—a help-yourself pile of statement sheets and, for no reason I could figure out, a battered eighties riot shield in one corner. There was yellowing linoleum on the floor and a smashed fly on one wall. No wonder Byrne looked the way he did.

I stayed out of sight behind the desk, with Byrne, while Sam tried to kick the interview room into some kind of shape. Byrne stashed his gum in his cheek and gave me a long depressed stare. "It'll never work," he informed me.

I wasn't sure where to go with this, but apparently it was no reply required; Byrne retrieved his gum and went back to gazing out the hatch. "There's Bannon now," he said. "The ugly great lump."

Sam has a lovely light touch with interviews, when he wants to, and he wanted to that day. He kept it easy, casual, nonthreatening. Would you have any ideas, any at all, about who might have stabbed Miss Madison? What are they like, those five up at Whitethorn House? Have you seen anyone you didn't recognize, hanging around Glenskehy? The impression he gave, subtly but clearly, was that the investigation was starting to wind down.

Bannon mainly answered in irritable grunts; McArdle was less Neanderthal and more bored. Both of them claimed to have no clue about anything, ever. I only half listened. If there was anything there, Sam would spot it; all I wanted was a look at John Naylor, and at the expression on his face when he saw me. I arranged myself in the cracked chair with my legs stretched out, trying to look like I'd been dragged in for more pointless questions, and waited.

Bannon was in fact an ugly great lump: a serious beer belly surrounded by muscles and topped off with a potato head. When Sam ushered him out of the interview room and he saw me, he did a double take and shot me a vicious, disgusted sneer; he knew who Lexie Madison was, all right, and he didn't like her. McArdle, on the other hand—he was a long skinny streak of a guy, with a straggly attempt at a beard—gave me a vague nod and shambled off. I got back behind the desk and waited for Naylor.

His interview was a lot like the others: seen nothing,

heard nothing, know nothing. He had a nice voice, a quick baritone with the Glenskehy accent I was starting to know—harsher than most of Wicklow, wilder—and an edge of tension. Then Sam wound it up and opened the interview-room door.

Naylor was average height, wiry, wearing jeans and a baggy, colorless sweater. He had a mop of tangled red-brown hair and a rough, bony face: high cheekbones, wide mouth, narrow green eyes under heavy eyebrows. I didn't know what Lexie's taste in men had been like, but there was no question, this guy was attractive.

Then he saw me. His eyes widened and he gave me a stare that almost slammed me back in my seat. The intensity of it: this could have been hatred, love, fury, terror, all of them at once, but it wasn't Bannon's narky little sneer, nothing like it. There was passion there, bright and roaring like an alarm flare.

"What do you think?" Sam asked, watching Naylor stride across the road towards a muddy '89 Ford that was worth maybe fifty quid in scrap metal, on a good day.

What I thought, mainly, was that I was pretty sure where that prickle at the back of my neck had been coming from. "Unless McArdle's very good at faking on his feet," I said, "I think you can move him to the bottom of the list. I'd bet money he didn't have a clue who I was—and even if your vandal's not our guy, he's been paying a lot of attention to the house. He'd know my face."

"Like Bannon and Naylor did," said Sam. "And they weren't one bit pleased to see you."

"They're from Glenskehy," Byrne said gloomily, behind us. "They're never pleased to see anyone, sure. And no one's ever pleased to see them."

"I'm starving," Sam said. "Come for lunch?"

I shook my head. "I can't. Rafe's already texted me, wanting to know if everything's OK. I told him I was still in the waiting room, but if I don't get into college soon, they're going to head down to Wicklow Hospital looking for me."

Sam took a breath, straightened his shoulders. "Right," he said. "We've knocked one out of the running, anyway; only two to go. I'll give you a lift into town."

Nobody asked, when I got into the library; the others nodded at me like I'd been out on a smoke break. My snit fit at Justin, the night before, had made its point.

He was still sulking at me. I ignored it all afternoon: the silent treatment makes me tense as hell, but Lexie's stubbornness would never have cracked, just her attention span. I finally snapped over dinner—stew, so thick that it barely counted as a liquid; the whole house smelled wonderful, rich and warm. "Is there enough for seconds?" I asked Justin.

He shrugged, not looking at me. "Drama queen," Rafe said, under his breath.

"*Justin,*" I said. "Are you still mad because I was a snotty cow last night?"

Another shrug. Abby, who had been reaching to pass me the stew pot, put it down.

"I was *scared,* Justin. I was worried I'd go in there today and the doctors would say there was something wrong and I'd need another operation or something." I saw him glance up, a quick anxious flick, before he went back to turning his bread into little pellets. "I couldn't handle you being scared as well. I'm really, really sorry. Forgive me?"

"Well," he said after a moment, with a tiny half smile. "I suppose so." He leaned over to put the stew pot beside my plate. "Now. Finish that off."

"And what did the doctors say?" Daniel asked. "You don't need more surgery, do you?"

"Nah," I said, ladling stew. "Just more antibiotics. It hasn't healed up all the way; they're scared I could still get an infection." Saying it out loud sent a twist through me, somewhere under the mike.

"Did they run tests? Do scans?"

I had no idea what doctors would have done. "I'm fine," I said. "Can we not talk about it?"

"Good girl," Justin said, nodding at my plate. "Does this mean we can use onions more than once a year, now?"

I got a horrible dropping feeling in my stomach. I gave Justin a blank look.

"Well, if you want more," he said primly, "then they don't make you gag after all, do they?"

Fuckfuckfuck. I'll eat just about anything; it hadn't occurred to me that Lexie might have food quirks, and it wasn't exactly something Frank could have found out in casual conversation. Daniel had lowered his spoon and was looking at me. "I didn't even taste them," I said. "I think the antibiotics are doing something weird to my mouth. Everything tastes the same."

"I thought it was the texture you didn't like," Daniel said.

Fuck. "It's the *thought* of them. Now that I know they're in there—"

"That happened to my granny," Abby said. "She was on antibiotics and she lost her sense of smell. Never came back. You should talk to the doctor about that."

"God, no," said Rafe. "If we've found something that makes her stop bitching about onions, I vote we let nature take its course. Are you having the rest of that, or can I?"

"I don't want to lose my sense of taste and eat onions," I said. "I'd rather get an infection."

"Good. Then pass it over here."

Daniel had gone back to his food. I prodded dubiously at mine; Rafe rolled his eyes. My heart was going ninety. *Sooner or later,* I thought, *I am going to make a mistake that I can't talk my way out of.*

"Nice save on the onions," Frank said, that night. "And when it comes time to pull you out, you've got it all set up and ready to go: the antibiotics were messing with your sense of taste, you quit taking them, and hey presto, you got an infection. I wish I'd thought of it myself."

I was up my tree, bundled in the communal jacket—it was a cloudy night, fine drizzle spattering the leaves, threatening to turn into full-on rain any minute—and keeping a very sharp ear out for John Naylor. "You heard that? Don't you ever go home?"

"Not much, these days. Plenty of time to sleep once we've got our man. Speaking of which, my weekend with Holly's coming up, so if we could start winding this up, I'd be a very happy camper."

"Me too," I said, "believe me."

"Yeah? I got the feeling you were starting to settle in very nicely."

I couldn't read his voice; no one does neutral like Frank. "It could be a lot worse, sure," I said carefully. "But tonight was a wake-up call. I can't keep this up forever. Anything useful on your end?"

"No luck on what sent May-Ruth running. Chad and her buddies can't remember anything unusual happening that week. But they might not anyway; it's been four and a half years."

This came as no surprise. "Oh, well," I said. "Worth a shot."

"Here's something that came up, though," Frank said. "Probably nothing to do with our case, but it's odd, and anything odd is worth thinking about, at this stage. Just on the surface, what kind of person did Lexie come across as, to you?"

I shrugged, even though he couldn't see me. There was something squirmy about this, too intimate, like being asked to describe myself. "I don't know. Bouncy, I guess. Cheerful. Confident. Lots of energy. A little childish, maybe."

"Yeah. Same here. That's what we got off the video clips, and that's what we got off all her mates. But that's not what my FBI boy's getting from May-Ruth's pals."

Something cold rippled through my stomach. I tucked my feet up higher into the branches and started chewing my knuckle.

"They're describing a shy kid, very quiet. Chad thought that had to do with her being from some nowhere town in the Appalachians; he said Raleigh was a huge adventure to her, she loved it but she was a little overwhelmed by it all. She was gentle, a daydreamer, loved animals, was thinking of maybe becoming a vet's assistant. Now tell me this: does that sound anything like our Lexie to you?"

I ran my hand through my hair and wished I were on solid ground; I needed to move. "So you're saying what? You think we're dealing with two different girls who both happen to look like me? Because I have to tell you, Frank, I've pretty much hit my limit for coincidences on this case." I had this insane vision of more and more doubles popping out of the woodwork, matching mes vanishing and reappearing all over the world like a huge Whack-a-Mole game, a me in every port. *This is what I get for wanting a sister when I was little,* I thought wildly, biting back a hysterical giggle, *be careful what you wish for—*

Frank laughed. "Nah. You know I love you, babe, but two of you are enough for me. Plus our girl's prints matched May-Ruth's. I'm just saying it's odd. I know people who've dealt with identity-swappers—protected witnesses, adult runaways like our girl—and they all say the same thing: these people were the same afterwards as they were before. It's one thing getting a new name and a new life; it's a whole other thing getting a new personality. Even for a trained undercover, it's a constant strain. You know what it was like, having to be Lexie Madison twenty-four seven—what it's like now, sure. It's not easy."

"I'm doing OK," I said. I had that wild urge to laugh again. This girl, whoever the hell she was, would have made a fantastic undercover. Maybe we should have swapped lives earlier.

"You are, of course," Frank said smoothly. "But so was

our girl, and that's worth looking into. Maybe she was just naturally gifted, but maybe she had training, somewhere— as an undercover, or as an actor. I'm putting out feelers; you have a little think and see if you've noticed any indicators that point in one direction or another. That sound like a plan?"

"Yeah," I said, slowly leaning back against the tree trunk. "Good thinking."

I didn't feel like laughing any more. That first afternoon in Frank's office had just flashed across my mind, so vivid that for an instant I smelled dust and leather and whiskeyed coffee, and for the first time I wondered if I had completely missed what was happening in that little sunlit room; if I had bounced blithely, unconsciously, past the most crucial moment of all. Here I had always believed the test had come in the first few minutes, with that couple on the street or when Frank asked me if I was afraid. It had never occurred to me that those were only the outer gates and that the real challenge had come much later, when I thought I was already safe inside; that the secret handshake I had given, without even realizing it, might have been the ease with which I helped come up with Lexie Madison.

"Does Chad know?" I asked suddenly, when Frank was about to hang up. "About May-Ruth not being May-Ruth?"

"Yep," Frank said cheerfully. "He does. I left him his illusions as long as I could, but this week I had my boy tell him. I needed to know if he was holding something back, out of loyalty or whatever. Apparently he wasn't."

The poor bastard. "How'd he take it?"

"He'll survive," Frank said. "I'll talk to you tomorrow." And he hung up. I sat in my tree, making patterns in the bark with my fingernail, for a long time.

I was starting to wonder if I'd been underestimating, not the killer, but the victim. I didn't want to think this, I'd been flinching off it, but I knew: there had been some- thing wrong with Lexie, way deep down. The flint of her, the way she had left Chad behind without a word and laughed while she got ready to leave Whitethorn House, like an animal biting off its own trapped paw with one snap and no whimper; that could have been just desperation. I understood that, all the way. But this, the seamlessness of that switch from sweet shy May-Ruth to bubbly clown Lexie: that had been something else, something wrong. No kind of fear or desperation could have demanded that. She had done it because she wanted to. A girl with that much hidden and that much dark could have sparked a very high caliber of anger in someone.

It's not easy, Frank had said. But that was the thing: for me, it always had been. Both times, being Lexie Madison had come as natural to me as breathing. I had slid into her like sliding into comfy old jeans, and this was what had scared me, all along.

It wasn't until I was getting into bed, that night, that I remembered: that day on the grass, when something had clicked into place and I had seen the five of them as a family, Lexie as the cheeky late-baby sister. Lexie's mind had gone along the same track as mine had, only a million times faster. She had taken one look and seen what they were and what they were missing, and fast as a blink she had made herself into that.

13

I had known, from the moment Sam said he was planning chats with his three potential vandals, that there would be consequences. If Mr. Baby-killers was in there, he wouldn't be one bit happy about being questioned by the cops, he would blame the whole thing on us, and there wasn't a chance in hell he would let it lie. What I missed was how fast the strike would come, and how straight. I felt so safe in that house, I had forgotten that that in itself should have been my warning.

It took him just one day. We were in the sitting room, Saturday night, not long before midnight. Abby and I had been doing our nails with Lexie's silver nail polish, sitting on the hearth rug, and were waving them around to dry them; Rafe and Daniel were balancing out the estrogen surge by cleaning Uncle Simon's Webley. It had been soaking in a casserole dish of solvent for two days, out on the patio, and Rafe had decided it was good to go. He and Daniel had turned the table into their armory zone—tool kit, kitchen towels, rags—and were happily cleaning the gun with old toothbrushes: Daniel was going at the crust of dirt on the grips, while Rafe tackled the actual gun. Justin was stretched out on the sofa, muttering at his thesis notes and eating cold popcorn out of a bowl beside him. Someone had put Purcell on the record player, a peaceful overture in a minor key. The room smelled of solvent and rust, a tough, reassuring, familiar smell.

"You know," Rafe said, putting down his toothbrush and examining the gun, "I think it's actually in pretty good shape, under all the crap. There's a decent chance it'll work." He reached across the table for the ammo box, slid a couple of bullets into place and clicked the cylinder home. "Russian roulette, anyone?"

"Don't," said Justin, with a shudder. "That's horrible."

"Here," Daniel said, holding his hand out for the gun. "Don't play with it."

"I'm *joking*, for God's sake," Rafe said, passing it across. "I'm just checking that everything works. Tomorrow morning I'll take it out on the patio and get us a rabbit for dinner."

"No," I said, snapping upright and glaring at him. "I *like* the rabbits. Leave them alone."

"Why? All they do is make more rabbits and shite all over the lawn. The little bastards would be a lot more use in a lovely fricassee, or a nice tasty stew—"

"You're disgusting. Didn't you ever see *Watership Down*?"

"You can't stick your fingers in your ears or you'll ruin your manicure. I could cook you a bunny *au vin* that would—"

"You're going to hell, you know that?"

"Oh, chill out, Lex, it's not like he'll do it," said Abby, blowing on a thumbnail. "The rabbits come out around dawn. At dawn, Rafe doesn't even count as *alive*."

"I don't see anything disgusting about shooting animals," Daniel said, carefully breaking the gun open, "provided you eat what you kill. We're predators, after all. In an ideal world, I'd love us to be completely self-sufficient— living off what we could grow and hunt, dependent on no one. In reality, of course, that's unlikely to happen, and in any case I wouldn't want to start with the rabbits. I've become fond of them. They go with the house."

"See?" I said to Rafe.

"See what? Stop being such a baby. How many times have I seen you stuff your face with steak, or—"

I was on my feet and into a shooter's brace, my hand grabbing at where my gun should have been, before I understood that I had heard a crash. There was a big jagged rock sitting on the hearth rug beside me and Abby, as if it had been there all along, surrounded by bright flecks of glass like ice crystals. Abby's mouth was open in a startled little O and a wide cold wind swept in through the broken window, swelling the curtains.

Then Rafe sprang out of his chair and threw himself towards the kitchen. I was half a pace behind him, with Justin's panicky wail—"Lexie, your stitches!"—in my ears. Somewhere Daniel was calling something, but I swung through the French doors after Rafe and as he leaped off the patio, hair flying, I heard the gate clang at the bottom of the garden.

The gate was still swinging crazily when we flung ourselves through it. In the lane Rafe froze, head up, one hand going back to clamp around my wrist: "Shhh."

We listened, not breathing. I felt something loom up behind me and spun round, but it was Daniel, swift and silent as a big cat on the grass.

Wind in leaves; then off to our right, towards Glenskehy and not far away, the tiny crack of a twig.

The last of the light from the house vanished behind us and we were flying down the lane in darkness, leaves whipping under my fingers as I reached out a hand to the hedge to guide myself, a sudden burst of running feet up ahead and a harsh triumphant shout from Rafe beside me. They were fast, Rafe and Daniel, faster than I would have believed. Our breathing savage as a hunting pack's in my ears, the hard beat of our feet and my pulse like war drums speeding me on; the moon waxed and waned as clouds skimmed past and I caught a glimpse of something black, only twenty or thirty yards ahead of us, hunched and grotesque in the strange white light and running hard. For a flash I saw Frank leaning over his desk, hands pressing his headphones on tighter, and I thought at him hard as a punch *Don't you dare, don't you dare send in your goons, this is ours.*

We swung round a kink in the lane, grabbing at the hedge for balance, and skidded to a stop at a crossroads. In the moonlight the little lanes stretched out in every direction, bare and equivocal, giving away nothing; piles of stones huddled in the fields like spellbound watchers.

"Where's he gone?" Rafe's voice was a cracking whisper; he whirled around, casting about like a hunting dog. "Where's the bastard gone?"

"He can't have got out of sight this fast," Daniel murmured. "He's nearby. He's gone to ground."

"*Shit!*" Rafe hissed. "*Shit,* that little *fuck,* that vile little—God, I'll *kill* him—"

The moon was slipping away again; the guys were barely shadows on either side of me, and fading fast. "Torch?" I whispered, stretching to get my mouth close by Daniel's ear, and saw the quick shake of his head against the sky.

Whoever this man was, he knew the hillsides like he knew his own hands. He could hide here all night if he wanted to, slip from cover to cover the way centuries of his rebel ancestors had done before him, nothing but narrow eyes watching among the leaves and then gone.

But he was cracking. That rock through the window straight at us, when he had to know we would come after him: his control was slipping, eroding to dust under Sam's questioning and the constant hard rub of his own rage. He could hide forever if he wanted to, but that right there was the catch: he didn't want to, not really.

Every detective, in all the world, knows that this is our best weapon: your heart's desire. Now that thumbscrews and red-hot pincers are off the menu, there's no way we can force anyone to confess to murder, lead us to the body, give up a loved one or rat out a crime lord, but still people do it all the time. They do it because there's something they want more than safety: a clear conscience, a chance to brag, an end to the tension, a fresh start, you name it and we'll find it. If we can just figure out what you want—secretly, hidden so deep you may never have glimpsed it yourself—and dangle it in front of you, you'll give us anything we ask for in exchange.

This guy was fed up to the back teeth of hiding on his own territory, skulking about with spray paint and rocks like a bratty teenager looking for attention. What he really wanted was a chance to kick some ass.

"Oh my God, he's *hiding*," I said, light and clear and amused into the wide waiting night, in my best snobby city-girl accent. Both of the guys grabbed me at the same time, but I grabbed them back and pinched, hard. "How pathetic is that? Such a big tough guy at a distance, but the second we get up close and personal, he's under some hedge shaking like a scared little bunny."

Daniel's hand loosened on my arm and I heard him exhale, a tiny ghost of a laugh—he was barely even panting. "And why not?" he said. "He may not have the guts to stand and fight, but at least he has enough intelligence to know when he's out of his depth."

I squeezed whatever bit of Rafe was nearest—if anything could flush this guy out of cover, it would be that lazy English sneer—and heard his fast, savage catch of breath as the penny dropped. "I doubt there's any intelligence involved," he drawled. "Too much sheep in the bloodline. He's probably forgotten all about us and wandered off to rejoin the flock."

A rustle, too faint and too quickly cut off to pinpoint; then nothing.

"Here, kitty," I crooned. "Here, kitty, kitty, kitty . . ." and let it trail off into a giggle.

"In my great-grandfather's day," Daniel said coolly, "we knew how to deal with peasants who got above themselves. A touch of the horsewhip, and they learned their place."

"Where your great-grandfather went wrong was letting them spawn at will," Rafe told him. "You're supposed to keep their breeding under control, the way you would with any other farm animal."

That rustle again, louder; then a tiny, distinct click, like one pebble hitting another, very close by.

"We had uses for them," Daniel said. His voice had a vague, abstracted note, the same note it got when he was concentrating on a book and someone asked him a question.

"Well, yes," Rafe said, "but look what you ended up

with. Reverse evolution. The shallow end of the gene pool. Hordes of drooling, half-witted, neckless, inbred—"

Something exploded out of the hedge, only a few yards away, shot past me so close that I felt the wind on my arms, and crashed into Rafe like a cannonball. He went down with a grunt and a hideous thud that shook the ground. For a split second I heard scuffling noises, wild rasping breath, the nasty smack of a fist hitting home; then I dived in.

We went over in a tangled heap, hard earth under my shoulder, Rafe gasping for air, someone's hair in my mouth and an arm twisting like steel cable out of my grip. The guy smelled like wet leaves and he was strong and he fought dirty, fingers groping for my eyes, feet jackknifing up and scrabbling to dig into my stomach. I hit out, heard a burst of breath and felt his hand fall away from my face. Then something slammed into us from the side, hard as a freight train: Daniel.

The weight of him sent all four of us rolling into bushes, branches clawing at my neck, breath hot on my cheek and somewhere the fast merciless rhythm of blows connecting with something soft, over and over. It was a vicious, nasty, messy fight, arms and legs everywhere, bony things jabbing, horrible muffled sounds like feral dogs worrying at a kill. It was three to one and we were every bit as furious as he was, but the dark gave this guy one advantage. We had no way of knowing who we were aiming at; he didn't have to care, any blow that hit home was a good one. And he was using it, slippery and corkscrewing, tumbling the heap of us over and over on the ground, no way to get our bearings, I was dizzy and breathless and hitting frantically into thin air. A body thumped onto me and I lashed backwards with my elbow, heard a bark of pain that could have come from Rafe.

Then those fingers went for my eyes again. I felt out, found a rough-stubbled jaw, got an arm free and punched with my whole body behind it. Something smashed into my ribs, hard, but it didn't hurt; nothing hurt, this guy could have ripped me wide open and I would never have felt it, all I wanted was to hit him and keep on hitting. A small cool voice far at the back of my head warned, *You could kill him, the three of you could kill him like this,* but I didn't care. My chest was a great burst of blinding white and I saw the final reckless arch of Lexie's throat, I saw the sweet glow of the sitting room defiled with that jagged spray of glass, I saw Rob's face cold and shuttered and I could have kept on punching forever, I wanted this guy's blood filling my mouth, I wanted to feel his face explode into pulp and splinters under my fist and just keep going.

He twisted like a cat and my knuckles hit dirt and rock, I couldn't find him. I grabbed in the dark, caught someone's shirt and heard it rip as he shouldered me away. There was a desperate, heaving scramble, pebbles flying; a dull sick thud like a boot hitting flesh, a furious animal snarl; then running footsteps, fast and irregular, fading.

"Where—" Someone got a fistful of my hair; I beat the arm away and felt wildly for that face, that rough battered jawline, found cloth and hot skin and then nothing. "Get *off*—" A grunt of effort, a weight coming off my back; then, sudden and sharp as an explosion, silence.

"Where—"

The moon came out from behind the clouds and we stared at each other: wild-eyed, dirty, panting. For a second I barely recognized the others. Rafe scrambling to his feet with his teeth bared and blood shining dark under his nose, Daniel's hair falling in his face and streaks of mud or blood like war paint across his cheeks: their eyes were black holes in the tricky white light and they looked like lethal strangers, ghost warriors from the last stand of some lost and savage tribe. "Where is he?" Rafe whispered, a low dangerous breath.

Nothing moved; just a coy little breeze flirting through the hawthorn. Daniel and Rafe were crouched like fighters, hands half curled and ready, and I realized I was too. In that moment I think we could have attacked each other.

Then the moon went in again. Something seemed to leach out of the air, some thrumming too high to hear. All of a sudden my muscles felt like they were turning to water, draining away into the earth; if I hadn't grabbed a handful of hedge I would have fallen over. There was a long ragged breath, like a sob, from one of the guys.

Footsteps pounded up the lane behind us—we all jumped—and skidded to a stop a few feet away. "Daniel?" Justin whispered, breathless and nervous. "Lexie?"

"We're over here," I said. I was shaking all over, violently as a seizure; my heart was clattering so high in my throat that for a second I thought I was going to throw up. Somewhere beside me, Rafe retched, doubled over coughing and then spat: "Dirt everywhere—"

"Oh my God. Are you all right? What happened? Did you get him?"

"We caught him," Daniel said, on a deep hard gasp, "but none of us could see a thing, and he got away in the confusion. There's no point in going after him; by now he's halfway to Glenskehy."

"God. Did he hurt you? Lexie! Are your stitches—"

Justin was on the verge of panicking. "I'm totally fine," I said, good and loud to make sure the mike could hear me. My ribs were starting to hurt like hell, but I couldn't risk anyone wanting to look. "Just my hands are killing me. I got a few punches in."

"I think one of them hit me, you little cow," Rafe said. His voice had a giddy, light-headed note. "I hope your hand swells up and turns blue."

"I'll hit you again if you're not careful," I told him. I felt along my ribs: my hand was trembling so hard I couldn't be sure, but I didn't think anything was broken. "Justin, you should've heard Daniel. He was brilliant."

"Oh, Jesus, yes," said Rafe, starting to laugh. "A touch of the *horsewhip*? Where the hell did that come from?"

"Horsewhip?" Justin asked wildly. "What horsewhip? Who had a horsewhip?"

Rafe and I were both laughing too hard to answer. "Oh, God," I managed. "'In my *great-grandfather's* day . . .'"

"'When the peasants knew their place . . .'"

"*What peasants?* What are you *talking* about?"

"It all made perfect sense at the time," said Daniel. "Where's Abby?"

"She stayed at the gate, in case he came back and—Oh God, you don't think he did, do you?"

"I doubt it very much," Daniel said. There was the edge of a laugh ready to burst through his voice, too. Adrenaline: we were all crackling with it. "I think he's had enough for one night. Is everyone all right?"

"No thanks to Little Miss Spitfire," said Rafe, trying to pull my hair and getting me in the ear instead.

"I'm fine," I said, batting Rafe's hand away. Justin, in the background, was still murmuring, "Oh my God, oh my God . . ."

"Good," Daniel said. "Then let's go home."

There was no sign of Abby at the back gate; nothing but the hawthorn trees shivering and the lazy, haunted creak of the gate in that small cool breeze. Justin was starting to hyperventilate when Daniel called into the darkness, "Abby, it's us," and she materialized out of the shadows, a white oval and a swish of skirt and a streak of bronze. She was holding the poker, in both hands.

"Did you get him?" she whispered, a low fierce hiss. "Did you get him?"

"My God, I'm surrounded by warrior women," Rafe said. "Remind me never to piss you two off." His voice sounded muffled, as if he was holding his nose.

"Joan of Arc and Boadicea," Daniel said, smiling; I felt his hand rest on my shoulder for a second and saw the other one stretch out to Abby's hair. "Fighting to defend their home. We got him; only temporarily, but I think we made our point clear."

"I wanted to bring him back and have him stuffed and mounted over the fireplace," I said, trying to dust muck off my jeans with my wrists, "but he got away."

"The little *fucker*," said Abby. She blew out a long, hard breath and lowered the poker. "I was actually hoping he'd come back."

"Let's get inside," said Justin, glancing over his shoulder.

"What did he throw, anyway?" Rafe wanted to know. "I didn't even look."

"A rock," said Abby. "And there's something taped to it."

"Oh, sweet Jesus in heaven," Justin said, horrified, the second we got into the kitchen. "*Look* at the state of you three."

"Wow," said Abby, eyebrows going up. "I'm impressed. I'd love to see the one that got away."

We looked just about as bad as I'd expected: shaking and skittery-eyed, covered in dirt and scrapes, great dramatic smears of blood in weird places. Daniel was leaning heavily on one leg and his shirt was ripped half off, a sleeve hanging loose. One knee was torn out of Rafe's trousers, I could see glossy red through the hole, and he was going to have a beauty of a shiner in the morning.

"Those *cuts*," said Justin. "They'll have to be disinfected; God only knows what you'd pick up from those lanes. The dirt of them, cows and sheep and all manner of—"

"In a minute," Daniel said, pushing his hair out of his eyes. He came up holding a twig, gave it a bemused look and laid it carefully on the kitchen counter. "Before we start on anything else, I think we need to see what's on that rock."

It was a folded piece of paper, the lined kind, torn out of a kid's school notebook. "Wait," Daniel said—Rafe and I had both moved forwards. He found two pens on the table, picked his way delicately through the broken glass to the rock, and used the pens to pull the paper free.

"Now," Justin said briskly, bustling in with a bowl of

water in one hand and a cloth in the other, "let's see the damage. Ladies first. Lexie, you said your hands?"

"Hang on," I said. Daniel had carried the piece of paper over to the table and was unfolding it carefully, still using the butts of the pens.

"Oh," Justin said. "Oh."

We moved in around Daniel, shoulder to shoulder. His face was bleeding—either a fist or the rim of his glasses had split his cheekbone open—but he didn't seem to have noticed.

The note was printed in furious block capitals, so hard that in places the pen had dug right through the paper. WE WILL BURN YOU OUT.

There was a second of absolute silence.

"Oh my God," Rafe said. He collapsed backwards onto the sofa and burst out laughing. "Brilliant. Actual torch-bearing villagers. How cool is that?"

Justin clicked his tongue disapprovingly. "Foolishness," he said. All his composure had come back now that he was in the house, with the four of us safely around him and something useful to do. "Lexie, your hands."

I held them out to him. They were a mess, covered with dirt and blood, knuckles split open and half my nails broken down to the quick—so much for my pretty silver manicure. Justin drew in his breath with a little hiss. "Good heavens, what did you *do* to the poor man? Not that he didn't deserve it. Come here, where I can see." He steered me into Abby's armchair, under the pole lamp, and knelt on the floor beside me. The bowl gave off a cloud of steam and disinfectant, a warm reassuring smell.

"Do we call the cops?" Abby asked Daniel.

"God, no," said Rafe, dabbing at his nose and checking his fingers for blood. "Are you mad? They'll just give us the same old spiel: 'Thanks for reporting it, there's not a chance in hell we'll ever catch the *perpetrator,* get a dog, bye.' This time they might even arrest *us*—one look and you can tell we've been in a fight. You think Laurel and Hardy will care who started it? Justin, can I have that cloth for a second?"

"In a minute." Justin was pressing the damp cloth against my knuckles, so gently I could barely feel it. "Does that sting?" I shook my head.

"I'll bleed on the sofa," Rafe threatened.

"You will not. Tip your head back and wait."

"Actually," Daniel said, still frowning thoughtfully at the note, "I think calling the police might not be a bad idea, at this point."

Rafe sat up fast, forgetting all about his nose. "Daniel. Are you serious? They're petrified of those apes down in the village. They'd do anything to get on Glenskehy's good side, and arresting us for assault would definitely do that."

"Well, I wasn't thinking of the local police," Daniel said. "Hardly. I meant Mackey or O'Neill—I'm not sure which would be better. What do you think?" he asked Abby.

"Daniel," Justin said. His hand had stopped moving on mine and that high, panicky note was seeping back into his voice. "Don't. I don't want—They've been leaving us alone, since Lexie got back—"

Daniel gave Justin a long, inquisitive look over his glasses. "They have, yes," he said. "But I seriously doubt that means they've dropped the investigation. I'm sure they're putting a considerable amount of energy into looking for a suspect, I think they would be very interested to hear about this one, and I think we have an obligation to tell them, whether it's convenient for us or not."

"I just want to go back to *normal*." Justin's voice was almost a wail.

"Yes, well, so do we all," Daniel said, a little testily. He winced, kneaded at his thigh muscle, winced again. "And the sooner all this is over and someone's charged, the sooner we can do exactly that. I'm sure Lexie, for example, would feel a lot better if this man were in custody. Wouldn't you, Lex?"

"Fuck custody, I'd feel a lot better if the little bastard hadn't got away so fast," I said. "I was having fun." Rafe grinned and leaned over to high-five my free hand.

"Regardless of the Lexie thing," Abby said, "this is a

threat. I don't know about you, Justin, but I don't particularly want to be burned out."

"Oh, for God's sake, he won't *do* it," Rafe said. "Arson takes a certain level of organizational ability. He'd blow himself up long before he got anywhere near us."

"You want to bet the house on that?"

The mood in the room had turned. The tight-knit, giddy exhilaration was gone, evaporated with a vicious sizzle like water hitting a hot stove; no one was having fun any more.

"I'd rather bet on this guy's stupidity than on the cops' brainpower. We need them like we need a hole in the head. If the moron comes back—and he *won't*, not after tonight— we sort him out ourselves."

"Because so far," Abby said tautly, "we've been doing such a brilliant job of dealing with our own problems by ourselves." She whipped the popcorn bowl off the floor with a tight, angry movement and squatted down to collect the glass.

"No, leave it; the police will want to see it all in situ," Daniel said, dropping heavily into an armchair. "Ouch." He grimaced, fished Uncle Simon's revolver out of his back pocket and put it on the coffee table.

Justin's hand froze in midair. Abby, straightening up fast, almost fell backwards.

If it had been anyone else I wouldn't have batted an eyelid. But Daniel: something cold as seawater surged over my whole body, whipped the breath out of me. It was like seeing your father drunk or your mother in hysterics: that freefall in your stomach, cables snapping as the elevator gets ready to plummet hundreds of sheer stories, unstoppable, already gone.

"You cannot be *serious*," Rafe said. He was on the edge of another fit of laughter.

"What the hell," Abby inquired, very quietly, "did you think you were going to do with that?"

"Really," Daniel said, giving the gun a faintly puzzled glance, "I'm not sure. I picked it up purely by instinct. Once we were out there, of course, it was much too dark and too chaotic to do anything sensible with it at all. It would have been dangerous."

"Heaven forbid," said Rafe.

"Would you have *used* it?" Abby demanded. She was staring at Daniel, her eyes huge, and holding the bowl like she was going to throw it.

"I'm not sure," Daniel said. "I had some vague idea of threatening him with it to prevent him from escaping, but I suppose one never really knows what one is capable of until the situation presents itself."

That click, in the dark lane.

"Oh God," Justin whispered, a tremulous breath. "What a mess."

"Not nearly as much of a mess as it could've been," Rafe pointed out cheerfully. "Blood-and-guts-wise, that is." He pulled off one of his shoes and shook a trickle of dirt and pebbles onto the floor. Not even Justin looked.

"Shut up," Abby snapped. "You shut up. This isn't a fucking joke. This is getting way out of hand. Daniel—"

"It's all right, Abby," Daniel said. "Really. Everything's under control."

Rafe collapsed back on the sofa and started to laugh again. There was a spiky, brittle edge to it, too near hysteria. "And you say this isn't a fucking joke?" he asked Abby. "Under *control*. Is that really the phrase you want, Daniel? Would you really, really say that this situation is under control?"

"I already have," Daniel said. His eyes on Rafe were watchful and very cold.

Abby slammed the bowl down on the table, popcorn scattering. "That's bollocks. Rafe's being a prick but he's right, Daniel. This is not under control any more. Someone could have got *killed*. The three of you running around in the dark chasing some psycho arsonist—"

"And when we got back," Daniel pointed out, "you were holding the poker."

"That's not the same thing at *all*. That was in case he came back; I didn't go *looking* for trouble. And what if he had managed to get that thing off you? Then what?"

Any second now someone was going to say the word "gun." As soon as Frank or Sam found out that Uncle Simon's revolver had evolved from a quaint little heirloom into Daniel's weapon of choice, we were into a whole new zone, one involving an Emergency Response Unit team on standby with bulletproof vests and rifles. The thought made my stomach twist. "Doesn't anyone want to hear what I think?" I demanded, thumping the arm of my chair.

Abby whipped around and stared at me as if she had forgotten I was there. "Why not," she said heavily, after a moment. "God." She dropped down on the floor, among the shards of glass, and clasped her hands around the back of her neck.

"I think we definitely tell the cops," I said. "This time they might actually get the guy. Before, they never had anything to go on, but now all they'll have to do is find the one who looks like he's been through a meat grinder."

"In this place," Rafe said, "that might not narrow it down very much."

"Excellent point," Daniel told me. "I hadn't thought of that. It would also be useful in a preemptive capacity, in case this man decides to accuse us of assault—which I think is unlikely, but you never know. So we're agreed? There's not really much point in dragging the detectives out here at this hour, but we call them in the morning?"

Justin had gone back to cleaning my hand, but his face was drawn and closed. "Anything to get this over with," he said tightly.

"I think you're bloody insane," Rafe said, "but then, I've thought that for a while now. And anyway, it doesn't really matter what I think, does it? You're going to do exactly what you want to, either way."

Daniel ignored that. "Mackey or O'Neill?"

"Mackey," Abby said, without looking up from the floor.

"Interesting," Daniel said, finding his cigarettes. "My first instinct would have been O'Neill, especially as he's the one who seems to have been exploring our relationship with Glenskehy, but you may be right. Does anyone have a light?"

"Can I make a suggestion?" Rafe asked sweetly. "When we're having our little chats with your cop friends, it might be an idea to leave that out." He nodded at the gun.

"Well, of course," said Daniel absently. He was still looking around for a lighter; I found Abby's, on the table beside me, and threw it to him. "It doesn't actually come into the story at all, anyway; there's no reason to mention it. I'll put it away."

"You do that," Abby said tonelessly, to the floor. "And then we can all just pretend it never happened."

Nobody answered. Justin finished cleaning my hands and wrapped Band-Aids around the split knuckles, carefully aligning the edges. Rafe swung his legs off the sofa, went into the kitchen and came back with a handful of wet paper towels, gave his nose a perfunctory scrub and tossed the towels into the fireplace. Abby didn't move. Daniel smoked meditatively, blood drying on his cheek and his eyes focused on something in the middle distance.

The wind picked up, swirled in the eaves and sent a high wail down the chimney, banked around and came rushing through the sitting room like a long cold ghost train. Daniel put out his cigarette, went upstairs—footsteps overhead, a long scraping noise, a thump—and came back with a scarred, jagged-edged piece of wood, maybe part of an old headboard. Abby held it for him while he hammered it into place over the broken window, the hammer blows echoing harshly through the house and outwards into the night.

14

Frank got there fast, the next morning; I got the feeling he'd been waiting by the phone with his car keys in his hand since dawn, ready to leap into action the second we made the call. He brought Doherty with him, to sit in the kitchen and make sure no one eavesdropped while Frank took our statements, one by one, in the sitting room. Doherty looked fascinated; he couldn't stop gawping, at the high ceilings, the patches of half-stripped wallpaper, the four of them in their spotless old-fashioned clothes, me. He shouldn't even have been there. This was Sam's line of investigation, plus Sam would have been out to the house like a shot if he'd had any idea that I'd been in a fight. Frank hadn't told him. I was very glad I wasn't going to be in the incident room when this one came out.

The others did beautifully. Their polished façade had gone up as soon as we heard tires on the drive, but it was a subtly different version from the one they used in college: less chilly, more engaging, a perfect balance between shocked victims and courteous hosts. Abby poured the tea and set out a carefully arranged plate of biscuits, Daniel brought an extra chair into the kitchen for Doherty; Rafe made self-deprecating jokes about his black eye. I was starting to get a taste of what the interviews must have been like, after Lexie died, and why they had driven Frank quite so far up the wall.

He started with me. "So," he said, when the sitting-room door shut behind us and the voices in the kitchen faded to a pleasant, muffled blur. "You got to see some action at last."

"And about time," I said. I was pulling up straight chairs to the card table, but Frank shook his head and dropped onto the sofa, waved me to an armchair.

"Nah, let's keep this cozy. You in one piece?"

"The nasty man's face ruined my manicure, but I'll survive." I fished in the pocket of my combats and pulled out a crumpled handful of notebook pages. "I wrote it up last night, in bed. Before anything could go fuzzy."

Frank sipped his tea and read, taking his time. "Good," he said finally, pocketing the pages. "That's nice and clear, or as clear as we're going to get with that kind of chaos." He put down his tea, found his own notebook and clicked his pen ready. "Could you ID the guy?"

I shook my head. "I didn't see his face. Too dark."

"It might've been an idea to bring a torch."

"There wasn't time. If I'd messed about looking for torches, he'd have been well gone. You don't need an ID, anyway. Just look for the guy with two black eyes."

"Ah," Frank said thoughtfully, nodding, "the fight. Of course. We'll get back to that in a minute. Just in case our boy claims he got his bruises falling downstairs, though, it would be useful to have some kind of corroborating description."

"I can only go on the feel of him," I said. "Assuming this was one of Sam's boys, Bannon's definitely out: he's way too chunky. This guy was wiry. Not very tall, but strong. I don't think it was McArdle, either; my hand came down straight on this guy's face at one stage, and I didn't feel any facial hair, just stubble. McArdle's beardy."

"That he is," Frank said, making a leisurely note. "That he is. So your vote goes to Naylor?"

"He'd fit. Right height, right build, right hair."

"That'll have to do. We take what we can get." He examined the page of his notebook thoughtfully, tapping his pen against his teeth. "Speaking of which," he said. "When you three went galloping off to fight for the cause, what did Danny Boy bring along?"

I was ready for this one. "Screwdriver," I said. "I didn't see him pick it up, but I left the room before he did. He had the tool kit out on the table."

"Because he and Rafe were cleaning Uncle Simon's gun. What kind of gun, by the way?"

"A Webley, early World War One issue. It's pretty beaten-up and rusty and all, but it's still a beauty. You'd love it."

"No doubt I would," Frank said amiably, making a little note. "With any luck I'll get a look at it, sometime. So Daniel's grabbing for a weapon in a big hurry, and there's a gun in front of him, but instead he goes for a screwdriver?"

"An unloaded, broken-open gun with the grips off. And I don't get the sense he knows his way around guns. Even if he didn't bother with the grips, it would've taken him a minute to sort it out." The sound of someone loading a revolver is unmistakable but small, and I had been across the room from Rafe when he did it; what with the music, there was a decent chance the mike hadn't picked it up.

"So he goes for the screwdriver instead," Frank said, nodding. "Makes sense. But for some reason, once he's got his man, it doesn't even occur to him to use it."

"He never got the chance. It was a mess out there, Frank: four of us rolling around on the ground, arms and legs everywhere, you couldn't tell what belonged to who—I'm pretty sure I gave Rafe that black eye. If Daniel had whipped out a screwdriver and started jabbing away, odds are he'd have got one of us." Frank was still nodding agreeably, writing all this down, but there was a bland, amused look on his face that I didn't like. "What? You'd rather he'd stabbed this guy?"

"It would certainly have made my life simpler," Frank said, cheerfully and cryptically. "So where was the famous— what was it again?—the famous screwdriver, during all the drama?"

"In Daniel's back pocket. At least, that's where he took it out of, when we got home."

Frank raised one eyebrow, all concern. "He's lucky he didn't stab himself with it. All that rolling around, I'd have expected at least a minor puncture wound or two."

He was right. I should have made it a wrench. "Maybe he did," I said, shrugging. "You can ask him to show you his arse, if you want."

"I think I'll pass, for now." Frank clicked his pen shut, tucked it away in his pocket and leaned back on the sofa, at ease. "What," he inquired pleasantly, "were you thinking?"

For a second I actually took it for a straight question about my thought process, instead of the opener for a major bollocking. I expected Sam to be pissed off at me, but Frank: he treats personal safety like a tetherball, he had begun this investigation by breaking every rule he could get his hands on, and I know for a fact that he once head-butted a dealer so hard that the guy had to be taken to the emergency room. It had never occurred to me that he might be in a snot about this. "This guy's escalated," I said. "He used to stay well away from people: he never did any damage to Simon March, last time he went out rock-throwing he picked a room that he could see was empty . . . This time, though, that rock missed me and Abby by inches—for all we know, he could actually have been aiming for one of us. These days he's more than willing to hurt people, not just property. He's looking more and more like a suspect."

"Of course," Frank said, crossing one ankle leisurely onto the other knee. "A suspect. The very thing we've been looking for. So let's think this through for a moment, will we? Let's say Sammy and I head down to Glenskehy today and pick up his three bright boys, and let's say, just for the hell of it, that we manage to get something useful out of one of them—enough for an arrest, maybe even a charge. What do you suggest I say when his solicitor and the Director of Public Prosecutions and the media ask me, and I think they will, why his face looks like hamburger? In the circumstances, I've got absolutely fuck-all choice except to explain that the damage was inflicted by two other suspects and one of my very own undercover officers. And what do you suppose happens next?"

I had never for a moment thought that far ahead. "You'll find a way round it."

"I may well," Frank said, in that same bland, pleasant voice, "but that's not really the point, is it? I guess what I'm asking is what exactly you went out there to do. It seems to me that, as a detective, your goal would have been to locate the suspect, identify him, and if possible either hold him or keep him under observation until you found a good way to get backup in there. Am I missing something?"

"Yeah, actually. You're missing the fact that it wasn't as simple as—"

"Because your actions suggest," Frank went on, as if I hadn't spoken, "that your main goal was to beat the living shite out of this guy. Which would have been just a tad unprofessional of you."

Out in the kitchen, Doherty said something shaped like a punchline and everyone laughed; the laughter was perfect, unforced and friendly, and it made me edgy as hell. "Oh, for fuck's sake, Frank," I said. "My goals were to keep hold of my suspect *and* not to blow my cover. How would you have liked me to do that? By dragging Daniel and Rafe off this guy and lecturing them on the correct treatment of suspects while I got on the phone to you?"

"You didn't have to throw punches of your own."

I shrugged. "Sam told me that last time Lexie went after this guy, she wanted to kick his nads into his esophagus. That's the kind of person she was. If I'd hung back and let the big brave boys protect me from the bad man, it would've looked dodgy as all hell. I didn't have time to consider the deeper implications here; I had to call it fast, and I called it in character. Are you seriously trying to claim you never got into a punch-up, when you were in the field?"

"Oh, God, no," Frank said easily. "Would I ever say such a thing? I've been in many a punch-up; I even won most of them, not to blow my own horn here. Here's the difference, though. I've got into fights because the other guy jumped me first—"

"Just like this guy jumped us."

"When you deliberately goaded him into it. You think I haven't heard that tape?"

"We'd *lost* him, Frank. If we hadn't made him break cover, he'd have got away clean as a whistle."

"Let me finish, babe. I've got into fights because the other guy started it, or because I couldn't get out of them without blowing my cover, or just to earn a little respect, bump up my place in the pecking order. But I can safely say that I've never got into a fight because I was so emotionally involved that I couldn't resist beating the holy crap out of someone. Not on the job, anyway. Can you say the same?"

Those wide blue eyes, amiable and mildly interested; that impeccable, disarming combo of openness and just a hint of steel. The edginess was building into a full-on danger signal, the electric warning animals get before thunder. Frank was questioning me the way he would question a suspect. I was one misstep away from being pulled off this case.

I forced myself to take my time: gave an embarrassed little shrug, shifted on the armchair. "It wasn't emotional involvement," I said at last, looking down at my fingers twisted in the fringe of a cushion. "Not like you mean, anyway. It's . . . Look, Frank, I know you were worried about my nerve, at the beginning of this. I don't blame you."

"What can I say," Frank said. He was slouching back and watching me with nothing at all on his face, but he was listening; I was still in with a chance. "People talk. The subject of Operation Vestal had come up, once or twice."

I grimaced. "I bet it had. And I bet I can guess what they said, too. Most people had me written off as a burnout before I'd even cleared out my desk. I know you took a chance sending me in here, Frank. I'm not sure how much you heard . . ."

"This and that."

"But you've got to know we fucked up royally, and there's someone on the streets right now who should be doing life." The hard catch in my voice: I didn't have to fake it. "And that sucks, Frank, it really does. I wasn't about to let that happen again, and I wasn't going to have you thinking I'd lost my nerve, because I *haven't*. I thought if I could just get this guy—"

Frank shot off the sofa like he'd been spring-loaded. "Get the—Jesus, Mary and Elvis, you're not here to *get* bloody *anyone*! What did I tell you, right from the beginning? The *one* thing you have to do is point me and O'Neill in the right direction, and we'll do the rest. What, was I not clear enough? Should I have fucking written it down for you? What?"

If it hadn't been for the others in the next room, the volume would have been through the roof—when Frank is mad, everyone knows all about it. I did a small quick flinch and got my head at an appropriately humble angle, but inside I was delighted: being bollocked out of it as a disobedient subordinate was a huge improvement on being batted around like a suspect. Getting overenthusiastic, needing to prove yourself after a bad slipup: those were things Frank could understand, things that happen all the time, and they're venial sins. "I'm sorry," I said. "Frank, I'm really sorry. I know I got carried away, and it won't happen again, but I couldn't stand the thought of blowing my cover and I couldn't stand the thought of you knowing I let him get away and Jesus, Frank, he was so close I could taste him . . ."

Frank stared at me for a long moment; then he sighed, collapsed back onto the sofa and cracked his neck. "Look," he said, "you brought another case with you onto this one. Everyone's done it. No one with half a brain does it twice. Sorry you caught a bad one, and all that, but if you want to prove something to me or anyone else, you'll do it by leaving your old cases at home and working this one properly."

He believed me. From the first minute of this case, Frank had had that other one hanging like a question mark in a corner of his mind; all I had needed to do was mirror it back to him at the right angle. For the first time ever, Operation Vestal, bless its sick dark heart, was actually coming in useful.

"I know," I said, looking down at my hands twisted together in my lap. "Believe me, I do."

"You could have blown this whole case, do you realize that?"

"Tell me I didn't fuck it up terminally," I said. "Are you going to pick the guy up anyway?"

Frank sighed. "Yeah, probably. We don't have much choice, at this point. It would be nice if you could join us for the interview—you might be able to contribute something good on the psychological front, and I think it could be useful to put our man face to face with Lexie and see what happens. Do you think you can manage to do that without leaping across the table and knocking his teeth in?"

I glanced up fast, but there was a wry grin at one corner of his mouth. "You've always been a funny guy," I said, hoping the wave of relief wouldn't leak into my voice. "I'll do my best. Get a big table, just in case."

"Your nerve is just fine, you know that?" Frank told me, picking up his notebook and fishing his pen back out of his pocket. "You've got enough bloody nerve for three people. Get out of my sight before you annoy me again, and send in someone who won't turn my hair gray. Send Abby."

I headed out to the kitchen and told Rafe that Frank wanted to see him next, just out of boldness and to show Frank I wasn't scared of him, even though I was; of course I was.

"Well," said Daniel, when Frank had finished doing his thing and steered Doherty off, presumably to break the good news to Sam. "I think that went well."

We were in the kitchen, tidying up the teacups and eating the leftover biscuits. "But that wasn't bad at all," Justin said, amazed. "I was expecting them to be horrible, but Mackey was actually *nice* this time."

"God, though, the local goon," Abby said, reaching over me for another biscuit. "He spent the whole time staring at Lex, did you see that? Cretin."

"He's not a cretin," I said. Doherty had amazed me by getting through a full two hours without calling me "Detective," so I was feeling charitable. "He just has good taste."

"I still say they'll do nothing," said Rafe, but not bitchily. Whether it was something Frank had said to them, or just the relief of getting his visit over with, they all looked better: looser, lighter. The sharp-edged tension of last night had faded away, at least for now.

"Let's wait and see," Daniel said, bending his head to a match to light his cigarette. "At least you'll have an exciting story to tell Four-Boobs Brenda, next time she backs you against the photocopier." Even Rafe laughed.

We were drinking wine and playing 110, that night, when my mobile rang. It startled the bejasus out of me—it wasn't like any of us got calls on a regular basis—and I almost missed the call, trying to find my phone; it was in the coat closet, still in the pocket of the communal jacket after last night's walk. "Hi," I said.

"Miss Madison?" said Sam, sounding deeply self-conscious. "It's Detective O'Neill here."

"Oh," I said. I had been heading back to the sitting room, but I reversed and leaned up against the front door, where there was no chance of the others picking up his voice. "Hi."

"Can you talk?"

"Sort of."

"Are you OK?"

"Yeah. Fine."

"For definite?"

"Totally."

"Jesus," Sam said, on a deep rush of breath. "Thank God. That prick Mackey heard the whole thing, did you know that? Didn't ring me, didn't say a word, just waited for this morning and headed down to you. Left me sitting on my arse in the incident room, like an eejit. If this case doesn't wind up soon, I'm going to end up splattering that fucker."

Sam almost never swears unless he's full-on furious. "Fair enough," I said. "I'm not surprised."

A moment's pause. "The others are there, right?"

"More or less."

"I'll keep it short. We sent Byrne to watch Naylor's house, have a look at him when he came home from work this evening, and the man's face is in bits—the three of ye did a good job, by the sound of things. He's my fella, all right. I'm pulling him in tomorrow morning—into the Murder squad, this time. I don't care about spooking him, not any more. If he gets itchy feet, I can hold him on breaking and entering. Do you want to come in, have a look?"

"Sure," I said. A big part of me wanted to wuss out: spend tomorrow in the library with the others around me, eat lunch in the Buttery watching rain fall outside the windows, forget all about what might be happening just up the road, while I still could. But whatever this interview turned out to be, I needed to be there for it. "What time?"

"I'll catch him before he goes to work, have him in here from about eight. Come whenever you like. Are you . . . You're OK with coming into the squad?"

I'd forgotten even to worry about that. "No problem."

"He fits the profile, doesn't he? Bang on."

"I guess," I said, "yeah." In the sitting room there was a comical groan from Rafe—he had obviously just made a mess of his hand—and a burst of laughter from the others. "You bastard," Rafe was saying, but he was laughing too, "you sly bastard, I fall for it every time . . ." Sam is a good interrogator. If there was something to get out of Naylor, odds were he would get it.

"This could be it," Sam said. The hope in his voice made me flinch, the intensity of it. "If I play my cards right tomorrow, this could be the end of it. You could be coming home."

"Yeah," I said. "Sounds good. I'll see you tomorrow."

"I love you," Sam said, keeping his voice down, right before he hung up. I stood there in the cool hallway for a long moment, biting down on my thumbnail and listening to the sounds from the sitting room—voices and the snap of cards, clink of glass, the crackle and whoosh of the fire—before I went back inside.

"Who was that?" Daniel asked, looking up from his hand.

"That detective," I said. "He wants me to come in to them."

"Which one?"

"The cute blond one. O'Neill."

"Why?"

Everyone was looking at me, motionless as startled animals; Abby had stopped with a card pulled halfway out of her hand. "They've found some guy," I said, sliding back into my chair. "About last night. They're going to question him tomorrow."

"You're joking," Abby said. "Already?"

"Go on, get it over with," Rafe told Daniel. "Say *I told you so*. You know you want to."

Daniel paid no attention. "But why you? What do they want?"

I shrugged. "They just want me to have a look at him. And O'Neill asked if I remembered anything more, about that night. I think he's hoping I'll take one look at this guy and point a trembling finger and go, 'That's him! The man who stabbed me!'"

"One of you has seen way too many made-for-TV movies," said Rafe.

"Have you?" Daniel asked. "Remembered anything more?"

"Sweet fuck-all," I said. My imagination, or did some

wire-fine tension drop out of the air? Abby changed her mind about her hand, tucked the card back in and pulled out another; Justin reached for the wine bottle. "Maybe he'll get someone to hypnotize me—do they do that in real life?"

"Get him to program you to get some work done every once in a while," Rafe said.

"Oo. Could he? Program me to get my thesis done faster?"

"Possibly he could, but I doubt he will," Daniel said. "I'm not sure evidence obtained under hypnosis is admissible in court. Where are you meeting O'Neill?"

"His work," I said. "I would have tried to get him to meet up in the pub, come for a pint in Brogan's, or something, but I don't think he'd go for it."

"I thought you hated Brogan's," Daniel said, surprised.

I was opening my mouth for a fast backpedal—*Duh, course I do, I was only messing* . . . It was nothing about Daniel that saved me; he was looking at me over his cards with calm, unblinking, owlish eyes. It was the puzzled little drop of Justin's eyebrows, the cock of Abby's head: they had no idea what he was talking about. Something was wrong.

"Me?" I said, puzzled. "I don't mind Brogan's. I never really think about it; I only said it 'cause it's right across from where he works."

Daniel shrugged. "I must have confused it with somewhere else," he said. He was smiling at me, that extraordinary sweet smile, and I felt it again: that sudden slackening in the air, the sigh of release. "You and your quirks; I can't keep track." I made a face at him.

"What are you doing flirting with cops, anyway?" Rafe demanded. "That's just wrong on so many levels."

"What? He's *cute*." My hands were shaking; I didn't dare pick up my cards. It had taken a second to sink in: Daniel had tried to trap me. I had been a fraction of a second from bouncing happily down his false trail.

"You're incorrigible," Justin said, topping up my wine.

"Anyway, the other one is much more attractive, in a bastard-y kind of way. Mackey."

"Oh, ewww," I said. Those fucking onions—I was sure, from that smile, that I had called this one right, but whether it had been enough to reassure Daniel; with him you could never tell . . . "No way. Bet you anything he's got a hairy back. Back me up here, Abby."

"Different strokes," Abby said comfortably. "And you're both incorrigible."

"Mackey's a prat," Rafe said. "And O'Neill's a yokel. And it's diamonds and it's Abby's go."

I managed to pick up my cards and tried to work out what the hell to do with them. I watched Daniel all evening, as carefully as I could without getting caught, but he was the same as always: gentle, polite, distant; paying no more attention to me than to anyone else. When I put my hand on his shoulder, on my way past to get another bottle of wine, he reached up and covered it with his own hand, squeezed hard.

15

I didn't get to Dublin Castle till almost eleven, the next morning. I wanted to let the daily routine kick in first—breakfast, the drive to town, everyone getting to work in the library; I figured it would settle the others, make them less likely to want to go with me. It worked. Daniel did ask, when I stood up and started putting on my jacket, "Would you like me to come along, for moral support?" but when I shook my head he nodded and went back to his book. "Do the trembling-finger-point either way," Rafe told me. "Give O'Neill a thrill."

Outside the door of the Murder squad's building, I chickened out. It was the entrance I couldn't do: checking in at reception like a visitor, making excruciating chirpy small talk with Bernadette the squad admin, waiting under fascinated passing eyes for someone to come steer me through the corridors like I'd never been there before. I phoned Frank and told him to come get me.

"Good timing," he said, when he stuck his head out the door. "We were just taking a little break, to re-evaluate the situation, shall we say."

"Re-evaluate what?" I asked.

He held the door open for me, stood back. "You'll see. It's been a fun morning all round. You really did a number on our boy's face, didn't you?"

He was right. John Naylor was sitting at an interview-room table with his arms folded, wearing the same colorless sweater and old jeans, and he wasn't good-looking any more. He had two black eyes; one cheek was lopsided, purple and swollen; there was a dark split in his bottom lip; the bridge of his nose had a horrible squashy look. I tried to remember his fingers going for my eyes, his knee in my stomach, but I couldn't square those with this battered guy rocking his chair on its back legs and humming "The Rising of the Moon" to himself. The sight of him, what we had done to him, made my throat close up.

Sam was in the observation room, leaning against the one-way glass with his hands shoved deep in his jacket pockets, watching Naylor. "Cassie," he said, blinking. He looked exhausted. "Hi."

"Jesus," I said, nodding at Naylor.

"You're telling me. He's saying he came off his bike, face first into a wall. And that's about all he's saying."

"I was just telling Cassie," Frank said, "we've got a bit of a situation on our hands."

"Yeah," Sam said. He rubbed at the corners of his eyes, like he was trying to wake up. "A situation, yeah. We pulled Naylor in around, what, eight o'clock? We've been going at him ever since, but he's giving us nothing; just stares at the wall and sings to himself. Rebel songs, mostly."

"He made an exception for me," said Frank. "Stopped the concert long enough to call me a dirty Dub bastard who should be ashamed of myself for licking West Brit arse. I think he fancies me. Here's the thing, though: we managed to get a warrant to search his place, and the Bureau just brought in what they found. Obviously we were hoping for a bloody knife or bloody clothing or what-have-you, but no such luck. Instead . . . surprise, surprise."

He picked up a handful of evidence bags from the table in the corner and waved them at me. "Check these out."

There was a set of ivory dice, a tortoiseshell-backed hand mirror, a small lousy watercolor of a country lane, and a silver sugar bowl. Even before I turned the bowl around and saw the monogram—a delicate, flourished M—I knew where these had come from. Only one place I knew of had this kind of tat variety: Uncle Simon's hoard.

"They were under Naylor's bed," Frank said, "prettily

packed away in a shoebox. I guarantee if you have a good look around Whitethorn House you'll find a cream pitcher to match. Which leaves us with the question: how did this lot end up in Naylor's bedroom?"

"He broke in," Sam said. He had gone back to staring at Naylor, who was slouched in his chair gazing at the ceiling. "Four times."

"Without taking anything."

"We don't know that. That's according to Simon March, who lived like a pig and spent most of his time legless drunk. Naylor could've filled up a *suitcase* with anything he fancied, and March would never have known the difference."

"Or," Frank said, "he could have bought it off Lexie."

"Sure," Sam said, "or off Daniel or Abby or what's-their-names, or off old Simon, come to that. Except that there's not one single speck of evidence to say he did."

"None of them ended up stabbed and searched half a mile from Naylor's home."

They had obviously been having this fight for a while; their voices had that heavy, well-practiced rhythm. I put the evidence bags back on the table, leaned against the wall and stayed well out of it. "Naylor's working for just over minimum wage and supporting two sick parents," Sam said. "Where the hell is he going to get the money to buy antique bits and bobs? And why the hell would he want to?"

"He'd want to," Frank said, "because he hates the March family's guts and he'd jump at the chance to screw them over—and because, just like you said, he's skint. He may not have the money himself, but there are plenty of people out there who do."

It took me that long to realize what they were fighting about, why the whole room was tight with that hard, bitten-down tension. Art and Antiques may sound like the nerd squad, a bunch of tweedy professors with badges, but what they do is no joke. The black market spreads worldwide, and it gets tangled up with a whole bunch of other kinds of organized crime along the way. People get hurt, in a swap network where the currencies range from Picassos to Kalashnikovs to heroin; people get killed."

Sam made a furious, frustrated noise, shook his head and slumped back against the glass. "All I want," he said, "is to find out whether this fella's a killer, and arrest him if he is. I don't give a damn what else he's been doing in his spare time. He could have fenced the *Mona Lisa* and I wouldn't care. If you seriously think he's been passing antiques, we can hand him over to A and A once we're done with him, but for now, he's a murder suspect. Nothing else."

Frank raised one eyebrow. "You're assuming there's no connection. Look at the pattern. Up until those five move in, Naylor's brick-throwing and spray-painting his little heart out. Once they're there, he takes one or two more shots and then, just like that"—he snapped his fingers—"all quiet on the western front. What, he thought those five were cute? He saw them renovating and didn't want to mess up the new decor?"

"They went after him," Sam said. The set of his mouth: he was inches from losing his temper. "He didn't fancy getting the shite kicked out of him."

Frank laughed. "You think that kind of grudge vanished overnight? Not a chance. Naylor found some other way to do damage to Whitethorn House—otherwise he wouldn't have quit the vandalism, not in a million years. And look what happens as soon as Lexie's not there to slip him antiques any more. He gives it a few weeks, in case she gets back in touch, and when she doesn't, he's right back to the rock through the window. He wasn't worried about getting the shite kicked out of him the other night, was he?"

"You want to talk about patterns? Here's a pattern for you. When the five of them chase him off, back in December, his grudge only gets worse. He's not going to take on all of them at once, but he keeps spying on them, he finds out that one of them makes a habit of going out walking during his window of opportunity, he stalks her for a while and then he kills her. When he finds out he didn't even get that right, the rage builds up again, till he loses control and bangs an arson threat through the window. How do you think he feels about what happened the other night? If one of those five keeps wandering around the lanes on her own, what do you think he's going to do about it?"

Frank ignored that. "The question," he told me, "is what we do with Little Johnny now. We can arrest him for burglary, vandalism, theft, whatever else we can come up with, and keep our fingers crossed that it loosens him up enough that he gives us something on the stabbing. Or we can stick this lot back under his bed, thank him kindly for helping us with our inquiries, send him home and see where he takes us."

In a way, this fight had probably been inevitable all along, from the second Frank and Sam showed up at the same crime scene. Murder detectives are single-minded, focused on narrowing the investigation slowly and inexorably till everything extraneous is gone and the only thing left in their sights is the killer. Undercovers thrive on extraneous, on spreading their bets and keeping all their options open: you never know where tangents might lead, what unexpected game might poke its head out of the bushes if you watch every angle for long enough. They light all the fuses they can find, and wait to see what goes boom.

"And then what, Mackey?" Sam demanded. "Just supposing for a second that you're right, Lexie was slipping the man antiques to sell, and Cassie gets their little operation going again. Then *what*?"

"Then," Frank said, "I have a nice chat with A and A, I head down to Francis Street and buy Cassie a handful of lovely shiny widgets, and we take it from there." He was smiling, but his eyes on Sam were narrow and watchful.

"For how long?"

"As long as it takes."

A and A uses undercovers all the time, undercovers posing as buyers, as fences, as sellers with nudge-and-a-wink sources, gradually working their way towards the big shots. Their operations last for months; they last for years.

"I'm investigating a fucking *murder* here," Sam said. "Remember that? And I can't arrest anyone for that murder while the victim's alive and well and messing about with silver sugar bowls."

"So? Get him after the antiques sting winds up, one way or the other. Best-case scenario, we establish a motive and a link between him and the victim, and we get to use them as leverage towards a confession. Worst-case scenario, we waste a little time. It's not like our statute of limitations is about to run out."

There wasn't a snowball's chance in hell that Lexie had spent the past three months selling John Naylor the contents of Whitethorn House just for kicks and giggles. Once that pregnancy test came up positive, she would have sold whatever it took to get out, but up until then: no.

I could have said so; should have. But the thing was that Frank was right on this much: Naylor would do anything that would damage Whitethorn House. He was going insane like a caged cat with his own helplessness, taking on that house charged with centuries of power, with no weapons in his hands but rocks and spray cans. If someone came up to him with a handful of spoils from Whitethorn House, a few bright ideas about where to sell the stuff and a promise of more, there was a good chance—an incredible chance—that he wouldn't know how to say no.

"I'll make you a deal," Frank said. "Have another go at Naylor—just you, this time; he and I aren't really clicking. Take as long as you need. If he gives you something on the murder—anything at all, even a hint—we arrest him, we forget the whole antiques question, we pull Cassie in and we shut the investigation down. If he gives you nothing . . ."

"Then what?" Sam demanded.

Frank shrugged. "If your way doesn't work, then you come back out here and we all have a little chat about my way."

Sam looked at him for a long time. "No tricks," he said.

"Tricks?"

"Coming in. Knocking on the door when I'm on the edge of getting something. That kind of thing."

I saw a muscle flick in Frank's jaw, but all he said was, blandly, "No tricks."

"OK," Sam said, on a deep breath. "I'll give it my best shot. Can you hang on here for a bit?"

He was talking to me. "Sure," I said.

"I might want to use you—bring you in, maybe. I'll figure it out as I go." His eyes went to Naylor, who had switched to singing "Follow Me Up to Carlow," just loud enough to be distracting. "Wish me luck," he said, straightening his tie, and he was gone.

"Did your boyfriend just insult my virtue?" Frank wanted to know, when the door of the observation room shut behind Sam.

"You can challenge him to a duel if you want," I said.

"I play fair. You know that."

"Don't we all," I said. "We've just got different ideas about what counts as fair. Sam isn't sure yours matches up all that well with his."

"So we won't buy a time share in the Med together," Frank said. "I'll live. What do you think of my little theory?"

I was watching Naylor, through the glass, but I could feel Frank's eyes raking the side of my head. "I don't know yet," I said. "I haven't really seen enough of this guy to have an opinion."

"But you've seen plenty of Lexie—secondhand, but still, you know as much about her as anyone does. Think she'd be capable of something like that?"

I shrugged. "Who knows? The whole thing about this girl is that no one has a clue what she was capable of."

"You were playing your cards very close to the chest, just now. It's not like you to keep your mouth shut for that long, not when you must have an opinion one way or the other. I'd like to have some idea which side you might be on, if your fella comes out of there with nothing and we have to pick up this argument again."

The interview-room door opened and Sam came in, juggling two mugs of tea and catching the door with his shoulder. He looked wide awake, almost jaunty: the fatigue falls off you, the second you're face to face with a suspect. "Shh," I said. "I want to watch this."

Sam sat down, with a comfortable grunt, and pushed one of the mugs across the table to Naylor. "Now," he said. His country accent had magically got a lot stronger: us against the city folk. "I've sent Detective Mackey off to do his paperwork. He was only annoying us."

Naylor stopped singing and considered this. "I don't like the cut of him," he said, finally.

I saw the corner of Sam's mouth twitch. "Neither do I, sure. But we're stuck with him." Frank laughed softly, beside me, and moved closer to the glass.

Naylor shrugged. "You are, maybe. I'm not. As long as he's here, I've nothing to say."

"Grand," Sam said easily. "He's gone, and I'm not asking you to talk, just to listen. There's something that I've been told happened in Glenskehy, a while back. As far as I can see, it could explain a lot. All I need you to do is tell me if it's true."

Naylor gave him a suspicious look, but he didn't start the concert again. "Right," Sam said, and took a swig of his tea. "There was a girl in Glenskehy, around the First World War . . ."

The story he told was a delicate blend of what he'd picked up in Rathowen, what I'd picked up from Uncle Simon's magnum opus, and something starring Lillian Gish. He pulled out all the stops: the girl's father had thrown her out of the house, she was begging in the streets of Glenskehy, locals spitting on her as they passed, kids throwing stones . . . He topped it all off with a semisubtle hint that the girl had been lynched by an angry mob from the village. The soundtrack here clearly involved a large string section.

By the time he finished his tearjerker, Naylor was rocking the chair back again and giving him a stony, disgusted stare. "No," he said. "Jesus, no. That's the biggest load of old shite I've heard in my life. Where did you get that?"

"So far," Sam said, shrugging, "that's the story I've heard. Unless someone else can correct it for me, I've no choice but to go on it."

The chair creaked, a monotonous, unsettling noise. "Tell me, Detective," Naylor said, "why would you be interested in the likes of us and our old stories? We're plain people around Glenskehy, you know. We're not used to getting the attention of important men like yourself."

"That's what he gave us all the way here, in the car," Frank told me, getting comfortable with a shoulder against the edge of the window. "Our boy's got a bit of a persecution complex."

"Shh."

"There's been some hassle up at Whitethorn House," Sam said. "Sure, I don't have to tell you that. We've received information that there's bad feeling between the house and the residents of Glenskehy. I need to establish the facts, so I can determine whether there's any connection."

Naylor laughed, a hard, humorless crack. "Bad feeling," he said. "I suppose you could call it that, yeah. Is that what they told you up at the House?"

Sam shrugged. "All they said was that they weren't welcome at the pub. No reason why they should be, sure. They're not locals."

"Lucky for them. They get a bit of hassle, and they've detectives crawling out of the woodwork to fix it. When it's *locals* getting the hassle, where are ye? Where were ye when that girl was hanged? Filing it as a suicide and heading back to the pub."

Sam's eyebrows went up. "It wasn't suicide?"

Naylor eyed him; those eyes swollen half shut made him look baleful, dangerous. "You want the true story?"

Sam made a small, easy gesture with one hand: *I'm listening.*

After a moment Naylor brought the chair down, reached out and wrapped his hands—broken nails, dark scabs on the knuckles—around the mug. "The girl worked as a maid up at Whitethorn House," he said. "And one of the young fellas up there, one of the Marches, he took a fancy to her. Maybe she was stupid enough to think he'd marry her and maybe she wasn't, but either way, she got into trouble."

He gave Sam a long bird-of-prey stare, making sure he understood. "There was no throwing her out of the house. I'd say her father was raging, and I'd say he talked about waiting for the March fella in the lanes some dark night, but he'd have been mad to do it. Pure mad. This was before the independence, d'you see? The Marches owned all round Glenskehy. Whoever the girl was, they owned her father's house; one word out of him, and his family would have been on the side of the road. So he did nothing."

"That can't have come easy," Sam said.

"Easier than you'd think. Most people then wouldn't deal with Whitethorn House any more than they had to. It had a bad name. Whitethorn's the fairy tree, d'you see? Belongs to the fairies." He gave Sam a grim, equivocal little smile. "There's still people won't walk under a hawthorn at night, though they wouldn't be able to tell you why. It's only leftovers now, scrapings, but back then there was superstition everywhere. It was the dark did it: no electricity and the long winter nights, you could see anything you liked in the shadows. There were plenty believed that them up at Whitethorn House had dealings with the fairies, or the devil, depending on what way your mind worked." That sideways, cold flick of a smile again. "What do you think, Detective? Were we all mad savages, back then?"

Sam shook his head. "There's a fairy ring on my uncle's farm," he said matter-of-factly. "He doesn't believe in the fairies, never did, but he plows around it."

Naylor nodded. "So that's what people said in Glenskehy, when this girl came up pregnant. They said she lay down with one of the fairy men from up at the House, and she got up with a fairy child. And serve her right."

"They thought the baby would be a changeling?"

"Yowza," Frank said. "It's life, Jim, but not as we know it." He was shaking with half-suppressed laughter. I wanted to kick him.

"They did, yeah," Naylor said coldly. "And don't be giving me that look, Detective. These are my great-grandparents we're talking about, mine and yours. Can you swear to me you wouldn't have believed the same, if you'd been born back then?"

"Different times," Sam said, nodding.

"Not everyone said it, now. Only a few—the older folk, mostly. But enough that, one way or another, it got back to your man, the child's father. Either he wanted rid of the child all along and he was only waiting for an excuse, or something wasn't right in his mind to start with. A lot of them were always what you might call a bit odd, up at the House; maybe that's one reason they got the name for having dealings with the fairies. He believed it, anyway. He thought there was something wrong with him, in his blood, that would wreck the child."

His broken mouth twisted sideways. "So he arranged to meet the girl one night, before the baby was born. She went along, not a worry on her: he was her lover, wasn't he? She thought he wanted to arrange to provide for her and the child. And instead he took a rope and he hanged her from a tree. That's the true story. Everyone in Glenskehy knows. She didn't kill herself, and no one from the village killed her. The baby's father killed her, because he was afraid of his own child."

"Bloody boggers," Frank said. "I swear to God, you get outside Dublin and it's a whole different universe. Jerry Springer, eat your heart out."

"God rest," Sam said quietly.

"Yeah," Naylor said. "God rest. Your lot called it a suicide, sooner than arrest one of the gentry from the Big

House. She went into unconsecrated ground, her and the child."

It could have been true. Any of the versions we'd heard could have been the true one, any or none; there was no way to tell, across a hundred years. What mattered was that Naylor believed what he was saying, every word. He wasn't acting like a guilty man, but this means less than you might think. He was consumed enough—that bitter intensity in his voice—that he might well believe he had nothing to feel guilty about. My heart was going fast and heavy. I thought of the others, heads bent in the library, expecting me to come back.

"Why would no one in the village tell me this?" Sam asked.

"Because it's none of your business. We don't want to be known for that: the mad village where the lunatic killed his bastard for being a fairy. We're decent people, in Glenskehy. We're plain people, but we're not savages and we're not eejits, and we're no one's freak show, d'you get me? We just want to be left alone."

"Someone's not leaving this alone, though," Sam pointed out. "Someone painted BABY KILLERS on Whitethorn House, twice. Someone put a rock through their window, two nights ago, and fought them like hell when they went after him. Someone doesn't want to leave that child to rest in peace."

A long silence. Naylor shifted in his chair, touched his split lip with a finger and checked for blood. Sam waited.

"It was never just the baby," he said, in the end. "That was bad enough, sure; but it only showed the way they are, that family. The cut of them. I didn't know what other way to say it."

He was halfway to putting his hand up for the graffiti, but Sam let that slide: he was after bigger game. "What way are they?" he asked. He was leaning back with his mug balanced on his knee, easy and interested, like a man settled in for a good long night at his local.

Naylor dabbed at his lip again, absently. He was think-ing hard, searching for words. "All your detective work about Glenskehy. Did you find out where it came from?"

Sam grinned. "My Irish is after getting awful rusty. Glen of the hawthorn, is it?"

Naylor gave a fast, impatient head-shake. "Ah, no, no, not the name. The place. The village. Glenskehy. Where d'you think it came from?"

Sam shook his head.

"The Marches. They made it, to suit themselves. When they were given the land and they built that house, they brought people in to work for them—maids, gardeners, stable hands, gamekeepers . . . They wanted their servants on their land, under their thumb, so they could keep them in line, but not too nearby; they didn't want to be smelling the stink of the peasants." There was a vicious, disgusted twist to the corner of his mouth. "So they built a village for the servants to live in. Like someone having a swimming pool put in, or a conservatory, or a stable full of ponies: just a little luxury, to make life more comfortable."

"That's no way to look at human beings," Sam agreed. "It's a long time ago, though."

"A long time ago, yeah. Back when the Marches had a use for Glenskehy. And now that it's not serving their plea-sure any more, they're standing by and watching it die." There was something building in Naylor's voice, something volatile and dangerous, and for the first time they came together in my mind, this man talking local history with Sam and the wild creature that had tried to gouge my eyes out in a dark lane. "It's falling to bits, that village. Another few years and there'll be nothing left of it. The only ones who stay are the ones trapped there, like myself, while the place dies and takes them along with it. Do you know why I never went to college?"

Sam shook his head.

"I'm no fool. I had the points for it. But I had to stay in

Glenskehy, to look after my parents, and there's no work there that needs an education. There's nothing but farming. What did I need a degree for, to dig muck on another man's farm? I started doing that the day after I left school. I'd no other choice. And there's dozens more like me."

"That's not the Marches' fault, sure," Sam said reasonably. "What could they do about it?"

That hard bark of a laugh again. "There's plenty they could do. Plenty. Four or five years back there was a fella came looking around the village, a Galway man, same as yourself. A property developer. He wanted to buy Whitethorn House, turn it into a fancy hotel. He was going to build it up—add new wings, new buildings round the grounds, a golf course, all the rest; he'd big plans, this fella. Do you know what that would have done for Glenskehy?"

Sam nodded. "A load of new jobs."

"More than that. Tourists coming through, new businesses coming in to look after them, people moving in to work for the new businesses. Young people staying on, instead of clearing out to Dublin as soon as they're able. New houses being built, and decent roads. A school of our own again, instead of sending the children up to Rathowen. Work for teachers, for a doctor, for estate agents maybe—educated people. Not all at once, like, it would've taken years, but once the ball starts rolling . . . That was all we needed: just that one push. That one chance. We'd have had Glenskehy coming back to life."

Four or five years back: just before the attacks on Whitethorn House began. He was matching my profile immaculately, piece by piece. The thought of Whitethorn House turned into a hotel made me feel a lot better about the state of Naylor's face, but still: you couldn't help being pulled in by the passion in his voice, seeing the vibrant vision he was in love with, the village turned bustling and hopeful again, alive.

"But Simon March wouldn't sell?" Sam asked.

Naylor shook his head, a slow angry roll; winced, touched his swollen jaw. "One man, on his own in a house that could fit dozens. What good was it to him? But he wouldn't sell. It's been nothing but bad news since the day it was built, that house, and he held onto it for dear life sooner than let it do anyone a scrap of good. And the same when he died: the young fella hadn't been near Glenskehy since he was a child, he has no family, he had no need for the place, but he held on. That's what they are, the Marches. That's what they've been all along. What they want, they keep, and the rest of the world be damned."

"It's the family home," Sam pointed out. "Maybe they love it."

Naylor's head came up and he stared at Sam, pale blazing eyes amid the swelling and the dark bruises. "If a man makes something," he said, "he has a duty to look after it. That's what a decent man does. If you make a child, it's yours to care for, as long as it lives; you've no right to kill it to suit yourself. If you make a village, it's yours to look after; you do what it takes to keep that place going. You don't have the right to stand by and watch it die, just so you can keep hold of a house."

"I'm actually with him on this one," Frank said, beside me. "Maybe we've got more in common than we thought."

I barely heard him. I had got one thing wrong in my profile, after all: this man would never have stabbed Lexie for being pregnant with his baby, or even for living in Whitethorn House. I had thought he was an avenger, obsessed with the past, but he was a lot more complicated and more ferocious than that. It was the future he was obsessed with, his home's future, seeping away like water. The past was the dark conjoined twin wrapped round that future, steering it, shaping it.

"Is that all you wanted from the Marches?" Sam asked quietly. "For them to do the decent thing—sell up, give Glenskehy a chance?"

After a long moment Naylor nodded, a stiff, reluctant jerk.

"And you thought the only way to make them do it was to put the frighteners on them."

Another nod. Frank whistled, softly, through his teeth. I was holding my breath.

"No better way to frighten them off," Sam said, thoughtful and matter-of-fact, "than to give one of them a little cut, one night. Nothing serious, not even meant to hurt her. Just to let them know: you're not welcome here."

Naylor's mug went down hard on the table and he shoved his chair back, arms folding tight across his chest. "I never hurt anyone. *Never.*"

Sam raised his eyebrows. "Someone handed out a fair old beating to three of the Whitethorn House people, the same night you got those bruises."

"That was a *fight*. An honest fight—and they were three to one against me. Do you not see the difference? I could have killed Simon March a dozen times over, if I'd wanted to. I never touched him."

"Simon March was old, sure. You knew he was bound to die within a few years, and you knew there was a decent chance his heirs would sell up, sooner than move out to Glenskehy. You could afford to wait."

Naylor started to say something, but Sam kept talking, level and heavy, cutting across him. "But once young Daniel and his mates arrived, it was a whole different story. They're going nowhere, and a bit of spray paint wasn't scaring them. So you had to up the stakes, didn't you?"

"*No.* I never—"

"You had to tell them, loud and clear: get out, if you know what's good for you. You'd seen Lexie Madison out walking, late at night—maybe you'd followed her before, had you?"

"I don't—"

"You were coming out of the pub. You were drunk. You

had a knife on you. You thought about the Marches letting Glenskehy die, and you went up there to end it once and for all. Maybe you were just going to threaten her, is that it?"

"No—"

"Then how did it happen, John? You tell me. How?"

Naylor shot forwards, his fists coming up and his lip pulling into a furious snarl; he was on the edge of going for Sam. "You give me the sick. They whistled for you, them up at the house, and you came running like a good dog. They go whining to you about the nasty peasant who doesn't know his place, and you bring me in here and accuse me of stabbing one of them—That's *shite*. I want them out of Glenskehy—and believe you me, they'll be out—but I never thought about hurting any of them. Never. I wouldn't give them the satisfaction. When they pack up their things and go, I want to be there to wave them good-bye."

It should have been a letdown, but it went like speed through my blood, pounded high up in my throat, took my breath away. It felt—and I shifted against the glass, kept my face angled away from Frank so he wouldn't see this—it felt like a reprieve.

Naylor was still going. "Those dirty bastards used you to put me in my place, just like they've been using the police and everyone else for three hundred years. I'll tell you this much for nothing, Detective, the same as I'd tell whoever gave you that load of old shite about a lynch mob. You can look in Glenskehy all you like, but you'll find nothing. It was no one from that village stabbed that young one. I know it comes hard to go after the rich instead of the poor, but if it's a criminal you're after and not a scapegoat, you look up at Whitethorn House. We don't breed them round my way."

He folded his arms, tilted his chair onto its back legs and started singing "The Wind That Shakes the Barley." Frank eased back away from the glass and laughed, quietly, to himself.

. . .

Sam tried for more than an hour. He went through every incident of vandalism, one by one, going back four and a half years; listed the evidence linking Naylor to the rock and the fight, some of it solid—the bruises, my description—and some invented, fingerprints, handwriting analysis; came into the observation room, grabbed the evidence bags without looking at me or at Frank, and tossed them on the table in front of Naylor; threatened to arrest him for burglary, assault with a deadly weapon, everything short of murder. In exchange he got "The Croppy Boy," "Four Green Fields" and, for a change of pace, "She Moved through the Fair."

In the end he had to give up. There was a long time between the moment when he left Naylor in the interview room and the moment when he came into the observation room, evidence bags dangling from one hand and the exhaustion back on his face, deeper than ever.

"I thought that went well," Frank said brightly. "You could even have got a confession on the vandalism, if you hadn't gone for the big prize."

Sam ignored him. "What do you think?" he asked me.

There was one off chance left, as far as I could see, one way Naylor could have snapped badly enough to stab Lexie: if he had been the baby's father, and she had told him she was going to have an abortion. "I don't know," I said. "I genuinely don't."

"I don't think he's our boy," Sam said. He dropped the evidence bags on the table and leaned heavily against it, head going back.

Frank did amazed. "You're giving up on him because he held out for one morning? From where I'm standing, he looks good enough to eat: motive, opportunity, mindset . . . Just because he tells a great story, you're going to arrest him on some pissant vandalism charge and throw away your chance to have him on murder?"

"I don't know," Sam said. He pressed the heels of his hands into his eyes. "I don't know what I'm going to do now."

"Now," Frank said, "we try it my way. Fair's fair; your way got us nowhere. Cut Naylor loose, let Cassie see what she can get out of him on the antiques deal, and see if that takes us any closer to the stabbing."

"This man doesn't give a damn about money," Sam said, without looking at Frank. "What he cares about is his town, and the damage that's been done to it by Whitethorn House."

"So he's got a cause. There's nothing in this world more dangerous than a true believer. How far do you think he'd go for that cause?"

This is one of the things about fighting with Frank: he moves the goalposts faster than you can catch up, you keep losing track of what you were originally arguing about. I couldn't tell whether he actually believed in this antiques caper, or whether it was just that he was ready to try anything, at this stage, to beat Sam.

Sam was starting to look dazed, like a boxer after taking too many punches. "I don't think he's a killer," he said doggedly. "And I don't see why you think he's a fence. There's nothing pointing to that."

"Let's ask Cassie," Frank suggested. He was watching me carefully. Frank's always been a gambler, but I wished I knew what was making him bet on this one. "What do you think, babe? Any chance I'm right about the antiques scam?"

In that second a million things went through my mind. The observation room I knew by heart, down to the stain on the carpet where I'd dropped a coffee cup two years back, and where I had become a visitor. My Detective Barbie clothes hanging in my wardrobe, Maher's juicy morning throat-clearing routine. The others, waiting for me in the library. The cool lily-of-the- valley smell of my room in Whitethorn House, wrapping around me soft as gauze.

"You could be," I said, "yeah. I wouldn't be surprised."

Sam, who in fairness had had a long day already, finally lost it. "Jesus, Cassie! What the *hell*? You can't seriously believe in that mad crap. What side are you on?"

"Let's try not to think in those terms," Frank put in, virtuously. He had arranged himself comfortably against a wall, hands in his pockets, to watch the action. "We're all on the same side here."

"Back off, Frank," I said sharply, before Sam could punch his lights out. "And Sam, I'm on Lexie's side. Not Frank's, not yours, just hers. OK?"

"That right there is exactly what I was afraid of." Sam caught the startled look on my face. "What, you thought it was just this tosspot"—Frank, who pointed to his chest and tried to look wounded—"that had me worried? He's bad enough, God knows, but at least I can keep an eye on him. But this girl—*On her side* is a bad, bad place to be. Her housemates were on her side all the way, and if Mackey's right, she was selling the lot of them down the river, not a bother on her. Her fella over in America was on her side, he *loved* her, and look what she did to him. The poor bastard's a wreck. Have you seen that letter?"

"Letter?" I said, to Frank. "What letter?"

He shrugged. "Chad sent her a letter, care of my FBI friend. Very moving and all, but I've been through it with a fine-tooth comb and there's nothing useful there. You don't need distractions."

"Jesus, Frank! If you've got something that tells me anything about her, anything at all—"

"We'll talk about it later."

"Read it," Sam said. His voice sounded raw at the edges and his face was white, white as it had been that first day at the crime scene. "You read that letter—I'll give you a copy, if Mackey won't. That fella Chad is bloody *devastated*. Four and a half years, it's been, and he hasn't gone out with another girl. He'll probably never trust a woman again. How could he? He woke up one morning with his whole life in bits around him. Everything he dreamed about, gone up in smoke."

"Unless you want that super of yours in here," Frank said silkily, "I'd keep it down."

Sam didn't even hear him. "And don't forget, she didn't fall into North Carolina out of the sky. She was somewhere else before that, and for all we know somewhere else before that. Somewhere out there, there's more people—God only knows how many—who'll never be able to stop wondering where she is, whether she's in a shallow grave in a dozen pieces, whether she went off the rails and ended up on the streets, whether she just never gave a damn about them to start with, what the hell *happened* to blow up their lives. All of them were on this girl's side, and look what it did to them. Everyone who's been on her side has ended up fucked, Cassie, everyone, and you're going the same way."

"I'm fine, Sam," I said. His voice rolled over me like the fine edge of dawn haze, barely there, barely real.

"Let me ask you this. Your last serious boyfriend was just before you first went undercover, am I right? Aidan something?"

"Yeah," I said. "Aidan O'Donovan." He was good news, Aidan: smart, high octane, going places, an offbeat sense of humor that could make me laugh no matter how crap my day had been. I hadn't thought about him in a long time.

"What happened to him?"

"We broke up," I said. "While I was under." For a second I saw Aidan's eyes, the evening he dumped me. I was in a hurry, had to get back to my flat in time for a late-night meeting with the speed-bunny who ended up stabbing me a few months later. Aidan waited with me at my bus stop and when I looked down at him from the top deck of the bus, I think he might have been crying.

"*Because* you were under. Because that's what *happens*." Sam spun round to Frank: "What about you, Mackey? Have you got a wife? A girlfriend? Anything?"

"Are you asking me out?" Frank inquired. His voice

sounded amused, but his eyes had narrowed. "Because I should warn you, I'm not a cheap date."

"That's a no. And that's what I figured." Sam whipped round to me again: "Just three weeks, Cassie, and look what's happening to us. Is this what you want? What do you think happens to us if you head off for a year to do this fucked-up *joke* of an idea?"

"Let's try this," Frank said softly, very still against the wall. "You decide if there's a problem on your side of the investigation, and I'll decide if there's a problem on mine. Is that OK with you?"

The look in his eyes had sent superintendents and drug lords scuttling for cover, but Sam didn't even seem to notice it. "*No*, it's not bloody OK. Your side of this investigation is a fucking disaster area, and if you can't see that, then thank Jesus I can. I've got a *suspect* in that room, whether he's our fella or not, and I found him through *police* work. What have you got? Three weeks of this insane bloody carry-on, all for nothing. And instead of cutting our losses, you're trying to force us to up the ante and do something even more insane—"

"I'm not forcing you to do anything. I'm asking Cassie— who's on this investigation as my undercover, remember, not your Murder detective—whether she'd be willing to take her assignment a step further."

Long summer afternoons on the grass, the hum of bees and the lazy creak of the swing seat. Kneeling in the herb garden picking our harvest, soft rain and leaf-smoke in the air, scent of bruised rosemary and lavender on my hands. Wrapping Christmas presents on Lexie's bedroom floor, snow falling past my window, while Rafe played carols on the piano and Abby harmonized from her room and the smell of gingerbread curled under my door.

Sam's eyes and Frank's on me, unblinking. Both of them had shut up; the silence in the room was sudden and deep and peaceful. "Sure," I said. "Why not?"

Naylor had moved on to "Avondale" and down the

corridor Quigley was being aggrieved about something. I thought of me and Rob watching suspects from this observation room, laughing shoulder to shoulder along the corridor, disintegrating like a meteor in Operation Vestal's poison air, crashing and burning, and I felt nothing at all, nothing except the walls opening up and falling away around me, light as petals. Sam's eyes were huge and dark as if I had hit him, and Frank was watching me in a way that made me think if I had any sense I'd be scared, but all I could feel was every muscle loosening like I was eight years old and cartwheeling myself dizzy on some green hillside, like I could dive a thousand miles through cool blue water without once needing to breathe. I had been right: freedom smelled like ozone and thunderstorms and gunpowder all at once, like snow and bonfires and cut grass, it tasted like seawater and oranges.

16

It was lunchtime when I got back to Trinity, but the others were still in their carrels. As soon as I turned into the long aisle of books that led to our corner they looked up, fast and almost simultaneously, pens going down.

"*Well,*" Justin said, on a big relieved sigh, as I reached them. "*There* you are. About time."

"Jesus," said Rafe. "What took so long? Justin thought you'd been arrested, but I told him you'd probably just eloped with O'Neill."

Rafe's hair was standing up in cowlicks and Abby had pen smudged on one cheekbone and they had no idea how beautiful they looked to me, how close we'd come to losing each other. I wanted to touch all four of them, hug them, grab their hands and hold on hard. "They kept me hanging around for ages," I said. "Are we going for lunch? I'm starving."

"What happened?" Daniel asked. "Were you able to identify this man?"

"Nah," I said, leaning across Abby to get my satchel. "He's definitely the guy from the other night, though. You should see his face. He looks like he went ten rounds with Muhammad Ali." Rafe laughed and held up his hand to me for a high-five.

"What are you laughing about?" Abby wanted to know. "The guy could have you charged with assault, if he wanted to. That's what Justin thought had happened, Lex."

"He won't press charges. He told the cops he fell off his bike. Everything's fine."

"Nothing jogged your memory?" Daniel inquired.

"Nope." I tugged Justin's coat off his chair and waved it at him. "Come *on*. Can we go to the Buttery? I want proper food. Cops make me hungry."

"Did you get any sense of what happens now? Do they think he's the man who attacked you? Did they arrest him?"

"Nah," I said. "They don't have enough evidence, or something. And they don't think he stabbed me."

I'd been so swept up by the thought that this was good news, I had forgotten that it might look very different from most other perspectives. There was a sudden flat silence, nobody looking at anyone else. Rafe's eyes closed for a second, like a flinch.

"Why not?" Daniel asked. "As far as I can see, he seems like a logical suspect."

I shrugged. "Who knows what goes on in their heads? That's all they told me."

"For fuck's *sake*," said Abby. She looked suddenly pale and heavy-eyed, in the glare of the fluorescent lights.

"So," Rafe said, "this whole thing was pointless, after all. We're back where we started."

"We don't know that yet," said Daniel.

"I think it's fairly clear. Call me a pessimist."

"Oh, God," Justin said softly. "I so hoped this was going to be over." No one answered him.

Daniel and Abby, talking late again, out on the patio. This time I didn't need to feel my way along the walls to the kitchen; I could have moved through that house blindfolded without putting a foot wrong, without creaking a floorboard.

"I don't know why," Daniel said. They were sitting on the swing seat, smoking, not touching. "I can't put my finger on it. Possibly I'm letting all the other tensions cloud my judgment . . . I'm just worried."

"She's been through a tough time," Abby said carefully.

"I think all she wants is to settle down and forget it ever happened."

Daniel watched her, moonlight reflecting off his glasses, screening his eyes. "What is it," he asked, "that you're not telling me?"

The baby. I bit down on my lip and prayed that Abby believed in loyalty among the sisterhood.

She shook her head. "You'll have to trust me on this one."

Daniel looked away, out over the grass, and I saw a flash of something—exhaustion, or grief—cross his face. "We used to tell one another everything," he said, "not so long ago. Didn't we? Or is that simply the way I remember it? The five of us against the world, and no secrets, ever."

Abby's eyebrows flicked up. "Did we? I'm not sure anyone tells anyone else everything. You don't, for example."

"I'd like to think," Daniel said, after a moment, "that I do my best. That, unless there's some pressing reason not to, I tell you and the others everything that really matters."

"But there's always some pressing reason, isn't there? With you." Abby's face was pale and shuttered.

"Possibly there is," Daniel said quietly, on a long sigh. "There didn't use to be."

"You and Lexie," Abby said. "Have you ever . . . ?"

A silence; the two of them watching each other, intent as enemies.

"Because that would matter."

"Would it? Why?"

Another silence. The moon went in; their faces faded into the night.

"No," Daniel said, finally. "We haven't. I would probably say the same thing either way, since I don't see how it would be important, so I don't expect you to believe me. But, for what it's worth, we haven't."

Silence, again. The tiny red glow of a cigarette butt, arcing into the dark like a meteor. I stood in the cold kitchen, watching them through the glass, and wished I could tell them: *It'll all be OK now. Everyone will settle; everything will go back to normal, given time, and now we've got time. I'm staying.*

A door banging, in the middle of the night; fast, careless footsteps thumping on wood; another slam, heavier this time, the front door.

I listened, sitting up in bed, my heart hammering. There was a shift somewhere in the house, so subtle that I felt it more than heard it, running through walls and floorboards into my bones: someone moving. It could have come from anywhere. It was a still night, no wind in the trees, only the cool deceptive call of an owl hunting far off in the lanes. I pulled my pillow up against the headboard, got comfortable and waited. I thought about having a cigarette, but I was pretty sure I wasn't the only one sitting upright, senses on full alert for the tiniest thing: the click of a lighter, the smell of smoke twisting in the dark air.

After about twenty minutes the front door opened and closed again, very quietly this time. A pause; then delicate, careful steps going up the stairs, into Justin's room, and the explosive creak of bedsprings below me.

I gave it five minutes. When nothing interesting happened, I slid out of bed and ran downstairs—there was no point in trying to be quiet. "Oh," Justin said, when I stuck my head round his door. "It's you."

He was sitting on the edge of his bed, half dressed: trousers, shoes but no socks, his shirt untucked and half buttoned. He looked awful.

"Are you OK?" I asked.

Justin ran his hands over his face, and I saw that they were trembling. "No," he said. "I'm really not."

"What happened?"

His hands came down and he stared at me, red-eyed. "Go to bed," he said. "Just go to bed, Lexie."

"Are you pissed off with me?"

"Not everything in this world is about you, you know," Justin said coldly. "Believe it or not."

"*Justin*," I said, after a second. "I just wanted to—"

"If you really want to help," Justin said, "then you can leave me alone."

He got up and started fussing with the bedsheets, pulling them tight in fast, clumsy little jerks, his back turned to me. When it was obvious he wasn't going to say anything more, I closed his door gently behind me and went back upstairs. There was no light from Daniel's room, but I could feel him there, only a few feet away in the darkness, listening and thinking.

The next day, when I came out of my five o'clock tutorial, Abby and Justin were waiting for me in the corridor. "Have you seen Rafe?" Abby asked.

"Not since lunch," I said. They were dressed for outdoors—Abby in her long gray coat, Justin's tweed jacket buttoned—and rain sparkled on their shoulders and in their hair. "Didn't he have a thesis meeting?"

"That's what he told us," said Abby, shifting back against the wall to let a bunch of yelling undergrads tumble by, "but thesis meetings don't last four hours, and anyway we checked Armstrong's office. It's locked. He's not in there."

"Maybe he went to the Buttery for a pint," I suggested. Justin winced. We all knew that Rafe had been drinking a little more than was good for him, but nobody mentioned it, ever.

"We checked there too," Abby said. "And he wouldn't go to the Pav, he says it's full of rugger-bugger wankers and it gives him boarding-school flashbacks. I don't know where else to look."

"What's wrong?" Daniel asked, coming out of his tutorial across the corridor.

"We can't find Rafe."

"Hmm," Daniel said, adjusting his armful of books and papers. "Have you tried ringing him?"

"Three times," said Abby. "The first time he hit Reject Call, and after that he turned his phone off."

"Are his things still in his carrel?"

"No," Justin said, slumping against the wall and picking at a cuticle. "Everything's gone."

"But that's a good sign, surely," Daniel said, giving him a look of mild surprise. "It means nothing unexpected's happened to him; he hasn't been hit by a car, or had some kind of health emergency and been taken to hospital. He's simply gone off on his own somewhere."

"Yes, but *where*?" Justin's voice was rising. "And what are we supposed to do now? He can't get home without us. Do we just *leave* him here?"

Daniel gazed down the corridor, over the milling heads. The air smelled of wet carpet; somewhere round the corner a girl shrieked, high and piercing, and Justin and Abby and I all jumped before we realized she was only playing at terrified, the scream had already dissolved into loud flirtatious scolding. Daniel, biting down thoughtfully on his lip, didn't seem to notice.

After a moment he sighed. "Rafe," he said, and gave a quick, exasperated shake of his head. "Honestly. Yes, of course we leave him here; there's really nothing else we can do. If he wants to come home, he can ring one of us, or take a taxi."

"To Glen*skehy*? And I'm not driving all the way back into town for him, just because he feels like being an idiot—"

"Well," Daniel said, "I'm sure he'll find a way." He tucked a stray sheet of paper into the pile he was carrying. "Let's go home."

By the end of dinner—a half-arsed dinner, chicken fillets from the freezer, rice, a bowl of fruit shoved into the middle

The Likeness · 371

of the table—Rafe hadn't rung. He had switched his phone back on, but he was still letting our calls go to voice mail. "It's not like him," Justin said. He was scraping compulsively, with one thumbnail, at the pattern on the edge of his plate.

"Sure it is," said Abby firmly. "He's gone on a bender and picked up some girl, just like he did that other time, remember? He was gone for two days."

"That was different. And what are you nodding about?" Justin added, sourly, to me. "You don't remember that. You weren't even *here* for that."

My adrenaline leaped, but no one looked suspicious; they were all too focused on Rafe to notice a slip that small. "I'm nodding because I've *heard* about it. There's this thing called communication, you should try it sometime—" Everyone was in a prickly mood, including me. I wasn't frantic with worry about Rafe, exactly, but the fact that he wasn't there was making me edgy, and so was the fact that I couldn't tell whether this was for solid investigative reasons—Frank's beloved intuition—or just because without him the balance of the room felt all wrong, off-kilter and precarious.

"How was that different?" Abby wanted to know.

Justin shrugged. "We didn't live together then."

"So? All the more reason. What's he supposed to do, if he wants to hook up with someone? Bring her here?"

"He's supposed to *ring* us. Or at least leave us a note."

"Saying what?" I demanded. I was chopping a peach into tiny bits. " 'Dear guys, I'm off to get laid. Will talk to you tomorrow, or later tonight if I can't score, or at three in the morning if she turns out to be a crap shag—' "

"Don't be vulgar," Justin snapped. "And for God's sake eat that bloody thing or stop messing about with it."

"I'm not being vulgar, I'm just *saying*. And I'll eat it when I'm ready. Do I tell you how to eat?"

"We should call the police," Justin said.

"No," Daniel said, tapping a cigarette on the back of his

wrist. "It wouldn't do any good at this point, anyway. The police wait a certain amount of time after someone goes missing—twenty-four hours, I think, although it may be more—before they set any kind of search in motion. Rafe's an adult—"

"In theory," said Abby.

"—and he has every right to stay out for the night."

"But what if he's done something stupid?" Justin's voice was rising towards a wail.

"One of the reasons I dislike euphemisms," Daniel said, shaking out his match and dropping it neatly into the ashtray, "is that they preclude any real communication. I think it's a safe bet that Rafe has in fact done something stupid, but that covers such a wide variety of possibilities. I assume you're worried that he's busy committing suicide, which frankly I think is extremely unlikely."

After a moment Justin said, without looking up, "Did he ever tell you about that time when he was sixteen? When his parents made him move school for the tenth time or whatever it was?"

"No pasts," Daniel said.

"He wasn't trying to kill himself," Abby said. "He was trying to get some attention from his dickhead dad, and it didn't work."

"I said *no pasts*."

"I'm *not*. I'm just saying this isn't the same, Justin. Hasn't Rafe been completely different, these last few months? Hasn't he been way happier?"

"These last few months," Justin said. "Not these last few weeks."

"Yeah, well," Abby said, and sliced an apple in half with a crisp snap, "we've none of us been at our best. It's still not the same. Rafe knows he's got a home, he knows he's got people who care about him, he's not about to hurt himself. He's just having a hard time, and he's gone off to get hammered and chase skirt. He'll be back when he's good and ready."

"What if he's . . ." Justin's voice trailed off. "I hate this, you know," he said softly, to his plate. "I really hate this."

"Well, so do we all," said Daniel briskly. "It's been a trying time for all of us. We need to accept that and have patience with ourselves, and with one another, while we recover."

"You said to just give it time and it would get better. It's not getting better, Daniel. It's getting *worse*."

"I was thinking," Daniel said, "of a little more time than three weeks. If you consider that unreasonable, then do by all means tell me."

"How can you be so *calm*?" Justin wasn't far off tears. "This is *Rafe* we're talking about."

"Whatever he's doing," Daniel said, turning his head politely to the side to blow smoke away from the rest of us, "I fail to see how it would make any difference if I became hysterical."

"I am not hysterical. This is how normal people react when one of their friends *vanishes*."

"Justin," Abby said, gently, "it's going to be fine," but Justin didn't hear her.

"Just because you're a bloody robot . . . My God, Daniel, just once, just *once* I'd like to see you act as if you *care* about the rest of us, about *anything*—"

"I think you have every reason to be aware," Daniel said coldly, "that I care very deeply about all four of you."

"I do not. *What* reason? I've got every reason to think that you don't give a damn—"

Abby made a small gesture, palm upturned to the ceiling, the room around us, the garden outside. There was something about it, about the way her hand fell back into her lap; something tired, almost resigned.

"That's right," Justin said, slumping down in his chair. The light caught him at a cruel angle, hollowing out his cheeks and raking a long vertical groove between his eyebrows, and for a second I saw like a time-slip overlaid on his face what he would look like in fifty years' time. "Of course. The house. And look where that's got us."

There was a tiny, sharp silence. "I have never claimed," Daniel said, and his voice had a dangerous depth of some emotion that I'd never heard there before, "to be infallible. All I've ever claimed is that I try, very hard, to do what's best for the five of us. If you believe I'm doing such a bad job of it, feel free to make decisions of your own. If you think we shouldn't be living together, then move out. If you think we need to report Rafe missing, then pick up the phone."

After a moment Justin shrugged miserably and went back to picking at his plate. Daniel smoked, gazing into the middle distance. Abby ate her apple; I turned my peach into purée. Nobody said anything for a long time.

"I see you've lost the lady boy," Frank said, when I rang him from my tree. We had apparently inspired him to have a health-food moment: he was eating something with seeds—I could hear him spitting them, attractively, into his hand or wherever. "If he turns up dead, then maybe everyone will start believing me about the mysterious stranger. I should've had money on it."

"Stop being a git, Frankie," I said.

Frank laughed. "You're not worried about him, are you? Seriously?"

I shrugged. "I'd rather know where he is, that's all."

"You can relax, babe. A lovely young lady of my acquaintance was trying to find out where her friend Martin was this evening, and just happened to dial little Rafe's number by mistake. Unfortunately, he didn't mention where he was before the misunderstanding got cleared up, but the background noise gave us a general idea. Abby was bang on: your boy's in a pub somewhere, getting gee-eyed and chasing the ladies. You'll get him back safe and sound, except for a five-star hangover."

So Frank had been worried, too; worried enough to dig out some woman floater with a sexy voice and get her making phone calls. Maybe Naylor hadn't been just a way for

Frank to get at Sam; maybe he had been serious about him as a suspect, all along. I pulled my feet farther up into the branches. "Great," I said. "That's good to know."

"So how come you sound like your cat just died?"

"They're in bad shape," I said, and I was glad Frank couldn't see my face. I thought I was about to fall out of the tree from sheer exhaustion. I grabbed a branch and held on. "For whatever reason—because they can't handle me getting stabbed, or because they can't deal with whatever it is they're not telling us—they're coming apart at the seams."

After a moment Frank said, very gently, "I know you're getting on well with them, babe. That's fine; they're not my cup of Earl Grey, but I've no objection to you feeling differently if it makes your job easier. But they're not your mates. Their problems aren't your problems; they're your opportunities."

"I know," I said. "I know that. It's just hard to watch."

"No harm in a bit of compassion," Frank said cheerfully, taking another big bite of whatever he was eating. "As long as it doesn't get out of hand. I've got something to take your mind off their troubles, though. Your Rafe's not the only one gone missing."

"What are you talking about?"

He spat out seeds. "I was planning on keeping tabs on Naylor, from a safe distance—get a handle on his routine, his associates, all the rest; give you a little more to work with. But it's not turning out that way. He didn't show for work today. His parents haven't seen him since last night, and they say this is out of character; the father's in a wheelchair, it's not like John to leave his mammy to do the heavy lifting on her own. Your Sammy and a couple of floaters are taking turns sitting on his house, and we've told Byrne and Doherty to keep an eye out. For whatever that's worth."

"He won't go far," I said. "This guy wouldn't leave Glenskehy unless he was dragged away kicking and screaming. He'll turn up."

"Yeah, that's what I figure. As far as the stabbing goes, I

don't think this cuts one way or the other; it's a myth that only the guilty ones run. But here's one thing I do know: whatever has Naylor running, it's not fear. Did he look scared to you?"

"No," I said. "Not for a second. He looked furious."

"To me, too. He wasn't one bit happy about that interview. I watched him leave, afterwards; two steps from the door, he turned around and he spat at it. That's one very pissed-off bogger, Cassie, and we already know he's got a temper problem—and, like you said, he's probably still in the area. I don't know whether he's gone missing because he doesn't want us surveilling him, or because he's got something up his sleeve, or what; but watch yourself."

I did. All the way home I kept to the middle of the lanes, with my gun cocked and ready in my hands. I didn't put it back into my girdle until the back gate had clanged behind me and I was safe in the garden, at the edge of the bright tracks of light from the windows.

I hadn't rung Sam. This time it wasn't because I'd forgotten. It was because I had no idea whether he would answer, or what either of us would have to say if he did.

Rafe showed up in the library the next morning, around eleven, with his coat buttoned wrong and his knapsack swinging carelessly from one hand. He stank of cigar smoke and stale Guinness, and he was still pretty unsteady on his feet. "Well," he said, swaying a little and surveying the four of us. "Hello, hello, hello."

"Where have you been?" Daniel hissed. His voice had a tense edge of anger, barely suppressed. He had been a lot more worried about Rafe than he'd let on.

"Here and there," Rafe told him. "Out and about. How are you?"

"We thought something had *happened* to you." Justin's whisper cracked, into something too loud and too sharp. "Why didn't you ring us? Even text us?"

Rafe turned to look at him. "I was otherwise occupied," he said, after considering this. "And I didn't feel like it." One of the Goon Squad, the mature students who always appoint themselves the Library Noise Vigilantes, looked up over his stack of philosophy books and went, "Shhh!"

"Your timing sucks," Abby said coldly. "This was not a good moment to take off on a skirt hunt, and even you should have been able to figure that out."

Rafe rocked backwards on his heels and gave her a deeply miffed look. "Fuck you," he said, loudly and haughtily. "I'll decide when I do what I want."

"Don't talk to her like that any more," Daniel said. He didn't even pretend to care about keeping his voice down. The entire Goon Squad went, "Shhh!" at once.

I tugged at Rafe's sleeve. "Sit down here and talk to me."

378 · Tana French

"Lexie," Rafe said, managing to focus on me. His eyes were bloodshot and his hair needed washing. "I shouldn't have left you on your own, should I?"

"I'm fine," I said. "I'm a happy camper. Want to sit down and tell me how your night went?"

He stretched out a hand; his fingers trailed down my cheek, my throat, slipped along the neckline of my top. I saw Abby's eyes widen behind him, heard a quick rustle from Justin's carrel. "God, you're so sweet," Rafe said. "You're not as delicate as you look, are you? Sometimes I think the rest of us are the other way around."

One of the Goon Squad had dug up Attila, who is the narkiest security guard in the known universe. He obviously went into the job in the hope of getting to crack the heads of dangerous criminals, but since these are thin on the ground in your average college library, he gets his kicks by making lost freshers cry. "Is this fella giving you any bother?" he asked me. He was trying to loom over Rafe, but the height difference was giving him trouble.

The wall went up straight away: Daniel and Abby and Justin snapped into attitudes of cool, poised ease, even Rafe straightened up and whipped his hand away from me and managed to look instantly, effortlessly sober. "Everything's fine," Abby said.

"I didn't ask you," Attila told her. "Do you know this fella?"

He was talking to me. I gave him an angelic smile and said, "Actually, Officer, he's my husband. I did have a barring order against him, but now I've changed my mind and we're off to shag deliriously in the Ladies." Rafe started to snicker.

"There's no fellas allowed in the Ladies," said Attila ominously. "And yous are causing a disturbance."

"It's all right," Daniel said. He stood up and took Rafe by the upper arm—the grip looked casual, but I could see his fingers digging in hard. "We were just leaving. All of us."

"Get *off* me," Rafe snapped, trying to shrug off Daniel's

hand. Daniel steered him briskly past Attila and down the long aisle of books, without looking back to see if the rest of us were following.

We gathered up our stuff, left in a hurry through Attila's awful warnings, and found Daniel and Rafe in the foyer. Daniel was swinging his car keys from one finger; Rafe was leaning lopsidedly against a pillar and sulking.

"Well done," Abby said to Rafe. "Really. That was classy."

"Don't start."

"But what are we doing?" Justin asked Daniel. He was carrying Daniel's stuff, as well as his own; he looked worried and overloaded. "We can't just *leave*."

"Why not?"

There was a brief, taken-aback silence. Our routine was so ingrained, I think it had stopped occurring to any of us that it wasn't actually a law of nature, that we could break it if we wanted to. "What'll we do instead?" I asked.

Daniel threw the car keys into the air and caught them. "We're going to go home and paint the sitting room," he said. "We've been spending far too much time in that library. A bit of work on the house will do us all good."

To any outsider this would have sounded deeply weird— I could hear Frank in my head, *God, they're rock 'n' roll, how do you stand the pace?* But everyone nodded, even, after a moment, Rafe. I had already noticed that the house was their safe zone: whenever things got tense, one of them would steer the conversation onto something that needed fixing or rearranging, and everyone would settle down again. We were going to be in big trouble once the house was all sorted out and we didn't have grouting or floor stains to use as our Happy Place.

It worked, too. Old sheets thrown over the furniture and cold bright air flooding through the open windows, crap clothes and hard work and the smell of paint, ragtime playing in the background, the naughty buzz of ditching college and the house swelling like an approving cat under the attention: it was exactly what we needed. By the time we finished the room, Rafe was starting to look sheepish instead of belligerent, Abby and Justin had relaxed enough to have a long comfortable argument about whether Scott Joplin sucked, and we were all in a much better mood.

"First dibs on the shower," I said.

"Let Rafe have it," said Abby. "To each according to his need." Rafe made a face at her. We were sprawled on the dust sheets, admiring our work and trying to get up the energy to move.

"Once this dries," Daniel said, "we'll need to decide what, if anything, we're putting on the walls."

"I saw these really old tin signs," said Abby, "up in the top spare room—"

"I am not living in a 1980s pub," said Rafe. He had sobered up along the way, or else the paint fumes had got the rest of us high enough that we didn't notice. "Aren't there paintings, or something *normal*?"

"The ones that are left are all horrible," Daniel said. He was leaning back against the edge of the sofa, with spatters of white paint in his hair and on his old plaid shirt, looking happier and more at ease than he had in days. "Landscape with Stag and Hounds, that kind of thing, and not particularly well done, either. Some great-great-aunt with artistic pretensions, I think."

"You've got no soul," Abby told him. "Things with sentimental value aren't *supposed* to have artistic merit as well. They're supposed to be crap. Otherwise, it's just showing off."

"Let's use those old newspapers," I said. I was flat on my back in the middle of the floor, waving my legs in the air to examine the new paint splashes on Lexie's work dungarees. "The ancient ones, with the article about the Dionne quintuplets and the ad for the thing that makes you gain weight. We can stick them all over the walls and varnish over them, like the photos on Justin's door."

"That's in my *bedroom*," Justin said. "A sitting room should have elegance. Grandeur. Not *ads*."

"You know," Rafe said, out of the blue, propping himself up on one elbow, "I do realize that I owe all of you an apology. I shouldn't have vanished, especially not without letting you know where I was. My only excuse, and it's not much of one, is that I was deeply pissed off about that guy getting off scot-free. I'm sorry."

He was at his most charming, and Rafe could be very charming when he felt like it. Daniel gave him a grave little nod. "You're an idiot," I said, "but we love you anyway."

"You're OK," Abby said, stretching up to get her cigarettes off the card table. "I'm not crazy about the idea of that guy running around loose, either."

"You know what I wonder?" Rafe said. "I wonder if Ned hired him to frighten us off."

There was an instant of absolute silence, Abby's hand stopped with a smoke halfway out of the pack, Justin frozen in the middle of sitting up.

Daniel snorted. "I seriously doubt that Ned has the intellect for anything that complex," he said acidly.

I had opened my mouth to ask, *Who's Ned?* but I had shut it again, fast; not just because I was obviously supposed to know this, but because I did. I could have kicked myself for not seeing it earlier. Frank has always thrown diminutives at people he doesn't like—Danny Boy, our Sammy—and like an idiot I had never considered the possibility that he might have picked the wrong one. They were talking about Slow Eddie. Slow Eddie, who had been wandering around the late-night laneways looking for someone, who had claimed he'd never met Lexie, was N. I was sure Frank could hear my heart punching the mike.

"Probably not," Rafe said, lying back on his elbows and contemplating the walls. "When we're done here, we should really invite him over for dinner."

"Over my dead body," said Abby. Her voice was tightening up. "You didn't have to deal with him. We did."

"And mine," said Justin. "The man's a Philistine. He drank Heineken all night, of course, and then he kept belching and naturally he thought that was hilarious, every single time. And all that droning about fitted kitchens and tax breaks and Section Whatever-it-is. Once was enough, thank you very much."

"You people have no heart," Rafe told them. "Ned *loves* this house. He told the judge so. I think we owe him a chance to see that the old family seat is in good hands. Give me a smoke."

"The only thing Ned loves," Daniel said, very sharply, "is the thought of six fully fitted *executive apartments* on extensive grounds with potential for further development. And over *my* dead body will he ever get a chance to see that."

Justin made a sudden jerky movement, covered it by reaching for an ashtray and shoving it across to Abby. There was a complicated, sharp-edged silence. Abby lit her smoke, shook out the match and threw the packet to Rafe, who caught it one-handed. Nobody was looking at anybody. An early bumblebee blundered in at the window, hovered over the piano in a slant of sun and eventually bumped back out again.

I wanted to say something—that was my job, defusing moments like this one—but I knew we had veered into some kind of treacherous and complicated swamp where one misstep could get me into big trouble. Ned was sounding like more and more of a wankstain—even if I didn't have the first clue what an executive apartment was, I got the general idea—but whatever was going on ran a lot deeper and darker than that.

Abby was watching me over her cigarette with cool, curious gray eyes. I shot her an agonized look, which didn't take much effort. After a moment she stretched for the ashtray and said, "If there's nothing decent to put up on the walls, maybe we should try something different. Rafe, if we found photos of old murals, do you think you could do something like that?"

Rafe shrugged. An edge of the belligerent don't-blame-me look was creeping back onto his face. That dark electric cloud had come down over the room again.

Silence was fine with me. My mind was doing cartwheels—not just because Lexie had for some reason been hanging out with the archenemy, but because Ned was clearly a taboo subject. For three weeks his name had never been mentioned, the first reference to him had fried everyone's heads, and I couldn't figure out why. He had lost, after all; the house was Daniel's, both Uncle Simon and a judge had said so, Ned should have triggered nothing more serious than a laugh and a few snide comments. I would have sold a major organ to find out what the hell was going on here, but I knew a lot better than to ask.

As it turned out, I didn't have to. Frank's mind—and I wasn't at all sure I liked this—had run parallel to mine, parallel and fast.

I went for my walk as early as I could. That cloud hadn't dissipated; if anything it had got thicker, pressing in from the walls and ceilings. Dinner had been painful. Justin and Abby and I had done our best to be chatty, but Rafe had gone into a sour sulk that you could practically see, and Daniel had withdrawn into himself, answering questions in monosyllables. I needed to get out of that house and think.

Lexie had met up with Ned at least three times, and she had gone to a lot of trouble to do it. The four big Ls of motive: lust, lucre, loathing and love. The chance of lust made my gag reflex kick in; the more I heard about Ned, the more I wanted to believe that Lexie wouldn't have touched him with someone else's. Lucre, though . . . She had needed money, fast, and a rich boy like Ned would have made a way better buyer than John Naylor and his crap farm job. If she had been meeting Ned to discuss what knickknacks he might want from Whitethorn House, how much he would be willing to pay, and then something had gone wrong . . .

It was a very strange night: huge and dark and gusty, snaps of wind roaring across the hillsides, a million high stars and no moon. I stuffed my gun back into my girdle, climbed up my tree and spent a long time there, watching the shadowy black surge of the bushes below me, listening hard for any faint sound that didn't belong; thinking about phoning Sam.

In the end I phoned Frank. "Naylor hasn't shown up yet," he said, no hello. "You keeping an eye out?"

"Yeah," I said. "No sign of him, as far as I can tell."

"Right." There was an absent note to his voice that told me his mind wasn't on Naylor either. "Good. Meanwhile, I've got something that might interest you. You know the way your new pals were bitching about Cousin Eddie and his executive apartments, this afternoon?"

For a second all my muscles jolted awake, till I remembered Frank didn't know about N. "Yep," I said. "Cousin Eddie sounds like a right little gem."

"Oh, yeah. One hundred percent pure brain-dead yuppie fuck, never had a thought in his life that didn't involve his dick or his wallet."

"You think Rafe was right about him hiring Naylor?"

"Not a chance. Eddie doesn't hobnob with the lower classes. You should've seen his face when he heard my accent; I think he was afraid I was going to mug him. But this afternoon reminded me. Remember how you said the Fantastic Four were weird about the house? Too attached?"

"Oh," I said. "Yeah." I had almost forgotten that, actually. "I think I overreacted. When you put a lot of work into a place, you do get attached to it. And it's a nice house."

"Oh, it is," Frank said. There was something in his tone that set my alarm bells jingling faintly, a fierce, sardonic grin. "It is that. I was bored today—Naylor's still in the wind and I'm getting nowhere on Lexie-May-Ruth-Princess-Anastasia-whoever, I've drawn a blank in about fourteen countries so far, I'm considering the possibility that she was built in a pod by mad scientists in 1997. So, just to show my homegirl Cassie that I trust her instincts, I put in a call to my mate in the Land Registry office and ask him for a rundown on Whitethorn House. Who loves you, baby?"

"You do," I said. Frank has always had a spectacular array of mates in unlikely places: my mate down at the docks, my mate on the County Council, my mate who runs the S&M shop. Back when we first began this whole Lexie Madison thing, My Mate At Births Deaths and Marriages made sure she was officially registered, in case anyone got suspicious and started sniffing around, while My Mate With The Van helped me move into her bedsit. I figure I'm happier not knowing about whatever complex barter system is going on there. "You bloody well should, after all this. And?"

"And remember saying they all act like they own the place?"

"Yeah. I guess."

"Your instincts hit the jackpot, babe. They do. So do you, actually."

"Quit being cute, Frankie," I said. My heart was pounding hard and slow and there was a strange dark shiver through the hedges: something was happening. "What are you on about?"

"Old Simon's will cleared probate and Daniel took possession of Whitethorn House on the tenth of September. On the fifteenth of December, ownership of the house was transferred into five names: Raphael Hyland, Alexandra Madison, Justin Mannering, Daniel March and Abigail Stone. Happy Christmas."

It was the sheer blazing courage of it that hit me first: the passion of trust it would take, to put your future where your mouth was, no half measures, scoop up all your tomorrows and put them so deliberately, so simply, in the hands of the people you loved best. I thought of Daniel at the table, broad-backed and solid in his crisp white shirt, the precise flick of his wrist as he turned a page; of Abby flipping bacon in her bathrobe, Justin singing out of tune while he got ready for bed, Rafe sprawled on the grass squinting up into the sun. And all the time, underpinning everything, this. I had had moments of envying them before, but this was something too deep for envy; something like awe.

And then I realized. N, plane fares, *Over my dead body will Ned get a chance.* Here I had been fucking about with music boxes and tin soldiers and trying to figure out how much your average family photo album was worth; here I had thought she had nothing to sell, this time.

If she had been negotiating with Ned, and the others had somehow found out: holy shit. No wonder his name had turned the room to ice, that afternoon. I couldn't breathe.

Frank was still going. I could hear him moving, pacing up and down the room, fast steps. "The paperwork on that would take months; Danny Boy must've started it almost the same day he got the keys. I know you like these people, Cassie, but you can't tell me that's not bizarre as all hell. That house is worth a cool couple of million, easy. What the fuck is he thinking? They're all going to live there forever in one big happy hippie commune? Actually, never mind what he's thinking, what the fuck is he *smoking*?"

He was taking it personally because he had missed it: all that investigation, and the middle-class student wimps had somehow slipped this right past him. "Yeah," I said, very carefully, "it's weird. They *are* weird, Frank. And yeah, it's going to get complicated down the road, when someone wants to get married or whatever. But, like you said your-self, they're young. They're not thinking that way yet."

"Yeah, well, little Justin won't be getting married any time soon, not without a major change in the legislation—"

"Stop being a cliché, Frank. What's the big deal?" This didn't mean it had to be one of the four of them, not neces-sarily; the evidence still added up to Lexie being stabbed by someone she had met outside the house. It didn't even mean she had actually been going to sell. If she had made a deal with Ned and then changed her mind, told him she was backing out; if she had just been playing with him all along—*loathing*—yanking his chain to pay him back for trying to take the house . . . He had wanted Whitethorn House badly enough to spit on his grandfather's memory; what would he have done if a share of it had been so close he could taste it, and then Lexie had snatched it away? I tried to shove the diary out of my mind: those dates, the first N just a few days after that missing circle; the hard scribble, pen almost digging through the paper, that said she hadn't been playing.

"Well," Frank said, with the lazy note to his voice that means he's at his most dangerous. "If you ask me, this could give us the motive we've been looking for. Me, I'd call that a big deal."

"No," I said promptly, maybe too promptly, but Frank didn't comment. "Not a chance. Where's the motive in that? If they all wanted to sell and she was blocking it, then maybe, but those four would rather pull out their own teeth with rusty pliers than sell that house. What have they got to gain by killing her?"

"One of them dies, his share—or hers—reverts back to the other four. Maybe someone figured a quarter of that lovely big house would be even nicer than a fifth. It more or less lets Danny Boy out—if he wanted the whole thing, he could've just kept it to start with. But that still leaves us with three little Indians."

I wriggled round the other way on my branch. I was very glad that Frank was off target, but, illogically, the extent to which he didn't get it was pissing me off. "What *for*? Like I said, they don't want to sell it. They want to *live* in it. They can do that just as well no matter what percentage they own. You think one of them killed her because he liked her bedroom better than his own?"

"Or her own. Abby's a good kid, but I'm not ruling her out. Or maybe it wasn't financial, for once; maybe Lexie was just plain driving someone nuts. People share a house, they get on each other's tits. And remember, there's a very good chance she was shagging one of the lads, and we all know how nasty that can turn. If you're renting, no big deal: some yelling, a few tears, a house meeting, one of you moves out. But what do you do if it's a co-owner? They can't throw her out, I doubt any of them can afford to buy her out—"

"Sure," I said, "except I haven't got one single whiff of any kind of major tension aimed at me. Rafe was pissed off with me at first for not realizing how shaken up they all were, but that's *it*. If Lexie had been getting up someone's nose to the point of murder, there's no way I could have missed it. These people *like* each other, Frank. They may be weird, but they like being weird together."

"So why didn't they tell us they all own the place? Why are they being so fucking secretive, unless they're hiding something?"

"They didn't tell you because you never asked them. If you were in their place, even if you were innocent as a baby, would you give the cops anything you didn't have to? Would you even spend hours answering questions, the way they have?"

"You know what you're talking like?" Frank said, after a pause. He had stopped pacing. "You're talking like a defense attorney."

I twisted round the other way again, swung my feet up against a branch. I was having a hard time staying still. "Oh, come on, Frank. I'm talking like a *detective*. And you're talking like a fucking obsessive. If you don't like these four, that's fine. If they twang your antennae, that's fine too. But it doesn't mean that every single thing you find is automatically evidence that they're stone-cold killers."

"I don't think you're in any position to question my objectivity, babe," Frank said. That lazy drawl had come back into his voice, and it made my back tense up against the tree trunk.

"What the hell is that supposed to mean?"

"It means I'm on the outside, keeping my perspective,

while you're neck-deep in all the action, and I'd like you to keep that in mind. It also means I think there's a limit to how far 'Oh, they're just charmingly eccentric' will go as an excuse for acting downright bloody squirrely."

"What brought this on, Frank? You've counted them out since the beginning, two days ago you were all over Naylor like a rash—"

"And I still am, or I will be as soon as we find the little bastard again. But I like spreading my bets. I'm not dropping anyone, anyone at all, until they're definitively ruled out. And these four haven't been. Don't forget that."

It was way past time for me to back off. "Fair enough," I said. "Until Naylor turns up again, I'll focus on them."

"You do that. So will I. And keep watching yourself, Cassie. Not just outside that house; inside, too. Talk tomorrow." And he was gone.

The fourth big L: love. I thought, suddenly, of the phone videos: a picnic on Bray Head, the summer before, all of them lying on the grass drinking wine out of plastic cups and eating strawberries and arguing lazily over whether Elvis was overrated. Daniel had gone into a long absorbed monologue about sociocultural context, until Rafe and Lexie decided everything was overrated except Elvis and chocolate and started throwing strawberries at him. They had been passing the camera phone around; the clips were disjointed and shaky. Lexie with her head in Justin's lap and him tucking a daisy behind her ear; Lexie and Abby sitting back to back and looking out at the sea, hair blowing, shoulders lifting in long matching breaths; Lexie laughing up into Daniel's face as she picked a ladybug out of his hair and held it out, him bending his head over her hand and smiling. I had seen the video so many times that it felt like my own memory, flickering and sweet. They had been happy, that day, all five of them.

There had been love there. It had looked solid and simple as bread; real. And it felt real to live in, a warm element through which we moved easily and which we breathed in with every breath. But Lexie had been ready and willing to blow all that sky-high. More than willing; hell-bent on it— that furious scrawl in the date book, while the phone video showed her climbing down from the attic laughing and covered in dust. If she had lived a couple of weeks longer, the others would have woken up one morning and found her gone, not a note, not a good-bye, not a second thought. It slid through a back corner of my mind that Lexie Madison had been dangerous, under that bright surface, and that maybe she still was.

I slid off my branch, hanging by my hands, dropped and landed in the lane with a thump. I dug my hands into my pockets and started walking—moving helps me think. The wind pulled at my cap and shoved into the small of my back, almost taking me off my feet.

I needed to talk to Ned, fast. Lexie had neglected to leave me instructions on how the hell they got in touch with each other. Not by mobile: Sam had pulled her phone records first thing, no unidentified numbers in or out. Carrier pigeon? Notes in the hollow tree? Smoke signals?

I didn't have much time. Frank had no idea that Lexie had ever met Ned and no idea that she had been getting ready to blow town—I knew there would turn out to be a good reason why I didn't want to tell him about that diary; just like he always says, your instincts work faster than your mind. But he wasn't about to let go of this. He would worry away at it like a pit bull, and sooner or later he was going to hit on this same possibility. I didn't know all that much about Ned, but enough to be pretty sure that, if he ended up in an interview room with Frank going at him full throttle, he would spill his guts inside five minutes. It never once occurred to me, not for a second, to sit back and let that happen. Whatever had been going on here, I needed to put my finger on it before Frank did.

If I wanted to make an appointment to meet Ned,

without any chance of the others finding out, how would I do it?

No phones. Mobiles keep a call register and they get itemized bills, she wouldn't have left anything like that lying around, and Whitethorn House didn't have a landline. There was no pay phone within walking distance, and the ones in college were risky: the Arts block phones were the only ones close enough to use on a fake bathroom break, and if one of the others had happened to walk by at the wrong moment, she would have been fucked—and this was too important for gambles. No calling in to see him, either. Frank had said Ned lived in Bray and worked in Killiney, there was no way she could have got there and back without the others missing her. And no letters or e-mails; she would never, not in a million years, have left a trail.

"How the hell, girl?" I said softly, into the air. I felt her like a shimmer over my shadow on the lane, the tilt of her chin and the mocking sideways flash of her eyes: *Not telling*.

Somewhere along the way I had stopped noticing just how seamlessly conjoined their five lives were. Into college together, all day in the library together, smoke break at noon with Abby and at four with Rafe, lunch together at one, home together for dinner: the routine of it was choreographed as precisely and tightly as a gavotte, never a minute left unaccounted for and never a minute to myself, except—

Except now. For one hour a night, like some spellbound girl in a fairy tale, I unwound my life from the others' and it was all my own again. If I were Lexie and I wanted to contact someone I should never have been contacting, I would use my late-night walk.

Not *would*: had. For weeks now I had been using it to phone Frank, phone Sam, keep my secrets safe. A fox skittered across the lane in front of me and vanished into the hedge, all bones and luminous eyes, and a shiver went down my back. Here I had thought this was my very own bright idea, I was making my own way step by step and alert through the dark. It was only now, when I turned around and looked back down the road, that I realized I had been blithely, blindly putting my feet smack in Lexie's footsteps, all the way.

"So?" I said aloud, like a challenge. "So what?" This was what Frank had sent me in for, to get close to the victim, get into her life, and—duh—I was doing it. A certain amount of creepy was not only beside the point but also pretty much par for the course on a murder investigation; they're not supposed to be one long round of laughs. I was getting spoiled, all these cozy candlelight dinners and handicrafts, turning jumpy when reality kicked back in.

One hour to get hold of Ned. How?

Notes in the hollow tree . . . I almost laughed out loud. Professional deformation: you've got the most esoteric possibilities all worked out, it's the simple ones that take forever to hit you. The higher the stakes, Frank once told me, the lower the technology. If you want to meet your mate for coffee, you can afford to arrange it by text message or e-mail; if you think the cops or the Mob or the Illuminati are closing in, you signal your contact with a blue towel on the washing line. For Lexie, days ticking away and morning sickness starting to kick in, the stakes must have felt like life and death.

Ned lived in Bray; only a fifteen-minute drive away, outside rush hour. Probably she had taken the risk of phoning him from college, the first time. After that, all she had needed was a safe drop spot, somewhere in these lanes, that both of them could check every couple of days. I must have walked straight past it a dozen times.

That shimmer again, in the corner of my eye: tip of a grin, there and tricky and then gone.

In the cottage? The Bureau gang had been all over it like flies on shite, dusted every inch for prints and found nothing. And he hadn't been parked anywhere near the cottage, that night I'd followed him. Allowing a little leeway for the fact that God forbid you should drive your Monster Truck on the kind of roads for which it was constructed, he would have parked as close to the drop spot as he could get. He had been on the main Rathowen road, nowhere near any turnoff. Wide verges, long grass and brambles, the dark road dropping away over the brow of the hill; and the milestone, worn and leaning like a tiny grave-marker.

I hardly realized I had turned around and was running hard. The others would be expecting me back any minute and the last thing I wanted was for them to get worried and come looking for me, but this couldn't wait till tomorrow night. I wasn't racing some hypothetical, infinitely flexible deadline any more; I was racing against Frank's mind, and Lexie's.

After the narrow lanes, the verge felt wide and bare and very exposed, but the road was deserted, not a glimmer of headlights in either direction. When I pulled out my torch, the letters on the stone marker jumped out at me, blurred with time and weather, throwing their own slanted shadows: *Glenskehy 1828*. The grass swirled and bent around it, in the high wind, with a sound like a long hiss of breath.

I caught the torch under my arm and parted the grass with both hands; it was wet and sharp-edged, tiny serrations pulling at my fingers. At the foot of the stone, something flashed crimson.

For a moment my mind couldn't take in what I was seeing. Sunk deep in the grass, colors glowed bright as jewels and minute figures scudded away from the torchlight: gloss of a horse's flank, flick of a red coat, toss of powdered curls and a dog's head turning as he leaped for cover. Then my hand touched wet, gritty metal and the figures shivered and clicked into place, and I laughed out loud, a small gasp that sounded strange even to me. A cigarette tin, old and rusty and probably nicked from Uncle Simon's stash; the rich, battered hunting scene was painted with a brush fine as an eyelash. The Bureau and the floaters had done a fingertip search for a mile around the cottage, but this was outside their perimeter. Lexie had beaten them, saved this for me.

The note was on lined paper torn out of some kind of

Filofax thing. The handwriting looked like a ten-year-old's, and apparently Ned hadn't been able to decide whether he was writing a business letter or a text message: *Dear Lexie, been trying 2 get hold of u in refrence 2 that matter we were talking about, Im still v v interested. Please let me know whenever u get a chance. Thanks, Ned.* I was willing to bet that Ned had gone to an insanely expensive private school. Daddy hadn't exactly got his money's worth.

Dear Lexie; Thanks, Ned . . . Lexie must have wanted to kick him for leaving that kind of thing lying around, no matter how well hidden. I took out my lighter, moved over to the road and set the note on fire; when it caught, I dropped it, waited for the quick flare to die down and crushed out the embers with my foot. Then I found my Biro and ripped a page out of my notebook.

By this stage Lexie's handwriting came easier than my own. *11 Thursday—talk then.* No need for fancy bait: Lexie had done all that for me, this guy was already well hooked. The tin shut with a neat, tiny click and I tucked it back into the long grass, feeling my fingerprints overlaying themselves perfectly on Lexie's, my feet planted carefully in the precise spots where her footprints had long since washed away.

18

The next day lasted about a week. The Arts block was too hot, dry and airless. My tutorial group were bored and fidgety; it was their last session, they hadn't read the material and couldn't be bothered to fake it, and I couldn't be bothered pretending I cared. All I could think about was Ned: whether he would show, what I would say if he did, what I would do if he didn't; how long I had before Frank caught up with us.

I knew that night was a long shot. Even assuming I was right about the cottage being their meeting place, Ned might easily have given up on Lexie altogether, after a month with no communication—he hadn't dated his note, it could have been weeks old. And even if he was the persistent type, the odds were against him checking the drop spot in time to make the meeting. A big part of me hoped he wouldn't. I needed to hear what he had to say, but anything I heard, Frank was going to hear too.

I got to the cottage early, around half past ten. At home, Rafe was playing stormy Beethoven with an awful lot of pedal, Justin was trying to read with his fingers in his ears, everyone was getting snippier by the minute and the whole thing showed every sign of spiralling into a vicious argument.

It was only the third time I had been inside that cottage. I was a little wary about angry farmers—the field had to belong to someone, after all, although apparently he wasn't too attached to it—but it was a still, bright night, nothing moving for miles around, just pale empty fields and the mountains black silhouettes against the stars. I got my back into a corner, where I could see the field and the road but where the shadows would mask me from anyone watching, and waited.

Just on the off chance that Ned did show up, I had to get this right; I only had one shot. I needed to let him lead, not just on everything I said, but on how I said it. Whatever Lexie had been for him, I needed to be the same. Going on past form, that could have been anything—breathy vamp, brave put-upon Cinderella, enigmatic Mata Hari—and, regardless of what Frank said about Ned's brainpower, if I hit the wrong note even he would probably notice. All I could do was play it quiet and hope he gave me some cue.

The road was white and mysterious, curling away downhill into deep black hedges. A few minutes before eleven there was a vibration somewhere, too deep or too far away to pinpoint, just a throb tugging at the edge of my hearing. Silence; then the faint crunch of footsteps, away down the lane. I pressed back into the corner and got one hand around my torch and the other up my sweater, on the butt of my gun.

That flash of fair hair, moving among the dark hedges. Ned had made it after all.

I let go of my gun and watched him haul himself awkwardly over the wall, inspect his trousers for contamination, brush off his hands and pick his way across the field with deep distaste. I waited till he was in the cottage, only a few feet away, before I switched on my torch.

"God," Ned said peevishly, throwing an arm up to shield his eyes. "Like, go ahead and totally blind me?"

That right there was, like, totally enough time for me to learn everything I needed to know about Ned in one easy lesson. Here I had been all freaked out about having one double; he must have run into a clone of himself on every street corner in south Dublin. He was so exactly like everyone else that there was no way to see him, through all those thousands of reflected images. Standard-issue trendy haircut, standard-issue good looks, standard-issue rugby build, standard-issue overpriced labels; I could have told you his whole life story on that one glance. I hoped to God I never had to pick him out of a lineup.

Lexie would have given him whatever he wanted to see, and there was no doubt in my mind that Ned liked his girls clichéd: sexy by numbers rather than by nature, humorless, not too bright and ever so slightly bitchy. It was a shame I didn't have a fake tan. "Ohmy*God*," I said, matching his peeved tone and doing the same geebag accent I'd used to get Naylor out of his hedge. "Don't have a thrombo. It's just a torch." This conversation wasn't starting out on a great note, but I was OK with that. There are some social circles where manners are a sign of weakness.

"Where have you been?" Ned demanded. "I've been leaving you notes, like, every other *day*. I've got better stuff to do than haul my arse down to bogland all the time, yah?"

If Lexie had been shagging this space waste, I was going to head over to the morgue and stab her myself. I rolled my eyes. "Um, hello? I got stabbed? I was in a *coma*?"

"Oh," Ned said. "Yah. Right." He gave me a pale-blue, vaguely put-out stare, like I'd done something tasteless. "Still, though. You could have got in touch. This is *business*."

That, at least, was good news. "Yah, well," I said. "We're in touch now, aren't we?"

"This total fucking low-life detective came and talked to me," Ned said, suddenly remembering. He looked as outraged as you can get without changing expression. "Like I was a suspect, or something. I told him this was so not my problem. I'm not from Bally*mun*. I don't *stab* people."

I decided I was with Frank on this one: Ned was not the brightest little bunny hopping through this forest. He was the type who was basically one big cluster of secondhand reflexes, no actual thought involved. I would have been willing to bet good money that he talked to working-class clients as though they were handicapped and said "Me love you long time" whenever he saw an Asian girl. "Did you tell him about this?" I asked, pulling myself up onto a broken bit of wall.

He gave me a horrified look. "No way. He'd have been all over me like a rash, and I couldn't be arsed trying to explain myself to him. I just want this sorted, yah?"

And civic-minded, too—not that I was complaining. "Good," I said. "I mean, it's not like this has anything to do with what happened to me, right?"

Ned didn't seem to have an opinion on that. He went to lean against the wall, examined it suspiciously and changed his mind. "So can we, like, move forwards?" he wanted to know.

I ducked my head and threw him a sideways poor-little-me glance, up under the lashes. "The coma totally messed up my memory. So you'll have to tell me where we were, and stuff?"

Ned stared at me. That impassive face, utterly expressionless, giving away nothing: for the first time I saw a resemblance to Daniel, even if it was Daniel after a frontal lobotomy. "We were on a hundred," he said, after a moment. "Cash."

A hundred quid for some family heirloom, a hundred grand for a share of the house? I didn't have to be sure what we were talking about to know he was lying. "Um, I don't think so," I told him, giving him a flirty smirk to soften the blow of being outsmarted by a girl. "The coma messed up my memory, not my *brain*."

Ned laughed, completely unembarrassed, stuffing his hands in his pockets and rocking back on his heels. "Well, hey, a guy's gotta try, right?"

I kept the smirk, since he seemed to like it. "Keep trying."

"OK," Ned said, sobering up and putting on his business face. "Seriously. So I said one eighty, right? And you told me I'd have to do better than that, which you're totally breaking my bollocks here but fair enough, and to get back to you. So I left you a note saying we can talk about two hundred K, right, but then you . . ." An uncomfortable shrug. "You know."

Two hundred K. For a second all I felt was the pure white high of triumph, the one every detective knows, when the cards turn over and you see that every bet you placed was pinpoint perfect, that flying blind you found your way straight home. Then I realized.

I had assumed Ned was the one holding things up, sorting out paperwork or trying to raise cash. Lexie had never needed serious money to run before. She had reached North Carolina with the deposit for a fleabag apartment and left it with what she got for her beaten-up car; all she had ever asked for was an open road and a few hours' head start. This time, she had been negotiating six-figure deals with Ned. Not just because she could; with the baby growing and Abby's sharp eyes in the background and an offer that size on the table, why hang around for weeks over a few grand either way? She would have signed on the dotted line, demanded small bills and been gone, unless she needed every penny she could get.

The more I had learned about Lexie, the more I had taken it for granted that she was planning on having an abortion, as soon as she got to wherever she was going. Abby—and Abby had known her, as well as anyone could— thought the same, after all. But an abortion only costs a few hundred quid. Lexie could have saved that much from her job by this time, nicked it out of the kitty one night, got a bank loan she would never repay; no need to mess around with Ned at all.

Raising a child costs a whole lot more. The princess of No Man's Land, the queen of a thousand castles between worlds, had crossed over. She had been about to open her hands and take hold of the biggest commitment of all. The wall felt like it was turning to water underneath me.

I must have been staring like I'd seen a ghost. "Seriously," Ned said, a little miffed, misreading the look. "I'm not messing you around. Two hundred Gs is my absolute best offer. I mean, I'm taking a major risk here. After we're sorted, I've still got to convince at least two of your mates. I'll get there in the end, obviously, once I've got the leverage, but that could take months and a shitload of hassle."

I pressed my free hand down on the wall, hard, feeling the rough stone dig into my palm, till my head cleared. "You think?"

Those pale eyes widened. "Oh, God, yah. I don't know what the fuck their damage is. I know they're your friends and Daniel's my cousin and shit, but, like, are they thick? Just the thought of doing something with that house had them squealing like a bunch of nuns at a flasher."

I shrugged. "They like the place."

"*Why?* I mean, it's a total dive, it doesn't even have *heating,* and they act like it's some kind of *palace.* Do they not realize what they could get out of it, if they just got a grip? That house has *potential.*"

Executive apartments on extensive grounds with potential for further development . . . For a second I despised Lexie and me both, for schmoozing this little skid mark for our own ends. "I'm the smart one," I said. "When you get the place, what are you going to do with all that potential?"

Ned gave me a baffled stare; presumably he and Lexie had already talked about this. I gave him back a blank look, which seemed to make him feel at home. "Depends on planning permission, yah? I mean, ideally, I'll go for a golf club or a spa hotel, something like that. That's where the serious long-term profit is, specially if I can get a helipad put in. Otherwise, we're talking major luxury apartments."

I considered kicking him in the nads and running. I had gone in there all ready to hate this guy's guts, and he wasn't letting me down. Ned didn't want Whitethorn House; he didn't give a flying fuck about it, no matter what he had said in court. What had him salivating wasn't the house but the thought of wrecking it, the chance to rip its throat out, scrape its ribs hollow and lick up every last taste of blood.

For a flash I saw John Naylor's face, swollen and discolored, lit up by those visionary eyes: *Do you know what that hotel would have done for Glenskehy?* Deep down, deeper and more powerful than the fact that they would loathe each other's guts, he and Ned were two sides of the same coin. *When they pack up their things and go,* Naylor had said, *I want to be there to wave them good-bye.* At least he had been willing to put his body, not just his bank account, on the line for what he wanted.

"Brilliant idea," I said. "I mean, it's so important not to let a house just sit there being lived in."

Ned missed the sarcasm. "Obviously," he said hastily, in case I started looking for a bigger cut, "it's going to take, like, a ton of investment cash just to get it off the ground. So two hundred's the best I can do. Are we good with that? Can I get the paperwork moving?"

I pursed up my mouth and pretended to mull that one over. "I'll have to have a little think about it."

"Ah, for fuck's *sake.*" Ned raked a hand through his quiff, frustrated, then smoothed it carefully back into shape. "Come on. This has been dragging on for, like, ever."

"Sor-*ry,*" I said, shrugging. "If you were in such a major hurry, you should've made me a decent offer to start with."

"Well, I am now, right? I've got investors lining up begging to get in on the ground floor of this, but they won't hang around forever. These are serious guys? With serious money?"

I gave him the smirk, with a bitchy little nose-wrinkle thrown in. "So I'll seriously let you know the exact second I decide. OK?" And I waved bye-bye.

Ned stayed put for another few seconds, shifting from foot to foot and looking majorly pissed off, but I kept the glassy smirk going. "Right," he said, finally. "Fine. Whatever. Let me know."

In the doorway he turned to tell me, impressively, "This could put me on the *map,* you know. This could have me playing with the *big* boys. So let's not fuck it up, OK?"

He was trying for a dramatic exit, but he lost his chance by tripping over something as he turned to flounce off. He tried to save it by breaking into a jaunty little jog across the field, not looking back.

I switched off my torch and waited there, in the cottage, while Ned sloshed through the grass and found his way back to his studmobile and Panzered off towards civilization, the throb of the SUV tiny and meaningless against the huge night hillsides. Then I sat down against the wall of the outer room and felt my heart beat where hers had finished beating. The air was soft and warm as cream; my arse went to sleep; tiny moths whirled around me like petals. There were things growing beside me out of the earth where she had bled, a pale clump of bluebells, a tiny sapling that looked like hawthorn: things made of her.

Even if Frank hadn't caught the live show, he would hear that conversation in just a few hours, as soon as he got into work the next morning. I should have been on the phone to him or Sam or both, working out the best ways to use this, but I felt like if I moved or tried to talk or breathed too hard my mind would spill over, soak away into the long grass.

I had been so sure. Can you blame me? This girl like a wildcat gnawing off her own limbs sooner than be trapped; I had been positive that *forever* was the one word she would never say. I tried to tell myself she might have been planning to give the baby up for adoption, ditch the hospital as soon as she could walk and vanish from the parking lot to the next promised land, but I knew: those numbers she had been throwing around with Ned weren't for any hospital, no matter how fancy. They were for a life; for two lives.

Just like she had let the others sculpt her delicately, unconsciously, into the little sister to round out their strange family, just like she had let Ned shape her into the clichés that were all he understood, she had let me make her into what I was longing to see. A master key to open every slamming door, a never-ending freeway to a million clean starts. There's no such thing. Even this girl who left lives behind like rest stops had found her exit, in the end, and had been ready to take it.

I sat in the cottage for a long time, with my fingers wrapped around the sapling—gently, it was so new, I didn't want to bruise it. I'm not sure how long it was before I managed to make myself stand up; I barely remember walking home. A part of me was actually hoping John Naylor would leap out of a hedge, blazing with his cause and looking for a screaming match or an all-out brawl, just to give me something I could fight.

The house was lit up like a Christmas tree, every window blazing, silhouettes flitting and a babble of voices pouring out, and for a moment I couldn't take it in: had something terrible happened, was someone dying, had the house tilted and sideslipped and tossed up some gay long-gone party, if I stepped onto the lawn would I tumble straight into 1910? Then the gate clanged shut behind me and Abby threw the French doors open, calling, "Lexie!" and came running down the grass, long white skirt streaming.

"I was keeping an eye out for you," she said. She was breathless and flushed, eyes sparkling and her hair starting to come loose from its clips; she had obviously been drinking. "We're being decadent. Rafe and Justin made this punch stuff with cognac and rum and I don't know what else is in it but it's *lethal,* and nobody has tutorials or anything tomorrow so fuck it, we're not going into college, we're staying up drinking and making eejits of ourselves till we all fall over. Sound good?"

"Sounds brilliant," I said. My voice came out strange, dislocated—it was taking me a while to pull myself together and catch up—but Abby didn't seem to notice.

"You think? See, at first I wasn't sure it was a good idea. But Rafe and Justin were already making the punch—Rafe set some kind of booze on *fire,* on purpose, like—and they yelled at me for always worrying about everything. And, I mean, at least for once they're not bitching at each other, right? So I figured what the hell, we need it. After the last few days—God, after the last few *weeks*. We've all been turning into crazy people, did you realize that? That thing the other night, with the rock and the fight and . . . Jesus."

Something crossed her face, a dark flicker, but before I could place it, it had vanished and the reckless, tipsy gaiety was back. "So I figure, if we go completely nuts for tonight and get everything out of our systems, then maybe we can all chill out and go back to normal. What do you think?"

Being this drunk made her seem much younger. Somewhere in Frank's bomber-paced war-game mind she and her three best friends were being lined up and inspected, one by one, inch by inch; he was evaluating them, cool as a surgeon or a torturer, deciding where to make the first test cut, where to insert the first delicate probe. "I would love that," I said. "God, I'd love that."

"We started without you," Abby said, rearing back on her heels to inspect me anxiously. "You don't mind, do you? That we didn't wait for you?"

"Course not," I said. "As long as there's some left." Far behind her, shadows crisscrossed on the living-room wall; Rafe bent with a glass in one hand and his hair gold as a mirage against the dark curtains, and Josephine Baker poured out through the open windows, sweet and scratchy and beckoning: *"Mon rêve c'était vous . . ."* In all my life I had seldom wanted anything as wildly as I wanted to be in there, get this gun and this phone off me, drink and dance until a fuse blew in my brain and there was nothing left in the world except the music and the blaze of lights and the four of them surrounding me, laughing, dazzling, untouchable.

"Well, of course there's some left. What do you think we are?" She caught my wrist and headed back towards the house, pulling me behind her, twisting her skirt up off the grass with her free hand. "You have to help me with Daniel. He's got this big glass, but he's *sipping* it. Tonight isn't about sipping. He's supposed to be *swigging*. I mean, I know he's getting enough into him to do some good, because he went off into this whole long speech about the labyrinth and the Minotaur and something with Bottom in *Midsummer Night's Dream*, so he's not *sober*. But still."

"Well, come on, then," I said, laughing—I couldn't wait to see Daniel really hammered—"what are we waiting for?" and we raced up the lawn together and swept into the kitchen hand in hand.

Justin was at the kitchen table, with a ladle in one hand and a glass in the other, bending over a big fruit bowl full of something red and dangerous-looking. "God, you're gorgeous," he told us. "You're like a pair of little wood nymphs, so you are."

"They are lovely," Daniel said, smiling at us from the doorway. "Give them some punch, so they'll think we're lovely too."

"We always think you're lovely," Abby told him, grabbing a glass from the table. "But we need punch anyway. Lexie needs *lots* of punch, so she can catch up."

"I'm lovely too!" Rafe shouted from the sitting room, over Josephine. "Come in here and tell me I'm lovely!"

"You're lovely!" Abby and I yelled at the top of our lungs, and Justin pushed a glass into my hand and we all headed into the sitting room, kicking off our shoes in the hall and licking off the punch that splashed onto our wrists and laughing.

Daniel stretched out in one of the armchairs and Justin lay on the sofa, and Rafe and Abby and I ended up sprawled on the floor because chairs felt too complicated. Abby had been right, the punch was lethal: lovely, tricky stuff that went down easy as fresh orange juice and then turned into a sweet wild lightness spreading like helium through every limb. I knew it would be a whole different story if I tried to do anything stupid, like stand up. I could hear Frank somewhere in the back of my head nagging about control, like one of the nuns from school droning on about the demon drink, but I was so bloody sick of Frank and his smart-arsed little sound bites and of being in control all the time. "More," I demanded, nudging Justin with my foot and waving my glass at him.

I don't remember big patches of that evening, not in detail. The second glass or maybe the third turned the whole night soft-edged and enchanted, something out of a dream. Somewhere in there I made some excuse to go up to my room and lock away my undercover paraphernalia— gun, phone, girdle—under the bed; someone turned off most of the lights, all that was left was one lamp and candles scattered around like stars. I remember an in-depth argument over who was the best James Bond, leading into an equally intense one over which of the three guys would make the best James Bond; a deeply crap attempt at some drinking game called "Fuzzy Duck" that Rafe had learned in boarding school and that ended when Justin snorted punch down his nose and had to rush out and sneeze booze into the sink; laughing so hard that my stomach hurt and I had to stick my fingers in my ears till I could get my breath back; Rafe's arm flung out under Abby's neck, my feet propped on Justin's ankles, Abby reaching up a hand to take Daniel's. It was as if none of the jagged edges had ever existed; it was close and warm and shining as that first week again, only better, a hundred times better, because this time I wasn't on the alert and fighting to get my bearings and stay in place. This time I knew them all by heart, their rhythms, their quirks, their inflections, I knew how to fit in with every one; this time I belonged.

What I remember most is a conversation—just a tangent, off something else, I don't know what—about Henry V. It didn't seem important at the time, but afterwards, after everything was over, it came back to me.

"The man was a raving psycho," Rafe said. He and I and Abby were lying on our backs on the floor again; he had his arm linked through mine. "All that heroic Shakespeare stuff was pure propaganda. Today Henry would be running a banana republic with serious border issues and a dodgy nuclear-weapons program."

"I like Henry," Daniel said through a cigarette. "A king like that is exactly what we need."

"Monarchist warmonger," said Abby, to the ceiling. "Come the revolution, you're up against the wall."

"Neither monarchy nor war has ever been the real problem," said Daniel. "Every society has always had war, it's intrinsic to humanity, and we've always had rulers—do you really see so much difference between a medieval king and a modern-day president or prime minister, except that the king was marginally more accessible to his subjects? The real problem comes when the two things, monarchy and war, become dislocated from each other. With Henry, there was no disconnect."

"You're babbling," Justin said. He was trying, with difficulty, to drink his punch without sitting up and without spilling it down his front.

"You know what you need?" Abby told him. "A straw. A bendy one."

"Yes!" said Justin, delighted. "I *do* need a bendy straw. Do we have any?"

"No," said Abby, surprised, which for some reason sent me and Rafe into helpless, undignified giggles.

"I'm not babbling," Daniel said. "Look at the old wars, centuries ago: the king led his men into battle. Always. That was what the ruler *was:* both on a practical level and on a mystical one, he was the one who stepped forwards to lead his tribe, put his life at stake for them, become the sacrifice for their safety. If he had refused to do that most crucial thing at that most crucial moment, they would have ripped him apart—and rightly so: he would have shown himself to be an impostor, with no right to the throne. The king *was* the country; how could he possibly expect it to go into battle without him? But now . . . Can you see any modern president or prime minister on the front line, leading his men into the war he's started? And once that physical and mystical link is broken, once the ruler is no longer willing to be the sacrifice for his people, he becomes not a leader but a leech, forcing others to take his risks while he sits in safety and battens on their losses. War becomes a hideous abstraction, a game for bureaucrats to play on paper; soldiers and civilians become mere pawns, to be sacrificed by the thousand for reasons that have no roots in any reality. As soon as rulers mean nothing, war means nothing; human life means nothing. We're ruled by venal little usurpers, all of us, and they make meaninglessness everywhere they go."

"Do you know something?" I told him, managing to lift my head a few inches off the floor. "I only have maybe a quarter of a clue what you're talking about. How are you this sober?"

"He's not sober," said Abby, with satisfaction. "Rants mean he's drunk. You should know that by now. Daniel is ossified."

"It's not a rant," Daniel said, but he was smiling at her, a mischievous flash of a grin. "It's a monologue. If Hamlet can have them, why can't I?"

"At least I *understand* the Hamlet rants," I said plaintively. "Mostly."

"What's he saying, basically," Rafe informed me, turning his head on the hearth rug so that those gold eyes were inches from mine, "is that politicians are overrated."

That picnic on the hill, months before, Rafe and me throwing strawberries to shut Daniel up in the middle of another rant. I swear I remembered it: the smell of the sea breeze, the ache of my thighs from climbing. "Everything's overrated except Elvis and chocolate," I announced, raising my glass precariously above my head, and heard Daniel's sudden, irresistible laugh.

Drink suited Daniel. It put a vivid flush on his cheekbones and a spark deep in his eyes, loosened his stiffness into a sure, animal grace. Usually Rafe was the resident eye candy, but that night it was Daniel I couldn't take my eyes off. Leaning back among the candle flames and the rich colors and the faded brocade of the chair, with the glass glowing red in his hand and dark hair falling across his forehead, he looked like some ancient war leader himself: a high king in his banquet hall, shining and reckless, celebrating between battles.

The sash windows flung open to the night garden; moths whirling at the lights, shadows crisscrossing, soft damp breeze playing in the curtains. "But it's *summer,*" Justin said suddenly, amazed, shooting up on the sofa. "Feel the wind, it's warm. It's summer. Come on, come outside," and he scrambled up, tugging Abby up by the hand as he went past, and clambered out the window onto the patio.

The garden was dark and scented and alive. I don't know how long we spent out there, under a huge wild moon. Rafe and me crossing hands and whirling on the lawn till we fell over in a panting giggling heap, Justin tossing a great double handful of hawthorn petals in the air so that they fell like snow onto our hair, Daniel and Abby dancing a slow barefoot waltz under the trees, like ghost lovers from some long-lost ball. I threw flips and cartwheels straight across the grass, fuck my imaginary stitches, fuck whether Lexie had done gymnastics, I couldn't remember the last time I had been this drunk and I loved it. I wanted to dive deeper into it and never come up for air, open my mouth and take a huge breath and drown on this night.

I lost the others, somewhere along the way; I was lying on my back in the herb garden, smelling crushed mint and looking up at a million dizzy stars, on my own. I could hear Rafe calling my name, faintly, at the front of the house. After a while I picked myself up and went to find him, but gravity had somehow gone slippery and it was hard to walk. I felt my way along the wall, keeping one hand on branches and ivy; I heard twigs snap under my bare feet, but there wasn't even a flicker of pain.

The lawn was white in the moonlight. Music streamed

out through the windows and Abby was dancing by herself on the grass, spinning slow circles, her arms outspread and her head back to the enormous night sky. I stood by the alcove, swinging a long trail of ivy with one hand, and watched her: the pale swirl and dip of her skirt, the turn of her wrist holding it up, the arch of her bare foot, the dreamy drunken sway of her neck, in and out of the whispering trees.

"Isn't she beautiful?" said a voice, softly, behind me. I was way too drunk even to be startled. It was Daniel, on one of the stone seats under the ivy, with a glass in his hand and a bottle on the flagstones beside him. The moon shadows turned him into carved marble. "When we're all old and gray and starting to slip away, even if I've forgotten everything else my life has ever held, I think I'll remember her like this."

A swift painful pang went through me, but I couldn't figure out why; it was much too complicated, too far away. "I want to remember tonight too," I said. "I want to tattoo it onto me so I don't forget."

"Come here," Daniel said. He put the glass down and moved sideways on the bench to make room, held out a hand to me. "Come here. We'll have thousands more nights like this. You can forget them by the dozen if you want to; we'll make more. We've got all the time in the world."

His hand around mine was warm, strong. He pulled me down on the seat and I leaned in against him, that solid shoulder, smell of cedar and clean wool, everything black and silver and shifting and the water murmuring on and on at our feet. "When I thought we'd lost you," Daniel said, "it was . . ." He shook his head, took a quick breath like a gasp. "I missed you; you have no idea how much. But it's all right now. Everything's going to be all right."

He turned towards me. His hand came up, fingers tangling in my hair, rough and tender, moving down across my cheek, tracing the line of my mouth.

The lights of the house spun blurred and magic as the

lights of a carousel, there was a high singing note above the trees and the ivy was whirling with music so sweet I could hardly bear it, and all I wanted in the world was to stay. Strip off the mike and the wire, into an envelope and down the postbox to Frank and gone, skim off my old life light as a bird and home straight here. *We didn't want to lose you, silly thing,* the others would be happy, the rest of our lives they would never need to know. I had as much right as the dead girl, I was Lexie Madison as much as she had ever been. My landlord throwing my awful work clothes into bin liners when the rent dried up, there was nothing there I would need now. Cherry blossom falling soft on the drive, quiet smell of old books, firelight sparkling on snow-crystalled windowpanes at Christmastime and nothing would ever change, only the five of us moving through this walled garden, neverending. Somewhere far in the back of my mind a drum was throbbing hard for danger, but I knew like a vision that this was why the dead girl had come a million miles to find me, this was why Lexie Madison all along: to wait for her moment to hold out her hand and take mine, lead me up those stone steps and in by that door, lead me home. Daniel's mouth tasted of ice and whiskey.

If I had thought about it, I would have expected Daniel to be a fairly crap kisser, in a meticulous kind of way. The fierceness of him took my breath away. When we pulled apart, I don't know how much later, my heart was running wild.

And now, I thought, with one tiny clear drop of my mind. *What happens now?*

Daniel's mouth, the corners curving in a tiny smile, was very close to mine. His hands were on my shoulders, his thumbs moving in long gentle strokes along the line of my collarbone.

Frank wouldn't have batted an eyelid; I know undercovers who've slept with gangsters, given out beatings and shot up heroin, all in the name of the job. I never said anything, not my business, but I knew well that was bollocks. There's always another way to what you're after, if you want to find it. They did those things because they wanted to and because the job gave them an excuse.

In that second I saw Sam's face in front of me, eyes wide and stunned, clear as if he were standing at Daniel's elbow. It should have made me cringe with shame, but all I felt was a wave of pure frustration, smashing over me so hard I wanted to scream. He was like this enormous feather duvet wrapped all around my life, smothering me to nothing with holidays and protective questions and gentle, inexorable warmth. I wanted to fling him off with one violent buck and take a huge breath of cold air, all my own again.

It was the wire that saved me. Not what it might pick up, I wasn't thinking that straight, but Daniel's hands: his thumbs were maybe three inches from the mike, clipped to my bra between my breasts. In one blink I was as sober as I've ever been in my life. I was three inches away from burned.

"*Well,*" I said, stalling, and gave Daniel a little grin. "It's always the quiet ones."

He didn't move. I thought I saw a flick of something in his eyes, but I couldn't tell what. My brain seemed to have seized up: I had no idea how Lexie would have got herself out of this one. I had a horrible feeling that she wouldn't have.

There was a crash inside the house, the French doors banged open and someone erupted onto the patio. Rafe was yelling. "—Always have to make such a huge fucking deal out of everything—"

"My God, that's rich, coming from you. *You* were the one who wanted to—"

It was Justin, and he was so furious his voice was shaking. I widened my eyes at Daniel, jumped up and peeped out through the ivy. Rafe was pacing up and down the patio and raking a hand through his hair; Justin was slumped against the wall, biting hard at a nail. They were still fighting, but their voices had dropped a notch and all I could hear was the fast, vicious rhythms. The angle of Justin's head, chin tucked into his chest, looked like he might be crying.

"Shit," I said, glancing back over my shoulder at Daniel. He was still on the bench. His face blurred into the patterns of leaf shadow; I couldn't see his expression. "I think they broke something inside. And Rafe looks like he might hit Justin. Maybe we should . . . ?"

He stood up, slowly. The black and white of him seemed to fill the alcove, tall and sharp and strange. "Yes," he said. "We probably should."

He moved me out of the way with a gentle, impersonal hand on my shoulder, and went out across the lawn. Abby had collapsed on her back in the grass in a whirl of white cotton, one arm flung out. She looked fast asleep.

Daniel knelt on one knee beside her and carefully hooked a lock of hair off her face; then he straightened up again, brushing bits of grass off his trousers, and went to the patio. Rafe yelled, "Jesus Christ!" spun round and stormed inside, slamming the door behind him. Justin was definitely crying now.

None of it made any sense. The whole incomprehensible scene seemed to be moving in slow, tilting circles, the house reeling helplessly, the garden heaving like water. I realized that I wasn't sober after all, in fact I was spectacularly drunk. I sat down on the bench and put my head between my knees till things stayed still.

I must have gone to sleep, or passed out, I don't know. I heard shouting, somewhere, but it didn't seem to have anything to do with me and I let it go by.

A crick in my neck woke me. It took me a long time to work out where I was: curled on the stone seat, with my head tilted back against the wall at an undignified angle. My clothes were clammy and cold and I was shivering.

I unfurled myself, in stages, and stood up. Bad move: my head went into a sickening spin, I had to grab at the ivy to stay vertical. Outside the alcove the garden had turned gray, a still, ghostly, predawn gray, not a leaf moving. For a second I was afraid to step out into it; it looked like a place that shouldn't be disturbed.

Abby was gone from the lawn. The grass was heavy with dew, soaking my feet and the hems of my jeans. Someone's socks, possibly mine, were tangled on the patio, but I didn't have the energy to pick them up. The French doors were swinging open and Rafe was asleep on the sofa, snoring, in a puddle of full ashtrays and empty glasses and scattered cushions and the smell of stale booze. The piano was speckled with shards of broken glass, curving and wicked on the glossy wood and the yellowing keys, and there was a deep fresh gouge on the wall above it: someone had thrown something, a glass or an ashtray, and meant it. I tiptoed upstairs and crawled into bed without bothering to take off my clothes. It was a long time before I could stop shivering and fall asleep.

19

Unsurprisingly, we all woke up late, with hangovers from hell and a collective foul mood. My head was killing me, even my hair hurt, and my mouth had that walk-of-shame feel, swollen and tender. I pulled a sweater over yesterday's clothes, checked the mirror for stubble burn—nothing—and dragged myself downstairs.

Abby was in the kitchen, smacking ice cubes into a glass. "Sorry," I said, in the doorway. "Did I miss breakfast?"

She threw the ice tray back into the freezer and slammed the door. "Nobody's hungry. I'm having a Bloody Mary. Daniel made coffee; if you want anything else, you can get it yourself." She brushed past me and went into the sitting room.

I figured if I tried to work out why she was pissed off at me, my head might explode. I poured myself a lot of coffee, buttered a slice of bread—toast felt way too complicated—and took them into the sitting room. Rafe was still unconscious on the sofa, with a cushion pulled over his head. Daniel was sitting on the windowsill, staring out at the garden, with a mug in one hand and a cigarette burning away forgotten in the other. He didn't look around.

"Can he breathe?" I asked, pointing at Rafe with my chin.

"Who cares?" said Abby. She was slumped in an armchair, with her eyes closed and her glass pressed to her forehead. The air smelled musty and overripe, cigarette butts and sweat and spilled booze. Someone had cleaned the shards of glass off the piano; they were in a corner of the floor, in a small, threatening pile. I sat down, carefully, and tried to eat without moving my head.

The afternoon oozed on, slow and sticky as treacle. Abby played halfhearted solitaire, giving up and starting over every few minutes; I dozed, off and on, curled in the armchair. Justin finally appeared, wrapped in his dressing gown, eyelids fluttering with pain at the light coming through the windows—it was sort of a nice day, if you were in the mood for that kind of thing. "Oh, God," he said faintly, shielding his eyes. "My *head*. I think I'm getting the flu; I ache *everywhere*."

"Night air," said Abby, dealing another hand. "Cold, damp, whatever. Not to mention enough punch to float a cruise ship."

"It is not the punch. My legs hurt; a hangover doesn't make your *legs* hurt. Can't we close the curtains?"

"No," said Daniel, without turning around. "Have some coffee."

"Maybe I'm having a brain hemorrhage. Don't they do things to your eyes?"

"You have a *hangover*," Rafe said, from the depths of the sofa. "And if you don't stop whining, I'm going to come over there and throttle you, even if it kills me too."

"Oh, great," Abby said, massaging the bridge of her nose. "It's alive." Justin ignored him, with an icy lift of his chin that said last night's fight wasn't over, and sank into a chair.

"Maybe we should think about going out, at some point," Daniel said, finally coming out of his reverie and looking around. "It might help to clear our heads."

"I can't go anywhere," Justin said, reaching for Abby's Bloody Mary. "I have the flu. If I go out I'll get pneumonia."

Abby slapped his hand away. "I'm drinking that. Make your own."

"The ancients would have said," Daniel told him, "that you were suffering from an imbalance of the humors: an excess of black bile, causing melancholy. Black bile is cold and dry, so to counter it, you need something warm and moist. I don't remember which foods are associated with sanguinity, but it seems logical that red meat, for example—"

"Sartre was right," Rafe said, through his cushion. "Hell is other people."

I felt the same way. All I wanted was for it to be evening so I could go for my walk, get out of this house and away from these people and try to wrap my head around the night before. I had never, in all my life, spent so much of my time surrounded by people. Up until that day it hadn't even registered, but all of a sudden everything they did—Justin's dying-swan act, the snap of Abby's cards—felt like a full-on assault. I pulled my sweater over my head, burrowed into the corner of the armchair and went to sleep.

When I woke up the room was empty. It looked like it had been abandoned fast, in some sudden emergency—lamps on, shades tilted at odd angles; chairs pushed back, half-empty mugs and sticky rings on the table. "Hi," I called, but my voice soaked away into the shadows and no one answered.

The house felt huge and unwelcoming, the way a house sometimes does when you come back downstairs after you've closed up for the night: alien, withdrawn, focused on its own private business. No note anywhere; the others had probably gone for a walk after all, to blow the hangovers away.

I poured myself a mug of cold coffee and drank it leaning against the kitchen sink, looking out the window. The light was just starting to turn gold and syrupy, and swallows were diving and chittering across the lawn. I left my mug in the sink and went up to my room, involuntarily walking quietly and skipping the creaky stair.

As I put my hand on the door handle I felt the house gather itself and tense around me. Even before I opened the door, before I smelt the faint wisp of tobacco smoke on the air and saw his silhouette sitting broad-shouldered and motionless on the bed, I knew Daniel was home.

The light through the curtains glinted blue on his glasses as he turned his head to me. "Who are you?" he asked.

I thought as fast as even Frank could ever want from me, I already had one finger on my mouth to shut him up while my other hand smacked the light switch, and then I called, "Hey, it's me, I'm out here," and thanked God Daniel was weird enough that we might just possibly get away with that *Who are you?* His eyes were intent on my face, and he was between me and my case. "Where is everyone?" I asked him, and ripped open the buttons of my top so he could see the tiny mike clipped to my bra, the wire running down into the white pad of bandage.

Daniel's eyebrows lifted, just a touch. "They went to see a film in town," he said calmly. "I had a few things I needed to do here. We decided not to wake you."

I nodded, gave him the thumbs-up and knelt down slowly to pull my case out from under the bed, not taking my eyes off him. The music box on the bedside table, solid and sharp-cornered and within reach: that should slow him down long enough to get me out of there if I needed it. But Daniel didn't move. I dialed the combination, opened the case, found my ID and threw it to him.

He inspected it closely. "Did you sleep well?" he asked formally.

He had his head bent over the ID, apparently absorbed in it, and my hand was on the bedside table, inches from my gun. But if I went to slip it into my waistband and he looked up; no. I zipped the case shut and locked it. "Not great," I said. "My head is still killing me. I'm going to go read for a while and hope it gets better. See you in a bit?" I waved a hand to get Daniel's attention; then I moved towards the door and beckoned.

He gave my ID one last look, then laid it carefully on the bedside table. "Yes," he said. "I'm sure I'll see you later." He got up from the bed and followed me downstairs.

He moved very silently, for such a big guy. I could feel him at my back all the way and I knew I should be scared—one push—but I wasn't: adrenaline was flying through me like wildfire and I've never been less afraid in my life. Rapture of the deep, Frank called it once, and warned me not to trust it: undercovers can drown like deep-sea divers on the ecstasy of weightlessness, but I didn't care.

Daniel stood in the sitting-room doorway, watching me with interest, while I hummed "Oh, Johnny, How You Can Love" under my breath and flipped through the records. I picked out Fauré's *Requiem*, stacked it up over the string sonatas—Frank might as well have something good to listen to, broaden his cultural horizons, and I doubted he'd notice the midstream switch—and turned it up to a nice solid volume. I flopped into my chair with a thump, sighed contentedly and flipped a few pages of my notebook. Then, very carefully, I peeled off the bandage strip by strip, unclipped the mike from my bra, and left the whole package on the chair to listen to music for a while.

Daniel followed me through the kitchen and out the French doors. I didn't like the idea of crossing the open lawn—*You won't have visual surveillance,* Frank had told me, but he would have said that either way—but we didn't have a choice. I skirted around the edge and got us in among the trees. Once we were out of view, I relaxed enough to remember my buttons and do them up again. If Frank did have someone watching, that would have given him something to think about.

The alcove was brighter than I had expected; the light slanted long and gold across the grass, slipped between the creepers and glowed in patches on the paving stones. The seat was cold even through my jeans. The ivy swayed back into place to hide us.

"OK," I said. "We can talk, but keep it down, just in case."

Daniel nodded. He brushed flecks of dirt off the other seat and sat down. "Lexie is dead, then," he said.

"I'm afraid so," I said. "I'm sorry." It sounded ludicrously, insanely inadequate on about a million levels.

"When?"

"The night she was stabbed. She wouldn't have suffered much, if that's any comfort."

He didn't respond. He clasped his hands in his lap and gazed out through the ivy. At our feet the trickle of water murmured.

"Cassandra Maddox," Daniel said eventually, trying out the sound of it. "I wondered quite a lot about that, you know: what your real name was. It suits you."

"I go by Cassie," I said.

He ignored that. "Why did you take off your microphone?"

With someone else I might have skated around this, parried it—*Why do you think?*—but not with Daniel. "I want to know what happened to Lexie. I don't care whether anyone else hears it or not. And I thought you would be more likely to tell me if I gave you a reason to trust me."

Either out of politeness or out of indifference, he didn't point out the irony. "And you think I know how she died?" he inquired.

"Yes," I said. "I do."

Daniel considered this. "Shouldn't you be afraid of me, in that case?"

"Maybe. But I'm not."

He scrutinized me for a long moment. "You're very like Lexie, you know," he said. "Not only physically, but temperamentally as well. At first I wondered if I simply wanted to believe that, to excuse the fact that I had been fooled for so long, but it's true. Lexie was fearless. She was like an ice skater balanced effortlessly on the edge of her own speed, throwing in joyous, elaborate twirls and leaps just for the hell of it. I always envied her that." His eyes were in shadow, and I couldn't read his expression. "Was this just for the hell of it? If I may ask."

"No," I said. "At first I didn't even want to do it. It was

Detective Mackey's idea. He thought it was necessary to the investigation."

Daniel nodded, unsurprised. "He suspected us from the beginning," he said, and I realized that he was right; of course he was right. All Frank's talk about the mysterious foreigner who followed Lexie halfway across the world, that was just a smoke screen: Sam would have thrown a blue fit if he thought I was going to share a roof with the killer. Frank's famous intuition had kicked in long before we ever got into that squad room. He had known, all along, that the answer was in this house.

"He's an interesting man, Detective Mackey," Daniel said. "He's like one of those charming murderers in Jacobean plays, the ones who get all the best monologues: Bosola, or De Flores. It's a pity you can't tell me anything; I would be fascinated to know how much he's guessed."

"So would I," I said. "Believe me."

Daniel took out his cigarette case, opened it and politely offered it to me. His face, bent over the lighter as I cupped my hand around the flame, was absorbed and untroubled.

"Now," he said, when he had lit his own smoke and put the case away, "I'm sure you have some questions you'd like to ask me."

"If I'm so much like Lexie," I said, "what gave me away?" I couldn't help it. It wasn't professional pride or anything; I just needed, badly, to know what that unmissable difference had been.

Daniel turned his head and looked at me. There was an expression on his face that I hadn't expected: something almost like affection, or sympathy. "You did extraordinarily well, you know," he said, kindly. "Even now, I don't think the others suspect anything. We'll have to decide what to do about that, you and I."

"I can't have done all that well," I said, "or we wouldn't be here."

He shook his head. "I think that underrates both of us, don't you? You were virtually flawless. I did know, almost immediately, that *something* was wrong—all of us did, just as you would sense something amiss if your partner were replaced by his identical twin. But there were so many possible reasons for that. At first I wondered if you might be faking the amnesia, for reasons of your own, but gradually it became clear that your memory was, in fact, damaged—there seemed to be no reason why you should pretend to forget about finding that photo album, for example, and it was obvious that you were genuinely disturbed by the fact that you didn't remember it. Once I was satisfied that that wasn't the problem, I thought perhaps you were planning to leave—which would have been understandable, in the circumstances, but Abby seemed very sure that you weren't, and I trust Abby's judgment. And you really did seem . . ."

His face turned towards me. "You really did seem happy, you know. More than happy: content; settled. Nested back in among us as if you had never been away. Perhaps this was deliberate, and you're even better at your job than I realize, but I find it hard to believe that both my instincts and Abby's could have been quite so wrong."

There was nothing I could say to that. For a split second I wanted to curl up in a ball and howl at the top of my lungs, like a kid devastated by the sheer ruthlessness of this world. I gave Daniel a noncommittal tilt of my chin, drew on my smoke and tapped ash onto the flagstones.

Daniel waited with a grave patience that sent a little warning chill through me. When it was clear that I wasn't going to answer, he nodded, a tiny, private, thoughtful nod. "At any rate," he said, "I decided you, or rather Lexie, must simply be traumatized. A profound trauma—and clearly this would qualify—can transform a person's entire character, you know: turn a strong person into a trembling wreck, a happy nature melancholic, a gentle one vicious. It can shatter you into a million pieces, and rearrange the remains in an utterly unrecognizable form."

His voice was even, calm; he was looking away from me again, out at the hawthorn flowers white and shivering in the breeze, and I couldn't see his eyes. "The changes in Lexie were so small, by comparison, so trivial; so easily accounted for. I assume Detective Mackey gave you the information you needed."

"Detective Mackey and Lexie. The video phone."

Daniel thought about that for so long that I thought he'd forgotten my question. There was an in-built immobility to his face—that square-cut jaw, maybe—that made it almost impossible to read. "'Everything's overrated except Elvis and chocolate,'" he said, in the end. "That was a nice touch."

"Was it the onions that did it?" I asked.

He drew in a breath and stirred, coming out of his reverie. "Those onions," he said, with a faint smile. "Lexie was fanatical about them: onions and cabbage. Fortunately none of the rest of us like cabbage either, but we had to reach a compromise on the onions: once a week. She still complained and picked them out and so on—mainly to tease Rafe and Justin, I think. So, when you ate them without a murmur and asked for more, I knew something was wrong. I didn't know what, exactly—you covered it very well—but I couldn't simply dismiss it. The only alternative explanation I could come up with was that, incredible though it seemed, you weren't Lexie."

"So you set a trap for me," I said. "The Brogan's thing."

"Well, I wouldn't call it a *trap*," Daniel said, with a touch of asperity. "More of a test. It was a spur-of-the-moment thing. Lexie had no particular feelings about Brogan's either way—I'm not sure she'd ever been there—which didn't seem like something an impostor would know; you might have found out her likes and dislikes, but hardly her indifferences. The fact that you got it right, and the Elvis comment, reassured me. But then there was last night. That kiss."

I went cold all over, till I remembered I didn't have the mike on me. "Lexie wouldn't have done that?" I asked coolly, leaning over to put out my smoke on the flagstones.

Daniel smiled at me, that slow sweet smile that made

him suddenly handsome. "Oh, she would have," he said. "The kiss was very much in character—and very nice, if I may say so." I didn't blink. "No, it was your reaction to it. For a split second, you looked stunned; utterly shocked at what you had done. Then you recovered and made some airy comment, and found an excuse to move away—but, you see, Lexie would never have been shaken by that kiss, not even for a second. And she would certainly never have drawn back at that point. She would have been . . ." He blew thoughtful smoke rings up into the ivy. "She would have been," he said, "triumphant."

"Why?" I asked. "Had she been trying to make something like that happen?" My mind was fast-forwarding through the video clips; there had been flirting with Rafe and Justin but never with Daniel, not a hint, but that could have been a bluff, to mislead the others—

"That," Daniel said, "is what gave you away."

I stared at him.

He ground out the cigarette under his foot. "Lexie was both incapable of thinking about the past," he said, "and incapable of thinking more than one step into the future. This may be one of the few things you overlooked. Not your fault; that level of simplicity is hard to imagine, and also hard to describe. It was as startling as a deformity. I seriously doubt that she would have been able to plan a seduction; but, once something had happened, she would have seen no reason to be shocked by it and certainly no reason to stop there. You, on the other hand, were clearly trying to gauge the consequences this might have. I'd guess that you have a boyfriend, or a partner, in your own life."

I didn't say anything. "So," Daniel said, "I rang the police headquarters this afternoon, once the others had gone out, and asked where I could find Detective Sam O'Neill. The woman I spoke to couldn't find an extension for him at first, but then she checked some directory and gave me a number to ring. She said, 'That's the Murder squad room.'"

He sighed, a small, tired, final sound. "Murder," he said quietly. "So then, you see, I knew."

"I'm sorry," I said, again. All day, while we drank coffee and got on each other's nerves and bitched about our hangovers, while he sent the others off to the pictures and sat in Lexie's small dimming bedroom waiting for me, he had been carrying this alone.

Daniel nodded. "Yes," he said. "I see that."

There was a long silence. Finally I said, "You know I need to ask you what happened."

Daniel took off his glasses and polished them on his handkerchief. Without them his eyes looked blank, blind. "There's a Spanish proverb," he said, "that's always fascinated me. 'Take what you want and pay for it, says God.'"

The words fell into the silence under the ivy like cool pebbles into water, sank without a ripple. "I don't believe in God," Daniel said, "but that principle seems, to me, to have a divinity of its own; a kind of blazing purity. What could possibly be simpler, or more crucial? You can have anything you want, as long as you accept that there is a price and that you will have to pay it."

He put the glasses on and looked at me calmly, tucking the handkerchief back into his shirt pocket. "It seems to me," he said, "that we as a society have come to overlook the second clause. We hear only 'Take what you want, says God'; nobody mentions a price, and when it comes time to settle the score, everyone's outraged. Take the national economic explosion, as the most obvious example: that's come at a price, and a very steep one, to my mind. We have sushi bars and SUVs, but people our age can't afford homes in the city where they grew up, so centuries-old communities are disintegrating like sand castles. People spend five or six hours a day in traffic; parents never see their children, because they both have to work overtime to make ends meet. We no longer have time for culture—theaters are closing, architecture is being wrecked to make way for office blocks. And so on and so forth."

He didn't sound even mildly indignant, only absorbed. "I don't consider this anything to become incensed about," he said, reading my look. "In fact, it shouldn't be remotely surprising to anyone. We've taken what we wanted and we're paying for it, and no doubt many people feel that on balance the deal is a good one. What I do find surprising is the frantic silence that surrounds this price. The politicians tell us, constantly, that we live in Utopia. If anyone with any visibility ever suggests that this bliss may not come free, then that dreadful little man—what's his name? the prime minister—comes on the television, not to point out that this toll is the law of nature, but to deny furiously that it exists and to scold us like children for mentioning it. I finally had to get rid of the television," he added, a little peevishly. "We've become a nation of defaulters: we buy on credit, and when the bill comes in, we're so deeply outraged that we refuse even to look at it."

He pushed his glasses up his nose with a knuckle and blinked at me through the lenses. "I have always accepted," he said simply, "that there is a price to pay."

"For what?" I said. "What do you want?"

Daniel considered this—not the answer itself, I think, but how best to explain it to me—in silence. "At first," he said eventually, "it was more a matter of what I *didn't* want. Well before I finished college, it had become clear to me that the standard deal—a modicum of luxury, in exchange for one's free time and comfort—wasn't for me. I was happy to live frugally, if that was what it took, in order to avoid the nine-to-five cubicle. I was more than willing to sacrifice the new car and the sun holidays and the—what are those things?—the iPod."

I was on the edge of my nerves already, and the thought of Daniel on a beach in Torremolinos, drinking a technicolor cocktail and bopping along to his iPod, almost made me lose it. He glanced up at me with a faint smile. "It wouldn't have been much of a sacrifice, no. But what I failed to take into account is that no man is an island; that I couldn't simply opt out of the prevailing mode. When a specific deal becomes standard throughout a society—reaches critical mass, so to speak—no alternatives are readily available. Living simply isn't actually an option these days; either one becomes a worker bee, or one lives on toast in a wretched bedsit with fourteen students directly overhead, and I wasn't particularly taken with that idea either. I did try it for a while, but it was practically impossible to work with all the noise, and the landlord was this sinister old countryman who kept coming into the flat at the oddest hours and wanting to chat, and . . . well, anyway. Freedom and comfort are at a high premium just now. If you want those, you have to be willing to pay a correspondingly high price."

"Didn't you have other options?" I said. "I thought you had money."

Daniel gave me a fishy stare; I gave him a bland one back. Eventually he sighed. "I believe I'd like a drink," he said. "I think I left—Yes, here it is." He had leaned sideways to feel under the bench, and I was braced and ready before I knew it—there was nothing handy that could make a weapon, but if I whipped ivy in his face, it might give me enough of a start to get to the mike and yell for backup—but he came back up with a half-full whiskey bottle. "I brought it out here last night, and then forgot it in all the excitement. And there should be—Yes." He brought out a glass. "Will you have some?"

It was good stuff, Jameson's Crested Ten, and God knows I could have used a drink. "No, thanks," I said. No unnecessary risks; this guy was a whole lot smarter than your average bear.

Daniel nodded, examined the glass and bent to rinse it in the trickle of water. "Have you ever considered," he inquired, "the sheer level of fear in this country?"

"Not on a regular basis," I said. I was having a hard time keeping track of the thread of this conversation, but I knew Daniel well enough to know that he was going somewhere with this and he would get there in his own sweet time. We had maybe forty-five minutes before Fauré ran out, and I've always been good at letting the suspect run the show. No matter how strong you are or how controlled, keeping a secret—I should know—gets heavy after a while, heavy and tiring and so lonely it feels lethal. If you let them talk, all you need to do is nudge them now and then, keep them pointing in the right direction; they'll do the rest.

He shook water droplets off the glass and pulled out his handkerchief again, to dry it. "Part of the debtor mentality is a constant, frantically suppressed undercurrent of terror. We have one of the highest debt-to-income ratios in the world, and apparently most of us are two paychecks from the street. Those in power—governments, employers— exploit this, to great effect. Frightened people are obedient— not just physically, but intellectually and emotionally. If your employer tells you to work overtime, and you know that refusing could jeopardize everything you have, then not only do you work the overtime, but you convince yourself that you're doing it voluntarily, out of loyalty to the company; because the alternative is to acknowledge that you are living in terror. Before you know it, you've persuaded yourself that you have a profound emotional attachment to some vast multinational corporation: you've indentured not just your working hours, but your entire thought process. The only people who are capable of either unfettered action or unfettered thought are those who—either because they're heroically brave, or because they're insane, or because they know themselves to be safe—are free from fear."

He poured himself three fingers of whiskey. "I'm not by any stretch of the imagination a hero," he said, "and I don't consider myself to be insane. I don't think any of the others are either of those things. And yet I wanted us all to have that chance at freedom." He put the bottle down and glanced across at me. "You asked me what I wanted. I spent a lot of time asking myself the same thing. By a year or two ago, I had come to the conclusion that I truly wanted only two things in this world: the company of my friends, and the opportunity for unfettered thought."

The words sent a slim knife of something like homesickness straight through me. "It doesn't seem like very much to ask," I said.

"Oh, but it was," Daniel said, and took a swallow of his drink. There was a rough edge to his voice. "It was a lot to ask. It followed, you see, that what we needed was safety—permanent safety. Which brings us back to your last question. My parents left investments that provide me with a small income—ample in the 1980s, now hardly enough for that bedsit. Rafe's trust fund gives him roughly the same amount. Justin's allowance will end as soon as he finishes his PhD; so will Abby's student grants, and Lexie's would have too. How many jobs do you think are available, in Dublin, for people who want only to study literature and to be together? In a few months, we would have been in precisely the same situation as the vast majority in this country: caught between poverty and slavery, two paychecks from the street, in thrall to the whims of landlords and employers. Perennially afraid."

He looked out through the ivy, up the grass to the patio, tilting his wrist slowly so that the whiskey slid circles round the glass. "All we needed," he said, "was a home."

"That's enough safety?" I asked. "A house?"

"Well, of course," he said, a little surprised. "Psychologically, the difference it makes is almost inexpressible. Once you own your home, free and clear, what is there left for anyone—landlords, employers, banks—to threaten you with? What hold does anyone have over you? One can do without practically anything else, if necessary. We would always be able to scrape together enough money for food, between us, and there is no other material fear as primal or as paralyzing as the thought of losing one's home. With that fear eliminated, we would be free. I'm not saying that owning a house makes life into some kind of blissful paradise; simply that it makes the difference between freedom and enslavement."

He must have read the look on my face. "We're in Ireland, for heaven's sake," he said, with a touch of impatience. "If you know any history at all, what could possibly be clearer? The one crucial thing the British did was to claim the land as their own, to turn the Irish from owners into tenants. Once that was done, then everything else followed naturally: confiscation of crops, abuse of tenants, eviction, emigration, famine, the whole litany of wretchedness and serfdom, all inflicted casually and unstoppably because the dispossessed had no solid ground on which to stand and fight. I'm sure my own family was as guilty as any. There may well be an element of poetic justice in the fact that I found myself looking at the other side of the coin. But I didn't feel the need simply to accept it as my just deserts."

"I rent," I said. "I'm probably two paychecks from the street. It doesn't bother me."

Daniel nodded, unsurprised. "Possibly you're braver than I am," he said. "Or possibly—forgive me—you simply haven't decided what you want from life yet; you haven't found anything that you truly want to hold onto. That changes everything, you know. Students and very young people can rent with no damage to their intellectual freedom, because it puts them under no threat: they have nothing, yet, to lose. Have you noticed how easily the very young die? They make the best martyrs for any cause, the best soldiers, the best suicides. It's because they're held here so lightly: they haven't yet accumulated loves and responsibilities and commitments and all the things that tie us securely to this world. They can let go of it as easily and simply as lifting a finger. But as you get older, you begin to find things that are worth holding onto, forever. All of a sudden you're playing for keeps, as children say, and it changes the very fabric of you."

The adrenaline, or the strange trembling light through the ivy, or the spirals of Daniel's mind, or just the sheer bizarreness of the situation, was making me feel as if I actually had been drinking. I thought of Lexie speeding through the night in poor Chad's stolen car, of Sam's face wearing that look of terrible patience, of the squad room in evening light with some other team's paperwork scattered across our desks; of my flat, empty and silent, dust starting to build up on the bookshelves and the standby light on the CD player glowing green in the darkness. I like my flat a lot, but it hit me that in all these weeks I hadn't missed it for a second, and that felt somehow horribly, horribly sad.

"I would venture to guess," Daniel said, "that you still have that first freedom—that you haven't yet found anything or anyone that you want for keeps."

Steady gray eyes and the hypnotic gold shimmer of the whiskey, sound of water, leaf shadows swaying like a darker wreath on his dark hair. "I used to have a partner," I said, "at work. Nobody you've met; he's not working this case. We were like you guys: we matched. People talked about us the way you do about twins, like we were one person—'That's MaddoxandRyan's case, get MaddoxandRyan to do it . . .' If anyone had asked me, I'd have said this was it: the two of us, for the rest of our careers, we'd retire on the same day so neither of us would ever have to work with anyone else and the squad would give us one gold watch between us. I didn't think about any of that at the time, mind. I just took it for granted. I couldn't imagine anything else."

I had never said this to anyone. Sam and I had never mentioned Rob, not once since he was transferred out, and when people asked how he was doing I gave them my sweetest smile and my best vague answers. Daniel and I were strangers and we were on opposite sides, under the civilized chitchat we were fighting each other tooth and nail and both of us knew it, but I said it to him. Now I think that should have been my first warning.

Daniel nodded. "But that was in another country," he said, "and besides, that wench is dead."

"That about sums it up," I said, "yeah." He was looking

at me with something in his eyes that went beyond kindness, beyond compassion: understanding. I think in that moment I loved him. If I could have dropped the whole case and stayed, I would have done it then.

"I see," Daniel said. He held out the glass to me. I started to shake my head automatically, but then I changed my mind and took it: what the hell. The whiskey was rich and smooth and it burned trails of light right down to my fingertips.

"Then you understand the difference it made to me," he said, "meeting the others. The world transformed itself around me: the stakes shot up, colors were so beautiful they hurt, life became almost unimaginably sweet and almost unimaginably frightening. It's so fragile, you know; things are so easily broken. I suppose this may be what it's like to fall in love, or to have a child, and to know that this could be taken from you at any moment. We were racing at breakneck speed towards the day when everything we had would be at the mercy of a merciless world, and every second was so beautiful and so precarious, it took my breath away."

He held out his hand for the glass and took a sip. "And then," he said, raising a palm towards the house, "this came along."

"Like a miracle," I said. I wasn't being snide; I meant it. For a second I felt the old wood of the banister under my palm, warm and sinuous as a muscle, as a living thing.

Daniel nodded. "Improbably," he said, "I believe in miracles, in the possibility of the impossible. Certainly the house has always felt like a miracle to me, materializing just at the moment when we needed it most. I saw straight away, the second my uncle's lawyer rang me with the news, what this could mean to us. The others had doubts, plenty of them; we argued for months. Lexie was—I suppose there's a kind of tragic irony in this—the only one who seemed perfectly happy with the idea. Abby was the hardest to convince—in spite of the fact that she was the one who most craved a home, or perhaps because of it, I don't know—but even she came round at last. I suppose, in the end, it came down to the fact that, if you are absolutely sure of something, it's almost inevitable that you'll eventually persuade people who aren't sure one way or the other. And I was sure. I've never been more sure of anything."

"Is that why you made the others co-owners?"

Daniel glanced sharply across at me, but I kept my face blandly interested and after a moment he went back to looking out through the ivy. "Well, not to win them over, or anything like that, if that's what you mean," he said. "Hardly. It was absolutely essential to what I had in mind. It wasn't the house itself I wanted—much as I love it. It was security, for all of us; a safe haven. If I had been the sole owner, then the crude truth of it is that I would have been the others' landlord, and they would have had no more safety than before. They would have been dependent on my whims, always waiting for me to decide to move or get married or sell up. This way it was all of our home, forever."

He lifted a hand and hooked the curtain of ivy aside. The stone of the house was rosy amber in the sunset light, glowing and sweet; the windows blazed like the inside was on fire. "It seemed like such a beautiful idea," he said. "Almost unthinkably so. The day we moved in, we cleaned the fireplace and washed up in freezing water and lit a fire, and sat in front of it drinking cold lumpy cocoa and trying to make toast—the cooker didn't work, the water heater didn't work, there were only two functioning lightbulbs in the whole house. Justin was wearing his entire wardrobe and complaining that we were all going to die of pneumonia or mold inhalation or both, and Rafe and Lexie were teasing him by claiming they'd heard rats in the attic; Abby threatened to make the pair of them sleep up there if they didn't behave. I kept burning the toast or dropping it into the fire, and we all found that ridiculously funny; we laughed until we could barely breathe. I've never been so happy in my life."

His gray eyes were calm, but the note in his voice, like a

deep bell tolling, hurt me somewhere under my breastbone. I had known for weeks that Daniel was unhappy, but that was the moment when I understood that, whatever had happened with Lexie, it had broken his heart. He had staked everything on this one shining idea, and he had lost. No matter what anyone says, a part of me believes that, on that day under the ivy, I should have seen everything that was coming, the pattern unrolling in front of me clean and quick and relentless, and I should have known how to stop it.

"What went wrong?" I asked quietly.

"The idea was flawed, of course," he said irritably. "Innately and fatally flawed. It depended on two of the human race's greatest myths: the possibility of permanence, and the simplicity of human nature. Both of which are all well and good in literature, but the purest fantasy outside the covers of a book. Our story should have stopped that night with the cold cocoa, the night we moved in: and they all lived happily ever after, the end. Inconveniently, however, real life demanded that we keep on living."

He finished his drink in one long swallow and grimaced. "This is foul. I wish we had ice."

I waited while he poured himself another one, gave it a look of faint distaste and set it down on the bench. "Can I ask you something?" I said.

Daniel inclined his head. "You talked about paying for what you want," I said. "How did you have to pay for this house? It looks to me like you got exactly what you wanted, for free."

He raised an eyebrow. "Do you think so? You've been living here for several weeks now. Surely you have a fair idea of the price involved."

I did, of course I did, but I wanted to hear it from him. "No pasts," I said. "For a start."

"No pasts," Daniel repeated, almost to himself. After a moment he shrugged. "That was part of it, certainly—this needed to be a fresh start for all of us, together—but it was the easy part. As you've probably gathered, none of us has the kind of past that one would want to retain in any case. The main difficulties there have been practical ones, really, rather than psychological: getting Rafe's father to stop ringing up and abusing him, Justin's father to stop accusing him of joining a cult and threatening to call the police, Abby's mother to stop showing up outside the library high as a kite on whatever it is she takes. But these were small problems, comparatively; technical difficulties that would have sorted themselves out, given time. The real price . . ."

He moved one finger absently around the rim of the glass, watching the gold of the whiskey bloom and dim as his shadow passed across it. "I suppose some people might call it a state of suspended animation," he said, at last. "Although I would consider that a highly simplistic definition. Marriage and children, for example, were no longer possibilities for any of us. The odds of finding an outsider who would be able to fit into what is, frankly, an unusual setup, even if he or she should want to, were negligible. And, although I won't deny that there have been elements of intimacy among us, for any two of us to enter into a serious romance would almost definitely have damaged our balance beyond repair."

"Elements of intimacy?" I asked. Lexie's baby—"Between who?"

"Well, really," Daniel said, with a touch of impatience, "I don't think that's the issue. The point is that, in order to make this house our shared home, we had to forfeit the possibility of many things that other people consider to be essential goals. We had to forfeit everything that Rafe's father would call the real world."

Maybe it was the whiskey, on a hangover and a half-empty stomach. Strange things spun in my mind, sprayed showers of light like prisms. I thought of ancient stories: battered travelers stumbling out of the storm into glowing banquet halls, losing hold of their old lives at the first taste of bread or honey wine; of that first night, the four of them smiling at me across the laden table and the lifted wine-glasses and the curls of ivy, smooth-skinned and beautiful, with candlelight in their eyes. I remembered the second before Daniel and I kissed, how the five of us had risen up in front of me breathtaking and eternal as ghosts, hanging sweet and gauzy over the drifts of grass; and that danger drum, somewhere behind my ears.

"This isn't as sinister as it sounds, you know," he added, catching something in my expression. "Regardless of what the advertising campaigns may tell us, we can't have it all. Sacrifice is not an option, or an anachronism; it's a fact of life. We all cut off our own limbs to burn on some altar. The crucial thing is to choose an altar that's worth it and a limb you can accept losing. To go consenting to the sacrifice."

"And you did," I said. I felt like the stone bench was rocking underneath me, swaying with the ivy in a slow dizzying rhythm. "You went consenting."

"I did, yes," Daniel said. "I understood all of the implications, very clearly. I had thought it all out before I ever embarked on this, and I had decided it was a price well worth paying—I doubt I would ever have wanted children in any case, and I've never placed much stock in the concept of one perfect soul mate. I assumed the others had done the same: weighed up the stakes and found the sacrifice worth making." He brought the glass to his lips and took a sip. "That," he said, "was my first mistake."

He was so calm. I didn't even hear it at the time, it wasn't until much later, when I went over the conversation in my head looking for clues, that I caught it: *was, would have.* Daniel used the past tense, all the way through. He understood that it was over, whether anyone else had noticed or not. He sat there under the ivy with a glass in his hand, serene as the Buddha, watching as the bow of his ship tilted and slid under the waves.

"They hadn't thought it through?" I asked. My mind was still sliding, weightless, everything was smooth as glass and I couldn't get a grip. For a second I wondered crazily if the whiskey had been drugged, but Daniel had had a lot more than me and he seemed fine—"Or they changed their minds?"

Daniel rubbed the bridge of his nose with finger and thumb. "Really," he said, a little wearily, "when I think about it, I made an astounding number of mistakes along the way. The hypothermia story, for instance: I should never have fallen for that. Initially, in fact, I didn't. I know very little about medicine, but when your colleague—Detective Mackey—told me that story, I didn't believe a word of it. I assumed he was hoping we'd be more likely to talk if we thought that it was a matter of assault, rather than murder, and that Lexie might at any minute tell him everything. All that week, I took it for granted that he was bluffing. But then . . ." He lifted his head and looked at me, blinking, as if he had almost forgotten I was there. "But then, you see," he said, "you arrived."

His eyes moved over my face. "The resemblance really is extraordinary. Are you—were you—related to Lexie?"

"No," I said. "Not as far as I know."

"No." Daniel went through his pockets methodically, took out his cigarette case and lighter. "She told us she had no family. This may be why the possibility of you didn't occur to me. The inherent unlikeliness of the situation was in your favor all along: any suspicion that you weren't Lexie would have had to be predicated on the improbable hypothesis of your existence. I should have remembered Conan Doyle: 'whatever remains, however improbable, must be the truth.'"

He flicked the lighter and tilted his head to the flame. "I knew, you see," he said, "that it was impossible Lexie should be alive. I checked her pulse myself."

The garden dumbstruck, in the fading gold light. The birds hushed, the branches caught in midsway; the house, a great silence poised over us, listening. I had stopped breathing. Lexie blew down the grass like a silver shower of wind, she rocked in the hawthorn trees and balanced light as a leaf on the wall beside me, she slipped along my shoulder and blazed down my back like fox fire.

"What happened?" I asked, very quietly.

"Well, really," Daniel said, "you know I can't tell you that. As you probably suspected, Lexie was stabbed in Whitethorn House; in the kitchen, to be exact. You won't find any blood—there was none at the time, although I know she bled later—and you won't find the knife. There was no premeditation and no intent to kill. We went after her, but by the time we found her it was already too late. I think that's all I can say."

"OK," I said, "OK." I pressed my feet down hard on the flagstones and tried to pull my head together. I wanted to dip a hand in the pond and splash cold water down the back of my neck, but I couldn't let Daniel see that, and anyway I doubted it would help. "Can I tell you what I think happened?"

Daniel inclined his head and made a small, courteous gesture with one hand: *Please do.*

"I think Lexie was planning to sell her share of the house."

He didn't rise to that, didn't even blink. He was watching me blandly, like a professor at an oral exam, flicking the ash off his cigarette, aiming it carefully into the water where it would wash away.

"And I'm pretty sure I know why."

I was sure he would bite on that one, positive—for a month now, he had to have been wondering—but he shook his head. "I don't need to know," he said. "It really doesn't matter, at this stage—if it ever did. I think, you know, that all five of us have a ruthless streak, in our different ways. Possibly it goes with the territory; with having crossed that river, into being sure of what you want. Certainly Lexie was capable of great ruthlessness. But not of cruelty. When you think of her, please, remember that. She was never cruel."

"She was going to sell up to your cousin Ned," I said.

"Mr. Executive Apartments himself. That sounds a lot like cruelty to me."

Daniel startled me by laughing, a hard, humorless little snort. "Ned," he said, with a wry twist to the corner of his mouth. "My God. I was far more worried about him than about Lexie. Lexie—like you—was strong-willed: if she decided to tell the police what had happened, then she would, but if she didn't want to talk, no amount of questioning would get anything out of her. Ned, on the other hand . . ."

He sighed, an exasperated puff that blew smoke out of his nose, and shook his head. "It's not just that Ned has a weak character," he said, "but that he has no character at all; he's essentially a cipher, composed entirely of the jumbled reflections of what he thinks other people want to see. We were talking earlier about knowing what you want . . . Ned was all fired up about this plan to turn the house into luxury apartments or a *golf* club, he had sheaves of complex financial projections showing how many hundreds of thousands we could each make over how many years, but he had *no idea* why he wanted to do it. Not a clue. When I asked him what on earth he wanted to *do* with all that money— it's not as though he's exactly on the breadline as it is—he stared at me as if I were speaking a foreign language. The question was completely unintelligible to him, light-years outside his frame of reference. It wasn't that he had some deep longing to travel the world, say, or to quit his job and focus on painting the Great Irish Masterwork. He wanted the money purely because everything around him has told him that it's what he should want. And he was utterly incapable of understanding that the five of us might have different priorities, priorities that we had established all by ourselves."

He stubbed out his cigarette. "So," he said, "you can see why I was worried about him. He had every reason in the world to keep his mouth shut about his dealings with

Lexie—talking would blow any possibility of a sale right out of the water, and besides, he lives alone, as far as I know he doesn't have an alibi; even he must realize that there's nothing to prevent him from becoming the prime suspect. But I knew that if Mackey and O'Neill were to give him anything more than a cursory interrogation, all that would fly straight out the window. He would become exactly what they wanted him to be: the helpful witness, the concerned citizen doing his duty. It wouldn't have been the end of the world, of course—he doesn't have anything to offer that would constitute solid evidence—but he could cause us an awful lot of trouble and tension, and that was the last thing we needed. And it wasn't as though I could gauge him, get some sense of what he was thinking, try to steer him away from disaster. Lexie—you—I could at least keep an eye on, to some extent, but Ned . . . I knew that getting in contact with him would be the worst thing I could possibly do, but, my God, it took everything I had not to do it anyway."

Ned was dangerous territory. I didn't want Daniel thinking too much about him, about my walks, about the possibilities. "You must have been raging," I said. "All of you, at both of them. I'm not surprised someone stabbed her." I meant it. In a lot of ways, the amazing thing was that Lexie had made it this far.

Daniel considered this; his face looked like it did in the evenings, in the sitting room, when he was deep in a book, lost to the world. "We were angry," he said, "at first. Furious; devastated; sabotaged, from within our own gates. But in a way, you know, the same thing that betrayed you in the end worked for you in the beginning: that crucial difference between Lexie and you. Only someone like Lexie—someone with no conception of action and consequence—would have been able to come home and settle back in as if nothing had ever happened. If she had been a slightly different kind of person, then none of us could ever have forgiven her, and you would never have made it in the door. But Lexie . . . We all knew that she had never for a moment intended to hurt us, and so it had never really occurred to her that we could be hurt; the devastation she was about to cause had truly never seemed like a reality to her. And so . . ." He drew in a long, tired breath. "And so," he said, "she could come home."

"As if nothing had ever happened," I said.

"I thought so. She never meant to hurt us; none of us ever meant to hurt her, let alone kill her. I still believe that should count for something."

"That's what I thought," I said. "That it just happened. She had been negotiating with Ned for a while, but before they could finalize anything, the four of you somehow found out." Actually, I had the beginnings of an idea how that part had gone down, too, but there was no reason to share that with Daniel. I was saving that one for when it would make the loudest bang. "I think there was a blazing row, and in the middle of it, someone stabbed Lexie. Probably no one, not even the two of them, was sure exactly what had happened; Lexie could well have thought she had just been punched. She slammed out and ran for the cottage—maybe she was supposed to meet Ned that night, maybe it was just blind instinct, I don't know. Either way, Ned never showed up. The ones who found her were you guys."

Daniel sighed. "Roughly," he said, "yes. In every essential, that's what happened. Can't you leave it at that? You know the gist of it; the other details would do no one the slightest bit of good and would do several people considerable harm. She was lovely, she was complicated and she is dead. What else is there that matters, now?"

"Well," I said. "There's the question of who killed her."

"Has it occurred to you," Daniel asked, and there was an undercurrent of some intense emotion building in his voice, "to wonder whether Lexie herself would want you to pursue this? No matter what she was considering doing, she loved us. Do you think she would want you setting out specifically to destroy us?"

Something still bending the air, rippling the stones

under my feet; something high as a needle against the sky and shivering just behind each leaf. "She found me," I said. "I didn't go looking for her. She came for me."

"Possibly she did," said Daniel. He was leaning towards me across the water, close, his elbows on his knees; behind the glasses his eyes were magnified, gray and bottomless. "But are you really so sure that what she wanted was revenge? She could so easily have run for the village, after all: knocked on a door, got someone to call an ambulance and the police. The villagers may not like us very much, but I doubt they would have denied help to an obviously wounded woman. Instead, she went straight to the cottage and simply stayed there, waiting. Haven't you ever wondered if she may have been a willing participant in her own death and in the concealment of her killer—if she went consenting, one of us to the end? Haven't you ever wondered if perhaps, for her sake, you should respect that?"

The air tasted strange, sweet, honey and salt. "Yeah," I said. It was hard to talk, the thoughts seemed to take forever moving between my mind and my tongue. "I have. I've wondered all the time. But I'm not doing this for Lexie. I'm doing this because it's my job."

It's such a cliché, and I said it so automatically; but the words seemed to whipcrack through the air startling and potent as electricity, rocketing down the ivy trails, burning white on the water. For a split second I was back in that first reeking stairwell with my hands in my pockets, looking up at that young junkie's dead bewildered face. I was stone cold sober again, that dreamlike dazzle had dissolved out of the air and the bench was solid and clammy under my arse. Daniel was watching me with a new alertness in his eyes, watching me like he had never seen me before. It was only in that second that it hit me: it was true, what I had said to him, and maybe it had been true all along.

"Well," he said, quietly. "In that case . . ."

He leaned back, slowly, away from me, against the wall. There was a long, humming silence.

"Where," Daniel said. He stopped for an instant, but his voice stayed perfectly even: "Where is Lexie now?"

"In the morgue," I said. "We haven't been able to reach her next of kin."

"We'll do whatever needs to be done. I think she would prefer that."

"The body is evidence in an open homicide case," I said. "I doubt anyone's going to release it to you. Until the investigation's closed, she'll have to stay where she is."

There was no need for me to get graphic. I knew what he was seeing; my mind had a full-color slide show of the same images ready and waiting to play. Something rippled over Daniel's face, a tiny spasm tightening his nose and lips.

"As soon as we know who did this to her," I said, "I can argue that the body should be released to the rest of you. That you count as her next of kin."

For a second his eyelids flickered; then his face turned blank. Looking back, I think—not that this is any excuse— that it was the easiest thing to miss about Daniel: how ruthlessly, lethally pragmatic he was, under the vague ivory-tower haze. An officer on the battlefield will leave his own dead brother behind without a second look, while the enemy's still circling, to get his live men safe away.

"Obviously," Daniel said, "I'd like you to leave this house. The others won't be back for an hour or so; that should give you ample time to pack your things and make any necessary arrangements."

This should hardly have come as a surprise, but it still felt like he'd slapped me straight across the face. He felt for his cigarette case. "I'd prefer that the others not find out who you are. I think you can imagine how badly it would upset them. I admit I'm not sure how to accomplish this, but surely you and Detective Mackey have a get-out clause in place, no? Some story you worked out to extricate you without raising any suspicions?"

It was the obvious thing to do, the only thing. You get burned, you get out, fast. And I had everything a girl could

444 · Tana French

ask for. I had narrowed our suspects down to four; Sam and Frank would be well able to take it from there. I could get around the fact that this wasn't on tape: disconnect the mike wire and claim it was accidental—Frank might not believe me, exactly, but he wouldn't care—report back the bits of this conversation that suited me, bounce back home immaculate and triumphant and take a bow.

I never even considered doing it. "We do, yeah," I said. "I can get out of here on a couple of hours' notice without blowing my cover. I'm not going to, though. Not till I find out who killed Lexie, and why."

Daniel turned his head and looked at me, and in that second I smelled danger, clear and cold as snow. Why not? I had invaded his home, his family, and I was trying to wreck them both for good. Either he or one of his own had already killed a woman for doing the same thing on a lesser scale. He was strong enough to do it and very possibly smart enough to get away with it, and I had left my gun in my bedroom. The trickle of water sang on at our feet and electricity fizzed through my back, down into the palms of my hands. I held his eyes and didn't move, didn't blink.

After a long moment his shoulders shifted, almost imperceptibly, and I saw his gaze turn inwards, abstracted. He had rejected that idea: he was moving towards some other plan, his mind clicking through options, sorting, classifying, connecting, faster than I could guess. "You won't do it, you know," he said. "You assume that my reluctance to hurt the others gives you an advantage—that, as they'll continue to believe you're Lexie, you have a chance at getting them to talk to you. But believe me, they're all very well aware of what's at stake. I'm not talking about the possibility of one or all of us going to jail; you have no evidence pointing towards any one of us in particular, no case against us either individually or collectively, or you'd have made your arrests long ago and this charade would never have been necessary. In fact, I'm willing to bet that, until a few minutes ago, you weren't actually certain that your target was within Whitethorn House."

"We kept all lines of inquiry open," I said.

He nodded. "As things stand, jail is the least of our worries. But take the situation, for a moment, from the others' point of view: assume that Lexie is alive and well and safely home again. If she were to find out what happened, it would mean the ruin of everything we've worked for. Suppose she were to learn that Rafe, to pick one of us at random, had stabbed her—had almost cost her her life. Do you think she could continue to share that life with him—without being afraid of him, without resenting him, without using this against him?"

"I thought you said she was incapable of thinking about the past," I said.

"Well, this is in a slightly different league," Daniel said, a little acidly. "He could hardly assume that she would dismiss this as if it were some spat over whose turn it was to buy milk. And even if she did, do you suppose he could look at her every day without seeing the constant risk she presented—the fact that at any moment, with one phone call to Mackey or O'Neill, she could send him to jail? This is Lexie, remember: she could make that call without realizing for a second the magnitude of that action. How could he treat her as he always has, tease her, argue with her, even disagree with her? And what about the rest of us, walking on eggshells, reading danger into every look and every word that passed between the two of them, always waiting for the tiniest misstep to detonate the land mine and blow everything to smithereens? How long do you think we'd last?"

His voice was very calm and even. Lazy curls of smoke were trickling from his cigarette, and he lifted his head to watch as they spread and wound upwards, through the fluttering bars of light. "We can survive the act itself," he said. "It's the shared knowledge of the act that would destroy us. This may sound odd, especially coming from an academic who prizes knowledge above almost anything, but read Genesis, or, even better, read the Jacobeans: they understood how too much knowledge can be lethal. Every time we were in the same room, it would be there among us like a bloody knife, and in the end it would slice us apart. And none of us will allow that to happen. Since the day you came into this house, we've put every drop of energy we have into preventing it, into restoring our lives to normality." He smiled slightly, one eyebrow lifting. "So to speak. And telling Lexie who stabbed her would end any hope of that normality. Believe me, the others won't do it."

When you're too close to people, when you spend too much time with them and love them too dearly, sometimes you can't see them. Unless Daniel was bluffing, he had made one last mistake, the same one he had been making all along. He was seeing the other four not as they were but as they should have been, could have been in some softer-edged and warmer world. He had missed the stark fact that Abby and Rafe and Justin were already disintegrating, they were running on empty; it stared him in the face every day, it passed him on the stairs like a cold breath and slipped into the car with us in the mornings and sat dark and hunched between us at the dinner table, but he had never once seen it. And he had missed the possibility that Lexie had had secret weapons of her own, and that she had willed them to me. He knew his world was falling apart, but somehow he was still seeing the inhabitants untouched amid the wreckage: five faces against drifting snow on a day in December, cool and luminous and pristine, timeless. It was the first time in all those weeks that I remembered he was much younger than me.

"Maybe not," I said. "But I've got to try."

Daniel leaned his head back against the stone of the wall and sighed. All of a sudden, he looked terribly tired. "Yes," he said. "Yes, I suppose you do."

"It's your call," I said. "You can tell me what happened right now, while I'm not wired: I'll be gone by the time the others get home, and if it comes to arrests it'll be your word against mine. Or I can stay here, and you can take the chance that I'll get something on tape."

He ran a hand over his face and straightened up, with an effort. "I'm perfectly aware, you know," he said, glancing at his cigarette as if he had forgotten he was holding it, "that a return to normality may not be possible for us, at this point. I'm aware, in fact, that our entire plan was probably unfeasible right from the start. But, like you, we have no choice but to try."

He dropped the smoke on the flagstones and put it out with the toe of his shoe. That frozen detachment was starting to slip into place over his face, the formal mask he used with outsiders, and there was a crisp note of finality in his voice. I was losing him. As long as we were talking like this, I had a chance, no matter how small; but any second now he was going to get up and go back indoors, and that would be the end of that.

If I had thought it would work, I would have got down on my knees on the flagstones and begged him to stay. But this was Daniel; my only chance was logic, cold hard reason. "Look," I said, keeping my voice even, "you're raising the stakes a whole lot higher than they need to be. If I get something on tape, then, depending what it is, it could mean jail time for all four of you—one on murder, and three on accessory or even conspiracy. Then what's left? What have you got to come back to? Given the way Glenskehy feels about you, what are the odds that the house will even be standing when you get out?"

"We'll have to take that chance."

"If you tell me what happened, I'll fight your corner all the way. You've got my word." Daniel would have had every right to give me a sardonic look for that, but he didn't. He was watching me with what appeared to be mild, polite interest. "Three of you can walk away from this, and the fourth can face manslaughter charges instead of murder. There wasn't any premeditation here: this happened during an argument, nobody wanted Lexie to die, and I can vouch for the fact that all of you cared about her and that whoever stabbed her was under extreme emotional duress. Manslaughter gets maybe five years, maybe even less. Then it's over, whoever it is gets out, and you can all four put this whole thing behind you and go back to normal."

"My knowledge of the law is patchy," Daniel said, leaning over to pick up his glass, "but as far as I know—and correct me if I'm wrong—nothing said by a suspect during questioning is admissible in evidence unless the suspect has been cautioned to that effect. Out of curiosity, how are you planning to administer a caution to three people who have no idea that you're a police officer?" He rinsed out the glass again and held it up to the light, squinting, to check that it was clean.

"I'm not," I said. "I don't need to. Whatever I get on tape was never going to be admissible in court, but it can be used to get an arrest warrant and it can be used in a formal interview. How long do you think Justin, for example, will hold out if he's arrested at two in the morning and questioned by Frank Mackey for twenty-four hours, with a tape of him describing Lexie's murder playing in the background?"

"An interesting question," Daniel said. He tightened the cap on the whiskey bottle, placed it carefully on the bench beside the glass.

My heart was going like hoofbeats. "Never go all in on a bad hand," I said, "unless you're absolutely positive you're a stronger player than your opponent. How sure are you?"

He gave me a vague look that could have meant anything. "We should go in now," he told me. "I suggest we tell the others that we spent the afternoon reading and recovering from our hangovers. Does that sound about right to you?"

"*Daniel,*" I said, and then my throat closed up; I could hardly breathe. Until he glanced down, I didn't even realize that my hand was on his sleeve.

"Detective," Daniel said. He was smiling at me, just a

little, but his eyes were very steady and very sad. "You can't have both. Don't you remember what we were talking about, just a few minutes ago—the inevitability of sacrifice? One of us, or a detective: you can't be both. If you had ever truly wanted to be one of us, wanted it more than anything else, you never would have made a single one of those mistakes, and we wouldn't be sitting here."

He laid his hand over mine, removed it from his sleeve and placed it in my lap, very gently. "In a way, you know," he said, "strange and impossible though it may seem, I very much wish you had chosen the other way."

"I'm not trying to ruin you," I said. "There's no way I can claim to be on your side, but compared to Detective Mackey, or even Detective O'Neill . . . If it's left up to them—and unless you and I work together, it will be; they're the ones running the investigation, not me—all four of you will be serving the maximum for murder. Life sentences. I'm doing my best here, Daniel, not to let that happen. I know it doesn't look like it, but I'm doing everything I can."

A leaf had fallen from the ivy into the trickle of water and got caught on one of the little steps, shaking against the current. Daniel picked it out carefully and turned it between his fingers. "I met Abby when I started Trinity," he said. "Quite literally; it was on registration day. We were in the exam hall, hundreds of students queuing for hours—I should have brought something to read, but it hadn't occurred to me that it would take so long—shuffling along under all those gloomy old paintings, and everyone whispering for some reason. Abby was in the next queue. She caught my eye, pointed to one of the portraits and said, 'If you let your eyes go loose, doesn't he look exactly like one of the old fellas out of the Muppets?'"

He shook water off the leaf: droplets flying, bright as fire in the crisscrossing sunbeams. "Even at that age," he said, "I was aware that people found me unapproachable. I had no problem with that. But Abby didn't seem to feel that way, and that intrigued me. She told me later that she was almost petrified with shyness, not of me in particular but of everyone and everything there—an inner-city girl from foster homes, thrown in amongst all those middle-class boys and girls who took college and privilege so completely for granted—and she decided that, if she was going to pluck up the courage to talk to someone, it might as well be the most forbidding-looking person she could find. We were very young then, you know.

"Once we'd finally got ourselves registered, she and I went for a coffee together, and then we arranged to meet again the next day—well, when I say *arranged,* Abby told me, 'I'm going on the library tour tomorrow at noon, see you there,' and walked off before I could answer either way. By that time I already knew that I admired her. It was a novel sensation, for me; I don't admire many people. But she was so determined, so vivid; she made everyone I had met before seem pale and shadowy by comparison. You've probably noticed"—Daniel smiled faintly, glancing up at me over his glasses—"that I have a tendency to keep myself at some distance from life. I had always felt that I was an observer, never a participant; that I was watching from behind a thick glass wall as people went about the business of living—and did it with such ease, with a skill that they took for granted and that I had never known. Then Abby reached straight through the glass and caught my hand. It was like an electric shock. I remember watching her walk off across Front Square—she was wearing this awful fringed skirt that was much too long for her, she looked drowned in it—and realizing that I was smiling . . .

"Justin was on the library tour the next day. He hung back a step or two behind the group, and I wouldn't even have noticed him if it hadn't been for the fact that he had a hideous cold. Every sixty seconds or so he came out with this enormous, explosive, wet sneeze, and everyone would jump and then snicker, and he would turn an extraordinary shade of beetroot and try to disappear into his handkerchief. He was obviously excruciatingly shy. At the end of the tour Abby turned around to him, as if we'd known one another all our lives, and said, 'We're going for lunch, are you coming?' I've seldom seen anyone look so startled. His mouth popped open and he mumbled something that could have meant anything, but he went over to the Buttery with us. By the end of lunch he was actually speaking in full sentences—and interesting ones, too. We'd read a lot of the same things, he had some insights into John Donne that had never occurred to me . . . It hit me, that afternoon, that I liked him; that I liked both of them. That, for the first time in my life, I was enjoying the company of others. You don't strike me as the kind of person who's ever had difficulty making friends; I'm not sure you can understand quite what a revelation that was.

"It took us until classes started, the next week, to find Rafe. The three of us were sitting at the back of a lecture room, waiting for the lecturer to show up, when all of a sudden the door beside us flew open and there was Rafe: dripping with rain, hair plastered to his head, fists clenched, obviously straight out of some traffic mess and in a horrible mood. It was a pretty dramatic entrance. Abby said, 'Check it out, it's King Lear,' and Rafe whipped around on her and snarled—you know how he gets—'How did you get here, then—in Daddy's limo? Or on your broomstick?' Justin and I were taken aback, but Abby just laughed and said, 'By hot-air balloon,' and pushed a chair towards him. And after a moment he sat down and muttered, 'Sorry.' And that was that."

Daniel smiled, down at the leaf, a private little smile as tender and amazed as a lover's. "How did we ever put up with one another? Abby talking nineteen to the dozen to hide her shyness, Justin half smothered under his, Rafe biting people's heads off right and left; and me. I was terribly serious, I know. It wasn't until that year, really, that I learned how to laugh . . ."

"And Lexie?" I asked, very softly. "How did you find her?"

"Lexie," Daniel said. The smile rippled across his face

like wind on water, deepened. "Do you know, I can't even remember the first time we met her? Abby probably can; you should ask her. All I remember is that, by the time we had been postgrads for a few weeks, she seemed to have been there forever."

He put the leaf down gently on the bench beside him and wiped his fingers on his handkerchief. "It always took my breath away," he said, "that the five of us could have found one another—against such odds, through all the layers of armored fortifications each of us had set up. A lot of it was Abby, of course; I've never known what instinct led her so unerringly, I'm not sure she knows herself, but you can see why I've trusted her judgment ever since. But still: it would have been so heart-stoppingly easy for us to miss one another, for me or Abby to show up an hour later for registration, for Justin to refuse our invitation, for Rafe to be just that little bit snippier so that we backed off and left him alone. Do you see now why I believe in miracles? I used to imagine time folding over, the shades of our future selves slipping back to the crucial moments to tap each of us on the shoulder and whisper: *Look, there, look! That man, that woman: they're for you; that's your life, your future, fidgeting in that line, dripping on the carpet, shuffling in that doorway. Don't miss it.* How else could such a thing have happened?"

He bent down and picked up our butts from the paving stones, one by one. "In all my life," he said simply, "these are the only four people I have ever loved." Then he stood up and walked off across the grass towards the house, with the bottle and the glass dangling from one hand and the cigarette butts cupped in the other.

The others came back still heavy-eyed and headachy and in a prickly mood. The film had been crap, they said, some awful thing with a random Baldwin brother having endless supposedly comic misunderstandings with someone who looked like Teri Hatcher but wasn't; the cinema had been full of kids who were clearly below the age limit and who had spent the whole two hours texting each other and eating crackly things and kicking the back of Justin's seat. Rafe and Justin were still very obviously not talking, and now Rafe and Abby apparently weren't either. Dinner was leftover lasagna, crunchy on top and scorched on the bottom and eaten in tense silence. No one had bothered to make a salad to go with it, or to light the fire.

Just when I was about ready to scream, Daniel said calmly, glancing up, "By the way, Lexie, I meant to ask you something. I thought I might touch on Anne Finch with my Monday group, but I'm awfully rusty. Would you mind giving me a quick rundown, after dinner?"

Anne Finch wrote a poem from the point of view of a bird, she showed up here and there in Lexie's thesis notes, and that, since there are only twenty-four hours in a day, was basically all I knew about her. Rafe would have pulled something like this out of pure malicious mischief, yanking my chain just because he could, but Daniel never opened his mouth without a solid reason. That brief, strange alliance in the garden was over. He was showing me, starting with the little things, that if I insisted on sticking around he could make my life very, very awkward.

There was no way I was going to make an eejit of myself

by spending my evening babbling about voice and identity to someone who knew I was talking rubbish. Lucky for me Lexie had been an unpredictable brat—although probably luck had nothing to do with it: I was pretty sure she had constructed that side of her personality specifically for moments a lot like this one. "I don't feel like it," I said, keeping my head down and jabbing at my crunchy lasagna with my fork.

There was an instant of silence. "Are you OK?" Justin asked.

I shrugged, not looking up. "I guess."

Something had just hit me. That silence and the fine thread of new tension through Justin's voice, and quick glances flicking back and forth across the table: the others were, instantly and so easily, worried about me. Here I'd spent weeks trying to get them to relax, drop their guard; I had never thought about how fast I could send them skidding in the opposite direction, and how serious a weapon that might make if I used it right.

"I helped you with Ovid when you needed it," Daniel reminded me. "Don't you remember? I spent ages finding you that quote—what was it?"

Obviously I wasn't about to rise to that one. "I'd only get mixed up and end up telling you about Mary Barber or someone. I can't think straight today. I keep . . ." I shoved lasagna bits aimlessly around my plate. "Never mind."

Nobody was eating any more. "You keep what?" Abby asked.

"Leave it," Rafe said. "God knows I'm not in the mood for Anne bloody Finch. If she's not either—"

"Is something bothering you?" Daniel asked me, politely.

"Leave her *alone*."

"Of course," Daniel said. "Get some rest, Lexie. We'll do it another night, when you're feeling better."

I risked a quick look up. He had picked up his fork and knife again and was eating steadily, with nothing on his face but thoughtful absorption. This move had backfired; he was calmly, intently considering his next one.

I went for a preemptive strike. After dinner we were all in the sitting room, reading, or anyway pretending to—no one had even suggested anything as social as a game of cards. The ashes from last night's fire were still in a dreary pile in the fireplace, and there was a soggy chill in the air; distant bits of the house kept letting out sharp cracks or ominous groans, making us all jump. Rafe was kicking the hearth-rail with the toe of one shoe, in a steady, irritable rhythm, and I was fidgeting, changing position in my chair every few seconds. Between the two of us, we were making both Justin and Abby tenser every second. Daniel, head bent over something with an awful lot of footnotes, didn't seem to have noticed.

Around eleven, like always, I went out to the hall and put on my outdoor stuff. Then I went back to the sitting room and hung in the doorway, looking unsure.

"Going for a walk?" Daniel asked.

"Yeah," I said. "It might help me relax. Justin, will you come with me?"

Justin started, stared at me like a rabbit in headlights. "Me? Why me?"

"Why anyone?" Daniel inquired, with mild curiosity.

I shrugged, an uneasy twitch. "I don't know, OK? My head feels weird. I keep thinking . . ." I twisted my scarf round my finger, bit my lip. "Maybe I had bad dreams last night."

"Nightmares," Rafe said, without looking up. "Not 'bad dreams.' You're not *six*."

"What kind of bad dreams?" Abby asked. There was a tiny, worried furrow between her eyebrows.

I shook my head. "I don't remember. Not properly. Just . . . I just don't feel like being out in the lanes alone."

"But I don't either," said Justin. He looked really upset.

"I hate it out there—really hate it, not just . . . It's *horrible*. Eerie. Can't someone else go?"

"Or," Daniel suggested helpfully, "if you're this anxious about going out, Lexie, why don't you stay at home?"

"Because. If I sit around in here any longer, I'm going to go crazy."

"I'll go with you," Abby said. "Girl chat."

"No offense," Daniel said, with a slight, affectionate smile at Abby, "but I think a homicidal maniac might be less intimidated by the two of you than he should be. If you're feeling nervous, Lexie, you should have someone large with you. Why don't you and I go?"

Rafe raised his head. "If you're going," he told Daniel, "then so am I."

There was a small, tight silence. Rafe stared coldly at Daniel, unblinking; Daniel gazed calmly back. "Why?" he asked.

"Because he's a moron," Abby said, to her book. "Ignore him and maybe he'll go away, or at least shut up. Wouldn't that be fun?"

"I don't *want* you guys," I said. I was all ready for this, Daniel trying to join the party. I hadn't counted on Justin having some weird unexplained phobia of country lanes, though. "All you'll do is bitch at each other, and I'm not in the mood. I want Justin. I never see him any more."

Rafe snorted. "You see him all *day*, every day. How much Justin can one person take?"

"That's different. We haven't talked in ages, not properly."

"I can't go out there in the middle of the night, Lexie," Justin said. He looked like he was actually in pain. "I would, honestly, but I just *can't*."

"Well," Daniel said to me and Rafe, putting his book down. There was a glint in his eye, something like a wry, tired triumph: one all. "Shall we go?"

"Forget it," I said, giving them all a disgusted glare. "Just forget it. Never mind. You can all stay here and bitch and complain, I'll go by myself, and if I get stabbed again, I hope you'll be happy."

Just before I slammed the kitchen door, panes of glass trembling, I heard Rafe starting to say something and Abby's voice cutting across his, low and fierce: "Shut up." When I turned back at the bottom of the garden, all four of them had their heads bent over their books again, in their pools of lamplight; glowing, enclosed, untouchable.

The night had turned cloudy, the air thick and immovable as a wet duvet dumped over the hills. I walked fast, trying to wear myself out, aiming for the point where I could fool myself that it was the exercise making my heart race. I thought of that great imaginary clock I'd felt somewhere in the background, my first couple of days, urging me faster. Sometime after that it had faded away into nothing, left me swaying to Whitethorn House's own sweet slow rhythms, with all the time in the world. Now it was back, ticking savagely and getting louder every minute, speeding towards some huge shadowy zero hour.

I rang Frank from down in one of the lanes—even the thought of climbing my tree, having to stay in one place, made me itch all over. "There you are," he said. "What were you doing, running a marathon?"

I leaned against a tree trunk and tried to get my breathing back to normal. "Trying to walk off my hangover. Clear my head."

"Always a good idea," Frank agreed. "First off, babe, well done last night. I'll buy you a fancy cocktail for that one, when you get home. I think you may just have got us the break we needed."

"Maybe. I'm not counting chickens. For all we know, Ned could be bullshitting me about the whole thing. He tries to buy Lexie's share of the house, she blows him off, he decides to give it one more go, then I mention the memory loss and he sees his chance to convince me we had a deal all along . . . He's no Einstein, but he's no idiot either, not when it comes to wheeling and dealing."

"Maybe not," Frank said. "Maybe not. How'd you manage to hook up with him, anyway?"

I had my answer to that one all ready. "I've been keeping an eye on that cottage, every night. I figured Lexie went there for a reason—and if she was meeting someone, that would be the logical place. So I thought there was a decent chance whoever it was would show up there again."

"And Slow Eddie wanders in," Frank said blandly, "just when I'd told you about the house, given the two of you something to talk about. He's got good timing. Why didn't you ring me, after he left?"

"My head was buzzing, Frankie. All I could think about was how this changes the case, how I can use it, what I do next, how to find out if Ned's bullshitting . . . I meant to phone you, but it went straight out of my head."

"Better late than never. So how was your day?"

His voice was pleasant, absolutely neutral, giving away nothing. "I know, I know, I'm a lazy cow," I said, giving it an apologetic cringe. "I should've tried to get something out of Daniel, while I had him to myself, but I just couldn't face it. My head was killing me, and you know what Daniel's like; he's not exactly light entertainment. Sorry."

"Hmm," said Frank, not very reassuringly. "And what's with the stroppy-bitch act? I'm assuming it was an act."

"I want to unsettle them," I said, which was true. "We've tried relaxing them into talking, and it hasn't worked. What with the new info, I think it's time to kick it up a gear."

"It didn't occur to you to talk that over with me before you swung into action?"

I left a small, startled pause. "I just figured you'd guess what I was at."

"OK," Frank said, in a mild voice that started sirens rising in my head. "You've done a great job, Cass. I know you didn't want to get involved, and I appreciate the fact that you did it anyway. You're a good cop."

It felt like something had hit me in the stomach. "What, Frank," I said, but I already knew.

He laughed. "Relax; it's good news. Time to wind it up, babe. I want you to go home and start complaining that you feel like you're getting the flu—dizzy, feverish, achy. Don't mention the wound hurting, or they'll want to look at it; just feel crap all over. Maybe wake one of them up during the night—Justin's the worrier, isn't he?—and tell him it's getting worse. If they haven't taken you to the emergency room by morning, make them. I'll handle it from there."

My nails were cutting into my hand. *"Why?"*

"I thought you'd be delighted," Frank said, doing taken aback and a little miffed. "You didn't want—"

"I didn't want to go in to start with. I know. But I'm in now, and I'm getting close. Why the hell would you want to pull the plug? Because I didn't ask you before I rattled these guys' cage?"

"God, no," said Frank, still all bland surprise. "Nothing to do with that. You went in to find a direction for this investigation, and you've done that beautifully. Congratulations, babe. Your work here is done."

"No," I said, "it's not. You sent me in to find a *suspect*, those were your exact words, and so far all I've found is a possible motive with four possible suspects attached—five, if you take into account that Ned could be lying his little head off. How does that move the investigation forwards, exactly? The four of them will stick to their story, just like you said at the beginning, and you're right back where you started. Let me do my fucking job."

"I'm looking out for you. That's *my* job. With what you've found out, you could be at risk here, and I can't just ignore—"

"Bull*shit*, Frank. If one of those four killed her, I've been in danger since Day One, and it never bothered you one bit till now—"

"Keep your voice down. Is that it? You're pissed off because I haven't been *protective* enough?"

I could practically see his hands flying up in outrage, the wide offended blue eyes. "Give me a break, Frank. I'm a big girl, I can take care of myself, and you've never had a problem with that idea before. So why the fuck are you pulling me out?"

There was a silence. Finally Frank sighed. "Fine," he said. "You want to know why, fine. I no longer feel that you're maintaining the objectivity required to serve this investigation."

"What are you talking about?" My heart was hammering. If he had surveillance on the house after all, or if he'd guessed that I'd taken off the mike—*I should never have left it for so long*, I thought wildly, *stupid, I should've gone back inside every few minutes and made some kind of noise*—

"You're way too emotionally involved. I'm not stupid, Cassie. I have a fair idea what happened last night, and I know there's shit you're not telling me. Those are warning signs, and I'm not going to ignore them."

He'd fallen for the Fauré; he didn't know I'd been burned. My heart rate went down a notch.

"You're losing your boundaries. Maybe I should never have pressured you to do this. I don't know the ins and outs of what happened to you on Murder and I'm not asking, but it clearly wrecked your head, and you obviously weren't ready for something like this just yet."

I have a flash-bang temper, and if I lost it now, the argument was over; I would have proved Frank's point. That was probably exactly what he was angling for. I kicked the tree trunk instead, hard enough that for a second I thought I'd broken my toe. When I could talk I said, coolly, "My head is doing just fine, Frank, and so are my boundaries. Every one of my actions has been directed towards achieving the goal of this investigation and finding a prime suspect in the murder of Lexie Madison. And I'd like to finish the job."

"Sorry, Cassie," Frank said, gently but very firmly. "Not this time."

There's one thing about undercover that no one mentions, ever. The rule is, the handler holds the brake: he's the one who decides when you need to pull back or come out. He's the one with the overview, after all, he may well have info that you don't, and you do what he says if you value either your life or your career. But here's the part we never talk about, the grenade you carry with you always: he can't make you. I had never known anyone to throw that grenade before, but every one of us knows it's there. If you were to say no, there would be—for a little while, at least, and that might be all you needed—fuck-all your handler could do about it.

That kind of breach of trust can't be repaired. In that second I saw the airport codes in Lexie's date book, that hard, ruthless scrawl.

"I'm staying," I said. A sharp wave of wind ran through the woods and I felt my tree shiver, a deep judder going up into my bones.

"No," Frank said, "you're not. Don't give me hassle on this, Cassie. The decision's been made; there's no point in us fighting about it. Go home, pack your stuff and start playing sick. I'll see you tomorrow."

"You put me in here to do a job," I said. "I'm not leaving till I get it done. I'm not fighting about it, Frank. I'm just telling you."

This time Frank understood. His voice didn't sharpen, but it had an undertow that made my shoulders go up. "Do you want me to pick you up off the street, find drugs on you and throw you in jail till you pull yourself together? Because I'll do it."

"No you won't. The others know Lexie doesn't do drugs, and if she gets dragged in on a bogus charge and then dies while in police custody, they'll kick up such a stink that this whole operation will go up in flames and you'll be cleaning up the mess for years."

There was a silence, while Frank evaluated the situation. "You know this could end your career, don't you?" he said eventually. "You're disobeying a direct order from a superior officer. You know I could haul you in, take your badge and your gun, and fire you on the spot."

"Yeah," I said. "I know." But he wouldn't do it, not Frank, and I knew I was taking advantage of that. I knew something else, too, I'm not sure how; maybe from the lack of shock in his voice. Sometime in his career, he had done this same thing himself.

"And you know you're making me miss my weekend with Holly. It's her birthday tomorrow. You want to explain to her why Daddy can't be there after all?"

I winced, but I reminded myself that this was Frank, Holly's birthday was probably months away. "So go. Let someone else monitor the mike feed."

"Not a chance. Even if I wanted to, I don't have anyone else. The budget's run out on this one. The brass are sick of paying officers to sit around listening to you drink wine and strip wallpaper."

"I don't blame them," I said. "What you do with the mike feed is your call; leave it to monitor itself, if you want. That's your half of the gig. I'm just doing mine."

"OK," Frank said, on a long-suffering sigh, "OK. Here's what we're going to do. You've got forty-eight hours, starting now, to wind this up—"

"Seventy-two."

"Seventy-two, on three conditions: you don't do anything stupid, you keep calling in, and you keep that mike on you at all times. I want your word."

Something prickled inside me. Maybe he did know, after all; with Frank you can never be sure. "Got it," I said. "I promise."

"Three days from now, even if you're an inch away from breaking the case, you come in. By"—watch check—"quarter to midnight on Monday, you're out of that house and in an emergency room, or at least on your way there. Until then, I'm going to hang on to this tape. If you stick to those conditions and you come in on time, I'll erase it, and no one else ever needs to know about this conversation. If you give me one more iota of hassle, I will haul your arse in, whatever that takes and whatever consequences it has, and I will fire you. We clear?"

"Yeah," I said. "We're crystal clear. I'm not trying to fuck you around, Frank. It's not about that."

"This, Cassie," Frank said, "was a really, really bad idea. I hope you know that."

There was a beep and then nothing, just waves of static in my ear. My hands were shaking so hard that I dropped the phone twice before I managed to hit End.

The irony of it: he was millimeters from right. Even twenty-four hours earlier, I hadn't been working this case; I'd been letting it work me, free-falling into it, full fathom five and swimming deeper. There were a thousand tiny phrases and glances and objects that had been scattered through this case like bread crumbs, going overlooked and unconnected because I had wanted—or thought I wanted—to be Lexie Madison so much more than I wanted to solve her murder. What Frank didn't know, and what I couldn't tell him, was that Ned of all people, without ever having a clue he was doing it, had pulled me back. I wanted to close this case, and I was ready—and this isn't something I say lightly—to do whatever it took.

Probably you could say I came back fighting because I had been suckered, almost fatally, and this was my last chance to make up for that; or because the only way I would ever get my career back—*It's my job,* I had said to Daniel, before I knew the words were going to come out—was if I got a solve here; or because our lost Operation Vestal had poisoned the air around me, and I needed an antidote. Maybe a little of all three. But this was the one I couldn't get away from: no matter what this woman had been or done, we had been built into each other since we were born. We had led each other to this life, this place. I knew things about her that no one else knew, in all the world. I couldn't leave her now. There was no one else to look through her eyes and read her mind, trace the silvery lines of runes she had left trailing behind her, tell the only story she had ever finished.

All I knew was that I needed the end of that story, that I needed to be the one who brought it home, and that I was frightened. I don't scare easy, but just like Daniel, I've always known that there's a price to pay. What Daniel didn't know, or didn't mention, is what I said right at the beginning: the price is a wildfire shape-changing thing, and you're not always the one who chooses, you're not always allowed to know in advance, what it's going to be.

The other thing hitting me over and over, with a horrible sick lurch every time: this could have been why she had come looking for me, this could have been what she had wanted all along. Someone to change places with her. Someone longing for the chance to toss away her own battered life, let it evaporate like morning mist over grass; someone who would gladly fade to a scent of bluebells and a green shoot, while this girl strengthened and bloomed and turned solid again, and lived.

I think it was only in that moment I believed she was dead, this girl I had never seen alive. I'll never be free of her. I wear her face; as I get older it'll stay her changing mirror, the one glimpse of all the ages she never had. I lived her life, for a few strange bright weeks; her blood went into making me what I am, the same way it went to make the bluebells and the hawthorn tree. But when I had the chance to take that final step over the border, lie down with Daniel among the ivy leaves and the sound of water, let go of my own life with all its scars and all its wreckage and start new, I turned it down.

The air was so still. Any minute now, I would have to go back to Whitethorn House and do my best to wreck it.

Out of nowhere I wanted to talk to Sam so badly it was like being hit in the stomach. It felt like the most urgent thing in the world, to tell him, before it was too late, that I was coming home; that, in the ways that mattered most, I was already back; that I was scared, terrified as a kid in the dark, and that I needed to hear his voice.

His phone was off. All I got was the voice-mail woman telling me, archly, to leave a message. Sam was working: taking his turn surveilling Naylor's house, going through statement sheets for the dozenth time in case he had missed something. If I'd been the crying type, I would have cried then.

Before I understood that I was doing it, I set my phone number to Private and dialed Rob's mobile. I pressed my free hand flat over the mike and felt my heart going slow and hard under my palm. I knew this was very possibly the stupidest thing I'd done in my life, but I didn't know how not to do it.

"Ryan," he said on the second ring, wide awake; Rob always had trouble sleeping. When I couldn't answer, he said, with a sudden new alertness in his voice, "Hello?"

I hung up. In the second before my thumb hit the button I thought I heard him say, fast and urgent, "Cassie?" but my hand was already moving and it was too late for me to pull it back even if I had wanted to. I slid down the side of the tree and sat there, with my arms wrapped tight around myself, for a long time.

There was this night, during our last case. At three in the morning I got on my Vespa and went down to the crime scene to pick Rob up. On the way back the roads were all ours, that late, and I was going fast; Rob leaned into the turns with me and the bike barely seemed to feel the extra weight. Two high beams came at us around a bend, brilliant and growing till they filled the whole road: a lorry, half over the center line and coming straight for us, but the bike swayed out of the way light as a stalk of grass and the lorry was past in a great whack of wind and dazzle. Rob's hands on my waist shook every now and then, a quick violent tremor, and I was thinking of home and warmth and whether I had anything in the fridge.

Neither of us knew it, but we were speeding through the last few hours we had. I leaned on that friendship loose and unthinking as if it were a wall six foot thick, but less than a day later it started to crumble and avalanche and there was nothing in the world I could do to hold it together. In the nights afterwards I used to wake up with my mind full of those headlights, brighter and deeper than the sun. I saw them again behind my eyelids in that dark lane, and I understood then that I could have just kept driving. I could have been like Lexie. I could have hit full speed and taken us soaring up off the road, into the vast silence at the heart of those lights and out on the other side where nothing could touch us, ever.

21

It only took Daniel a couple of hours to come up with his next move. I was sitting up in bed, staring at the Brothers Grimm and reading the same sentence over and over without taking in a word of it, when there was a quick, discreet rap on my door.

"Come in," I called.

Daniel put his head in the door. He was still dressed, spotless in his white shirt and shining shoes. "Do you have a minute?" he inquired politely.

"Of course," I said, just as politely, putting down the book. There was no way this was a surrender or even a truce, but I couldn't think of anything either of us could try, not without the others there for weapons.

"I just wanted," Daniel said, turning to close the door behind him, "a quick word with you. In private."

My body thought faster than my mind. In that second when his back was to me, before I knew why I was doing it, I grabbed the mike wire through my pajama top, gave it a hard upwards yank and felt the pop as the jack came free. By the time he looked around again, my hands were lying innocently on the book. "About what?" I asked.

"There are a few things," Daniel said, smoothing the bottom of the duvet and sitting down, "that have been bothering me."

"Oh?"

"Yes. Almost since you . . . well, let's say arrived. Small inconsistencies, growing more troubling as time went on. By the time you asked for more onions, the other evening, I had serious questions."

He left a polite pause, in case I wanted to contribute anything to the conversation. I stared at him. I couldn't believe I hadn't seen this one coming.

"And then, of course," he said, when it was obvious that I wasn't going to answer, "we come to last night. As you may or may not know, on a few occasions you and I—or, at any rate, Lexie and I—have . . . Well, suffice it to say that a kiss can be as individual and unmistakable as a laugh. When we kissed, last night, it left me more or less positive that you're not Lexie."

He gazed at me blandly, across the bed. He was burning me all over again, every way he knew how: with my boss, with the boyfriend he'd guessed at, with the brass who would not approve of an undercover smooching a suspect. They were his brand-new remote-controlled weapons. If that mike had been plugged in, I would have been a few hours away from a grim trip home and a one-way ticket to a desk in Offaly.

"Absurd though this may sound," Daniel said tranquilly, "I'd like to see this supposed stab wound. Simply to reassure myself that you're actually who you're claiming to be."

"Sure," I said cheerfully, "why not?" and saw the startled flicker in his eyes. I pulled up my pajama top and tugged the bandage free to show him the jack and the battery pack, separate.

"Nice shot," I told him, "but no dice. And if you do get me pulled out, do you think I'll go quietly? I'll have nothing to lose. Even if all I've got is five minutes, I'll use them to tell the others who I am and that you've known for weeks. How well do you think that'll go down with, say, Rafe?"

Daniel leaned forwards to inspect the mike. "Ah," he said. "Well, it was worth a try."

"My time's almost up on this case anyway," I said. I was talking fast: Frank would have started getting suspicious the instant the mike feed died, I had maybe a minute before his head went up in smoke. "I've only got a few days left. But I want those few days. If you try to take them away from me,

I'll go down all guns blazing. If you don't, you still have a good chance that I won't get anything worthwhile, and we can work it so the others never have to know who I was."

He watched me, expressionless, those big square hands tidily clasped in his lap. "My friends are my responsibility. I'm not going to stand back and let you sweep them off into corners for interrogation."

I shrugged. "Fair enough. Try and stop me any way you can; you didn't have any trouble tonight. Just don't mess with my last few days. Deal?"

"How many days," Daniel asked, "exactly?"

I shook my head. "Not in the deal. In about ten seconds I'm going to plug this in again, so it sounds like an accidental disconnect, and we're going to have a harmless little chat about why I was in a mood at dinner. OK?"

He nodded absently, still examining the mike. "Great," I said. "Here goes. I don't feel like"—I plugged the wire back in halfway through the sentence, for an extra touch of realism—"talking about it. My head's a mess, everything feels sucky, I just want everyone to leave me alone. OK?"

"You're probably just hungover," Daniel said, obligingly. "You've always had a hard time with red wine, haven't you?"

Everything sounded like a trap. "Whatever," I said, giving him an irritable teenager shrug and sticking my bandage back down. "Maybe it was the punch. Rafe probably put meths in it. He's drinking a lot more these days, have you noticed?"

"Rafe is fine," Daniel said coolly. "And so will you be, I hope, after a good night's sleep."

Quick footsteps downstairs, and a door opening. "Lexie?" Justin called anxiously, up the stairs. "Is everything OK?"

"Daniel's annoying me," I shouted back.

"Daniel? How are you annoying her?"

"I'm not."

"He wants to know why I feel crap," I called. "I feel crap because I just do, and I want him to leave me alone."

"You feel crap because what?" Justin had come out of his room, to the bottom of the stairs; I could picture him, in his striped pyjamas, clutching the banister and peering short-sightedly upwards. Daniel was giving me an intent, thought-ful gaze that made me edgy as hell.

"Shut *up!*" yelled Abby, furious enough that we could hear her right through her door. "Some of us are trying to *sleep* here."

"Lexie? You feel crap because what?"

A thud: Abby had thrown something. "Justin, I said shut *up! Jesus!*"

Faintly, from the ground floor, Rafe shouted something irritable that sounded like "What the hell is going *on?*"

"I'll come down and explain, Justin," Daniel called. "Everyone go back to bed." To me: "Good night." He stood up and smoothed the duvet again. "Sleep well. I hope you'll feel better in the morning."

"Yeah," I said. "Thanks. Don't count on it."

The steady rhythm of his footsteps going downstairs, then hushed voices below me: at first a lot of Justin and an occasional brief interjection from Daniel, shifting gradually till it was the other way round. I got out of bed, carefully, and put my ear to the floor, but they were talking barely above whispers and I couldn't make out the words.

It was twenty minutes before Daniel came back upstairs, softly, pausing for a long few seconds on the landing. I didn't start shaking until his bedroom door closed behind him.

I stayed awake for hours that night, flipping pages and pretending to read, rustling the covers and doing deep breaths and pretending to be asleep, unplugging the mike for a few seconds or a few minutes every now and then. I think I created a pretty good impression of a jack come loose, disconnecting and reconnecting itself as I moved, but it didn't reassure me. Frank is very far from stupid, and he was in no humor to give me the benefit of any doubts.

Frank to the left of me, Daniel to the right, and here I

was, stuck in the middle with Lexie. I passed the time, while I played my mike-jack game, by trying to work out how it was logistically possible for me to have ended up on the opposite side from absolutely everyone else involved in this case, including people who were on opposite sides from each other. Before I finally went to sleep I took the chair from Lexie's dressing table, for the first time in weeks, and braced it against my door.

Saturday went fast, in a helpless nightmare daze. Daniel had decided—partly because working on the house always settled them all down, presumably, and partly to keep everyone in one room and under his eye—that we needed to spend the day sanding floors: "We've been neglecting the dining room," he told us, at breakfast. "It's starting to look terribly shabby, next to the sitting room. I think today we should start bringing it up to scratch. What do you think?"

"Good idea," said Abby, sliding eggs onto his plate and giving him a tired, determinedly positive smile. Justin shrugged and went back to picking at toast; I said, "Whatever," into the frying pan; Rafe took his coffee and left without a word. "Good," Daniel said serenely, going back to his book. "That's a plan, then."

The rest of the day was just about as excruciating as I'd expected. The Happy Place magic was apparently on its day off. Rafe was in a silent, fuming rage with the whole world; he kept banging the sander into the walls, making everyone jump, till Daniel took it out of his hands without a word and passed him a sheet of sandpaper instead. I turned up my sulk as loud as I could and hoped it would have some effect on someone, and that sooner or later—not too much later—I would find a way to use it.

Outside the windows it was raining, thin petulant rain. We didn't talk. Once or twice I saw Abby wipe her face, but she always had her back to the rest of us and I couldn't tell if she was crying or if it was just the sawdust. It got everywhere: drifting up our noses, down our necks, working its way into the skin of our hands. Justin wheezed ostentatiously and had great dramatic coughing fits into a handkerchief until finally Daniel put down the sander, stalked out, and came back with an ancient, hideous gas mask, which he held out to Justin in silence. No one laughed.

"They've got asbestos in them," Rafe said, scrubbing viciously at an awkward corner of floor. "Are you actually trying to kill him, or do you just want to give that impression?"

Justin gave the mask a horrified look. "I don't want to breathe asbestos."

"If you'd prefer to tie your handkerchief around your mouth," said Daniel, "then do that instead. Just stop moaning." He shoved the mask into Justin's hands, went back to the sander and fired it up again.

The gas mask that had sent me and Rafe into a giddy fit, that night on the patio. *Daniel can wear it into college, we'll get Abby to embroider it* . . . Justin dumped it gingerly in a bare corner, where it sat for the rest of the day, staring at us all with huge, empty, desolate eyes.

"And what's been going on with your mike?" Frank inquired, that night. "Just out of curiosity."

"Ah, fuck," I said. "What, it's doing it again? I thought I'd fixed it."

A skeptical pause. "Doing what again?"

"This morning when I went to change my bandage, the jack was out. I think I put the bandage on wrong, after my shower last night, and the jack pulled out when I moved. How much did you miss? Is it working now?" I stuck a hand down my top and tapped the mike. "Can you hear that?"

"Loud and clear," Frank said dryly. "It popped out a few times during the night, but I doubt I missed anything significant there—I certainly hope not, anyway. I lost a minute or two of your midnight chat with Daniel, though."

I put a grin in my voice. "Oh, that? He was edgy because of the stroppy-bitch act. He wanted to know what was wrong, so I told him to leave me alone. Then the others heard us and got in on the action, and he gave up and went to bed. I told you it would work, Frankie. They're going up the walls."

"Right," Frank said, after a moment. "So apparently I didn't miss anything educational. And as long as I'm working this case, I suppose I can't say I don't believe in coincidences. But if that wire happens to come loose again, even for one second, I'm coming down there and dragging you in by the scruff of your neck. So get out your Super Glue." And he hung up.

I walked home trying to work out what I would do next if I were in Daniel's shoes, but as it turned out he wasn't the one I should have been worrying about. I knew, even before I got into the house, that something had happened. They were all in the kitchen—the guys had obviously been halfway through the washing up, Rafe was holding a spatula like a weapon and Justin was dripping suds all over the floor—and they were all talking at once.

"—doing their job," Daniel was saying flatly, as I opened the French doors. "If we don't let them—"

"But *why*?" Justin wailed, over him. "Why would they—"

Then they saw me. There was a second of absolute silence, all of them staring at me, voices sliced off in mid-word.

"What's going on?" I asked.

"The cops want us to come in," said Rafe. He threw the spatula into the sink, with a clang and a splash. Water spattered on Daniel's shirt, but he didn't seem to notice.

"I can't go through that again," Justin said, sagging back against the counter. "I can't."

"Come in where? What for?"

"Mackey rang Daniel," said Abby. "They want us to come talk to them, first thing tomorrow morning. All of us."

"*Why?*" That toerag Frank. He had known, when I phoned him, that he was going to pull this crap. He hadn't even bothered to hint at it.

Rafe shrugged. "He didn't share. Just that he, quote, wants a *chat* with us. Unquote."

"But why there?" Justin demanded frantically. He was staring at Daniel's phone, on the kitchen table, like it might pounce. "Before, they always came here. Why do we have to—"

"Where does he want us to go?" I asked.

"Dublin Castle," Abby said. "The Serious Crime office, or squad, or whatever they call it."

Serious and Organized Crime work downstairs from Murder; all Frank had to do was whisk us up an extra flight of stairs. S&O do not investigate your average stabbing, not unless there's a crime lord involved, but the others didn't know that, and it sounded impressive.

"Did you know about this?" Daniel asked me. He was giving me a cold stare that I didn't like one bit. Rafe raised his eyes to the ceiling and muttered something that included the words "paranoid freak."

"No. How would I?"

"I thought your friend Mackey might have rung you as well. While you were out."

"He didn't. And he's not my *friend*." I didn't bother hiding the pissed-off look; let Daniel try to figure out whether it was genuine. I had two days left, and Frank was going to eat away one of them with endless pointless nothing questions about what we put in our sandwiches and how we felt about Four-Boobs Brenda. He wanted us first thing in the morning: he was planning to stretch this out for as long as he could, eight hours, twelve. I wondered if it would be in character for Lexie to kick him in the goolies.

"I knew we shouldn't have rung them about that rock," Justin said wretchedly. "I knew it. They were leaving us *alone*."

"So let's not go," I said. Probably Frank would class this as doing something stupid, breaking one of his conditions, but I was too annoyed to care. "They can't make us."

A startled pause. "Is that true?" Abby asked Daniel.

"I think so, actually," Daniel said. He was examining me speculatively; I could almost hear the wheels spinning. "We're not under arrest. This was a request, not a command, although that's not how Mackey made it sound. All the same, I think we need to go."

"Oh, do you?" Rafe inquired, not nicely. "Do you really? And what if I think we should let Mackey go fuck himself?"

Daniel turned to look at him. "I plan to continue cooperating fully with the investigation," he said calmly. "Partly because I think it's wise, but mainly because I'd like to know who did this terrible thing. If any of you would prefer to stand in the way and raise Mackey's suspicions by refusing to cooperate, I can't stop you; but remember, the person who stabbed Lexie is still out there, and I for one think we should do our best to help catch him." The smart-arsed bastard: he was using my mike to feed Frank exactly what he wanted him to hear, which apparently was a heap of pious clichés. The two of them were perfect for each other.

Daniel glanced inquiringly around the kitchen. No one answered. Rafe started to say something, checked himself and shook his head in disgust.

"Good," said Daniel. "In that case, let's finish up here and get to bed. Tomorrow's going to be a long day." And he picked up the dishcloth.

I was in the sitting room with Abby, pretending to read and thinking up creative new words for Frank and listening to the tense silence coming from the kitchen, when I realized something. Given the choice, Daniel had decided he'd prefer to spend one of my last few days with Frank, rather than with me. I figured, in its own dangerous way, that was probably a compliment.

What I remember most about Sunday morning is that we did the whole breakfast routine, every step of it. Abby's quick tap on my door; the two of us making breakfast side by side, her face flushed from the heat of the stove. We moved easily around each other, passing things back and forth without having to ask. I remembered that first evening, the pang as I'd seen how closely woven together they were: somehow, along the way, I had become part of that. Justin frowning at his toast as he sliced it into triangles, Rafe's autopilot maneuver with the coffee, Daniel with the edge of a book caught under the corner of his plate. I didn't let myself think, even for a splinter of a second, about the fact that in thirty-six hours I would be gone; the fact that, even if I were to see them again, someday, it would never be like this.

We took our time. Even Rafe resurfaced once he'd finished his coffee, nudging me sideways with his hip so he could share my chair and nick bites of my toast. Dew ran down the windowpanes, and the rabbits—they were getting cheekier and closer every day—were nibbling the grass outside.

Something had changed, during the night. The jagged cutting edges between the four of them had melted away; they were gentle with one another, careful, almost tender. Sometimes I wonder if they took such care with that breakfast because, at some level deeper and surer than logic, they knew.

"We should go," Daniel said, finally. He closed his book, reached to put it on the counter. I felt a breath, something between a catch and a sigh, ripple around the table. Rafe's chest rose, quickly, against my shoulder.

"Right," Abby said softly, almost to herself. "Let's do this."

"There's something I'd like to discuss with you, Lexie," Daniel said. "Why don't you and I ride into town together?"

"Discuss what?" Rafe asked sharply. His fingers dug into my arm.

"If it were any of your business," Daniel said, taking his plate to the sink, "I would have invited you to join us." The jagged edges crystallized again, out of nowhere, fine and slicing the air.

"So," Daniel said, when he had pulled up his car in front of the house and I got in beside him, "here we are."

Something smoky curled through me: a warning. It was the way he was looking not at me but out the car window, at the house in cool morning mist, at Justin rubbing his windscreen fussily with a folded rag and Rafe slumping down the stairs with his chin tucked deep into his scarf; it was the expression on his face, intent and thoughtful and just a touch sad.

I had no way of knowing what this guy's limits were, or if he had any. My gun was behind Lexie's bedside table— Murder has a metal detector. *The only time you'll be out of coverage,* Frank had said, *is on the drive to and from town.*

Daniel smiled, a small private smile up at the hazy blue sky. "It's going to be a beautiful day," he said.

I was about to slam out of the car, stamp over to Justin and tell him Daniel was being horrible and demand to ride with him and the others—it seemed to be the week for complicated vicious spats, nobody would be suspicious of one more—when the door behind me flew open and Abby slid into the back seat, flushed and tangle-haired, in a tumble of gloves and hat and coat. "Hey," she said, slamming the door. "Can I come with you guys?"

"Sure," I said. I'd seldom been that glad to see anyone.

Daniel turned to look at her over his shoulder. "I thought we said you were going with Justin and Rafe."

"You must be joking. The mood they're in? It'd be like riding with Stalin and Pol Pot, only less cheerful."

Unexpectedly, Daniel smiled at her, a real smile, warm and amused. "They are being ridiculous. Yes, let's leave them to it; an hour or two stuck in a car together might be exactly what they need."

"Maybe," Abby said, sounding unconvinced. "That or they'll just kill each other." She pulled a folding hairbrush out of her bag and attacked her hair. In front of us, Justin got his car off to a jerky, irritable start and peeled off down the drive, way too fast.

Daniel put his hand back over his shoulder, palm up, towards Abby. He wasn't looking at her, or at me; he was gazing out the windscreen, unseeing, at the cherry trees. Abby lowered her brush and laid her hand in his, squeezed his fingers. She didn't let go until Daniel sighed and detached his hand from hers, gently, and started the car.

22

Frank, the utter fuckbucket, dumped me in an interview room ("We'll have someone with you in a minute, Miss Madison") and left me there for two hours. It wasn't even one of the good interview rooms, with a watercooler and comfy chairs; it was the crap little one that's two steps up from a holding cell, the one we use to make people nervous. It worked: I got edgier every minute. Frank could be doing anything out there, blowing my cover, telling the others about the baby, that we knew about Ned, anything. I knew I was reacting exactly the way he wanted me to, exactly like a suspect, but instead of snapping me out of it this just made me madder. I couldn't even tell the camera what I thought about this situation, since for all I knew he had one of the others watching and was banking on me doing exactly that.

I swapped the chairs around—Frank had of course given me the one with the cap taken off the end of one leg, the one meant to make suspects uncomfortable. I felt like yelling at the camera, *I used to work here, dickhead, this is my turf, don't try that shit on me.* Instead I found a pen in my jacket pocket and kept myself amused by writing LEXIE WAS HERE ON THE WALL, in fancy letters. This didn't get anyone's attention, but then I hadn't expected it to: the walls were already scattered with years' worth of tags and drawings and anatomically difficult suggestions. I recognized a couple of the names.

I hated this. I had been in this room so many times, me and Rob working suspects with the flawless, telepathic coordination of two hunters circling their moment; being there without him made me feel like someone had scooped out all my organs and I was about to cave in on myself, too hollow to stand. Eventually I dug my pen into the wall so hard that the point snapped off. I threw the rest of it across the room at the camera and got it with a crack, but even that didn't make me feel any better.

By the time Frank decided to make his big entrance, I was seething in about seven different ways. "Well well well," he said, reaching up and switching off the camera. "Fancy meeting you here. Have a seat."

I stayed standing. "What the fuck are you playing at?"

His eyebrows went up. "I'm interviewing suspects. What, I need your permission now?"

"You need to bloody well talk to me before you throw a curveball straight at my head. I'm not just having a laugh out there, Frank, I'm *working*, and this could wreck everything I'm trying to do."

"Working? Is that what the kids are calling it these days?"

"That's what *you* called it. I'm doing exactly what you sent me in there to do, I'm finally getting somewhere, why the hell are you shoving a spoke in my wheels?"

Frank leaned back against the wall and folded his arms. "If you want to play dirty, Cass, I can play too. Not as much fun when you're on the receiving end, is it?"

The thing was that I knew he wasn't playing dirty, not really. Making me sit in the naughty corner and think about what I'd done was one thing: he was furious enough—and with good reason—that he probably wanted to punch me in the eye, and I knew well that unless I pulled off a spectacular last-minute save I was going to be in big trouble when I came in the next day. But he would never, no matter how angry he was, do anything that might jeopardize the case. And I knew, cool as snow under all the spitting mad, that I could use that.

"OK," I said, taking a breath and running my hands over my hair, "OK. Fair enough. I deserved that."

He laughed, a short, tight bark. "You don't want to get me started on what you deserve, babe. Trust me on that one."

"I know, Frank," I said. "And when we've got the time, I'll let you give me hell for as long as you want, but not now. How're you doing with the others?"

He shrugged. "As well as could be expected."

"In other words, you've got nowhere."

"You think?"

"Yeah, I do. I know those four. You can keep going at them till you have to retire, and you'll still get nowhere."

"It's possible," Frank said blandly. "We'll have to wait and see, won't we? I've got a few years left in me."

"Come on, Frank. You're the one who's said that, right from the beginning: those four stick together like glue, there's no point in going at them from the outside. Wasn't that why you wanted me on the inside to start with?"

A noncommittal little tilt of his chin, like a shrug.

"You know well you're not going to get anything good out of them. You just want to rattle them, right? So let's rattle them together. I know you're pissed off with me, but that'll keep till tomorrow. For now, we're still on the same side."

One of Frank's eyebrows flickered. "We are?"

"Yeah, Frank, we are. And the two of us together can do a lot more damage than you can on your own."

"Sounds fun," Frank said. He was lounging against the wall with his hands in his pockets, eyes hooded lazily to hide the sharp, assessing glint. "What kind of damage did you have in mind?"

I moved round the table and sat on the edge, leaning in towards him, as close as I could get. "Interview me and let the others eavesdrop. Not Daniel—he doesn't rattle, all that'll happen if we push him is he'll walk out—but the other three. Switch on their intercoms to pick up this room, put them near monitors, whatever—if you can make it look accidental, great, but if you can't it doesn't matter. If you want to keep an eye on their reactions, then let Sam do the interview."

"While you say what, exactly?"

"I'll let it slip that my memory's starting to come back. I'll keep it vague, stick to stuff I can't get wrong—running for the cottage, blood, that kind of thing. If that doesn't rattle them, nothing will."

"Ah," Frank said, with a wry tip of a grin. "So that's what you were setting up, with the sulks and the temper tantrums and the whole prima-donna bit. I should have guessed. Silly me."

I shrugged. "Yeah, sure, I was going to do it anyway. But this way's even better. Like I said, we can do a lot more damage together. I can get edgy, make it obvious that there's more I'm not telling you . . . If you want to script it for me, then fine, do it, I'll say whatever you want. Come on, Frankie, what do you say? You and me?"

Frank thought this over. "And what do you want in exchange?" he inquired. "Just so I know."

I gave him my best wicked grin. "Relax, Frank. Nothing that'll jeopardize your professional soul. I just need to know how much you've told them, so I don't shove my foot in my mouth. And you were planning to share that with me anyway, right? Since we're on the same side and all."

"Yeah," Frank said dryly, on a sigh. "Naturally. I've told them sweet fuck-all, Cass. Your arsenal is still intact. That being the case, it would make me a very happy camper if you were to actually use some of it, sooner or later."

"I'm going to, believe me. Which reminds me," I added, as an afterthought. "The other thing I need: can you keep Daniel out of my hair for a while? Whenever you've finished with us, send the rest of us home—don't tell him we're gone, though, or he'll be out of here faster than a speeding bullet. Then give me an hour, two if you can, before you cut him loose. Don't spook him, just keep it routine and keep him talking. OK?"

"Interesting," Frank said. "Why?"

"I want to have a chat with the others without him around."

"That much I got. Why?"

"Because I think it'll work, is why. He's the one in charge there, you know that; he decides what they say and don't say. If the others are shaken up and they don't have him around to keep a lid on them, who knows what they'll come out with?"

Frank picked at something between his front teeth, examined his thumbnail. "What exactly are you aiming for?" he asked.

"I won't know till I hear it. But we've always said they were hiding something, right? I don't want to walk off this case without doing my best to get it out of them. I'm going to hit them with everything I've got—guilt trips, tears, tantrums, threats, the kid, Slow Eddie, you name it. Maybe I'll get a confession—"

"Which I've said from the beginning," Frank pointed out, "is not what we need from you. What with that annoying little admissibility rule, and all."

"You're telling me you'd turn down a confession if I brought you one on a silver platter? Even if it's not admissible, that doesn't mean it's not useful. You pull them in, play them the tape, go at them hard—Justin's cracking already, one good tap and he'll fall apart." It took me a second to realize where the déjà vu was coming from. The fact that I was having the exact same argument with Frank that I had had with Daniel gave me a strange cold twist in my stomach. "A confession may not be exactly what you asked Santy to bring you, but at this stage, Frankie, we can't afford to pick and choose."

"I'll admit it would be better than what we've got now. Which is a big heaping plate of fuck-all."

"There you go. And I could end up with something a lot better than that. Maybe they'll give us the weapon, the crime scene, who knows?"

"The old ketchup technique," Frank said, still inspecting

his thumbnail with interest. "Turn 'em upside down, give 'em a good shake and hope something comes out."

"*Frank*," I said, and waited till he glanced up at me. "This is my last shot. Tomorrow I come in. Let me have it."

Frank sighed, leaned his head back against the wall and had a leisurely look around the room; I saw him take in the new graffiti, the bits of exploded pen in the corner. "What I'm curious about," he said eventually, "is how you're so sure that one of them did it."

My blood stopped moving for a second. All Frank had ever wanted from me was one solid lead. If he found out I had that already, I was toast: off the case and into big trouble, faster than you can say Up Shit Creek. I would never even make it back to Glenskehy. "Well, I'm not *sure*," I said easily. "But, like you said, they've got motive."

"Yeah, they've got motive. Of a kind. But then, so do Naylor and Eddie and a whole bunch of other people, some of whom we presumably haven't even identified yet. This girl put herself in harm's way on a regular basis, Cass. She may not have ripped people off financially—although that's debatable: you could argue that she got her share of Whitethorn House under false pretenses—but she ripped them off emotionally. That's a dangerous thing to do. She lived at risk. And yet you're very, very sure which risk caught up with her."

I shrugged, hands going out. "This is the only one I can go after. I've got one day left; I don't want to ditch this case without giving it everything I've got. What are you bitching about, anyway? You've always liked them for it."

"Oh, you picked up on that? I underestimated you, babe. Yeah, I've always liked them. But you haven't. A few days ago you were claiming these four were a bunch of fluffy little bunnies who wouldn't hurt a fly between them, and now you've got that steel-trap look in your eye and you're working out the best way for us to fuck with their heads. So I'm wondering what it is that you're not telling me."

His eyes were on me, level and unblinking. I gave it a

second, ran my hands through my hair like I was trying to figure out how to put this. "It's not like that," I said, in the end. "I've just got a feeling, Frank. Just a feeling."

Frank watched me for a long minute; I swung my legs and tried to look open and sincere. Then: "OK," he said, suddenly all business, shoving himself off the wall and heading over to switch the camera back on. "You've got a deal. Did you lot bring two cars, or am I going to have to drive Danny Boy all the way back to Glenarsefuck when I'm done with him?"

"We brought both cars," I said. Relief and adrenaline were making me giddy; my mind was racing through how to work this interview and I wanted to shoot straight up in the air like a firework. "Thanks, Frank. You won't regret it."

"Yeah," Frank said, "well." He swapped the chairs back around. "Sit. Stay. I'll get back to you."

He left me there for another couple of hours, presumably while he gave the others everything he'd got, in the hope that one of them would crack and he wouldn't need to use me after all. I spent the time smoking illegal cigarettes—no one seemed to care—and working out the details of how to do this. I knew Frank would be coming back. From the outside, the others were impregnable, seamless; even Justin would be holding up cool as ice in the face of Frank's worst. Outsiders were too far away to shake them. They were like one of those medieval fortresses built with such fierce, intricate, defensive care that they could only ever be taken from the inside, by treachery.

Finally the door flew open and Frank stuck his head in. "I'm about to link you up to the other interview rooms, so get in character. Five minutes to curtain."

"Don't link Daniel in," I said, sitting up fast.

"Don't fuck up," Frank said, and vanished again.

When he came back I was perched on the table, bending the ink tube of the Biro into a catapult and flipping the broken bits at the camera. "Hey," I said, brightening up at the sight of him. "I thought you'd forgotten all about me."

"Now how could I ever do that?" Frank asked, giving me his very best grin. "I even brought you coffee—milk and two sugars, am I right? No, no, don't worry about that"—as I hopped off the table and went for the Biro bits—"someone'll get them later. Sit down and we'll have a chat. How've you been?" He pulled out a chair and shoved one of the Styrofoam cups across to me.

He started out sweet as honey—I'd forgotten what a charmer Frank can be, when he feels like it. You're looking wonderful, Miss Madison, and how's the old war wound getting on, and—when I played up to him, gave a stretch to show him how well the stitches had healed—isn't that a lovely sight, and just the right amount of flirtation in his grin. I threw in eyelash-and-giggle touches, just little ones, to piss Rafe off.

Frank took me through the whole John Naylor saga, or anyway a version of it—not exactly the version that had originally happened, but definitely a version that made Naylor sound like a good suspect: soothing the others down, before we started detonating things. "I'm all impressed now," I told him, tilting my chair back and giving him a mischievous sideways look. "I thought you'd given up ages ago."

Frank shook his head. "We don't give up," he said soberly. "Not on something as serious as this. No matter how long it takes. We don't always want to be obvious about it, but we're always working away, putting the pieces together." It was impressive; he should have come with his own soundtrack. "We're getting there. And right now, Miss Madison, we need a little help from you."

"Sure," I said, bringing my chair down and doing focused. "Do you want me to look at that guy Naylor again?"

"Nothing like that. It's your mind we need this time, not your eyes. You remember how the doctors said your memory might start coming back, as you recovered?"

"Yeah," I said, uncertainly, after a pause.

"Anything you remember, anything at all, could help us a lot. I want you to have a think and tell me: has anything come back to you?"

I left it a beat too long before I said, almost convincingly, "No. Nothing. Just what I told you before."

Frank clasped his hands on the table and leaned towards me. Those attentive blue eyes, that gentle, coaxing voice: if I'd been a genuine civilian, I'd have been melting all over my chair. "See, I'm not so sure. I'm getting the impression you've remembered something new, Miss Madison, but you're worried about telling me. Maybe you think I might misinterpret it, and the wrong person could get in trouble? Is that it?"

I threw him a quick looking-for-reassurance glance. "Sort of. I guess."

He smiled at me, all crinkling crow's-feet. "Trust me, Miss Madison. We don't go around charging people with serious crimes unless we have serious evidence. You're not about to get anyone arrested all by yourself."

I shrugged, made a face at my coffee cup. "It's nothing big. It probably doesn't mean anything anyway."

"You let me worry about that, OK?" Frank said soothingly. He was about one step from patting my hand and calling me "love." "You'd be surprised what can come in useful. And if it doesn't, then there's no harm done, am I right?"

"OK," I said, on a breath. "It's just . . . OK. I remember blood, on my hands. All over my hands."

"There you go," Frank said, keeping that reassuring smile switched on. "Well done. That wasn't so hard, was it?" I shook my head. "Can you remember what you were doing? Were you standing up? Sitting down?"

"Standing up," I said. I didn't have to put the shake in my voice. A few feet away, in the interview rooms I knew inside out, Daniel was waiting patiently for someone to come back and the other three were slowly, silently, beginning to wind tighter. "Leaning against a hedge—it was prickly. I was . . ." I mimed twisting up my top, pressing it against my ribs. "Like that. Because of the blood, to make it stop. But it didn't help."

"Were you in pain?"

"Yeah," I said, low. "It hurt. A lot. I thought . . . I was scared I was going to die."

We were good together, me and Frank; we were on the same page. We were working together as smoothly as Abby and me making breakfast, as smoothly as a pair of professional torturers. *You can't be both,* Daniel had told me. And: *She was never cruel.*

"You're doing great," Frank told me. "Now that it's started coming back to you, you'll have the whole lot remembered in no time, you'll see. That's what the doctors told us, isn't it? Once the floodgates open . . ." He flipped through the file and pulled out a map, one of the ones we'd used during our training week. "Do you think you could show me where you were?"

I took my time, picked a spot about three-quarters of the way from the house to the cottage and put my finger on it. "Maybe there, I think. I'm not sure."

"Great," Frank said, doing a careful little scribble in his notebook. "Now I want you to do something else for me. You're leaning against that hedge, and you're bleeding, and you're scared. Can you try and think backwards? Just before that, what had you been doing?"

I kept my eyes on the map. "I was all out of breath, like . . . Running. I was running. So fast I fell over. I hurt my knee."

"From where? Think hard. What were you running away from?"

"I don't—" I shook my head, hard. "No. I can't tell what bits happened, and what bits I just . . . dreamed, or something. I could've dreamed all of it, even the blood."

"It's possible," Frank said, nodding easily. "We'll keep that in mind. But, just in case, I think you need to tell me everything—even the parts you probably dreamed. We'll sort them out as we go. OK?"

I left a long pause. "That's all," I said at last, too weakly. "Running, and falling over. And the blood. That's it."

"Are you sure?"

"Yeah. I'm positive. There's nothing else."

Frank sighed. "Here's the problem, Miss Madison," he said. A fine, steely sediment was slowly building up in his voice. "Just a few minutes ago, you were worried about getting the wrong person into trouble. But nothing you've said so far points towards anyone at all. That tells me you're skipping something, along the way."

I gave him my defiant Lexie glare, chin out. "No I'm not."

"Sure you are. And the really interesting question, as far as I'm concerned, is why." Frank shoved his chair back and started a leisurely stroll around the interview room, hands in his pockets, making me shift again and again to watch him. "See, call me crazy, but I figured we were on the same side here, you and me. I thought both of us were trying to find out who stabbed you and put that person away. Am I crazy? Does that sound crazy to you?"

I shrugged, twisting to keep an eye on him. He kept circling. "Back when you were in hospital, you answered every question I asked—not a bother, no hesitation, no messing about. You were a lovely witness, Miss Madison, lovely and helpful. But now, all of a sudden, you're not interested any more. So either you've decided to turn the other cheek on someone who almost killed you—and forgive me if I'm wrong, but you don't look like a saint to me—or there's something else, something more important, getting in the way."

He leaned against the wall behind me. I gave up on watching him and started picking nail polish off my thumbnail. "So I have to ask myself," Frank said softly, "what could possibly be more important to you than putting this person away? You tell me, Miss Madison. What's important to you?"

"Good chocolate," I said, to my thumbnail.

Frank's tone didn't change. "I think I've got to know you pretty well. When you were in hospital, what did you talk about, every day, the second I got in your door? What was the one thing you kept asking for, even when you knew you couldn't have it? What was the one thing you were dying to see, the day you got out? What had you so excited you nearly burst your stitches jumping around at the thought?"

I kept my head down, bit at the nail polish. "Your friends," Frank said, very quietly. "Your housemates. They matter to you, Miss Madison. More than anything else I can think of. Maybe more than getting the person who stabbed you. Don't they?"

I shrugged. "Course they matter to me. So?"

"If you had to make that choice, Miss Madison. If, let's just say, just for the hell of it, you remembered that one of them had stabbed you. What would you do?"

"I wouldn't *have* to make that choice, because none of them would hurt me. Ever. They're my *friends*."

"That's exactly my point. You're protecting someone, and I don't see that being John Naylor. Who is there that you'd protect, except your *friends*?"

"I'm not protecting—"

Before I even heard him move he had come off the wall and slammed both hands down on the table beside me, his face inches from mine. I flinched harder than I meant to. "You're lying to me, Miss Madison. Do you honestly not realize how bloody obvious that is? You know something important, something that could blow this case wide open, and you're hiding it. That's obstruction. It's a crime. It can land you in *jail*."

I jerked my head back, shoved my chair away from him. "You're going to arrest me? For *what*? Jesus, I'm the one who got hurt here! If I just want to forget all about it—"

"If you want to get yourself stabbed every day of the

week and twice on Sunday, I don't give a flying fuck. But when you waste my time and my officers' time, that's my business. Do you know how many people have been working this case for the past month, Miss Madison? Do you have the faintest clue how much time and energy and money we've put into this? There's not a chance I'm going to let all that go down the toilet because some spoiled little girl is too wrapped up in her *friends* to give a fuck about anything or anyone else. Not a chance in hell."

He wasn't faking. His face thrust hard up to mine, the hot blue sizzle in his eyes: he was raging and he meant every word, to me, to Lexie, probably even he didn't know which. This girl: she bent reality around her like a lens bending light, she pleated it into so many flickering layers that you could never tell which one you were looking at, the longer you stared the dizzier you got. "I'm going to break this case," Frank said. "I don't care how long it takes: the person who did this is going down. And if you don't pull your head out of your arse and realize how important this is, if you keep playing stupid little games with me, you're going down right alongside him. Is that clear?"

"Get out of my face," I said. My forearm was up between us, blocking him. In that second I realized that my fist was clenched and that I was as angry as he was.

"Who stabbed you, Miss Madison? Can you look me in the eye and tell me you don't know? Let's see you do it. Tell me you don't know. Come on."

"*Fuck* that. I don't have to prove anything to you. I remember running, and blood on my hands, and you can do whatever you want with that. Now leave me *alone*." I slumped down in my chair, shoved my hands in my pockets and stared at the wall in front of me.

I felt Frank's eyes on the side of my face, his fast breathing, for a long time. "Right," he said, at last. He eased back slowly, away from the table. "We'll leave it at that, then. For now." And he left.

. . .

It was a long time before he came back—another hour, maybe, I'd stopped watching the clock. I picked up the Biro bits, one by one, and arranged them in pretty patterns on the edge of the table.

"Well," Frank said, when he finally decided to join me. "You were right: that was fun."

"Poetry in motion," I said. "Did it do the job?"

He shrugged. "It rattled them, all right; they're antsy as hell. But they're not cracking, not yet. Another couple of hours might do it, I don't know, but Daniel's starting to get restless—oh, very politely, of course, but he's been asking how much longer we think this might take. I figure if you want any time with the other three before he walks out, you'd better take them now."

"Thanks, Frank," I said, and meant it. "Thank you."

"I'll keep him as long as I can, but I'm not guaranteeing anything." He took my coat off the back of the door and held it for me. As I slid into it he said, "I'm playing fair with you, Cassie. Now let's see you play fair with me."

The others were downstairs in the lobby. They all looked gray and eye-baggy. Rafe was at the window, jiggling one knee; Justin was huddled in a chair like a big miserable stork. Only Abby, sitting up straight with her hands cupped in her lap, looked anything like composed.

"Thanks for coming in," Frank said cheerfully. "You've all been very, very helpful. Your mate Daniel is just finishing up a few things for us; he said you should go ahead, he'll catch you on the way."

Justin started upright, like he'd just been woken up. "But why—" he began, but Abby cut him off, her fingers coming down across his wrist.

"Thanks, Detective. Call us if there's anything else you need."

"Will do," Frank said, giving her a wink. He had the door open for us, and was holding out his other hand to shake good-bye, before anyone caught up enough to argue. "See you soon," he said to each of us, as we passed.

"Why did you do that?" Justin demanded, as soon as the door closed behind us. "I don't *want* to leave without Daniel."

"Shut up," Abby said, giving his arm a squeeze that looked casual, "and keep walking. Don't turn around. Mackey's probably watching us."

In the car, nobody said anything for a very long time.

"So," Rafe said, after a silence that felt like it was filing my teeth. "What did you talk about this time?" He braced himself, a tiny jerk of his head, before he turned to look at me.

"Leave it," Abby said, from the front.

"Why Daniel?" Justin wanted to know. He was driving like someone's lunatic granny, switching back and forth between bursts of suicidal speed—I was praying we wouldn't run into a traffic cop—and patches of obsessive carefulness, and his voice sounded like he might be about to cry. "What do they want? Have they *arrested* him?"

"No," Abby said firmly. There was obviously no way she could have known that, but Justin's shoulders dropped a fraction of an inch. "He'll be fine. Don't worry."

"He always is," Rafe said, to the window.

"He figured this would happen," Abby said. "He wasn't sure which one of us they'd hang onto—he thought probably Justin or Lexie, maybe both of you—but he figured they'd split us up."

"*Me?* Why me?" Justin's voice was getting a hysterical edge.

"Oh for God's sake, Justin, act like you have a pair," Rafe snapped.

"Slow down," Abby said, "or we'll get pulled over. They're just trying to shake us up, in case we know anything we're not telling them."

"But why do they think—"

"Don't get into that. That's what they want us doing: wondering what they're thinking, why they're doing stuff, getting all freaked out. Don't play into their hands."

"If we let those apes outwit us," Rafe said, "then we deserve to go to jail. Surely to God we're smarter than—"

"Stop it!" I yelled, banging my fist against the back of Abby's seat. Justin gasped and nearly sent the car off the road, but I didn't care. "You stop it! This isn't a *competition*! This is my *life* and it's not a fucking game and I hate all of you!"

Then I startled the living hell out of myself by bursting into tears. I hadn't cried in months, not for Rob, not for my lost life in Murder, not for any of the terrible fallout of Operation Vestal, but I cried then. I pressed the sleeve of my sweater over my mouth and bawled my eyes out, for Lexie in every one of her changing faces, for the baby whose face no one would ever see, for Abby spinning on moonlit grass and Daniel smiling as he watched her, for Rafe's expert hands on the piano and Justin kissing my forehead, for what I had done to them and what I was about to do, for a million lost things; for the wild speed of that car, how mercilessly fast it was taking us where we were going.

After a while Abby reached into the glove compartment and passed me a packet of tissues. She had her window open and the long roar of the air sounded like high wind in trees, and it was so peaceful, in there, that I just kept crying.

23

As soon as Justin pulled up in the stables, I jumped out of the car and ran for the house, pebbles flying up under my feet. Nobody called after me. I jammed my key into the lock, left the door swinging open and thumped upstairs to my room.

It felt like ages before I heard the others coming in (door closing, fast overlapping undertones moving into the sitting room), but actually it was less than sixty seconds—I had an eye on my watch. I figured I needed to give them about ten minutes. Any less, and they wouldn't have time to compare notes—their first chance all day—and work themselves into a full-on panic; any more, and Abby would pull herself together and start bringing the guys back into line.

During those ten minutes I listened to the voices downstairs, taut and muffled and fringed with hysteria, and I got ready. Late-afternoon sun was flooding through my bedroom window and the air blazed so bright that I felt weightless, suspended in amber, every movement I made as clear and rhythmic and measured as part of some ritual that I had been preparing for all my life. My hands felt like they were moving on their own, smoothing out my girdle—it was starting to get grubby by this time, it wasn't exactly something I could stick in the washing machine—pulling it on, tucking the hem into my jeans, easing my gun into place, as calmly and precisely as if I had forever and a day. I thought about that afternoon a million miles away, in my flat, when I had put on Lexie's clothes for the first time: how they had felt like armor, like ceremonial robes; how they had made me want to laugh out loud from something like happiness.

When the ten minutes were up I pulled the door closed behind me, on that little room full of light and lily-of-the-valley smell, and listened as the voices downstairs trailed off into silence. I washed my face in the bathroom, dried it carefully and straightened my towel between Abby's and Daniel's. My face in the mirror looked very strange, pale and huge-eyed, staring out at me with some crucial, unreadable warning. I tugged my sweater down and checked to make sure the bulge of the gun didn't show. Then I went downstairs.

They were in the sitting room, all three of them. For a second, before they saw me, I stood in the doorway watching them. Rafe was sprawled on the sofa, snapping a pack of cards from hand to hand in a fast restless arc. Abby, curled in her chair, had her head bent over the doll and her bottom lip caught hard between her teeth; she was trying to sew, but every stitch took her about three stabs. Justin was in one of the wingbacked chairs with a book, and for some reason he was the one who almost broke my heart: those narrow hunched shoulders, the darn in the sleeve of his sweater, those long hands on wrists as thin and vulnerable as a little boy's. The coffee table was scattered with glasses and bottles—vodka, tonic, orange juice; something had splashed onto the table as they poured, but no one had bothered to clean it up. On the floor, shadows of ivy curled like cut-outs through the sunlight.

Then their heads came up, one by one, and their faces turned towards me, expressionless and watchful as they had been that first day on the steps. "How're you doing?" Abby asked.

I shrugged.

"Have a drink," Rafe said, nodding at the table. "If you want anything that's not vodka, you'll have to get it yourself."

"I'm getting bits back," I said. There was a long slant of sun lying across the floorboards at my feet, making the new varnish shine like water. I kept my eyes on that. "Bits of that night. They said that might happen, the doctors did."

Trill and snap of the cards, again. "We know," Rafe said.

"They let us watch," Abby said softly. "While you talked to Mackey."

I jerked my head up and stared at them, open-mouthed. "Well, *Jesus*," I said, after a moment. "Were you going to tell me that? Ever?"

"We're telling you now," said Rafe.

"Fuck you," I said, and the shake in my voice sounded like I was an inch from more tears. "Fuck the lot of you. How stupid do you think I am? Mackey was a total dickhead to me and I still kept my mouth shut, because I didn't want to get you into trouble. But you were just going to let me keep being the idiot, for the rest of our lives, while all of you knew—" I pressed the back of my wrist over my mouth.

Abby said, very quietly and very carefully, "You kept your mouth shut."

"I shouldn't have," I said, into my wrist. "I should've just told him everything I remember and let you bloody well deal with it."

"What else," Abby asked, "what else do you remember?"

My heart felt like it was about to slam straight out of my chest. If I had this wrong, then I was going down in flames, and every second of this month had been for nothing at all—crashing through these four lives, hurting Sam, staking my job: all for nothing. I was throwing every chip I had onto the table, without the slimmest clue how good my hand was. In that instant I thought of Lexie: how she had lived her whole life like this, all in on the blind; what it had cost her, in the end.

"The jacket," I said. "The note, in the jacket pocket."

For a second I thought I had lost. Their faces, upturned to me, were so utterly blank, as if what I had said meant nothing at all. I was already whipping through ways to backpedal (coma dream? morphine hallucination?) when Justin whispered, a tiny devastated breath, "Oh God."

You didn't usually bring your cigarettes on your walk, Daniel had said. I had been so focused on covering the slipup, it had taken me days to realize: I had burned Ned's note. If Lexie didn't have a lighter on her, then—short of eating the notes, which was a little extreme even for her— she had no quick way of getting rid of them. Maybe she had ripped them to tiny pieces on her way home, thrown the bits into hedges as she passed, like a dark Hansel-and-Gretel trail; or maybe she hadn't wanted to leave even that much trace, maybe she had shoved them into her pocket to flush or burn later, at home.

She had been so fiercely careful, standing guard over her secrets. There was only one mistake I could imagine her making. Just once, hurrying home in the dark and the lashing rain—because it had to have been raining—with the baby already turning the edges of her mind to cotton wool and escape hammering through every vein, she had pushed the note into her pocket without remembering that the jacket she was wearing wasn't all hers. She had been betrayed by the same thing she was betraying: the closeness of them, how much they had shared.

"Well," Rafe said, reaching for his glass, one eyebrow arching up. He was trying for his best world-weary look, but his nostrils flared, just slightly, with each breath. "Nicely done, Justin my friend. This should be interesting."

"What? What are you talking about, nicely done? She already *knew*—"

"Shut up," said Abby. She had gone white, freckles standing out like face paint.

Rafe ignored her. "Well, if she didn't, she does now."

"It's *not my fault*. Why do you always, always blame me for everything?"

Justin was very close to losing it. Rafe raised his eyes to

the ceiling. "Do you hear me complaining? As far as I'm concerned, it's about bloody time we got this over with."

"We are not discussing this," Abby said, "until Daniel gets home."

Rafe started to laugh. "Oh, Abby," he said. "I do love you, but sometimes I wonder about you. You have to know that, once Daniel gets home, we won't be discussing this at all."

"This is about all five of us. We don't talk about it till we're all here."

"That's crap," I said. My voice was rising and I let it. "It's such crap I can't even listen to it. If this is about all five of us, then why didn't you tell me weeks ago? If you can talk about it behind my back, then surely to God we can talk about it without Daniel."

"Oh God," Justin whispered again. His mouth was open, one hand trembling inches from it.

Abby's mobile started to ring, in her bag. I had been listening for that sound all the way home, all the time in my room. Frank had let Daniel go.

"Leave it!" I yelled, loud enough to stop her hand mid-reach. "It's Daniel, and I know exactly what he's going to say anyway. He'll just order you not to tell me anything, and I am so fucking *sick* of him treating me like I'm six! If anyone has a right to know exactly what happened here, it's me. If you try to answer that bloody phone I swear I'm going to *stamp* on it!" I meant it, too. Sunday afternoon, all the traffic was headed into Dublin, not out; if Daniel floored it—and he would—and managed not to get pulled over, he could be home in maybe half an hour. I needed every second of that.

Rafe laughed, a small rough sound. "Attagirl," he said, raising his glass to me.

Abby stared at me, her hand still halfway to her bag.

"If you guys don't tell me what's going on," I said, "I'm phoning the cops right now and I'm telling them everything I remember. I am."

"Jesus," Justin whispered. "Abby . . ."

The phone stopped ringing.

"Abby," I said, taking a deep breath. I could feel my nails digging into my hands. "I can't do this if you guys keep leaving me out. This is *important*. I can't . . . we can't work this way. Either we're all in this together or we're not."

Justin's phone rang.

"You don't even have to tell me who actually did it, if you don't want to." I was pretty sure that if I listened hard enough I'd hear Frank banging his head off a wall, somewhere, but I didn't care: one step at a time. "I just want to know what happened. I'm so sick of everyone knowing but me. I'm so sick of it. Please."

"She's got every right to know," Rafe said. "And personally, I'm also pretty sick of living my life on the basis of 'Because Daniel said so.' How well has that been working out for us, so far?"

The ringing stopped. "We should call him back," Justin said, half out of his chair. "Shouldn't we? What if he's been arrested and he needs bail money, or something?"

"He hasn't been arrested," Abby said automatically. She dropped back into the chair and ran her hands over her face, blew out a long breath. "I keep telling you, they need evidence to arrest someone. He's fine. Lexie, sit down."

I stayed where I was. "Oh, God, sit *down*," Rafe said, on a long-suffering sigh. "I'm going to tell you this whole pathetic saga anyway, whether anyone else likes it or not, and you're getting on my nerves, fidgeting there. And Abby, chill out. We should have done this weeks ago."

After a moment I went to my chair, by the fireplace. "Much better," Rafe said, grinning at me. There was a reckless, risky gaiety in his face; he looked happier than he had in weeks. "Have a drink."

"I don't want one."

He swung his legs off the sofa, poured a big sloppy vodka and orange and passed it to me. "Actually, I think we should all have another drink. We're going to need it." He topped up glasses with a flourish—Abby and Justin didn't seem to notice—and raised his to the room. "Here's to full disclosure."

"OK," Abby said, on a deep breath. "OK. If you really want to do this, and it's coming back to you anyway, then I guess . . . what the hell."

Justin opened his mouth, then shut it again and bit his lips.

Abby ran her hands through her hair, smoothing it hard. "Where do you want us to . . . ? I mean, I don't know how much you remember, or . . ."

"Bits," I said. "They don't fit together or anything. Just go from the beginning." All the adrenaline had dissolved out of my blood and I felt so calm, all of a sudden. This was the last thing I would ever do in Whitethorn House. I could feel it all around me, every inch of it singing with sun and dust motes and memory, waiting to hear what came next. I felt like we had all the time in the world.

"You were heading out for your walk," Rafe said helpfully, flopping back onto the sofa, "around, what, just after eleven? And Abby and I discovered we were both out of smokes. Funny, isn't it, what little things make all the difference? If we'd been nonsmokers, this might never have happened. When they talk about the evils of tobacco, they never mention this."

"You said you'd pick some up on your way," Abby said. She was watching me carefully, hands clasped tight in her lap. "But you're always gone for at least an hour, so I figured I might as well run out and get them at the petrol station. It looked like it was going to rain, so I threw on the jacket— I mean, it didn't seem like you wanted it, you were already putting your coat on. I stuck my wallet in the pocket, and . . ."

Her voice trailed off and she made a small, tense gesture that could have meant anything. I kept my mouth shut. No more leading, if I could help it. The rest of this story had to come from them.

"And she pulled out this piece of paper," Rafe said, through a cigarette, "and went, 'What's this?' Nobody paid much attention, at first. We were all in the kitchen; we were doing the washing up, me and Justin and Daniel, and arguing about something or other—"

"Stevenson," Justin said, softly and very sadly. "Remember? Jekyll and Hyde. Daniel was going on about them; something to do with reason and instinct. You were in a silly mood, Lexie, you said you'd had enough shop talk for the night and anyway Jekyll and Hyde would both have been crap in bed, and Rafe said, 'A one-track mind, and it's a dirt track . . .' We were all laughing."

"And then Abby said, 'Lexie, what the hell?'" said Rafe. "A whole lot louder. We all stopped messing about and turned around, and she was holding out this ratty bit of paper and looking like someone had slapped her across the face—I've never seen her look like that, ever."

"That's the part I remember," I said. My hands felt like they'd been melted onto the arms of the chair by some blast of heat. "Then it goes fuzzy again."

"Luckily for you," Rafe said, "we can help you with that. I think the rest of us will remember every second for the rest of our lives. You said, 'Give me that,' and grabbed for the piece of paper, but Abby jumped back, fast, and passed it to Daniel."

"I think," Justin said, in a low voice, "that was when we started to realize there was something serious happening. I'd been about to say something silly about a love letter— just teasing you, Lexie—but you were so . . . You *lunged* at Daniel, trying to get it away from him. He shot out his other hand to hold you off, sort of reflexively, but you were fighting him, really fighting—punching at his arm, trying to kick him, grabbing for that thing. You didn't make a single sound. That's what frightened me most, I think: the silence. It seemed like people should be shouting or screaming or *something*, like then I might be able to *do* something, but it was so quiet—just you and Daniel breathing hard, and the tap still running . . ."

"Abby caught hold of your arm," Rafe said, "but you whipped round, with your fists up; I honestly thought you were about to go for her. Justin and I were standing there gawping like a pair of morons, trying to figure out what the fuck—I mean, two seconds ago we'd been on Jekyll sex, for God's sake. As soon as you let go of Daniel, he shoved the paper at me, caught your wrists from behind and told me, 'Read that.'"

"I didn't like it," Justin said softly. "You were *flinging* yourself back and forth, trying to pull away from Daniel, but he wouldn't let go. It was . . . You tried to bite him, his arm. I thought he shouldn't be doing that, if it was your paper then he should let you have it, but I just couldn't catch up enough to say anything."

I wasn't surprised. These were not men of action here; their currencies were thoughts and words, and they had been catapulted into something that blew both of those right out of the water. What did surprise me, what set warning lights flashing at the back of my mind, was the speed and ease with which Daniel had snapped into action.

"So," Rafe said, "I read the thing out loud. It said, 'Dear Lexie, have thought it over and OK we can talk about 200K. Please get in touch 'cause I know we both want to get this deal wrapped up. Best regards, Ned.'"

"Surely to God," Justin said softly and bitterly, into the airless silence, "you remember that."

"The spelling was shit," said Rafe, through his cigarette. "He actually had a number two for 'to,' like a fucking *fourteen*-year-old. What an utter moron. Apart from anything else, I would've expected you to have better taste than to mess about making shoddy little deals with someone like that."

"Would you have?" Abby asked. Her eyes were very steady on mine, searching, and her hands had gone still in her lap. "If none of this had happened, would you really have sold out to Ned?"

When I think about how breathtakingly cruel I was to those four, this is one of the few things that make me feel any better: I could have said yes, then. I could have told them exactly what Lexie was planning to do to them, to everything they had put their hearts and minds and bodies into building. Maybe that would have hurt them less, in the end, than thinking it had all been over nothing; I don't know. All I know is that the last time I had a choice, and much too late to make any difference, I lied for the right reasons.

"No," I said. "I just . . . God. I just needed to know I could. I freaked out, Abby. I started feeling trapped and I panicked. It was never about actually leaving. I just had to know I could leave, if I wanted to."

"Trapped," Justin said, and his head moved in a quick, hurt jerk. "With us," but I saw Abby's fast blink as she realized: the baby.

"You were going to stay."

"Oh God, I wanted to stay," I said, and I still don't know and never will whether this one was a lie at all. "So much, Abby. I really did."

After a long moment she nodded, almost imperceptibly.

"I told you," Rafe said, tipping his head back and blowing smoke at the ceiling. "Fucking Daniel. Up until last *week* he was still practically hysterical with paranoia about that. I told him I'd talked to you and you had no intention of going anywhere, but God forbid he should listen to anyone."

Abby didn't react to that, didn't move; it looked like she wasn't even breathing. "And now?" she asked me. "Now what?"

For a light-headed second I lost the thread, thought she had made me and was asking if I wanted to stay anyway. "What do you mean?"

"She means," Rafe said, his voice cool and clipped and very level, "when this conversation is over, are you going to phone Mackey or O'Neill or the village idiots and turn us in. Shop us. Rat us out. Whatever the appropriate expression is, in these circumstances."

You'd think this would have sent guilt shooting through me like pins and needles, spreading from that mike red-hot against my skin, but the only thing I felt was sad: a huge, final, dragging sadness, like an ebb tide down in my bones. "I'm not going to say anything to anyone," I said, and felt Frank, off in his little humming circle of electronics, approve. "I don't want you guys going to jail. No matter what happened."

"Well," Abby said softly, almost to herself. She sat back in her chair and smoothed her skirt, absently, with both hands. "Well, then . . ."

"Well, then," Rafe said, and drew hard on his smoke, "we made this whole thing an awful lot more complicated than it needed to be. Somehow, I'm not surprised."

"Then what?" I said. "After the note. Then what happened?"

A small, tense shift through the room. None of them were looking at each other. I searched for some tiny difference between their faces, anything that would hint that this conversation was hitting one of them harder than the others, that someone was protecting, being protected, guilty, defensive: nothing.

"Then," Abby said, on a big breath. "Lex, I don't know if you'd thought about what it would mean, if you sold your share to Ned. You don't always . . . I don't know. Think things through."

A vicious snort from Rafe. "That's putting it mildly. My God, Lexie, what the hell did you think would happen? You'd sell up, buy yourself a nice little apartment somewhere, and everything would be just ducky? What did you expect to get when you walked into college every morning? Hugs and kisses and your sandwich all ready for you? We would never have *spoken* to you again. We would have hated your guts."

"Ned would have been at the rest of us," Abby said, "all the time, every day, to sell out to some developer and turn this house into apartments or a golf club or whatever the hell it was that he wanted. He could have moved *in* here, *lived* with us, and there would've been nothing we could do about it. Sooner or later, we would have given up. We would have lost the house. This house."

Something stirred, subtle and waking: a tiny ripple in the walls, a creak of floorboards upstairs, a draft spinning down the stairwell.

"We all started shouting," Justin said, low. "Screaming, everyone at once—I don't even know what I was saying. You got away from Daniel, and Rafe grabbed you, and you hit him—*hard,* Lexie, you punched him in the stomach—"

"It was a fight," Rafe said. "We can call it whatever we want, but the fact is we were fighting like a bunch of scum-bags on a street corner. Another thirty seconds and we would all have been rolling around on the kitchen floor beating the living shit out of each other. Except that before we got that far—"

"Except," Abby said, her voice slicing his off clean as a slammed door, "we never got that far."

She met Rafe's eyes calmly, unblinking. After a second he shrugged and slumped back on the sofa, one foot jiggling restlessly.

"It could have been any of us," Abby said, to me or to Rafe, I couldn't tell. There was a depth of passion in her voice that startled me. "We were all raging—I've never been that angry in my life. The rest was just chance; just the way things happened. Every one of us was ready to kill you, Lexie, and you can't blame us."

That stirring again, somewhere off the far edge of my hearing: a whisk across the landing, a humming in the chimneys. "I don't," I said. I wondered—I should have known a whole lot better, I must have read too many cheesy ghost stories as a kid—if this was all Lexie had wanted from me: to let them know it was OK. "You had every right to be mad. Even afterwards, you would've had every right to throw me out."

"We talked about it," Abby said. Rafe raised an eyebrow. "Me and Daniel. Whether we could all still live together, after . . . But it would have been complicated, and anyway, it was *you*. No matter what, it was still you."

"The next thing I remember," Justin said, very quietly, "is the back door slamming and this knife lying in the middle of the kitchen floor. With *blood* on it. I couldn't believe it. I couldn't believe this was actually happening."

"And you just let me *go*?" I said, to my hands. "You didn't even bother to find out if—"

"No," said Abby, leaning forwards, trying to catch my eye. "No, Lex. Of *course* we bothered. It took us all a minute to catch up with what had happened, but the second we did . . . It was Daniel, mostly; the rest of us were basically paralyzed. By the time I could move again, he was already getting the torch out. He told me and Rafe to stay put in case you came home, burn the note and get hot water and disinfectant and bandages ready—"

"Which would have come in useful," Rafe said, lighting another cigarette, "if we'd been delivering a baby in *Gone with the Wind*. What on earth was he picturing? Home surgery on the kitchen table with Abby's embroidery needle?"

"—and he and Justin went looking for you. Straight away."

It had been a good call. Daniel had known he could trust Abby to keep it together; if anyone flaked out, it would be Rafe or Justin. He had got them separated, put them both under supervision and come up with a plan that kept them both busy, all within seconds. The guy was wasted on academia.

"I'm not sure we were really as quick off the mark as we think," Justin said. "We could have been standing there in a daze for a good five or ten minutes, for all I know. I can barely remember that part; my mind's wiped it out. The first thing I'm clear on is that, by the time Daniel and I got to the back gate, you were gone. We didn't know if you'd headed for the village to get help, or collapsed somewhere, or—"

"I just ran," I said quietly. "I just remember running. I didn't even notice I was bleeding for ages." Justin flinched.

"I don't think you were, at first," Abby said gently. "There wasn't any blood on the kitchen floor, or on the patio."

They had checked. I wondered when, and whether that had been Daniel's idea or Abby's. "That was the other thing," Justin said. "We didn't know . . . well, how bad it was. You were gone so fast, we hadn't had a chance to . . . We thought—I mean, I thought, anyway—since you had got out of sight so quickly, it couldn't be all that serious, could it? It might have been just a nick, for all we knew."

"Ha," said Rafe, reaching for an ashtray.

"We didn't *know*. It might have been. I said so to Daniel, but he just gave me a look that could have meant anything. So we . . . God. We started looking for you. Daniel said the most urgent thing was to find out if you'd gone to the village, but it was all locked up and dark, just the odd light on in bedrooms; there was obviously nothing going on. So we started working our way back towards the house, going back and forth in these big arcs, hoping we'd cross paths with you somewhere along the way."

He stared down at the glass in his hands. "At least, that's what I assume we were doing. I was just following Daniel on and on and on through this pitch-black *labyrinth* of lanes; I had no idea where we were, my sense of direction was completely gone. We were afraid to switch on the torch and afraid to call you—I'm not even sure why, it just seemed too dangerous: in case someone in a farmhouse noticed or in case you hid from us, I suppose, I don't know which. So Daniel just flicked on the torch for a second every few minutes, cupped his hand around it and did a quick sweep, then switched it off again. The rest of the time we felt our way by the hedges. It was *freezing*, like winter—we hadn't even thought of coats. It didn't seem to bother Daniel, you know what he's like, but I couldn't feel my toes; I was sure I was getting frostbite. We wandered around for *hours*—"

"You didn't," Rafe said. "Trust me. We were stuck here with a bottle of disinfectant and a bloody knife and nothing to do but stare at the clock and go out of our minds. You were only gone about forty-five minutes."

Justin shrugged, a tense twitch. "Well, it felt like hours. Finally Daniel stopped dead—I bumped straight into the back of him, like something out of Laurel and Hardy—and he said, 'This is absurd. We'll never find her like this.' I asked him what else he suggested we should do, but he ignored me. He just stood there, staring up at the sky like he was waiting for divine inspiration; it was starting to cloud over, but the moon had come up, I could see his profile against it. After a moment he said—perfectly normally, as if we were in the middle of some dinner-table discussion—'Well, let's assume she's headed for a specific place, rather than simply wandering around in the dark. She must have been meeting Ned *somewhere*. Somewhere sheltered, surely; the weather's so unpredictable. Is there anywhere nearby that she—' And then he *took off*. He was running, flat out, and *fast*, I didn't know he could run like that—I don't think I'd ever seen Daniel run before, have you?"

"He ran the other night," Rafe said, grinding out his cigarette. "After the torch-bearing villager. He's fast, all right, when he needs to be."

"I didn't have a clue where he was going; all I could think about was trying to keep up. For some reason the idea of being out there by myself sent me into a complete panic—I mean, I know we were only a few hundred yards from home, but that's not what it felt like. It felt . . ." Justin shivered. "It felt dangerous," he said. "Like something was happening, all round us, and we couldn't see it, but if I was on my own . . ."

"That was shock, hon," Abby said gently. "It's normal."

Justin shook his head, still staring down at his glass. "No," he said. "It wasn't like that." He took a quick, hard swig of his drink and grimaced. "Then Daniel switched the torch on and swung it around—it was like a lighthouse beam, I was sure everyone for miles around would come running—and he stopped on that cottage. I only saw it for a second, just a corner of broken-down wall. Then the torch went out again, and Daniel *threw* himself over the wall into the field. There was all this long wet grass tangling round my ankles, it was like trying to run through porridge . . ." He blinked at his glass and pushed it away from him on the bookshelf; a little of his drink splashed out, staining someone's notes with sickly orange splotches. "Can I have a cigarette?"

"You don't smoke," Rafe said. "You're the good one."

"If I have to tell this story," said Justin, "I want a fucking *cigarette.*"

There was a high, precarious wobble in his voice. "Knock it off, Rafe," Abby said. She stretched over to pass Justin her smoke packet; as he took it, she caught his hand and squeezed.

Justin lit the cigarette clumsily, holding it high up between stiff fingers, inhaled too hard and choked. No one said anything while he coughed, caught his breath, wiped his eyes with a knuckle under his glasses.

"Lexie," Abby said. "Can't we just . . . You've got the important part. Can't we leave it?"

"I want to hear," I said. I could hardly breathe.

"So do I," said Rafe. "I've never heard this part either, and I've got a feeling it might be interesting. Aren't you curious, Abby? Or do you already know this story?"

Abby shrugged. "All *right,*" said Justin. His eyes were pressed shut and his jaw was so tense he could barely get the cigarette between his lips. "I'm . . . Just give me a second. *God.*"

He took another drag, retched a little, managed to hold

it. "OK," he said. He had his voice under control again. "So we got to the cottage. There was just enough moonlight that I could see outlines—the walls, the doorway. Daniel switched on the torch, with his other hand partway over it, and . . ."

His eyes opened, skated away from us to the window. "You were sitting in a corner, against the wall. I shouted something—called you, maybe, I don't know—and I started to run over to you, but Daniel grabbed my arm, *hard,* he *hurt* me, and pulled me back. He put his mouth right up against my ear and hissed, 'Shut up,' and then, 'Don't move. You stay right here. You stay still.' He shook my arm—I had *bruises*—and then he let go of me and went over to you. He put his fingers on your throat, like this, checking your pulse—he had the torch on you, and you looked . . ."

Justin's eyes were still on the window. "You looked like a wee girl asleep," he said, and the grief in his voice was soft and relentless as rain. "And then Daniel said, 'She's dead.' That's what we thought, Lexie. We thought you had died."

"You must have already been in the coma," Abby said gently. "The cops told us it would have slowed down your heartbeat, your breathing, stuff like that. If it hadn't been so cold—"

"Daniel straightened up," Justin said, "and wiped his hand on the front of his shirt—I'm not sure why, it wasn't *bloody* or anything, but that was all I could see: him rubbing his hand down his chest, over and over, as if he didn't even know he was doing it. I couldn't—I couldn't look at you. I went to hold myself up against the wall—I mean, I was hyperventilating, I thought I was going to *faint*—but he said, very sharply, 'Don't touch anything. Put your hands in your pockets. And hold your breath for a count of ten.' I didn't understand what he was talking about, none of it made any sense, but I did it anyway."

"We always do," Rafe said, in an undertone. Abby gave him a quick glance.

"After a minute Daniel said, 'If she had gone for her walk as usual, she would have her keys and wallet on her, and that torch she uses. One of us needs to go home and get them. The other one should stay here. It's unlikely that anyone will pass by, at this hour, but we don't know the full extent of her arrangements with Ned, and if someone does happen to pass, we need to know about it. Which would you prefer to do?'"

Justin made a tentative move to stretch out a hand to me, took it back and clasped it tightly around his other elbow. "I told him I couldn't stay there. I'm sorry, Lexie. I'm so sorry. I shouldn't have been . . . I mean, it was *you;* it was still you, even if you had been . . . But I couldn't. I was—I was shaking all over, I think I must have been gibbering at him . . . Finally he said—and he didn't even seem *upset,* not any more, just impatient—he said, 'For heaven's sake, shut up. I'll stay. Get home as fast as you can. Put your gloves on and get Lexie's keys, her wallet and her torch. Tell the others what's happened. They'll want to come back with you; don't let them, whatever you do. The last thing we need is more people trampling all over the place, and anyway there's no point in giving them more to forget. Come straight back here. Take the torch with you, but don't use it unless you really need to, and try to be quiet. Can you remember all that?'"

He drew hard on the cigarette. "I said yes—I'd have said yes if he'd asked me whether I could *fly* home, as long as it meant getting out of there. He made me repeat it all back to him. Then he sat down on the ground, beside you—not too close, I suppose in case he got . . . you know. Blood on his trousers. And he looked up at me and said, 'Well? Go on. Hurry.'

"So I went home. It was horrible. It took—well, if Rafe's right, it can't have actually taken that long. I don't know. I got lost. There were places where I *knew* I should have been able to see the lights from the house, but I couldn't; just black, for miles around. I knew for sure, like a fact, that the house wasn't even there any more; there was nothing left but hedges and lanes, on and on, this huge maze and I would never get out of it, it would never be daylight again. That there were things watching me, up in the trees and hidden in the hedges—I don't know what kind of things, but . . . watching me, and laughing. I was terrified. When I finally saw the house—just this faint gold glow, over the bushes—it was such a relief I almost screamed. The next thing I remember is pushing the back door open—"

"He looked like *The Scream*," Rafe said, "only muddier. And he was making absolutely no sense; half what came out of his mouth was pure gibberish, like he was speaking in tongues. All we could make out was that he had to go back, and that Daniel said we should stay where we were. Personally, I thought fuck that, I wanted to go find out what the hell was going on, but when I started getting my coat, Justin and Abby both went into such hysterics that I gave up."

"And a good thing too," Abby said coolly. She had gone back to the doll; her hair fell across her face, hiding it, and even from across the room I could tell that her stitches were huge and sloppy and useless. "What possible use do you think you could have been?"

Rafe shrugged. "We'll never know, will we? I know that cottage; if Justin had just told me where he was going, I could have gone instead, and he could have stayed here and pulled himself together. But apparently that's not what Daniel had in mind."

"Presumably he had reasons."

"Oh, I'm sure," Rafe said. "I'm sure he did. So Justin flapped around for a bit, grabbing things and babbling at us, and then he dashed out again."

"I don't remember getting back to the cottage," Justin said. "Afterwards I was absolutely covered in mud, up to my knees—maybe I fell over, I don't know—and I had all these little scratches on my hands; I think I must have been holding onto the hedges to stay standing. Daniel was still sitting beside you; I'm not sure he'd moved since I left. He looked up at me—there was rain on his glasses—and do you know what he said? He said, 'This rain should come in useful. If it keeps up, any blood or footprints will be gone by the time the police arrive.'"

Rafe moved, a sudden restless shift that made the sofa springs grate.

"I just stood there staring at him. All I heard was 'police' and I honestly couldn't think what the police had to do with anything, but it terrified me just the same. He looked me up and down and then he said, 'You're not wearing gloves.'"

"With Lexie right there beside him," Rafe said, to nobody in particular. "Lovely."

"I'd forgotten all about the gloves. I mean, I was . . . well, you get the idea. Daniel sighed and got up—he didn't even seem to be in a hurry—and wiped his glasses on his handkerchief. Then he held out the handkerchief to me and I tried to take it, I thought he meant for me to clean my glasses as well, but he whipped it away and said, sort of irritably, 'Keys?' So I brought them out, and he took them and wiped them off—that was when I finally figured out what the handkerchief was all about. Then he . . ." Justin moved in the chair, as if he was looking for something but wasn't sure what. "Do you really not remember any of this?"

"I don't *know*," I said, giving a convulsive little shrug. I still wasn't looking at him, except out of the corner of my eye, and it was making him nervous. "If I remembered, I wouldn't have to ask you, would I?"

"OK. OK." Justin pushed his glasses up his nose. "Well. Then Daniel . . . Your hands were sort of in your lap, and they were all . . . He picked one of your arms up by the sleeve, so he could get the keys into your coat pocket. Then he let go, and your arm—it just *fell*, Lexie, like a rag doll's, with this awful thud . . . I couldn't watch any more after that, I really couldn't. I kept the torch on—on you, so he could see, but I turned around and looked out at the field— I hoped maybe Daniel would think I was watching in case anyone came. He said, 'Wallet' and then 'torch' and I passed them back to him, but I don't know what he did with them—I heard scuffly noises, but I was trying not to picture . . ."

He took a deep, shaky breath. "It took him forever. The wind was getting up and there were noises everywhere, rustles and creaks and little skittering sounds . . . I don't know how you do it, wandering around there at night. The rain was coming down harder but only in patches, there were these huge clouds blowing fast, and every time the moon came out the whole field looked *alive*. Maybe it was just shock, like Abby says, but I think . . . I don't know. Maybe there are some places that just aren't right. They're not good for you. For your mind."

He was staring somewhere in the middle of the room, eyes unfocused, remembering. I thought of that small unmistakable shot of current up the back of my neck and I wondered, for the first time, how often John Naylor had really been following me.

"Finally Daniel straightened up and said, 'That should do it. Let's go.' So I turned around, and . . ." Justin swallowed. "I still had the torch on you. Your head had sort of fallen on one shoulder, and it was raining on you, there was rain on your face; it looked like you were crying in your sleep, like you'd had a bad dream . . . I couldn't—God. I couldn't stand the thought of just *leaving* you there like that. I wanted to stay with you till it got light, or at least till it stopped raining, but when I said that to Daniel he looked at me like I had lost my mind. So I told him at least, at the very least, we had to get you out of the rain. At first he said no to that, too; but when he realized that I wasn't going to leave otherwise, that he'd have to physically drag me all the way home, he gave in. He was absolutely furious—all this stuff about how it would be my fault if we all ended up in jail—but I didn't care. So we . . ."

Wetness shone on Justin's cheek, but he didn't seem to notice. "You were so *heavy*," he said. "You're such a little slip

of a thing, I've picked you up a million times; I thought . . .
But it was like dragging a huge sack of wet sand. And you
were so cold, and so . . . your face felt like something else;
like that doll. I couldn't believe it was really you.

"We got you into that room with the roof, and I tried to
make you—make it less . . . It was so *cold*. I wanted to put
my cardigan over you, but I knew Daniel would do something if I tried; hit me, I don't know. He was rubbing things
off with his handkerchief—even your face, where I'd
touched you, and your neck where he'd felt for . . . He broke
off a branch from those bushes at the door, and he swept out
the whole place. Footprints, I suppose. He looked . . . God.
Grotesque. Walking backwards in that awful eerie room,
hunched over with this branch, *sweeping*. The torch shining
through his fingers, and these huge shadows swinging on
the walls . . ."

He wiped his face, stared down at his fingertips. "I said
a prayer over you, before we left. I know that's not much,
but . . ." His face was wet again. "May perpetual light shine
upon her," he said.

"Justin," Abby said, gently. "She's right here."

Justin shook his head. "Then," he said, "we went home."

After a moment Rafe clicked his lighter, hard—all three
of us jumped. "They showed up on the patio," he said.
"Looking like something out of *Night of the Living Dead*."

"We were both practically screaming at them, trying to
find out what had happened," Abby said, "but Daniel just
stared past us; he had this terrible glassy look, I don't think
he really saw us. He put out one arm to stop Justin going
inside, and he said, 'Does anyone have any washing to do?'"

"I don't think any of us had the foggiest clue what he
was talking about," Rafe said. "It was not a good moment
to go all cryptic. I tried to grab him, to make him tell us
what the fuck had *happened* out there, but he jumped back
and snapped, 'Don't touch me.' The way he said it—I almost
fell over backwards. It wasn't that he shouted at me or anything, he was practically whispering, but his face . . . He

didn't look like Daniel any more; he didn't even look human. He was *snarling* at me."

"He was covered with blood," Abby said bluntly, "and he didn't want you to get it on yourself. And he was traumatized. You and I had it easy that night, Rafe. No"—as Rafe snorted—"we did. Would you have wanted to be in that cottage?"

"It might not have been a bad idea."

"You wouldn't have," Justin said, with an edge to his voice. "Believe me. Abby's right: you had it easy." Rafe shrugged elaborately.

"Anyway," said Abby, after a tense second. "Daniel took a deep breath and rubbed his hand over his forehead and said, 'Abby, get us each a full change of clothes and a towel, please. Rafe, get me a plastic bag, a big one. Justin, take your clothes off.' He was already unbuttoning his shirt—"

"By the time I got back with the bag, he and Justin were both standing on the patio in their boxers," Rafe said, brushing ash off his shirt. "Not a pretty sight."

"I was *freezing*," Justin said. He sounded a lot better, now that the worst part was over: shaky, drained, released. "It was lashing rain, it was about seven million degrees below zero, the wind was like ice and we were standing on the patio in our underwear. I had no idea why we were doing this; my mind had gone numb, I was just doing whatever I was told. Daniel threw all our clothes into the bag and said something about lucky we weren't wearing coats— I started to put my shoes in, I was trying to help, but he said, 'No, leave those here; I'll deal with them later.' Sometime around then Abby got back with the towels and the clothes, and we dried off and got dressed—"

"I tried again to ask what was going on," said Rafe, "from a safe distance this time. Justin gave me this deer-in-headlights stare and Daniel didn't even look at me; he just tucked his shirt into his trousers and said, 'Rafe, Abby, bring your washing, please. If you don't have any dirty clothes, clean ones will do.' Then he scooped up the bag in his arms and marched off into the kitchen, barefoot, with Justin tagging after him like a puppy. For some reason I actually went and *got* my washing."

"He was right," Abby said. "If the police had got there before we had the washing done, it needed to look like a normal load, not getting rid of evidence."

Rafe gave a one-shouldered shrug. "Whatever. Daniel got the washing machine started and stood there frowning at it, like it was some fascinating mystery object. We were all in the kitchen, standing around like a bunch of spare pricks, waiting for I don't know what; for Daniel to say something, I suppose, although—"

"All I could see was the knife," Justin said, low. "Rafe and Abby had just *left* it there, on the kitchen floor—"

Rafe raised his eyes to the ceiling, jerked his head at Abby. "Yeah," she said, "that was me. I figured we'd better not touch anything, not until the others came back and we knew what the plan was."

"Because of course," Rafe told me, in a drawling pseudo-undertone, "there was bound to be a plan. With Daniel, isn't there always a plan? Isn't it nice to know there's a plan?"

"Abby yelled at us," said Justin. "She shouted, 'Where the hell is Lexie?' In my ear. I almost fainted."

"Daniel turned around and stared," Rafe said, "like he had no idea who we were. Justin tried to say something and made this awful choking noise, and Daniel jumped about a mile and blinked at him. Then he said, 'Lexie is in that ruined cottage she likes. She's dead. I assumed Justin had told you.' And he started putting his socks on."

"Justin had told us," Abby said quietly, "but I guess we had been hoping he'd got it wrong, somehow . . ."

A long silence. Upstairs the clock on the landing was ticking, slow and heavy. Somewhere Daniel had his foot on the accelerator and I thought I could feel him out there, coming closer every second, the dizzying speed of the road under his tyres.

"And then?" I asked. "Did you just go to *bed*?"

They looked at each other. Justin started to laugh, a high, helpless sound, and after a moment the others joined in.

"What?" I said.

"I don't know what we're laughing about," Abby said, wiping her eyes and trying to compose herself and look stern, which sent them all into fresh spurts of giggles. "Oh, God . . . It wasn't funny; really, it wasn't. It's just . . ."

"You're not going to believe this," Rafe said. "We played poker."

"We did. We sat at that table—"

"—practically having heart attacks every time the rain hit the window—"

"Justin's teeth wouldn't stop chattering, it was like sitting next to a maraca player—"

"And when the wind did that thing with the door? And Daniel knocked his chair over?"

"Look who's talking. About ninety percent of the time I could see every card in your hand. You're lucky I was in no mood for cheating, I could've cleaned you out—"

They were talking over each other, chattering like a bunch of teenagers bursting out of some huge exam, giddy with relief. "Oh, my God," Justin said, closing his eyes and pressing his glass against his temple. "That fucking, fucking *card* game. My jaw still drops when I think about it. Daniel kept saying, 'The only reliable alibi is an actual sequence of events—'"

"The rest of us could barely talk in sentences," said Rafe, "and he's waxing philosophical about the art of the alibi. I couldn't have *said* 'reliable alibi.'"

"—so he made us turn all the clocks back to eleven, just before it all went horrible, and go back into the kitchen and finish the washing up, and then he made us come in here and play *cards*. As if nothing had happened."

"He played your hand as well as his," Abby told me. "The first time you had a decent hand and he had a better one, he went all in for you and then knocked you out. It was surreal."

520 · Tana French

"And he kept *narrating,*" Rafe said. He stretched for the vodka bottle and topped up his glass. In the hazy afternoon light through the windows he looked beautiful and dissolute, shirt open at the collar and streaks of golden hair falling in his eyes, like some Regency buck after a long night's dancing. "'Lexie's raising, Lexie folds, Lexie would need another drink at this point, could someone please pass her the wine . . .' He was like some nutcase who sits next to you in the park and feeds bites of sandwich to his imaginary friend. Once he'd got you out of the game he made us act out this little *scene,* you heading off on your walk and all of us waving bye-bye to thin air . . . I thought we were losing our minds. I remember sitting there, in that chair, politely saying good-bye to the door and thinking very clearly and calmly, *So this is what insanity feels like.*"

"It must have been three in the morning by then," Justin said, "but Daniel wouldn't let us go to bed. We had to sit there and keep playing Texas bloody Hold-'em, to the bitter end—Daniel won, of course, he was the only one who could concentrate, but it took him *forever* to wipe the rest of us out. Honestly, the cops must think we're the worst poker players in history, I was folding on flush draws and raising on a ten high . . . I was so exhausted I was seeing double, and it all felt like a hideous nightmare, I kept thinking I had to wake up. We hung the clothes in front of the fire to dry and the room was like something out of *The Fog,* clothes steaming and the fire spitting and everyone chain-smoking Daniel's horrible unfiltered things—"

"He wouldn't let me go get normal ones," said Abby. "He said we all needed to stay together, and anyway the cameras at the petrol station would show what time I'd come in and it would mess everything up . . . He was like a general." Rafe snorted. "He was. The rest of us were shaking so much we could barely hold our cards—"

"Justin got sick at one stage," Rafe said through a cigarette, waving out the match. "In the kitchen sink, charmingly enough."

"I couldn't help it," Justin said. "All I could think of was you, lying there in the dark, all by yourself—" He reached out and squeezed my arm. I put up a hand to cover his for a second; his was cool and bony and trembling hard.

"That was all any of us could think about," Abby said, "but Daniel . . . I could see how much it was taking out of him—his *face* had fallen in under the cheekbones, like he'd lost a stone since dinner, and his eyes looked wrong, all huge and black—but he was so calm, as if nothing had happened. Justin started cleaning up the sink—"

"He was still gagging," Rafe said. "I could hear him. Out of the five of us, Lexie, I think you may have had the nicest evening."

"—but Daniel told him to leave it; he said it would skew the timeline in our minds."

"Apparently," Rafe informed me, "the essence of the alibi is simplicity; the fewer steps one has to omit or invent, the less likely one is to make a mistake. He kept saying, 'As it stands, all we need to do is remember that we went from the washing up to the card game, and eliminate the intervening events from our minds. They never happened.' In other words, get back here and play your hand, Justin. The poor bastard was *green*."

Daniel had been right, about the alibi. He was good at this; too good. In that second I thought of my flat, Sam scribbling and the air outside the windows dimming to purple and me profiling the killer: someone with previous criminal experience.

Sam had run background checks on every one of them, found nothing worse than a couple of speeding tickets. I had no way of knowing what checks Frank might have run, in his private, complex, off-the-record world; how much he had found and kept to himself, and how much had slipped past even him; who, out of all the contenders, was the best secret keeper of us all.

"He wouldn't even let us move the knife," Justin said. "It was there the whole time we were playing cards. I had my back to the kitchen and I swear I could *feel* it behind me, like something out of Poe, or the Jacobeans. Rafe was across from me, and he kept doing this little jump and blink, like a tic—"

Rafe threw him an incredulous grimace. "I did not."

"You did. You were *twitching,* every minute, like clockwork. It looked exactly like you had seen something terrifying over my shoulder, and every time you did it I was too afraid to turn around in case the knife was hanging there in midair, glowing or throbbing or I don't know what—"

"Oh, for God's sake. Bloody Lady Macbeth—"

"Jesus," I said suddenly. "The knife. Is it still—I mean, have we been *eating* with . . ." I flipped a hand vaguely towards the kitchen, then shoved a knuckle in my mouth and bit down. I wasn't faking; the thought of every meal I'd eaten here streaked with invisible traces of Lexie's blood did slow somersaults across my mind.

"No," Abby said quickly. "God, no. Daniel got rid of it. After we'd all gone to bed, or anyway to our bedrooms—"

"Good night, Mary Ellen," said Rafe. "Good night, Jim Bob. Sleep tight. Jesus."

"—he went straight down again—I heard him on the stairs. I don't know exactly what he did down there, but next morning the clocks were back to normal, the sink was spotless, the kitchen floor was clean—it looked like it had been scrubbed, the whole thing, not just that one patch. The shoes, Daniel's and Justin's that they'd left on the patio, they were in the coat closet and they were clean too—not squeaky clean, just the way we always do them—and dry, like he'd put them by the fire. The clothes were all ironed and folded, and the knife was gone."

"What one was it?" I asked, a little shakily, around my knuckle.

"It was just one of those manky old steak knives with the wooden handles," Abby said gently. "It's OK, Lex. It's gone."

"I don't want it to be in the house," I said.

"I know. Me neither. I'm pretty sure Daniel got rid of it, though. I'm not positive how many we had to start with, but I heard the front door, so I figure he must have been taking it outside."

"Where to? I don't want it in the garden either. I don't want it anywhere around." My voice was shaking harder. Frank, somewhere, listening and whispering, *Go girl go.*

Abby shook her head. "I'm not sure. He was gone a few minutes, and I don't think he'd have left it in the grounds, but do you want me to ask? I can tell him to move it if it's anywhere nearby."

I twitched one shoulder. "Whatever. Yeah, I guess. Tell him." Daniel would never in a million years do it, but I had to go through the motions, and he would have a lot of fun leading surveillance on wild-goose chases; if things ever got that far.

"I didn't even hear him go downstairs," Justin said. "I was . . . Christ. I don't even want to think about it. I was sitting on the edge of my bed with the lights out, *rocking.* All through the card game I wanted to get away so badly I could have screamed, I just wanted to be by myself, but as soon as I was, it was even worse. The house kept creaking—all that wind and rain—but I swear to God it sounded exactly like you were moving around upstairs, getting ready for bed. Once"—he swallowed, jaw muscles clenching—"once I heard you humming. 'Black Velvet Band,' of all things. It was that clear. I wanted to—If I look out my window I can see whether your light is on, it shines onto the lawn, and I wanted to check, just to reassure myself—oh God, I don't mean *reassure,* you know what I mean—but I couldn't. I couldn't make myself stand up. I was absolutely positive that if I pulled that curtain I would see your light on the grass. And then what? Then what could I *do?*"

He was shaking. "Justin," Abby said gently. "It's OK."

Justin pressed his fingers across his mouth, hard, and took a deep breath. "Well," he said. "Anyway. Daniel could have been *thundering* up and down those stairs and I wouldn't have noticed."

"I heard him," Rafe said. "I think I heard every single thing for a mile around, that night; even the tiniest noise somewhere down at the bottom of the garden practically made me jump out of my skin. The joy of criminal activity is that it gives you ears like a bat's." He shook his smoke packet, tossed it into the fireplace—Justin opened his mouth automatically and then closed it again—and took Abby's off the coffee table. "Some of it made for very interesting listening."

Abby's eyebrows went up. She stuck her needle carefully into a hem, put the doll down and gave Rafe a long cool look. "Do you really want to go there?" she inquired. "Because I can't stop you, but if I were you I'd think very, very hard before I opened that particular Pandora's box."

There was a long, fizzing silence. Abby folded her hands in her lap and watched Rafe calmly.

"I was drunk," Rafe said, suddenly and sharply, into the silence. "Banjoed."

After a second Justin said, to the coffee table, "You weren't that drunk."

"I was. I was legless. I don't think I've ever been that drunk in my life."

"No you weren't. If you had been that drunk—"

"We had all been drinking pretty solidly for most of the night," Abby said evenly, cutting him off. "Not surprisingly. It didn't help; I don't think any of us got much sleep. The next morning was pure nightmare. We were so upset and wrecked and hungover that we were practically dizzy, couldn't think straight, couldn't even *see* straight. We couldn't decide whether to call the cops and report you missing, or what. Rafe and Justin wanted to do it—"

"Rather than leave you lying in a rat-infested hovel till some local yokel happened to stumble on you," Rafe said through a cigarette, shaking Abby's lighter. "Call us crazy."

"—but Daniel said it would look weird; you were old

enough to go for an early-morning walk or even skive off college for the day if you wanted to. He phoned your mobile—it was right there in the kitchen, obviously, but still, he figured there should be a call on it."

"He made us have *breakfast*," Justin said.

"Justin managed to get as far as the bathroom, that time," said Rafe.

"We couldn't stop fighting," Abby said. She had picked up the doll again and was methodically, unconsciously plaiting its hair, over and over. "Whether we had to eat breakfast, whether to call the cops, whether we should leave for college like normal or wait for you to come back—I mean, the natural thing would have been for Daniel or Justin to wait for you while the rest of us headed in, but we couldn't do it. The thought of splitting up—I don't know if I can explain it, how badly that idea freaked us out. We were ready to kill each other—Rafe and I were screaming at each other, actually screaming—but the second someone suggested doing separate stuff, I literally went weak at the knees."

"Do you know what I thought?" Justin said, very quietly. "I was standing there, listening to you three argue and looking out the window waiting for the police or someone to come, and I realized: it could be days. It could be weeks; this could go on for weeks, the waiting. Lexie could be there for . . . I knew there wasn't a chance in hell I could get through that day at college, never mind weeks. And I thought what we should really do was stop fighting and get a duvet and curl up under it, all four of us together, and turn the gas on. That was what I wanted to do."

"We don't even *have* gas," Rafe snapped. "Don't be such a bloody drama queen."

"I think that was on all our minds—what we would do if you weren't found right away—but nobody wanted to mention it," Abby said. "It was actually a huge relief when the police showed up. Justin saw them first, out the window; he said, 'Someone's here,' and we all froze, right in the middle of yelling at each other. Rafe and I started to go for the window, but Daniel said, 'Everyone sit down. Now.' So we all sat at the kitchen table, like we had just finished breakfast, and waited for the bell to ring."

"Daniel answered it," Rafe said, "of course. He was cool as ice. I could hear him out in the hall: Yes, Alexandra Madison lives here, and no we haven't seen her since last night, and no there's been no argument, and no we're not worried about her, just unsure whether she's coming to college today, and is there a problem, Officers, and this note of concern gradually seeping into his voice . . . He was *perfect*. It was absolutely terrifying."

Abby's eyebrows went up. "Would you have preferred him to be a babbling mess?" she inquired. "What do you think would have happened if *you* had answered that door?"

Rafe shrugged. He had started fiddling with the cards again.

"In the end," Abby said, when it was obvious he wasn't going to answer, "I realized we could go out there—actually, it would look weird if we didn't. It was Mackey and O'Neill—Mackey was leaning up against the wall and O'Neill was taking notes—and they scared the living shit out of me. The plain clothes, these expressions that told you absolutely nothing, the way they talked—like there was no hurry, they could take all the time they wanted . . . I'd been expecting those two eejits from Rathowen, and it was obvious straight away that these guys were not the same thing at all. They were so much smarter and so, so much more dangerous. I'd been thinking the worst was over, nothing could ever be as bad as that night. When I saw those two, that was when it hit me that this was only just beginning."

"They were cruel," Justin said suddenly. "Horribly, horribly cruel. They stretched it out forever, before they told us. We kept asking what had happened, and they just stared at us with these smug blank faces and wouldn't give a straight answer—"

" 'What makes you think something might have happened to her?'" Rafe put in, doing a viciously accurate send-up of Frank's lazy Dublin. "'Did someone have a reason to hurt her? Was she afraid of someone?'"

"—and even when they did, the bastards didn't tell us you were *alive*. Mackey just said something like, 'She was found a few hours ago, not far from here. Sometime last night, she was stabbed.' He *deliberately* made it sound like you were dead."

"Daniel was the only one who kept his head," Abby said. "I was about a second from bursting into tears; I'd been holding it back all morning in case it made my eyes look funny, and it was such a relief to finally be *allowed* to know what had happened . . . But Daniel said straight off, like a shot, 'Is she alive?'"

"And they just left it," Justin said. "They didn't say a word, for what felt like forever; just stood there watching us, and waiting. I told you they were cruel."

"*Finally,*" Rafe said, "Mackey shrugged and said, 'Barely.' It was like all of our heads had exploded. I mean, we had been primed for . . . well, the worst; we just wanted to get it over with, so we could go have our nervous breakdowns in peace. We were not ready for this. God knows what we might have come out with—we could have blown the whole thing right there—except that Abby, with impeccable timing, threw a fainting fit. I've been meaning to ask you, actually, was that real? Or was it all part of the *plan*?"

"Very little of this was part of anyone's plan," Abby said tartly, "and I did not faint. I got dizzy for a second. If you remember, I hadn't had a lot of sleep." Rafe laughed, nastily.

"Everyone jumped to catch her and sit her down and get water," said Justin, "and by the time she was all right, we had pulled ourselves together—"

"Oh, *we* had, had we?" Rafe inquired, eyebrows going up. "You were still standing there opening and shutting your mouth like a goldfish. I was so terrified you would say something idiotic, I was *babbling*, the cops must have thought I was a total moron: where did you find her, where is she, when can we see her . . . Not that they answered, but at least I tried."

"I did my best," said Justin. His voice was rising; he was starting to get upset again. "It was easy for you, getting your head around it: oh, she's alive, isn't that lovely. You weren't there. You weren't remembering that awful cottage—"

"Where, as far as I can see, you were about as much use as tits on a bull. Again."

"You're drunk," Abby said coldly.

"Do you know," Rafe said, like a kid pleased at shocking the grown-ups, "I think I am. And I think I might just keep getting drunker. Unless anyone has a problem with that?"

No one answered. He stretched for the bottle, eyes sliding sideways to me: "You missed some night, Lexie. If you were wondering why Abby thinks everything Daniel says is the Word of God—"

Abby didn't move. "I've warned you once, Rafe. This is twice. You don't get a third chance."

After a moment Rafe shrugged and buried his face in his glass. In the silence I realized Justin had flushed deep red, right up to his hairline.

"The next few days," Abby said, "were pure hell. They told us you were in intensive care in a coma, the doctors weren't sure whether you were going to make it, but they wouldn't let us go see you—even getting them to tell us how you were doing was like pulling teeth. The most we could get out of them was that you weren't dead yet, which wasn't exactly comforting."

"The place was *swarming* with cops," said Rafe. "Cops searching your room, searching the lanes, pulling out bits of the *carpet* . . . They interviewed us so many times that I started repeating myself, I couldn't remember what I'd already said to who. Even when they weren't there, we were on guard all the time—Daniel said they couldn't bug the house, not legally, but Mackey doesn't strike me as the type to worry too much about technicalities; and anyway, having cops is like having rats, or fleas, or something. Even when you can't see them, you can *feel* them somewhere, crawling."

"It was awful," Abby said. "And Rafe can bitch all he wants about that poker game, but it's a damn good thing Daniel made us do it. If I'd even thought about it before, I would've figured giving an alibi took about five minutes: I was here, everyone else says the same thing, the end. But the cops grilled us for *hours,* over and over, about every single tiny detail—what time did you start the game? Who sat where? How much money did you each start with? Who dealt first? Were you drinking? Who drank what? Which *ashtray* were you using?"

"And they kept trying to trap us," Justin said. He reached for the bottle; his hand shook, just a little. "I'd give a perfectly simple answer—we started playing around quarter past eleven, that kind of thing—and Mackey or O'Neill or whoever it was that day would get this worried look and say, 'Are you sure about that? Because I think one of your friends said it was at quarter past ten,' and start rummaging through notes, and I would just *freeze.* I mean, I didn't know whether one of the others had made a mistake—it would have been easy to do, we were all such a mess we could barely think straight—and whether I should back them up, say, 'Oh, that's right, I must have got mixed up,' or something. In the end I always stuck to the story, which turned out to be the right thing to do—nobody had made any mistakes, the cops were just bluffing—but that was sheer luck: I was too paralyzed with terror to do anything else. If it had gone on any longer, I think we would all have lost our minds."

"And all for what?" Rafe demanded. He sat up suddenly, almost spilling the cards off his lap, and plucked his cigarette out of the ashtray. "Here's the part that still amazes me: we took Daniel's word for it. He has all the medical knowledge of a cheese soufflé, but he told us Lexie was dead and we just assumed he was right. Why do we always *believe* him?"

"Habit," said Abby. "He usually is right."

"You think so?" Rafe asked. He was lounging back against the arm of the sofa again, but there was an edge to his voice, something dangerous and spiraling. "He certainly wasn't right this time. We could have simply phoned for an ambulance like normal people and everything would have been *fine*. Lexie would never press charges or whatever they call it, and if any of us had *thought* about it for a single second, we'd have known that. But no, we let Daniel call all the shots; we had to sit here having the Mad Hatter's tea party—"

"He didn't know everything would be fine," Abby said sharply. "What do you think he should have done? He thought Lexie was *dead,* Rafe."

Rafe shrugged, one-shouldered. "So he says."

"What's that supposed to mean?"

"I'm just saying. Remember when that wanker showed up to tell us she was out of the coma? The three of us," he told me, "we were so relieved we almost collapsed; I thought Justin was actually going to faint."

"Thank you for that, Rafe," Justin said, reaching for the bottle.

"But did Daniel look relieved to you? Like hell he did. He looked like someone had hit him in the gut with a bat. Even the cop noticed, for God's sake. Remember?" Abby shrugged coldly and bent her head over the doll, fumbled for her needle.

"Hey," I said, kicking the sofa to get Rafe's attention. "*I* don't remember. What happened?"

"It was that prat Mackey," Rafe said. He took the vodka bottle from Justin and topped up his glass, not bothering with tonic. "Bright and early on the Monday morning, he's at the door, telling us he's got news and asking if he can come in. Personally I would have told him to fuck himself, I'd seen enough cops that weekend to last me a lifetime, but Daniel answered the door and he had this crackpot theory that we shouldn't do anything that might antagonize the police—I mean, Mackey was *already* antagonized, he hated us all on sight, what was the point of cozying up to him?—so he let him in. I came out of my room to see what the story was, and Justin and Abby were coming out of the kitchen, and Mackey stood there in the hall looking round at us all and said, 'Your friend's going to make it. She's awake and asking for breakfast.'"

"And we were all overjoyed," Abby said. She had found the needle and was stabbing at the doll's dress with short, angry stitches.

"Well," Rafe said. "Some of us were. Justin was clutching onto the door handle grinning like an idiot and sagging as if his knees had gone out from under him, and Abby started laughing and jumped on him and gave him this huge hug, and I think I made some kind of weird whooping noise. But Daniel . . . he just stood there. He looked—"

"He looked young," Justin said suddenly. "He looked really young and really scared."

"You," Abby told him sharply, "were in no state to notice anything."

"I *was*. I was looking at him *specifically*. He was so white he looked sick."

"Then he turned round and walked in here," Rafe said, "and leaned on the window frame, looking out at the garden. Not a word. Mackey gave the rest of us the eyebrow and asked, 'What's up with your mate? Isn't he pleased?'"

Frank had never mentioned any of this. I should have been annoyed—he was one to talk about playing dirty—but he seemed like some half-forgotten person from another world, a million miles away.

"Abby disentangled herself from Justin and said something about Daniel being all emotional—"

"Which he was," Abby said, and bit off a thread with a snap.

"—but Mackey just smiled this cynical little smirk and then left. As soon as I was sure he was actually gone—he's the type who would hang around eavesdropping in shrubberies—I went in to Daniel and asked him what the fuck his problem was. He was still at the window, he hadn't moved. He pushed his hair off his face—he was sweating—and he said, 'There isn't a problem. He's lying, of course; I should have realized that immediately, but he caught me off guard.' I just stared at him. I thought he had finally lost it."

"Or you have," Abby said crisply. "I don't remember any of this."

"You and Justin were busy dancing around hugging each other and making squeaky noises, like a pair of Teletubbies. Daniel gave me this irritated look and said, 'Don't be naïve, Rafe. If Mackey were telling the truth, do you honestly believe that would be unadulterated good news? Hasn't it even occurred to you just how serious the consequences could have been?'"

He took a long swallow of his drink. "You tell me, Abby. Does that sound *overjoyed* to you?"

"Jesus *Christ*, Rafe," Abby said. She was sitting up straight, eyes snapping: she was getting angry. "What are you babbling about? Are you losing your mind? Nobody wanted Lexie to die."

"You didn't, I didn't, Justin didn't. Maybe Daniel didn't. All I'm saying is that I've got no way of knowing what he felt when he checked Lexie's pulse; I wasn't there. And I can't swear I know what he'd have done if he realized she was alive. Can you, Abby? After these last few weeks, can you swear, hand on heart, that you're absolutely positive what Daniel would have done?"

Something cold slipped across the back of my neck, riffled the curtains, spiraled off to nose delicately in corners. All Cooper and the Bureau had been able to tell us was that she had been moved after she died; not how long after. For at least twenty minutes they had been alone together in the cottage, Lexie and Daniel. I thought of her fists, clenched tight—*extreme emotional stress*, Cooper had said—and then of Daniel sitting quietly beside her, carefully tapping ash into his smoke packet, droplets of soft rain catching in his dark hair. If there had been anything more than that—a hand twitching, a gasp; wide brown eyes staring up at him, a whisper almost too faint to hear—no one would ever know.

Long night wind sweeping across the hillside, owl calls fading. The other thing Cooper had said: doctors could have saved her.

Daniel could have made Justin stay in the cottage, if he had really wanted to. It would have been the logical thing to do. The one who stayed had nothing to do, if Lexie was dead, except keep still and not touch anything; the one who went back to the house had to break the news to the others, find the wallet and the keys and the Maglite, stay calm and work fast. Daniel had sent Justin, who could barely stand up.

"Right up until the night before you came home," Rafe told me, "he *insisted* you were dead. According to him, the cops were just bluffing, claiming you were alive so we'd think you were talking to them. He said all we had to do was keep our heads and they'd back down sooner or later, they'd come up with some story about how you'd relapsed and died in hospital. It wasn't until Mackey phoned to ask if he could drop you off the next day, if we'd be home—that was when it hit Daniel that, duh, there might not actually be some huge conspiracy going on; this might actually be as simple as it looked. Lightbulb moment."

He took another big swig of his drink. "Overjoyed, my shiny white arse. I'll tell you what he was: he was *petrified*. All he could think about was whether Lexie had really lost her memory or whether she'd just said that to the cops, and what she might do about it once she got home."

"So?" Abby demanded. "Big deal. We were all worried about that, if we're honest. Why not? If she did remember, she'd have had every right to be raging with the lot of us. That evening you came home, Lex, we'd been like a bunch of cats on hot bricks all day. Once we realized you weren't angry or anything, we were OK—but when you got out of that cop car . . . Jesus. I thought my head was going to explode." For one last second, I saw them again the way I had that evening: a golden apparition on the front steps, shining and poised like young warriors stepped out of some lost myth, heads lifted, too bright to be real.

"Worried," Rafe said, "yes. But Daniel was a lot more than worried. He was so hysterically nervous that it was making me nervous too. Finally I cornered him—I had to sneak up to his room late at night, like we were having an affair or something; he was bloody careful not to let me get him alone—and I asked him what the hell was up. Do you know what he said to me? He said, 'We have to accept the fact that this may not be over so easily. I think I have a plan that should cover all eventualities, but a few of the details are still unclear. Try not to worry about it for the moment; it may never come to that.' What do you suppose he meant by that?"

"Not being a mind reader," Abby said crisply, "I haven't a clue. I assume he was trying to reassure you."

A dark lane and a tiny click, and that note in Daniel's voice: focused, absorbed, so calm. I could feel my hair lifting. It had never occurred to me, not once, that the gun might not have been pointing at Naylor.

Rafe snorted. "Oh, please. Daniel didn't give a damn about how any of us felt—including Lexie. All he cared about was finding out whether she remembered anything and what she was going to do next. He wasn't even subtle about it; he was *blatantly* pumping her for information, every chance he got. Do you remember what route you took that night, are you taking the jacket or would you rather not, oh Lexie do you want to *talk* about it . . . It made me *sick*."

"He was trying to *protect* you, Rafe. Us."

"I don't need protecting, thanks very much. I'm not a bloody child. And I definitely, definitely don't need protecting by *Daniel*."

"Well, good for you," said Abby. "Congratulations, big

man. Whether you feel you needed it or not, he was doing his best. If that's not good enough for you—"

Rafe gave a jerky, one-shouldered shrug. "Maybe he was. Like I said, I've got no way to know for sure. But if he was, then his best is pretty crap, for such a smart guy. These last few weeks have been hell, Abby, living hell, and they didn't *need* to be. If Daniel had just listened to us, instead of doing *his best* . . . We wanted to tell you," he said, swinging round to me. "All three of us. When we found out you were coming home."

"We really did, Lexie," said Justin, leaning over the arm of his chair towards me. "You don't know how many times I almost . . . God. I thought I was going to explode, or disintegrate or something, if I didn't tell you."

"But Daniel," Rafe said, "wouldn't let us. And look how well that's turned out. Look how well *every single one* of his ideas has turned out. *Look* at us; where he's got us." His hand flying up to all of us, to the room, bright and desperate and cracking at the seams. "None of this needed to happen. We could've called an ambulance, we could've told Lexie straight off—"

"No," Abby said. "No. *You* could have called an ambulance. *You* could have told Lexie. Or I could have, or Justin. Don't you dare put this all on Daniel. You're a grown man, Rafe. Nobody held a gun to your head and made you keep your mouth shut. You did it all by yourself."

"Maybe. But I did it because Daniel told me to, and so did you. You and I were on our own here for how long, that night? An hour? More? And the only thing you could talk about was how badly you wanted to get help. But when I said yeah, OK, let's do it, you said no. Daniel said not to do anything. Daniel had a plan. Daniel would handle it."

"Because I *trust* him. I owe him that, that much at *least,* and so do you. This—everything we've got—it's because of Daniel. If it weren't for him, I'd be on my own in a scary underground bedsit right this minute. Maybe that doesn't mean anything to you—"

Rafe laughed, a loud, harsh, startling sound. "This fucking house," he said. "Every time anyone hints that your precious Daniel might not be perfect, you throw the house in our faces. I've been keeping my mouth shut because I thought maybe you were right, maybe I owed him, but now . . . I've just about had it up to my tits with this house. Another of Daniel's brilliant ideas, and how well has this one worked out? Justin's a wreck, you're six feet deep in denial, I'm drinking like my father, Lexie almost *died,* and most of the time we all hate one another's guts. All because of this fucking house."

Abby's head came up and she stared at him. "That's *not Daniel's fault.* He just wanted—"

"Wanted what, Abby? What? Why do you think he gave us all shares in the house to start with?"

"Because," Abby said, low and dangerous, "he cares about us. Because, right or wrong, he figured this was the best way to make sure all five of us were happy."

I expected Rafe to laugh out loud at that, too, but he didn't. "You know," he said after a moment, staring down into his glass, "I thought that too, at first. I really did. That he was doing it because he loved us." The vicious edge had fallen out of his voice; all that was left was a simple, tired melancholy. "It made me happy, thinking that. There was a time when I would've done anything for Daniel. Anything."

"And then you saw the light," Abby said. Her voice was hard and brittle, but she couldn't keep the shake out of it. She was more upset than I'd ever seen her, more upset even than when I'd brought up the note in the jacket. "Someone who gives his best friends most of a seven-figure house is obviously doing it for purely selfish reasons. Paranoid much?"

"I thought about that. I've thought about this a lot, the last few weeks. I didn't want to—God . . . But I couldn't help it. Like picking at a scab." Rafe looked up at Abby, shaking his hair out of his face; the booze was soaking in and his eyes were bloodshot and puffy, as if he'd been crying. "Say we'd all ended up in different colleges, Abby. Say we'd never met. What do you think we'd be doing now?"

"I don't have the foggiest clue what you're talking about."

"We'd be OK, the four of us. Maybe we would've had a tough first few months, maybe it would've taken us a while to get to know people, but we'd have done it. I know none of us were the outgoing type, but we'd have learned. That's what people *do,* in college: they learn to function in the big scary world. By now we'd have friends, social lives—"

"I wouldn't," Justin said, quietly and definitely. "I wouldn't be OK. Not without you guys."

"Yes you would, Justin. You would. You'd have a boyfriend—you too, Abby. Not just someone who shares a bed with you occasionally, when the day's been too much to take. A boyfriend. A partner." He gave me a sad little smile. "You, silly thing, I'm not so sure. But you'd be having a lot of fun, either way."

"Thanks for sorting out our love lives," Abby said coldly, "you patronizing prick. The fact that Justin doesn't have a fella doesn't make Daniel the Antichrist."

Rafe didn't rise to that, and for some reason that frightened me. "No," he said. "But think about this for a second. If we'd never met, what do you think Daniel would be doing now?"

Abby gave him a blank stare. "Climbing the Matterhorn. Running for office. Living right here. How the hell do I know?"

"Can you see him going to the Freshers' Ball? Joining college societies? Chatting up some girl in American Poetry class? Seriously, Abby. I'm asking. Can you?"

"I don't *know.* It's all *if,* Rafe. *If* doesn't mean anything. I've got no idea what would have happened if everything had gone differently, because I'm not bloody clairvoyant, and neither are you."

"Maybe not," Rafe said, "but I know this much. Daniel

would never, no matter what, *never* have learned how to deal with the outside world. I don't know if he was born this way or if he was dropped on his head as a baby or what, but he's just not capable of living a normal human life."

"There's nothing wrong with Daniel," Abby said, cold fine syllables like chips of ice splintering. "Nothing."

"There is, Abby. I love him—yes, I do, I still do—but there's always been something wrong with him. Always. You have to know that."

"He's right," Justin said, softly. "There has. I never told you, but back when we first met, back in first year—"

"Shut up," Abby snapped viciously, whirling on him. "You shut your mouth. What makes you any different? If Daniel's fucked up, then you're just as fucked up as he is, and you, Rafe—"

"No," Rafe said. He stared down at his finger tracing patterns in the condensation on his glass. "That's what I'm trying to tell you. The rest of us—when we want to, we can hold conversations with other people, for God's sake. I picked up a girl, the other night. Your tutorial brats love you. Justin flirts with that blond guy who works in the library—you do, Justin, I've seen you; Lexie had a laugh with the people in that awful café. We can connect with the rest of the world, if we put in the effort. But Daniel . . . There are only four people on the planet who don't think he's a full-on freak show, and all four of them are in this room. We'd have been OK without him, one way or another, but he wouldn't have been OK without us. If it weren't for us, Daniel would be lonelier than God."

"So?" Abby demanded, after a long second. "So what?"

"So," Rafe said, "if you ask me, that's why he gave us shares in the house. Not to make our lives all sunshiny. To have company, here in his private universe. To keep us, for good."

"You," Abby said. She was breathless. "You nasty-minded little piece of work. Where you get the sheer brass neck—"

"It was never us he was protecting, Abby. Never. It was this: his own ready-made little world. Tell me this: why did you ride in to the cop shop with Daniel, this morning? Why didn't you want him to be alone with Lexie?"

"I didn't want to be anywhere near you. The way you've been acting, you make me *sick*—"

"Bullshit. What do you think he was going to do to Lexie, if she even hinted that she might still sell up, or talk to the cops? You keep saying I could have told her any time, but what do you think Daniel would have done to me, if he thought I was going to step out of line? He had a plan, Abby. He told me he had a plan to cover all eventualities. *What the hell do you think his plan was?*"

Justin gasped, a terrified, childlike sound. The light in the room had changed; the air had tilted, pressure shifting, all those little eddies gathering themselves together and whirling around some huge focal point.

Daniel filled the doorway, tall and unmoving, hands in the pockets of his long dark coat. "All I ever wanted," he said quietly, "was here in this house."

24

"Daniel," Abby said, and I saw her whole body loosen with relief. "Thank God."

Rafe eased back, slowly, on the sofa. "Cute entrance," he said coldly. "How long have you been listening at the door?"

Daniel didn't move. "What have you told her?"

"She was remembering *anyway*," Justin said. His voice was shaking. "Didn't you hear? In the police station? If we didn't tell her the rest, she was going to ring them and—"

"Ah," Daniel said. His eyes went to me, one small expressionless flick, and then away again. "I should have guessed. How much did you tell her?"

"She was upset, Daniel," said Abby. "Stuff was coming back to her, she was having a hard time dealing with it, she needed to know. We told her what happened. Not who . . . you know. Did it. But the rest."

"It was a highly educational conversation," Rafe said. "All round."

Daniel took this in with a brief nod. "All right," he said. "Here's what we're going to do. Everyone's emotions are running high"—Rafe rolled his eyes and made a disgusted noise; Daniel ignored him—"and I don't think there's anything to be gained by continuing this discussion right now. Let's leave it for a few days, really leave it, while the dust settles and we take in what's happened. Then we can talk about it again."

Once I and my mike were out of the house. Before I could say anything, Rafe asked, "Why?" Something in the roll of his head, the slow lift of his eyelids, as he turned to stare at Daniel: it hit me, with a vague shapeless warning, just how drunk he was.

I saw Daniel realize the same thing. "If you'd prefer not to resurrect it," he said coolly, "believe me, that's fine with me. I'd be delighted never to have to think about this again."

"No. Why leave it?"

"I told you. Because I don't think any of us are in any state to discuss this rationally. It's been an excruciatingly long day—"

"What if I don't give a fuck what you think?"

"I am asking you," Daniel said, "to trust me. I don't often ask you for anything. Please do me this favor."

"Actually," Rafe said, "you've asked us to do a lot of trusting you, this last while." He put down his glass on the table with a sharp little click.

"Possibly I have," said Daniel. For a fraction of a second he looked exhausted, drained to the last drop, and I wondered how exactly Frank had kept him for so long; what they had talked about, the two of them alone in a room. "So a few more days can't really do that much harm, can they?"

"And you were listening behind that door, like some gossip-starved housewife, for long enough to work out exactly how far I trust you. What are you afraid will happen, if we keep talking about this? Are you afraid Lexie won't be the only one who wants to leave? What will you do then, Daniel? How many of us are you prepared to kill off?"

"Daniel's right," Abby said crisply. Daniel coming home had calmed her down: her voice sounded strong again, certain. "All our heads are wrecked; we're not making sense. In a few days' time—"

"On the contrary," said Rafe, "I think I may be making sense for the first time in years."

"Leave it," said Justin, barely above a whisper. "Please, Rafe. Leave it."

Rafe didn't even hear him. "You can believe every word

542   ·   Tana French

he says is gospel, Abby. You can come running when he snaps his fingers. You think he cares that you're in love with him? He doesn't give a damn. He'd get rid of you in a heartbeat, if he had to, just like he was ready to—"

Abby finally lost her temper. "*Fuck* you, you self-righteous bloody—" She shot up off her chair and fired the doll straight at Rafe, one fast vicious move; he threw up a forearm reflexively and smashed it away, into a corner. "I warned you. What about *you*? Using Justin when you need him—you think I didn't hear him going downstairs, that night? Your bedroom's under mine, genius. And then when you don't need him, you treat him like shit, break his heart over and over and—"

"Stop it!" Justin shouted. His eyes were squeezed tight and his hands were pressed over his ears; his face looked like he was in agony. "God, stop it, *stop*—"

Daniel said, "That's enough." His voice was starting to rise.

"It's *not!*" I yelled, loud enough to cut straight across everyone. I'd been so quiet the last while, letting them run with it and waiting for my moment, that all of them shut up and whipped round to look at me, blinking, as if they'd almost forgotten I was there. "It's not enough. *I* don't want to leave it."

"Why not?" Daniel inquired. He had his voice back under control; that perfect, immovable calm had slammed down across his face the instant I opened my mouth. "I would have thought you of all people, Lexie, would want to get back to normal as quickly as possible. It's not like you to obsess over the past."

"I want to know who stabbed me. I need to know."

Those cool, curious gray eyes, examining me with detached interest. "Why?" he repeated. "It's over, after all. We're all still here. There's been no permanent harm done. Has there?"

Your arsenal, Frank had said. The lethal last-resort grenade Lexie had left me, passed from her hand to Cooper's to mine; the jewel-colored flash in the dark, bright and then gone; the tiny switch that had set all this in motion. My throat closed up tight till it ached even to breathe, and I shouted through it, "I was pregnant!"

They all stared at me. It was so quiet all of a sudden, and their faces were so absolutely still and blank, I thought they hadn't understood. "I was going to have a baby," I said. I felt light-headed; maybe I was swaying on my feet, I don't know. I didn't remember standing up. The sun streaming across the room turned the air a strange, holy, impossible gold. "It died."

Silence, still.

"That's not true," Daniel said, but he wasn't even looking to see how the others had taken it. His eyes were fixed on me.

"It is," I said. "Daniel, it is."

"No," said Justin. His breath was coming as if he had been running. "Oh, Lexie, no. Please."

"It's true," Abby said. She sounded terribly tired. "I knew, before any of this even happened."

Daniel's head tipped back, just a fraction. His lips parted and he let out a long breath, soft and immensely sad.

Rafe said softly, almost gently, "You bastard fuck." He was standing up, in slow motion, with his hands curled in front of him as if they were frozen there.

For a second, taking in what that meant—my money had been on Daniel, no matter what he claimed to Abby—used up all my mind. It was only when Rafe said again, louder, "You fuck," that I realized he wasn't talking to Daniel. Daniel, still framed in the doorway, was behind Justin's chair. Rafe was talking to Justin.

"Rafe," Daniel said, very sharply. "Shut up. *Now.* Sit down and pull yourself together."

It was the worst possible thing he could have done. Rafe's fists snapped closed; he was bone white and his top lip was pulled back in a snarl, and his eyes were gold and mindless as a lynx's. "Don't you ever," he said, low. "Don't you *ever* tell me what to do again. *Look* at us. Look at what you've done. Are you pleased with yourself? Are you happy now? If it hadn't been for you—"

"*Rafe,*" Abby said. "Listen to me. I know you're upset—"

"My—Oh, God. That was my *child.* Dead. Because of him."

"I told you to be quiet," Daniel said, and there was something dangerous growing in his voice.

Abby's eyes flicked to me, intent and urgent. I was the only one Rafe would listen to. If I had gone to him then, put my arms around him, made this into his and Lexie's private grief instead of a public war, I could have ended it there. He would have had no choice. For a second I could feel it, strong as reality: his shoulders slackening against me, his hands coming up to circle me tight, his shirt warm and clean-smelling against my face.

I didn't move. "You," Rafe said, to Daniel or to Justin, I couldn't tell which. "You."

In my memory it happened so neatly, clean distinct steps, as if it had been choreographed to perfection. Maybe that's just because I had to tell the story so many times, to Frank, Sam, O'Kelly, over and over to the Internal Affairs investigators; maybe it wasn't like that at all. But the way I remember it, this is what happened.

Rafe went for Justin or Daniel or both, a straight headlong charge like a fighting stag's. His leg hit the table and it toppled, high arcs of liquid glittering through the air, bottles and glasses rolling everywhere. Rafe caught himself with a hand on the floor and kept going. I got in front of him and grabbed his wrist, but he threw me off with one huge fling of his arm. My feet slid on spilled vodka and I went down hard. Justin was up and out of his chair, hands outstretched to keep Rafe off, but Rafe slammed into him full force and they both crashed back onto the chair, skidding backwards, Justin letting out a terrified moan, Rafe on top and scrabbling for traction. Abby got one hand twisted in his hair and the other in his shirt collar and tried to haul him off; Rafe shouted and heaved her away. He had his fist pulled back to punch Justin in the face, I was coming up off the floor and somehow Abby had a bottle in her hand.

Then I was on my feet and Rafe had leapt backwards off Justin and Abby was pressed against the wall, as if we had been blown apart by a bomb blast. The house was frozen, stunned into silence; the only sound was all of us breathing, hard fast gasps.

"There," Daniel said. "That's better."

He had moved forwards, into the sitting room. There was a dark gash in the ceiling above him; a trickle of plaster fell onto the floorboards, with a light pattering sound. He was holding the World War I Webley in both hands, easily, like someone who knew how to use it. He had it trained on me.

"Drop that *now*," I said. My voice came out loud enough that Justin let out a wild little whimper.

Daniel's eyes met mine and he shrugged, one eyebrow going up ruefully. He looked lighter and looser than I had ever seen him; he almost looked relieved. We both knew: that bang had flown down the mike straight to Frank and Sam, inside five minutes the house would be surrounded by cops with guns that made Uncle Simon's banjaxed revolver look like a kid's toy. There was nothing left to hold onto. Daniel's hair was falling in his eyes and I swear he was smiling.

"Lexie?" said Justin, a high incredulous breath. I followed his eyes, down to my side. My sweater was rucked up, showing the bandage and the girdle, and I had my gun in my hands. I didn't remember pulling it out.

"What the *hell*?" said Rafe, panting and wild-eyed. "Lexie, what the hell?"

Abby said, "*Daniel.*"

"Shh," he said gently. "It's all right, Abby."

"Where the hell did you *get* that? Lexie!"

"Daniel, *listen.*"

Sirens, somewhere far off in the lanes; more than one.

"The *cops*," Abby said. "Daniel, the cops followed you."

Daniel pushed his hair out of his face with the back of a

wrist. "I doubt it's that simple," he said. "But yes, they're on their way. We don't have long."

"You need to put that away," Abby said. "*Right now.* You too, Lexie. If they see those—"

"Again," Daniel said, "it's not that simple."

He was right behind Justin's chair, the high-backed armchair. It and Justin—petrified, staring, hands clamped on the armrests—shielded him to chest height. Above them was the barrel of the gun, small and dark and wicked, pointed straight at me. The only clear shot I had was a head shot.

"She's right, Daniel," I said. I couldn't even try to take cover behind a chair, not with all these civilians in the room. As long as he had the gun on me, it wasn't on them. "Put it away. How do you think this is going to end best? If the police find us all sitting here peacefully waiting for them, or if they have to bring in a full SWAT team?"

Justin tried to get up, feet scrabbling limply at the floorboards. Daniel took a hand off the gun and shoved him down, hard, into the chair. "Stay there," he said. "You're not going to get hurt. I got you into this; I'll get you out."

"What do you think you're *doing*?" Rafe demanded. "If you have some idea about all of us going down in a blaze of glory, you can stick it—"

"Be quiet," said Daniel.

"Put down yours," I said, "and I'll put down mine. OK?"

In the second when Daniel's attention went to me, Rafe made a grab at his arm. Daniel sidestepped, fast and neatly, and elbowed him in the ribs without ever taking the gun off me. Rafe doubled over with a rough whoosh of breath. "If you do that again," Daniel said, "I'll have to shoot you in the leg. I need to get this done and I don't have time to deal with your distractions. Sit down."

Rafe collapsed on the sofa. "You're insane," he said, between painful wheezes. "You have to know you're insane."

"Please," Abby said. "They're coming. Daniel, Lexie, *please.*"

The sirens were getting closer. A dull clang of metal, booming off the hillsides: Daniel had closed the gates, and someone's car had just rammed them open.

"Lexie," Daniel said, very clearly, for the mike. His glasses were slipping down his nose, but he didn't seem to notice. "I was the one who stabbed you. As the others will have told you, it wasn't premeditated—"

"Daniel," Abby said, high and twisted and breathless. "Don't do this."

I don't think he heard her. "The argument broke out," he told me, "it turned into a fight, and . . . honestly, I don't remember exactly how it happened. I had been doing the washing up, I had a knife in my hand, I was terribly upset at the thought that you wanted to sell your share of the house; I'm sure you can understand that. I wanted to hit you, and I did—with consequences that none of us ever, for one moment, could have foreseen. I'm sorry for any and every wrong I did you. All of you."

Screech of brakes, rush of pebbles scattering; the sirens, howling and mindless outside.

"Put it down, Daniel," I said. He had to know: that I only had a head shot, that I couldn't miss. "It'll be OK. We'll sort everything out, I swear we will. Just put it down."

Daniel looked around at the others: Abby poised ready and helpless, Rafe hunched glaring on the sofa, Justin twisted round to stare up at him with huge frightened eyes. "Shh," he said to them, and put a finger to his lips. I had never seen that much love and tenderness and incredible urgency in anyone's face, ever. "Not one word. No matter what."

They stared at him. "It'll be all right," he said. "Really, it will. It's going to be fine." He was smiling.

Then he turned to me and his head moved, a tiny private nod I'd seen a thousand times before. Me and Rob, eyes catching across a door that wouldn't open, an interview-room table, and that almost invisible nod passing between us: *Go.*

It took so long. Daniel's free hand coming up in slow motion, a long fluid arc, to brace the gun. An immense underwater silence filling the room, all the sirens had fallen away, Justin's mouth was stretched wide but I couldn't hear anything coming out; the only sound in the world was the flat click of Daniel cocking the revolver. Abby's hands going out to him, starfished, her hair swinging up. I had so much time, time to see Justin's head going towards his knees and to swing my gun down to the chest shot opening up, time to watch Daniel's hands tightening around the Webley and to remember what they had felt like on my shoulders, those hands, big and warm and capable. I had time to recognize this feeling from so long ago, remember the acrid smell of panic off Dealer Boy, the steady rush of blood between my fingers; the realization of how easy it was, bleeding to death, how simple, how effortless. Then the world exploded.

I read somewhere that the last word on every crashed airplane's black box, the last thing the pilot says when he knows he's about to die, is "Mammy." When all the world and all your life are ripping away from you at the speed of light, that's the one thing that stays yours. It terrified me, the thought that if someday a suspect got a knife to my throat, if my life shrank to one split second, there might be nothing left inside me to say, no one to call. But what I said, small in the hair-thin silence between Daniel's shot and mine, was "Sam."

Daniel didn't say a word. The impact sent him stagger-ing backwards and the gun dropped from his hand, hit the floor with an ugly thud. Somewhere broken glass was fall-ing, a sweet impervious tinkle. I thought I saw a hole like a cigarette burn, in his white shirt, but I was looking at his face. There was no pain on it, no fear, nothing like that; he didn't even look startled. His eyes were focused on something—I'll never know what—behind my shoulder.

He looked like a steeplechaser or a gymnast, landing perfectly out of the final death-defying leap: intent, tranquil, gone past every limit, holding back nothing; certain.

"No," Abby said, flat and final as an order. Her skirt fluttered, gay in the sunlight, as she leaped for him. Then Daniel blinked and crumpled sideways, slowly, and there was nothing behind Justin except a clean white wall.

25

The next few minutes are shreds of nightmare spliced together with great blank patches. I know I ran, slid on fallen glass and kept running, trying to get to Daniel. I know Abby, crouched over him, fought like a cat to keep me off, wild-eyed, clawing. I remember blood smeared down her T-shirt, the boom echoing through the house as someone broke the front door open, men's voices shouting, feet pounding. Hands under my arms, pulling me back; I twisted and kicked till they gave me a hard shake and my eyes cleared and I recognized Frank's face close to mine, *Cassie it's me stop relax it's over.* Sam shoving him away, his hands rough with panic all over me, checking for bullet holes, fingers coming away bloody *Is that yours is that yours?* I didn't know. Sam turning me, grabbing at me, his voice finally sagging with relief: *You're grand, you're OK, he missed . . .* Someone said something about the window. Someone sobbing. Too much light, colors so bright you could cut yourself, too many voices, *ambulance, get an—*

Finally someone steered me out front and into a marked car, slammed the door. I sat there for a long time, looking at the cherry trees, at the quiet sky slowly dimming, at the distant dark curves of the hills. I didn't think about anything at all.

There are procedures for this, for officer-involved shootings. There are procedures for everything, in the force, going carefully unmentioned till the day they're needed at last and the keeper turns the rusty key, blows dust off the file. I had never met a cop who had shot anyone. There was no one who could have told me what to expect, or how to do this, or that it was all going to be OK.

Byrne and Doherty got stuck taking me to headquarters, in Phoenix Park, where Internal Affairs work in showroom offices and a thick puffy cloud of defensiveness. Byrne drove; the slump of his shoulders said, clear as a voice balloon coming out of his head, *I knew something like this would happen.* I sat in the back like a suspect and Doherty tried to be surreptitious about watching me in the rearview mirror. He was practically drooling: this was probably the most exciting thing that had ever happened to him, plus gossip is good currency in our world and he had just won the lottery. My legs were so cold I could barely move them; I was cold right down to my bones, as if I'd fallen into a freezing lake. At every traffic light Byrne stalled the car and swore morosely.

Everyone hates IA—the Rat Squad, people call them, the quislings, various other less flattering things—but they were good to me, that day at least. They were detached and professional and very gentle, like nurses going through their expert rituals around some patient who had been in a terrible, disfiguring accident. They took my badge—"for the duration of the investigation," someone said soothingly; it felt like they had shaved my head. They peeled off the bandage and unclipped the mike. They took my gun like evidence, which of course it was, careful latex fingers dropping it into an evidence bag, sealing it, labeling it with neat marker strokes. A Bureau tech with her hair in a smooth brown bun like a Victorian maid's stuck a needle in my arm, deftly, and took a blood sample to test for alcohol and drugs; I remembered, vaguely, Rafe pouring and the smooth cool of the glass, but I couldn't remember taking even one sip, and I thought this had to be a good thing. She swabbed my hands for gunshot residue and I noticed, as if I were watching someone else from a long way away, that my hands weren't shaking, they were rock steady, and that a month of Whitethorn House cooking had softened the hollows by my wrist bones. "There," the tech said comfortingly, "quick and painless," but I was busy staring at my hands and it wasn't till hours later, when I was sitting on a neutral-colored lobby sofa under innocuous art waiting for someone to come take me somewhere else, that I realized where I'd heard that tone before: out of my own mouth. Not to victims, not to families; to the others. To men who'd left their wives half blinded, to women who'd scalded their toddlers with boiling water, to killers, in the light-headed disbelieving moments after everything came pouring out, I had said in that infinitely gentle voice, *It's OK, you're OK. Breathe. The worst part's over.*

Outside the lab window the sky had gone black, a tainted rusty black smeared orange with city lights, and there was a thin breakable moon riding low among the treetops in the park. A shiver rocked my spine like a long cold wind. Cop cars speeding through Glenskehy and then away again, John Naylor's eyes pure with rage, and night coming down hard.

I wasn't supposed to talk to Sam or Frank, not till all of us had been interviewed. I told the tech I had to go to the bathroom and gave her a woman-to-woman look to explain why I was taking my jacket with me. In the cubicle I flushed the jacks and while the water was still running—everything about IA makes you paranoid, the thick carpets, the hush—I texted Frank and Sam, fast. *Someone NEEDS to keep an eye on the house.*

I set my phone to silent and sat on the toilet lid, smelling sick fake-flower air freshener and waiting, for as long as I could get away with, but neither of them answered. Their phones were probably off; they would be doing furious full-on interviewing of their own, expertly juggling Abby and Rafe and Justin between them, having quick undertone conferences in corridors, asking questions over and over again with relentless, ferocious patience. Maybe—my heart flipped upwards, punched at the base of my throat—maybe one of them was at the hospital, talking to Daniel. White face, IV lines, people in scrubs moving fast. I tried to remember exactly where the bullet had hit him, ran through it over and over in my head, but the film blinked and stuttered and I couldn't see. That tiny nod; the leap of his gun barrel; recoil slamming up my arms; those grave gray eyes, pupils only a little dilated. Then there was just Abby's voice flat and adamant *No;* the blank wall where Daniel had been standing, and silence, huge and roaring in my ears.

The tech handed me back to the IA guys and they told me that if I was feeling a little shaken up I could wait till the next day to give my statement, but I said no, thanks, I was fine. They explained to me that I had the right to have a lawyer or a union rep present and I said no, thanks, I was fine. Their interview room was smaller than ours, barely room to push your chair back from the table, and cleaner: no graffiti, no cigarette burns in the carpet, no gouges in the walls where someone had gone alpha gorilla with a chair. Both of the IA guys looked like cartoon accountants: gray suits, bald spots, no lips, matching rimless glasses. One of them leaned against the wall behind my shoulder—even if you know all the tactics inside out, they still work on you— and the other one sat across from me. He adjusted his notebook fussily so that it lined up with the edge of the table, turned on his tape recorder and did the preliminary spiel. "Now," he said. "In your own words, Detective."

"Daniel March," I said; they were the only words that would come out. "Is he going to be all right?" and I knew even before he told me, I knew when his eyelids flickered and his eyes slid away from mine.

The Bureau tech—her name was Gillian—drove me home sometime late that night, when the IA twins had finished taking my statement. I told them what you'd expect: the truth, as well as I could put it into words, nothing but the truth, not the whole truth. No, I didn't feel that I'd had any option except to fire my weapon. No, I had had no opportunity to attempt a nonlethal disabling shot. Yes, I had believed my life was in danger. No, there had been no prior indication that Daniel was dangerous. No, he hadn't been our prime suspect, long list of reasons why not—it took me a second to remember them, they felt so long ago and far away, part of a different life. No, I didn't believe it had been remiss of me or Frank or Sam to leave a gun in the house, it was standard undercover practice to leave illegal materials in place for the duration of the investigation, we had had no way to remove it without blowing the whole operation. Yes, in retrospect that decision did appear to have been unwise. They told me we'd talk again soon—they made it sound like a threat—and set up an appointment for me with the shrink, who was going to just about wet his polyester blend over this one.

Gillian needed my clothes—Lexie's clothes—to test for gunshot residue. She stood at the door of my flat, hands folded, watching me while I changed: she had to be sure that what she saw was what she got, no switching out the T-shirt for a clean one. My own clothes felt cold and too stiff, like they didn't belong to me. The flat was cold too, it had a faint dank smell, and there was a thin film of dust on all the surfaces. Sam hadn't come by in a while.

I gave Gillian my clothes and she folded them away, efficiently, in big evidence bags. At the door she hesitated, hands full; for the first time she looked unsure, and I realized she was probably younger than me. "Are you going to be all right on your own?" she asked.

"I'm fine," I said. I had said it enough times, that day, that I was thinking of getting a T-shirt printed.

"Is there anyone who could come stay with you?"

"I'll ring my boyfriend," I said, "he'll come over," even though I wasn't sure that was true; I wasn't sure at all.

When Gillian left carrying the last of Lexie Madison, I sat on my windowsill with a glass of brandy—I hate brandy, but I was pretty sure I was officially in shock in about four different ways, and besides it was the only booze in the flat—and watched the lighthouse beam blinking, serene and regular as a heartbeat, out over the bay. It was some ungodly hour of the night, but I couldn't imagine sleeping; in the faint yellow light from my bedside lamp the futon looked vaguely threatening, overstuffed with squashy heat and bad dreams. I wanted to ring Sam so badly it was like being dehydrated, but I didn't have anything left inside me to handle it, not that night, if he didn't answer.

Somewhere far away a house alarm screamed briefly, till someone switched it off and the silence swelled up again and hissed at me. Off to the south the lights of Dun Laoghaire pier were strung out neat as Christmas lights; beyond them I thought I saw, for a second—trick of the eyes—the silhouette of the Wicklow mountains, against the dark sky. There were only a few stray cars passing down the strand road, that time of night. The smooth sweeps of their headlights grew and faded and I wondered where those people were going, late and solitary, what they were thinking about in the warm bubbles of their cars; what delicate, hard-won, irreplaceable layers of lives were wrapped around them.

I don't think about my parents much. I've only got a handful of memories, and I don't want them wearing away, textures rubbing smooth, colors fading from overexposure. When I take them out, once in a blue moon, I need them bright enough to catch my breath and sharp enough to cut. That night, though, I spread them all on the windowsill like frail pictures cut from tissue paper and went through them, one by one. My mother a nightlight shadow on the side of my bed, just a slim waist and a ponytailed fall of curls, a hand on my forehead and a smell I've never found anywhere else and a low sweet voice singing me to sleep: *A la claire fontaine, m'en allant promener, j'ai trouvé l'eau si belle que je m'y suis baignée . . .* She was younger then than I am now; she never made thirty. My father sitting on a green hill with me and teaching me to tie my shoelaces, his worn brown shoes, his strong hands with a scrape on one knuckle, taste of cherry ice pop on my mouth and both of us giggling at the mess I made. The three of us lying on the sofa under a duvet watching *Bagpuss* on TV, my father's arms holding us together in a big warm tangled bundle, my mother's head nudged under his chin and my ear on his chest so I could feel the buzz of his laugh in my bones. My mother putting on her makeup on her way out to a gig, me sprawled on their bed watching her and twisting the duvet cover around my thumb and asking, *How did you find Daddy?* And her smiling, in the mirror, a small private smile into her own smoky eyes: *I'll tell you that story when you're older. When you've got a little girl of your own. Someday.*

The sky was just starting to turn gray, far out over the horizon, and I was wishing I had a gun to take to the firing range and wondering whether a really serious swig of brandy would let me doze off on the windowsill, when my buzzer rang; a tiny, tentative flick of a ring, so quick I thought I'd imagined it.

It was Sam. He didn't take his hands out of his coat pockets and I didn't touch him. "I didn't want to wake you," he said, "but I figured, if you were awake anyway . . ."

"I can't sleep," I said. "How did it go?"

"Like you'd expect. They're in bits, they hate our guts and they'll be giving us nothing."

"Yeah," I said. "I figured that."

"Are you all right?"

"I'm fine," I said, automatically.

He glanced around the room—too tidy, no plates in the sink, futon still folded up—and blinked hard, like his eyelids were scratchy. "That text you sent me," he said. "I did get on to Byrne, soon as I found the message. He said he'd keep an eye on the place, but . . . You know what he's like. All he did was drive by when he got around to it, on his night round."

Something gauzy and dark swept up behind me,

looming, trembling at my shoulder like a great cat ready to pounce. "John Naylor," I said. "What did he do?"

Sam rubbed his eyes with the heels of his hands. "The firemen think it was petrol. We left crime-scene tape all around the house, but . . . The door was broken in, sure; and that window at the back, the one Daniel shot out. Your man just walked through the tape and straight in."

A pillar of fire on the mountainside. Abby and Rafe and Justin alone in grimy interview rooms, Daniel and Lexie on cold steel. "Did they save anything?"

"By the time Byrne spotted it, and then by the time the fire service got there . . . It's miles from anything."

"I know," I said. Somehow I was sitting down on the futon. I could feel the map of Whitethorn House branded on my bones: the shape of the newel post printed in my palm, the curves of Lexie's bedstead down my spine, the slants and turns of the staircase in my feet, my body turned into a shimmering treasure map for a lost island. What Lexie had started, I had finished for her. Between the two of us, we had razed Whitethorn House to rubble and smoking ash. Maybe that was what she had wanted me for, all along.

"Anyway," Sam said. "I just thought you'd better hear it from me, instead of . . . I don't know, on the morning news. I know the way you felt about that house." Even then, there wasn't a spark of bitterness in his voice, but he didn't come to me and he didn't sit down. He still had his coat on.

"The others," I said. "Do they know?" For a dizzy second, before I remembered how much they hated me now and how much right they had, I thought: *I should tell them. They should hear it from me.*

"Yeah. I told them. They're not mad about me, but Mackey . . . I figured I'd better do it. They . . ." Sam shook his head. The tight twist to one corner of his mouth told me how it had gone. "They'll be all right," he said. "Sooner or later."

"They don't have families," I said. "They don't have friends, nothing. Where are they staying?"

Sam sighed. "They're in custody, sure. Conspiracy to commit murder. It won't stick—we've nothing admissible on them, unless they talk, and they won't—but . . . well. We have to give it a go. Tomorrow, once they're released, Victim Support'll give them a hand finding somewhere to stay."

"What about Whatsisname?" I asked; I could see the name in my head, but it wouldn't come out. "For the fire. Did you pull him in yet?"

"Naylor? Byrne and Doherty went looking for him, but he hasn't shown up yet. No point in chasing after him; he knows those hills like the back of his hand. He'll come home sooner or later. We'll pick him up then."

"What a mess," I said. The dim, unfocused yellow light made the flat feel underground, suffocating. "What a five-star, twenty-four-carat, all-out mess."

"Yeah," Sam said, "well . . ." and hitched vaguely at the shoulders of his coat. He was looking past me, at the last stars fading in the window. "She was bad news from the beginning, that girl. It'll all sort itself out in the end, I suppose. I'd better head. I've to be in early, have another go at those three, for all the good it'll do. I just thought you should know."

"Sam," I said. I couldn't stand up; it took all the guts I had left just to hold out my hand to him. "Stay."

I saw him bite down on the inside of his lip. He still wouldn't meet my eyes. "You should get some sleep too; you must be shattered. And I shouldn't even be here, sure. IA said . . ."

I couldn't say to him, *When I was sure I was about to be shot, you were what I thought in my last second.* I couldn't even say *Please.* All I could do was sit there on the futon with my hand stretched out, not breathing, and hope to God that I hadn't left it too late.

Sam ran a hand over his mouth. "I need to know something," he said. "Are you transferring back to Undercover?"

"*No,*" I said. "Jesus, no. Not a chance in hell. This was different, Sam. This was a once-off."

"Your man Mackey said—" Sam caught himself, shook his head in disgust. "That tosser," he said.

"What did he say?"

"Ah, a load of old shite." Sam sat down on the sofa with a thud, as if someone had cut his strings. "Once an undercover, always an undercover; you'd be back, now you'd had a taste of it. That kind of thing. I couldn't . . . It was bad enough for a few weeks, Cassie. If you went back full-time . . . I can't handle that. I can't."

I was too tired to get properly angry. "Frank was bullshitting," I said. "It's what he does best. He wouldn't have me on his squad even if I wanted to be there—which I don't. He just didn't want you trying to get me to come home. He figured, if you thought I was where I belonged . . ."

"Sounds about right," Sam said, "yeah." He stared down at the coffee table, rubbed dust off it with his fingertips. "So you're staying in DV? For definite?"

"If I've still got a job after yesterday, you mean?"

"Yesterday was Mackey's fault," Sam said, and even through all the exhaustion I saw the hard flare of anger across his face. "Not yours. Every single bloody bit of this is on Mackey. IA aren't eejits; they'll see that, same as everyone else does."

"It wasn't just Frank's fault," I said. "I was there, Sam. I let things get out of control, I let Daniel get his hands on a gun, and then I shot him. I can't put that on Frank."

"And I let him run with his lunatic bloody idea, and I've to live with that. But he's the one who was in charge. When you take that on, you have to take responsibility for whatever comes out of it. If he tries to dump this mess on you—"

"He won't," I said. "Not his style."

"Seems to me it's exactly his style," Sam said. He shook his head, shaking off the thought of Frank. "We'll deal with that when it comes. But say you're right, and he doesn't shaft you to save his own arse; you're staying in DV?"

"For now," I said, "yeah. But down the line . . ." I hadn't even known I was going to say this, it was the last thing I'd ever expected to come out of my mouth, but once I heard the words it seemed to me that they'd been waiting for me to find them ever since that luminous afternoon with Daniel, under the ivy. "I miss Murder, Sam. I miss it like hell, all the time. I want to come back."

"Right," Sam said. His head went back and he took a breath. "Yeah, I thought that, all right. That's the end of us, then."

You're not allowed to go out with anyone on your squad—as O'Kelly elegantly puts it, no shagging on the company copier. "No," I said. "Sam, no; it doesn't have to be. Even if O'Kelly's on for taking me back, there might not be an opening for years, and who knows where we'll be by then? You could be running a squad of your own." He didn't smile. "If it comes down to it, we'll just stay under the radar. It happens all the time, Sam. You know it does. Barry Norton and Elaine Leahy—" Norton and Leahy have been on Motor Vehicles for ten years and living together for eight of them. They pretend to carpool, and everyone including their super pretends not to know.

Sam shook his head, like a big dog waking up. "That's not what I want," he said. "All the best to them, and all, but I want this to be real. Maybe you'd be grand with having what they've got—I always figured that was one reason why you didn't want to tell people about us, sure: so you could maybe come back to Murder, someday. But I'm not after a shag, or a fling, or some half-arsed part-time thing where we have to act like we're . . ." He fumbled inside his coat; he was so exhausted that he was pawing at it as if he were drunk. "I've been carrying this around with me since two weeks after we started going out. Remember, we went for that walk round Howth Head? It was a Sunday?"

I remembered. A cool gray day, soft rain weightless in the air, wide smell of sea filling my chest; Sam's mouth tasted of wild salt. We walked on the edges of high cliffs all afternoon and ate fish and chips on a bench for dinner, my legs were killing me, and it was the first time after Operation Vestal that I can remember feeling like me.

"The day after," Sam said, "I bought this. On my lunch break." He found what he'd been looking for and dropped it on the coffee table. It was a blue velvet ring box.

"Oh, Sam," I said. "Oh, Sam."

"I meant it," Sam said. "This. You; us. I wasn't just having a laugh."

"Neither was I," I said. That observation room; the look in his eyes. *Was.* "Never. I just . . . I got lost along the way, for a while. I'm so sorry, Sam. I fucked up every way there is, and I'm so sorry."

"I *love* you, for Christ's sake. You going off undercover like that, I nearly went mental—and I couldn't even talk to anyone about it, because no one knew. I can't . . ."

He trailed off, rubbed his eyes with the heels of his hands. I knew there had to be some delicate way of asking this, but the edges of my vision kept warping and flicking and I couldn't think straight. I wondered if there could have been a worse time for this conversation. "Sam," I said, "I killed a person today. Yesterday; whatever. I don't have any brain cells left. You're going to have to spell it out: are you breaking up with me or proposing to me?" I was pretty sure which one it was. All I wanted was to get it over with, do the good-bye routine, and chug the rest of the brandy till I knocked myself out.

Sam gave the ring box a baffled look, as if he wasn't sure how it had got there. "Jesus," he said. "I didn't . . . I'd it all planned: dinner somewhere nice, with a view, like. And champagne. But I suppose—I mean, now that . . ."

He picked up the box, opened it. I couldn't catch up; the only thing that registered was that he didn't seem to be dumping me, and that the relief was purer and more painful than I could have imagined. Sam disentangled himself from the sofa and got down on one knee, clumsily, on the floor.

"Right," he said, and held out the box to me. He was

white and wide-eyed; he looked as stunned as I was. "Will you marry me?"

The only thing I wanted to do was laugh—not at him, just at the sheer screaming pitch of crazy that day had managed to hit. I was scared that if I started I wouldn't be able to stop. "I know," Sam said, and swallowed, "I know it'd mean you couldn't come back to Murder—not without special permission, and . . ."

"And neither of us is going to get any special treatment any time soon," I said. Daniel's voice brushed along my cheek like dark feathers, like a long night wind coming down from some far mountain. *Take what you want and pay for it, says God.*

"Yeah. If . . . God. If you want to think about it . . ." Another swallow. "You don't need to decide right now, sure. I know tonight's not the best moment for . . . But maybe it needed doing. Sooner or later, I need to know."

The ring was a simple one, a slim hoop with one round diamond glittering like a dewdrop. I had never in my life pictured an engagement ring on my finger. I thought of Lexie slipping hers off in a dark room, leaving it beside the bed she had shared with Chad, and I felt the difference slide into the crack between us like a narrow blade: I couldn't put this on without knowing that it would stay on, for good.

"I want you to be happy," Sam said. That stunned look had faded out of his eyes; they were clear and unfaltering on mine. "Whatever that takes. There's no point if you're not going to be . . . If you can't be happy without coming back on the squad, then tell me."

There's so little mercy in this world. Lexie sliced straight through everyone who got between her and the door, people she had laughed with, worked with, lain down with. Daniel, who loved her like his blood, sat beside her and watched her die, sooner than allow a siege on his spellbound castle. Frank took me by the shoulders and steered me straight into something that he knew could eat me alive. Whitethorn House let me into its secret chambers and healed my wounds, and in exchange I set my careful charges and I blew it to smithereens. Rob, my partner, my shield-mate, my closest friend, ripped me out of his life and threw me away because he wanted me to sleep with him and I did it. And when we had all finished clawing chunks off each other, Sam, who had every right to give me the finger and walk away for good, stayed because I held out my hand and asked him to.

"I want to go back to Murder," I said, "but it doesn't need to be now. It doesn't even need to be soon. Someday, sooner or later, one of us will do something brilliant and we'll have all the brownie points in the world, and then we'll ask for special permission."

"And if we don't? If we never do anything brilliant, or if they say no anyway. Then what?"

That wing brush again, along the line of my jaw. *To go consenting.*

"Then," I said, "I'll survive. And you'll have to put up with me bitching about Maher for the rest of our lives." I stretched out my hand to Sam and I saw the look that was dawning in his eyes, and as he reached over to put the ring on my finger I realized there was no jagged black terror falling through me this time, no wild scream at the irrevocable thing inches away and rising, I wasn't frightened at all; the only thing I felt was sure.

Later, when we were cocooned in the duvet and the sky outside was turning salmon-colored, Sam said, "There's one more thing I need to ask you, and I'm not sure how to do it."

"Ask away," I said. "Comes with the territory." I waved my left hand at him. The ring looked good on there. It even fit.

"No," Sam said. "Something serious."

I figured at this point I was ready for anything. I turned over on my stomach and propped myself up so I could look at him properly.

"Rob," he said. "You and Rob. I saw the way you were together, the two of ye; how close you were. I always expected . . . I never thought I had a look in."

This one I had not been ready for.

"I don't know what went wrong between ye," Sam said, "and I'm not asking. I've no right to know. Just . . . I've some idea what you went through, during Operation Vestal. And after. I wasn't trying to be nosy, nothing like that; but I was there."

He looked up at me, steady gray eyes, unblinking. There was nothing I could say; my breath was gone.

It was that night with the headlights, the night I went to get Rob at the crime scene. I knew him well enough to know that otherwise he would disintegrate, just smash into a million pieces, but not well enough to guess that he would do it anyway, and that all I had done was draw the flak my way. We did something good; I thought that meant no damage could come of it. It's occurred to me since that I may be a lot dumber than I look. If I learned one thing in Murder, it's that innocence isn't enough.

I'm not Lexie, I'm not clockwork, specially not when I'm wrecked and stressed and wretched. By the time the terrible sinking feeling kicked in, I had moved to DV, Rob had been bounced into bureaucratic limbo somewhere and all our bridges were burned to bitter ash; he had gone so far away I couldn't even see him on the other side. I didn't tell anyone. I got the boat to England before dawn one sleety Saturday and was back in my dark flat that night—the plane would have been faster but I couldn't take it, the thought of sitting still for an hour each way, squashed elbow to elbow between strangers. I walked up and down the deck of the boat instead. On the way back the sleet came down harder, soaked me to the bone; if there had been anyone else on deck they would have thought I was crying, but I wasn't, not even once.

Sam was the only person I could stand to be around,

then. Everyone else was on the other side of a thick, wavy glass wall, they yammered and gestured and pulled faces and it took all the energy I had to work out what they wanted from me and make the right noises back. Sam was the only one I could hear. He has a beautiful voice: a country voice, slow and calm, deep and rich as earth. That voice was the one thing that made it through the glass and felt real.

When we met for coffee that Monday after work, he gave me a long intent look and then said, "You look like you've the flu; it's going around. I'll bring you home, will I?" He tucked me into bed, went to the shops to buy food, came back and cooked me stew. Every night that week he made me dinner and told terrible jokes till I laughed just at the hopeful look on his face. Six weeks later, I was the one who kissed him first. When those square gentle hands touched my skin I could feel ripped cells healing. I never fell for Sam's big-thick-bogger act, I was always sure there was more; but it had never once occurred to me—I told you I'm dumber than I look—that he had known, every step of the way, and known to leave it.

"The only bit I need to know," Sam said, "is whether it's over, for you; the whole thing. Whether . . . I can't be wondering, our whole lives, what would happen if Rob got his head together and came back wanting to . . . I know how hard it was for you. I tried to—give you space, I suppose they call it; to figure things out. But now, if we're really engaged . . . I just need to know."

The first sunlight was exploding onto his face, turning him grave and clear-eyed as some tired apostle in a window. "It's over," I said. "It really is, Sam. It's all over now."

I laid a hand on his cheek; it was so bright that for a second I thought it was burning me, a pure painless fire. "Good," he said, on a sigh, and his hand came up to cup the back of my head and pull me down on his chest. "That's good," and his eyes were closing before he finished the sentence.

. . .

I slept till two in the afternoon. Sometime in there Sam dragged himself out of bed and kissed me good-bye and closed the door softly behind him, but nobody rang to tell me to get my arse into work, presumably because nobody had managed to disentangle what squad I was on right then or whether I was suspended or whether I still had a job at all. When I finally woke up I considered calling in sick, but I wasn't sure who to call—Frank, probably, but he was unlikely to be in a conversational mood. I decided to let someone else figure this one out. Instead I headed up to Sandymount village, kept my eyes off the newspaper headlines, bought food, went home and ate most of it, and then took a very long walk on the beach.

It was a sunny, lazy afternoon. The promenade was full of old people wandering along with their faces turned up to the sun, couples leaning into each other, overexcited toddlers tumbling along like big sweet bumblebees. I recognized a lot of people. Sandymount's still holding onto being that kind of place, where you know faces and swap smiles and buy homemade perfume from the neighbors' kids; it's one of the reasons I live there, but that evening it felt strange and disconcerting all the same. I felt like I had been away too long for that, long enough that the shop fronts should all have been different, the houses painted new colors, the familiar faces grown up, grown old, gone.

The tide was out. I took off my shoes, rolled up my jeans and walked out onto the sand till the water was ankle-deep. One moment from the day before fell through my head, over and over: Rafe's voice, soft and dangerous as snow, saying to Justin, *You bastard fuck.*

This is what I could have done, in that last second before it all exploded: I could have said, "Justin? *You* stabbed me?" He would have answered. It would have been there on the tape, and sooner or later Frank or Sam would have found a way to make him say it again, under caution this time.

Probably I'll never know why I didn't do it. Mercy, maybe; one drop of it, too little and too late. Or—this is the one Frank would have picked—too much emotional involvement, even then: Whitethorn House and the five of them still dusted over me like pollen, still turning me glittering and defiant, *us against the world.* Or maybe, and I like to hope it was this one, because the truth is more intricate and less attainable than I used to understand, a bright illusive place reached by twisting back roads as often as by straight avenues, and this was the closest I could come.

When I got home Frank was sitting on my front steps with one leg stretched out, teasing the next-door cat with an untied shoelace and whistling "Leave Her, Johnny, Leave Her" through his front teeth. He looked terrible, crumpled and bleary-eyed and in serious need of a shave. When he saw me he folded his leg back under him and stood up, sending the cat whisking off into the bushes.

"Detective Maddox," he said. "You didn't show for work today. Is there a problem?"

"I wasn't sure who I work for right now," I said. "If anyone. Plus I slept it out. I'm owed a few days' holiday; I'll take one of those."

Frank sighed. "Never mind. I'll sort something out—you can count as one of mine for another day. Starting tomorrow, though, you're DV again." He stood aside to let me open the door. "It's been very."

"Yeah," I said. "That it has."

He followed me up the stairs into my flat and headed straight for the cooker—there was still half a pot of coffee left over from my unidentified meal earlier on. "That's what I like to see," he said, finding a mug on the draining board. "A detective who's always prepared. You having some?"

"I've had loads," I said. "Go for it." I couldn't work out what he was there for: to debrief me, kick my arse, kiss and make up, what. I hung up my jacket and started pulling the sheets off the futon, so we could both sit down without having to get too close.

"So," Frank said, shoving his mug into the microwave and hitting buttons. "You hear about the house?"

"Sam told me."

I felt his head turn; I kept my back to him, hauling the futon into its sofa version. After a moment he started the microwave whirring. "Well," he said. "Easy come, easy go. It was probably insured. You talk to IA yet?"

"Oh yeah," I said. "They're thorough."

"They come down hard on you?"

I shrugged. "No more than you'd expect. How about you?"

"We've got history," Frank said, without elaborating. The microwave beeped; he got the sugar bowl out of its cupboard and dumped three spoons in his coffee. Frank doesn't take sugar; he was fighting hard to stay awake. "The shoot'll come back good. I had a listen to the tapes: three shots, the first two a fair distance from you—the computer lads will be able to work out exactly how far—and then the third right by the mike, nearly blew my eardrums. And I had a little chat with my mate in the Bureau, too, once they'd finished with the scene. Apparently the trajectory of one of Daniel's bullets came up almost a perfect mirror image of yours. No question: you only fired after he'd shot directly at you."

"I know," I said. I folded the sheets and threw them in the wardrobe. "I was there."

He leaned back against the counter, took a mouthful of coffee and watched me. "Don't let the IA boys rattle you."

"This was a mess, Frank," I said. "The media are going to be all over it, and the brass are going to want someone to take the fall."

"For what? The shoot was textbook. The house is on Byrne: he was warned to look after it, he didn't follow through. Everything else along the way, we've got the ultimate defense: it worked. We got our man, even if we didn't get a chance to arrest him. Just as long as you don't do anything stupid—anything else stupid—we should all be able to walk away from this."

I sat down on the futon and found my smokes. I couldn't tell whether he was reassuring me or threatening me, or maybe a little of both. "What about you?" I asked, carefully. "If you've got history with IA . . ."

Flick of an eyebrow. "Nice to know you care. I've also got leverage, if it comes down to that."

That tape—me disobeying a direct order, telling him I wasn't coming in—flashed between us, solid as if he had tossed it onto the table. It wouldn't get him off the hook— you're supposed to be able to control your squad—but it would drag me in there with him, and it might muddy the waters enough to let him wriggle away. In that moment I knew that if Frank wanted to pin this whole mess on me, blast me right out of my career, he could do it; and that he probably had every right.

I saw the tiny flash of amusement, in those bloodshot eyes: he knew what I was thinking. "Leverage," I said.

"Don't I always," said Frank, and just for a second he sounded tired and old. "Listen, IA need to throw their weight around, makes them feel like they can get it up, but as of now, they're not out to get you—or your Sammy, come to that. They'll give me a fun few weeks, but we'll all be fine in the end."

The shot of anger startled me. Whether or not Frank decided to throw me to the wolves—and I knew nothing I could say would sway him one way or the other—*fine* was not the word I personally would have picked for anything about this situation. "Right," I said. "That's good to hear."

"Then why the long face? As the bartender said to the horse."

I almost threw the lighter at his head. "Jesus Christ, Frank! I killed Daniel. I lived under his roof, I sat next to him at his table, I ate his food"—I didn't say, *I kissed him*—"and then I killed him. Every day for what should have been the rest of his life, he won't be here, and it'll be because of me. I went in there to *catch* a murderer, I spent

570 · Tana French

years throwing my heart and soul into doing that, and now
I'm—" I shut up because my voice was shaking.

"You know something?" Frank said, after a moment.
"You've got a bad habit of taking too much credit for the
stuff other people do around you." He brought his mug over
to the sofa and collapsed, legs spread wide. "Daniel March
was no idiot. He knew exactly what he was doing, and he
deliberately forced you into a position where you had absolutely no choice except to take him down. That wasn't
homicide, Cassie. It wasn't even self-defense. That right
there was suicide by cop."

"I know," I said. "I know that."

"He knew he was cornered, he had no intention of going
to prison—and I don't blame him; can you see him making
friends with the boys on the cell block? So he picked his way
out and he went for it. I'll give the guy this: he had guts. I
underestimated him."

"Frank," I said. "Have you ever killed anyone?"

He reached for my smoke packet, watched the flame as
he lit his cigarette one-handed. "Yesterday was a good
shoot," he said, when he'd put his lighter away. "It happened, it was no fun, in a few weeks it'll be over. The end."

I didn't answer. Frank blew a long trail of smoke at the
ceiling. "Look, you closed the case. If you had to shoot
someone along the way, it might as well have been Daniel.
I never liked the little fucker."

I was in no mood to keep a lid on my temper, not with
him. "Yeah, Frankie, I spotted that. Everyone within a mile
of this case spotted that. And you know why you didn't like
him? Because he was exactly like you."

"Well well well," Frank drawled. There was an amused
twist to his mouth, but his eyes were ice blue and unblinking and I couldn't tell whether he was furious or not. "And
here I almost forgot you'd studied the old psychology."

"The spitting image, Frank."

"Bull*shit*. That guy was wrong, Cassie. Remember what

you said, in your profile? Prior criminal experience. Remember that?"

"What, Frank," I said. I realized my feet had come out from under me and were braced, hard, on the floor. "What did you find on Daniel?"

Frank shook his head, one small ambiguous jerk, over his cigarette. "I didn't need to find anything. I know when someone smells wrong, and so do you. There's a line, Cassie. You and me, we live on one side of it. Even when we fuck up and wander over to the other side, we've got that line to keep us from getting lost. Daniel didn't have it."

He leaned over the coffee table to tap ash. "There's a line," he said. "Don't ever forget there's a line."

There was a long silence. The window was starting to dim again. I wondered about Abby and Rafe and Justin, where they would spend tonight; whether John Naylor would sleep sprawled in moonlight on the ruins of Whitethorn House, the one-night king of all our wreckage. I knew what Frank would say: *Not your problem, not any more.*

"What I'd love to know," Frank said after a while, and his tone had changed, "is when Daniel made you. Because he did, you know." Fast glint of blue, as he glanced up at me. "From the way he talked, I'm pretty sure he knew you were wired—but that's not what's bothering me. We could have wired Lexie, if we'd had her; the wire wasn't enough to tell him you were a cop. But when Daniel walked into that house yesterday, he knew for definite that you had a gun on you, and that you'd use it." He settled into the sofa, one arm spread along the back, and drew on his smoke. "Any idea what gave you away?"

I shrugged. "I'd bet on the onions. I know we figured I'd saved that, but apparently Daniel played better poker than we thought."

"No kidding," said Frank. "And you're sure that's all it was? He didn't have a problem with, for example, your taste in music?"

He knew; he knew about the Fauré. There was no way he could be certain, but all his instincts were telling him something was there. I made myself meet his eyes, look puzzled and a little rueful. "Nothing springs to mind."

Curls of smoke hanging in the sunlight. "Right," Frank said, at last. "Well. They say the devil's in the details. There's nothing you could have done about those onions—which means there's nothing you could have done to prevent yourself getting burned. Right?"

"Right," I said, and that at least came easy. "I did everything I could, Frank. I was Lexie Madison as hard as I knew how."

"And if, just say, you'd figured out a couple of days ago that Daniel had made you, is there anything you could have done that might have made this end better?"

"No," I said, and I knew that was true too. This day had begun years before, in Frank's office, over burnt coffee and chocolate biscuits. By the time I tucked that timeline into my uniform shirt and walked back to the bus station, this day had been ready and waiting for us all. "I think this was the happiest ending we were ever going to get."

He nodded. "Then you did your job. Leave it at that. You can't blame yourself for the stuff other people do."

I didn't even try to explain to him what I was seeing, the fine spreading web through which we had all tugged one another to this place, the multiple innocences that make up guilt. I thought of Daniel with that unutterable sadness like a brand on his face, telling me, *Lexie had no conception of action and consequence,* and I felt that slim blade slide deeper between her and me, twisting.

"Which," Frank said, "brings me to my reason for coming over here. I've got one more question left about this case, and I've got a funny feeling you might know the answer." He glanced up from picking something out of his mug. "Did Daniel really stab our girl? Or was he just taking the rap, for some fucked-up reason all his own?"

Those level blue eyes, across the coffee table. "You heard

what I heard," I said. "He's the only one who got specific; the other three never gave me a name. Are they saying it wasn't him?"

"They're saying sweet fuck-all. We've been going at them all today and most of last night, and we've yet to get a word out of them beyond 'I want a glass of water.' Justin did a fair bit of crying, and Rafe threw a chair when he found out he'd been nursing a viper in his bosom for the past month— we had to slap him in cuffs till he settled down—but that's as far as the communication goes. They're like bloody prisoners of war."

Daniel's finger pressed to his lips, his eyes moving among the others with an intensity I hadn't understood, then. Even for this point beyond the farthest horizon of his own life, he had had a plan. And the other three, whether out of faith in him or out of habit or just because they had nothing else left to hold on to, were still doing what he had told them to do.

"One reason I ask," Frank said, "is because the stories don't quite match. Almost, but not quite. Daniel told you he happened to have a knife in his hand, because he was washing up; but on the tape, Rafe and Justin both describe Daniel using two hands in the struggle with Lexie. *Before* she got stabbed."

"Maybe they're confused," I said. "It happened fast; you know what eyewitness accounts are worth. Or maybe Daniel was minimizing: trying to claim he just happened to have the knife, when actually he picked it up specifically to stab Lexie. We'll probably never know exactly what happened."

Frank drew on his cigarette, watching the tiny red glow. "As far as I can tell," he said, "there's only one person who was washing up, and who wasn't doing something else with his hands between the point when the note came out and the point when Lexie got stabbed."

"Daniel killed her," I said, and it didn't feel like a lie then and it doesn't now. "I'm positive, Frank. He was telling the truth."

Frank watched my face for a long minute, searching. Then: "OK," he said, on a sigh. "I'll take your word for it. I'm never going to think he was the type to snap like that, no plan, no organization; but hey, maybe we had less in common than you think. My money was on someone else from the start, but if everyone wants it to be Daniel . . ." A small backwards jerk of his head, like a shrug. "There's not a lot I can do about it."

He stubbed out his smoke and stood up. "Here," he said, fishing in a jacket pocket. "I figure you might as well have this."

He tossed something across the table to me; it flashed in the sunlight and I caught it reflexively, one-handed. It was a minicassette, the kind Undercover uses to record a mike feed.

"That's you flushing your career down the jacks. I seem to have stepped on a cable while I was on the phone to you that day, disconnected something. The official tape has about fifteen minutes of nothing, before I caught the problem and plugged everything back in. The techs want me drawn and quartered for abusing their beloved gadgetry, but they'll just have to get in the queue."

Not his style, I had said to Sam the night before; not Frank's style, to let me take the fall. And before that, way back at the beginning: Lexie Madison was Frank's responsibility when he made her from nothing, she stayed his responsibility when she turned up dead. It wasn't that he felt guilty about this godawful mess, nothing like that—once IA got off his back, he would probably never think about it again. But some people take care of their own, no matter what that turns out to mean.

"No copies," Frank said. "You'll be fine."

"When I said you're a lot like Daniel," I said, "that wasn't an insult."

I saw the flick of something complicated in his eyes as he took that in. After a long moment, he nodded. "Fair enough," he said.

"Thanks, Frank," I said, and closed my hand over the tape. "Thank you."

"Whoa," Frank said suddenly. His hand shot out, across the table, and grabbed my wrist. "And what's this?"

The ring. I'd forgotten; my head was still getting used to it. It took an effort not to giggle at the look on his face. I'd never seen Frank Mackey truly gobsmacked before. "I think it suits me," I said. "You like?"

"Is this new? Or did I miss something before?"

"Pretty new," I said, "yeah."

That lazy, malicious grin, tongue stretching his cheek; all of a sudden he looked wide awake and sparking with energy, ready to roll. "Well, fuck me sideways with a broomstick," he said. "I don't know which of you two just surprised me more. I've got to say, hand on heart, I take my hat off to your Sammy. Wish him good luck from me, will you?"

He started to laugh. "Holy Mother of the Divine," he said, "if this hasn't just about made my day. Cassie Maddox getting married! Sweet Jesus! Wish that man luck from me!" and he ran off down the stairs, still laughing at the top of his lungs.

I sat there on the futon for a long time, turning the tape in my hands and trying to remember what else was on there—what I had done, that day, besides go all in and dare Frank to fire me. Hangovers, coffee and Bloody Marys and all of us sniping at each other. Daniel's voice saying, in Lexie's darkened bedroom, *Who are you?* Fauré.

I think Frank expected me to destroy the tape, unspool it and stick it through a home shredder—I don't have one, but I bet he does. Instead I climbed up on the kitchen counter, got my Official Stuff shoebox off the cupboard and put the tape inside, in with my passport and my birth cert and my medical records and my Visa bills. I want to listen to it, someday.

26

A few weeks after the end of Operation Mirror, while I was still fucking about with paper and waiting for somebody somewhere to decide something, Frank phoned me. "I've got Lexie's dad on the line," he said. "He wants to talk to you." A click, and then nothing but the little red light on my phone blinking, for a call waiting to be picked up.

I was driving a desk in the DV squad room. It was lunchtime, a still blue-sky summer day; everyone else had headed out to lie in Stephen's Green with their sleeves rolled up and hope for some kind of tan, but I was avoiding Maher, who kept edging his chair closer to mine and asking me conspiratorially what it felt like to shoot someone, so most days I invented urgent paperwork and then took a very late lunch.

It had been this simple, in the end: half the world away, a very young cop called Ray Hawkins had gone to work one morning and forgotten his house keys. His dad had dropped them in to him at the station. The father was a retired detective, and he had automatically scanned the notice board behind the desk—alerts, stolen cars, missing persons— while he handed over the keys and reminded Ray to pick up fish for dinner on the way home. And then he'd said, *Hang on a sec; I've seen that girl somewhere.* After that, all they had had to do was go back through years of missing-person files till that face leaped out at them, one last time.

Her name was Grace Audrey Corrigan and she had been two years younger than me. Her father was called Albert. He worked a small cattle station called Merrigullan, somewhere out in the huge nameless spaces of Western Australia. He hadn't seen her in thirteen years.

Frank had told him that I was the detective who had spent most time on the case, the one who had cracked it in the end. His accent was so blunt that it took a while for my ear to catch up. I expected a million questions but he didn't ask me anything, not at first. Instead he told me things: all the things I could never have asked him for. His voice— deep, gruff-edged, a big man's voice—moved slowly, with big gaps like he wasn't used to talking, but he talked for a long time. He had saved up thirteen years' worth of words, waiting for this day to come find him.

Gracie had been a good kid, he said, when she was little. Sharp as a knife, smart enough for college twice over, but she wasn't interested. A homebody, Albert Corrigan said; eight years old and explaining to him how as soon as she was eighteen she was going to marry one of the jackaroos, so they could take over the place and look after him and her mum when they got old. "She had it all planned out," he said. Through it all, there were the leftovers of an old smile in his voice. "Told me that in a few years I should start keeping that in mind when I was hiring—keep an eye out for someone she could marry. Said she liked tall blokes with blond hair, and she didn't mind blokes who shouted but she didn't like the ones who got drunk. She always did know what she wanted, Gracie."

But when she was nine her mother had hemorrhaged, giving birth to Grace's baby brother, and bled out before a doctor could get there. "Gracie was too young to hear that," he said. I knew from the simple, heavy fall of his voice that he had thought this a million times, it had worn a long groove in his mind. "I knew as soon as I told her. The look in her eyes: she was too young to hear it. It cracked her straight across. If she'd been even a couple of years older, she might've been all right. But she changed, after that. Nothing you could put your finger on. She was still a great kid, still did her schoolwork and all that, didn't talk back. Took over running the house—little slip of a thing making beef stew for dinner like she'd seen her mum do, on a stove bigger than her. But I never knew what was going on in her head again."

In the gaps the static roared in my ear, a long muted sound like a seashell. I wished I knew more about Australia. I thought of red earth and sun that hit you like a shout, twisted plants stubborn enough to pull life out of nothing, spaces that could dizzy you, swallow you whole.

She had been ten the first time she ran away. They found her inside a few hours, out of water and crying with fury by the side of the road, but she did it again the next year, and the next. She got a little farther each time. In between she never mentioned it, gave him a blank stare when he tried to talk about it. He never knew what morning he would wake up and find her gone. He put blankets on his bed in summer and none in winter, trying to make himself sleep lightly enough to wake at the click of a door.

"She got it right when she was sixteen," he said, and I heard him swallow. "Nicked three hundred quid from under my mattress and a Land Rover from the farm, let the air out of the tires on all the other cars to slow us down. By the time we got after her she'd made it to town, ditched the Land Rover at the service station and got a lift from some truckie headed east. The coppers said they'd do their best, but if she didn't want to be found . . . It's a big country."

He'd heard nothing for four months, while he dreamed of her thrown away on some roadside, picked clean by dingoes under a huge red moon. Then, the day before his birthday, he'd got a card.

"Hang on," he said. Rustling, a bump; a dog barking, somewhere far off. "Here we go. Says, 'Dear Dad, happy birthday. I'm fine. I've got a job and I've got good mates. I'm not coming back but I wanted to say hi. Love, Grace. P.S. Don't worry, I'm not a pro.'" He laughed, that gruff little breath again. "Isn't that something? She was right, you know, I'd been worrying about that—pretty girl with no qualifications . . . But she wouldn't have bothered saying that if it wasn't true. Not Gracie."

The postmark said Sydney. He had dropped everything, driven to the nearest airfield and caught the mail plane east to put crappy photocopied fliers on lampposts, HAVE YOU SEEN THIS GIRL? Nobody had called. Next year's card had come from New Zealand: "Dear Dad, happy birthday. Please quit looking for me. I had to move because I saw a poster of me. I AM FINE so knock it off. Love, Grace. P.S. I don't actually live in Wellington, I just came here to post this, so don't bother."

He didn't have a passport, didn't even know how to set about getting one. Grace was only a few weeks off eighteen, and the Wellington cops pointed out, reasonably enough, that there wasn't much they could do if a healthy adult decided to move out of home. There had been two more cards from there—she'd got a dog, and a guitar—and then, in 1996, one from San Francisco. "So she made it to America in the end," he said. "God only knows how she got herself over there. I guess Gracie never did let anything stand in her way." She had liked it there—she took the tram car to work, and her flatmate was a sculptor who was teaching her how to throw pottery—but the next year she was in North Carolina, no explanation. Four cards from there, one from Liverpool with a picture of the Beatles on it, then the three from Dublin.

"She had your birthday marked in her date book," I said. "I know she would have sent you one this year too."

"Yeah," he said. "Probably she would." Somewhere in the background, something—a bird—gave a loud witless yelp. I thought of him sitting on a battered wooden veranda, thousands of miles of wild stretching all around him, with their own pure and merciless rules.

There was a long silence. I realized I had slid my free hand, elegantly, into the neck of my top, to touch Sam's engagement ring. Until Operation Mirror was officially closed out and we could tell people without giving IA a collective aneurysm, I was wearing it on a fine gold chain that used to be my mother's. It hung between my breasts, just about where the mike had been. Even on cold days, it felt warmer than my skin.

"How'd she turn out?" he asked, at last. "What was she like?"

His voice had gone lower, rough at the edges. He needed to know. I thought about May-Ruth bringing her fiancé's parents a house plant, Lexie throwing strawberries at Daniel and giggling, Lexie shoving that cigarette case deep into the long grass, and I had absolutely no clue what the answer was.

"She was still smart," I said. "She was doing a postgrad in English. She still didn't let anything get in her way. Her friends loved her, and she loved them. They were happy together." In spite of everything the five of them had done to one another in the end, I believed that. I still do.

"That's my girl," he said, absently. "That's my girl . . ."

He was thinking about things I had no way of knowing. After a while he took a fast breath, coming out of his reverie. "One of them killed her, though, didn't he?"

It had taken him a long time to ask. "Yes," I said, "he did. If it's any comfort, he didn't mean to do it. It wasn't planned, nothing like that. They just had an argument. He happened to have a knife in his hand, because he was doing the washing up, and he lost his temper."

"She suffer?"

"No," I said. "No, Mr. Corrigan. The pathologist says all she would have felt before she lost consciousness is shortness of breath and a fast heartbeat, as if she'd been running too hard." *It was peaceful,* I almost said; but those hands.

He said nothing for so long that I wondered if the line had gone or if he had walked away, just put the phone down and left the room; if he was leaning on a railing somewhere, taking deep breaths of wild cool evening air. People were starting to come back from lunch: footsteps thumping up the stairs, someone in the corridor bitching about paperwork, Maher's big belligerent laugh. *Hurry,* I wanted to say; *we don't have much time.*

Finally he sighed, one long slow breath. "Do you know what I remember?" he said. "The night before she ran away, that last time. We were sitting out on the veranda after dinner, Gracie was having sips of my beer. She looked so beautiful. More like her mum than ever: calm, for once. Smiling at me. I thought it meant . . . well, I thought she'd settled, finally. Maybe taken a fancy to one of the jackaroos—she looked like that, like a girl does when she's in love. I thought, *That's our baby, Rachel. Isn't she gorgeous? She turned out all right, in the end.*"

It sent strange things fluttering in my head, frail as moths circling. Frank hadn't told him: not about the undercover angle, not about me. "She did, Mr. Corrigan," I said. "In her own way, she did."

"Maybe," he said. "Sounds like. I just wish . . ." Somewhere that bird screamed again, a long desolate alarm call fading off into the distance. "What I'm saying is, I reckon you're right: that fella didn't mean to kill her. I reckon it was always going to happen, one way or another. She wasn't made right for this world. She'd been running away from it since she was nine."

Maher slammed into the squad room, bellowed something at me, whapped a big piece of sticky-looking cake onto his desk and started disemboweling it. I listened to the static echoing in my ear and thought of those herds of horses you get in the vast wild spaces of America and Australia, the ones running free, fighting off bobcats or dingoes and living lean on what they find, gold and tangled in the fierce sun. My friend Alan from when I was a kid, he worked on a ranch in Wyoming one summer, on a J1 visa. He watched guys breaking those horses. He told me that every now and then there was one that couldn't be broken, one wild to the bone. Those horses fought the bridle and the fence till they were ripped up and streaming blood, till they smashed their legs or their necks to splinters, till they died of fighting to run.

Frank turned out to be right: we all came out of Operation Mirror just fine, or at least no one ended up fired or in jail, which I think probably meets Frank's standard for "fine." He got docked three days' holiday and got a reprimand on his file, officially for letting his investigation get out of control—with a mess this size, IA needed someone's head to go on the block, and I got the feeling they were delighted to let it be Frank's. The media had a shot at whipping up some kind of frenzy about police brutality, but nobody would talk to them—the most they got was a shot of Rafe giving a photographer the finger, which showed up in a tabloid, complete with morally upright pixilation to protect the children. I did my compulsory time with the shrink, who was over the moon to see me again; I gave him a bunch of mild trauma symptoms, let them vanish miraculously over a few weeks under his expert guidance, got my clearance and dealt with Operation Mirror my own way, in private.

Once we knew where those cards had been posted, she was easy enough to track down. There was no need to bother—anything she had done before she hit our patch and got herself killed wasn't our problem—but Frank did it anyway. He sent me over the file, stamped CLOSED, with no note.

They never found her in Sydney—the nearest they got was a surf stud who thought he had seen her selling ice cream at Manly Beach and had a feeling her name was Hazel, but he was too unsure and too thick to count as a reliable witness—but in New Zealand she had been Naomi Ballantine, the most efficient office receptionist on her temp agency's books, until a satisfied customer started pushing her to go full-time. In San Francisco she was a hippie chick called Alanna Goldman, who worked in a beach-supplies shop and spent a lot of time smoking pot around campfires;

friends' photos showed waist-length curls whipping in ocean breeze, bare feet and seashell necklaces and brown legs in cutoff jeans. In Liverpool she was Mags Mackenzie, an aspiring hat designer who served drinks in a quirky cocktail bar all week and sold her hats from a market stall at weekends; the photo had her wearing a wide-brimmed red-velvet swirl with a puff of old silk and lace over one ear, and laughing. Her housemates—a bunch of high-octane late-night girls who did the same general kind of thing, fashion, backing vocals, something called "urban art"— said that two weeks before she split, she had been offered a contract to design for a trendy boutique label. They hadn't been all that worried when they woke up and found her gone. Mags would be all right, they said; she always was.

The letter from Chad was paper-clipped to a blurry snapshot of the two of them in front of a lake, on a shimmering-hot day. She had a long plait and an oversized T-shirt and a shy smile, head ducking away from the camera; Chad was tall and tan and gangly, with a floppy gold forelock. He had his arm around her and he was looking down at her like he couldn't believe his luck. *I just wish you would of given me a chance to come with you,* the letter said, *just a chance, May. I would of gone anywhere. Whatever you wanted I really hope you found it now. I just wish I could know what it was and why it wasn't me.*

I photocopied the pictures and the interviews and sent the file back to Frank with a Post-it that said "Thank you." The next afternoon I left work early and went to see Abby.

Her new address was on file: she was living in Ranelagh, Student Central, in a tattered little house with weeds in the front lawn and too many bells beside the door. I stayed out on the pavement, leaning on the railing. It was five o'clock, she would be coming home soon—routine dies hard—and I wanted to let her see me from far off, be braced and ready before she reached me.

584 · Tana French

It was about half an hour before she came around the corner, wearing her long gray coat and carrying two supermarket bags. She was too far away for me to see her face, but I knew that brisk, neat walk by heart. I saw the second when she spotted me, the wild rock backwards, the grab as her bags almost slipped out of her hands; the long pause, after she realized, when she stood in the middle of the empty pavement deciding whether to turn around and go somewhere else, anywhere else; the lift of her shoulders as she took a deep breath and started walking again, towards me. I remembered that first morning, around the kitchen table: how I had thought that, if things had been different, the two of us could have been friends.

She stopped at the gate and stood still, scanning every detail of my face, deliberate and unflinching. "I should kick the living shite out of you," she said, eventually.

She didn't look like she could do it. She had lost a lot of weight and her hair was pulled up in a knot that made her face look even thinner, but it was more than that. Something had gone out of her skin: a luminosity, a resilience. For the first time I got a flash of what she would be like as an old woman, erect and sharp-tongued and wiry, with tired eyes.

"You'd have every right," I said.

"What do you want?"

"Five minutes," I said. "We've found out some stuff about Lexie. I thought you might want to know. It might . . . I don't know. It might help."

A lanky kid in Docs and an iPod brushed past us, let himself into the house and slammed the door behind him. "Can I come in?" I asked. "Or if you'd rather I didn't, we can stay out here. Just five minutes."

"What's your name again? They told us, but I forget."

"Cassie Maddox."

"Detective Cassie Maddox," Abby said. After a moment she shifted one bag up onto her wrist and found her keys. "OK. You might as well come in. When I tell you to leave, you leave." I nodded.

Her flat was one room, at the back of the first floor, smaller than mine and barer: a single bed, an armchair, a boarded-up fireplace, a minifridge, a tiny table and chair pulled up to the window; no door to a kitchen or a bathroom, nothing on the walls, no knickknacks on the mantelpiece. Outside it was a warm evening, but the air in the flat was cool as water. There were faint damp-stains on the ceiling, but every inch of the place was scrubbed clean and a big sash window looked out to the west, giving the room a long melancholy glow. I thought of her room in Whitethorn House, that rich, ornate nest.

Abby dumped the bags on the floor, shook off her coat and hung it on the back of the door. The bags had left red grooves on her wrists, like handcuff marks. "It's not as crap as you think," she said; defiantly, but there was a weary undertone there. "It does have its own bathroom. Out on the landing, but what can you do."

"I don't think it's crap," I said, which was actually sort of true; I've lived in worse. "I just expected . . . I thought there would be insurance money, or something. From the house."

Abby's lips tightened for a second. "We weren't insured," she said. "We always figured, the house had lasted this long; we'd rather put our money into doing it up. More fools us." She pulled open what looked like a wardrobe; inside were a tiny sink, a two-ring cooker and a couple of cupboards. "So we sold up. To Ned. We didn't have much choice. He won—or maybe Lexie won, or your lot, or the guy who burned us out, I don't know. Someone else won, anyway."

"Then why live here," I asked, "if you don't like it?"

Abby shrugged. She had her back to me, putting stuff away in the cupboards—baked beans, tinned tomatoes, a bag of off-brand cornflakes; her shoulder blades, sharp through the thin gray sweater, looked fine as a child's. "First place I saw. I needed somewhere to live. After your lot let us go, the people from Victim Support found us this horrible B and B in Summerhill; we didn't have any money, we put most of our cash into the kitty—as you know, obviously—and it all went up in the fire. The landlady made us get out by ten in the morning, come back in by ten at night, I spent all day in the library staring at nothing and all night sitting in my room by myself—the three of us weren't really talking . . . I got out as fast as I could. Now that we've sold up, the logical thing would be to use my share for a deposit on an apartment, but for that I'd need a job that can pay the mortgage, and until I finish my PhD . . . The whole damn thing just feels too complicated. I have a hard time making decisions, these days. If I leave it long enough, my rent will eat up all the money and the decision'll take care of itself."

"You're still in Trinity?" I wanted to scream. This tight, strange, eggshells conversation, when I'd danced to her singing, when we'd sat on my bed eating chocolate biscuits and swapping worst-kiss stories; this was more than I had any right to, and I couldn't break through it and find her.

"I've started. I might as well finish."

"What about Rafe and Justin?"

Abby slammed the cupboard doors and ran her hands through her hair, that gesture I'd seen a thousand times. "I don't know what to do about you," she said abruptly. "You ask me something like that, and part of me wants to fill you in on every detail, and part of me wants to give you hell for putting us through this when we were supposed to be your best friends, and part of me wants to tell you to mind your own fucking business, cop, don't you dare even mention their names. I can't . . . I don't know how to talk to you. I don't know how to *look* at you. What do you *want*?"

She was about two seconds from throwing me out. "I brought this," I said, fast, and found the sheaf of photocopies in my satchel. "You know Lexie was going under a fake name, don't you?"

Abby folded her arms at her waist and watched me, wary and expressionless. "One of your friends told us. Whatsisname, who was all over us from the start. Stocky blond guy, Galway accent?"

"Sam O'Neill," I said. I was wearing the ring on my finger, these days—the slagging, which had ranged from affectionate to deeply bitchy, had more or less died down; the Murder squad even gave us some mystifying silver dish thing, for an engagement present—but there was no reason why she should make the connection.

"Him. I think he expected it to shock us into spilling our guts, or something. So?"

"We traced her," I said, and held out the photocopies.

Abby took them and ran a thumbnail through the pages, one fast flip; I thought of that expert, effortless shuffle. "What's all this?"

"Places she lived. Other IDs she used. Photos. Interviews." She was still giving me that look, flat and final as a slap in the face. "I figured you should have the choice. The chance to have them, if you want them."

Abby tossed the papers onto the table and went back to her shopping bags, slotting things into the tiny fridge: a pint of milk, a little plastic serving of some chocolate-mousse thing. "I don't. I already know everything I need to know about Lexie."

"I thought it might help explain some stuff. Why she did what she did. Maybe you'd rather not know, but—"

She whipped upright, fridge door swinging wildly. "What the hell do you know about it? You never even *met* Lexie. I don't give a flying fuck if she was going under a fake name, if she was a dozen different people in a dozen different places. None of that matters. I *knew* her. I *lived* with her. That wasn't fake. You're like Rafe's father, all that bullshit about the real world—*That was the real world*. It was a whole lot more real than *this*." A fierce jerk of her chin, at the room around us.

"That's not what I mean," I said. "I just don't think she ever wanted to hurt you, any of you. It wasn't like that."

After a moment the air went out of her; her spine sagged. "That's what you said, that day. That you—she—just panicked. Because of the baby."

588 · Tana French

"I believed that," I said. "I still do."

"Yeah," said Abby. "Me too. That's the only reason I let you in." She shoved something more firmly onto one of the fridge shelves, shut the door.

"Rafe and Justin," I said. "Would they want to see this stuff?"

Abby balled up the plastic bags and stuffed them into another bag, hanging off the chair. "Rafe's in London," she said. "He left as soon as your lot would let us travel. His father found him a job—I don't know what, exactly; something to do with finance. He's totally unqualified for it and he's probably crap at it, but he won't get fired, not as long as Daddy's around."

"Oh, God," I said, before I could stop myself. "He must be miserable."

She shrugged and shot me a quick, unfathomable look. "We don't talk a lot. I've phoned him a few times, stuff about the sale—not that he gives a damn, he just tells me to do whatever I want and send him the papers to sign, but I have to check. I rang him in the evenings, and it mostly sounded like he was in some fancy pub, or a nightclub— loud music, people yelling. They call him 'Raffy.' He was always about three-quarters drunk, which I doubt comes as any surprise to you, but no, he didn't sound miserable. If that helps you feel better."

Rafe in moonlight, smiling, eyes slanted sideways at me; his fingers warm on my cheek. Rafe with Lexie, somewhere—I still wondered about that alcove. "What about Justin?"

"He went back up North. He tried to stick it out at Trinity, but he couldn't take it—not just the staring and whispering, although that was pretty bad, but . . . nothing being the same. A couple of times I heard him crying, in his carrel. One day he tried to go into the library and he couldn't do it; he had a panic attack, right there in the Arts block, in front of everyone. They had to take him away in an ambulance. He didn't come back."

She took a coin from a neat stack on the fridge and fed it into the electricity meter, turned the knob. "I've talked to him a couple of times. He's teaching English in a boys' school, filling in for some woman on maternity leave. He says the kids are spoiled little monsters and they write 'Mr. Mannering is a faggot' on the board most mornings, but at least it's peaceful—it's out in the countryside—and the other teachers leave him alone. I doubt either he or Rafe would want that stuff." She flicked her head at the table. "And I'm not going to ask them. You want to talk to them, do your own dirty work. I should warn you, I don't think they'll be overjoyed to hear from you."

"I don't blame them," I said. I went to the table, tapped the bundle of paper into shape. Below the window, the back garden was overgrown, strewn with bright crisp packets and empty bottles.

Abby said, behind me, with no inflection in her voice at all, "We're always going to hate you, you know."

I didn't turn around. Whether I liked it or not, in this one small room my face was still a weapon, a bare blade laid between her and me; it was easier for her to talk when she couldn't see it. "I know," I said.

"If you're looking for some kind of absolution, you're in the wrong place."

"I'm not," I said. "This stuff is the only thing I've got to offer you, so I figured I had to try. I owe you that."

After a second, I heard her sigh. "It's not that we think this was all your fault. We're not stupid. Even before you came . . ." A movement: her shifting, pushing back hair, something. "Daniel believed, right up to the end, that we could still fix things; that there was still a way for it to be OK again. I didn't. Even if Lexie had made it . . . I think, by the time your mates showed up at our door, it was already too late. Too much had changed."

"You and Daniel," I said. "Rafe and Justin."

Another beat. "I guess it was that obvious. That night, the night Lexie died . . . we couldn't have made it through, otherwise. And it shouldn't have been a big deal. Various stuff had happened before, here and there along the way; everyone was always fine about it. But that night . . ."

I heard her swallow. "Before that, we had a balance, you know? Everyone knew Justin was in love with Rafe, but it was just there, in the background. I didn't even realize that I . . . Call me stupid, but I really didn't; I just thought Daniel was the best friend I could ever want. I think we could all have gone on like that, maybe forever—or maybe not. But that night was different. The second Daniel said, 'She's dead,' things changed. Everything got clearer, too clear to bear, like some huge light had been switched on and you could never close your eyes again, not even for a second. Do you know what I mean?"

"Yeah," I said. "I do."

"After that, even if Lexie had come home after all, I don't know if we . . ."

Her voice trailed off. I turned round and found her watching me, closer than I'd expected. "You don't sound like her," she said. "You don't even move like her. Are you anything like her at all?"

"We had some things in common," I said. "Not everything."

Abby nodded. After a moment she said, "I'd like you to leave now."

I had my hand on the doorknob when she said, suddenly and almost unwillingly, "You want to hear something strange?"

It was getting dark; her face looked like it was fading away, into the dim room. "One of the times I rang Rafe, he wasn't in that club or whatever; he was home, on the balcony of his apartment. It was late. We talked for a while. I said something about Lexie—that I still miss her, even though . . . in spite of everything. Rafe made some flip comment about having too much fun to miss anyone; but before he said it, before he answered, there was this little pause. Baffled. Like it took him a second to figure out who I was talking about. I know Rafe, and I swear to God he almost said, 'Who?'"

Upstairs, half muffled by the ceiling, a phone burst into "Baby Got Back" and someone thumped across the floor to answer it. "He was pretty drunk," Abby said. "Like I told you. Still, though . . . I can't stop wondering. If we're forgetting each other. If in another year or two we'll all have been wiped right out of each other's minds; gone, like we never met. If we could pass on the street, within inches, and not even blink."

"No pasts," I said.

"No pasts. Sometimes"—a quick breath—"I can't see their faces. Rafe and Justin, I can handle it; but Lexie. And Daniel."

I saw her head turn, her profile against the window: that snub nose, a stray strand of hair. "I loved him, you know," she said. "I would have loved him as hard as he'd let me, for the rest of my life."

"I know," I said. I wanted to tell her that being loved is a talent too, that it takes as much guts and as much work as loving; that some people, for whatever reason, never learn the knack. Instead I got the photocopies back out of my bag and flipped through them—I practically had to hold them against my nose, to see—until I found the streaky color copy of that snapshot: the five of them, smiling, wrapped in falling snow and silence, outside Whitethorn House. "Here," I said, and held it out to Abby.

Her hand, pale in the near-darkness, reaching out. She went to the window, tilted the page to the last of the light.

"Thanks," she said, after a moment. "I'll keep this." She was still there, looking at it, when I closed the door.

After that I hoped I'd dream about Lexie, just every now and then. She's fading from the others' minds, day by day; soon she'll be gone for good, she'll be only bluebells and a hawthorn tree, in a ruined cottage where no one goes. I figured I owed her my dreams. But she never came. Whatever it was that she wanted from me, I must have brought it to her, somewhere along the way. The only thing I dream of is the house, empty, open to sun and dust and ivy; scuffles and whispers, always just one corner away; and one of us, her or me, in the mirror, laughing.

This is the one thing I hope: that she never stopped. I hope when her body couldn't run any farther she left it behind like everything else that tried to hold her down, she floored the pedal and she went like wildfire, streamed down night freeways with both hands off the wheel and her head back screaming to the sky like a lynx, white lines and green lights whipping away into the dark, her tires inches off the ground and freedom crashing up her spine. I hope every second she could have had came flooding through that cottage like speed wind: ribbons and sea spray, a wedding ring and Chad's mother crying, sun-wrinkles and gallops through wild red brush, a baby's first tooth and its shoulder blades like tiny wings in Amsterdam Toronto Dubai; hawthorn flowers spinning through summer air, Daniel's hair turning gray under high ceilings and candle flames and the sweet cadences of Abby's singing. Time works so hard for us, Daniel told me once. I hope those last few minutes worked like hell for her. I hope in that half hour she lived all her million lives.

Acknowledgments

I owe huge thank-yous to more people every time. The amazing Darley Anderson and everyone at the agency, especially Zoë, Emma, Lucie and Maddie; three incredible editors, Kendra Harpster at Viking Penguin, Sue Fletcher at Hodder & Stoughton and Ciara Considine at Hodder Headline Ireland, for making this book so many times better; Clare Ferraro, Ben Petrone, Kate Lloyd and all at Viking; Breda Purdue, Ruth Shern, Ciara Doorley, Peter McNulty and all at Hodder Headline Ireland; Swati Gamble, Tara Gladden, Emma Knight and all at Hodder & Stoughton; Jennie Cotter at Plunkett Communications; Rachel Burd, for the razor-sharp copy-edit; David Walsh, for answering a wild variety of questions about police procedure; Jody Burgess, for Australia-related info, corrections and ideas, not to mention Tim Tams; Fearghas Ó Cochláin, for medical info; my brother, Alex French, for tech and other support; Oonagh Montague, for generally being great; Ann-Marie Hardiman, for her academic input; David Ryan, for his completely academic input; Helena Burling; all at PurpleHeart Theatre Company; the BB, for helping me to bridge the culture gap again; and, of course, my parents, David French and Elena Hvostoff-Lombardi, for a lifetime's worth of support and faith.

In some places, where the story seemed to require it, I've taken liberties with facts (Ireland doesn't, for example, have a Murder squad). All errors, deliberate or otherwise, are mine.

Read on for a selection from
Tana French's novel *The Searcher*,
now available . . .

New York Times bestselling author of
THE WITCH ELM

TANA
FRENCH

The Searcher

A NOVEL

Chapter 1

When Cal comes out of the house, the rooks have got hold of something. Six of them are clustered on the back lawn, amid the long wet grass and the yellow-flowered weeds, jabbing and hopping. Whatever the thing is, it's on the small side and still moving.

Cal sets down his garbage bag of wallpaper. He considers getting his knife and putting the creature out of its suffering, but the rooks have been here a lot longer than he has. It would be pretty impertinent of him to waltz in and start interfering with their ways. Instead he eases himself down to sit on the mossy step next to the trash bag.

He likes the rooks. He read somewhere that they're smart as hell; they can get to know you, bring you presents even. For nearly three months now he's been trying to butter them up with scraps left on the big stump towards the bottom of the garden. They watch him trudge up and down through the grass, from the ivy-loaded oak where they have their colony, and as soon as he's a safe distance away they swoop down to squabble and comment raucously over the scraps; but they keep a cynical eye on Cal, and if he tries to move closer they're gone, back into the oak to jeer down at him and drop twigs on his head. Yesterday afternoon he was in his living room, stripping away the mildewed wallpaper, and a sleek mid-sized rook landed on the sill of the open window, yelled what was obviously an insult, and then flapped off laughing.

The thing on the lawn twists wildly, shaking the long grass. A big daddy rook jumps closer, aims one neat ferocious stab of his beak, and the thing goes still.

Rabbit, maybe. Cal has seen them out there in the early mornings, nibbling and dashing in the dew. Their holes are somewhere in his back field, down by the broad copse of hazels and rowans. Once his firearm license comes through, he's planning to see if he remembers what his grandpa taught him about skinning game, and if the mule-tempered broadband will deign to find him a recipe for rabbit stew. The rooks crowd in, pecking hard and bracing their feet to jerk out bites of flesh, more of them zooming down from the tree to jostle in on the action.

Cal watches them for a while, stretching out his legs and rolling one shoulder in circles. Working on the house is using muscles he'd forgotten he had. He finds new aches every morning, although some of that is likely from sleeping on a cheap mattress on the floor. Cal is too old and too big for that, but there's no point in bringing good furniture into the dust and damp and mold. He'll buy that stuff once he has the house in shape, and once he figures out where you buy it—all that was Donna's department. Meanwhile, he doesn't mind the aches. They satisfy him; along with the blisters and thickening calluses, they're solid, earned proof of what his life is now.

It's headed into the long cool September stretch of evening, but cloudy enough that there's no trace of a sunset. The sky, dappled in subtle gradations of gray, goes on forever; so do the fields, coded in shades of green by their different uses, divided up by sprawling hedges, dry-stone walls and the odd narrow back road. Away to the north, a line of low mountains rolls along the horizon. Cal's eyes are still getting used to looking this far, after all those years of city blocks. Landscape is one of the few things he knows of where the reality doesn't let you down. The West of Ireland looked beautiful on the internet; from right smack in the middle of it, it looks even better. The air is rich as fruitcake, like you should do more with it than just breathe it; bite off a big mouthful, maybe, or rub handfuls of it over your face.

After a while the rooks slow down, getting towards the end of their meal. Cal stands up and picks up the trash bag again. The rooks cock smart, instant glances at him and, when he starts down the garden, heave themselves into the air and flap their full bellies back to their tree. He hauls the bag down to a corner beside the creeper-covered tumble-down stone shed, pausing along the way to check out the rooks' dinner. Rabbit, all right, a young one, although barely recognizable now.

He leaves the trash bag with the rest and heads back to the house. He's almost there when the rooks kick off, jostling leaves and yelling cuss words at something. Cal doesn't turn around or break stride. He says very softly through his teeth, as he closes the back door behind him, "Mother-*fucker.*"

For the last week and a half, someone has been watching Cal. Probably longer, but he had his mind on his own business and he took for granted, like anyone would have a right to do amid all this empty space, that he was alone. His mental alarm systems were switched off, the way he wanted them. Then one night he was cooking dinner—frying a hamburger on the rust-pocked stove's one working burner, Steve Earle good and loud on the iPod speaker, Cal adding in the occasional crash of air drums—when the back of his neck flared.

The back of Cal's neck got trained over twenty-five years in the Chicago PD. He takes it seriously. He ambled casually across the kitchen, nodding along to the music and examining the counters like he was missing something, and then made a sudden lunge to the window: no one outside. He turned off the burner and headed for the door fast, but the garden was empty. He walked the perimeter, under a million savage stars and a howler's moon, fields laid out white all around him and owls yelping: nothing.

Some animal noise, Cal told himself, drowned out by the music so that only his subconscious picked it up. The dark is busy around here. He's sat out on his step well past midnight, a few times, drinking a couple of beers and getting the hang of the nighttime. He's seen hedgehogs bustling across the garden, a sleek fox stopping on its route to give him a challenge of a stare. One time a badger, bigger and more muscular than Cal would have expected, trundled along the hedge and disappeared into it; a minute later there was one high shriek, and then the rustle of the badger moving off. Anything could have been going about its business out there.

Before Cal went to bed that night, he stacked his two mugs and two plates on the bedroom windowsill and dragged an old desk up against the bedroom door. Then he called himself a dumbass and put them away.

A couple of mornings later he was stripping wallpaper, window open to let out the dust, when the rooks exploded up out of their tree, shouting at something underneath. The fast trail of rustles heading away behind the hedge was too big and noisy for a hedgehog or a fox, too big even for a badger. By the time Cal got out there, he was too late again.

Probably bored kids spying on the newcomer. Not much else to do around here, with the village no bigger than the little end of nothing, and the closest two-horse town fifteen miles away. Cal feels dumb for even considering anything else. Mart, his nearest neighbor up the road, doesn't even lock his door except at night. When Cal raised an eyebrow at that, Mart's high-boned face creased up and he laughed till he wheezed. "The state of that there," he said, pointing towards the house. "What would anyone rob off you? And who'd rob it? Am I going to sneak in some morning and go through your washing, looking for something to spruce up my fashion sense?" And Cal laughed too and told him he could do with it, and Mart informed him that his own wardrobe would do him grand, seeing as he had no plans to go courting, and started explaining why not.

But there have been things. No big deal, just stuff that

flicks at the edges of Cal's cop sense. Engines revving, three a.m. down faraway back roads, deep-chested bubbling snarls. A huddle of guys in the back corner of the pub some nights, too young and dressed wrong, talking too loud and too fast in accents that don't fit in; the snap of their heads towards the door when Cal walks in, the stares that last a second too long. He's been careful not to tell anyone what he used to do, but just being a stranger could be plenty, depending.

Dumb, Cal tells himself, turning on the burner under his frying pan and looking out the kitchen window at the dimming green fields, Mart's dog trotting beside the sheep as they plod peacefully towards their pen. Too many years on the beat in bad hoods, now farmhands look like gang-bangers.

Bored kids, ten to one. All the same, Cal has started keeping his music down so he won't miss anything, he's thinking about getting an alarm system, and this pisses him off. Years of Donna lunging for the volume knob, *Cal, that baby next door is trying to sleep! Cal, Mrs. Scapanski just had surgery, you think she needs that blowing her eardrums? Cal, what are the neighbors gonna think, we're savages?* He wanted land partly so he could blast Steve Earle loud enough to knock squirrels out of the trees, and he wanted buttfuck nowhere partly so he wouldn't have to set alarms any more. He feels like he can't even, for example, adjust his balls without looking over his shoulder, which is something a man ought to be able to do in his own kitchen. Kids or not, he needs this put to bed.

At home he would have solved this with a couple of good, discreet cameras that uploaded straight to the cloud. Here, even if his Wi-Fi could handle that, which he doubts, the idea of taking his footage down to the nearest station doesn't sit well. He doesn't know what he might start: neighbor feud, or the watcher could be the officer's cousin, or who knows what.

He's considered tripwires. These are presumably illegal, but Cal is pretty sure this in itself wouldn't be a big deal: Mart has already offered twice to sell him an unregistered shotgun that he's got lying around, and everyone drives home from the pub. The problem is, again, that Cal is in the dark on what he might set in motion.

Or what he might have set in motion already. Listening to Mart, Cal has started to get an inkling of how tangled up things get, around here, and how carefully you have to watch where you put your feet. Noreen, who runs the shop in the brief double line of buildings that counts as Ardnakelty village, won't order the cookies Mart likes because of a complicated saga that took place in the 1980s and involved her uncles, Mart's father and grazing rights; Mart doesn't speak to an unpronounceable farmer on the other side of the mountains because the guy bought a pup that was sired by Mart's dog when it somehow shouldn't have been. There are other stories like that, although Cal doesn't have them all straight, because Mart talks in big sweeping loops and because Cal doesn't fully have the hang of the local accent. He likes it—rich as the air, with a needle-fine point that makes him think of cold river water or mountain wind— but chunks of the conversation go right over his head, and he gets distracted listening to the rhythms and misses more. But he's gathered enough to know that he could have sat on someone's stool in the pub, or cut across the wrong piece of land on one of his walks, and that that could mean something.

When he arrived here, he was ready for closed ranks against the stranger. He was OK with that, as long as no one set his place on fire; he wasn't looking for golf buddies and dinner parties. But it didn't turn out that way. People were neighborly. The day Cal arrived and started hauling stuff into and out of the house, Mart wandered down to lean on the gate and probe for information, and ended up bringing over an old mini-fridge and recommending a good building supplies store. Noreen explained who was what kind of cousin to who and how to get onto the group water scheme, and—later, once Cal had made her laugh a few times—started offering, only halfway joking, to set Cal up with her widowed sister. The old guys who apparently live in the pub have moved from nods to weather comments to passionate explanations of a sport called hurling, which to Cal looks like what you might get if you kept the speed, dexterity and ferocity of ice hockey but took away the ice and most of the protective equipment. Up until last week he felt that he had been, if not exactly welcomed with open arms, at least accepted as a mildly interesting natural phenomenon, like maybe a seal that had taken up residence in the river. Obviously he was always going to be an outsider, but he was getting the feeling that that wasn't a big deal. He's no longer so sure.

So, four days ago, Cal drove into town and bought a big bag of garden soil. He's aware of the irony of buying more dirt, when he just spent most of his savings on ten acres of it, but his personal dirt is rough and chunky, shot through with grass roots and small sharp rocks. For this he needed fine, moist, even stuff. The next day he got up before dawn and spread a layer of it by the outside wall of his house, under each of the windows. He had to pull weeds and creepers and scrape back pebbles to get a decent surface. The air was cold right down to the bottom of his lungs. Slowly the fields lightened around him; the rooks woke up and started bickering. When the sky got bright and he heard Mart's faint peremptory whistle to his sheepdog, Cal crumpled up the soil bag to stuff at the bottom of the trash, and went inside to make breakfast.

Next morning, nothing; morning after that, nothing. He must have got closer than he thought, the last time, must have given them a scare. He went about his business and kept his eyes off the windows and the hedges.

This morning, footprints, in the dirt under his living-room window. Sneakers, going by the fragments of tread,

but the prints were too scuffed up and overlapped to tell
how big or how many.

The frying pan is hot. Cal throws in four slices of bacon,
meatier and tastier than what he's used to, and, once the fat
sizzles cracks in two eggs. He saunters over to his iPod,
which lives on the same left-behind wooden table where he
eats his meals—the sum total of Cal's current furniture is
that table, a left-behind wooden desk with a busted side,
two scrawny left-behind Formica chairs, and a fat green
armchair that Mart's cousin was throwing out—and puts
on some Johnny Cash, not too loud.

If he's done something that pissed someone off, the
prime candidate has got to be buying this house. He picked
it off a website, on the basis that it came with some land,
there was good fishing nearby, the roof looked sound, and
he wanted to check out the papers sticking out of that old
desk. It had been a long time since Cal had got a wild hare
like that and chased after it, which seemed like an extra
reason for doing it. The estate agents were asking 35K. Cal
offered thirty, cash. They about bit his hand off.

It didn't occur to him at the time that anyone else might
want the place. It's a low, gray, undistinguished house built
sometime in the 1930s, five hundred and some square feet,
slate-roofed and sash-windowed; only the big cornerstones
and the broad stone fireplace give it a touch of grace. Going
by the website photos, it had been abandoned for years,
probably decades: paint peeling in big streaks and mottles,
rooms strewn with upended dark-brown furniture and rot-
ting flowered curtains, saplings springing up in front of the
door and creepers trailing in at a broken window. But he's
learned enough since then to understand that someone else
might in fact have wanted this place, even if the reasons
aren't immediately apparent, and that anyone who felt they
had a claim on it was likely to take that seriously.

Cal scoops his food onto a couple of thick slices of bread,
adds ketchup, gets a beer out of the mini-fridge and takes
his meal to the table. Donna would give him shit about the

way he's been eating, which doesn't include a whole lot of fiber and fresh vegetables, but the fact is that even living out of a frying pan and a microwave he's dropped a few pounds, maybe more than a few. He can feel it, not just in his waist-band but in his movements: everything he does has a sur-prising new lightness to it. That was unsettling at first, like he had come unhitched from gravity, but it's growing on him.

The exercise is what's doing it. Just about every day Cal goes walking for an hour or two, nowhere particular, just following his nose and getting the lie of his new land. A lot of days it rains on him, but this is OK: he has a big wax jacket and the rain is like nothing he's felt before, a fine soft haze that seems to hang motionless in the air. Mostly he leaves his hood down just so he can feel that haze against his face. As well as seeing farther than he's used to, he can hear farther: the occasional sheep's bleat or cow's bawl, or farmer's shout, comes to him from what seems like miles away, thinned and gentled by the distance. Sometimes he sees one of the farmers, going about his business away across the fields, or chugging down a narrow lane in a tractor so that Cal has to press back into the unruly hedge as he goes past, lifting a hand in greeting. He's passed strong-built women hauling heavy things around cluttered farmyards, red-cheeked toddlers staring at him through gates and sucking on the bars while the rangy dogs bark up a storm at him. Sometimes a bird calls a wild high streak above his head, or a pheasant explodes out of the undergrowth as he comes close. He gets back to the house feeling like he made the right call, throwing everything up in the air and coming here.

In between walks, with nothing else to call on his atten-tion, Cal pretty much works on the house from morning till night. The first thing he did when he arrived was sweep away the thick cocoon of cobwebs and dust and dead bugs and what-have-you that was patiently working to fill every inch of the place. Next he put new glass in the windows, and replaced the toilet and the bath—both of which had been smashed up pretty good by someone with a lump hammer and a deep-seated grudge against bathroom fixtures—so he could stop shitting in a hole in the ground and washing out of a bucket. Cal is no plumber, but he's always been handy and he has YouTube how-to videos, when the internet doesn't crap out on him; it worked out OK.

After that he spent a while going through the left-behind stuff that littered the rooms, taking his time, giving each piece his full attention. Whoever lived here last was serious about religion: they had pictures of Saint Bernadette, a disappointed-looking Virgin Mary, and someone called Padre Pio, all in thin cheap frames and all left to yellow in corners by less devout heirs. They liked condensed milk, of which there were five tins in the kitchen cupboard, all of them fifteen years out of date. They had pink-printed china cups, rusted-out saucepans, rolled-up oilcloth tablecloths, a figurine of a kid in a red robe and crown with the head glued back on, and a shoebox holding a pair of old-fashioned men's dress shoes, worn to creases and polished to a shine that still shows. Cal was a little surprised to find no evidence of teenage occupation, no empty beer cans or cigarette butts or used condoms, no graffiti. He figured this place must be too remote for them. At the time, that seemed like a good thing. Now he's less sure. The possibility of teenagers checking on their old hangout is something he'd prefer to have on the menu.

The papers in the desk turned out to be nothing much: articles torn out of newspapers and magazines, folded into neat rectangles. Cal tried to find some unifying thread among the articles, but failed: they involved, among other things, the history of the Boy Scouts, how to grow sweet peas, tin whistle tunes, the Irish peacekeeping forces in the Lebanon, and a recipe for something called Welsh rarebit. Cal kept them, seeing as they were in a way the thing that had brought him here. He tossed most of the other stuff, including the curtains, which now seems like a bad call.

He's considered digging them back out of the heap of trash bags that's growing behind the shed, but some animal has probably either chewed them up or pissed on them by now.

He's replaced gutters and downpipes, climbed up on his roof to evict a sturdy crop of yellow-flowered weeds from his chimney, sanded and polished the old oak floorboards, and these days he's working on the walls. The last inhabitant had surprisingly unconventional tastes in decoration, that or a few buckets of cheap paint. Cal's bedroom used to be a deep, rich indigo, till the damp mottled it with streaks of mold and pale patches of bare plaster. The smaller bedroom was a light minty green. The living-room part of the front room was rusty red-brown, slapped on top of layers of buckling wallpaper. It's unclear what exactly was going on in the kitchen area, which looks like someone might have been aiming to tile it and then got sidetracked, and nobody made even that much effort with the bathroom: it's a tiny tacked-on cube at the back of the house, with plaster walls and a remnant of green carpet more or less covering the raw floorboards, like it was made by aliens who had heard about this thing called a bathroom but weren't exactly clear on the details. Cal, at six foot four, has to squeeze himself into the bath with his knees practically under his chin. Once he's tiled the room he'll put in a shower fixture, but that can wait. He wants to get the painting done while the weather is good enough that he can leave the windows open. Already there have been days, just one or two of them, with the sky a dense gray and the cold rising up from the ground and the wind riding straight across hundreds of miles and through his house like it's not there, to warn him of what winter's going to be. Nothing approaching the snowbanks and sub-zero of Chicago winters—he knows that from the internet—but something in its own right, something steely and intractable, with a tricky side.

Cal takes a look at his day's work while he eats. The

wallpaper melded into the wall in places over the years, which makes this slow going, but he's got more than half the room stripped to bare plaster; the wall around the chunky stone arch of the fireplace is still a scuffed red-brown. An unexpected part of him likes the room this way. It implies things. Cal is no artist, but if he was, he'd be inclined to leave it like this for a while, paint a few pictures.

He's halfway through his food and still considering this when the back of his neck flares again. This time he even hears the signal that triggered it: a small, clumsy scramble, almost instantly cut off, like someone started to trip into the undergrowth outside the window and then caught themselves.

Cal takes another big, leisurely mouthful of sandwich, washes it down with a long gulp of beer, and wipes foam off his tache. Then he grimaces and leans forwards, with a belch, to put his plate on the table. He pulls himself out of the chair, cracks his neck and heads for the john, already fumbling at his belt buckle.

The bathroom window opens as smoothly and silently as if it's been sprayed with WD-40, which it has. Cal has also practiced the climb onto the toilet cistern and out the window, and he manages it a lot more deftly than anyone could expect of someone his size, but that doesn't change the fact that one reason he quit being a beat cop was because he had had it with climbing unreasonable objects in pursuit of mopes doing gratuitous crap, and he had no plans to go back to that. He lands on the ground outside with his heart speeding in the old familiar hunting rhythm, his ass scraped up by the window frame, and a rising sense of aggravation.

The best he's got is a piece of pipe, left over from the bathroom work and stashed in a bush. Even holding it, he feels empty-handed and too light, without his gun. He stands still for a minute, letting his eyes adjust and listening, but the night is speckled all over with small noises and he can't pick out any one that seems more relevant than the others. It's got dark; the moon is up, a sharp slice chased over by ragged clouds, casting only a faint unreliable light and too many shadows. Cal adjusts his grip on the pipe and moves, with the old practiced compromise between speed and silence, towards the corner of the house.

Below the living-room window a huddle of denser darkness crouches, motionless, head just high enough to peer over the sill. Cal scans carefully, as best he can, but the grass all around is clear: looks like just the one. In the spill of light from the window he catches a buzz cut and a smudge of red.

Cal drops the pipe and charges. He's going for a full tackle, planning on flattening the guy and figuring out the rest from there, but his foot turns on a rock. In the second while he's flailing for his balance, the guy leaps up and away. Cal lunges into the near-darkness, grabs hold of an arm and hauls with all his might.

The guy flies towards him too easily, and the arm is small enough that his hand wraps right around it. It's a kid. The realization loosens Cal's grip a notch. The kid twists like a bobcat, with a hiss of breath, and sinks his teeth into Cal's hand.

Cal roars. The kid yanks free and takes off across the garden like a rocket, feet almost noiseless on the grass. Cal starts after him, but in seconds he's disappeared into the scribble of shadow by the roadside hedge, and by the time Cal reaches it, he's gone. Cal shoves his way through the hedge and looks up and down the road, narrowed to a faint ribbon by the moon-shadows of the hedges crowding in. Nothing. He tosses a couple of stones into the bushes in various directions, trying to flush the kid out: no.

He doubts the kid had reinforcements—he would have yelled out, either for help or to warn them—but he jogs a circle around the garden just in case. The rooks are asleep, undisturbed. New footprints in the soil below the living-room window, same tread as last time; nowhere else. Cal backs himself up in the heavy shadow of the shed and waits for a long time, trying to quiet his panting, but there's no rustle in any hedge and no shadow sneaking away across any field. Just the one, and just a kid. And not coming back, at least not tonight.

Inside, he takes a look at his hand. The kid got him good: three teeth broke the skin, and one place is bleeding. Cal got bit once before, on the job, which led to a maelstrom of paperwork, interviews, blood tests, legal wrangling, pills and court appearances that went on for months, till Cal got fed up keeping track of what was for what and just handed over his arm or his signature on request. He finds his first-aid kit and soaks his hand in disinfectant for a while, then sticks on a Band-Aid.

His food has gone cold. He nukes it up and takes it back to the table. Johnny Cash is still going, mourning his lost Rose and his lost boy, in a deep broken quaver like he's already a ghost.

Cal isn't feeling the way he would have expected. Kids spying on the new guy were the thing he was hoping to find, the best-case scenario. He figured he would shout vague threats after them while they zoomed away yelling and laughing and calling insults over their shoulders, and then he would shake his head and go back indoors bitching about kids nowadays like some old geezer, and that would be the end of that. Maybe they would come back for another round, every now and then, but Cal was basically OK with that. Meanwhile, he could return to doing his renovation and playing his music loud and adjusting his balls whenever he damn well pleased, with his police sense put back to bed where it belongs.

Except he doesn't feel like that was the end of that, and his police sense isn't going back to sleep. Kids screwing with the stranger for kicks should have come in a bunch, and they should have been rowdy, hopped up on their own daring like it was caffeine. He thinks of this kid's stillness under the window, his silence when Cal grabbed him, the snake-strike ferocity of his bite. This kid wasn't having fun. He was here for a purpose. He'll be back.

Once Ed Buck, sports reporter, and Adam Benson, star quarterback for the Chicago Bears, played football on the same college team. Years later, they are still close friends. In New York for a game against the Giants, Benson hands Buck the biggest story of his career.

Gambling on football is one of the country's leading "industries," and the mob's been forcing Benson to throw games. The quarterback has had enough. Sunday, he tells Buck, he's playing to win, and to hell with the mob. After the game, Buck can run with the story.

Adam Benson never makes it off the field alive, and Ed Buck suspects his friend was murdered. Buck knows barely enough to convince a police detective to look into Benson's death—but more than enough to set the mob on his tail.

As Lt. Gerry Keegan probes the tangled connections between the dead quarterback and the head of an organized crime family, uncovering drug dealing, murder, blackmail, prostitution, and double- and triple-crosses, Ed Buck and his fiancée run for their lives.

BOOKS BY DAVE KLEIN

Blindside
Hit and Run
Leonard Marshal: The End of the Line
Big Blue: A Giant Year
The Game of Their Lives
Great Infielders of the Major Leagues
Great Moments in Baseball
Great Moments in Golf
On the Way Up: What It's Like in the Minor Leagues
Pro Basketball's Big Men
Pro Football Mystique
Stars of the Major Leagues
Tom and the Boys
The Vince Lombardi Story

FOURTH DOWN

Dave Klein

TOR®

A TOM DOHERTY ASSOCIATES BOOK
NEW YORK

This is a work of fiction. All the characters and events portrayed in this book are either products of the author's imagination or are used fictitiously.

FOURTH DOWN

A Tor Book
Published by Tom Doherty Associates, LLC
175 Fifth Avenue
New York, NY 10010

www.tor.com

Tor® is a registered trademark of Tom Doherty Associates, LLC.

ISBN: 0-812-57103-7
Library of Congress Catalog Card Number: 99-22196

First edition: September 1999
First mass market edition: September 2000

Printed in the United States of America

0 9 8 7 6 5 4 3 2 1

ACKNOWLEDGMENTS

For the help I received, with great doses of love and friendship, I would like to thank 323. Both the love and the friendship are there—then, now, and always.

The early help provided by Michael Seidman is gratefully appreciated.

The later help, from Tom Doherty and Melissa Ann Singer, even more so.

And the nicest thing about this book is that in its writing not a single animal was harmed.

January 1999

ONE

. . . **ABOVE** all, no matter what else would come to mind seconds after anybody asked him how he felt about football, his first thought, his first visceral memory, was the heat.

And the grass drills.

He had never experienced heat like that, but even if he had, he absolutely never would have considered putting himself through such intense physical strain in the midst of the worst of it. Grass drills? Devised, clearly, by some equally warped and perverted descendent of the Marquis de Sade.

The football players, already having gone through intense strength-draining practice sessions for up to three hours, were lined up in sweating, panting rows and, at the sound of a shrill, nerve-jangling whistle, began to jog in place. The leader of this little experiment in terror would suddenly shriek, "Hit the grass!," which required all the sweating young men to throw their bodies to the ground, belly first, and jump right back up again, almost as soon as contact had been made, to resume jogging in place.

The torturer would then scream, "On three!," meaning on every third jog-step the "hit the grass" procedure would be repeated. But then he'd change it to "on four," or "on six," sometimes "on two," and those who

failed to keep up not only physically but also with the
math would be forced to go through extra sessions of
grass drills before they would be allowed to stagger off
into the nearby woods and puke.

But that was the way things were in 1968. It seemed
college campuses slightly out of the way, like the University of Oklahoma at Norman, were divided into two
groups of male underclassmen—those who couldn't
play football and therefore spent their time either studying or protesting (rarely both) and those who did play
football and didn't have time for much else, especially
to give a damn one way or another about their nation's
involvement in Vietnam, which was some obscure
country halfway around the world that specialized in
growing rice while starving its young.

It was hot because preseason practice was held in
August, when the temperature and humidity both
fooled around with and finally married each other, becoming, for all time, the nineties twins. And Ed Buck
played football at Oklahoma. This was truly surprising,
since he was a walk-on, no-scholarship unknown whom
nobody from Oklahoma had scouted or even heard of
and, of all things, a Jewish kid from the streets of New
York. Neither category, walk-on nor New York Jew,
had been represented in the storied Oklahoma football
program for nearly a decade, and never had both af-
flictions been present at the same time in one athlete.

The fact that Ed Buck was matriculating at OU at
all was equally inexplicable. He had attended Boys
High in Brooklyn, played football there only because
he had been able to hide it from his parents, and
through a variety of subterfuges somehow managed to
deal with the problem of being too good until the *Daily
News* named him to its All-City team. In itself, this
didn't really present an insurmountable problem, be-

cause the only newspaper ever read in the Buck household was the *Times*. But then too many of his parents' friends began calling to congratulate them, and he was able to save himself from eternal Jewish Parent Purgatory only because he had found time to earn sufficiently high grades to rank ninth in his graduating class and soon after was accepted by Cornell, Colgate, and Tufts, three of the four colleges to which he had applied at his parents' urging. Princeton had turned him down, thereby reinforcing their solid conviction that Albert Einstein had been the only Jew to spend any time there, because the desperate White Anglo-Saxon Protestants had harbored a sinister plot to mystically excise a few of his intelligence genes while he slept.

Ed was also accepted by the University of Oklahoma, to which he had applied on his own. His father, Sheldon Kalman Buck, whose father's last name had been Buchhalter, had with predictable precision determined that Cornell produced more doctors than Tufts, which in turn produced more lawyers than Cornell, and that both produced more of both than Colgate. So he and Ed's mother, Dora, during one of their "official" meetings in the kitchen of their apartment on Avenue J, decided, after long and soul-searching study, that Ed accept the admission offered by Cornell.

Which was exactly when Ed said, "Oklahoma."

The battle raged for a month. Ed wanted to go somewhere else, to see some other part of the country. Besides, in a truth known only to himself, standing six-four and weighing 250, he harbored just enough ego to want to try his hand at major college football. But that could never be mentioned as a factor, for he had barely begun to convince his parents that he had not already suffered irreparable brain damage from his bout with high school athletic insanity. Instead, he argued that it didn't matter where he went to college because he wanted to be neither doctor nor lawyer but writer, author, a man of words like his two heroes, Ernest Hemingway and Jack Kerouac. It was undeniable that writers learned by doing, by traveling, by coping with unusual, perhaps even threatening, situations.

Sheldon Buck, a certified public accountant, was convinced that writers wound up broke and depressed, probably drunk, certainly divorced, and alone. Dora Buck said she had known only one other woman to have raised a lunatic son, Molly Goldman, whose Nathan had turned down the chance to use his hard-earned dentist's degree by going in as a partner with Dr. Paul Katz, a family friend. Instead, Nathan had run away to Southern California, where he sold paper tax shelters to rich actors and actresses, an endeavor that invariably made them less rich while at the same time adding to Nathan Goldman's clearly ill-gotten gains. Dora sulked, pleaded, and finally settled on old-fashioned, healthy mourning, convinced beyond a doubt that her Edward was going to be killed and eaten by Christians or Indians, after which they would sell his typewriter and electric shaver for far less than they were worth.

Sheldon persevered, correlating for his confused son Cornell with a guaranteed high future income, Tufts with permanent financial security, Colgate with at least a chance at professionalism. Ed listened patiently because he loved his parents, tolerated all their arguments and all their threats and all their warnings of doom, and wound up leaving by train for Norman, by way of Oklahoma City, ten days before the fall semester of 1968 was to begin. Sheldon formally shook his hand at the platform in Penn Station and surreptitiously slipped Ed five twenties neatly folded in half.

Dora, wiping her reddened eyes with a finely embroidered handkerchief made decades ago by her mother in Russia, managed to insert two twenties and a ten in her only son's jacket pocket when he bent for a final kiss, knowing in her heart that he would discover it in times of great need, hopefully before he ever thought to send the jacket to a dry cleaner.

The freshman year was a piece of cake. The high school education he had mastered under the then-strict guidelines of the New York City Board of Education had put him at least a year ahead of the demands placed on college freshmen by OU. Freshman English was a cupcake; basic algebra was almost embarrassingly easy. The American history professor was well ahead of the class, which added some interest to that course, and Introduction to the Novel, which Ed had to beg to be allowed to take as a freshman, was his favorite. But Ed's high point came as a result of spotting a notice on the bulletin board in the student union center, which he had started visiting to earn quick money at the snooker tables.

FOOTBALL TRYOUTS. OWEN FIELD. MONDAY SEPT. 2. 9 A.M.

OU did not need to conduct tryouts—indeed, did not want to—and seldom, if ever, were any real players ever turned up during such charades. The team was stocked with High School All-American types from Oklahoma, Tennessee, Texas, California, Arkansas, and Nebraska. In addition, the nation's most highly prized high school quarterback, Adam Benson of Oliphant, Pennsylvania, had broken recruiters' hearts at Penn State, Syracuse, Florida State, Ohio State, Notre Dame, and Miami by deciding, as Ed had, to see what Oklahoma was all about.

But since the university had been founded under federal land-grant conditions, certain formalities had to be maintained, just as the Grambling University sports program, traditionally all-black, had to have at least one white athlete on scholarship to satisfy state of Louisiana requirements. At OU sports teams had to hold open tryouts, all male students were required to participate in some form of ROTC training, and blacks had to be accepted according to some nebulous but nevertheless quite real formula. It was argued by some students that the one overriding factor in the formula was overwhelming athletic ability. No one disputed the theory.

So the morning arrived and, armed with nothing more than shorts and a pair of low-cut cleats, Ed Buck jogged the two miles to the field, found the open gate, and approached the first man he saw with a clipboard, an assistant coach named Harvey Joe Bigelow.

"Buck, Ed, freshman," he said.

"Ah don't seem to find your name on my list heah," said Harvey Joe, nervously eyeing this obviously fit, visibly well-built freshman. "What's your position, son?"

"Offensive line, sir. I mostly played tackle in high school, but I spent some time at center."

Harvey Joe shrugged. "Well, it sure don't matter. I'll find your name sooner or later. Get over there with the offensive line; ask for Coach Johnson."

Coach Frank "Pop" Johnson didn't have Buck's name on his list, either, and didn't like being surprised. But what he did like was the size of this kid, the clear eyes, and the implied toughness in that New York accent.

"Do we know about you?" Johnson asked, his sun-leathered, weather-beaten, lined face creasing easily into a smile. "Do we know you're here?"

"No, sir, but it said you were holding tryouts and I just got here and I'd like to try out. OK?"

"You play?"

"High school."

"Any good?"

It was Ed's turn to smile. "Yes, sir. Real good."

Pop Johnson had been around the whole thing twice. He was sixty-two years old and had played pro football when it was little more than a barnstorming carnival. He had coached high school teams and college teams, at the highest levels and at those places where football was still just a game. He even coached for a while in the National Football League, but that wasn't what he wanted. Pop Johnson loved to work with kids, make them better, watch them improve. Right now, he was getting a tingle, a feeling, about Ed Buck.

"Look, son. We have to hold these tryouts, you understand? Every year a couple of kids show up, mostly just for the fun of it, and we let 'em work out with the team and take a few hits and then they go back to being students and they leave the football players alone. From the look of you, you'd have to play offensive tackle on the freshman team. Now, in addition to being the offensive line coach for the varsity, I am the freshman coach, and I make damn sure to take care of myself, you understand? I have got one freshman tackle who was a Scholastic All-American and three more who were All-State. The All-American is six-six and weighs two hundred and seventy pounds and he has a thirty-eight-inch waist and a fifty-four-inch chest.

"So, now I'm gonna ask you again. You any good?"

Ed Buck looked the old man right in his eyes. "Damn good, coach. Watch me."

Pop Johnson watched. When the daylong workout had ended, he ambled over to Ed, who had more than held his own, who had even blocked Raymond Mc-Clelland, the Sooners' junior All-American defensive end, four consecutive times during skeleton passing drills. McClelland didn't like that, especially from a freshman nobody knew about, so after the third time he jumped up, threw a roundhouse right, and caught Ed just under the breastbone.

"Don't you fuck with me, you freshman piece of shit," snarled Raymond McClelland, standing tall and lean and almost religiously outraged over the prone body of the upstart maverick.

When the five-man offensive line and the two receivers shuttled back to the impromptu huddle, Ed was seething. "Call the same play," he hissed to the freshman quarterback, the prized recruit from Pennsylvania, the heroic Adam Benson.

"You got it," smiled the rock-hard coal country kid, who was thinking that he might have just made a friend.

Same formation, same objective: to free a receiver over the middle. Raymond McClelland, who had guffawed with his friends in the defensive huddle, now smiled benignly, and with great confidence, across the line of scrimmage.

"Watch me, boy; I'm comin' through."

Ed said nothing at all. His face was white, his body taut. The ball was snapped, Ed stutter-stepped backward, setting up for pass-blocking duties, and Mc-Clelland came roaring across the line—to be met by Ed Buck's left hand, an uppercut that seemed to start from the ground. It caught the All-American smack on the point of the chin and lifted him about six inches off his

feet before he fell to the ground in a heap, an unconscious heap.

Everything stopped. Jim Lee Hudson, the nation-
ally famous head coach of the annually powerful
Sooners, rushed toward the scene to see whether his
defensive star was all right and to kick the ass of this
unknown freshman, but Pop Johnson caught him by
the elbow.

"Hold on, Jim Lee; I got a feelin' about that boy.
You been watchin' his feet? He's quick. He's smart.
You just saw that he's tough. And he won't back down.
Before you get all over him, maybe you ought to find
out how come your All-American is pukin' on the
ground, you know?"

Hudson smiled. "You're right, Pop. Who is that
kid?"

"Walk-on. Named Buck, Ed Buck. Freshman. From
Brooklyn-New-Yawk, if you please."

The smile broadened. "Get him signed up, Pop, and
if anybody asks, tell 'em we knew about him all along,
that a friend, maybe some high school coach up there,
tipped us off. Who do we know in Brooklyn? Some
scout?"

Johnson nodded his head. "We'll find somebody.
Golly, coach, you sure are one smart sumbitch, ain't
you?"

Jim Lee Hudson smiled broadly. After all their years
together, he kept finding new reasons to like old Pop
Johnson.

Ed Buck made the freshman team. He started, then
spent the next three seasons with the varsity; he could
not hide from his parents the fact that he played football because he was a junior and senior All-American
selection and was drafted by the Chicago Bears in the
third round of the 1972 draft. He signed a contract, got

a $50,000 signing bonus, was prepared to earn $105,000 in his rookie season, and then, playing in the now-extinct College All-Star game against that year's defending NFL champions, the Green Bay Packers, tore his right knee, suffering extreme damage to the medial collateral and cruciate ligaments, and knew with absolute certainty that his football career had come to a tragic, premature but unquestioned end.

So he came home and became a sportswriter for the *New York Express*. It came as no surprise to him or anyone else that he was assigned to cover pro football in general and the New York Giants in particular.

Now, a dozen years later, his weight down to 240, his reputation as one of the nation's best sportswriters assured, the author of half a dozen "airplane book" novels that probably would have pleased Hemingway and infuriated Kerouac, with enough money to do what he wanted to do, a divorce now seven years old, and completely healed, he was comfortable, secure, pleased with his life. Sheldon Kalman Buck, had he lived, would have been happy, not to mention surprised, that all writers do not end up desolate and drunk. Dora Buck, had she lived, would have continued to insist that Ed got out of Oklahoma just in time.

It was football season. The Chicago Bears were coming to town, and that meant a long-awaited visit with their star quarterback, Adam Benson, the six-time Pro Bowl selection, holder of many NFL career records, the "old man" of the league's quarterbacks, the Scholastic All-American from Oliphant, Pennsylvania, and OU— and Ed Buck's best friend.

As a professional, Benson had made as much of an impact off the field as on it. He had taken the Bears to their first-ever Super Bowl championship three years earlier despite having been picked up and booked for disorderly conduct in Miami Beach and spending four hours in a one-man cell, providing the *Miami Herald* with a prizewinning photograph of Benson signing autographs for the local police while sitting on the cell's threadbare cot next to three as-yet undrunk bottles of beer. He and one of the second-string defensive linemen had decided that Super Bowl Week had made too much of an imposition on their social lives. So they got themselves roaring drunk and before being arrested were cruising down Collins Avenue in a convertible, throwing official NFL footballs through storefront plate glass windows.

The league commissioner had considered ruling Benson ineligible to play that day. For about three seconds. Then wiser heads prevailed, advisers who reminded the commissioner of the television ratings, the enormous amounts of money at stake, and the almost certain publicity damage, the fact that this was going to be, beyond doubt, the biggest Super Bowl attraction since the underdog New York Jets had stunned the haughty Baltimore Colts in premerger days.

The official announcement at noon on Super Sunday, five hours prior to the game, was that Adam Benson, released and in the care of his team, would be summoned to New York the following week for a "frank discussion" with Commissioner Paul A. Davis. The unfortunate second-string defensive tackle, however, would not be allowed to play that day. It had been "learned" that he (and the commissioner had managed this with a straight face) had been the one to "lead Benson astray" in the first place.

The media chuckled, convinced that "frank discussion" meant another attempt by another authority figure to show Benson the "proper" way to represent himself and the league. Ed Buck, who had spent four years with Adam, chuckled most of all. Ed knew it was hopeless, that a capricious, uninhibited spirit like Benson's would never respond well to society's bonds. If at all.

Adam had finally married, three years ago when he was thirty, to a legitimate centerfold girl, tall and willowy and flat-out gorgeous. Her name was Sherri Novak, and with her looks and his reputation they immediately became a celebrity couple for the entertainment pages, invited to the California and New York parties and offered off-season roles in movies that wouldn't demand too much in the way of acting skills.

Adam had called Ed late the previous Wednesday night, eager for their reunion—it had been almost a year, and they hadn't gone that long since leaving Oklahoma together—and while Ed thought Adam's old bubbling enthusiasm was missing, he chalked it off to the pressures of the game, the recent slump that had dropped him to the lower half of the NFL's quarterback-efficiency charts the previous season, which had never happened before, and his obvious struggle so far through the seven games of the current season.

Sherri wasn't going to make the trip. The Bears would arrive in New York late Friday afternoon. Ed would meet Adam at the team hotel, and Saturday night would be dinner, just the two of them, at an out-of-the-way but exceptional steak house on Manhattan's Lower West Side, the Old Homestead.

Pro football weekends in New York City, with the weather crisp and clear, were among Ed Buck's favorite things, and adding to that the pleasure of seeing his old friend again simply heightened the anticipation.

Ed even started to feel some of that old football excitement that had been missing lately. All things considered, Ed was anxiously looking ahead to this meeting.

TWO

ADAM Benson looked terrible.

Haggard was the first word that came to mind; *pale and drawn* followed almost immediately.

They sat at the bar of the Metro-Plaza Hotel, two old friends pulling at their drinks. Ed smiled and nodded and feigned interest in what Adam was saying, but his mind was casting about for some explanation. *He's not old,* Ed thought, *and he's not sick, because he's playing regularly. It can't be emotional, because that would affect his performance, and even if he was struggling, what was a struggle for Adam Benson represented a high-quality season for most other quarterbacks in the league.*

But he looked so awful.

Finally, Ed had to ask. "Adam, what's wrong? You look like two trucks have been taking turns running you over at night. Man, I mean, you look like hell. You losin' weight, too?"

A shrug of the shoulders, and the Benson smile flashed through. "Hey, it's a jungle out there, Jane," he laughed. "This is the National Football League, Eddie, and my offensive line sucks. I need you at one of the tackles, you know? That big kid, the first-round draft choice, Lange? Well, my friend, he's a turkey. They made a mistake and they know it, but they can't cut him loose yet because it would make them look stupid in public. He's got no heart, Eddie, just a lot of size and no balls. I told 'em if I can't count on a guy I can't play with him, and they know that, but then the owner tells the coach to keep him in and that's the way it's going to be.

"Also, Bill Jillian, the center? He's workin' with a bad back. The guy's got all the heart in the world, but he can't move because of the back. But Michael Lee Reasons, the guy who plays behind him, is a coward. Can't do the long snap, either. So Jilly has to play, and he gets the ball to me and most of the time he gets the job done, but then there are certain nose tackles . . . like the guy the Giants have, Blake? . . . the small, quick ones . . . who show him one move and then cut across and get past him the other way, and he can't do anything but scream in pain. So now I'm keepin' both backs in to block, and that cuts down my passing choices."

Talking about the Bears' deficiencies visibly depressed Adam. "I been thinkin' it's gettin' time to retire, maybe," he said. "I mean, two years ago I had the best damn offensive line in the entire league, and then Slaby and Webster retire, Jamieson gets smart with the coach and winds up in Buffalo, for God's sake, and Pownall gets himself elected union president and they cut his ass the next week. All I got left is Jillian and a bunch of shit. This is takin' more out of me than it's worth, Eddie. Even the game we won, it took me three days to shake the aches. I am really taking one unbelievable pounding, you know?"

Having worked himself up, apparently getting a rare chance to bitch to somebody who would understand, Benson made a fast emotional comeback. Wiping his sweating forehead with a cocktail napkin, snapping his fingers for another round, he laughed.

"Did I tell you I got to meet Burt Reynolds, at his

house, and he had my picture waitin' for me to autograph? I did, down in Florida; guy's got a house like a
small town. We sat around all afternoon, maybe half a
dozen of us, talkin' football. He knows something about
this game, you know? Oh, and Sherri isn't here because
she's auditioning for a part in one of those horror movies for teenagers. You know, like *Halloween*? She says
there's a pretty good chance she'll get it, too."

He rambled on for a while, drinking three more
beers, growing more animated. Color flooded his
cheeks, his eyes sparkled again, and he looked just like
Adam Benson was supposed to look.

"Hey, Ed, I'm gonna be late for another team meeting," he suddenly said, glancing at his watch, slapping
two twenties on the bar, pushing the stool away behind
him. "Tomorrow night, the Homestead, eight o'clock.
Right?"

They shook hands and he was gone, hitting the hotel
lobby in a half-skipping, half-running motion, just slipping into an elevator car as the door began to slide
silently shut.

Ed was smiling as he left the hotel, and a little flushed
from the beer, too. Since it was reasonably warm for
late October, he decided to walk the twenty blocks back
to his apartment. Tomorrow he would knock off his
Sunday column, put the finishing touches on the advance story for the Giants–Bears game—using exclusive
quotes from the star quarterback, of course—and maybe
see Leigh for a few hours in the afternoon. Usually,
Saturday nights at home were for her, but she knew
that when Adam Benson hit town she'd better find
other plans. Still, Ed had thought about taking her with
him, to meet Adam, because he felt it had come time
to do that. But the mysterious way Adam was behaving
convinced him to let it wait for the next opportunity.

He felt a twinge when he opened the door to the apartment, for maybe the thousandth time, knowing no one was home. Maybe he'd think a little harder about what Leigh had been trying to sell him. Marriage. Lord, he swore he'd never marry again, not after the ordeal that was spelled *Suzanne,* as in Suzanne Chait-Buck; now, thank God, Suzanne Chait-Feldman. No kids, no alimony, but best of all, no Suzanne. No wondering who she was with when he was on the road, who had been sleeping with and sweating on and fucking his wife in his own bed. There was an old line from the late Hugh Vanbrock, Hall of Fame quarterback, later a head coach, offered when someone asked if he cheated on the road:

"Cheat on the road? Son, when I close my suitcase I get a hard-on," he had said, laughing.

In Suzanne's case it had been slightly different. When Ed closed his suitcase, she got horny.

Saturday morning woke up raining. Ugly, dirty gray clouds spitting down on the streets of New York City. Always a good day to work. Ed brewed coffee first. Coffee was one of his great weaknesses, and so he allowed it to be one of his great extravagances, like Knockando, the best of the single-malt scotches, and Ketel One, the top of the vodka line. He bought the coffee in compact eight-ounce boxes from a specialty company that imported it from Holland. Sure it was expensive, but the powdery rich brown grinds, which resembled talcum powder more than coffee, made the best cup he'd ever had. At the equivalent of eighteen bucks a pound, it better be good. The Knockando and Ketel One he got in the biggest bottles he could find. Same story. Expensive but worth it.

Something in Adam's behavior still bothered him,

still hovered just beyond awareness, taunting and teasing. He was . . . what? Too changeable, too unpredictable? Just different, a new Adam Benson that Ed simply wasn't accustomed to seeing? How often did they really see each other, three, four times a year? It was the past that bonded them together, a comfortable, familiar friendship grounded in what life had been, not in what it was now. So Adam was different. So what? The last time they had met was in January, at the Super Bowl in Phoenix. Ed was there to work, Adam to party, mostly, to represent a beer company at the cocktail hours and NFL-related functions. *That was ten months ago. So he's different now. Who isn't?*

Ed shrugged, poured the first of what would be many mugs of hot, black coffee, flipped on the switch of his laptop computer—hooked right in, it was, to the newspaper's system; instant story, without an editor, even, in Ed's case—and began to work. Shortly after, he sat back and smiled, wondering how he could ever work during the day without coffee and Marlboros and how he could ever work at night without vodka and Marlboros.

It was simple and easy, a smooth transition between the column, opinion—remember, the readers want to know what you think so they don't have to think for themselves—and the game advance, which was as useless as all game advances, free publicity for the team, in effect.

The Giants are playing the Bears today, at the stadium, at one o'clock, here are the starting players, here is the situation as it affects both teams in their divisional standings, here are a few of the more noteworthy statistics achieved so far by some of the individual players, and here, you should pardon the expression, is the way I have chosen to present this information to you, in the form of some gimmicky, often contrived hook:

"The difference between the Giants' 6–1 record and the Chicago Bears' 1–6 is only eighteen points," he wrote. "The Giants have won five games by a total of nine points, while the hard-luck Bears have lost five by the identical margin. The fact that both teams are virtually even in talent and experience will become obvious on the field, where it should be a far better and more closely fought game than the two records might indicate."

Once, as a community service to the team's owners, in a time when stadiums weren't always sold out, the city newspapers, as in the rest of the country, ran these advances as an attempt to spur some last-minute Sunday-morning ticket sales. Now advances were real crap, but the copy filled the hole, and it was precisely what the sports editor. Willie Moss, who had been in the position for almost half a century and was the best newspaperman Ed would ever know, insisted was part of the paper's job in covering the team.

"You can't just ignore a game and then go cover the damned thing and come in with a front-page story and a column," Willie had always said. "If it deserves that kind of treatment when they play it, then it deserves some kind of announcement that it's going to be played that day. Final. That's it. Anybody who covers a New York team for this paper while I'm the sports editor, any team, any sport, is going to do game advances or wind up taking high school box scores on the telephone Friday night. And remember to always fill in with the good kind of crap between commas. That's what the readers want, even if they don't know it."

The point was well made and well-taken. Game advances had become a way of life. Boring, perhaps, but nevertheless automatic, and the trivial material that made the players turn from names on a broadsheet into real people became part of Ed's writing.

The fourth mug of coffee and maybe the fifteenth Marlboro later, at four in the afternoon, Ed punched the key to "SAVE" what he had written, picked up the desk telephone, dialed the newspaper's incoming transmission number, got the required *beep,* and pushed the transmit button on the minicomputer. The answering beep told him the machines had joined in perfect, if only temporary, union, and since he had written the equivalent of seven old-fashioned pages of paper, the transmission process would continue for approximately four minutes.

He leaned back, watched as each line blinked and disappeared (not forever, though the first time he had watched the process in operation it had almost brought his heart to a stop), put a match to yet another Marlboro, and closed his eyes. *Beep . . . beep . . . beep . . .* Line after line went whirring into the telephone cable, to be gobbled up by the monster at the other end, to be turned into type of a preprogrammed style and face, to be made ready, justified, balanced, and paginated, for the editor who would be in soon to study Ed's offerings, as well as those of all the other writers on the staff, on his video display terminal for final changes and headline work.

Old-fashioned typewriters were still in his blood, but Ed had quickly come to rely on the speed and ease of editing offered by these new machines. You don't like it, you just push a button and everything disappears, electronically erased, and you don't have to roll fresh blank paper into the carriage, type all the same headers and codes, then find you made the same error again and had to go through the process yet another time. Still, typewriters were real; these things were probably produced by George Lucas and used by Mark Hamill or R2D2. Or maybe they *were* R2D2.

The final *beep* told him that both files had been successfully transmitted. Glancing at his watch, he figured one of the editors would already be in the office, since all deadlines were earlier on Saturday nights to handle the rush of extra Sunday editions. He pushed the proper combination of number-buttons, heard two rings and then: "Spawwwts."

That was Howard Weiss, the best editor in the city, the guy who could turn sows' ears into silk paragraphs.

"Hey, Howard, Buck here."

"We got 'em both," Weiss snapped. Conversational amenities had never been part of his repertoire. "Column's real good; advance is a piece of shit."

"Advances are always a piece of shit, my prizewinning editor friend," Ed said. "Let Moss say the word and there won't be a dry eye in the house when we kill the bastards."

"I'll fix it, save your ass another day. It's busy. You done?"

"Yeah. And my compliments to your speech teacher, you silver-tongued devil, you."

Flipping on the television, Ed had the chance to see the tail end of the UCLA–Ohio State game, unconsciously hoping UCLA was winning because the coach, a nice guy named Walter Raye, used to coach the Giants, winced when the announcer's voice told him there were three minutes to play and the Buckeyes held a two-touchdown lead, turned down the volume, and made a mental note to call Los Angeles sometime the next week to talk to Walter Raye, find out what he thought about the Giants from his new vantage point. He had virtually handpicked his successor, the current Giants' coach, Duane Charles, who had been not only his defensive coordinator for four years but also his closest friend, best man, and godfather to his first child.

However, in the past few months, with the Giants doing better and better, it became obvious to those who knew how to look that Charles was growing more sensitive to the references that this was "Raye's team," seeing as how it was virtually unchanged in terms of the offensive and defensive units put in place—especially over the last two years.

Charles was visibly uncomfortable when asked to talk about Raye or to explain just how things were different when the cast of characters had remained virtually unchanged. Perhaps that would be an interesting dimension to explore.

But now it was past five, and it remained for Ed to shave, shower, make a few telephone calls, perhaps sit back with his feet up and his legs propped for thirty minutes, carefully nursing the first Ketel One of the day (with shaved ice, of course, in a fat-bodied, squat pony glass).

At seven-fifteen he strode out of his apartment on East 72d Street, waited no more than five minutes before a taxicab cruised past and stopped, and was in the lobby of the Old Homestead at seven-fifty, shaking hands with the owner, Mike Muldowney, an old friend, looking around for Benson, then telling Mike that tonight's guest was the noted quarterback Adam Benson and that a slightly out-of-the-way table, like in a corner or against a wall, would make the night much easier for his neatly uniformed waiters, who would not have to wait while a small crowd of autograph seekers clogged the aisles.

Mike understood perfectly, made a few marking-pen flourishes on the oversize desk blotter used as the reservations chart, and smiled. "All done, Ed." Snapping his fingers at the nearest waiter, Mike added: "Take Mr. Buck to table seven, Mario, and nothing he or his guest orders is to be billed, do you understand?"

Mario not only understood but smiled. He knew, since this had happened the last time, and because Ed really didn't like the no-charge courtesy, that Buck was going to leave sufficient cash on the table, after he argued with Muldowney, who would refuse to accept payment. And one way or another, that cash, which figured to be about a hundred bucks, was going to wind up in the pocket of the extremely grateful Mario Cress.

He led Ed to the table, assured him that he would bring his guest as soon as he arrived, and asked whether Mr. Buck would like his Knockando mist. Mr. Buck would, and Mr. Buck was impressed that Mario remembered.

But it wasn't until Mario delivered the second Knockando that Adam arrived, twenty minutes late. "Sorry," he said, easing himself into the chair against the wall. "Meeting ran late. Damn coach thinks we can beat this losing streak by having meetings. Been here long?"

Ed shook his head. "Nah, couple of minutes. You drinking?"

It was Adam's turn to shake his head. "Game tomorrow. Just a light beer."

Mario heard, and it arrived, in a frosted mug, moments later. "You gonna beat our Giants tomorrow, Mr. Benson?" He smiled. "I remember last year, you beat us good, and I had a hundred bucks on the Giants. But I don't hold a grudge. Just lay down tomorrow so I can get my money back, OK?"

Adam's practiced public smile vanished as quickly as Mario did, and he turned to Ed, his face devoid of color.

Now Ed was sure something was wrong. He looked directly into his friend's eyes and quietly spoke two words: "Tell me."

Adam nodded, almost imperceptibly. "OK, I will. I have to. This is as far as I go." He paused, drew a deep breath, motioned with his head over his right shoulder in the direction in the waiter had gone. "What he said, that waiter? He was right. It's in the bag. I am gonna lay down tomorrow. The Giants are gonna win. I have made the Bears losers in three of the seven games we have lost this season, and tomorrow is supposed to be another one. I am supposed to throw at least three interceptions, and if we get inside the Giants' twenty-yard line I am supposed to fumble a snap. I have been throwing games for two years, Eddie. I think I'd be a lot happier dead."

A humorless, dry laugh. "And if I don't do it, I *will* be dead. Worse yet, if I don't do it, Sherri will be dead. I don't know what else to say. Shit, what else could be this bad?"

Ed stood up, pushed back his chair, and dropped some money on the table. "Not here, Adam. My apartment. Now."

Benson nodded, also rose, and followed his friend out to the entrance hall, where Mike Muldowney grew panicky. They assured him nothing was wrong, that they'd be back soon, that Benson had forgotten an important errand that had to be done immediately.

In less than thirty minutes they were in Ed Buck's apartment, sitting on facing chairs separated by a glass coffee table.

"The whole thing, Adam. All of it, now. We got all night, and the hell with your curfew."

Another ironic smile played with Benson's lips. "No curfew this trip," he murmured. "Coach Parr thinks we need to kick our heels a little, stay out late, maybe get laid, get loose, and win one. It's OK. Shit, it's expected of me, considering my reputation, you know? Funny, nobody really knows what they're saying when they talk about Adam Benson's reputation."

For the next hour, almost without pause, the quarterback spun out a story of sensational partying, random sex, high-level gambling, multimillion-dollar drug deals, addiction, manipulation, intimidation, and, finally, fear. Adam dealt with a man called Whistle, a common thug, who told him which games were to be fixed, how much he was going to receive, and what would happen to him and his wife, especially his wife, if he changed his mind or if, for whatever reason, things didn't come out the way they had been structured.

"I made six hundred thousand a game last year. We arranged three games. It's easy. I fumble the snap, or I change my cadence, just once a game, to draw one of my own linemen offsides, or I throw the ball just a foot too far or to the wrong side. Simple. Nobody knows; nobody suspects. It's a game of inches and breaks, and who can blame the quarterback for those things? I feel lousy, Eddie. I've been crapping on the game and my career and everything I ever got out of football."

Ed nodded in agreement. "You're right, Adam, and nothing anybody says is gonna make that come out any different. But why do it at all? What made it something to even consider? You didn't really do it just for the money, did you?"

"Hell, no. I make too damned much and I'd probably play for expenses, food, and a place to live if somebody asked. It was the cocaine, Eddie. I got myself an addiction, and that costs more, and the longer you do it the more you need, and that runs up the price, and it's absolutely true that if you can get all you need without worrying you can play well enough so that nobody will think anything's wrong. I use an untraceable masking agent when we take the urine tests. I couldn't do this for another whole season, and I am cutting way down, but this is no problem at all."

"So what happened? Why the guilt now, after all the damage has been done? This is starting to sound like some fucking soap opera, you know?" Ed knew he sounded more indignant than he wanted to, than he had intended, and was still trying to remember that Adam Benson was his friend, that they went back a long way, that according to his ever-increasing sense of perspective that seemed to go hand in glove with the years old friendships were to be cherished and preserved.

"I just don't want to do it anymore," Adam whispered. "I don't want to lose; I don't want to be on somebody's string. I'm still a great quarterback, and I want to go out as one. Not like this. Not like some slug that crawls back under a rock after he dirties something good and clean. I'm going to be putting my ass on the line, and worse yet, I'm going to be jeopardizing Sherri, but I can't live with myself anymore. That's it. I am going back to playing quarterback, and the bad guys are going to have to find themselves another boy. I told them. Last week. I said we will probably lose the game to the Giants, but if we do, it won't be because I didn't try to beat their brains out first. Hey, what can they do, sue me? Report me to the police?"

"No, you asshole, they can kill you."

"Never. They're gamblers, not murderers, not Mafia

guys with flat noses. Forget them; it's over. All I want to be able to do now is play football and get out of this without people knowing what a shit I've been."

"They can and they will kill you."

"I know none of this gets in the papers, Ed. I know that. It's why I decided to tell you. You're my friend and I had to get this out, had to share it with someone I trust. I hope you don't think I'm just another prick, but I am and if you did, you'd be right. And I'm sorry. I know what football means to you, and believe it or not, but it's my life and I don't want to fuck it up. It just happened. I got trapped by the good times and then it was too late and I was in too deep to get out. Or so I thought. But I'm out of it now and I'm going to stay out of it. I'm going to be the best damned quarterback you ever saw."

Ed shook his head. "You always were, Adam. You always were."

Adam nodded, moved as if to leave, then suddenly grabbed Ed in an impulsive bear hug before turning and walking out of the apartment.

Ed walked aimlessly from room to room, the silence painfully loud, his mind swirling with confusion as he tried to fit things into the logical, newspaper style of organization that was the only way he could ever feel comfortable. Finally he went to the counter between the kitchen and the dining room that he used as a bar and poured a vodka, straight. It didn't much help; it was without taste. He sat on the couch, staring at nothing but the dark. It wasn't over. Things were never that simple, especially with such danger present and so much at stake. Where were the responsibilities and obligations this time? According to the rules by which he lived, he should have had no problem. He should have called his boss, the department head, and demanded a meeting with the overall editor of the newspaper, perhaps with the publisher and the corporate lawyers as well, to determine a course of action, since such a story had to be printed.

Had to be printed.

But it wouldn't be, not yet, anyway, because Adam Benson was his friend, because he felt his friend's life was at risk, and because he would do nothing to adversely affect that. It was a long time before Ed slept, and when he did, it was fitful at best.

THREE

IT was October 29, the anniversary of the crash of the New York Stock Exchange, but unlike that suicidal day in 1929, this one was sunny and crisp, the morning light more golden than pastel, extending the promise of that special kind of autumn day so rare as to perfectly define the season.

Ed had slept poorly, but sitting on the couch staring out into the blackness of Manhattan had done nothing to provide answers to those questions concerning his professional ethics and responsibilities. He had no idea how he would handle the story of this game, but in the end that was of secondary significance. He was still worried for his friend, now more than ever.

But perhaps things would work out just as Adam had suggested. A game scheduled to be fixed would instead be played honestly, and by the best quarterback in the league. To whom, indeed, would the fixers complain? Besides, as Adam had also posed, there was a chance no one would ever know. The Giants were far superior to Chicago, and even if Benson was able to call upon his magic again, even if the offensive line suddenly became capable of blocking and protecting him, the Giants had more than enough offense, more than enough defense, and there seemed no doubt that they were going to make this season one for their fans to remember.

Maybe the Bears would lose by more than the required margin; maybe the man Adam called Whistle would shrug, convinced that the quarterback had merely been shooting off his mouth and wouldn't have the nerve, at crunch time, to really renege against such dangerous men. Maybe.

Being a New Yorker, a status conferred only on those who live and work in four of the five boroughs that make up the largest city in the nation—Staten Island is far too suburban and removed to count and should be part of New Jersey anyway—Ed Buck didn't own a car. In fact, he had allowed his New York State driver's license to lapse several years ago. So going to a game at Yankee Stadium meant using the subway, the IRT train from the Lexington Avenue stop at 77th Street for the forty-five-minute trip.

There was no commuter crowd at ten o'clock Sunday morning, few suspicious-looking travelers whom Ed would associate with muggings and violence, and certainly no reason for delay. The trip was without incident, but the unusual peace and quiet of the underground, although it gave Ed more time to think, got him no closer to resolving his personal conflict. Adam Benson had put him in an untenable position, and he resented it.

By eleven-fifteen he was sitting in a quiet corner of the press lounge, sipping coffee from a plastic cup, thumbing through a week-old copy of the *Giant,* an independently produced tabloid-sized fan's newspaper that had dramatically increased in circulation and impact over the last few years. Most of the sportswriters assigned to cover the team were paid for freelance feature articles, and six months earlier the owners had managed to lure one of the best newspapermen in the area, an unrelenting Giant fan from the *Daily News* named Al Savill, to become the publication's first full-time editor. He had immediately injected a new look and verve, as well as some controversial content, to the extent that the team had begun to pay attention and show annoyance at editorial opinion with which it didn't agree. That was par for the course.

Vinnie Gordo and Stan Bradley, the "Double-Team Team" from the *Daily News* who spent the entire season with the Giants, on the road and at home, wandered into Ed's corner, carrying briefcases, portable computers, and cups of coffee.

"Hey, reading up on what's new and breaking?" asked Bradley, a tall gangly black man who had played basketball at Fordham while majoring in Obnoxious 101.

Ed smiled. "You bet, Stanley. I tried to find out what's new and breaking in the *Daily News* this morning, but then I made a mistake and read your story. So I didn't learn a thing."

Gordo laughed. He was short and stout, a student of the game who still, down deep, was in awe of Ed Buck the former All-American football player. "They win today by four touchdowns, Ed," Vinnie said. "The way the Bears are playing, we can start writing our leads by halftime."

"What? And miss those vintage hot dogs? Today's are from 1958. You remember what a great year that was for dog meat, don't you?"

The repartee was forced. Ed was uncharacteristically silent, and as soon as his two visitors realized it, they drifted off to find better company until the game started. Ed went back to the *Giant*, not even knowing what he was reading, just marking time until the next part of the day, the one he felt might turn out to be far more important than the game but one he wished he didn't have to view, began to take shape.

At twelve-forty-five he took the elevator to the press box on the fourth level, which actually was too high. But the Boland brothers, who owned the team, weren't about to pass up the chance to rake in exorbitant prices from three thousand of the best seats in the old stadium they had arranged for the city to renovate into luxury suites at the taxpayers' expense by holding out the threat of taking the team to the Jersey Meadowlands. Besides, the Bolands had never much cared about the newspapers, and it was universally felt that this lack of concern was easily explained: they couldn't read them, so why help them?

The high school band of the week, invited without an offer of expenses and "paid" with the worst, field-level, end zone seats, tooted its way through the national anthem. Four Chicago captains met at midfield with six New York captains, and after introductions were completed the Giants won the coin toss and chose to receive. Harland Vares kicked off for the Bears, Spider Keyes took it at the fifteen-yard line and returned it to the forty-five, great field position, and the capacity crowd, even before most had reached their seats, began its rhythmic, patented chant of: *"Score . . . score . . . score . . . "*

The Giants' quarterback, Gary Feller, went for it all on the first play. And he got it, throwing a deep sideline pass to the right flanker, Billy Joe Booker, who snatched the ball away from the Bears' left cornerback, Horace Jacobs, recklessly cutting across the receiver's path, looking for the interception. Booker, who possessed world-class sprinter's speed and had been an Olympic silver medalist three years earlier, had no trouble losing the frantic outside linebacker as well as the free safety, who had been caught totally unaware and never had a chance to catch the speedster despite having the angle. Jacobs simply stood at the sideline, head down, kicking at an imaginary divot in one of the league's last real grass-dirt fields, nothing artificial, not AstroTurf or TartanTurf or SmurfTurf.

With just fifty-three seconds elapsed in the game, Vares' extra point made the score 7–0. The anticipated rout evidently had begun. Ed relaxed, certain that Adam Benson, even on his greatest day, couldn't stem this tide.

The Giants kicked off. Chicago's James Truman took the ball at the goal line, eluded one tackler at the ten, sidestepped another at the thirty-three, and suddenly, impossibly, streaked between two Giants at midfield and was untouched, alone, uncatchable, all the way into the end zone. The scoreboard clock, which had read 14:07 when Feller threw the fifty-five-yard touchdown pass to Booker, showed 13:40. The score was tied.

Now the Bears kicked off. Keyes was snowed under by a gang of tacklers at the Giants' twenty-four, and three plays later Billy Anderson had to punt out of trouble. Finally, with possession on the Bears' forty, Adam Benson took the field.

Ed had seen Adam play for too long, had been there when the fire began to stoke itself, had been part of the electricity when he got himself psyched to play, and was able to tell, just from the bounce in his step and the almost spastic motion of his hands, that this was going to be one of those days. Ed had often ruminated over a theory he knew he would put into practice if ever he coached Adam Benson. He had even mentioned it once to Walter Raye when he took over as the Giants' head coach. They were talking about Ed's days at Oklahoma and Raye's at Alabama—they were approximately the same age, and in fact, Raye had been a senior at Alabama when Ed was a freshman at Oklahoma—on a late-night coast-to-coast flight. "Honest, Walter, I remember when we got a good quick start," Ed said, "he'd get all excited and damned near jump up and down and play his ass off the rest of the game."

"Yeah, I remember, especially when you guys beat the piss out of us in the Orange Bowl. I thought that was about the best game I ever saw a quarterback play, you know?"

Ed had smiled, clearly recalling that 30–27 victory so long ago, when Alabama had taken a 24–9 lead into the fourth quarter.

"So what would you do, Ed, if you were his coach?"

"Shit, Walter, the first play I'd call would be a short pass, a little baby pass, two yards to the sideline. Just so he gets to complete his first one. I mean, the man goes absolutely out of his fucking mind. You can see it. He comes back to the huddle talkin' a mile a minute and jumping up and down and all excited to get the next play called. I mean, he almost fucking stutters and wets his pants, he's so keyed up."

Raye had nodded and, like all coaches, filed away the information for possible future use, either for the day he might find himself coaching Adam Benson or, more likely, for a day when he might have to coach against Benson in a crucial game. Besides, it was a tip from another football player, someone who had been there, who knew, who wasn't just another asshole reporter.

Ed saw the signs. He knew Adam had decided to forget that this game was supposed to be lost. He knew, with a mixture of excitement and fear, that Adam Benson was about to stick it to the gamblers, the guys who control the money and the drugs and who sometimes choose to put an end to a life without feeling a twinge of conscience.

Adam knelt on one knee in the huddle, one of his trademarks. Ed could see Adam's hands drawing diagrams in the air, his head bobbing, his body tensing and relaxing, tensing and relaxing. *He's going to have one of those games,* Ed thought. *He's going to tell the bad guys to shove it.*

The Bears broke the huddle. Benson crouched behind the center, barked signals, barked again, again. The forty-second clock counted itself down, and just before it would have expired Adam took the snap, dropped back, faked a handoff to the fullback slamming up the middle to buy another few seconds, then veered to his right, apparently heading for the sideline, suddenly braking, almost skidding to a quick stop, and firing a line drive across his body, to his left, to the other side of the field.

It is the most difficult pass for a quarterback to throw, demanding not only timing and touch but also incredible arm strength and a large dollop of acting skill. Benson had it. Benson had also fooled the entire Giants' defense, because no one was there to defend against Ronnie Barnes, the halfback, who had slipped off to the left sideline and virtually walked downfield, waiting for the play to break.

Barnes caught the pass in stride, suddenly running full-speed, and was in the end zone before half the Giants knew what had happened. The play was so spectacular that the crowd, almost involuntarily, began to cheer, then, as if realizing it had happened against the Giants, choked off the noise. Ed Buck, sitting at his press station, felt his legs tighten, as if he were on the field, sharing in the excitement, basking again in the glow of a magical Adam Benson performance, feeling almost grateful to be allowed to be a part of it.

The Bears held the lead, and after a deep kickoff and some inspired defense they had the ball again, too, on their forty-seven. The first quarter was winding down, but Benson wanted another touchdown. He was having fun again, enjoying the lead, pleased with the play he had called to catch the league's best defense in high school embarrassment.

Adam handed off to Barnes after faking a toss to the fullback, and the play gained seven yards. Now Adam dropped back, stumbled, seemed about to be covered by hard-charging Giant defenders, and suddenly threw the screen pass to Barnes, who had stationed himself at the line of scrimmage. The right guard and the tackle, having allowed the defensive players to crash through, suddenly pulled out and set up a convoy for Barnes, who took the ball down to the Giants' eight-yard line before a desperate ankle-high tackle brought him down short of the goal line.

There was very little noise in the stadium now, although those who appreciated the rare talent they were watching were too enrapt to make any noise. They were studying Adam Benson, because few men had ever been able to lift quarterbacking to this particular state-of-the-art level.

From the eight, hands cupped tightly together underneath the center, Benson bellowed the signals. Ed could almost hear him on the field in Lincoln, Nebraska, or the Los Angeles Coliseum, or the Orange Bowl in Miami, could picture those games with the Sooners when Benson's genius hushed the crowds, when those rabid fans of the home team were forced to pay their respects to a genius. And it was happening again, right here in Yankee Stadium, in a game that should have been a pushover for the home team. Against their will, against their wishes, more than sixty thousand fans found they were forced to recognize a master.

Lifting his head from the possession chart he was filling in, Ed studied the Giants' defensive formation. Benson was spitting out signals, staccato, shrill, a voice Buck would have recognized anywhere in the world, anytime. And suddenly, perhaps because of nothing more than a gut feeling, perhaps because of the way Benson was almost fighting to keep his feet planted, Ed knew what he was going to do. It was a bootleg, the naked bootleg that even Benson's own players didn't know was coming, for that was the only way to keep it pure, to make it work. He had done it against Georgia once, and another time against Oklahoma State.

Jillian, the center, snapped the ball. Barnes, the half-back, had been set in motion, cutting back across the grain, just behind Benson, moving right, and Ed knew how surprised he was when Adam put the ball in his belly and then pulled it back. But Barnes was a professional, and it didn't take a fraction of a second for him to know he was the unsuspecting decoy. He never broke stride but clutched the imaginary football to his stomach and kept right on running.

The linemen, aware only of the play that had been called, a misdirection comebacker to the halfback in motion, had taken that first false step to their left and then cut-block the Giants by color, mowing down any blue uniform in their area of responsibility, generally no bigger than one yard square. It was called zone blocking, and it was especially effective in short-yardage situations. Nevertheless, what made it work was the natural execution by the other players, who sincerely believed in the play and therefore had no reason to show any brief glimpse of nervousness, which as a result would almost certainly tip off the real intent.

Adam Benson had the ball. Now, with the nerve of a gambler and the guts of a cat burglar, he tucked it tight to his right buttock and just for a second stood there, motionless, watching Barnes move to what everyone thought was going to be an attempt to score.

And then Benson began to amble to his left, gradually gaining speed. There was an instant flash of recognition on the face of the Giants' right outside linebacker, Tommy Taylor, when Benson swept past him. Right then, but forever too late, Taylor knew he had been duped, knew the entire defense had been duped, knew that Adam Benson had the ball and was going in for the touchdown, and knew there wasn't a thing in the world any of them could do about it. They had been suckered by an expert. For the second time in two consecutive series they had been set up by the master, then chopped in half by a classic opportunist.

Benson scored, and the Giants, reacting that split second too late, charged after him. So, too, did his own linemen, suddenly aware that they held a two-touchdown lead and now concerned with protecting their quarterback from the kind of punishment meted out by those who have been made to look foolish in front of their own.

The pileup was gigantic. It took a full minute to clear it, the officials pulling and tugging at the bodies, helping them off, getting them away, breaking up one minor skirmish between a Giant linebacker and Chicago's tight end.

But Adam Benson loved it, rolling over on the grass in the end zone just over the goal line, laughing so loud the paying customers in the first few rows of the end zone seats could hear him distinctly. Football hadn't been fun in a long time, but today everything was right. Today beating the heavily favored Giants in New York, not only making it look easy but also subjecting the Giants to some real humiliation in front of their fans, made everything right. He had reason to laugh. It was the joy of a boy coming through the frustrations and worries of a man.

In the press box, the noise level grew as the clock ticked off the final seconds of the first half, and the grin on Ed Buck's face was hard to wipe off, even when fat Fred Harris, the Giants' business manager and an old friend of the owners, walked past.

"Hey, Buck, you rootin'?" he asked. "I don't see anything that damned funny."

"You wouldn't, Fred, because it's happening to you. Don't you see? Adam Benson is the best quarterback in the league. Remember three years ago, when the Bears were trying to trade him? Might have been a good idea if you had said yes, you know?"

Harris walked off grumbling about the front-running, ungrateful sportswriters who don't give a shit about the team but eat the free food and drink the free beer. Fat Fred was primarily concerned with that food and beer and, in fact, related most things in his life to a stuffed face and a bloated belly. That he knew next to nothing about football, that most of the other teams in the league wanted to trade with the Giants because they could almost always fool the guy, was a truth that didn't seem to matter, because he worked cheap and did exactly what the Boland brothers told him to do, and they really didn't care that much about whether the team finished as champions or in fourth place, just so long as the television revenue kept escalating. Besides, Fat Fred had played for the Giants years earlier, and the Bolands always rewarded such men, assuming it didn't cost much.

The Bears held a 21–7 lead, but there was ample reason to believe that the Giants would be able to come back and perhaps still win with convincing superiority, so there seemed no sense in starting to write the first-edition story. Ed confined himself to doing the running account of the first half, storing it in the computer for use only if the game should go into overtime and some type was necessary to fill the space for the street sales. The running was little more than a play-by-play recap of the four scoring drives plus some of the more note-worthy individual statistics. The afternoon-paper re-porters didn't have to deal with such tedium; they had taken the elevator back to the lounge area, watching halftime highlights from other games on the television monitor or snacking on fat Fred Harris's cheap hot dogs.

Benson had gone through the roof, statistically, showing seven completions in eleven attempts for 204 yards, scored the two touchdowns, and thrown no in-terceptions. It had been a long time since Ed had seen his friend this good, perhaps not since that Super Bowl year when he won every award possible and set a league completion percentage record—78.2—that might stand forever. This was going to be a fun game to write, and because there was no one in the press corps who knew Benson (or football) nearly as well as Ed did, no one was aware that Adam had found all the glitches and holes in the Giants' highly publicized (and too unbending) semirevolutionary three-two-six defensive alignment and that such a masterful job of "industrial espionage" couldn't be wiped out during a brief half-time meeting. The Bears were going to win this game. That was guaranteed.

The second half had already started when the last few stragglers returned, mostly the radio guys whose microphones weren't necessary until afterward (and then just barely), who really showed up at the games to look for jobs and, of course, to see the action from the vantage point of "privileged citizen." The Giants kicked off, Chicago took over deep in its own territory, and Benson's problems with his offensive line became apparent. Jillian let the nose tackle through almost untouched, and Burton leveled Adam with a nine-yard sack.

Then the rookie tackle, Billy Lange, showed why he wouldn't stay long in the game, flat-out quitting (Ed saw it, but then Ed had been a tackle and knew what to look for) when the Giants' left defensive end, M. T. Marshall, hurt him with the only forearm shiver he was allowed, as part of his initial move at the snap of the ball. Marshall sluiced past the kid, showing incredible speed for a near-three-hundred-pounder, and Adam was down again, this time just as he was setting up seven yards deep in the backfield.

With third and twenty-six on the Bears' four-yard line, Adam chose caution as the greater part of valor, calling a simple fullback slam into the middle and giving the huddle up to the punter. The ball went to the Giants' forty-eight, Keyes wrestled for two yards on the return and Feller set the Giants in formation at midfield. It took five plays, the longest being the thirty-one-yard touchdown reception by the rookie halfback, Phil King, who had come in on third-and-seven as a blocking back but set off on a short circle pattern out of the backfield when the Bears didn't blitz but dropped into a seven-man coverage umbrella.

The score was thus narrowed to 21–14. The Giants' offense, at least, had made the proper adjustments. It was about to become evident whether the defense had a clue as to what it would take to cool off the white-hot Adam Benson. The Giants kicked off; Truman took it on the Chicago eleven and was cut down at the twenty-one. The crowd began to come alive, realizing that if the defense held here, the offense seemed more than capable of getting the tying touchdown.

The Bears' offensive players took the field, their orange-and-white uniforms already bearing the ex-pected "Christmas tree" stains—green for grass, red for blood.

Benson was still on fire. On second-and-ten, he found the tight end clear across the middle for a twenty-one-yard gain to the Bears' thirty-two. On first down he threw a strike to Barnes, circling out of the backfield, and it was a twenty-two-yard gain, to the Giants' forty-six. Ed watched as Benson bounced and jumped and grew hotter still, keeping the ball on first down—almost unheard of in the NFL, considering the low-percentage nature of the call—and made six yards behind Lange, the rookie who couldn't play offensive tackle.

The ball was on the Giants' forty. The defense had been no more effective than tissue paper in a hurricane. This latest Bears' drive was the easiest yet, almost hu-miliating in its thoroughness, and the crowd had begun to boo. From the forty, Adam crouched behind the cen-ter, barked his signals, built in a long pause in an at-tempt to draw somebody offsides and get a bonus of five free yards, then took the snap and darted back on his toes, eyes scanning the defensive formation as it unfolded before him. He pump-faked once and took the Giants' left cornerback out of the play, waited for the wide receiver to make the cut to the inside, a deep, diagonal pattern, and let it fly. Connection! Comple-tion! Only a spectacular knee-high tackle by a swiftly pursuing Taylor saved the touchdown, on the Giants' two.

No matter. A touchdown was inevitable, and the crowd knew it. A pallor fell across the field, giving Adam the chance to bark signals in such quiet that his voice could be heard in the press box: "On two, bingo, fourteen, six, twenty-eight, hut-hut-hut." On the final "hut," Jillian snapped the ball. Lange came down on the defensive tackle, jammed him laterally across the line of scrimmage; Jillian hesitated to allow the traffic to clear in front of him and then went searching for a blue shirt, finding the middle linebacker and mowing him down, creating the beginning of a massive pileup in the end zone. Adam Benson had the ball, of course, had followed Jillian's block, had waited with unnatural patience while Lange made his clearing, sealing block, and then drove headfirst into the end zone, realizing that he had scored when he saw the white goal line marker under his right shoulder.

The players on the Bears' sideline were up on their feet, jumping and waving upheld fists, knowing now for certain that they were part of a stunning upset.

The officials had blown their whistles, stopping the clock, and with the help of a few of them the players had begun to get back on their feet and allow those underneath to do the same. One by one they unpiled, the Bears running joyously to their bench, the Giant defenders, thoroughly confused, trudging with heads down to their sideline.

Ed Buck felt an inner satisfaction for his friend and watched the end zone to see how Adam was going to react now. He had taken the game by the nape of the neck and shook and shook until it came out right. There was virtually no chance that the Giants would be able to mount a comeback; one more Bears' score, even a field goal, would put this one out of reach. The gamblers and the fixers were fucked. Benson had told them that he was going to do it and he was doing it.

Adam was still lying across Bill Jillian's legs, motion-less. Jillian was saying something to the official, old Jack Reader, hovering over them, who then bent and stared into Benson's face. Reader turned to the head linesman; Jillian scrambled out from under the quarterback and then gently turned him over on his back. Adam still hadn't moved. Ed saw the rolling gurney being trun-dled out from under the stadium tunnel in the opposite end zone, pushed by two white-coated paramedics, while the two team doctors sprinted for the end zone and arrived almost simultaneously, almost comically, to kneel on either side of the motionless player. Now they helped move him—gently, gently—to the stretcher, which had been lowered almost to ground level and was raised only after Benson had been carefully strapped in, helmet removed.

Ed thought it might be a spinal or head injury, con-sidering the care with which the doctors had supervised the movement of his body. Now even thoughts of the fix, of the point-rigging scandals, of the threat to his friend's life were gone. This was injury, that most dreaded of events to a football player, and this seemed to be serious injury, perhaps career-threatening, espe-cially at Benson's age. But Buck couldn't storm down to the training room; he was a member of the media and thus was expressly banned from the training room or the locker room proper, for that matter, when play-ers and coaches were on the field. He would have to wait along with the others until an announcement was made.

The score was 28–14 when Vares kicked off for the Bears, and the ball bounced once at the Giants' nine before skidding into the end zone, where it was downed. Feller put the team in play from the twenty and netted only six yards in three plays against the fired-up Bears' defense, and the Giants had to punt.

But Ed's concentration was slipping. He had to know what was wrong with Benson, but repeated requests to both the Giants' publicity director, Don Carson, and his Chicago counterpart, Rick O'Donnell, had been fruitless.

"We'll make an announcement as soon as we know something, Ed," Carson said. "We can't get any word from their locker room yet."

"Fucking phone not working again?"

"No, it's working fine. They're just not answering it."

Ed went back to his seat, tried to pay attention, tried to keep up his charts, but his interest had waned appreciably. There was an undercurrent of unease throughout the press box; Ed could feel it.

Gordo, sitting near him, leaned over and put it into words: "The longer it takes, the more serious it must be, you know?"

"Yeah, I know, and there's nothing we can do. Drives me up the wall."

On the field, both teams had reached that point—which seems to arrive at least once in every football game—of total inertia. The Giants' defense had stiffened, or so it would appear, but the Bears' offense had flattened out, with a young and rarely used quarterback, Solomon Black, trying his best not to throw a pass, to keep the ball on the ground, clearly under orders, and allow the clock to finish the job that Adam Benson had started.

The fourth quarter was halfway over, the Bears still holding the 28–14 lead and moving downfield slowly

but inexorably. The crowd had already begun to thin
out, and with each first down in the ground-dominated
drive more of the faithful got to their feet and made
for the exit ramps. Ed stood up, perhaps for the first
time in a year deciding not to wait for the end of the
game and a complete chart. He was going downstairs,
into the catacombs under the old stadium, to wait outside the visitors' locker room until he could get in and
see what had happened to his friend.

There was already a crowd queued at the elevator,
the "PRESS ONLY POSTGAME ELEVATOR" that
the working press almost never got to use, it being
crammed with friends of the Boland brothers, such as
a local (not network) news anchorman, prematurely
gray and prematurely senile, and his five friends, at
least half a dozen of the more extravagant spenders
among the advertisers, girlfriends (and their friends) of
the Bolands (both of whom were married), and as
many television cameramen and day-off personalities as
could squeeze into the overworked car.

"Hey, Ed, how are you?" bellowed the news anchorman. "Come on. Push in here; we'll make room
for you."

"Nah, thanks, Jim, I'll just hit the steps. You know I
don't like to interfere with your parties," Ed snapped.
"Have a safe trip."

There were three sets of stairs and two ramps that
one could use to get to the basement entrance to the
stadium, and Ed knew the route by heart. The paying
customers seldom used this way out, even those few
who were aware of it, and so there was no delay at all
in reaching the ground floor. Pushing open the small
door at the base of the final set of stairs, Ed half-trotted
down the ramp and was in the corridor under the stadium, a roughly circular passageway off of which were

locker rooms, ushers' changing rooms, ticket-counting facilities, support areas, three darkrooms for the photographers, and a large press working room, complete with folding wooden chairs and cinder-block walls.

About fifty feet past the press room was the visiting team's locker room, where a small cluster of press had already gathered, mostly the sidebar writers, the columnists, and a few photographers and cameramen.

Ed sidled up to Chuck Nolan, the Newark paper's rotund little columnist. "What's going on?" he asked.

"Not a damned thing, Eddie. It's spooky. No noise, nothing."

"Anything? Anybody come in, go out? Nothing?"

"Not a fucking thing. It's like the damned room is empty, you know? They're gonna open the door and there won't even be stools."

The sound of the crowd insinuated its way into the basement corridors, and Ed always marveled at the fact that the officials' whistles sounded louder down here, echoing and reverberating, than they ever did on the field. Finally the gun—the game was over. In a few minutes, the Bears came tramping down the field ramp, yelling, clapping backs, clapping hands, dirty and scuffed, uniforms grass-stained and blood-blotched, whooping with the thrill of a soundly administered beating of a heavily favored team.

Behind them came the coaches, the trainers, the equipment men, then O'Donnell, the publicist.

"Just give us a minute, guys," he said. "I'm sure this door will open soon. We won, right?"

The door closed. For a few more seconds there were the normal sounds of a team shedding gear, popping beer cans. Then, at once, silence, followed almost immediately with a keening, moaning sound that reached its icy fingers out into the corridor through the door and chilled the heart and marrow.

Ed knew.

The door opened and it was O'Donnell, accompanied by the team's owner, Johnson Dillard, a good-old-boy type with a red face and a broad girth, but now his eyes were red, his speech tentative.

"Gentlemen," he began, "it is with the utmost sadness that I must inform you that Adam Benson has suffered a fatal heart attack. He died the way he would have wanted, as a winner, with the ball in his hands and a touchdown on his final play." With that, Dillard broke down completely, leaving it to the equally red-eyed O'Donnell to fill in some of the necessary details.

"Dr. Thomas Mannion examined Benson on the field when the players realized he wasn't moving and exhibited no signs of life. Dr. Mannion was unable to get a pulse, determined that Adam was not breathing, and administered mouth-to-mouth resuscitation. To no avail. Oxygen was administered in the locker room, as was a derivative of adrenaline, by injection directly into the heart. At 4:34 P.M., Eastern Standard Time, Adam Benson was pronounced dead of cardiac arrest. His body has been taken to St. Vincent's Hospital, where an autopsy will be performed tonight. His widow, Sherri Benson, has been notified and will arrive at seven o'clock tomorrow morning from Los Angeles. Funeral arrangements are incomplete at this time."

The ground began to sway, and Ed fought for balance and control. *Adam Benson dead? Never. No man had ever been more alive, more in love with life. Dead of a heart attack? A joke, a macabre joke played by a fiend. Adam Benson dead? No one with such skills, with such verve and daring, could just stop living. No one, especially not Adam Benson. Remember? The games won when all was lost? The special magic that poured out of him and enclosed everyone around him? Come on, God, stop screwing around. A bad joke, baby. Make him live again. Make this nightmare stop. Adam Benson can't be dead. He's thirty-seven years old, an athlete, a man for whom such things as the Hall of Fame and megadollar contracts were invented. Dead?* "Bullshit!" Ed Buck screamed, and then the pain wrenched his body and the sobs constricted his chest and he wailed at the loss of a friend.

Gordo, who knew the relationship, who knew the closeness, came to Ed and put an arm around him. "Come on, Ed; let's go get a drink. Come on; I'll drive you home."

"No, I want to go to the hospital. I want to wait there until somebody he knows gets there. I'll call his father. I knew him pretty well. Vinnie, can you get me to St. Vincent's?"

Vinnie nodded. "Sure, Ed, but aren't you going to write?"

Like he had been slapped in the face, like ice water had been poured on him while he was sunbathing asleep, Ed Buck was jolted into control and composure. "Yeah, first we write; then the hospital. If Adam is really dead, he's gonna be that way a long time. Thanks, Vinnie. Let's go upstairs."

The story was of the death, not the game. But the story of the death in no way mentioned the information Adam Benson had given Ed the night before. This was not the time. This was not the way to bury a friend. There would be time for investigation and research, but not now. Now was time to mourn.

FOUR

LEIGH Crespino knew better. She had been involved with bachelors before—several of them, in fact—and she recognized that the longer they lived with themselves and their bachelor status, the better they liked it, the more accustomed to it they grew, and the harder it was to convince them that marriage was even a semiviable alternative.

But while those others all had been nice guys with something decent or meaningful to bring to a relationship, Leigh had escaped being stricken with that malady called love—until Ed Buck. She knew she was in deep trouble with this one, because she wanted to be with him no matter what, marriage or no marriage.

That wasn't how it all started out, of course. But so what? It was exactly how things were now. She knew where she was with him, knew all about the weird hours and the unexpected trips and the hardening status of his bachelorhood. It wasn't her idea of satisfying, but she had already told herself that whatever the structure of their relationship, she had no choice but to accept it. She did love him, and somehow, she hoped, there would be marriage in their future.

He called at two in the morning, but when the telephone rang she already knew who it was and what it was about. She had heard about Adam Benson, of

course, and had tried to reach Ed with no success, realizing after an hour of dialing his apartment that he'd
still be at the stadium or the office or even the hospital
or morgue. She knew he was hurting, knew he was in
pain, had no idea where to find him, and so she waited.
Just waited. Leigh Crespino had been doing a lot of
waiting for the past year, all in the name of Ed Buck.

She reached for the phone, also knowing that she
was the first person to whom he had reached out, and
that pleased her very much.

"Ed? Where are you?"

"Downstairs, here. Can I come up?" His voice was
thin, fragile, shaky.

"Of course. Wait a minute." Leigh put the receiver
back in its cradle, then dialed 0323, the code built in
to the apartment's security system that opened the double doors, extra-thick and bullet-proof, to the elevators.
She tugged on jeans, slipped on a sweater, left her feet
bare, and walked into the living room, arriving at the
door almost at the second Ed did, opening it and then
her arms, holding him close, tightly, while silent sobs,
without tears, more like muscle spasms, took control of
him.

Then it was over. Abruptly, as if he had once again
looked at himself and, despising weakness, pulled himself away from his emotions, creating an artificial sense
of calm and dispassionate involvement.

"You heard?"

"Yes, I heard," Leigh said. "The radio said heart attack. Is that what it was?"

"So far that's all we know." Ed headed for the overstuffed soft leather couch, kicking off his shoes as he
fell back into it. "I waited until his father showed up.
You remember me talking about Andy Benson? The
toughest old man I ever met? He wasn't so tough when

he saw me at the hospital, Leigh. That old guy just fell apart, cried like a baby, held onto me, and . . . damn, it was terrible. I was trying so hard not to do that, not to come apart, and then that old man broke up and I went with him. We just held onto each other in the lobby and cried and cried. He's alone, old Andy Benson. His wife died about six years ago and he moved from the farm they had to Scranton and now he's got nobody. Adam's brother lives in Florida, and his sister is married to some Oregon dentist. They put him in a room there, gave him something to make him sleep. I'll go back tomorrow when Sherri gets in from California."

Leigh went to him again, sat next to him, and just held on, saying nothing, just being there. Ed gripped her hard, embracing her warmth, her silence, a confirmation of sorts that life and breath still existed.

"Coffee?" she asked. "Or a drink?"

He managed a wan smile. "Coffee, baby. I've had enough tonight."

She padded into the small kitchen, her jet-black hair tumbling around her shoulders and partially across her face, found the coffee canister without turning on the overhead light, and measured enough for a full pot. She had a feeling this was going to be an all-night catharsis, and she was ready for it, for it meant drawing even closer to Ed. While the coffee was dripping into the pot, she took a bottle of Ketel One, ice cubes, and two pony glasses, stacked them on a tray, then grabbed two mugs from the cabinet over the sink. By the time she had collected spoons, the sugar bowl, napkins, and the mugs, the coffee had finished dripping, and balancing the whole assortment, she arrived back in the living room to find Ed staring into space, looking out at nothing.

She poured, and still he said nothing. She pushed the mug at him, touched his arm, and caused him to look around; just for a fraction of a second, he was surprised to find her there, confused at where he was. It was just a fleeting look, crossing his face the way a shadow might, and then he seemed to register his contacts and looked at her with a sad, small smile.

"I've got to talk to you about something," he said softly. "I don't really want to, and I probably shouldn't, but I've got to tell somebody and you're it."

"Shoot," Leigh said. "I can take anything."

He shook his head. "No, this isn't funny. This is dead serious, and I don't know why I just don't go to the police, which I probably will. But I need your opinion. You have the best mind I know, and I want your input. This is dangerous, and before I start, I want to you know that it's OK if you tell me not to say anything, that you don't want to hear this stuff, any of it. I love you, Leigh, and I want to include you, but I love you so much I don't want to be the cause of you getting hurt, either. So quickly, say it, before I start talking."

It was her turn to shake her head. "You look here, you dope," and her voice was louder and more strident than she wanted it to be, and her voice shook with more emotion and frustration than she could have expected. "You look here, you fucking idiot. I love you. I want to marry you. I don't want to be your girlfriend, you moron, I want to be your wife, and that means for the whole deal. If there's something you can't tell anybody in the world, you can tell it to me. If there's something you want to do so awful and so horrible that nobody in the world will let you do it, I'll let you. I love you, you idiot. Now tell me what you have to say so that you can be finished and I can take you into my bed and fuck your eyes out."

That, finally, brought the smile to his face.

"On one condition."

"Oh, you infuriating man. OK, what?"

He smiled again. "The condition is, that if I tell you all this terrible stuff, and if I tell you what I'm going to do about it, then you have to marry me, because a wife can't be forced to testify against her husband. OK?"

She was totally without the ability to speak, but a shriek came from her lips and she clutched him around the neck so tightly that for a minute he feared for his windpipe. "Marry you? What the hell do you think I've been talking about for a year? Marry you? Only somebody as crazy as I am would even consider it. Marry you? Yes. When? Tomorrow? Wednesday?"

Their next embrace was for a much longer period of time, and it wasn't necessary for them to speak, yet in that fearful, trembling embrace both of them said all that can ever be said and all that ever need be said.

They withdrew then, took their coffee mugs in hand, and with Leigh staring directly into his eyes, Ed Buck told her everything Adam Benson had told him. Everything.

"And so maybe you can see," Ed said hours later, when he had finally finished, when he had cried and remembered the old times at Oklahoma, when he had cried and admitted that his best years were gone, when he had cried and lamented his lost youth, "so you can see, maybe, why I don't think I can believe a heart attack. Adam was beating the shit out of the Giants, but more important, he was doing a million-dollar number on some very bad people. I know, I know. It's impossible to kill a football player on the field during a game. It's impossible. He wasn't shot and he wasn't stabbed and I know it's absolutely impossible, but he's dead and he was too young to die and not that way, for sure, and it's just too much of a fucking coincidence."

His voice was hoarse by now, his words cracking, barely audible. He paused, drew in one more large gulp of air, and said, "Leigh, somebody killed my friend. I'm going to find out who, and how, and you have to help me."

She nodded her head, her cheeks damp with tears. "Yes, I will," she said. "Now let's go to bed, and one day soon, when this is over, let's go and get ourselves married. OK?"

"OK," he said.

They cried again, together. And then they made love, and it was never that good before, and as Ed drifted into sleep, as the sky over Manhattan was turning pink-orange, he heard Leigh say, "Good night, my husband," and he thought he'd never heard anything quite that perfect in his life.

They slept for only a few hours and felt more tired than before when they awoke, and with a gripping sadness Ed realized that all of what had happened the day before was not only real but forever. Adam Benson was still dead.

FIVE

HER face streaked with dry and drying tears, Sherri Novak Benson looked across at the man sitting behind an ornate mahogany desk.

"He didn't have to die, Billy. He didn't have to die."

The man was short and squat, a fire hydrant with arms and legs, no more than five-feet-five, but he weighed every bit of 250 pounds. He fiddled with an enormous gold pinkie ring, twisting it around and around his stubby finger while he talked.

"Yeah, he did. He was gonna turn us in. He made a deal with us, he took the money, he knew how it was, and he was gonna fuck it all up and turn us in. You know that. He told you." He looked up at her, smiled a chilling smile, and added: "He told you, and then you told us. Remember?"

Adam Benson's widow began to cry again and started to get up from the chair to leave, but the big man standing behind her, the only other person in the room, reached out and put a hand on her shoulder. She sat back down.

"You have to go to New York," the man, Billy DeSalvo, continued, pretending not to hear her cry or to have seen her attempt to leave. "You have to be the perfect widow. You are going to get your husband's body and bring it to wherever you want it buried, and there is gonna be a funeral and all the newspapers and television and the radio stations are going to be there and you are going to cry and look pretty and keep your mouth shut and that is going to be the end of it. You knew what he was going to do, and you know what you want, what you need from us. You know it wasn't really a personal thing; he just made a mistake and we had to stop him from making a bigger one. Hey, chickie, you didn't have much of a marriage anyway, remember?"

Sherri Novak nodded slowly, still crying, as much for her complicity and her charade with Adam as for the death of the man to whom she had been married for just three years. He was dead. That was fact. But she still had needs, and Billy DeSalvo was going to meet them. All she had to do was mourn, and then keep quiet. But Adam was dead, the most exciting man she had ever met, ever, in all her twenty-six years. He was kind and decent, too, and she hadn't known a man like that since her father died. She had been seventeen then, and in less than six months she was out of the house in Buffalo, first going to Miami Beach, then Las Vegas, finally Los Angeles, always trading with her body, eventually meeting up with people like Billy DeSalvo, ultimately finding her answers in the drugs that made her need more and tied her to DeSalvo and all the ones before him.

In the last year, she had come to admit to four needs in her life, and three were still within reach if she played her cards right: she wanted to be in the movies; she wanted all the cocaine she would ever need without worrying about how she was going to pay for it; she wanted lots and lots of money, fuck-you kind of money; and she wanted to stay married to Adam Benson. Now he was gone, but the other three goals were there, right in front of her, close enough to touch. She nodded her head again, reached out for the airplane tickets DeSalvo held out to her, as well as a small plastic bag filled with white powder and a set of credit cards. But for a long moment he kept them just out of her reach.

"It's nine o'clock now," DeSalvo said, grinning again. "The red-eye leaves at twelve. The credit cards are in your name, the tickets are first class, there's enough shit in the bag to last you two weeks . . . even you, baby . . . and in the ticket envelope you got ten thousand bucks in cash." He completed the short instructions and leaned back in the reclining leather chair. "You go to New York, buy whatever you need, spend whatever you want, take care of all the questions, but don't really say nuthin' to nobody and get back here as soon as you can. First thing, no fuckin' around or stopping off someplace. We got what you want, the movie deal is about to get made, and you may have to start workin' in less than a month. You know, you might be a star yet, and with a dead football hero for a husband it could happen even sooner. You got all that?"

Sherri nodded. "Yeah, Billy, I got it," she said, her voice tight, controlled. "I got the money and the tickets and the shit. And I got no husband now, but I got you, and dipshit over here"—she nodded at the big man still hovering behind her chair—"and I got whoever you want me to have, right? What else do I need, right, Billy?"

He said nothing.

"I also got more on you than you want anybody to know, Billy, so how do I know you don't plan to blow up the damned plane tonight? How do I know that, Billy? How do I know that, my friend?"

The chill become a real and palpable presence in the

room. "You don't, you stupid broad; you don't. But it wouldn't look good to make you dead now, see? Too soon. It wouldn't be smart. The fucking football player drops dead in a game and the same night the widow's plane explodes when she goes cross-country for the body? Too soon, too stupid. Maybe we'll get around to you in a month, two months, six. Maybe a year. You know, we got people who can make you wish we only wanted you dead, especially a nice head like you. You know why else we ain't gonna kill you? Because we can use you. Because you are the nicest-looking piece of ass I have ever seen and guys will turn over their mothers to us just to get close to you. Because you can even act. Because we have already invested a bunch of dollars in your ass.

"But mostly, because Mr. Assante likes you. Me, I could kill you in a minute. I could watch somebody else kill you. I could take fuckin' Polaroid pictures of it and save 'em. You know why? Because to me you're just another broad. There are great broads all over, you know? Prettier, sexier, bigger tits, great legs, and they would do anything, and I mean anything, to get where you're goin'. And they have. You know what else? There are even great broads who don't have to put shit in their noses every four fuckin' hours, too. But see, we got you to need it, we made you need it, and now we know you're comin' back, and we know you're gonna keep your mouth shut, too. We own you, and you know it."

He stood, walked around the desk to the chair where Sherri Benson was sitting. He leaned down and spoke right into her face, inches away, close enough for her to smell his breath, to feel the flecks of spittle as he raised his voice, to see the dilated pupils in his black, hateful eyes. "We own you, don't we?"

She nodded her head, weeping.

"Answer me."

"Yes, Billy, you do. You own me. Mr. Assante owns me. Anybody else you want to own me owns me. Billy, please, I'm hurting; can I use some now?"

Billy DeSalvo smiled. It was going to get worse. She knew it. "Not yet. First there's something I want you to do for me, now, here." He nodded at the big man, and big, stupid Rico Scalzi walked around to the front of the chair.

"Billy, for God's sake, Adam's dead. Today. Billy, not now. Please, Billy, don't make me."

"Now, damn it!" he barked.

Sherri Novak Benson stood, the silk dress clinging to her body. She reached her hands up behind her neck, unbuttoned the collar, and shrugged the dress off her shoulders to the floor. She wore no bra, and her breasts, nipples already hardening, thrust upward, as fine as any Billy had ever seen. She stood in her high heels and skimpy bikini panties, then bent, hooked her thumbs in the elastic and slipped off the whispering fabric, it, too, falling to the carpeted floor.

DeSalvo stood back and gazed at this most erotic of bodies, the front of his trousers already tenting. With no expression showing on her face, Sherri Novak Benson began to pinch her breasts, then lifted them gently, pushing them together, then dropped her hands to the wispy blond curls at her pelvis and softly inserted a finger into her vagina, the fingers of her other hand caressing herself.

"Sit down," he said, and she did.

Billy nodded again, and Rico Scalzi undid his trousers, letting them fall around his ankles.

DeSalvo handed Sherri Benson the small plastic bag. With one hand she worked Scalzi's already-rising organ into a full erection; with the other, she tapped out a measure of the white powder onto its purplish, rigid head.

"Go ahead, Mrs. Benson, snort your coke," DeSalvo said, "and when you get the high, make sure you show Rico just how grateful you are."

Sherri Benson bent to her task, and neither man noted or would have cared about the new flood of tears that blurred her vision. In a minute, neither did she. The rush, the high, was all she wanted. The rest would pass.

SIX

"I'VE got a friend in the police department," Ed said, turning to Leigh in bed shortly after seven o'clock.

They had managed to sleep for a couple of hours. She looked up, saw his drawn, pale face, and realized nothing was going to be all right until his friend was buried and the murderer identified and caught; although she had serious doubts that it was murder, she kept them to herself. She also realized that getting married would have to wait, but that was all right. They were going to be married, and that was all that counted for the time being.

"Are you going to call him?" she asked.

"Yeah, I think so. But that's not the first thing. I have to go to the hospital and check on Adam's father, and his wife should be landing any minute. She might need a place to stay, somebody to be with. I don't know what to do first. The hospital, I guess."

"Do you want me to go with you?"

"I'd love it. But don't. Stay here. I need to know I can call you. Can you stay home today? Not go to work?"

"Of course. How about your friend? The policeman?"

Buck nodded. "He's not a cop, exactly; he's a detective. Not exactly a detective, either, but he used to be.

He's assistant to the chief of detectives. I think he can pull enough strings to find out what happened."

"Should I call him?"

Ed nodded. "Yeah, that's a good idea. See if he can meet me tonight, at my place. His name is Gerry Keegan. Lieutenant Joseph Gerard Keegan, working out of the Foley Square headquarters building."

"OK, darling. But let's make it here tonight, not your place. In fact, let's make this place your place. Permanently. How about if I go over to your apartment later and find some clothes and stuff?"

He smiled, nodding his assent.

They got out of bed then, showered together, and while Leigh set up the coffee machine Ed shaved and dressed. She was on the telephone, her back to him, when he walked into the kitchen.

"Tell Dirty Dave that I can't come in today, or tomorrow, or maybe the rest of the week, Doris. Tell him I don't want to get fired, but if that's how he feels, maybe I'll just quit. This is more important."

But she was smiling. David Drexler, founder and president of one of New York's most successful advertising agencies, might not even realize that Leigh Crespino was missing for a day or two. She was one of his staff of four secretaries, but he was so seldom in the suite of offices that her absence might be covered for a week. On the other hand, the last thing he'd want to do would be fire Leigh Crespino. With her quick mind and natural instinct for where to advertise which product she had quickly become a valuable asset to DD Ads, Inc.

"I'm here for as long as you need me to be here," she said, smiling, when Ed walked up behind her. "Coffee?"

He gulped half a mug while standing at the window,

looking out at Second Avenue and the cords of traffic already coiling and snarling. "I just can't believe he's dead," he said. "I'll call," he added, returning from wherever he had so briefly been, and was gone.

Leigh sat at the small pedestal kitchen table, sipping coffee, trying to sort through at least those things near the surface of her consciousness. Ed's friend was dead, a spectacular event in terms of who he was and where it had happened. Ed had been privy to confidential information about gambling and game fixing, and in his mind the coincidence was too neat, too pat.

He was going to need her over the next few weeks, for both emotional support and help. She wouldn't fail him.

Leigh reached for the phone and dialed 411 for information. "Yes, operator, New York Police, Foley Square precinct, please. No, this is not an emergency."

She waited, finally heard the electronic, metallic voice, and copied down the number spit out by the computer. She dialed, and a male voice, interspersed with the intentionally audible regulated beeps of a recording device, informed her that she had, indeed, reached "Foley Square, New York Police Department, Sergeant Quinn."

"Is Lieutenant Joseph Keegan in, please?" she asked.

"Hold, please. Who's calling?"

"My name is Crespino. Leigh Crespino. He won't know me, but tell him I'm calling for Ed Buck. They know each other."

A pause. Static hummed in her ear, as well as the faint sound of someone else's conversation, not loud enough to make out the words but, because of the extremely overworked and overloaded New York telephone system, not an uncommon occurrence.

"Keegan," a man said, deep-voiced, cutting through

the not-quite-noiseless silence of holding on.

"This is Leigh Crespino, Lieutenant Keegan. Ed Buck asked me to call. He thinks we're going to need your help. Unofficially, at least for now."

"We? Miss Crespino, have you finally gotten Big Ed to pair up? Congratulations. Tell that jerk it's about time. Now, what can I do? What does he . . . I'm sorry; what do the two of you need?"

"I don't know, Lieutenant," she began, thinking that he had the timbre of voice that made you like him, at least at first, "not exactly—"

He cut through her sentence. "It's Gerry," he said. "If you're the girl who has finally put a collar on Eddie Buck, we've got to be on a first-name basis. OK, Leigh?"

She smiled. She was sure she liked this man. "OK, Gerry. I'm not sure what Ed has in mind, but you heard about the football player who died yesterday?"

"Yes, Adam Benson. I imagine the whole country has heard about that. How is Ed involved?"

"Well, he isn't, Gerry, except that he and Benson were good friends. They played together at Oklahoma, stayed in touch all these years, and had dinner the night before the game. Saturday night. And Adam told Ed some things that make him suspicious now, after the death. I think he wants to see you, but off-the-record. Can we set that up?"

"Sure. Where and when?"

"Tonight, nine o'clock, my place. It's 200 East 68th Street, fifth floor, Apartment 515-B. And yes, Gerry, it's about to be our place."

She could hear him smile. "Just invite me to the wedding, and make sure it's Orthodox. His grandmother will refuse to come unless the food's kosher."

Leigh Crespino was Italian, but she had already promised herself that if Ed Buck wanted to live in a Jewish home, under Hebrew laws, or Hindu or Buddhist or WASP, it would be her pleasure to learn the rules and put them into practice.

"We believe in great vodka and scotch, imported beer, and dinner, if you like," she said, smiling into the phone, "Gerry," she added.

He laughed. "I'm pleased to know that Ed found a girl without going outside his religion, either," he said. "Nine it is, but don't bother with the dinner."

SEVEN

BILLY DeSalvo was frightened, but not physically, not the way he used to be in the neighborhood when the big kids went after him.

This fear was different. This was the kind that comes when somebody very important is angry at something you did, when that important man can inflict severe pain and humiliation and can even instruct others to end your life.

Billy was stricken by that kind of fear because Adam Benson wasn't supposed to die, because Adam Benson wasn't supposed to do anything but continue to arrange the proper results of certain selected NFL games involving the Chicago Bears.

Billy was afraid of a man he had never met, whose real name he didn't know, and a man he would never know. But in the world in which Billy lived everybody knew of this man, a mystery to all but a few, a man truly to be feared because of who he was and the power he commanded.

The only name ever needed was Assante, and it was enough to cause even the most arrogant to pause and reflect. Once, only once, Billy had received a telephone call from Assante. It was almost seven years ago, when Billy had moved into the Los Angeles sports betting circle and made a few quick hits, reaching a few of the pro basketball players and realizing enormous profits from their subsequent efforts. What had amazed him the most was the relatively inexpensive toys and inducements he really needed.

The center of the Los Angeles Hoops, a seven-footer named Marcellus Malone, wanted $25,000 a game for each game in which he would be asked to shave a few points. Billy DeSalvo, who had learned the art on the streets of Brooklyn, stalled. "It's too damned much, Marcellus; my people can't afford it. Come on; you'll make an extra grand a game and nobody is gonna know nuthin'. What's so bad about that?"

Marcellus was adamant. Billy allowed him to convince him to try, to let him believe that there was another "boss," a shadowy figure who had the power to make the decision, when in reality it was just Billy.

"I'll have to make a call," he said, finally, allowing himself to show just a trace of fear and a lot of reluctance. "You stand next to me. We'll either do it right now or it's no deal, never."

Malone couldn't wait. The two of them went into Billy's private office in the no-profit bar he had bought in a rundown section of LA, never intending for it to make money, and dialed, with great show, the local number for weather information. While the electronic voice droned on about clouds and humidity, he spoke to those anonymous people of his. "Yeah, that's right, Mr. Spencer. Marcellus says he won't do it for less than $25,000 a game. . . . Yeah, I know; we'll have to cut down the games. . . . I know. . . . No, sir, I don't think he'll do it for less." At this point, Billy looked over at Malone, who shook his head. "Right, that's what he says. . . . Well, OK. I think it's the right decision, Mr. Spencer. . . . Yes, sir, absolutely. We can trust this man."

He put the phone down slowly, looked at Marcellus Malone for a long, silent moment, then smiled broadly. "Well, you did it, big guy!" he shouted. "You got him to back down. Good job, 'Cell."

The fix stayed in place for two seasons, during which time Billy DeSalvo arranged for a total of ten games to be fixed. It wasn't too many, because Billy had learned a long time ago the penalties of greed. It cost him, as the sole operator of the scam, a total of $250,000 for Marcellus Malone. Billy made that much the first game, and by the time all ten had been played out, with only one "accident" along the way when Malone shot so badly he had been taken out of the game near the end and his replacement, trying to impress the coach, had scored the last eight points, Billy DeSalvo had taken in just short of $1 million bucks.

And the beauty part was that nobody else knew. Just Billy and the big spade, who finally crumbled under his cocaine habit and now was pushing a rag in a car wash.

It had been Billy's deal, Billy's plan to meet the player, to get friendly, to slowly work in the thought that there was money to be made, big money, without the Hoops even losing a game. "Just don't win by the spread," Billy had explained. "I'll tell you which games we want, I'll tell you what the number is, and you make sure the other team loses by less than that number. That's all. Nobody gets hurt; nobody has to lose a chance at a championship; nobody knows nuthin' but peace and quiet."

He sealed it by arranging regular visits by one of the most beautiful young girls he had ever seen, an eighteen-year-old named Sherri Novak, whom he had led into a major-league coke and heroin habit, and who, as a result, had developed an incredible lack of conscience and inhibitions.

And even she had no idea what was happening. She
just did what she was told and Billy DeSalvo made sure
she had enough shit. It was the sweetest deal ever. Big,
big money and nobody knew.

Then Billy's telephone rang. Somebody knew.

"Billy DeSalvo?" a deep, hoarse voice nearly whispered.

"Yeah, who wants to know?"

"This is a friend of your father's, from New York.
My name is Assante. I want you to stop dealing with
the black, the basketball player."

Billy could still remember the way his hand shook.
Damn, Assante. Everybody in the business knew of the
Boss. Billy was no different. He knew all the things
everybody else knew, had heard all the stories of violent, absolute vengeance, and had no interest in finding
out whether he was "important" enough for Assante to
assign someone to convince him.

"Yes. I understand," he said. "How can I show my
friendship?"

Assante was pleased. Very pleased. The exercise of
power always pleased him because it, too, was an absolute. "We will share this," he said, the voice soothing
now, calmer, less strident. "We will share this not because I desire the money, but because you will prove
yourself to me with this sacrifice. Later, you will see,
this gift of yours will be repaid several times over."

Of that Billy DeSalvo was certain, and he knew that
the telephone call was, all things considered, a blessing.
Better to swim with the shark and benefit by its protection than to be pursued and devoured.

So the deal with Marcellus Malone was split, 75 percent of the take going to the mysterious Assante, the
remaining 25 percent staying with Billy. But Assante's
people had managed to infiltrate another team, had

"bought" another player and presented Billy with 25 percent of that money, too. A bond had been established, a tie had been formed, and when Billy really thought about it, which wasn't often, he knew that the Assante organization had hundreds like him on the streets, around the country, turning in huge sums of money only because of the implied threat so subtly framed in explaining what might happen if an agreement wasn't reached.

"The best day of my life," he had once said to his bodyguard and only friend, Rico Scalzi. "It was the best day of my life when Mr. Assante called."

There was no reason to assume that Assante was a surname, that it was even a true name, but Billy felt better, more comfortable, by making it appear to be a business arrangement between two men, not between a man and an organization so large and so powerful that no one, no person, no corporation, no police department, no government, could mount a serious threat.

Rico had nodded, his trust in Billy DeSalvo almost religious. He had been brought up in the slums of New York City, his people were Assante people, and when there was trouble one prayed first to Assante, then to God. To work for a man who worked for Assante, who received money from him, who shared in business transactions with him, was all too much, much more than Rico Scalzi could have expected. It was unimportant to say that he would kill for Billy DeSalvo, because he already had. Twice. For Assante. It was more important, more significant, to say that Rico loved DeSalvo, beyond any reluctance to act instantly to satisfy any of his whims, to fulfill any assignment, and, if necessary, to die in the effort. Gladly. With honor.

Gradually, Assante's sources moved DeSalvo higher

in the organization. He was trustworthy, if not overly intelligent. He was loyal, if only because of fear. He was dependable, because he knew the consequences of irresponsibility. He loved money, more than anything but food, gargantuan amounts of it. He was ruthless in his own way, or perhaps *without conscience* was more accurate. Women were unimportant to him, except as tools, as currency, and he was clever enough to know how to use them properly. The young blonde he had used to nail down the basketball player was more than just useful. Assante had plans for her—rather, for what she was able to make others do.

In all, Billy DeSalvo, the runny-nosed kid from middle-class Brooklyn Heights, had carved a considerable niche for himself in Los Angeles. He lived in Bel Air, secluded, in a house valued at more than $4 million. He drove a Bentley, kept an old Rolls Corniche in the garage, had a small fortune on deposit in a bank on Grand Cayman Island, and, of course, offered to do anything he could for the Assante organization.

Billy brought a smile of amusement to Assante's face on the few occasions he and Scalzi spoke of him. He was insignificant but for the things he could arrange, the money he produced, the loyalty he displayed at every opportunity. Assante knew he was rock-solid—Scalzi told him, once a month, in a private home overlooking the ocean on Pacific Highway in Malibu Beach. He liked Rico. He had liked Rico's two older brothers, who had been equally loyal soldiers in New York, both of whom, sadly, had died in the service of the organization.

Maria Scalzi, the bereaved mother, had been sent to Florida, had been set up in a palatial home in Golden Beach. She was part of Assante's history, part of his childhood, and she was among the few who knew everything there was to know about him, about his business, about who his boss, his only boss, really was. Her husband, Enrico, had served well as a master engraver, had worked for six full years engraving the plates that produced the AT&T bearer bonds with which Assante had almost brought Wall Street to its knees, flooding the financial marketplace with $100 million of the virtually flawless, as well as worthless, copies.

When old Enrico died, before the two sons had met their bullet-riddled destinies, those in attendance at the High Mass funeral service in St. Joseph's Church caught the law-enforcement clowns off guard. They never expected the superstars who appeared, and even had they staked out the High Mass, which they did not, there wouldn't have been time to properly arrange the kind of surveillance needed.

They had no idea Enrico Scalzi was that well respected in the organization, and so they spent the next year trying to find out exactly what it was he did. They failed, as they usually did when they began to dig into the Assante organization.

Rico Scalzi had been brought to Assante himself after the death of his brothers, when he was already a man of twenty-five. He trembled with awe. He stammered his words. He mumbled, mostly, eyes cast down at his shoes, at the ground, anywhere but at Assante.

"I have a new interest in Los Angeles," Assante had said to Rico, his voice friendly but also full, powerful, resonant. "There is a man there, a fat man, a stupid man, but he has proven his loyalty and his respect and he is going to do business with me. For me. For now. I want you to be his right hand, and my eyes. I owe much to your family. Your father was a great man; your brothers were loyal and brave. It would honor me to have another Scalzi in my employ. Will you take the job?"

Rico knelt on one knee, reached for the old man's right hand, and gently pressed his lips to the large ring. His acquiescence promised all that it implied. He was employed for life. He would never reveal any information about the organization, and especially, above all else, he would never reveal anything he knew about Assante. Death itself carried less fear—much less—than the shame of informing, the disgrace of weakness.

Two years earlier, Assante's spokesman had reached Billy DeSalvo at his home, ringing his unlisted telephone at 3:00 A.M. It was not as if Billy had been wakened. He and Rico were counting money, money in tens and twenties, the old-fashioned way. It was for the laundry, and the next night Rico would fly to Grand Cayman, to deposit the wrinkled bills collected from Billy's drug salesmen in the Grand Cayman National Trust and Bank and watch it turn into perfectly clean, absolutely untraceable entries on anonymous ledgers for some anonymous empty corporation that listed fictitious people as its officers and a post office box in Sante Fe, New Mexico, as its home office.

"Yeah, hello," Billy said, annoyed at the disrespect of some people.

"It is a message from Assante," said a cool, cultured voice. "We must discuss something important."

"When?" Not why. Just when.

"In the morning. At ten. Please keep an appointment you have made at the Key Systems Building on Wilshire Boulevard. Your appointment is with Arthur McDonald, and his office is on the nineteenth floor, Suite Forty. Thank you, and good night."

Billy didn't sleep. Not at all. No chance. This was his first contact since the Malone thing, the first opportunity to serve as more than just a collector of money and a dispatcher of same. He was ready well before ten o'clock, shaved and bathed, neatly dressed, Rico sitting downstairs in the Bentley, not his own anonymous gray Chevrolet.

The directory in the entrance lobby listed some of Southern California's most prestigious firms. Under "M" was the entry for "McDonald, Arthur R., Investment Counseling." The elevator whispered its way up to the nineteenth floor; an arrow clearly visible upon emerging from the car pointed to the right for Suites 1930–1955. Billy DeSalvō opened the door, was greeted by a middle-aged woman who smiled at him. "Good morning, Mr. DeSalvo. Mr. McDonald is waiting for you in his office. Thank you for being on time. He has an extremely busy day today."

She rose, led him down a corridor, and opened a large mahogany door, unmarked, letting it swing open as she stepped back. DeSalvo entered. The woman reached for the doorknob and silently swung the door shut.

Seated at a large desk, bare but for a telephone, was a man Billy DeSalvo did not know and had never seen. Behind the desk, drapes fully open, was a floor-to-ceiling glass wall, and the glare from the streaming sun temporarily blinded Billy and made a full study of the man's face impossible.

"Hello, Billy," he said. "I believe you know Miss Novak."

Billy glanced to his left, in the direction of the man's extended arm, and saw the peachcake he had used to get Marcellus Malone's attention. "Yeah, I know her," he said, strangely uncomfortable, annoyed that the girl should be there before he was, that he wasn't told she'd be there at all. "You McDonald?"

The man smiled. "If you like, yes, I am Arthur R. McDonald. I deal in investments. Please have a seat," and he gestured at a maroon leather armchair to the right of the desk. Billy DeSalvo sat quickly, already aware that he had been rude, that this might, in fact, be Assante himself. "I'm sorry for my behavior, Mr. McDonald," he said. "It wasn't an easy night, and we found some traffic before we could get here."

McDonald smiled broadly, openly. There was genuine warmth in his face. "Yes, of course. I know how Rico dislikes traffic. When you leave, please be sure to give him my best wishes."

It had to be Assante. How the hell could he know so much?

"Well, we are here to discuss a business venture in which our friend has a very strong conviction," the man began. "Miss Novak has been promised a role in a major motion picture for her time and certain of her sacrifices. Not to mention, how shall we say, the continuation of supply of certain chemical substances her system requires. You, Mr. DeSalvo, will profit in amounts of money thus far withheld from your activities with our friend. He has been highly pleased by your continued support and allegiance. He is now prepared to show his gratitude, in return for your efforts as the, shall we say, manager of this particular project."

Billy's hands were shaking. This was it, the major kill, the big time for sure, say good-bye to the penny shit forever, Billy Boy.

"Hey, you know I'll do anything, Mr.—our friend, I mean—asks me to do. Just lay it out for me, OK?"

McDonald smiled again, clearly pleased. "I can tell you that our friend is going to be very happy, Billy," he said. "Fine, then, let us begin."

They began talking about Adam Benson, the National Football League, the Chicago Bears, Sherri Novak's film career and her drug habit, and how Billy DeSalvo and Rico Scalzi were going to manage the entire affair.

Only Sherri, of the three people present, seemed less than agreeable, but at one point, when her voice had become strident in its refusal, the elegant, splendid Arthur R. McDonald had half-stood, reached out, and slapped her face with the palm of his hand, a crack so loud it echoed in the still office. That this man had done such a thing, that it was so totally out of character, surprised her more than the blow.

She would nod her mute agreement to everything that was said after that.

Two hours later, when they all left the empty shell of an office, the deal was set, the arrangements had been made, Billy DeSalvo was going to run the operation (and be solely responsible for the heat, although he couldn't know that), Sherri Novak was going to ensure her success in the film world and her ability to acquire all the money and drugs she'd ever need by marrying this football player, and Assante was going to make millions more dollars through the tried but until then unsuccessful method of fixing the results of NFL games.

And Adam Benson didn't know a thing about it or any of the people involved.

EIGHT

DETECTIVE Joseph Gerard Keegan, just Gerry Keegan when he was with friends, was ... well ... with friends.

He had arrived promptly at nine o'clock, liked Leigh from the minute she opened the door and smiled at him as if they had been meeting each other like this for years, and was further pleased to see just how close she and Eddie Buck seemed to be. The casual brush of a hand on his cheek, the straightening of a lock of hair that had slipped down on her forehead, Gerry was sure he had never seen this kind of natural togetherness when Eddie was married to Suzanne, a woman who had a decided leaning to the shrewish, who was able to express disappointment and bitter disapproval with a look and a glance, a motion of her head, that no one in the room could mistake.

He remembered that from the time he had been married to Marsha, and even though that was a lifetime ago, his stomach still tightened just a little when he thought of that sad, unhappy woman.

He entered the apartment and gave Leigh his jacket, and Ed appeared from the kitchen, pony glass in his hand, just the right mix of vodka and shaved ice. Gerry Keegan, at least in Ed's mind, was the inventor of the "Ketel Mist," and while he thought the fast dilution of such an outstanding vodka was somehow to be avoided, it was what Gerry Keegan drank, and after all, how much worse was it than those millions of amateurs who took one of the great single-malt scotches and mixed it with tap water?

"Well, it's not the best of times, and I'm sorry I haven't tried to get us together when there was no other reason but social," Buck began when they were seated, "but my friend is dead and I'm convinced he was murdered."

Keegan put down his glass, empty, and when Leigh moved to refill it he motioned her away. "One for now," he said. "More when it's strictly social, OK?"

She nodded, silent, allowing the two men to conduct what she was certain would be a quick discussion of Ed's almost irrational conviction that Adam Benson was somehow murdered.

"Gerry, they killed him. They had reasons, and I know they did it, but they are so damned smart that nobody could even think it was anything but accidental. But I know it was done to him and I need you to help me prove it."

Keegan nodded, and because he was unusually tall and unusually thin, and because one leg was crossed over the other and his arms folded across his chest, the simple action of nodding his head seemed to cause all his extremities to move as if they weren't all connected to a common torso. "Tell me what you know."

Ed told him.

"You got a tape of this, in his voice?" Keegan asked.

Ed shook his head from side to side. "No, no tapes. Shit, Gerry, I didn't know what he was gonna be telling me. He was my best friend and I promised him it would just be something between us. He came to my apartment Saturday night, before the game, spilled it all, and felt like he had a friend he could admit anything to without worrying about the guy's memory, you know? I didn't even take notes. I wasn't working, you understand? I was busy being his friend."

Keegan looked disappointed. "Shame," was all he said, so quietly that it was barely audible.

"Why?"

"Because if I had a concrete reason, if I had evidence, then what I'd want to do would be a lot easier to accomplish. Because if I go to the coroner's office and demand a full work-up autopsy his family is going to complain, and maybe somebody in the family is mixed up with what you think got him killed, and if they bitch loud enough I'm going to look like an asshole because he isn't a guy found murdered someplace, because it really isn't any of my business and sure isn't in my jurisdiction, and because then I'll have to explain about my friend the sportswriter and his crazy theory that nobody can prove or even think of a way to try to prove. That's why it's a damned shame, Eddie, because if you had a tape or if you had been wired or something, anything I could hold in my hands and show the official jerkoffs, it would be possible. As it stands now, I can't do a damned thing. And even if I thought you had a chance of being right, which I'm not sure I can say, I'm afraid my hands are tied."

"But, Gerry, what if he was murdered? Just for a second, for the hell of it, let's pretend we both know for sure that it was a murder. What would you do then, with no proof, no evidence, nothing else but what you feel? How would you deal with it then, if you were absolutely, positively sure-as-shit convinced that Adam Benson was wiped out because he told the gambling syndicate in this country to fuck off?"

Keegan said nothing. He stared out at some point

above Ed Buck, silent. Then Keegan said, "Well, if I had that sure a gut feeling, I guess I'd tell the coroner to do the full work-up autopsy and not give a shit who bitched, because he's an old friend and I think if I made it the one all-important favor I was ever going to ask him he'd find a way to do it without anybody else knowing and then cover it all up so nothing would ever be known if he didn't find anything. And if he did, of course, then it wouldn't matter who knew what we had done because it would be legal and there'd be an investigation and all that stuff. But that's only what I'd do if I had a strong, 100 percent feeling. I don't, Eddie, and you haven't convinced me I should."

He paused, saw the tight, stubborn cast to his friend's face.

"OK, I asked you to tell me why I should be as sure as you are, and you told me. Now convince me you're right, Ed. Tell me how a guy could be murdered in front of seventy-four thousand fans in a public stadium in broad daylight, on a field with twenty-one other football players and six officials and sidelines full of coaches and players and photographers and television technicians? Tell me who did it? How? There was no bullet hole, no knife wound. He wasn't poisoned, because every player on the team ate the same pregame meal and it was served in the hotel at a buffet table—yeah, we did that much asking, anyway.

"So we have ruled out guns, knives, and poison. He was not involved in a hit-and-run auto death. A fucking safe didn't fall on his head. He wasn't caught in a fire; he didn't die of smoke inhalation. What did it to him, Eddie? Some incantation mumbled by some mafioso's mother sitting on her veranda in Italy looking out at the Mediterranean? Who did it? How was it done? I don't even give a shit why, because if you can make

me think there's even a chance you're right . . . Yeah,
you don't have to convince me, just make me think
there's a one-in-a-thousand chance that you're right.
Well, go ahead. Give me a reason to put my ass on
the line after twenty-five years of unblemished service.
How did they kill Adam Benson? You don't even have
to tell me who 'they' are. Just how did they do it?"

Ed began to lose his temper, not at Keegan but at
the futility of proving something that was apparently
impossible to begin with. How, indeed, could a guy be
killed on a football field, in Yankee Stadium, without a
mark on him?

"Damn it, Gerry, I'm not the detective. I'm not the
cop. And I'm sure not some kind of mystic psychic
weirdo you guys sometimes use when nothing else
seems like it makes any sense. Maybe that's what we
need, some kind of Uri Geller doll, a guy who's
gonna smell Adam's coffee cup or comb or something
and tell you exactly who had him killed and exactly
how they did it. I don't know. How the hell am I
supposed to know how? All I know is what he told
me, that yesterday was the day he was gonna shove it
up their asses, and now he's dead. I know that my
friend is dead and I'm the only one he told this story
to and I can't even find anybody who wants to help
me get him some justice. I'm sorry I asked. Thanks
for coming, and maybe next time we'll be at some
silly cocktail party and we'll talk about the fucking
Giants and the Super Bowl. You know, something
important."

Keegan blew up. "You damned fool, why do you
think I'm here? Because I want your fucking autograph? Because I want inside information on which
games you're gonna pick the wrong way Sunday? I'm
here because I'm your friend, because I know you

longer than you knew Adam Benson, because you asked for help in an area in which I am an acknowledged goddamned expert, and so here I am. Cocktail parties? You don't get invited to the important cocktail parties. How could I see you at one of those? Now talk to me, you stupid shit, or I am going home. I'm tired."

For the first time in the conversation, Ed smiled. His face relaxed, he laughed. "Important cocktail parties? My, my, you are going places in the crooked New York City poli-pol circles, aren't you? I'm sorry. You're right. I'm a shit."

Leigh couldn't restrain herself. "Gentlemen," she said softly, "without trying to sound overly feminine or stupid, what the hell is poli-pol?"

Keegan smiled back at her. "That's his word," he said, nodding at Ed. "See, paranoid old Buck here is sure that the police and the political animals in this city are in collusion and have been since the city got running water and flush toilets, that nothing goes on or is allowed to go on, which is probably the point of his argument, unless the mayor and the police commissioner, who has to blow the mayor because that's who gave him the job in the first place, first have a little meeting and exchange promises and get about six nephews and cousins easy jobs. I used to laugh like hell. Now, as I move up a little higher. I'm not so sure he's wrong. Anyway, that's poli-pol."

Leigh smiled, satisfied, and leaned back. Ed, too, leaned back, looked at his friend the detective, and began speaking.

"Gerry, you know there are ways of killing somebody without leaving a trace, not a goddamned hint that anything wrong happened. I read a novel once where some Japanese guy visited his friend in jail and the guy was really unhappy about being there, you know? He had lost face, and he was an old guy to whom face was everything. So he asked his friend to kill him, but not to have to pay the price or get caught."

He paused, and Keegan could see the brightness in his eyes, as if he had just unlocked a wondrous secret. "Gerry, this guy took a pencil from his pocket, just a regular everyday pencil, and pressed it against his friend's temple, in some special spot only these Japanese ninjas knew about, and in like fifteen seconds this old guy smiles, nods his head, and keels over, dead as a fucking mackerel. And the friend gets up, bows his farewells, and leaves the old guy neatly arranged on his bed, looking just like he was asleep. No wound, no blood, no sign. Just an old guy who died in his sleep. It was perfect."

Gerry Keegan suddenly became Detective Joseph Gerard Keegan. "So what are you saying? That the bad guys dressed up like football players and carried a pencil in their uniforms, and when there was this big pileup they pressed it against Adam Benson's temple and made him to go sleep forever? How about Tinkerbell shows up and nobody can see her and she fucks him to death on the goal line? Come on, Eddie; isn't that a bit contrived?"

"Sure it is, and you're right," Buck said. "But something like that is possible, and I think you know it, and all you asked me to do was convince you there was maybe a one-in-a-thousand shot and you'd try to find somebody or something. I did, damn it; I did."

Keegan nodded. "Yeah, you did," he said. "Maybe there's something I can do, ask around, call in a favor, something. Give me a day to think about it, Eddie. I need to think about it."

He rose from the couch, clearly no longer in a social frame of mind. "Leigh," he said, "it was nice to meet you. If you are really going to marry this guy, I'm a little suspicious of your taste in men, but perhaps you'll invite me to the wedding anyway, so I can have one final chance to make you see the light." The smile on his face was genuine but fleeting.

"Ed," he said, turning to his friend. "I don't know if you have anything right going for you except this woman, but I agree what you've given me does have a one-in-a-thousand chance of being accurate and I am going to try to find out something. I'll call. You stay out of it, don't bother me, and above all don't call anybody else to find out what I'm doing, because anything I do right now is going to be unofficial. Don't get my ass in trouble by being a prying reporter. OK?"

Ed Buck smiled. "OK, Gerry. No trouble, I promise. But let me know what's happening, because I can't keep a promise like this forever, you know?"

Keegan left the apartment, got into his private nondescript black Ford sedan, and drove home slowly, thinking about where to start, what to do, how to handle this special favor, and whether there really could be anything to it. Hey, fixed games in the NFL would be too massive a story to handle quietly. A star quarterback getting killed because of it, and because he was involved, would only make it worse.

By the time Keegan reached home in newly safe Brooklyn Heights, he had decided that the first thing to do would be speak with George Laskey, the assistant medical examiner under whose temporary care rested the body of the late Adam Benson, quarterback. George owed him a favor, a big one. He was going to ask for something in return, finally, six years after he had made a record of a homosexual pandering arrest disappear, one concerning Scott Laskey, George's son and only child.

NINE

THERE were two things Dr. George Laskey did probably better than anyone else. He was as clever and gifted a forensics expert as could be found in New York City, where all the good ones worked. He also could drink more vodka than any man alive, at least in the opinion of those who had tried to drink with him, and it might well have been the reason that he was the assistant medical examiner and not in charge of the department. The guy who was, Dr. Kenneth Huff, should have retired by now, but the mayor was reluctant to pull that particular trigger because he'd have no choice but to elevate George Laskey to the position. The mayor had been at an important political gathering two years ago at the dedication of the newest wing at St. Vincent's, and George had picked that night to get drunk for the first time in a decade.

"Cheap vodka," he said the next day.

But George Laskey was reliable, consistent, and dependable, an aging Boy Scout with pallid complexion, wispy light brown hair that failed miserably in his attempt to cover an ever-widening bald spot. The perpetual smirk on his face, coupled with his lack of height, too many pounds, and the bald spot, reminded most people he met of an aging leprechaun. The fact that George was forty-seven came as a surprise; he looked older. He was quick to laugh and smart as a whip, and if he drank ... well, so did a lot of people who couldn't hide it nearly as well and because of it were totally unable to function anywhere near George's level.

Detective Joseph Gerard Keegan always deserved Laskey's attention. He owed Keegan for saving his son from a stupid mistake, saving the embarrassment and probable career-killing reaction his "accident" would have brought about. The kid was twenty-three now, certifiably gay, and so what? He was bright, attentive, and on his way to first-year residency at Manhattan Memorial, a huge private hospital on the Upper East Side. Scott Laskey was going to be a surgeon, and as George would say to his friends, "the only difference is that he cuts open live people and I cut open dead ones."

None of it would have been possible had Gerry Keegan not intervened, not put his own career on the line and somehow found a way to squash the stupidity. Scott, then eighteen, and his friend Chuck Grossi, both of them newly thrilled with the bravado they had exhibited by admitting to their homosexuality, had been picked up for soliciting an undercover detective on Third Avenue, offering the services of both for a hundred bucks. The second they described what they had in mind and said how much they wanted for their services the handcuffs came out and the two were taken into custody.

Keegan made the incident disappear.

George Laskey owed him. Big-time.

So when Keegan's voice turned up on Laskey's answering machine, he called right back. And when Keegan said he needed some time, Laskey told him to come right over, meet him in the lobby of the New

York City Police Forensics Lab on Varick Street near the Holland Tunnel.

Half an hour later, they were shaking hands.

"Gerry, how can I help?" George asked when they were seated in his tiny cubicle of an office just beyond the huge room with more than fifty stainless-steel operating tables lined up, complete with the stainless-steel sinklike drains to suck away the blood, a rolling cart of surgical instruments, a scale to weigh various organs, a computer terminal and screen, and an overhead microphone/tape recorder with a foot-pedal activation switch.

Keegan always had trouble drinking coffee when he could look through the glass door and see all this, but it never bothered Laskey, nor did it ever dawn on him that it might bother someone else.

"I need a favor, George."

"Name it, Gerry. Scott starts his internship next month."

Uncomfortable, Keegan tried to shake that debt. "George, look, it was just a favor, an easy one. I'm glad for you both. I did what I would do for any friend in the department. Nobody was hurt; nobody had charges to press. The kid made a mistake. Done. Let's drop it. You've done fifteen favors for me that might have put you in a spot since then. We're more than even. OK?"

Laskey smiled. "Fine, so how can I help?"

"I need you to do an autopsy without anybody knowing you're doing it." he said. "This is a major-league favor. You could lose your job and your license. If it was me, I wouldn't do it. But if I'm right, we'll all come out of this with citations and maybe promotions."

Laskey brightened. "Gerry, the only promotion I can get I can't get, at least until Mayor Moron is out is out of office." That was what most of the city employees called Mario Marone. "But if you need it done, then consider it done. Where's the body?"

"You have it. Came in last night."

"Yeah. So did sixteen others. You got a name or should I cut up all of them until we find the Easter eggs?"

"Adam Benson."

"Holy shit. The quarterback? What am I looking for?"

"I don't know."

"Well, that's helpful. What happened?"

"Don't know."

"What do you think happened?"

"Murder."

"Yeah, right. On a football field in the middle of a game. In full view of . . . Jesus, Gerry, what do I look for? Where do I start?"

"That's why you get the big bucks, George. But remember, nothing to nobody. This is just between us."

"Yeah, sure. Then I'll tell his widow somebody got him confused with the floater we found in the river and cut him all apart before the mistake was . . . oh, shit, I'll find a way. Call me tonight."

Keegan stood, again those long limbs making him appear more like a marionette than a man. "Thanks, George. May your scalpels always be sharp."

"Get the hell out of here," Laskey said, laughing.

It was later that day, well past six, which was later than George Laskey ever liked to stay in what he called the Vault, that he put down his scalpel, surveyed the results of an exhaustive autopsy, and virtually whispered into the overhead microphone something that he had never had to say before.

"The guy is still alive," he said. "Nothing killed him. He's not dead and he is as healthy as a horse."

There had been no sign of the easy symptoms. No heart attack. No drug overdose, although there were obvious signs of what the medical fraternity calls "extended recreational cocaine usage." No severe trauma to the head or the neck. No aneurysm in his brain, no embolism anywhere else in his body. No internal injury from a sudden impact during the game that might have punctured a lung or cracked his larynx.

Nothing.

Adam Benson wasn't dead, except for the inescapable fact that he was. He was the healthiest corpse George Laskey had ever seen.

He didn't call Gerry Keegan until he got home and had a drink, which put the time at about nine.

"What do you mean, nothing killed him?" the detective yelped. "He's dead; something must've killed him. What do you think he's doing, sleeping?"

"I know," Laskey said. "I know. But I don't know. To find out, I'll have to run much more sophisticated tests than we normally do for the drunks and the vein poppers. But nobody is supposed to know I did this. The widow said no autopsy. So what am I supposed to do, Gerry?"

All detective now, Keegan studied his options. "Make it official," he said. "This is an autopsy ordered by the New York Police Department. Do whatever you have to do, but find out what killed the guy, and for God's sake keep it away from the press."

He slammed the receiver down, picked it up again, and dialed Ed Buck's apartment.

"Listen; this is Keegan," he said when Buck picked up. "We've got a case. Sort of. I asked for a favor and we did an autopsy. Your friend shouldn't be dead. Nothing killed him. The only way to find out what really happened is a much more intense study, and I authorized it. If I have to, I'll put this under suspicion of first-degree murder. I'll keep you informed."

"Thanks, Gerry. I'll try not to be a pest."

"Yeah. Sure you will. Talk to you tomorrow."

TEN

SHERRI Novak arrived the next morning, her face tearstained, haggard, grieving. She hugged Ed when she arrived at the hospital, in the lounge area reserved for VIP attendance, and Ed was struck again by her beauty.

"Eddie, what am I going to do? I don't know how to bury a person; I don't know how to be a widow. What do I do first?"

Forced to set aside his own mourning for the moment, Ed Buck became friend of the family, that one efficient person who seems to materialize when a crisis bursts open.

"His dad is coming in today," Ed told Sherri. "I would think he'd want Adam buried in Oliphant, unless you and he had already decided things like that." As he said "he," he realized how foolish it sounded. People as beautiful and alive as Adam and Sherri Benson didn't think about burial plots and wills and estate planning. Normal people did that. Ordinary people.

"No, we didn't have any plans," Sherri said. "Whatever Mr. Benson wants is fine. Ed, where is he? Where is Adam? I want to see him."

Where indeed? Did Ed tell the newly minted widow that her husband's body had already been opened by a police order? Did he tell her that the New York City

Police Department, at his urging, had begun handling this case as if it was premeditated murder?

"He's in the morgue," Ed managed to say. "They did an autopsy. Standard procedure for this kind of thing. But now that you're here, they'll release the body to you, arrange for you to have someone pick him up. Or we can just wait for his father."

Sherri stiffened, almost imperceptibly. Her eyes opened wide. "Autopsy? Why would they need an autopsy?" she asked, and Ed Buck wondered whether that was shock or fear just on the other edge of her voice.

"Any public death, Sherri. Anything like that. Anything suspicious. They just automatically do an autopsy. Routine."

"Suspicious? What's suspicious about it?"

"Sherri, the guy is the quarterback of a team and right there during a game he just dies? He scores a touchdown and he doesn't get up when they unpile? Don't you think that looks a little suspicious, that some people might be a little suspicious about why he died, how he died?"

She looked thoughtful for a moment, her mind frantically racing, then nodded her head. "Well, yeah, of course it does," she said, "but how else could he have died except from something like a heart attack?"

"I don't know, but the detective I spoke to said that's why they do these things."

Sherri looked at Ed, right into his eyes. "Did they find anything? Anything at all?"

He shook his head. "No, and that's why it's still suspicious. No sign of a heart attack, an aneurysm, a stroke. No head injury. No broken rib that punctured a lung. He didn't swallow his tongue and suffocate. Nothing. He's just dead and nobody knows why, or

even how it happened. They can't just let it hang like that, you know?"

"Well, I can," Sherri Benson snapped, angry now, the grief fled from her face. "They aren't going to do anything else to Adam. Nothing. That's it. I'm the wife . . . and I can stop it, can't I?"

Gerry Keegan appeared at her side. He introduced himself and, taking her hand, said, "I'm afraid not, Mrs. Benson. You can't actually stop the procedure now. Once we get involved in something like this, it has to run its course. We'll release the body as soon as we can. I've asked the doctor to meet us. And I am very sorry at what happened. I was a fan of your husband's for a long time."

Ed and Keegan led Sherri Benson to a couch and tried to answer questions for her while they waited.

George Laskey finally came across the lounge and was introduced to Ed and Sherri. "My deepest condolences," he said to her, bowing ever so slightly, an almost European touch. "I conducted the autopsy myself. I was the only one who touched him. I am truly sorry, Mrs. Benson. Your husband seemed to be a man in better than reasonable condition, a little wear and tear, a few old scars, but nothing out of the ordinary for a professional athlete."

"Then who—I mean what—killed him?"

"We don't know yet," he said. "Detective Keegan has authorized a more complete examination, the kind we conduct only when foul play is suspected. To tell the truth, though, I don't know what to expect to find. I did a normally thorough job and I couldn't find a thing to attribute his death to. That in itself is suspicious, of course. People just don't die without a reason, without a cause. It is not within the parameters of the definition of death."

Sherri looked stricken. Ed was puzzled. Keegan nodded, stared at the woman for a long minute, then turned to explain in layman's terms.

"Look, a man dies of a heart attack, there is evidence of damage to the heart. A man has a stroke, you find the spot. Gunshot, poisoning, bludgeoning, choking . . . all those more normal causes of death are easily found, targeted, and studied.

"But Adam Benson shouldn't be dead. There isn't a mark on him. There is no evidence of foul play. No poison. His oxygen wasn't cut off. Nothing, nothing, nothing. And then more of the same. Nobody dies from being too healthy. Dr. Laskey here will find it. He will need more time, and when he is finished we will have an answer. We owe it to your husband, Mrs. Benson, to find out exactly what happened. It is a little difficult to imagine a man being killed in front of a packed Yankee Stadium crowd and not finding a mark on him, wouldn't you agree?"

She nodded, face pale, lips thin. "Do what you have to do, Detective Keegan," she said. "I will be . . . Jesus, I don't know where I will be. Probably in a hotel. The Warwick, probably. I'll let Ed know."

They said good-bye. Keegan got into his unmarked car and dissolved into the steady flow of traffic. Ed and Sherri went back inside to wait for Adam's father.

They didn't have long to wait. Andy Benson arrived, nearly filling the doorway to the waiting lounge. He knew Ed from all those years ago, of course, and grabbed him in a great, burly bear hug, tears running down his cheeks. "All the way up here on the train I couldn't stop crying, Eddie," he said. "I'm a grown man. A tough old man. And I couldn't stop crying."

He turned and saw Sherri.

"I am Andy Benson," he said. "It is nice to meet you."

For a second Ed thought the old man, who he knew to be well past seventy, had simply blocked a memory. Of course he would have met his daughter-in-law by now. Of course he would.

But Sherri nodded, extended her hand, and said, "Hello, Mr. Benson. I'm so sorry we couldn't have met under different circumstances."

Adam and Sherri had been married for three years and he had never brought his new wife to see his father? Had never flown the old man out to California or down to Florida or wherever the hell it was they lived to see his new wife?

Ed was stunned.

"Mr. Benson," Sherri said, "I understand you have a family burial plot back in Oliphant. I'd like to have Ed buried there, if it's all right with you."

He nodded. "Sure," he said gruffly. "He'll rest next to his mother. Thank you for that. Who do I see to make arrangements?"

"We can't do anything yet, Andy," Ed said. "They aren't finished with his body yet. They don't know what killed him. I asked a detective friend to look into it and they're treating it like a suspicious death. As soon as they're done, they'll let us know and we can take the body."

Andy Benson nodded. "I'll wait," he said.

"Andy, it could take days. You can't wait. Why don't you come home with me?"

He stood, hat in his hand, pain on his face. "I won't be in anybody's way? You're sure? I don't think I'd like to be alone in New York City right now. Thank you."

"I'll call Leigh," Ed said to Sherri, "my fiancée. She'll

come and take you back to her place until you get settled."

Sherri nodded.

"I'd like to see you tonight, for dinner," Ed said to her. "I'll bring Andy to Leigh's place and we'll stay there for a while. Is that all right with everybody?"

They both nodded their assent. Ed went to the pay phone, and half an hour later Sherri Benson was on her way. Ed sat with Andy Benson for a long time, neither man talking. Finally the old man, eyes still red, looked over at his son's friend.

"You think it's kind of strange that I never met her, don't you?"

"Yes, Andy. I do. I know Adam was proud of her, and I know how much he loved you. I don't understand it at all. Do you?"

Andy nodded. "It was her," he said. "Adam told me she didn't want to get involved in any family stuff. That she had grown up alone, that her father and her brother had left as soon as they could, and that she had lived with her mother for a while, until the woman killed herself with drink and drugs. So she didn't want to get too close to another family, even her husband's. And she told him, too, that she never wanted to have a kid. Imagine that."

His shoulders started shaking again and that awful sound of a proud old man's heart breaking came through in muffled sobs.

"I never met her until today, Ed," he said. "I don't like her and I don't trust her."

With that, they got up, wordlessly, and walked out onto the street to hail a cab.

ELEVEN

ED helped Andy Benson, with his one overnight suitcase, out of the taxi and into his apartment building. They spoke mostly about Adam and their college days at Oklahoma; Adam's high school exploits, which Ed had heard about in the time they had spent together; and a few things he never knew and never would have known had this tragedy not happened.

For instance, that Adam had named him, Ed Buck, as executor of his will. Not his father. Not his wife. That the will was in Andy Benson's possession, not in his wife's; that there was more than $3 million in Adam's estate, which included property on Cape Cod and Key West.

"He gave you the real estate," Andy said. "Adam had a problem telling people how much he loved them. I always had the same problem. But, Ed, you were his best friend. I don't think he had another."

Pouring another pony glass of Ketel One, with Andy Benson nursing a second beer, Ed learned more about his friend, the kinds of things that Andy, without knowing why, had to talk about to provide some sort of catharsis for his grief. That once, at the age of sixteen, Adam got into a fight over a girl and sent the other guy to the hospital with a fractured skull and that his mother was so upset at the thought that the boy might die that she refused to sleep or eat for six days, until the doctors said a full recovery was likely. That by the time Adam was thirteen everybody in Oliphant and soon the entire state of Pennsylvania knew he was one of those miracle athletes and that he could have gone to college to play basketball or baseball, not just football.

But he said he didn't want baseball because he didn't think he could make it to the major leagues as a pitcher, "and if I can't have the ball every play, be in charge, I'm not interested."

The old man finally went to take a nap and left Ed sitting in the living room, staring out at the busy street, holding a half-full glass of watered-down vodka and wondering what the rest of the story would be by the time the mystery of Adam Benson's death was solved.

And why didn't Andy Benson like Sherri? What was there? What had happened? Or was it just an old man's instinct, a dislike of the flashy and the extravagant?

TWELVE

ED must have dozed off, too. The jangle of the telephone woke him an hour later, and in reaching for it he toppled the glass that had been set down on the table next to his chair.

"Ed, it's Sherri. I have to talk to you. I'm at Leigh's, but I can't talk to you here. Or on the telephone. Will you meet me?"

"Sure. Listen, if you just go out and turn left, there's a place on the corner, kind of a pub called the Knickerbocker. Go there. Get a booth in the back. Tell the guy at the bar, probably Rob Knox, that you're expecting me. I'll be there in half an hour."

Quickly showered and dressed, Ed hailed a taxi and in twenty minutes was at the Knick, as all the locals called it. Sherri was there, in the back booth, and considering the time of day, the middle of the afternoon, there wasn't much in the way of a crowd.

He slid in opposite her, told Knox to bring him a mug of black coffee, and sat studying Sherri's face.

She was gorgeous, the rare kind of beauty that cosmetics cannot create and often obscure. She was beautiful but hard, no softness in her face, rather angles and sculpted lines, and although Ed never knew her and had never really spoken to her, he sensed more of an intelligence than she would ever allow to be seen.

"What's up, Sherri? What do you need that needs to be secret? Is there something I can do, something I can help you do?"

She stared at him and the sadness in her eyes was palpable. "I want to ask you to find the bastards who had him killed," she said. "But that isn't necessary. I know who they are. I need you to prove it and to make them pay. I don't know how it was done, but I know who ordered it done, and I'll tell you everything I can to find a way to get even for Adam."

Was that the floor opening under him? "So you know—"

"Yes, of course. It's why he's dead, Ed. There's another reason, too. Me. He's dead because of me. Our marriage was arranged. They needed him to help them make a lot of money; I needed them to get where I thought I wanted to go. I didn't love Adam when we married. Oh, he loved me. He was crazy in love with me. And I kind of liked him, too."

Ed's left hand shot out, and he had to stop its motion at the last second before it crashed into the side of her face. All the pent-up anger and anguish at the death of his friend was threatening to boil to the surface, unleashed. How could this woman so casually address the death of the man she had married with, "And I kind of liked him, too." Ed was unsuccessful at hiding the motion of his left hand; Sherri noticed and flinched.

"You kind of liked him? You kind of liked him?" he said, voice hard and rigidly in control. "You kind of liked the guy? He was your husband. He loved you. What the fuck does that mean?"

Sherri began to sob, very quietly, almost unnoticed but for the erratic movement of her shoulders and the fact that she had turned her face away from him, toward the wall. "It means," she whispered, "that I married Adam because they told me I had to, and it means that once I did, I fell in love with him. I knew about the gambling; I knew about the cocaine. I hooked him. I got him into it. And I agreed that gambling, fixing the games, was the best way for him to keep it coming and stay out of trouble. But I never, never thought they'd kill him, Ed. He told me he was going to stop it and I begged him not to. I knew what they were capable of doing. And they did it, in the one place in the world where no one can commit a murder. Witnesses? There were almost seventy thousand of them, and not one of them saw a thing."

She looked up at him, face tear-tracked.

"Please, Ed. Think whatever you want to about me, but help bring these people down. Do it for Adam. Not for me. I don't count here and I think maybe I never counted at all, to anybody. Not ever. And especially not to myself. But I loved him. So did you. Please help me."

THIRTEEN

ED told her about the conversation with Adam Saturday night. My God, was it only that, only two days ago? He told her that Adam had been both frightened and belligerent, embarrassed for what he had done to the game that had provided him with everything and in fear of what his sudden reversal would do to her, to his wife.

"He loved you very much and always seemed to consider himself especially lucky that you would even agree to talk to him. When you said you'd marry him, I swear he thought it was some kind of joke."

Sherri's eyes misted again. "It was, at least at first," she whispered.

Sherri Novak Benson was twenty-six years old. She had been born Sheila Novaczenski in Buffalo, New York, to a mother who drank and a father who worked too hard to have much time for her.

Sheila had a brother, Johnny, two years older, and by the time she was fourteen Johnny had sexually abused her and, worse, humiliated her by forcing her to make it with his friends, each watching and taking turns. The news that Johnny Novaczenski had been killed in a botched holdup of a convenience store came as no surprise and brought little regret to Sheila. By then her mother had been institutionalized and her father, working harder than ever, had mourned for a day or two and then gone back to his job as a maintenance man for the big hospital, Saint Theresa of Mercy.

Sheila left Buffalo as soon as she graduated from high school, hitched to New York City with a truck driver who said he would charge her twenty bucks but took a blow job instead. Sheila knew that was coming and was surprised the guy didn't insist on the money, too.

It took less than a week to change her name and get work in the big city. She became Sherri Novak, an escort girl, and learned one thing, that her looks made up for everything, her beauty and sexuality were her tickets out of the garbage can, and, above all, she had to preserve her looks and her body.

Her pride went first; her sensitivity followed. There was nothing she wouldn't do for the money, less she wouldn't do for someone she thought might be of help later on down the road. Which was exactly how she met Billy DeSalvo.

It was a Christmas party in Queens, and the local low-level hoods had hired several girls to spice up the festivities. It was a celebration of sorts; more money had been made that year in prostitution, gambling, and drug sales than ever in their little group; more than $5 million by the end of December would be salted away for sharing later on.

So Sherri, hired along with three other girls from the escort company, agreed to earn 1,000 bucks for the night's work. What work? "Anything any of the guys asks you to do," said Dominick Valentine, who put the party and all other "major" deals together. "If you don't think you can handle that, back out now."

For a thousand bucks Sherri would do most anything, and by 5:00 A.M. she had. But by far the sickest and most perverted of them all had been this short, fat guy from California, a local hero who went to Hollywood and made good and now came home to visit his mother for Christmas.

Sherri could tell right away that DeSalvo didn't really like women; he liked watching them have sex, usually in submissive, subservient positions, as if being taken advantage of by men and, oddly, by "tougher" women. He would have objected violently to the phrase *more masculine women,* but there it was, regardless. Billy DeSalvo was not a homosexual, but he wasn't quite heterosexual, either. He had been cursed with a tiny dick, and that was a lifelong source of embarrassment and humiliation to him, and so he got aroused watching beautiful girls "naked and in heat," as he called it.

He zeroed in on Sherri, and because he was the visiting celebrity, an old friend who might soon be able to help the others take a few more steps up the ladder, anything he wanted was the way things were going to be. Sherri found herself making love to one of the other girls while one of DeSalvo's friends was anally fucking her. DeSalvo filmed the whole scene with his camcorder.

Sherri found herself naked and on her knees in front of a row of five of these cheap hoods, Billy holding a stopwatch to determine which one came the quickest. The winner got another blow job, courtesy of Sherri.

Of course it was demeaning. But it wasn't any different from blowing her brother or his friends, or that fat, smelly truck driver, and this was a grand for the night. She had long ago learned to block out her feelings and her objections to almost anything. Hell, there were times when she wasn't even aware of where she was, whom she was with, and, most critically, what she was doing.

DeSalvo liked her. He liked her looks and her sex-producer make additional hundreds of thousands of dollars through the judicious use of information allowing him to bet on the right Los Angeles Hoops games and only the right games.

Billy DeSalvo.

They were, in a strange way, glad to see each other again.

Billy laughed at the recollection of the Christmas party in Brooklyn eight months earlier, then turned to Teddy Corr, the producer, and said, "Hey, this broad is the best cocksucker I have ever seen, anywhere. She's a fucking artist."

Corr had to see for himself, and Billy DeSalvo proved to be accurate. "There are people you have to get to know in Hollywood," he breathed, "important people who can help you. A talent like yours should never go to waste."

It didn't go to waste that night, for certain. While Billy watched, which was his favorite thing of all, Teddy Corr availed himself of the talent three times; Bobby Moska once, although against his wishes; and Judy Brett most of the rest of the time, much to her delight. In fact, it was she who suggested that Sherri come to Hollywood soon and stay with her at the beach house in Malibu "for as long as you need before you find your own place." At the same time she made it clear to Corr that finding work for Sherri would be a great idea.

But DeSalvo put a stop to that instantly. He knew the value Sherri Novak would have in his particular world and wasn't about to allow an empty suit from Hollywood to stand in the way.

"I have already arranged for Sherri to work for my people," he said, growing suddenly and strangely quiet and formal. None of those present misunderstood the change in persona, not even Sherri, who recognized that an offer, a lucrative one, had just been made and that her silence was acceptance.

"Hey, great," chirped the ever-alert Corr. "That way, we can get to see a lot of Miss Novak anyway."

It was left at that. She never saw any of those people again, although Judy Brett tried several times to find her in the next few months.

Sherri did go to Los Angeles, about two months later. She called a number DeSalvo had left her and in two days had an apartment, a job as a special escort to select individuals, and a thousand dollars a week, plus whatever she could raise on her own. But she was to never, absolutely never, try to get any money out of DeSalvo's special friends. For them, she was bought and paid for.

She understood perfectly.

Three weeks after going to work for DeSalvo, she also picked up a cocaine habit, courtesy of her employer. For her, life was much, much better than it had ever been before. Now she wanted to look into the possibility of an acting career, and when she mentioned it to DeSalvo he readily promised to help her. "We have friends in the business, more important than that asshole Corr," he said, cackling at the memory of that night in Vegas. "We can arrange that. You do what we ask, and one day you won't need us. You'll be a star."

For a smart girl like Sherri, she was unbelievably stupid to believe the little fat man.

FOURTEEN

THEY decided to go through with the funeral first and spare Andy Benson the anguish of knowing about the dark, ugly side of his son's life. It would be better, they decided, if he could remember Adam as a golden, somehow blessed athlete, a quarterback with ethereal skills and magnetism who was better and cleaner and more close to perfect.

But Ed did call Gerry Keegan late that night to tell him what he had learned and that they wanted to put everything else aside until the funeral was done and the man was buried. Keegan, understanding that no one had an inkling of what had been uncovered, agreed to wait. But when he hung up he did make one call, and when he got Laskey he told him to look extra carefully.

"The man died from being healthy," the doctor said. "Of course I'll be careful—"

Keegan cut him short. "No, he didn't die naturally. Find out how they killed him, and don't say anything to anybody until I talk to you again. Nothing, to nobody. Oh, and, George? He was a hard cocaine user. You should be able to find that with a blood screen procedure, right?"

George Laskey nodded, then realized Keegan couldn't see that reaction. "Right, Gerry, I understand. I'm still holding the body; this may take time. Tell his family not to make any strong commitments yet for a funeral and burial."

Keegan put the receiver down and stared into space. Laskey put his receiver down and stared at his hands. He owed Gerry Keegan big-time, and this might be his only chance to square the debt. No matter how Keegan shrugged it off, covering for Scott had been an incredible piece of work. The kid was going to be a doctor. Almost there. And he was still a fag. Well, sure. These days it was acceptable. But you have to call them gays, not fags. George Laskey would have to remember that.

Ed, assured Leigh that it was really over, that nothing more could be expected.

"Well, there may be one more little inconvenience," he said.

"Such as?"

"I need you two to be witnesses. Sherri and I are getting married."

Leigh, her eyes moist, looked up at him and said, "I know a great place. It's down at the Jersey shore. It's called Ship Bottom. And there's a wonderful little hotel. It's called the St. Rita. And...oh, damn it, Gerry, what a wonderful thing."

EPILOGUE

ABOUT thirty miles north of George Town, the capital of Grand Cayman and the Cayman Islands, is an area called Rum Point. It is the northernmost tip of the island, situated at the junction of Bowse Bluff and Cayman Kai, well past Sparrowhawk Point and Long Coconut Point, Old Man Bay and Grape Tree Point, past Spanish Bay and Boatswains Point.

The ocean cracks against the shoreline, its breaking waves and frisky whitecaps belying its Caribbean identity. It is perhaps one of the most peaceful, isolated spots in the Western Hemisphere. The weather, which is almost always placid, ranges between sixty-five and ninety degrees. There is almost always a prevailing west wind, offshore breezes that flog the ocean, and the sun's coloring is, impossibly, closest to washed-out pastels. In eternal spring, but with a small break for torrid summer, this part of Grand Cayman has an idyllic quality not found anywhere else.

There are only a dozen homes there, each built into the beach on a small, protected hillock, each parcel of land no less than twenty acres. Each of the palatial homes, built by expatriates, mostly from the States and Great Britain, bears a nameplate, a shingle swinging in the mild tropical breezes, identifying themselves to the precious few motorists who wander out that far. The nameplates bear names such as Road's End and Heaven's Gate and Windfall.

One of the homes, the most simple yet somehow the most elegant, all startling white and, to the knowing eye, clearly the most expensive, is called My Father's House.

No one ever came to visit its single occupant, and only an occasional glance at the local newspaper, the *Daily Caymanian*, told him of the continuing upheaval in the United States—famous politicians resigning in disgrace or being indicted or both, banks being forced to close, organized crime leaders being arrested and, for a change, having the charges stick, at least two major New York Stock Exchange brokerages being forced to liquidate and close.

He learned, weeks after the fact, of the promotion of Detective First Class Joseph Gerard Keegan to assistant police commissioner of New York, his invaluable help in bringing down the corruption boosting him rapidly up the ladder.

He learned of a Pulitzer Prize being awarded to Edward Kalman Buck of the *New York Express* for his investigative reporting leading to the disclosure of much of the incendiary information.

Only occasionally did the single occupant venture into George Town, usually stopping at one of the banks and then for a solitary dinner at one of only two restaurants, the Brasserie or Hooks. He never needed a reservation. When he appeared, a table was made ready for him. It seemed many people knew him, welcomed him, and fought for him to sit with them. He almost always declined, politely, and with a smile, choosing to sit alone, on the periphery of the crowded dining room.

Once, he was seen with an old man, white-haired,

stooped over, feeble, and infirm. They assumed it was his father. When they left, the two embraced, as if having just seen each other for the last time.

Mostly, those who sought his company were bankers and real estate brokers. Banking, as everyone knew, comprised the single most profitable industry in the country, one that made the tiny Caribbean nation the fourth-wealthiest in the world. Caymanian banking rules demanded confidentiality and offered no exchange of information with any other country in the world. Monies deposited in Cayman banks were totally and completely safe from prying eyes. It was a criminal offense for any banking official to discuss any client's finances with anyone, even other bank employees. The banking system was billed as a tax haven, and it was. There was no income tax on the island, nor was any contemplated.

Every once in a while someone was arrested and charged with violation of the Cayman Banking Laws, the result of a sting operation conducted by the banking commission to ensure the integrity of this unique financial structure.

The solitary occupant had learned, from sources he never lost in the States, that Ed and Leigh Buck owned property on Key West. There were a few times he was tempted to call one of the old guard, to see if they could be found. No malice was intended, just a curiosity about how their lives were going, since he, and he alone, was responsible for them being alive at all.

But he resisted the impulse. He had disappeared. It was better that way. He had a lifetime of atonement to earn for all he had done. He would forever be grateful to Keegan and Buck and, in a way, to Assante.

He was Rico Impelliteri, and he was alone.

FIFTEEN

BILLY DeSalvo wasn't exactly nervous, but he had enjoyed better days and he knew there had been many times when his mind was more clear and relaxed. He hadn't heard from Sherri in three days. He knew she got there. He knew she was staying with the sportswriter's girlfriend. Buck had played with Benson in college. They had stayed friends; Benson gave him some stories, nothing much. Big fucking deal.

DeSalvo also knew, through the scores of pipelines he had in New York and could never, would never, lose, that the Buck guy was handling the burial arrangements, that he had met with Benson the Friday night and the Saturday night before the game, that they had gone to his apartment and kind of in a hurry, the waiter said to Tony the Freak, who felt he had to call one of the bookies he knew, who in turn told his boss, and, eventually, that guy thought it was important enough to tell Billy. Not that he knew anything about any of the plans, just that Billy was a major player in pro football gambling and would probably appreciate the information.

"The waiter said that they didn't even order dinner, just had a drink, talked for a while, and then got up and raced out," said the guy from the right-hand side of the country. Billy thanked him, told him to thank

Tony the Freak, and said he'd take a look at the line when it got close to kickoff and if he learned anything he'd get back in time for the guy to take advantage.

Done. A favor given, unbidden. Now a favor owed.

But Billy was a little nervous about the thing. The killing had gone perfectly. The rat was dead, before he could fuck up a major money deal. Before he could run to the cops. Before he could bring ruin and, more seriously, shame and ridicule to the Assante family. But before he could tell the fucking sportswriter? Nobody knew. Billy had to have somebody close, somebody watching. Sportswriters in New York know a lot of people. Cops and politicians could be bought, and cheap. But the people in the NFL office, which had a better security crew for investigating gambling than the fucking FBI, they were the dangerous ones. They still believed in honesty and straight games, and the dumb bastards wouldn't even let the casino owners build a $300 million stadium in Vegas to hold the Super Bowl every year. For free. Why? Because you could bet on organized sports in Nevada, on the NFL games. It was a fucking joke. Didn't they think people all around the country bet on NFL games every week? Didn't they know that the Super Bowl was the greatest single-game betting action in history, that more people bet on the sixteen-game NFL season than they did on the eight-fucking-million-game major-league baseball season?

Of course they knew, and when it was "the right time" Billy was sure the NFL would suddenly recognize "its friends" in Las Vegas and among certain of the politicians, but it wasn't the right time and that was that.

Big fucking deal.

More important, did Benson and this sportswriter

just talk about old times, the games they played and the broads they fucked, or did he spill his guts to his buddy just before he got ready to suit up and die? This bothered Billy DeSalvo, this not knowing, and it was important that he find out. Critically important. After all, Mr. Assante had put him in charge of this operation. The last thing in the world he wanted was for it to get fucked up. Getting whacked would be a blessing compared to things Billy had heard happened when Mr. Assante really got angry.

So someone had to go to New York, to be there, be aware. Billy couldn't send Rico Scalzi, even though the big man was the perfect choice, because the broad knew him—and blew him, wasn't that an old punch line to an old joke?—and the second she saw him she'd flip out. Whoever went had to be able to hang around, just on the edge, someone who, if Sherri noticed him, wouldn't matter, wouldn't set off any bells and sirens.

Also, Billy would prefer not to have Mr. Assante know that the situation was cloudy. The man would probably find out anyway. He had a way of knowing everything. But Billy had to make every effort to keep it a secret. And if Assante learned? Well, not a real problem, Billy felt. "Just making sure, Mr. Assante. Just making sure we were covered everywhere. Nobody likes surprises, right, Mr. Assante?"

Hell, Billy might even earn points for being extra careful, and that couldn't hurt him when it came time for another big job, another slow but definite move up the ladder. Billy DeSalvo was ambitious, but it was ambition mixed with caution and animal street cunning. He knew when to bow and scrape, and he felt the big shots who suddenly woke up dead, almost every one of them, had never learned how to do that. It was important, to his way of thinking, a critical part of the overall intelligence with which a guy had to approach his goals. If people thought you were sucking up to them, they might not respect you a hell of a lot, but guys like Billy never expected respect. What he wanted was success, money, recognition in that small circle in which he wanted to travel.

If it was ass kissing, then he was an ass kisser, and he had refined it to an art form.

He needed someone he could trust, or someone who was afraid of him, which would be even better. Because while Billy knew he was relatively low on the list of important people in his world, he also knew he had climbed out of the muck at the bottom and there were lots of people he could step on. And he enjoyed that, possessing a knack for zeroing in on people who had something to lose, something that would be catastrophic if it was made public or if it was suddenly snatched away. If Billy DeSalvo was a bottom feeder, he had learned to be a very skilled one.

In his particular business, finding someone he could trust was not a goal easily achieved. He trusted no one and didn't expect anyone to trust him. Such a man would be marked as a fool, and fools were not to be easily suffered. No one really trusted anyone in this life, not even at the top. They all worked together because of the common goal of substantial profits and the other common bond, fear of the bigger and more powerful bottom feeders.

So Billy DeSalvo had to be smart. He had to find somebody to act as his eyes and ears. A reporter, sort of, and he giggled when he thought of that. A reporter to spy on the reporter and the new widow piece of ass.

First he had to get some information, and this was incredibly easy; all he had to do was work through the good old NYPD.

He dialed a number. On the third ring a voice said, "Detective Quinn."

"Hey, jerkoff. You still peepin' through keyholes?"

A half-second of silence, followed by a high cackle. "Billy, you fat fuck, how are things in California?"

"Shit, it's easy out here, Patty. These LA cops couldn't find their dicks if they were in their hands. You guys are the real goods back home."

"Yeah, yeah. You fucked us pretty good, too, Billy. You know somethin'? I miss you. I do."

Now it was Billy's turn to laugh. "Yeah, bullshit. You miss the money I used to lay on you to leave my bookies alone. Can't find another source these days?"

"Nah. Shit, it's all dried up, Billy. Hey, I know you didn't call to say hello. What do you need?"

"Nuthin' much. I'm interested in that quarterback who bought it during the game the other day. Benson? I'm just curious. What happened? That cost me a bundle out here, and now I think everybody in the country is gonna be bettin' down on whoever the Bears play the rest of the season. I may take Chicago right off the board."

"Yeah. Makes sense. They don't have anybody even close to bein' a suspect. They don't even think it was anything but the poor bastard getting wiped out by a heart attack. Strange, the guy just dropped dead, just like that, during the game. Medical examiner couldn't find shit. Said the guy was too fucking healthy, that's what killed him. Some shit, huh? Hey, he went out a hero. Ball in his hands, just scored a touchdown. Perfect for him. Me? I wanna go in the saddle, but not with my old lady. Those new saddles are a lot better, you know?"

Billy laughed, a hearty laugh only he knew was forced. "Yeah. New saddles are the best, especially the ones that suck, too. So what I want to know is what his friend has been writing. You know, the guy he played with in college? The sportswriter."

"Oh, Eddie Buck? Shit, he's like shattered. He hasn't been in the paper since it happened. Damned good writer, too. I miss his stuff. He's takin' care of the arrangements, you know? Benson's wife came in from Hollywood. Man, what a looker that one is. I'd give a month's pay to get her in the sack."

Billy laughed. "A month's pay for you doesn't even buy her a good vibrator, Patty. But yeah, I know what you mean. Super good-lookin' cunt. Best I ever saw. Met her once at a party." He giggled silently at his private joke.

"Yeah, you're livin' the life, Billy. So this guy is handling the funeral as soon as they release the body. The broad is stayin' with his girlfriend, some chick named . . . hold on. I'll look at Keegan's book . . . named Leigh Janice Crespino. Lives on East 72d. Works for some major big-hitter advertising agency, DD Ads. That's about all I know, Billy. Hey, when you come home to visit your mother stop up and say hello. You left a lotta empty pockets in this precinct."

"Yeah, right, Patty. Right. I'll do that. Hey, thanks. Keep it hard."

It wasn't often you hit a home run the first time up, you know? DD Ads? The guy who owned that . . . what the fuck was his name? Oh, right. Drexler. David Drexler. In the hole for over four hundred thousand to Tony the Freak's boss, Philly Gags. Favor for favor, right. Now he was going to call in an old one.

He dialed Philip Gagliardi's number.

One ring.

"Yeah?"

"Put Gags on the phone," he said.

"Who the fuck is this?" A gruff, deep voice. Probably Louie Donato.

"It's DeSalvo, Louie, you piece of shit."

"Oh, hey, Billy. How's it hangin'? Gotta be careful, you know?"

"Yeah. I know. Put him on."

"Right away."

A few minutes, duly noted.

Then, "Billy? Hey. What's up?"

"I need something, Gags. It's important."

"Sure, Billy. What I got, you got."

"I want you to put that asshole Drexler's tab on me. And I want you to have him call me today. Tell him if he thought bein' in a deep fuckin' hole with you was trouble, now he's got so much grief he won't be able to sleep even if I let him off the hook. But first fax me everything you got on him. Do it now."

"Can I ask why?"

"You know better."

"Yeah, I do. Where should he call you?"

Billy spoke a phone number, his private number. Then he gave Gagliardi the fax machine number. Then Billy hung up, without saying a good-bye or thanks, and waited for his newest pigeon to fly into the coop.

Philly Gags was prompt, probably because he was nervous. He had asked DeSalvo for information and was offhandedly dismissed, shrugged off like some piece of garbage. That always made him nervous. DeSalvo was moving up, and Philly seemed to be headed in the other direction.

Two minutes later the fax started beeping, then sheets of paper spewed out. In all, eight of them, and it showed a guy up to his balls in money trouble, wife trouble, and business trouble.

David Drexler was forty-seven, a pushy Jew from the

Bronx who had made it on nerve and lies. He had moved up through three different advertising agencies, taking clients with him whenever he got a better offer. In fact, those better offers came after he had sworn he could get the clients. But there wasn't much integrity in any of the advertising agencies in New York City anyway, so nobody thought he was necessarily a bad guy, just another asshole with some money, a few contacts, and the nerve to pull the trigger when a chance came along. The major difference, Drexler always felt, between him and hundreds of others was that they thought too much about which way to go, what was right, who would they hurt, should they, shouldn't they? Fuck it. Just do it. If it was wrong, you could always fix it later.

Finally, armed with other agencies' accounts, money from his parents' estate, which was considerable, a gift for lying and fixing things, and a long list of the absolutely most gorgeous call girls in New York from which he selected those to use as party favors, Drexler opened his own agency. DD Ads flew right from the start, with such accounts as Hertz, Burger King, Ford, Panasonic, Merrill Lynch, and those less impressive in terms of name recognition but just as lucrative when it came to billing, like automobile parts manufacturers, airline caterers, the people who made the fabric for the clothes but you never saw their name on the labels.

Drexler hired more than fifty staff members, stealing the best account execs from the other top agencies, including his vice president in charge of dirty deeds, Andrew Mosca, one of the world's true creeps and backbiters, from Johnson, Gaskill, Henderson and Ziebart, the second-biggest agency in the world.

Drexler found a gem named Leigh Janice Crespino working as the executive secretary to Harry Olsen, the president of Smith, Slocum and Jensen, where Drexler had started as a junior account executive right out of Syracuse University.

Right now, DD Ads was moving up in the marketplace, moving up fast. But like all these guys, Drexler had a bunch of weaknesses, the kind that people like Billy DeSalvo lived to find out about, then lived off the knowledge. Billy was going to be the salt on an open wound, a whole fucking bag of salt for a long list of gaping wounds that were so easily exposed.

For instance, Drexler kept a penthouse apartment on East 86th Street for a broad named Jennifer Robinoff, a cosmetics model whose face was on almost as many covers as her body was under them. She latched onto Drexler, and he to her, and they fed off each other in a vicious symbiotic relationship. It was his money and prestige and her body and class. It was Drexler at all the major events that New York City could muster and this five-foot, ten-inch former model draped on his arm like the world's most expensive hood ornament. She would drop him in a New York heartbeat—it was inevitable and they both knew that—but as long as the money kept rolling in, his money, because while she earned upward of a million bucks a year that was hers, all hers, she would indulge every one of the little Jew's sexual fantasies.

Drexler's wife, the former Karen Schneider, lived on Long Island with their three children. She had long since abandoned all hope of their marriage working. Resigned to living in empty luxury, she spent all the money she could spend, fucked people like her tennis instructor and her personal fitness trainer and half the semiretired stockbroker millionaires in Sands Point, and took three or four very expensive vacations a year. She and her husband barely spoke. He seldom slept home, preferring the surroundings of the East 86th Street apartment and the erotic embraces of Jennifer Robinoff—Jenny Bird to an adoring public as well as the ultimate wet dream of every straight male under fifty. Make that eighty.

Drexler's high-living finances had begun to put a crimp even in such a cash-flow fortune as he had established. Trips to Las Vegas, Reno, and the Caribbean almost always turned into financial nightmares. The cars, the clothes, the estate on the Island, and the penthouse on the Upper East Side, everything together, wound up putting Drexler in a position of needing slightly more than five million bucks a year, from profits or expenses or his overblown salary and every other way he could find to take it out of the company.

He usually found the way by simply writing checks, leaving it to his comptroller and accountants and lawyers to find a way to explain it or, short of that, cover it up and make it go away. His perception of that money was that it was all his anyway, and let other people explain it or make it right with the government. He always smiled at a slogan on a sticky pad he once had: "I can't be overdrawn; I still have checks left."

But expenditures like that weren't easily covered and did not easily disappear. There were records. Some people knew how to get them. Philly Gags was one of them, especially since the cocksucker was into Drexler for almost half a million bucks.

Gags didn't want to cut Drexler off, because he brought with him lots of other high rollers who didn't know a football from a dildo but managed to fuck themselves pretty good anyway. They all seemed to lose nine out of ten bets. Big bets. But Gags couldn't let the guy skate, so he was really happy when Billy DeSalvo called to broker the debt. Thrilled. Off the hook. He would reduce the nut by half for DeSalvo. It's good luck to do favors for guys on their way up.

Good riddance. Wash the hands and get rid of the prick.

Billy picked up his telephone and placed a call to a man named Eugene Medici, another kid from the streets of Brooklyn who turned up as vice president of advertising at the Skeezixs Candy Company, not as big as some of the other accounts tied to DD Ads but enough to put a hurting on Drexler should he lose it. Skeezixs Candy billed $25 million a year.

Past tense.

"Gino, it's Billy DeSalvo," he said when he had finished being passed off from one secretary to another. "How the hell are you, goombah?"

"Great, Billy. This isn't a social call. I know that. What do you need, ten tons of Milky Way bars? Tell me."

DeSalvo laughed. "Gino, I would like you to find another advertising agency. Today."

"Why?"

"Because the Boss would like you to do him this favor, Gino."

"Done. The kike got himself in deep shit, didn't he?"

"Yeah. The deepest kind, Gino. Hey thanks. Regards to Angela."

End of phone call.

Beginning of the end for David Drexler.

Almost as DeSalvo put the receiver back in the cradle, the phone rang again. He smiled. Damn, it was a rush to have this kind of power. It always got him a hard-on.

"Hello?"

"Who the hell is this?" asked a man trying to keep

strength and authority in his voice and losing the battle every second.

"My name is not important," Billy said. "But what I am about to tell you is very important."

"Fuck you."

"If you hang up, there is nothing in this world that can stop what will happen next," DeSalvo said. "You will stay on the line and listen to me. I am the man who just assumed the debt you have run up with Philip Gagliardi. By my reckoning, you now owe me almost half a million dollars. Let's make it seven hundred thousand, which includes interest and the fact that you intended to fuck my friend Philly Gags and for the inconvenience of me having to spend this time with you on the telephone."

"What?"

"There is no way for you to get out of this debt, and I want the money tomorrow. All of it. In cash. I am aware of the fact that your son, Michael, attends the Adams-Osborne Day School. I know that your two girls, Michele and Amy, attend the Harriet Douglass School. I know your wife, Karen, goes to the tennis club for lessons almost every day and that four mornings a week somebody named Joseph comes to your house to act as her personal trainer. I have photographs of Karen giving each of these men blow jobs.

"Oh, and more bad news, Mr. Drexler. You will receive a call later this afternoon from Gene Medici. You know him, don't you? He will tell you that the Skeezixs Candy Company advertising will no longer be handled by DD Ads. And I am totally confident that with one more telephone call I can convince Revlon that Jenny Bird is no longer their ideal model, now that she has AIDS and all.

"Mr. Drexler, do I have your attention now?"

"Yes. What can I do for you?" There was no bravado in his voice now, no power and no influence, just the whining of a desperate man waiting to be told exactly what to do.

Billy smiled. God, he loved it. "I want to arrange a meeting with Leigh Janice Crespino of your office. I want it to be ... let's see, this is Tuesday? Friday. In New York. At a place I will decide on later. You will tell her it is about a possible advertising account. You can say whatever the hell you want about the kind of advertising. It doesn't matter. I don't care and it isn't important. I just want to talk to her and I want her to meet me, which is probably more important. It may take the entire day. We are to be alone. Is all this perfectly understandable to you?"

"Yes."

"Thank you. Arrange this meeting, you will have bought yourself another week to come up with the money. And at bargain rates. Six hundred thousand. Cash."

"Yes. I understand. I will do everything you asked. But what about the Skeezixs account? Is that still gone?"

Billy almost burst out laughing. "Don't sweat it, Mr. Drexler. Sugar is bad for you anyway."

SIXTEEN

THE funeral was scheduled for Thursday or Friday at St. Matthew's Roman Catholic Church in Oliphant, depending on when Dr. Laskey was able to complete the second autopsy. Sherri had agreed to allow anything Ed and Gerry Keegan advised. She was still staying with Leigh and had decided not to call Billy DeSalvo. She knew he'd be looking for her because she hadn't called yet and making a call now would only open up several questions that she did not want to have to answer. Besides, she was done with him, with all of them. It was time to take another route, time to care about herself just a little. She had met some nice people here. She wanted to be one of them.

She was going to work with the police, tell them what she knew, and if it was discovered that Adam had indeed been murdered—with enough clarity that the police would be able to call it that—then she would agree to become an informant and go into hiding until the case was made and arrests had been completed.

But for now, while Dr. Laskey worked on her husband's corpse, while she took comfort from the newness of having friends like Ed and Gerry and Leigh, there was nothing to do but wait.

And talk. It was Tuesday night they had met at Leigh's apartment for a quick, light dinner. Gerry Kee-

gan had agreed to work on an anonymous basis for
now. Nothing Sherri, or any of them, said would be
written or recorded. Or remembered. So Sherri began
to talk, and she talked for hours, chronicling the beginnings in Buffalo, the move to New York, then to Las
Vegas, finally to Billy DeSalvo and the Hollywood
scene.

She told them everything and with each word grew
more and more convinced that she was killing any
chance of forming real friendships with these three people, but they reacted with sympathy and understanding
for her and contempt for the people who had combined
to turn her life into the hell it had been, and for one of
the rare times in her life she knew what it felt like to
have the genuine support of people who really didn't
want anything from her, only for her. Leigh reached
out and touched Sherri's hand, taking it and gently
squeezing it, smiling at her with what looked almost
like tears in her eyes.

"Sherri, the first major problem we have to deal
with," Gerry Keegan was saying, "is that we have to
prove it was murder. There is just no way we can do
that. The autopsy shows a perfectly normal man,
healthy and fit, who just happens to be dead. The doctor has no idea why Adam is lying there and not getting
ready for next week's game. There is no explanation
for his death, other than that he simply stopped living.

"We know what you've told us. We have no reason
not to believe you. So Adam was involved in some
crooked games. Well, that's more of a National Football League problem than it is ours now. If he was alive
and we found out, we'd have to arrest him. But he's
not, and we only have your word that DeSalvo actually
arranged for Adam to be killed. There is no way on
earth to figure out how he did it. If it was done."

"They did it. I know they did it. DeSalvo arranged it, with the help of this guy Assante and the scary one, McDonald. They told me they did it. I told you all that. There is no question, no doubt. Adam was murdered."

Keegan held up his hand to calm her and quiet her. "Stop. I'm talking like a cop now. I said I believed you. When the little slime said he had your husband killed I believed he did it, and I believe he told you he did it. I knew that little bastard when he was here, a nickel-and-dime crook, and telling you about it and forcing you to do what you told us the day after Adam was killed was just up his alley. He probably got off telling you, too, and I don't think he gets off doing anything else except watching."

Sherri's startled glance and reaction told Keegan he had touched a nerve.

"So all I have to do now is learn how it was done. But until then, we don't have a damned thing. Not a damned thing. And I want to get something on this piece of shit. Anything. I want to make this case airtight and get you off the hook and away from these people once and for all. And get that little bastard on murder one. But frankly, right now I don't know how to proceed."

Leigh, who had been listening quietly, suggested that Dr. Laskey be called again. Gerry Keegan shook his head. "No, he knows where I am. If he finds something, he'll call."

Ed turned to his friend. "Have you been able to turn anything up? Anything at all, Gerry? Did you question the guys who were on the field when Adam was killed? Did you find out about the doctors on the sidelines, the food the team ate that morning? Anything look suspicious? Different?"

Keegan shook his head. "Ed, that's been done, or it's in the process of being done. That and a lot more. You know I'm not going to be able to sit here and tell you step-by-step what's been taking place, how we've been working. Can't do that. I'm not even sure who I can talk to in my precinct anymore. There are so many dirty cops I think they make up the majority now, at least here in New York. Too much money, too many bad guys walking because of too many scumbag lawyers and a legal system that is a hundred years outdated, with more holes and escape hatches than ever before. The good guys are losing ground every day, and I don't see how it's going to get better anytime soon. Cops don't get paid what they need for the risks they take. And more than anybody else in this society, they see how easy it is to make staggering amounts of money. And you know something else? Nobody really gives a shit. Drug dealers, if they do it with class, are like American heroes, for God's sake."

Leigh shook her head violently, angrier than Ed had ever seen her before. "No, that's not true. They're scum. They're killers. They sell that shit to kids and they are killing an entire generation. It's in the rock music and the rap music and that hip-hop shit and it's in the schools and it's in the fact that the middle and upper classes don't want to know. They've got what they wanted and now they don't want to hear about the problems. And when those problems reach out and touch them, they buy their way out of it. Except, of course, for all those well-to-do kids who wind up dead because of drugs. Then the idiot parents blame the cops."

Gerry Keegan looked at her with something approaching reverence. "Well said, lady," he whispered. "Now if you were the police commissioner or the mayor or somebody who could make something happen, we'd all be a hell of a lot better off."

But Leigh wasn't finished. "Gerry, look, when I was in high school, the boy I was dating, maybe someone I could have had a life with, decided to try to be 'cool' and use drugs. He got some bad stuff. He had a violent reaction to it. And he died. Poor, sweet Howard Irving died because of one mistake."

She took a deep breath, lips flecked with spittle, eyes wide, cheeks flushed. "It's important to me, more than just important. It's critical. The stuff's pervasive. It's all over. Look at those commercials, the ones that preach, 'Just say no'? That's bullshit. The ones the kids are listening to are the Nike things, the ones that say, 'Just do it.' And they do. They put shit in their noses and they shoot it into their veins and they kill themselves with dirty needles and they think it's cool. There are gangs of kids on the streets in this city, and in lots of other cities, that 'initiate' their girls by making them shoot heroin into their bodies or have sex with guys who already have AIDS. To prove that they want to belong, you see? Belong? They're proving they want to die, and for being that fucking stupid they deserve to."

Suddenly, as if touched with a hot electric wire, Leigh realized that Sherri was silently sobbing. "I'm sorry; I'm sorry; I didn't mean that. It wasn't about you, Sherri."

"No, you're right. It was stupid and I was stupid and I liked it too much to stop. I didn't have anything except my body, and that helped me get where I thought I wanted to be. Trouble is, once I got there I couldn't think of anything except getting out. But I can't. And now I wound up killing Adam, or getting him killed, because I couldn't say no to the same kind of people you are talking about, Leigh. Except you have no idea just how vicious Billy DeSalvo can be, and he isn't even in charge of much. He works for men who would just as soon kill someone as say good morning to them."

Keegan said, "We know the chain. We know which animal is higher than the last. We know it moves all the way up to Anthony Assante, and there has never been a thing we've learned that could directly tie him to anything. But we know it's him. He knows that we know, and he knows we can't do anything about it. He laughs at us, and it drives me crazy. If this can lead to him, if we can tie him to this thing, then whatever we do to get there is worth the ride, don't you see? If we can stop him, we stop hundreds of people underneath him, at least for a while. If we can cut off the head, it will take a while until the snake can grow another one."

Sherri nodded. "I'll tell you everything I know," she said, "and I know a hell of a lot more than they think I do."

SEVENTEEN

WEDNESDAY morning, midweek except for the fact that it was Leigh's first day at work since the previous Friday. She planned to finish the week and then drive with Ed to Oliphant for Adam Benson's funeral Saturday morning.

There was a note taped to her computer screen: "See me when you get in. DD."

From the boss. Maybe it was good news. Maybe they had just landed that Donna Karan account. Maybe even the PSI Network billing. Or maybe he just wanted to say he was sorry, knowing that Adam Benson was Ed's best friend.

So she carried her coffee mug with her to David's door, knocked once, and entered.

He was seated behind his desk, one of those ornate old mahogany monsters his wife had found years ago in an antique shop in Cos Cob and had repaired, restained, recoated, and shipped down to his office. He thought he hated it until one day, quite accidentally, he discovered three secret compartments opened only by pressing a hidden button underneath the desktop, inside the top drawer. For a man like David Drexler, something like that, under lock and key, was an invaluable security blanket.

"Leigh," he said, getting to his feet and stepping

around the desk. "I'm sorry about what happened. I know what a difficult time it must be for Ed, and naturally for you. Is there anything I can do?"

"No, David, but thank you for asking. Yes, it was a shock, a terrible thing that will take him a long time to get over. But thank you for your concern. Is there anything else? I'm two days behind, and with the funeral this weekend I hope I can be back on Monday and try to get into the normal routine again."

Drexler sat back behind his desk. "Yes, an assignment. We are trying to get a major account managed out of Southern California by a company called Interim Basis. It controls a large portion of tourism advertising in California, Washington, Oregon, Alaska, and Hawaii. We're looking at upwards of $30 million in initial annual billing. The guy is coming in to meet with Barnes, Ralph, and Barry on Thursday and then with us Friday. I want to you to handle the negotiations. You'll meet a man named Edward Small. I'll have more details for you tomorrow. It's very important, Leigh. A major responsibility, and it will mean a huge bonus if we get the account."

Leigh was at first flattered and surprised—flattered that David would hand her such a plum, surprised that she had not known of any preliminary contact or ongoing, if premature, negotiations. But he had always been straight with her, so there was no reason to suspect that he had wanted to give it to someone else first, as well as no reason to be annoyed that he hadn't seen fit to fill her, his chief assistant, in on the project from the start. In addition to being terminally unpredictable, David was often secretive. He didn't trust anybody in the advertising or communications world, and there was probably great validity in subscribing to such a theory.

"Well, thank you, thank you very much," she managed, unusually flustered. "I'm excited about this. If you can fill me in on some of the details, I'll prepare the next few nights at home. There are so many things cooking here . . . I don't suppose you want me to hand off anything to Robert or to Kimberly, do you?"

Drexler smiled. "If it's important stuff, why would you want either of those two to handle it? They're fine as assistants, but I don't think they'll ever be really qualified to manage their own major billing accounts, do you?"

"No, I guess not. Anyway, get me something to study, and maybe I can talk to this guy Small before he flies in. All right?"

"No. He doesn't want telephone contact. He's a little eccentric, I suppose. He wants to walk in and find prepared proposals. He has culled about six agencies from his short list, leaving just the two of us. And we kind of have to guess at what he wants to see."

Leigh bridled. "David, that's insane. How can I prepare a major advertising proposal when I don't know what the client wants, what the client is looking to spend, where the client wants the message aimed, or any of about another hundred or so things? Are you sure this Interim group isn't just jerking you off?"

Drexler smiled. "Leigh, please. Who jerks me off is my business."

She smiled, a bit tightly. "OK, then. I have two days, you're telling me. Not even. To come up with a major proposal for a major advertiser and I don't even know what he wants. Any chance we can postpone the meeting?"

"None."

"David, this is crazy."

"I know, Leigh. But we meet all kinds. Who knows?

He might just want to see how you work under pressure. How we work, I should say. Let's meet later and I'll throw a few ideas at you and we'll brainstorm for a while. Tell Ed you're going to be late tonight."

Bad timing, Eddie, but I have to do this.

"All right. I'll talk with you later today. I'm going to try to clear everything off my desk in record time."

She left the office and Drexler leaned back in the rich leather chair, put his feet up on the desk, and looked out the glass wall/window. *What the fuck am I going to tell her?* he wondered. *I don't know what this guy DeSalvo wants, but it ain't advertising and I don't think it's pussy. All I know is I made a hundred grand by arranging this meeting between them. Great. Now all I have to do is find 600 more big ones for this Mafia guinea prick who sounds like he'd just as soon kill me as take my money. Maybe both. Shit. Shit. Shit.*

EIGHTEEN

GERRY Keegan figured that Sherri Novak Benson would be better off in a safe house somewhere, managed by the New York Police, not in Leigh Crespino's apartment on the Upper West Side. She hadn't made contact with DeSalvo in three days, and it was too late for her to suddenly call now. It was done. He had to be beyond suspicious by now, had to be wondering where she was and whom she was with, who was talking to her. And what she was saying.

Keegan made the arrangements, and he hadn't been just scaring the general public when he told Ed, Leigh, and Sherri that the crooked cops outnumbered the honest ones these days. He got in touch with Homicide Detective Mike Herbert, a gold shield who had been on the force longer than anyone and still drove a ten-year-old Ford. "Mike, I need a safe place," Keegan said when he called Herbert at his home in Queens. It was near midnight, but he decided he would rather wake him than risk the usual office listeners' snooping on this kind of call.

Herbert didn't have to guess at the voice. He viewed Keegan as one of the few untouched and uncorrupted members of the force. "Where and who?" was all he said.

"I don't care where. For the widow of the football player."

"Drugs?"

"Right again, Mike. I think we can get a line on DeSalvo and through him we can hook that Assante asshole, maybe for good."

A deep intake of breath, followed by the calm, methodical planning of a veteran policeman.

"We are not supposed to have this place, and nobody knows we do, and if anybody asks we don't know a fucking thing about it, Gerry. It's in an apartment building right across the fucking street from Gracie Mansion that only a few of us know about. Nobody from city hall even has a clue. The damned police commissioner doesn't know about it, either. All told, I think maybe twenty guys are aware of it. You want to use that?"

"Yes. I'm going to have to tell two other people where she is, though. Is that all right?"

"You trust them?"

"You know I do."

"Then it's OK. It's the Venture Arms, sixteenth floor, Apartment 323. You'll find the keys in your top left-hand drawer tomorrow morning. It's stocked. The telephone is on and it can't be tapped. No bugs. We sweep it once a week. Use it as long as you need. There's recording equipment built right into the entertainment center in the living room. The button to start recording is on the floor at the edge of carpet in front of the fireplace. Just walk to it and step hard. You'll feel it. And it won't make a sound when it clicks on. It's self-loading, self-rewinding, and you can't record over it. You can't erase anything, in other words."

"Thanks, Mike. Owe you one."

"Just get that fucker and we're even," Herbert said,

and then he placed the receiver back on its cradle, picked it up again, and arranged for the keys to find their way into Keegan's desk before morning.

And then Herbert made one more call—to Anthony Assante in the posh suburb of Bedford Hills, in West-chester County.

NINETEEN

PAUL Boland got a phone call from Detective Joseph Gerard Keegan asking for an appointment later that day, two days before the funeral would be held for Adam Benson.

Of course, Boland complied.

Three hours later he was answering questions about the previous Sunday, what had happened that was different, who was hanging around the locker room who didn't usually make an appearance, something that was said or overheard. Anything.

Paul couldn't really be of much help. He generally had no idea what went on during the hours before a game, except for the numbers of friends and/or business associates he was drinking with in the upstairs and very private Stadium Club. His brother, Peter, would not have been any more help, even if he had been available and had not taken the company jet to the Bahamas for the week, from where he would fly to Dallas in time for the Giants' next game and the Boland brothers' next staggering party.

Keegan quickly realized he was talking with an empty suit of Hall of Fame proportions, so he politely exited from the conversation by offering his thanks for the cooperation and for permission to speak with Duane Charles, the Giants' head coach.

To Paul Boland's mind, he couldn't have cared less if the detective spoke with Charles or had him electrocuted. Boland didn't like the coach very much. It was probably a combination of two things: he had to pay him too much money and he resented that deeply, and he didn't understand Charles's speech, had always harbored a deep distrust of the southern drawl, and was disappointed that Charles treated him much the same as everyone else did—that is to say, with no respect and an all too obvious superior attitude, which Paul Boland interpreted as "he's the boss and he owns the team so we might as well be nice to him, but he's a fucking moron and who gives a shit about him anyway?"

He reached over and pushed the intercom button. His secretary, a good-looking unmarried woman in her late thirties, answered immediately. "Yes, Mr. Boland."

"Jacqui, call Coach Charles downstairs. Tell him Detective Keegan needs some time. Now. And tell him to drop everything else."

Jacqueline Appleton, who enjoyed the relatively easy job she had taking care of these two idiot brothers, would have gladly fucked either or both of them had they asked, which they never had. She thought Peter Boland was gay, and while nobody had ever seen him in such a situation, women sometimes sensed that better than men. She hung up, depressed the intercom button, and pressed another, punching in the numbers that caused the phone to ring on Coach Charles's desk.

"Hey, Duane, it's Jacqui," she said.

"Hey, baby, what's it like upstairs?"

Jacqueline Appleton had fucked Coach Charles, many times. Lately, in fact, on a weekly schedule. She liked him and thought his gifts were cute, mostly coming in the form of checks. And unlike many other men she had known, his checks never bounced.

"A detective is coming downstairs to talk with you," she said. "Pretty Paul said to tell you it's important, you have to do it, and no arguments. The guy's name is Keegan. I guess it has something to do with the terrible thing that happened last Sunday."

"Shit. Damn. Fuckin' waste of time. All right. Tell him to come down. Tell him I'll meet him at the basement elevator. Damned stupid mule-fucking New York City detective might get himself lost between there and the damned locker room. I knew a cop whose hand used to get lost between thinking about jerking off and reaching for his pecker."

Jacqueline smiled. She also loved the down-home kind of cussing Duane did, creating almost another language of the profane. She was waiting for the right Thursday night to tell him how it turned her on.

Keegan emerged from Pretty Paul Boland's office. "Follow me, Detective Keegan," Jacqui said, swaying just enough to let him examine the terrain as she led him to the interstadium elevator. "Coach is waiting for you. He'll show you into his locker-room office."

She flashed him a bright smile and swayed her way back to the executive offices, knowing that he was watching her.

He was. *Silly-looking broad,* Gerry Keegan thought. *Kind of a fat ass, too.*

When the elevator doors slid open in the basement, there stood head coach Duane Charles, once an All-American middle linebacker at the University of Nebraska who broke the University of Alabama's heart by leaving his home state. He then embarked on an All-Pro career at the same position for the Atlanta Falcons. Generally considered to be a horse's ass with a wide mean streak, he didn't make many friends during his career, but he was recognized for having a down-home football-smarts intelligence that boded well for a career in coaching just as long as he didn't ask for too much money.

And he didn't. Charles thought money wasn't nearly as important as winning, and as long as he had enough to pay the bills, afford the nice house in Connecticut and the one he called home on the panhandle of Alabama—the Redneck Riviera he loved so much—he was not going to worry about which new young coach had signed a contract for how many millions of dollars.

Charles had made $400,000 for the last six years, never thought about asking for more, and felt strongly that football players made a hell of a lot more money than they should. He was violently against contracts that ran more than one year in duration. "Kid gets three years not to worry about his money, he sure as hell won't worry about football, neither," he moaned. "Pay 'em all the same and pay 'em all for one year. Then fire the ones who didn't play well and double the salaries of the ones who did."

The old school, of course, would not be listened to in these days of megadollars and the television networks running the league. But it was what Duane Charles was all about, and he had no problem telling people exactly how he felt, whether the people were his players, other coaches, the press, the electronic interviewers, or the various women he enjoyed.

Coach Charles shook hands with Gerry Keegan and led him into his office, which was a neat but not overly large room cut off the main locker room. The door closed, which was good, but it couldn't possibly shut out Duane's deep booming voice when he had to explain things to a player who had played badly or not taken well to on-the-field criticism.

But now voices were modulated and the door was

closed and those players straggling in early for afternoon practice had no way to know if the coach was in
or not, which led more than a few of them to flip the
finger at the closed door.

"Coach, I'm investigating the death of Adam Benson," Keegan began. "It happened right here on the
field and it happened in a pileup involving players on
your team, and that's about the only reason I have for
being here today at all. This is mostly background, I
guess. Was there anything unusual that day? Did any
of the players or your assistant coaches say anything
or see anything different? Do you remember anything
out of the ordinary?"

Charles thought. "No, sir. Can't say that anything
sits up and bites me about Sunday. Just the usual nerves
and guys pukin' in the john and punchin' lockers and
so forth. The game? I thought the game was well
played, close. That Adam Benson, my God, when he
had it workin' there just wasn't anybody better. Never.
Nobody, not even Joe Willie Namath, who beat us in
the Orange Bowl. But unusual? Nothin' really. We let
them move pretty well down the field, which is not
something teams usually do against us. And he fooled
us a couple of times really good, especially on that
touchdown. Nobody knew he was going to keep it, not
even his own guys. That's what makes it work. When
nobody knows it's coming."

Keegan had heard that several times. But it was better to just let Charles keep talking. Most people, Keegan
had found, don't know when they're saying something
that might be important to an experienced interrogator,
and whether it was gentle or harsh, when a detective
talks to a civilian about a crime it isn't an interview;
it's an interrogation.

"So that play, nothing unusual? Except, of course,

that Benson didn't do what you expected."

"Nope. We had a three-fill defense. That's a coverage that concentrates on the run but allows some of our faster guys to be there just in case the quarterback decides to throw. The three-fill is, well, a defense we use a lot."

"Same people?"

The coach looked up, just for a second, but it was a reaction that could be read. Not many civilians knew that certain defenses used different players, that the same eleven starters don't play all the time, the way most fans think. "Yeah, I think so. No, wait. Robbie Banks twisted an ankle in warm-ups. He didn't play. We used Parks, the kid from Florida State, pretty good draft choice for the third round. Kid likes to hit. Mean bastard. But he wasn't in on that play. No, sir. That would have been . . . let's see; Benson ran right, then cut back, so he finally wound up being hit by the left end. That would be Marshall. The left tackle, Johnson. The left outside linebacker, Simpson. The left corner-back, St. John. And the free safety, Harrison. No. Not Harrison. That dumb bastard missed the assignment. He was back on the right side of the end zone playing with his dick. So those were the guys. Marshall, Johnson, Simpson, St. John. Those four. You want them in here?"

"No, coach. That won't be necessary. Nobody was hurt on that play? Nobody on the Giants?"

"No, sir. I don't think so. I'll check with Sid Marr. He's the trainer. He'd know for sure. But nothing was serious, or I'd know that."

Marshall. Johnson. Simpson. St. John. They were the four Giants closest to the scene of the murder, however unlikely that word seemed when applied to the death of Adam Benson. Larry Marshall, Melvin Johnson,

Jackie Simpson, Eldon St. John. Buck would help him build preliminary profiles on these four, background information, anything that might lead to a suspicion, a doubt, a connection to anything that had to do with Billy DeSalvo, Anthony Assante, or the organization that hid and protected them.

Marshall, Johnson, Simpson, St. John. Could one of them be not only a professional football player but also a murderer?

Keegan drove back to his precinct office, sat at the desk, and dialed the number he had previously obtained for the Bears office. He dialed, asked the switchboard operator for Rick O'Donnell, the public relations director, and when he answered introduced himself.

"Yes, sir," said O'Donnell. "How can I help?"

"I would like to know if anybody can provide me with the names of the players who were closest to Benson on that play," Keegan responded. "We have the videotape shot. We have played it back and forth, over and over, but some of the players are hidden. There's an arm we can't identify. Somebody's ass. You know."

"Right. I have that. The coaches broke it down as soon as they got back Sunday night. God, I don't know how they're going to manage this next game or two. The players are in shock. One of the team doctors called in a psychiatrist to treat them for the posttrauma disorientation. The coaches are just wandering back and forth. Nobody wants to go near Adam's locker. What a nightmare."

"Yeah," said Keegan.

"Oh, OK. Hold on. I'll get the list." Keegan could hear the receiver being put down on the desk, not on hold. He heard a muffled voice. "Anita, where's that damned list of players who were on the ground with Benson?" then heard O'Donnell pick up the phone again.

"Detective Keegan? The players closest to Adam when he ran that play were the right tackle, Bill Jillian, the tight end, Mark Tucker, the wide receiver, Thomas McNeely, and the fullback, Harlan Ellsworth. But none of them were absolutely next to him, you know? It was a surprise. He didn't tell anybody he was keeping the ball. So he ran into the end zone kind of on his own. That's why they call it a naked reverse."

"Yeah, or a bootleg," Keegan said, remembering a little bit more from his college football days and his long conversations with Ed Buck each day he spent tracking down this mystery. "I understand just enough to know what you're saying. But what about when your players realized he had scored? Didn't somebody jump on him? That always seems to happen."

"Yeah. Tucker did. The fullback, Harlan Ellsworth, he did, too. And the center, Michael Lee Reasons. Then everybody else joined the pile. It was an electric sort of moment."

Yeah, right. What crap. All public relations people must be cut from the same flawed cloth.

Great. Mark Tucker. Bill Jillian. Thomas McNeely. Harlan Ellsworth. Michael Lee Reasons. Five more to add to the list of those players who were near or underneath or on top of Adam Benson when he drew his last breath.

Keegan needed to talk to George Laskey, so he picked up the phone and dialed the interoffice system exchange that put him in touch with the medical examiner's office. He asked for Laskey, heard the connection being made, and then heard his friend's voice.

"Keegan here, George," he said. "What's up? Anything?"

There was a lift, a lilt, to Laskey's voice. "You must have ESP, Gerry. I just finished dictating a report to you. We got it. We found what killed Adam Benson, and I'll be double damned if it isn't the smartest piece of murder I've seen in years."

"Tell me."

"Well, if you just stay with me," Laskey said, "I'll try to explain it in layman's terms."

"Damn it, George. I've been doing this for twenty-something fucking years. I have heard enough medical examiners give me their findings. I am not a fucking idiot. Now tell me what happened."

"Somebody poked a long, very thin needlelike object into Adam Benson's heart," he said. "Like an old-fashioned hat pin, maybe six inches long, but thinner. It was a direct hit, but if administered properly, or just through blind luck, that's all the heart needs to have a momentary seizure. It's exactly like a muscle cramp, like when you wake up at night with your calf muscle all knotted and it hurts like hell. Except this produces a heart attack with no signs, no warning, no symptoms, no traceable evidence unless you really look hard for a puncture mark. We found it. That's how he died, and it most definitely was murder. Intentional, clever, and absolutely premeditated. And the guy was lucky, too, because he could have hit a rib with the thing and nothing would have happened. Or he could have missed the heart and just given Benson a bruise. But it went in exactly the right place and at the right angle. He was either very lucky or well coached."

Keegan paused, carefully measuring what he knew and what he had to do.

"Don't say a word," he finally told the doctor. "Fill out the report. File it. But take your time. And don't get yourself in any trouble. And keep quiet about it. Don't say anything. Can you tell me anything else about the murder weapon, George? Anything at all?"

"Not really. Just a long, very thin instrument. Easily hidden, just as easily disposed of. I mean, whoever did it could have simply pushed it into the ground. Maybe a hundred pairs of feet have stomped over it since then, with shoes, cleats, boots, whatever. That's if it's there, Gerry."

"Yeah. The guy could have stuck it in, made sure it worked, then pulled it back and hid it in his uniform. If he did that, it's long gone by now. And forever."

Dr. Laskey interrupted the conversation, which was really Gerry Keegan talking to himself out loud. "Gerry, I've got to go. I have to fill out this report. I've got to put the guy back together again. I've got to tell the funeral parlor the body is ready to be claimed. I'll talk to you tomorrow."

"OK, George. Thanks. I'll be in touch."

Keegan put the telephone down and stared at the wall in the precinct house. He didn't really see anything. He was just staring.

One of the players on the field last Sunday was a murderer. One of the players killed Adam Benson. But who? And why? And exactly how?

TWENTY

THE call Billy DeSalvo didn't want to get, not now and not ever, came that night. DeSalvo was home in his Bel Air mansion. The bodyguards were there, of course, positioned intelligently and unobtrusively, but they didn't count. They weren't supposed to be seen, and certainly they weren't supposed to bother Mr. DeSalvo. To his mind, they were just vicious two-legged Dobermans used to patrol the grounds and the house and trained to kill on command. Nothing more.

Rico Scalzi was there, too. Naturally. The big man didn't live with DeSalvo, but he spent enough time there so that he might as well get his mail delivered to the Harlene Hill Road address. He was there that night, near midnight, to go over with DeSalvo the impending trip to New York and the meeting with the broad from the advertising agency who was close to the sports-writer, Benson's closest friend.

The agency guy was clever. He told the girl, Leigh Crespino, that she was going to meet a businessman from the West Coast who had control over more than 30 million bucks in advertising for tourism to the Coast and Hawaii.

Good. Fine. Who the fuck cared? She agreed to meet with him Friday, and that's when she'd know who he really was and what this really was all about. She'd find out just how important it was for her boyfriend to back off, to drop the questions, and to get the detective, Keegan, to do the same.

Billy had told Scalzi to stay in Los Angeles. There were things to do, things to oversee. Rico was becoming increasingly more crucial to the daily operation of DeSalvo's little empire, one that existed with the blessing of Anthony Assante, and only because of that.

And the telephone call was from Assante.

"Boss, it's him, Mr. Assante," said Rico, and DeSalvo wasn't comfortable with how long and how apparently friendly the preliminary conversation between Assante and Rico had been.

"Yes sir, Mr. Assante," DeSalvo said. "How can I help you?"

The voice, disembodied as it was, three thousand miles away, still carried with it a threatening, ominous tone all the more frightening because it was never raised.

"You are coming home this week, Billy?"

"Yes, sir. I am flying in Thursday night. I am going to meet with a woman who lives with the sportswriter. He is the one who was friendly with Adam Benson and he is the one who called in the detective. We don't know yet if they know how Benson died—"

"They do," Assante interrupted. "They know exactly how it was done. Billy, it wasn't that clever. It was too easy to discern."

Beads of perspiration began to line up in little rows of buttons up and down the back of Billy DeSalvo's neck.

"The fix in the National Football League was brilliant, Billy, and I gave you much credit for arranging it. Bringing in the Novak girl, getting her to marry Benson, addicting her, and thereby putting a hook up his ass, that was all brilliant, Billy."

"Thank you, sir," DeSalvo said, although at the same time wondering where the conversation was going.

"But, Billy, Benson decided to back out of his deal. I understand that. So he had to be killed. I understand that, too. A man should live or die by his word."

"Yes, sir."

"The detective, Keegan, is not going to change his mind and go looking for something else to keep him busy, Billy. The sportswriter is too close. His girlfriend knows too much. You have created a dangerous situation for me, Billy. I hope you can find a way out of it quickly and cleanly. I cannot have things like this going on in my business."

"I understand that, Mr. Assante," Billy murmured, and now the droplets of perspiration had turned into rivulets down his back. "I am going to take care of it all. I promise that to you. I guarantee it, Mr. Assante. No one will ever know what really happened."

A silence.

"Billy, that is not entirely correct. In truth, you are never going to know how this comes out. Do you understand?"

Billy DeSalvo began to formulate an answer, which was really a question, but the words never got out. They were blocked, as was his oxygen supply, by the tightly wound silk scarf wrapped around his neck, held there by Rico Scalzi's powerful, hammerlike hands. Oddly, the most interesting part of dying an agonizing, asphyxiating death was watching the veins pop in Rico's massive forearms as he tightened his grip and pulled the scarf ever tighter. Billy was fighting for breath now, struggling for air. There was a buzzing in his ears growing louder, the room was spinning, and then it went all black, and all he had left to see was Rico's forearms and one of the corners of the Fendi scarf.

Billy still didn't believe he was going to die. Hey, he had been in worse spots before. Surely Rico would relent. They were friends. It was a joke. Mr. Assante would change his mind. Mr. Assante had told Rico to almost kill him, just to show how angry he was at the way Billy had fucked this thing up.

But die? No, not him. There was too much left on his plate.

Then, suddenly, one last light. It turned from bright to opaque and then quickly to a swirling black fog. A final, frantic gasp for air died hopelessly in his throat. And then he died, and the last flash of awareness he had was one of great surprise.

Billy DeSalvo was no longer a player in the world of Anthony Assante.

Rico, hardly exerted, stepped over the body, mildly offended by the stench of feces that had been released when all muscle control left DeSalvo, and he picked up the telephone.

Assante was waiting.

"It is done," Rico said.

"Good, come home," said Assante.

Rico smiled. He had never liked Los Angeles.

The next call he placed was to a number he had been given just two days ago. He did not know who would answer, and it really didn't matter.

"I am calling for a friend from New York," he said. "There is a house here in Bel Air that needs cleaning."

"We'll be right there," said a woman on the other end. "Leave the front door unlocked but not open. Go now. Touch nothing. Have a pleasant trip."

Once again Rico smiled. Assante had everything covat their groin? What was there about men, and about women, that made this all so ridiculously easy?

Love? She never loved anyone. She was without emotion, except for that most basic sensation of exquisitely good sex, those rare times when a man found her secret spot and actually enabled her to feel.

Like Adam Benson had done.

And the men she knew never understood what that secret was. It had nothing to do with sex or physical appearance. She had enjoyed sex more with men who had small penises than with those whose organs were so gigantic it was a struggle just to get them to fit someplace.

One night she was involved in a party in a penthouse suite at the MGM Grand, one of the top-floor extravaganzas that cost $2,500 a night and came complete with, well, with everything.

Including women.

Or men, if the occupants so desired.

Or boys and girls.

This group was the party of a successful, and therefore wealthy, Hollywood movie producer, celebrating the premiere of his latest box office smash, a stereotypical collection of shootings, explosions, sex, drugs, lots of near-naked women, and the all-around all-American violence that played successfully before 80 percent of the public.

He brought his girlfriend, Harmony Hunter, a starlet hoping to fuck her way even higher; the supporting actor Bobby Moska, whose legendary sexual exploits almost always involved men; the studio's publicity head, Judy Brett, an ordinary-looking shrew with an acid tongue and a liking for beautiful women, which she had in common with her boss; and a sloppy little gambler, a converted New Yorker who had helped the uality and her resignation to his orders. "Best piece of ass I've ever seen," he cackled most of the night, running a tongue around her nipple or slipping a finger into her vagina to watch her squirm, shift her weight from one foot to the other while she smiled, to make him think she was enjoying herself. "If you want to come to California, you look me up," he said when the night was finally finished. "I can set you up with some guys and a job and you'll do all right. With that body and that mouth, you can own the fucking world."

He liked that. He laughed. So did the rest of the morons, because he did. And Sherri smiled through her hatred, because this fat piece of shit was, indeed, going to be her ticket to moving up.

From there she went to Vegas, tried going legit for a while, working as a waitress in one of the casino coffee shops, but soon discovered that six bucks an hour and tips couldn't even bring her what one night in bed with a high roller pulled in, and not a penny of that was anybody's business.

So she began hooking, and it was easy. She was a knockout, and the more money she made the more she had for the right clothing, the right grooming. The people with whom she had sex were nameless, faceless men and women who represented nothing more than an income, a way to make a living that escaped 99 percent of the rest of the world, mostly because she had the looks that no one else had, sometimes because she didn't have the conscience others possessed. And that was something she simply couldn't understand. Why was sex so important to men? Why were her breasts enough to drive guys crazy? Why were they all so absolutely crazed by the thought of making love to her? What was it that made them drool when she slowly licked her lips while looking directly in their eyes, or

ered. By morning the house would be empty and the
two bodyguards would have been sent elsewhere.
Nothing was ever left to chance. Billy DeSalvo would
simply have disappeared, and the house, which had
been purchased by a man named Arthur McDonald,
who did not exist, would be sold through a real estate
company owned by Assante.

The money from the sale would be deposited in a
bank in the Cayman Islands, in the name of Maria
Scalzi, Rico's mother. Even as a bargain, priced to
move cheaply for the sake of a quick sale, it would net
slightly more than $2.5 million, which was more than
a fair price to be paid for three minutes' work, to rid
the world of another animal dirtying the name of Anthony Assante.

Rico made his exit, returned to his beachfront home
in Malibu, and threw his few personal items into a
small duffel bag. He was going to miss the place, with
its privacy and the nymphomaniac woman next door
whose husband was never there, but New York was
better. It was home. And maybe, if it looked like he'd
be staying long enough, he'd bring his mother back, at
least for the spring and summer months when it wasn't
so cold.

Rico climbed back into the new Buick Park Avenue
black four-door, exactly the same kind of car that had
been left for him each year since he had been told to
move to Los Angeles three years ago. He would leave
it at the airport, and it would disappear, just like Billy
DeSalvo. If Rico couldn't get a red-eye flight to New
York or Newark, he'd sleep at the airport Marriott and
get the first one out in the morning. He was going to
be needed to brief the man who would be keeping
DeSalvo's appointment with Leigh Crespino.

TWENTY
ONE

THE four of them sat in Ed's living room. Adam's father had made the lonely trip back to Oliphant to handle funeral arrangements for Saturday. Ed and Leigh and Sherri, who wanted to go to Oliphant but was convinced to stay and help, listened as Gerry Keegan outlined the cause of death and the probable method of its infliction.

"I don't understand," Ed said. "A long needlelike thing just slipping into the heart and he's dead? The heart is a muscle. I can stab my bicep with a needle and it won't stop working. I can puncture my pecs, damned near put a needle into any muscle, and not have it stop. I don't understand."

Gerry nodded. "Right, except for the fact that the heart is more or less electronically regulated. It needs to keep its beat, its rhythm. That's why hearts can be started again with electrical impulses. Inserting the needle, even twisting it around some, caused the heart muscle to contract. When it contracted, it stopped. But it would have been simple to get it going again—if Adam had been in a hospital or even near any kind of paramedic treatment. But he wasn't. So it contracted, stopped for a second, and . . . well, it stayed that way. Stopped.

"According to George Laskey, he suffered a heart

attack, but it was more like a trauma to the heart. There have been fighters killed by a direct, powerful punch to the heart area. It stops that muscle for a second, and when nothing comes along to revive it the heart stops pumping. That stops the blood flow and that's it. Dead."

Leigh shook her head. "So what you're saying is that one of the players involved in that particular play, in that pileup, was carrying a needlelike instrument, that he had the chance to use it and so he did, under orders from somebody. Wouldn't all that gear players use have prevented it from getting through? Shoulder pads, something?"

"No, only if he had been wearing something for bruised or cracked ribs, and then a kind of corset would have been in place. But Adam wasn't hurt. He wore his shoulder pads, and they come down only to a point just below the front of the shoulders, like halfway down to the sternum. And the pads are longer on each side than in the middle of the chest. The guy didn't even have to be very educated in the human body. He would have needed one lesson, someone to show him just once approximately where to jab it in, and the length of it would have taken care of the rest. Laskey said it could even have been more sophisticated, somewhat thicker around on the handle to contain a small chip that emitted a charge of electricity when the tip met some resistance. A small electrical charge, he said, would have made sure the heart would stop."

"Well, so now we know how," Ed said. "But we don't know why and we don't know who. I suppose we know why, come to think of it. Bad break for the bad guys, sure, but then he said he would blow the whistle. And I guess even if he never said it, they would have had to do this just in case he ever decided it would be a good idea. So we need to know who did it. Do you have any idea, Gerry?"

Keegan shook his head. "Nope, but we're working on it. Sherri, I got you into a safe place. I'd like to move you in tonight. It's a great apartment, right across from Gracie Mansion, the mayor's official residence. There are more cops around there than at a rally for Louis Farrakhan. We know Billy DeSalvo engineered this thing, but we don't know who directed him. I know him. He isn't smart enough to get this NFL-fixing thing into operation. He's a soldier. He gets told what to do and then he does it. I have my suspicions, but I doubt that I'll ever be able to make anything stick."

She nodded and got up from her seat. "I have to go to the bathroom for a minute," she said. "Be right back."

Keegan shook his head. "Sherri. Don't go. I know why you're going and what you're going to do. Let us help you beat it. You can, you know. Let me see what's in your purse."

She barely resisted but handed him the small purse and watched as he pulled from it a cellophane packet of white powder. Cocaine. Watched as he opened it, emptied it into the ashtray, and poured some of his drink on it. She nodded. "I'll go where you say, Gerry, and I'll do whatever you say. I want to be off this. I want to get the people who killed Adam. I don't want to live the kind of life I've been living." Her eyes watered over, and she sat down again, putting her face in her hands.

"I don't know if I told you everything I know, but I keep thinking of new things," she said, after drawing a few deep breaths. "Billy had a lieutenant. Rico. Rico Scalzi. Big, mean, does anything he says. Mostly his dirty work. And you're right. Billy didn't put this football deal together, but he was in charge of it. I don't know who was his boss. I only met one other guy, some older man everyone was afraid of. And I met him just once, with Billy, in some office building in downtown Los Angeles."

Keegan's eyebrows raised ever so slightly. "You remember his name?"

"Yes. McDonald. Arthur McDonald. Maybe seventy, seventy-five. Could have been even older. Silvergray hair. Good shape. Not too tall, but he looked taller. And lean. He slapped me when I said something he didn't like. Just reached over the desk and slapped me in the face. Hard. I could feel his power. And Billy never moved a muscle. I know he was scared to death of him. It was this guy, McDonald, who laid it all out for Billy. Told him to use me to get to Adam, told him to keep me supplied with coke, told him to cut me off if I didn't cooperate.

"Gerry, he promised me a movie role. It was all set. And you know what? I'm a good actress. I really can do this work. But it's like, well, you don't get a chance unless you know somebody. Once you have the work, it's easy to get more. I'm not stupid, not some dumb blonde, but I didn't have anything when I got out there and I had to do all the demeaning, garbage things to get closer to some of the important people. This guy McDonald, he was as important as I ever met, and I think maybe one of the most important men in Hollywood."

Keegan nodded. "Or New York," he said softly. "The man I think you met was Anthony Assante, who almost never goes anywhere. This must have been very important to him, or somebody out there was."

Keegan was right. And Keegan was wrong.

TWENTY
TWO

THERE were probably no more than half a dozen people in the world who knew the man called McDonald, and they lived with this burden uncomfortably. Several others had met strange and mysterious ends, and although McDonald was clearly the reason and none of the people with whom he did business found it mysterious at all, not once was he ever even suspected.

One time, just disappoint him one time, and there was no second chance. He was reluctant to the point of intractable to add anyone to the list of those who knew who he was and those to whom he might extend a small bit of friendship. Once someone was accepted, McDonald expected total and complete loyalty, unswerving, unquestioned. There was no other choice, not family and not friendship, not business, and not even religion. McDonald was the most important person in their lives, their most crucial consideration, and the fount of incredible sources of nontaxable income in the lives of those few who knew him; he was almost as critical in the lives of hundreds of thousands who did not and never would know him.

Arthur McDonald was eighty-three years old, officially. Actually, he was almost eighty-six, except only he knew that and there was no one left who could provide similar information. Those with whom he did business did not know his real name, although they thought they did.

They thought he was Salvatore Posilipo.

He wasn't. Salvatore Posilipo was the first man McDonald had murdered, on a battlefield in Europe in 1944. It was a necessary action. He needed a new identity.

It was the perfect time. The confusion was chaotic. The visibility was almost zero because of smoke and flames and black, sucking fire. The guttural bark of machine guns and the sharp cracking sound of rifles and the almost incessant rocking of exploding hand grenades and the sickly yellow-green fumes produced by the bombs that fell from the air and dismembered friend and foe alike combined to create a nightmarish, surreal setting in which nothing anyone did could be seen or chronicled or even remembered. Too many men were fighting for their lives, and it was a fight most of them would lose.

So Salvatore Posilipo became a sacrifice. He was a twenty-six-year-old man with a young wife and a son waiting and praying for him at home in Philadelphia. He was fighting because they told him he had to. He didn't mind, of course. He was a first-generation American citizen, and he was inordinately proud of that. He would have willingly laid down his life to protect those things that his father, also Salvatore, had told him were the most important in life.

But no one ever would know that he hadn't been killed by a German bullet or run down by a German tank or blown up by a German land mine. It would have been incomprehensible to learn that he had been shot in the back by his own kind, a man named Giovanni Impelliteri, who was the same age, who had no family, who had listened to the news of the Japanese attack on Pearl Harbor with a grim smile on his face. This would be a war that lasted for a long time, he thought, and it would provide a chance for those who saw it to become rich and powerful and, most important of all, to become invisible.

So Giovanni Impelliteri had enlisted at the Church Street recruiting center in lower Manhattan three days after the bombing. He requested immediate action, on the front, so that he might help defeat the enemy. He was a natural, a fighter with no fear, a killer with a flair and absolutely no remorse or hesitation. He would do whatever needed to be done.

Six months later, when he boarded a ship and set sail with fifteen hundred others for the European continent, he had gone through basic training at Fort Dix in New Jersey and earned grudging respect from the instructors and officers. He was totally ruthless, hard to know, but not a single man at Dix would hesitate to go into battle with Giovanni Impelliteri.

They had started to call him Johnny Imp, but he glared the first time someone said it to his face, eyes boring painful holes in the guilty party, and after that they never called him Johnny Imp to his face. As his legend grew, most never even used it behind his back, certain somehow that he would know and be angry.

Giovanni was not a big man, perhaps five-feet-nine. Hard as metal, lean as bone, he weighed 155 pounds and never moved an ounce from that number. He was handsome in a hard way, like a stone replica of a human being, and as far as anyone knew he never went out with the others to drink, to search for women, to use the increasingly available whores who set up shop just outside Dix.

He had no friends. He had no vices. He had no hobbies or interests.

He simply wanted to be taught to kill.

He learned quickly and well.

But in his mind, where he had formulated his plan, one that would have made a chess master proud for its far-reaching and incredibly logical thought processes, he could not remain Giovanni Impelliteri. Not for long, anyway. He had to start a new life, create a new identity, and he was going to use the war, this unexpected and welcome opportunity, to set his career in motion.

So the ship disgorged yet another load of American boys in England, and Impelliteri's group, the Eighty-first, was dispatched almost immediately to Poland. In the spring of 1944 slow, painful advances were being made that brought the Americans to the German border. That assault stalled for six months or more, a holding action that was nevertheless deadly. And then the breakthrough. It was in early November of 1944. Impelliteri and his platoon were part of a massive charge through the Rhine Valley and finally, inexorably, found themselves on German soil.

They watered that soil with German blood. They left German bodies to become fertilizer for that German soil. They swept through the countryside with the violence and effectiveness of a new strain of uncontrollable airborne sickness. Impelliteri's group—he had already received a battle promotion to sergeant—was particularly forceful, which is the way the higher-ranking officers put it. They were, in truth, frightened of this man, this cold and ruthless man who seemed to derive more pleasure than any man should from taking the lives of others, although those who had "liberated" the concentration camps silently and sometimes even vocally praised Impelliteri's intensity and dedication.

And then it was time for him to disappear. He had looked long and hard before he found Salvatore Posilipo. They were the same size, had the same general features, exhibited bravery and determination that would see them successfully through life-threatening situations. Giovanni cultivated Salvatore, "Sally," he called him, "the toughest girl I ever knew." Posilipo, who had grown to admire Impelliteri for his courage and had come to respect him, was pleased at the friendship and the good-natured teasing. No one else ever got close to Johnny Imp. No one.

It was a gray, cold, and bitter day. Approximately fifty U.S. soldiers had broken through a shoulder-high stone wall outside Munich and were greeted, from the other side of the field, by intense fire. Everyone began shooting in the general direction of the attack. Men on radios frantically screamed for air cover, shrieked out locations, and then fell. Giovanni Impelliteri kept his eye on Posilipo and, when the carnage was at its peak, calmly shot him in the back, between and slightly above the shoulder blades. Sally Posilipo fell, dead instantly. No one noticed.

Impelliteri crawled to the body, swapped dog tags, said a brusque farewell to his friend, and then planted a hand grenade under Posilipo's face, rolling out of the way just as the explosion ripped off Sally's head, rendering him totally and forever unidentifiable.

But, of course, once Impelliteri had assumed the identity of Salvatore Posilipo, there would be those who would know him. Those who would meet him, do business with him, and therefore know his name. That could not be, for Sally Posilipo was dead and, as his personal sacrifice, so was Giovanni Impelliteri.

He would never be Giovanni Impelliteri, and he could not be Salvatore Posilipo.

It was another two steps removed from his real identity. Men like Giovanni/Salvatore need to distance themselves from whatever it was they planned to do, as well as from reality.

Impelliteri had made one more switch of dog tags, later that night, and had "traded identities" with another young man, lying dead on the side of the road, his face blown away by a mortar round. His name had been Arthur R. McDonald.

Impelliteri became Arthur R. McDonald.

The war ended.

The body bearing the dog tags of Giovanni Impelliteri, the body that had once been christened Salvatore Posilipo, was buried, unmourned, in a cemetery in France. The grave was unmarked save for a small white cross. The name scratched into the cross in rudimentary lettering was Impelliteri's.

The body of Arthur R. McDonald, which had been identified as that of Salvatore Posilipo, was buried with honor and ceremony in St. Vincent's Reform Catholic Cemetery outside Philadelphia, by the proud and grieving Posilipo family.

Arthur R. McDonald's parents never understood why their son stopped writing to them and never came home. They mourned his loss as surely as if he had died.

Impelliteri was safe.

TWENTY
THREE

ONE of the few men in the world who knew this story, and therefore knew that McDonald was Posilipo and that Posilipo was Impelliteri, was Anthony Assante. They had been doing business since the early 1950s. It was Assante, a high-ranking member of one of the most feared organized crime families, who made the introductions that brought McDonald/Impelliteri into the same inner circle. Since McDonald wasn't Italian, at least to the outside world, he could never become a "made man," could never be as close as the others. That was fine. He never wanted that kind of association. It meant giving away too much personal information, and that was what he guarded most zealously.

But McDonald showed the powerful families how to make more money than they had ever thought possible, and they responded with respect and information of their own. It was a magnificent association: McDonald was a perfect front man, white-haired and genteel, educated, and impossibly wealthy. The families needed someone like him and never expected he would be so productive for them. What they didn't know until it was far too late was the sinister danger he represented.

Success came faster and more successfully than anyone could have imagined, and it was the kind of business—banking, stocks, legitimate—that became increasingly more difficult for the authorities to trace, to chart. McDonald's genius, coupled with a predator's ruthlessness, was made to reflect off Assante. He was impregnable, untouchable, directing business deals and takeovers, administering life lessons and death with the impunity of a man protected by layers and layers of alibis and shell corporations and, as well, by the absence of anyone who knew more than a small part of the overall operation.

It was safe and foolproof, Assante realizing early on that any investigation could be squashed by money, that any group of law-and-order civil servants could be bought, at a price so ridiculously low it inspired only disdain in the minds of those who wielded the power.

Police were nothing, politicians even less, and the more important the politician, the easier it was to buy him. Construction and corporate swindles were almost too easy. Brokering for state- and federal-level lobbyists became simple. Millions upon millions of dollars were flowing into the carefully structured cobwebs of revenue depositories, but the action was gone. If it can be imagined that generating more than a billion dollars over a four-year period was boring, then that is exactly how Assante felt.

McDonald did not feel the same. He was content. He had done all that he had started out to do, in the streets as a child and on the battlefields of Europe as a young man. Every conquest, every success, was a powerful incentive to do more, to make more, to bring another man to his knees.

He had little need for the money, and he had shunned public displays of recognition and power all his life. His desires were simple and mostly revolved around privacy and comforts. He had no family, no children. He was not a charitable man. The money simply accumulated and had reached a point where no one could count it, not McDonald and not any of his accountants and financial advisers and attorneys.

McDonald had no close friends, save for Anthony Assante, and when Assante came to him with the idea of "arranging" NFL games he gave his reluctant approval because it was something everyone knew about, something glamorous and romantic, and it sparked just a touch of excitement in this old man's dull life.

"Get me the best," he told Assante, "and make it foolproof."

So Assante arranged for Adam Benson, clearly the best and most visible. It was as if some earlier McDonald had turned Joe DiMaggio or Mickey Mantle. It was impossible, so much so that no one would even dream that it might happen.

But Assante knew the lure of sex, drugs, and money and the effect of the implied threat of power and force. Once in, the hook was forever. No exit. And Adam Benson had become another example.

McDonald was angry, for a short while, because of the resultant media frenzy, even when the fools didn't know the truth but thought the quarterback had simply died of heart failure on the field. But he had seen enough of this television/advertising/season-ticket bonanza to realize that there might be something huge, financially speaking, in getting the game under the control of one of the "organizations" he headed. So he forgave Assante for his indiscretion, counted the small amount of money the project produced as a bonus instead of a liability, and forgot the entire nuisance.

So did all his people, those who knew, and there had been that termination of the one who had managed it.

The project was over, as dead as Adam Benson.

But one of the most dangerous men in the world had made one small mistake. He had underestimated the power of genuine friendships.

TWENTY FOUR

GERRY Keegan sat alone in a small office the day after Adam Benson's funeral. It was a circus in the little town of Oliphant, with dignitaries from the various sports worlds present, not to mention headline-famous athletes and coaches. In all, more than five hundred people tried to jam into the small Miller & Sons Mortuary on Front Street, which of course didn't work.

Keegan was bothered by the funeral at several levels. Sherri Novak, for instance, and there was no hiding the fact, at least to himself, that he was attracted to her.

He was also disturbed by the inescapable fact of the murder. Benson had been killed, with intent, on the football field in Yankee Stadium. The murderer was more than clever; he was diabolically gifted. But there were only football players as suspects, and none of them had any serious hook to Benson or to the organized crime animals who had clearly orchestrated this killing.

So how to get more from Sherri, and how to get a lead on which one of the players might have actually done the deed? There would never be a murder weapon found. Keegan was as sure as he was about anything in the world that the needle, the hat pin, whatever it was, had been secreted back into the player's uniform and taken away, and if it had been disposed of later on somewhere in Manhattan or the Bronx this indeed would be a case of searching for a needle in a haystack.

But the basic rule of any crime still applied. Somebody did it. Somebody was out there waiting to be discovered, then arrested, then prosecuted. It was merely a case of finding the guilty party, and almost never did a crime of this magnitude simply disappear. Someone did it because someone else had ordered it done, and in between there had to be another handful of culpable enablers.

Keegan was convinced that the actual murderer was the least important person in the chain and would bet that the incentive there was money or drugs or both.

Who ordered it done and why were of far greater importance.

But detectives began at the beginning, at the point of the crime, and then worked out from there in ever-widening circles of involvement.

So once again Keegan went over the names of the players not only on the field but also in the pileup in the end zone.

The players for the Bears were Bill Jillian, the center; Mark Tucker, the tight end; Thomas McNeely, the wide receiver; Harlan Ellsworth, the fullback; and Michael Lee Reasons, the center.

The Giants were Larry Marshall, the defensive left end; Melvin Johnson, the defensive left tackle; Jackie Simpson, the left outside linebacker; and Eldon St. John, the left cornerback.

Nine men.

One of them was a murderer.

But who? And how to find the answer?

As in any investigation, Keegan had to start with the experts. He had already visited with the Giants' head coach. He would do that again, almost certainly. But this particular man was a Cro-Magnon type. If he couldn't talk about football, he had nothing to talk about. Duane Charles reminded Keegan of the joke about the scientist at Rice who built the first interactive computer and wanted to show it off to his colleagues. So he called in the head of the math department and said, "Hey, Harold, ask him a question."

Humoring his friend, the mathematician asked, "What is the obverse of the triple gain of a quantum equation moved to unidentifiable sectors?"

Whirr. Buzz. "It would have to be six trillion minus the unidentifiable portion of the sector, sir, but probably no greater than a plus-minus of twenty nanoseconds."

Harold was amazed.

Now the professor called in the head of the English department and said, "Hey, Ralph, ask him a question."

Another case of humoring a friend. "Machine," said Ralph, "when one combines the best parts of the structural verse of Russian sonnets and the influence of the early Moorish poets, how does that combination best reflect in modern poetry?"

Bells and whistles. One minute, tops. "Most opinions offered to date identify e. e. cummings, but the stronger case can be made for Ezra Pound."

Ralph was amazed.

And now the professor spotted the football coach walking down the hall. "Billy Joe, come in here; ask my machine a question."

The coach looked warily at the computer. "I'm the football coach; what do you know about defense?"

Less than five seconds passed, and the computer

said, in a high-pitched, nasal twang-drawl, "How 'bout them Cowboys?"

That joke always made Keegan laugh.

Ed Buck had first told it to him.

So now Ed was going to do profiles on the four Giant players involved. He was home when Keegan called.

After listening to the request, Ed readily accepted but asked his friend if he could bring someone else in on the investigation.

"Who would that be?" Keegan wondered.

"The Giants' psychological profile guy, a really good guy named David Silverman. He sits on about six different boards of directors, does all the employment profiles for most of the major corporations in the area, and works with the Giants on an almost daily basis, especially when it's time for the college player draft. They won't take a kid unless Dr. Silverman has passed on him, and he interviews about two hundred of them at the tryouts and workouts. The coaches hate him because they'll take anybody who can play, but David won't approve certain guys. Why? I don't know for sure. That's why he does what he does."

Keegan had no problem with the involvement of Dr. Silverman. The more experts the better, and this was absolutely on the money in terms of the man fitting the job.

"Call him. Give him Marshall, Johnson, Simpson, and St. John. I guess you'll have to tell him why we're interested, too. Fill him in."

"Why these four?"

"Because they were the four Giants in the pileup," Keegan said. "I have five Bears I need to get work-ups on. Do you know if anybody like this Silverman guy does the same job for them?"

"Yeah. David Silverman."

A break, if even the smallest kind. "Call him," Keegan said.

"Who are the Bears?"

"Jillian, Tucker, McNeely, Ellsworth, and Reasons."

Buck put the telephone down. Something was starting to happen, and it was encouraging enough to lift him slightly out of the depression that lingered from the funeral the day before.

Most of Adam's high school friends, now prematurely potbellied, wore on their faces the look of the loss of a very close friend. Many of the NFL players had tears on their cheeks. The idiot Boland brothers, in an uncharacteristic fit of generosity, had chartered a bus to bring the entire team and all the front office personnel to Oliphant. Most of the Bears were there, too.

Services were short. The local priest, who had seen Adam through all his religious passages as a boy, officiated. "We miss him mostly because of who he was here in Oliphant," intoned the Reverend Louis Asher, "and we were proud of who he was after he left us. Adam Benson will be missed by those who knew him then and by those who knew him after he left."

Done. Benson's father shook hands, tears streaming silently down his cheeks. Sherri stayed at his arm, black dress and black veil only adding to her unintentional sexuality. Ed and Leigh were with the official mourning party, too. A short stop at a local restaurant, too quiet and too sad, finished the day. Andy Benson went home to be alone, while Sherri accompanied Ed, Leigh, and Gerry Keegan to the limousine that would take them back to New York.

Adam Benson was dead and buried.

Now Keegan wanted to be able to say the same about whoever killed him.

TWENTY FIVE

DR. David Silverman sat at his desk in his office on Park Avenue, intentionally selected to be near both the NFL and the Giants' offices—walking distance, actually. He was sketching abstract designs around the list of nine names, drawing circles around a few of them, squares around others. That he was shocked to hear that players were being investigated, that one of them almost certainly had to be implicated in the murder of Adam Benson, was a gross understatement. But shock was not surprise. Nothing much surprised Dr. Silverman anymore. Professional football players, as well at athletes in other pro sports, had been allowed for way too long to live in their own world, with their own rules and too much money and virtually no supervision. The teams "arranged" to get them out of trouble. All they needed was a jump shot or the ability to hit a baseball or pitch it.

And in the case of football, with which he was mainly involved, any of the world-class skills that could be translated into winning and, therefore, profits for the team were worth preserving, even if it meant breaking a few silly laws along the way.

Three of the names earned a circle or a square as well as an asterisk. Dr. Silverman knew all the players, of course. They hadn't been in the league that long. It seemed as though no players stayed around too long in these days of salary caps and ever-increasing demands to be faster and bigger and stronger. He had run through all nine during the various free-agent tryouts held each February in Indianapolis, where upward of three hundred college athletes were poked, prodded, timed, asked to lift weights and jump vertically as well as horizontally, and measured and, in more recent years, tested psychologically.

"We do not expect to find any potential rocket scientists," David had said once, over a long dinner with Ed at Le Cirque 2000 (Silverman paid), "but we don't want to draft any psychotics, either. We understand the football aspect of colleges in this country. It's as though they have two groups of student bodies, the ones who have to earn passable grades to stay in school and the athletes, who can do anything they damned well please short of murdering someone as long as they can help the team win games."

Silverman's track record had been nearly flawless over the years. He didn't reject too many potential draft choices, but those he did had turned out to justify his negative feelings. Three were already out of the league because of drug abuse, uncontrollable drug abuse. Another was serving time in jail for operating a ring that sold cocaine in the streets of Miami. Two others were currently under suspension.

Yet another had been signed by the Giants after being released by two other teams because of allegations of sexual and physical abuse of women and an alcohol problem out of control.

"If we can get him off the booze, we can keep him away from the women," Silverman had told the Giants' personnel director, an intelligent, thoughtful man named Henry Olden. "He is an intelligent, relatively

decent young man who cannot be allowed to go anywhere near alcohol. I think he's worth the cost of re-
habilitation."

That was four years ago. He had played well for the
Giants, once being voted to the Pro Bowl, and had
never again been involved in anything seamy. Nor, for
that matter, had he ever again touched a drop of alcohol. On the other hand, Silverman's wife, Roberta,
had refused to soften her view of this gargantuan kid
and refused to discuss it in public or even quietly with
friends. She was offended that her husband could have
acted in such a "feminine unfriendly" manner, all in the
interest of providing a football team with another good
player.

Of course, Silverman's recommendations were just
that. Opinions. He had no real control over which players the teams' personnel and coaching staffs finally isolated as their draft picks. But more and more, his input
was being considered as a necessary ingredient in making an intelligent decision.

So there he sat, nine names scrawled on paper, being
asked by a good friend, on behalf of an official police
investigation of homicide, to decide which one, or
more, of the nine could have actually agreed to commit
murder.

Silverman knew, from his years of study and experience with infinitely more dangerous men than football
players, that anyone could commit a murder. "If the
right buttons are pushed," he had written in a University of Pennsylvania doctoral thesis, "then the basest
emotions and instincts are released. Most people have
found ways to guard against those buttons being
pushed. Some don't have the necessary protective devices, and so we must all hope they don't find themselves in those specific situations."

Football, especially on the professional level, strips
away layers of social behavior and does, in a real and
valid sense, expose the basest emotions and instincts. It
would be easier, Silverman had always felt, to turn a
pro football player, rather than an ordinary man, into
a murderer. And defensive players were more likely to
slip into that role. Their game was far less controlled
and far more vicious. Just go get the ball, and the man
with the ball, and do whatever you can, even going
beyond the scope of the far too lenient rules, to get the
job done.

He started with the four Giants. Marshall was a
three-year veteran; Johnson and Simpson had been in
the NFL five years; St. John was playing in his sixth
season. Perhaps as a partial testimony to Silverman's
input, all four had been drafted by the Giants and had
remained with them. None of them had been a problem, although Silverman had been slightly less than absolutely confident in the futures of Marshall and St.
John. Both of them had been in trouble in high school
and college. Nothing serious, just the antics of young
blue-chip athletes exercising their strength and superiority. Silverman had passed both of them because the
infractions were physical, no drugs involved, no criminal mentality noticeable. Marshall was simply a bully
with a mean streak, which is almost mandatory for one
who would play defensive end at this world-class level.
St. John was quiet, moody, extremely intelligent, and
just slightly unbalanced. Again, for those who play cornerback that is recommended.

The cornerback is out there all alone. The receiver
knows where he's going, knows the route he's going to
run, while the cornerback has to guess. And if he makes
one mistake, one false step, one split-second stumble,
the receiver is downfield with the football in his arms,

blurring his way into the end zone, while the cornerback is trudging off, head down, kicking at the ground, totally and completely embarrassed and exposed.

"You have to have the mentality of an assassin to play cornerback," an earlier team psychologist, Dr. Arnold Mandell in San Diego, then doing a profile of the Chargers, had written. "Cornerbacks get no help and never get much credit, but they get all the blame, and it's there for millions of people to see."

Dr. Mandell had provided the definitive profile of linebackers, too, calling them "the ideal soldiers in war, the ones who have enough cunning to slip behind enemy lines and enough innate violence to coolly murder the enemy."

But he had identified the cornerbacks as the latently psychotic, the ones most likely to murder, to take a life in a premeditated and cold-blooded fashion. Silverman remembered interviewing St. John at the Indianapolis tryouts, looking into his dark, deep stare, noticing, almost surprised, the high level of intelligence. And he remembered the critical response to what he highlighted as the most important question he would ask this young man.

"How would you feel about playing offense, if the Giants were to try to make you a wide receiver?" Silverman had asked.

St. John had looked him hard in the face. "No, man. No offense," he had replied. "I like hitting too much to play offense."

"Like it? Why?"

"I get excited, man. Like aroused. You know, like when I'm with a girl."

David Silverman knew this kid was highly rated. He knew the Giants liked St. John a lot. He knew that they needed a cornerback. And here he was, six-two and 210 pounds, ran the forty in 4.35 seconds, had a forty-one-inch vertical jump, went off the charts on the watered-down intelligence test generally administered to football players.

And yet Silverman recommended that they pass him up in the draft, let another team take him.

"Why?" asked Tom Royster, the assistant personnel director.

"I don't know," Dr. Silverman had answered, for the first time in all the years he had been judging the personalities and psyches of prospective draft choices. "I don't know, but he frightens me."

Royster and the team had taken this into consideration, but without specific points of discontent they chose to pass on the negative evaluation. They drafted St. John in that year's first round, and he had played with exceptional skill.

Silverman still wasn't sure why he had felt uneasy. Now, perhaps, he would come closer to fingering his source of concern.

He had been slightly upset by Marshall, too, but never suggested avoiding him. Marshall was simply a bully, strong and quick, agile, and without conscience. He could be controlled, managed, manipulated, and, in all, coerced into playing well for three or four years, maybe more, until his inability to discipline himself led to obesity and eventual early retirement.

But St. John made Silverman nervous, then and now.

Could he murder? Absolutely. Was he clever enough to pull it off? Definitely. Given the proper circumstances, would he be a viable suspect? Certainly.

But why? How? And what did he have to gain? Maybe more to the point, what did he stand to lose if he refused to do this?

Well, the entire list Buck had given Silverman would

have to be checked. Never leave a job undone; never do a job less than completely. He had all his files at hand, nine folders, one of which may have held an answer.

Of the nine, Silverman was absolutely convinced that Jillian, Tucker, Reasons, Johnson, and Simpson could not have been involved. Not possibly. He would stake his reputation, not to mention his high six-figure salary based on that reputation with teams and major corporations, on that feeling.

That left four. McNeely, Ellsworth, Marshall, and St. John.

He would get to work immediately.

TWENTY
SIX

THOMAS McNeely, who had attended but did not graduate from Clemson University, had been evaluated by Dr. Silverman as a nondangerous, nonpsychotic, not overly intelligent person. His work ethic soared in direct proportion to the amount of incentive placed just ahead of him, within his reach but only with great effort.

He was perfect as a wide receiver, stretching that extra foot, finding one more burst of speed, not so much in celebration of his athletic skills but for the inherent glory in making a big play. He liked that such things called attention to himself.

There had been only one incident at Clemson, when McNeely and three other men, two of whom had been football players, were arrested on rather common charges of drunk and disorderly one Saturday night following an unexpected victory over heated rival Auburn. McNeely had punched one of the policemen, which in turn got him a billy club on the side of his head, but he and the school agreed not to prolong the incident. For their part, the Clemson police (the town, not the campus, cops) dropped the matter. No record, no problem.

McNeely was genuinely contrite. His fear of authority had kept him clean until then, and he was not going to become a chronic offender. He was not a problem, but reports at the scene indicated that he had lost control when the police officer struck him with the club and was consumed by his rage, threatening to kill the man, promising to return with a gun. It was the alcohol, nothing more. But there was a tendency toward violence.

· David Silverman studied his notes carefully and then rejected McNeely as a possible suspect.

Harlan Ellsworth, possibly the best blocking fullback in the NFL, had been a linebacker at Penn State, one of those players moved by legendary head coach Joe Paterno into a position he needed and not necessarily what was in the best interests of the player. Paterno recruited several quarterbacks and tailbacks each year, arguably getting the pick of the nation's high school kids because of his reputation and Penn State's decades-long history as a contender for the national championship. Each one was promised that the starting job would be his. The mothers and the fathers urged their sons to take kindly old Joe's offer and, of course, the free, full-ride scholarship.

Then the boys would show up for summer practice and find eight quarterbacks and ten tailbacks, discover they were in a competition for the job among the best the nation's high schools could produce. The losers became second-and third-teamers. Some were told to "look elsewhere," because there wasn't much chance of any change in their immediate futures.

Others were offered the chance to change positions, to compete at a new position that might take advantage of their skills and athleticism. One example was quarterback Jim Kelly, recently retired after a certain Hall of Fame career with the Buffalo Bills. He attended Penn State, was told he would not, after all, win the quarterback job, and was offered the chance to move to line-backer.

Kelly told Paterno to stuff it, transferred to the University of Miami, and became an All-American player and a first-round draft choice.

Well, Ellsworth had been given that choice, one of moving from linebacker (where Paterno was well stocked) to fullback, where he needed someone to make way for his next custom-tailored All-American, Brian Wharton (who, in fact, did become an All-American, largely due to the ferocity of Ellsworth's blocking).

So here was Ellsworth, with the temperament of a defensive player, having been switched to perhaps the only offensive position that allowed, condoned, and encouraged a player's ability to generate that kind of unbridled defensive fury.

Ellsworth had to be kept in school by some complex manipulations on the part of the office of the dean of students, activities that the NCAA, the colleges' governing body of all things athletic, would have found not only reprehensible but also illegal and in direct and blatant violation of its often-sanctimonious rules. Ellsworth was not much of a scholar. He did not believe in attending many classes. But he was so good, so valuable, that certain allowances were made, with season tickets to the Nittany Lions' home games (ranging from hard-to-find to absolutely rare) offered to various professors for a minimally passing grade. Such tickets in the hands of such underpaid men of academe could produce up to five hundred dollars a pair for each home game. Certainly, it was a reward well worth the incidental action of changing a grade of 68 to 70; even 58 to 70 was not out of the question.

Ellsworth was a bully and a braggart. He had been in numerous fights while in school, had been picked up once in a scheme to use stolen telephone calling cards, but all of his indiscretions were without that seething rage that Silverman looked for as one of the basic symptoms of possible psychosis. It was probably all he looked for, since the young man wasn't mentally or emotionally capable of suppressing those feelings and then successfully hiding them from society.

But Silverman could not arbitrarily discount Ellsworth as one of the suspects. He put that file aside.

As for the two Giants remaining on his list, he, frankly, did not like either one of them very much. He had told the scouting department as much, although failing to absolutely reject Marshall. So far, the big lineman had been kept under control. There had been a few incidents—he had been ejected three times from games for palpably unfair acts of violence—but he had stayed away from the real trouble, the career-ending kind of trouble.

St. John was a different matter. He had become articulate, poised in public, popular with his teammates and the public, and three times a Pro Bowl nominee. He now earned more than $750,000 a year, with built-in performance clauses that provided another $100,000 or so. He was successful, in both football and his social adjustment. Maybe he'd been wrong about him.

But not so fast. St. John wasn't off the list of candidates, not yet and perhaps not ever. Something lurked there, just under the surface. His new face, his new image, his new persona didn't ring true. In Silverman's considered opinion, the same bad seed still lay dormant, but far from dead.

Eldon St. John, one of nine children produced by four different fathers, had been raised by his mother, Jessie, and his three older sisters. It was a meager existence, punctuated by trips to the welfare office in Chicago, highlighted by gang fights and dead friends and drugs being sold rampant on the streets. But Eldon could play sports. He was a quality basketball player, the fastest sprinter on the high school's track team, but he really excelled in football.

From the minute he learned the game, he knew it was what he wanted. It was the only way he could imagine being able to hit other people and not be hauled off to the local police station, where the white cops would take him and others like him into a back room and play tattoo on his back with rubberized crowd control clubs. It all came to him naturally, the ability to see where the receiver was going while at the same time keep his eye on the ball, the gift of running backward almost as fast as others ran forward, the boiling, roiling sensation of pure pleasure when he crashed into a receiver, especially when the unfortunate player had just jumped for the ball and was coming down.

The scout from Ohio State saw St. John play four times in his senior year at James Polk High School, and that was enough. He told the head coach, Jake Maddock, that "Eldon St. John is the best high school cornerback in the country, and right now he may be the best cornerback in college football, too." So all the stops were pulled for this six-two, 200-pound blue-chipper. His mother got a job that paid her three times what it was worth. His oldest sister got one, too. One of his younger brothers was guaranteed a scholarship to Ohio State when he got out of high school. Eldon got so much undisclosed, untraceable money from Ohio State alumni groups that he never even considered other offers, many of them equally illegal, from the other thirty or forty colleges that wanted him to play for them.

While in college, Eldon got one girl pregnant, and when she asked if he would marry her or at least take his share of the responsibility he beat her so badly that she lost the child. But only a handful of people knew that happened: her story, once she deposited the $25,000 in cash handed to her in an envelope by a used car dealer in Columbus, was that she fell down a long flight of metal steps in the girls' dorm.

One major problem had been handled, but not with sufficient secrecy to prevent Dr. Silverman from finding out.

There were other incidents, all of them stemming from a violent nature, uncontrollable in its fury and unpredictable in its emergence, but they were all handled, dealt with in such a way that the career of Eldon St. John would not be interrupted, nor would the winning tradition he helped instill in the Buckeyes' football program.

Without being able to prove the girl-falling-down-the-flight-of-steps incident was a heinous fabrication, Dr. Silverman could not, ethically would not, present that as a matter of truth to the Giants. He alluded to it, referred to the questionable situation that had occurred with the girl who had been St. John's close acquaintance, but had to disavow any claim of absolute knowledge. Silverman did, however, mention it to St. John one day, long after the Giants had drafted the athlete.

He got, in return, a cold, hard stare.

"I felt real bad for Darika," St. John said. "She really got hurt, I understand, and I was sorry. I really liked her for a while, you know? You know what she's doing these days?"

St. John's folder went on top of the pile.

TWENTY
SEVEN

DAVID Drexler got a phone call the day before Billy DeSalvo was to arrive for his meeting with Leigh Crespino, from someone he didn't know, to whom he had never spoken, but who knew the number to his private telephone, the single unit that sat on his desk.

"The meeting with DeSalvo and the broad is off," said the man, in a hard, clipped voice. "Someone else will be there tomorrow."

"Why?" Drexler asked.

"Billy's dead, that's why."

Click.

Drexler found himself wondering, just for a fleeting second, if this meant he could get the candy account back. Then he picked up his interoffice phone and dialed Leigh's number.

"Yes?"

"It's David. The meeting with the guy from California is still on tomorrow, but not with the guy you were going to see. That shouldn't make any difference to you."

"No, it doesn't. What happened to the first guy?"

"He died suddenly. Tough to keep appointments after that happens."

Leigh thought this new development was interesting, and that night at home, over dinner with Ed, she mentioned it. He thought it was a little odd, too, and phoned Gerry Keegan to tell him.

"Just to keep everything on the record," Ed said to Leigh.

Keegan, too, thought the news had some peripheral interest, that it might somehow pertain to the case under investigation, so he called one of the Madison Avenue guys he knew and asked if the name David Drexler was familiar.

"Sure, owns a big ad agency. Kind of a prick but gets some major billing. Why?"

"He had a meeting, with some guy who represents the tourist Boards of California and Hawaii, scheduled for tomorrow. Wanted to give Drexler a major account. Now the meeting is still on but not with this guy. He's dead."

Aside from wondering whether this could allow his firm to steal the account not yet awarded, Ralph Johnson had little interest. Guys died every day, especially in this business.

"Yeah. Shit happens. So what, Gerry?"

"Find out who the dead guy was, Ralph? OK? I'll owe you one."

Johnson placed a call to one of David Drexler's private secretaries, a girl he had fucked a few years ago and one of the few such past-tense lovers with whom he still had a friendly relationship.

"Hi, Kathy, it's Ralph Johnson. Sorry for calling so late."

Kathy Layton's interest flickered. Johnson was only a fair fuck but made a lot of money. "Don't worry about it, baby. What's up?"

"I've been thinking about you, Kath," Johnson said, absolutely unable to stop himself. "Thought we might get together for a drink Friday night."

"You still married, Ralph?"

"No, but my wife thinks I am," he said.

She smiled. Same old Johnson. But why not? "Sure, the Crown, maybe seven?"

"Done. I'm excited. Oh, by the way, how's business at DD Ads?"

"Good, as far as I know."

"Kathy, I know Drexler had a meeting scheduled tomorrow with some California and Hawaii tourist board guy with a bunch of money to spend and he's dead. The meeting is still on, and I'm interested in the account, too, you know? And with the guy dead, maybe they need more time to work it out? You know? Do you know who the dead guy was, or his company?"

"Hold on, Ralph. Let me get my book."

A pause. One minute. Two. Then she returned.

"A man named DeSalvo," she said. "William De-Salvo. That's all I have, Ralph. I don't know the company."

"Thanks, love. I'll see you Friday night."

He put the receiver down, aware he had built half a hard-on and realizing he'd get the rest of the way there, and then some, Friday night. It was a good thing Keegan had called.

Johnson returned the favor. Keegan picked up on the second ring.

"Gerry, Ralph Johnson. The dead guy was named William DeSalvo."

Bingo, thought Keegan. "Thanks," he said to Johnson. "Doesn't mean a thing to me. But thanks anyway."

A mistake, Keegan thought. The big guy, and Keegan had a feeling who it was, had made a mistake. He had had DeSalvo killed without canceling the meeting with Drexler's company first. Now someone else would have to show up. And Keegan was absolutely convinced that it had nothing to do with advertising; it was to get somebody close to Leigh, to frighten her, to pump her for information, or, conceivably but not likely, to kill her right there as a warning to Ed Buck.

But something tickled in the back of Keegan's mind. If everybody was crooked, and as a good cop you learned to make that assumption early in your career, then how could he absolutely, positively trust Mike Herbert, the guy who had arranged for Sherri to stay in the Venture Arms apartment? She had been there for a few days now and nothing had gone wrong, but it was time to move her. Especially with DeSalvo dead, somebody was going to have to clean up his mess, tie together all his loose strings, and certainly getting Sherri to stop breathing had to be high on every agenda and every list of priorities. She knew too much, had clearly demonstrated that she no longer wanted to be a part of the situation, and had become dangerous. Hazardous material.

So both women were in danger, to one extent or another. Keegan had to tell Ed about Leigh's jeopardy; he knew that. He did consider not doing so but got past that immediately. Ed had to know, and Gerry had to tell him. The situation with Sherri was more delicate. If Gerry was right and someone had found out where she was staying, even if it wasn't Herbert but someone else in that office, then there was no safe place in New York. And the scumbags had things tied up in Jersey, too.

But who could possibly guess that Sherri Novak would move in with Gerry Keegan's mother in Brooklyn, right under their noses?

He would see to that right now, not wait for morning, and the cover story would be that Novak had left to go back to California. Or something, somewhere, some other place. After all, she was not a suspect, simply a grieving widow. And personally, he would deal with what he thought was totally out of the question for him at this stage of his life, a budding emotional feeling for a woman.

Even though it was late, he called Sherri. She answered on the second ring, and her voice did not sound as though he had awakened her.

"Hello?"

Remember the tape, he reminded himself. *It's always running. Don't say anything stupid.* There was a woman officer living with Sherri, and if you don't trust one, you don't trust any.

"Hello?" she asked again.

"Hi, Mrs. Benson. It's Detective Keegan. I know it's late, but I have a few things to talk to you about. I'll pick you up in an hour, if you don't mind going out this late. It's kind of important."

She had been around subterfuge and mystery long enough to know he was speaking in code. He had stopped calling her Mrs. Benson a long time ago.

"Sure, Detective Keegan, if you think it's important. I'll be ready." She paused and decided to make it even easier. "I'll wait for you at the front door," she added. "No reason for you to come up."

Good girl, he thought, smiling. "That's fine. In half an hour. Put Officer Pearson on the phone. I'll get her off the hook."

He cleared it with the woman cop; then he called Ed.

"It's late," Gerry said, "but it's important. Leigh has a meeting tomorrow and we aren't sure who it's going to be with. It was supposed to be with a guy named DeSalvo, who has as much to do with advertising as Mother Cabrini. He's a mob guy. Or was.

He's dead. I think it was somebody who wanted to get a message to you. To shut you up. To make you think about sports and not dead quarterbacks. Is she there?"

"Yes, I'll get her. How serious is this, Gerry?"

"I won't bullshit you with fairy stories, Ed. It's about as serious as it gets. I would rather not have her keep the meeting, but it would be the best thing to do, to solve this, to nail the guys who did it."

"Gerry, I can't tell her what to do. I'll put her on. Just be careful. You know how important she is."

Leigh came to the phone, wasting no time. "What's going on, Gerry? Ed looks a little scared."

He told her. Almost everything.

"Of course I'll go to the meeting," she said. "You want me wired?"

He laughed. "You've been reading too many mystery novels," he said. "We don't really do that anymore. It's primitive. In twenty minutes, someone will leave a newspaper wrapped in a plastic bag at your door. He'll rap on the door a few times just to let you know he was there. You won't see him. Don't even try. Take the newspaper out of the plastic bag and feel along the center fold. You'll find a small coin-shaped item, like a quarter, no thicker. And it will look like a quarter, just like one. When you have your meeting tomorrow, just keep it in your pocket. Just make sure it's with you. Body heat activates it. When you get back home, leave the coin in the same place you found it. Just put it in a newspaper, then ring my private desk number three times. No one will answer, but the third ring will trigger a message and the device will be picked up within an hour."

"I'll put it in my bra," she said.

Keegan smiled. "I don't need to know that, and I'll

never tell the tech who works with it later where it was."

He would call no one, assign no one to this job. On his way to pick up Sherri, he'd make the drop himself. If you do it yourself, you know it gets done, and you know nobody else gets involved.

He retrieved a recording wafer from the supply he kept in the small steel box under his bed. It was safe there. He had the only key. He kept two other handguns in there (one registered, one a mystery guest), along with the recording devices, three passports (one of which was his), and other assorted items of interest and use to him.

He dressed, took his copy of the *New York Times*, which he had not had time to open, inserted the wafer recorder exactly at the center-fold crease, and slid it back into the plastic sleeve. One long strip of clear sealing tape ensured that the disk would stay where it was.

He drove over to Ed's apartment, dropped the paper so that it leaned against the door, and rapped a few times, to let them know something had been delivered. Then he ducked into a small alcove down the hall and waited until Ed came out, picked up the paper, and looked around, and Gerry Keegan was on his way when the apartment door closed again.

He drove toward Gracie Mansion, turned left at the next corner, and found himself in front of the Venture Arms. He didn't have to tap the horn. Sherri was there, waiting, and quickly slid in. He smiled when he noticed that she had her small overnight bag with her.

"Good thinking," he said.

"I didn't think you'd be picking me up to ask questions," she replied. "Am I in trouble?"

"Yes, you probably were, but no, you aren't now. We're moving you to another location."

"Where, Gerry?"

"I'm taking you home to see Mother," he said.

She smiled.

TWENTY
EIGHT

ED handed the coin recorder to Leigh, who smiled thinly, put it in her pocketbook, and went back to bed. So did he, and neither of them slept. Nor did either of them feel any magic. No sex on this night. No contact, at least physically, but Ed never felt closer to Leigh than he did right now. She was going to risk a great deal, perhaps even her life, in order to help get the people who had had Adam Benson killed.

Ed could never tell her how much it meant to him, nor, he feared, could he ever tell her how much she did, either.

They were quiet for most of the rest of the night, except to occasionally blurt out, unsolicited and almost unexpected, things like, "I love you, Leigh," and, "Just hold me, Eddie; make me feel safe."

At six in the morning, as she was leaving the bed to shower and prepare for the day, he asked, "What are you doing next weekend?"

"Why?"

"Well, if you aren't busy and don't have anything planned, how about we drive down to . . . oh, I don't know, someplace like Long Beach Island in Jersey and get married?"

"I'll let you know," she said, voice cracking and catching, and then she began to cry.

They held each other for another thirty minutes, which caused her to rush the rest of the morning until she was ready to leave the apartment. "I decided," she said as she left. "The answer is yes, and the question is why did you wait so damned long?"

A huge grin plastered itself across his face. "Hey, you know that old line about why buy the cow—"

"Pig!" she exploded, and he laughed even after she kicked him in the shins.

TWENTY
NINE

DR. Silverman had put out all his lines, left the appropriately disguised messages to colleagues around the league, spoken to those who had already called back, and gathered as much information as possible by telephone. He found himself wanting the guilty party to be St. John but found, as well, more and more evidence that Eldon was not a monster, even if he was someone Silverman would fight to the death to keep away from his family and friends.

Dr. Aaron Pierce, under whom Silverman had studied for two doctoral semesters at Northwestern, offered another insight. "Someone who has already disguised himself is likely to do it more effectively the next time, and the time after that, and the time after that."

St. John had disguised himself, certainly, in the cloak of a respectable citizen. But he wasn't attempting to prove to be something else. He still was an arrogant, ego-centered man, flashy and garish.

But whole.

At least on the surface.

What about Harlan Ellsworth, who had once played defense, who had once borne the label of "probable assassin profile" that psychologists affix to a segment of the professional football population? The High School All-American linebacker had latent violence ingrained

in his football persona. It was what enabled him to ex-
cel at both positions, as an All-American fullback/block-
ing back at Penn State (who stepped in for three games
in his senior year when the middle linebacker was injured and played both ways) and now as a budding
Pro Bowl fullback with the Bears. He was huge and
powerful, his six-foot-two body layered with 240
pounds of muscle, but there were hundreds of players
that size and bigger. The difference, which always
amazed Dr. Silverman, was the emotional output generated when a few of them, a sparse handful, were
placed in a highly competitive situation.

"Some players refuse to fail," he once told Ed, "and
others are simply satisfied with doing well, reveling in
their own physical gifts, if you will. That represents a
huge difference. It can take a player, or a businessman
or anybody else who deals with competition, well past
what his normal physical barriers would be."

Was Ellsworth a possibility, somewhat overlooked
because of the garishness and visibility of St. John? It
was worth some investigating.

Dr. Silverman called the Bears' offices and asked for
Louis Jerome, the team's head trainer and an old friend.

"David, what's up?" Jerome asked, clearly pleased to
hear from his mentor.

"Terrible thing about Benson," Silverman answered.
"Just a nightmare."

"Yes, and shocking. I mean, he was a little older, but
I worked with him every day. The guy was in great
shape. His annual physical showed no heart problem
at all. Nothing except normal range everywhere."

"Lou, I have to ask you something that I'd like to
see doesn't go any further. Is that acceptable?"

Pause. "Sure, David. We go back too many years for
me not to trust you now."

"Lou, what's going on with Ellsworth? Anything different? Anything strange?"

"You mean is he on anything?"

"Yes, that, too. Is he?"

Pause. "David, I thought he was last off-season, but we can't just spot-check for substance abuse unless there's a reason, you know? Once they reported to camp, we gave him the standard blood screen and urinalysis and nothing showed. I don't think the bad guys have come up with a better, super masking drug yet, so no, I can't say he's on anything."

"Does he hang with that type?"

"David, he's a thug, not a nice man, nobody you'd want to have dinner with. I think there are some psychological warts on him, too, things that don't look good in sunlight, if you know what I mean."

"Yeah, so what makes him different from three-quarters of the players in this league, Lou? This isn't a game for sane people."

Jerome took a long time before answering.

"I think Harlan Ellsworth is dangerous. I think he can really hurt somebody. And he has no fuse at all when it comes to temper. He explodes, instantly. I guess that's what makes him such a great blocker, that plus the fact that he actually, literally hates the people he's playing against. He's a frightening man, David. He scares the shit out of me."

Was that a tingle?

"Lou, find out what you can about what he does off the field, in the off-season. I can't tell you why. Not yet. But it's important."

"Does it have anything to do with poor Adam?"

"I can't tell you anything, Lou. Trust me for now."

"Done. I'll call tomorrow. Maybe tonight. Still have the same home number?"

"Yep."

"Good. And say hello to Bobbi."

St. John could have done it. So, too, could Ellsworth. Silverman figured he had the final two candidates for the grand prize.

THIRTY

LEIGH was scared, really, truly scared, and she was not the type of woman to get that way very easily, without considerable prodding. Ed and Gerry both insisted this meeting had nothing to do with advertising, that whatever it was, with whomever she met, it was about Adam Benson's murder and she was going to be far more of a focal point than she could ever have dreamed. To say it made her nervous, frightened, and fearful would have been to seriously understate her situation.

But she was going to do it, and walking the ten blocks to the office she ran it over and over in her mind. What to say? How to react? How to respond? Was she in actual physical danger? Would the little recorder work? Did David Drexler know what was going on or was he just an innocent pawn in all of this? Was Ed in danger? Was something going to happen to her?

The recorder felt heavy in her bra, as though everyone on the street could see it, although she knew that was ridiculous. She clutched her handbag tightly, tighter than usual, and the click of her heels on the sidewalks of Manhattan sounded loud, ominous, louder than the noise of the other pedestrians, louder than the blaring of the horns and the shouts of the cabdrivers and the roaring of the trucks and buses streaming up and down Madison Avenue.

At the same time, David Drexler sat in his office, having arrived far earlier than he usually made his appearance. He was talking to someone he didn't know, someone with whom he had never spoken before.

His hands were filmy with perspiration. He heard the words, spoken in a soft, unhurried, cultured tone. He got the meaning, which was as direct as the voice was soft, and the insinuations were subtle. But all he could think of was that his business, his little empire, was about to crumble, that all he had worked for, at first, and then enjoyed to the fullest was about to explode in his face.

"Yes, sir. I understand," he said. "I will speak with Miss Crespino as soon as she gets in. I will make it clear what it is you want, Mr. McDonald. Absolutely clear. No question. And thank you for this opportunity to help."

There was no response. For a few seconds, which seemed like long minutes, there was just silence. Then he heard, soft but distinct, the click of someone breaking the connection. Hanging up.

He put his receiver back in its cradle, took a deep breath, and reached for his handkerchief to wipe his forehead. He didn't know the man who had been on the other end of the conversation, and was sure he didn't want to, either. A voice so soft that it sent daggers of fear piercing through him. Whatever this man wanted to know he learned. Whomever he wanted to hurt he did so easily, by lifting a telephone, perhaps, just as he had done this morning. Drexler's hands were still shaking, although less noticeably, when he rang for his secretary and asked if Leigh had arrived yet.

"No, not yet, but she should be in any minute," Kathy Layton said. "She usually gets in around nine-thirty."

"Tell her to see me first thing," he said.

"Sure, Mr. Drexler."

He sounded nervous, she thought, and wondered whether it had anything to do with that call from Ralph Johnson last night and this guy DeSalvo.

Fifteen minutes later, Leigh Crespino walked in and passed Kathy's desk. "Oh, Leigh, Drexler wants to see you. First thing, he said!" she called out.

"Thanks, Kath. Just going to put my stuff down. Tell him I'll be right in."

Leigh sat in the soft chair opposite David Drexler's desk, notepad in her hands, assuming he wanted to see her to somehow prep her for this meeting. Instead, she sat in stunned silence as he stammered and stuttered his way through the delivery of this cryptic but absolutely real message.

"Leigh, the man you were going to meet with this morning—the guy who died—I don't know who he was, only that he was on the phone last week and insisted on seeing you. He controlled a lot of people, some of them very important to DD Ads. Just to prove to me how important he was and how much he could do to hurt us, he caused us to lose the Skeezixs candy account.

"Nobody knows this yet. But we have lost it, just because this guy DeSalvo called somebody and asked for this favor."

He paused.

"The word *favor* should imply what I think is going on here. He asked for a favor, and somebody else important readily agreed. So we lost an account, for no good reason. In fact, I heard yesterday that it's already been picked up by Huff and DeCicco. But that's not important. It's gone and we have no choice but to accept that."

Another long pause, as he played with his ballpoint pen.

"What I am going to tell you now has nothing to do with advertising or business or accounts or any of that, but it has a lot to do with this business and you, personally. Me, too, I think. I received a call earlier this morning from a man named McDonald. That's all I was told. McDonald. How he got my private phone number I don't know, but honestly, I wasn't surprised. This DeSalvo had it, too. These people get whatever they want.

"Leigh, DeSalvo was coming in today to warn you, in no uncertain terms, that any more probing into the death of that football player—what was his name, Benson?—will result in your boyfriend getting hurt, possibly you getting hurt, maybe the both of you winding up dead. This was a very scary man, Leigh. It was made very clear to me that you are to tell Ed that he should stop the investigation. That he should tell the detective, and I was told the guy's name is Keegan, that he is no longer interested in pursuing this. That he is in fear for his life, and yours, and that no one can protect the two of you should you ignore this warning.

"And this McDonald said that if the detective stops, nothing will ever happen to any of you, that it will be forgotten, and, most important, that it will be considered a favor done for him by the both of you. Those kinds of favors to these kind of people are often repaid handsomely."

Drexler didn't bother to add that should the police be called off and the matter dropped, DD Ads would receive a replacement account for the lost candy billing, one that would be far larger and more profitable.

Which account he didn't know, nor the extent of the dollar value, but he realized that the favor he had done for this man would be repaid and the parameters for the payback had already been established.

He simply had to see to it that Leigh Crespino did as she had been told: actually, that she did as he had been told.

Leigh thought carefully as to her response, her first response. It would be critical, because Gerry had instructed her to see if she could extract more information from the man sent to interview her.

"David, let me see if I understand this. Somebody is in effect claiming responsibility for the death of Adam Benson, and that somebody doesn't want any police investigation to go forward. That's murder, isn't it? Are you telling me to ignore a murder, to just forget it, make believe it just didn't happen, and then to tell Ed and Detective Keegan that it doesn't matter, just go on with something else?"

Drexler stirred uncomfortably in his chair. "Yes, I guess that's it. The guy's dead; wouldn't make sense for other people to wind up the same way, would it?"

"Who was this guy? Who called you? Who was supposed to be here today and what happened to him?"

"Leigh, the guy who called me this morning said his name was McDonald. Arthur McDonald. A businessman out in California with offices and interests here in New York and many other places. He said the guy who was supposed to be here, William DeSalvo, had been killed. I don't know how. I don't know what happened. But he was going to deliver this same message in person. I think this way was a lot safer for you, you know?"

She nodded. "I guess so. Look, David; I'll give this message to Ed. What he decides to do about Detective

Keegan is up to him. I know what a strain this has been for you, and losing Skeezixs is going to hurt. I'll do what I can. Do you mind if I take the rest of the day? I'm a little shaken by all this. OK?"

Relieved, Drexler nodded. He stood, offered Leigh his hand. "Sure, go, home. Go shopping. Just remember, these guys mean business and I hope we can not only do what they want but keep it quiet. Just us, OK?"

She nodded, turned, and left, hoping beyond hope that the coin-sized tape recorder had captured it all.

As it turned out, it had.

Gerry Keegan was delighted.

Now there were two major assignments remaining, one for him, one for Ed Buck.

Keegan had to find out who Arthur McDonald was, who he really was. Buck, with the help of Dr. Silverman, had to come up with the player who had committed the murder.

THIRTY
ONE

ELDON St. John was concerned. It was not something he could put a finger on, nothing specific, no reason for this silent alarm. He was just stricken by a feeling of unrest, nerves and malaise. It felt like something undone, unsaid, seen but not remembered. Kind of strange, kind of odd, and definitely unsettling.

Did it have something to do with Sunday's game, with the death of Adam Benson? St. John was sure it did, certain beyond question that whatever was bothering him had something to do with the game, had everything to do with the death.

How could Adam Benson be dead? How could a guy like that just die? He was a pro football player, man, in top condition. He had passed his team's physical that summer; he had played in every game, done all the running, gone through all the practices. Why would he suddenly fall down and be dead, man?

St. John remembered the play, of course. Strong-side right, power sweep. Except Benson had fooled even his own guys, faked the handoff to the halfback and kept the ball, wheeling to his left. He had a lineman there, maybe two. He had the fullback. The Giants were fooled, even though four or five of the defensive guys made a strong adjustment and came back to the ball, himself included.

He got in on the hit, but Benson was already in the end zone. Eldon was pretty sure of that. And he heard the usual noises you'd hear in that kind of a pileup. The groans, the screaming, the cussing. Normal stuff you don't even really register, just part of the game.

Except he thought he heard a little something else. Not a scream, not exactly. More like a sharp intake of breath, like from a quick pain, like when you had the wind knocked out of you and couldn't catch your breath, like maybe when you fell on the ball and somebody piled hard on top of you.

Just that one sound, man, a kind of deep breath. But in reverse. Like it was all going out. And he heard the fullback, Ellsworth, yelling, "Man, what's the matter? Benson? Hey, Adam, what is it, man?"

Except that was what Eldon had heard first.

Then he had heard that funny noise.

Ah, shit. Must be in his head.

You know?

But nobody had asked him anything. Beside, what did it matter? The cat was dead, man. Cold. And that noise, that sound, it was just in his mind anyway, right?

THIRTY
TWO

FOR the first time in his life, Anthony Assante was terrified.

Absolutely, positively terrified.

He had made the decision to have DeSalvo killed, and to him it was entirely logical, devoid of any emotion at all. It was a business decision, and he had made many in the years since he had ascended to second in power. This was no different. There were many credible reasons for the act. It was important that this thing take place. It would serve the best interests of many people. And so it was done.

Rico Scalzi was the perfect choice. He was more than just loyal. An order from Assante was tantamount to a commandment from heaven, and Rico was a very religious man. He was also ready to die for Assante should that be requested, for favors long owed on behalf of his parents and for providing him with an income and a job and a feeling of importance and respect.

But for some reason, which Assante could not fathom, Arthur McDonald was furious. Seldom, if ever, had Assante known him to be this angry, and it was obvious in the icy response he received when he told him that the decision had been made, the execution carried out.

"Who told you to do that?"

Short, staccato bursts of barely restrained anger, delivered in a cold fury, followed by the telephone connection being broken.

That had never happened before. Assante was terrified.

But because he had not survived these many years by allowing himself the luxury of acting foolishly or rashly, he tried to understand the anger. McDonald was overreacting. That much was obvious to Assante, who knew McDonald perhaps not well but better than any other living human being, and he never overreacted. Never.

So what was it that suddenly made him act this way? Did DeSalvo mean anything to him? No. Assante was sure of that. Was it the meeting with the advertising agency woman that McDonald did not want to cancel? Perhaps, but why? It didn't mean anything, not really. It was a front, a scam.

The fact that Assante had used Rico was of no consequence. Rico belonged to Assante. There was nothing personal there.

The quarterback? He couldn't possibly have mattered. He was simply the tool through which a small inroad to the NFL had been made, and that it turned out badly didn't change the fact that there had been a lot of money made with no way of tracing the fixes back to the key parties.

No, it was something else. Fear of the media? Never. Something personal? McDonald had no personal attachments, not to anyone or anything, and every indication through all these years was that he feared no one.

So what could have happened? Did Assante overstep his authority? Did he go beyond what was within his area of responsibility? It had never come up before.

Assante made decisions as if he had to answer only to himself, which was almost always the case.

So what had happened?

Why was the killing of Billy DeSalvo such a mistake? Why did Assante have the growing feeling that he had committed a grievous error? He had to know. He had to solve the puzzle, because it was not out of the question that his life could depend on it.

Was it something to do with Rico? He couldn't see how, because Scalzi belonged to him, to Assante. Rico's whole family did, and he was indebted to the point of giving up his life if that was requested.

Was it DeSalvo? How could it be? DeSalvo was a piece of garbage, an insect who got as far as he did with a few lucky breaks and the time-honored trick of being in the right place at the right time, of being in possession of a professional athlete at a time when they wanted to move into that market.

But DeSalvo didn't count. He was more trouble than he was worth. He was nothing. Why would anyone be so upset that it was done? That he was whacked? Why?

Getting the answer was more important than anyone else could realize.

THIRTY
THREE

A lot of otherwise secretive people, many of them members of New York's Finest, were looking for Sherri Novak. To no avail. She had vanished from her "safe house" in the middle of the night and hadn't returned.

Detective Keegan said he had no idea where she had gone, and he expressed great indignation and concern at her unexplained absence. Several telephone calls had been placed to those who were paid to know the answers to otherwise unanswerable questions, and there was no positive response to be found. Assante was livid. He had received a telephone call, and the tone in the old man's voice was at least as ominous as it had been when he inquired as to why DeSalvo was killed.

Mike Herbert got a telephone call from a man he had never spoken to but knew only too well. By reputation.

"This is Anthony Assante," said the voice. "I am interested in a person who is no longer living where we were told she was living. I understand it was you who made the arrangements. I would consider it a personal favor if you could help me find her."

Herbert felt that cold, chilling know in his gut. "Mr. Assante, I didn't know until this minute that she was no longer where we had placed her—for her own safety, of course. I don't know how she could have disappeared, but I'll find her. I'm sure there's nothing to it."

A long pause.

Then the connection was broken.

Mike Herbert had good reason to be in fear.

Keegan called Ed Buck, told him where Sherri was, told him why she had been moved, told him that the guy who had been scheduled to visit Leigh was not an advertising client and, in fact, had no connection with advertising at all. He was a known member of organized crime, and he obviously had been told to come in to scare Leigh.

Or worse.

"You're in more danger than you can imagine," Keegan said. "I would like to know you're going away somewhere. Like today."

"Gerry, I can't. What about my job?"

"What about your life?"

"OK. I get it."

"Go away, Eddie. Just take Leigh and go someplace. I'll leave a message on your answering machine. Check once a day. From a pay phone."

Buck put down the receiver, then picked it up again and dialed New Jersey Information. "Police department, Ship Bottom," he asked.

He wrote down the number, dialed.

"Do you know of a place in town where a guy could get married without a big fuss?" he asked the desk sergeant who answered.

"Yes, sir. The courthouse. It's in the police department building."

"What do I need to get it done fast?"

The sergeant chuckled. "Well, you need a license. You can get that here. You need the blood tests. You can get them here. You need to find out if they'll be open when you want them to be, and if you're thinking about any time between nine in the morning and four in the afternoon they're open."

It was Ed's turn to chuckle. "See you tomorrow," he said.

He called Leigh's office.

"Come home," he said.

"I was just leaving," she said, a catch in her voice. "I just had a frightening conversation with Drexler. I'm taking the rest of the day off."

"No, you're taking a few days off. I'll pack. I'll rent a car. We're going away."

"Where?

"Ship Bottom, New Jersey, I'm going to make an honest woman out of you, remember?"

"I'll be right there."

By four, they hit the New Jersey Turnpike, then switched to the Garden State Parkway, followed directions from the toll booth guy, and left the picturesque highway at Exit 63. Down the causeway, heading east, until greater Long Beach Island was reached.

"The man said to turn right," Leigh said.

They did, and about half an hour down the ocean road they found the St. Rita Hotel, which was actually more of a boarding house, once recommended by old friends, Mindy and Scott Rittenhouse.

They checked in. Dinner was acquired at a neat little "Jersey Shore" place called the Hook and Sinker, all seafood, heavy plastic dishes and fresh salt air supplied with every breath at no extra cost.

It was, indeed, a special pre-wedding dinner, followed by their first restful night in weeks, and at nine o'clock the next morning they showed up at the police station/courthouse/volunteer fire department.

"Oh, you must be the man who called yesterday," said Sgt. Andrew Rollo, blond and young, red-faced, and friendly. "Doc Adams will take the blood. He'll run it through the screening in an hour. We aren't real busy right now, looks like. Soon as you're cleared, Fred Hanson in the Hall of Records will issue the marriage license. Fifty bucks. Fred will also perform the ceremony. Fifty bucks more. You got a witness?"

They shook their heads.

"I'll stand up for you, sir, no charge," Andrew Rollo said, and Leigh had a feeling he actually blushed.

Leigh Crespino and Edward Buck were married at one o'clock in the afternoon. Ship Bottom police sergeant Andrew Rollo served as the best man. Fred Hanson performed the civil ceremony.

But the best thing about it was that no one knew where they were, and there were a lot of people looking.

THIRTY
FOUR

AFTER talking to his coach, Eldon St. John called Gerry Keegan.

"This is Eldon St. John," he said. "I play for the Giants and I think I have something that might help you."

"Regarding?"

"That Adam Benson thing."

"I'll meet you at the stadium."

"No, man, no good. Too many people here. You know the Grand Concourse?"

"Near the stadium?"

"Right, that's it. There's a restaurant, Livingston's, corner 161st Street and Lenox Hill Avenue. An hour."

Keegan found it, seamy and dark, with its own particular odor wafting from floor to ceiling, and then he found St. John in a booth in the back. There were three patrons at the bar, all of them telling very important secrets to their glasses of beer.

"Hi, I'm Keegan," he said, sliding in and shaking hands. "I admire your skills."

St. John shook Keegan's hand, then shook his head. "Fuck that," he said. "This isn't about football and fan shit. You ain't gettin' my autograph. This is about something I know that I know you want to know. Need to know. About the play when Benson came up dead.

I just don't want anybody to know I'm talkin' to you. I ain't spent much time in my life being sociable with the police. You understand?"

"Done."

So Eldon St. John told Keegan about the funny noise, about the sharp release of breath, about Harlan Ellsworth, the Chicago fullback, asking Benson if he was all right seconds before St. John heard that strange breathing sound.

"I won't release your name," Keegan said, "but you're going to have to sign a statement, and you may have to testify in court."

St. John nodded. "I know, I know. And I don't like it. But, man, I'll do what I have to do. But I don't want you to use my name unless we can't help it."

Again Gerry Keegan nodded. "We'll find a way to do this without you being seen. I'll prepare the statement. I'll get it ready for you to sign. Then we'll get it to you somehow. You want a lawyer to be there with you?"

"No, man. I like lawyers even less then I like cops. But how do you know what I said? How do you remember everything?"

Keegan smiled. "One of the reasons you don't like cops, Eldon. I just taped you."

Gears were meshing. The pace was picking up. Keegan could feel it. He returned to the precinct, told his superior officer, Capt. Nelson Edwards, that he had to issue an arrest warrant to hold Harlan Ellsworth of the Chicago Bears until someone from New York could get out there and question him. Keegan said that Ellsworth was the newly identified suspect in the murder of Adam Benson.

Edwards picked up the phone immediately and got the Chicago police, and the necessary steps were taken.

"Go," he said, and Keegan left the office to return home, pack a bag, and get on the next flight to Chicago.

He had one stop to make. His mother's apartment in Brooklyn. He wanted to see Sherri, not only because there were some questions he had to ask but also simply because he wanted to see her.

It would be nice to see his mom, too.

They both smiled when he opened the door, although he scowled at his mother because it had been left unlocked.

"Hi, Mom. Is Sherri being a good girl?"

Mrs. Keegan beamed. It was enough of an answer, and it implied a question, too, one that he didn't feel like addressing even to himself yet, much less his mother.

"Mom, I have to talk to Sherri. It's police business. I don't want to take her out, so could we have a little privacy?"

She beamed again. "Why don't you go into your old room?" Mrs. Keegan suggested sweetly, and that caused both Gerry and Sherri to blush, just a little.

Gerry closed the door. Sherri sat on the leather recliner, and he plopped down on the bed. She looked around and took in the old-fashioned bookcase, from which was hanging a New York Yankees banner, a baseball glove with a baseball tucked into the pocket and held forever in perfect position by a wide, thick rubber band, a trophy with the figure of an athlete leaping high and straight into nowhere.

"What's the award for, Gerry?" she asked, her voice taking on just a slightly teasing edge.

She was right. The tough guy actually blushed.

"High school basketball team," he said softly. "We won the city championship."

"But you have the trophy?"

"Well, no, the school has that trophy. I have this one."

"Why?"

"I was named the tournament's Most Valuable Player," he said, now beet red.

He had to get away from the personal questioning, so he put on his most stern face and said, "Sherri, do you know the name Harlan Ellsworth?"

"Yes. He's a football player, isn't he?"

"He is. Do you remember his name ever coming up with DeSalvo or Scalzi or McDonald? Have you ever heard it before?"

"Adam talked about him, how he really didn't like him or trust him, but how good a player he was and how much the team needed him. I don't think he trusted him much."

"How do you mean?"

"He said that Billy told him if he didn't keep cooperating, they'd get Ellsworth to do it, because he knew what was happening and he was interested in the money."

"You'll sign this? Testify to it?"

"Of course, Gerry. You don't have to ask."

Closer, closer.

"Sherri, I'm flying to Chicago in about an hour. I just have time to get to La Guardia. You stay here. Please, please stay here. Don't go anywhere; don't take any phone calls, don't do a damned thing. Just stay here. This thing might be over soon, but we'll move on from there. Do you know what I'm trying to say?"

She smiled. "Yes, I do, Gerry. I'll be here. It might be a long time before you can get rid of me."

The pace, he thought happily, was definitely picking up.

* * *

"Sergeant Keegan, I'm Randy Miller, I'm to take you directly to the precinct. I don't think it's a secret that you have set off a shit storm down there, sir."

Keegan smiled. "I take it, then, that Ellsworth has been placed under arrest?"

"Oh, yes, sir. And the owner of the team is about to have a stroke. The newspapers are all over us. The radio station, QYK, is calling everywhere, the players, the coaches, the police, even the mayor's office. Just what is going on, Sergeant, if I'm allowed to know?"

"Son, you are not allowed to know. Not yet. So why don't we just get to the house and maybe this will all get unwrapped."

"Yes, sir," he said, and Officer Miller didn't say another word during the drive from the airport to the downtown police headquarters building.

Capt. Amos Logan, a big, burly man with a weathered, wrinkled face browned by years of sun and heat, was waiting for Keegan.

"Sergeant, I've done everything your captain asked. I have had Harlan Ellsworth arrested. At the Bears' practice field, no less. I have him isolated. I have read him his rights, but he has not yet had the opportunity to seek counsel, and that's going to happen in just a short while, because we simply can't hold him like this. I'm sure you know all this."

"I do, Captain, and I appreciate the cooperation. Where is he? I have to talk to him immediately, and if it goes well then this is all over quickly."

Logan nodded and motioned for Keegan to follow.

They went to the elevator, took it down three floors, walked along a well-lighted corridor to a sign that read: LOCK UP. A guard at a gate nodded at Logan and pushed a button from inside, and the gates swung open electronically. There was a row of cells. They stopped at one that had no residents on either side of it, and there was Harlan Ellsworth, still in jeans and a Chicago Bears T-shirt, glaring at his visitors.

Logan unlocked the cell door with a key hanging from his belt loop and motioned Ellsworth outside, and the three of them walked down to another room, empty but for a long table, which was bolted to the floor, and four chairs. There were metal rings affixed to the floor and the table, to handle handcuffs or leg irons, but Ellsworth wasn't cuffed, nor was there any evidence of resistance.

Ellsworth was smoldering, a huge, muscular man with an easy athletic gait and eyes burning like black coals. "I want my lawyer," he said.

"In a minute, Harlan," said Captain Logan. "This is Sergeant Gerard Keegan from the New York City Police Department. He'd like to ask you a few questions."

"Go ahead," Ellsworth mumbled.

Logan held up his hand. "You're willing to answer questions, even without your lawyer being here?"

Ellsworth nodded.

Keegan looked at Logan, who raised an eyebrow and mouthed, "Mirandized."

"Harlan, do you know a man named Billy DeSalvo?"

"Yes."

"Do you know a man named Rico Scalzi?"

"Yes."

"Have you ever met a man named Anthony Assante?"

"Yes."

"Were you involved in a plan to fix the scores of games?"

"Yes."

"Did you kill Adam Benson?"

A pause. A last flight from hope.

Then, "Yes, I had to."

Keegan turned to Logan. "Captain, this man is to be arraigned on charges of first-degree murder in the death of Adam Benson last Sunday in New York City. He is allowed to seek legal advice, and I will ask if I can use your telephone so that we can begin extradition proceedings. The murder took place in New York. It's ours."

Logan nodded, clearly shaken.

Keegan turned back to Ellsworth, who was staring at the ground. "Harlan, you don't have to answer me, but I'd like to ask one more question for now. Why did you do it?"

Ellsworth looked up, and now his eyes weren't blazing; they were damp. Fear and realization had sunk in.

"I had to," he murmured, "or they would have killed me. I was in too deep. So was Adam; so are a dozen other guys. It was my way out, and they told me I would never get caught. Never."

Keegan nodded. "What did you kill him with, Harlan?"

"It was a long sticker thing, like an ice pick. Steel. I slipped it into my jersey, in my shoulder pads, and when we had the pileup I just reached in and slipped it out and stuck him in the chest. Somebody showed me where and how. Some big dude. Mean. Good shape. I didn't know if it would work, but it was a chance I had to take. You don't know those people, what they do, what they can do."

"Who showed you how to do it, Harlan?"

"The big guy. Rico."

"Where is the murder weapon, Harlan?"

"Man, I don't know. I threw it in the trash in the locker room when we came in. Long gone, I guess."

Indeed, long gone. But a confession in the presence of Logan as well as a detective sergeant of the New York City Police would almost certainly suffice.

Logan stared at the man. "I'll have a statement prepared, Harlan. Then you'll sign it. Right?"

"I will. I need this to be over. I didn't mind killin' the white dude. It was me or him. But these people, man, I won't be worth an hour on the street now."

Keegan wondered how long Harlan would live in jail but kept that question to himself.

THIRTY
FIVE

WHEN Keegan got to his hotel, he called Ed's apartment, waited for the recorder to pick up, and then said, "It's half-over. We arrested and charged Harlan Ellsworth with Adam's murder. He was ordered to do it, frightened into doing it, and we don't yet know who made the decision. He knew all the names we knew, met them and talked to them, but he doesn't know who's over them. Stay wherever you are. Don't come home."

It took less than twenty-four hours for the courts to clear the way for Ellsworth's transportation to New York, and Keegan was pleasantly surprised that Ellsworth's attorney, appointed by the team, was absolutely no trouble. Though Keegan had to remain in Chicago overnight, he turned down Captain Logan's invitation to take in a Bulls game. Keegan would have loved to see Michael Jordan once more, with the great athlete's retirement so close and so certain, but didn't much feel like enjoying a basketball game. He did, however, accept a dinner invitation at Eli's, one of the grand old stockyard-style steak houses in Chicago.

The next morning Ellsworth was escorted, handcuffed to a local detective, to the airport. There, officially, he was handed over, and cuffed, to Keegan and they boarded the plane for the trip east. The flight went uneventfully, without much conversation.

At one point, Ellsworth looked up and said, "I didn't want to do it, you know? I didn't care much about Benson, not either way, but I didn't want to kill him. Or anyone else. But when they told me it was going to be me if it wasn't him, man, what choice did I have?"

"You could have gone to the police. You could have done a lot of things."

"Yeah, but me and the police . . . well, no, that couldn't happen."

Keegan stared at him for a long minute. "So what do you have now, Harlan? You've got a murder rap. You knew what you were doing. You planned it. You carried it through. You are going away for life, if you're lucky, maybe even execution. You know how they do it these days, Harlan? They strap you to a cold metal table, they inject a poison so strong you're dead in three minutes, and you don't even have much time to think about how fucking sorry you were and what kind of a fucking moron you were to do it at all. You like that, Harlan? Sounds good to you? So was it worth it? Did those people scare you more than this?"

"The old guy did," he said. "I never met anybody like that. I never talked to anybody like that. Man, he, like, looked inside me and turned my shit into soup, you know?"

Carefully, slowly, Keegan asked, "What old guy? You didn't mention an old guy."

"Hey, you didn't ask me. You just asked me names, if I knew those people. This dude, that dude. And I said I did. They all . . . like . . . seemed to work for this old guy. In Los Angeles, end of last season, when we played the Rams."

"Where?"

"I don't know. Some big office building. All white,

lots of glass. Near the top floor, maybe the top floor. I don't remember. I got picked up by a limo at the hotel Saturday morning, met with this guy and DeSalvo and Rico, made our deal, and the limo took me back."

"This old guy, Harlan. What was his name?"

"McDonald. They called him Mr. McDonald."

McDonald. The guy Leigh said her boss had talked to on the phone, the one who said DeSalvo was dead and couldn't make the trip, the meeting. The guy who told Drexler what to say. McDonald. Who the hell was McDonald?

"What do you remember about him, Harlan? This is important. If you give him to us, we could do something for you. Anything is better than execution. You know what I'm saying?"

A flicker of interest. "What do I remember? Just that he was cold. I never met a man with such cold eyes. Like nobody mattered, like everybody he saw was a piece of shit. He scared me, man, and I haven't been scared since I was little and one of my mother's boyfriends used to beat on me just for fun."

The arrest of Ellsworth had become a media sensation. Keegan's name had been linked to the arrest, so he, too, was suddenly much in demand. He hated it, chose not to answer questions put to him as he left the airport, his prisoner in tow, and later when he entered and then exited the courthouse. He pleaded with his captain to assume all such duties "so that I have the time I need to work."

Ellsworth's attorney, H. Elliott Brechner, one of several on retainer to the team, came in on a later flight and checked into a midtown hotel. He was licensed to practice in the state of New York and so would remain as the player's counsel. Brechner was more than agree-

able to Keegan's request that he be given all the time
he needed to speak with Ellsworth, the obvious assumption being that all the help Harlan could provide
would probably work in his favor at the end.

For the next two days Keegan spent most of his time
with Ellsworth and Brechner. He began to see an in-
tricately woven web of corruption that led to several
players and several teams. Ellsworth incriminated eight
athletes, most of them well-known, not only on the
Bears, but also the Dallas Cowboys, Oakland Raiders,
Arizona Cardinals, Miami Dolphins, and New York
Jets. He knew most of them, and they spoke about their
situation on occasion. To the best of Ellsworth's knowledge, all the players were receiving between fifty thousand and two hundred thousand a game. All were
offensive players. All had met with DeSalvo and Scalzi
and, only once each, had been brought to a meeting
with McDonald.

"Will you identify them for the record?" Keegan
asked.

Ellsworth looked at his attorney.

"Harlan, you are facing a murder rap," Brechner
said. "They could decide to execute you. I'll give you
the best defense I can, if that's what you want. I will
plead not guilty for you. But my best advice is to take
whatever deal you can get; you won't get squat without
cooperating. Do you owe these other players your
life?"

"No. It's just me now. I'll identify them. I'll swear to
all of it."

THIRTY
SIX

GIOVANNI Impelliteri was busy on the telephone. He had lots of people to find, including Ed Buck, Leigh Crespino, the detective Keegan, Assante, Sherri Novak, and the cop Michael Herbert, who had let her slip away.

Impelliteri was in his home in Pound Ridge, New York, one of the most elegant of the posh Westchester County area. It was a ten-acre estate, guarded beyond all remote chances of an intruder getting through. The home itself, more than twenty rooms with a four-car garage, was more than one hundred years old, but everything was new, the wiring and the plumbing and the security system and even the protected telephone lines. No one got in or out physically, and no one got in or out electronically without Impelliteri knowing.

Few people lived there. The cook, the driver, the three who cleaned and kept things arranged carefully, because Impelliteri was a meticulous man whose compulsion for neatness bordered on the obsessive. He had been married, but Maria, the only woman he had ever loved, had died eighteen years ago, the cancer eating her up, it seemed, even as he watched it happen. From one day to the next she was thinner, more drawn, in greater pain. She pleaded to be set free. One day she stared up at him from her bed, from her pain, and said,

"Nanni, please let it happen; please let me go."

He nodded, cold because that's what he had trained himself to be, but not dispassionate, not uncaring, at least not for this one woman, and he smothered her. She had closed her eyes as he bent over her, and when he lifted the pillow from her face he saw peace in her expression, an almost invisible hint of a smile gently curving her mouth. She had gone off to wait for him, who knew where? He was convinced she was waiting, just as he was convinced there was something next, something beyond this adventure, and he wondered, from time to time, if his independence and strength would be rewarded in the next place or if the cruelty he had had to inflict would be punished.

No matter, there was no longer any time to think about changing, no time at all.

Maria had borne him one son. He was a handsome, strapping, strong young man now. But Maria had never known the boy had lived. While she was carrying the child, Giovanni Impelliteri decided he could not be burdened with family. He could not allow himself to be weakened by the presence of a child. It was a difficult, hard, and cold decision, but one he had to make. So much was at stake; so much else remained to be done. No strings, no hold on him. A child would be a weapon to use against him.

So he arranged for the child to be taken the night he was born. Impelliteri told the doctor to tell Maria that it had been stillborn. He paid handsomely for the favor. The doctor knew who he was, what he was, only partially, but it was sufficient knowledge to frighten him. He did as he was told. Maria wept, because she knew Giovanni hadn't wanted a child in the first place and that this was to be her only chance at motherhood. An accident, carefully planned, had taken root, taken hold.

Except now the child was dead, was born dead, and that vital part of her life was gone. There had been a funeral, incredibly well attended, and that had been the end of it.

Giovanni would not speak of it with her, forbade her from speaking of it at all, and after a while she stopped mentioning it. But she never stopped grieving, and often she sobbed herself to sleep. It became her cross, her sorrow.

The boy was taken to the family of an old friend and raised there, with two other young sons who never realized he was not their own flesh and blood.

His name was Enrico. The family name was Scalzi. Rico had never known his father. No strings, no attachments, no danger. But Giovanni had made sure, beyond all normal considerations and cautions, that Rico would be cared for and taken care of and looked after by his friend Scalzi. There was enough money in secret accounts around the world to keep Rico a rich man if he lived to be 1000. There was real estate, jewelry, stocks, and bonds. Rico Scalzi didn't know it, but he was worth in excess of $100 million. He thought old Scalzi was his father, and that was fine. Rico worshiped Assante, and that was as Impelliteri had managed things.

He watched with joy and pride as Rico grew to manhood, became part of the organization, showed courage and bravery and cunning. There were times when Impelliteri had almost told him about his history, times when he wanted Rico to know just who he was and just how proud of him his real father had grown.

But the life, the duties, the obligations . . . it all prevented such disclosure.

Until now. Rico had been summoned. He had to be told everything. Giovanni Impelliteri was furious that

Assante had involved Rico in the murder of that piece
of slime named DeSalvo. Impellteri knew that Rico
had murdered before, but those were absolutely and
totally untraceable killings. This one was too close to
the police, to the newspapers. This one had to do with
nonfamily matters. This one was too public. Giovanni
had learned long ago that when another gangster gets
himself killed nobody really cares. But when this football player had to go, when the murder was done, it
caused a public outrage. Bad enough. But now De-
Salvo, who had already been tied to it, had been killed
by Rico. That was too close.

Impelliteri was furious. He would now be forced to
do what he had never wanted to do, acknowledge to
Rico that he was more than a member of the extended
family, more than the son of an old and trusted friend.

That he, himself, was next in line.

Where to start? How to tell him? Should he be told?
What were the options? How should they be implemented? How could they be implemented at such a late
date, with so much to be explained, with a fortune ri-
valing those of the most powerful men in the world
soon to be at the disposal of this simple man?

Impelliteri loved his son, the son he had never pub-
licly embraced or privately acknowledged. But he also
realized the enormity of his responsibilities to his colleagues and to the thousands of those who worked for
him, without really knowing who he was, and to the
vast sums of money and property he had assembled
through the years.

The detective and the newspaperman were going to
continue the investigation. There would be no way to
stop them, and even killing them, which would be a
normal reaction in this situation, would not serve Impelliteri's cause. It had already become too public, too

notorious, and there was no way to stop it unless the authorities were given a guilty party.

There was only one solution, painful and final. But there was much to protect, much to preserve.

Impelliteri picked up the telephone, the one that was a single, direct-dial line and as clean as a connection could ever be, and dialed a number known only to him.

"Yes?"

It was Anthony Assante.

"You have created a situation that is unacceptable. You must now provide the solution."

"I understand."

"Who is your best man?"

"Rico."

"No."

A pause.

"Nicholas Conti."

"For certain?"

"Yes."

"Contact him. I have a contract. Immediate."

"Who?"

"Rico Scalzi."

The sharp intake of breath gave away the shock.

"It is your fault, Anthony. I will not forget it."

"I understand."

From the moment Giovanni Impelliteri put the telephone back on its cradle, Rico Scalzi was a dead man. So, too, was Anthony Assante.

But there was a difference. Assante knew it.

THIRTY
SEVEN

ASSANTE picked up the phone, hands shaking. He had been pushed to the brink of terror more than a few times. He had cried out in abject horror on three separate occasions, fortunately not in anyone's presence. Only to himself would he admit he had wet his pants once from fear, as a grown man, and he held onto that memory as a sign that never again would he allow himself to lose control.

But Impelliteri's calm, his detachment in the face of the unthinkable assignment he had just issued, the contract he had just ordered, was as cold a piece of business as this cold, cruel man had ever experienced.

He knew in his heart that when he arranged to complete this contract he, too, would be somebody's target. Nick Conti himself, perhaps. Conti, assuredly the most heartless of all the killers Assante had ever known, would have no more compunction at killing him than he would at killing Rico Scalzi or an old woman in a wheelchair or a small child skipping home from grade school. Conti was one of those rare people born without a conscience, a man who neither enjoyed nor detested the killing of another person. It was a job. His job. And he did it with remarkable and terrifying efficiency. Scalzi had killed, and killed efficiently and cleverly, but he did it out of loyalty and love for the man he viewed as his patron and protector. He probably did have a conscience. Some of the deaths he administered certainly must have caused him remorse.

Assante dialed a number known only to a few. There were the usual four rings, then a click, then a recorded message.

"Try your party at the fifth number," it said.

Assante knew all eight numbers by heart. He redialed a number that, like all the others, was totally untraceable. It rang once.

"Yes?"

"This is Assante."

"Yes?"

"I have a contract for you."

"How much?"

Assante noted that the first question was not "who?" but "how much?"

"One hundred thousand."

"Acceptable. Who is it?"

"Rico Scalzi."

"When?"

"Now."

"It's done. And, Anthony, are you sure he would approve?"

Assante knew what Conti meant. "Nick, he is the one who issued the contract."

"It's done. Payment in the usual manner?"

"Yes. It will be done today."

Both ends of the connection went dead.

Assante would wire the money to the Cayman National Bank in Grand Cayman Island, to a numbered account accessible only by one person. Nick Conti. When Assante received confirmation that it had been done, by calling a man at the bank, J. C. Calhoun, who was the best he had ever known at keeping secrets, he would fulfill his part of the bargain—neatly, cleanly, and ruthlessly.

Now Anthony Assante had to see about his own safety.

He picked up the telephone again and dialed another number plucked from memory. All his life he had been able to remember telephone numbers, bank account numbers, anything to do with numbers, and if he had ever dialed a number even once it was somehow recorded in his mind's Rolodex.

"Who is it?"

"Rico, this is Anthony Assante."

"It is my pleasure to hear from you. How may I help you?"

"Leave. Leave now. Go away. Do not return. Do you still have that bank account in Grand Cayman?"

"Yes."

"I will put money in it. Go away. It is important that no one knows where you are. Even me. Contact me in a month."

"This is all right with the don?"

"It is his instruction."

"Then I am gone."

Assante rang off, to pick up the receiver a moment later and dial yet another number.

"Yeah?"

"This is Assante. I want to talk to the commissioner."

"Yes, sir. Hold on, please."

If Nick Conti found Rico Scalzi before Rico got away, so be it. There was nothing further Assante could do. More to the point, he had just sealed his own fate. But by bartering everything he knew about the transactions and businesses run by this one particular subject, Assante would become a most important person and would, as such, be protected, hidden, made comfortable for the rest of his life, and, most important, taken out of the spotlight.

He had just arranged for whatever remained of his life to be spent in hiding or under constant surveillance, but it would provide a far longer life than had he done nothing. He was among the walking dead.

"Mr. Assante? This is James Fox."

"Commissioner, I would like to arrange a meeting. I have some information you have wanted for years."

"At your convenience."

"Today. Your office. Three o'clock. I know there is a side door to the building. I will enter that way."

"We'll be waiting, and you will be safe."

"I would expect nothing less, Commissioner. I am about to make you a famous man."

It was done.

THIRTY
EIGHT

CAPT. Nelson Edwards got a call moments later. "It's from Commissioner Fox," said the desk sergeant.

"I'll take it in my office." Edwards snapped, striding to his glassed-in cubicle, closing the door, and sitting down before picking up the phone. The rare occasions when Fox had called him directly always required him to be sitting.

"Yes, Commissioner. This is Nelson Edwards. How can I help?"

"Good afternoon, Captain. I would like you here, at my office, at two-thirty today. With Detective Keegan."

"Yes, sir. May I ask why?"

"No."

"We'll be there, sir."

Keegan was somewhat disturbed at the command performance. "I had an interview set up for today," he said.

"It's the commissioner; he wants us there and we'll be there," Edwards replied. "There is absolutely no question in my mind that we will be there. And we will go there together, so I won't worry that one of us might forget to attend."

"Damn it, Captain, I just—"

"Forget it, Gerry. It's not up for discussion."

Keegan went back to his desk and phoned his

mother's house. "Hi, Mom; is Sherri there?"

"Yes, Joseph," she said. "Hold on. She's right here. We were talking."

He smiled.

"Hi, Joseph," she said, brightly.

Her, too? He smiled.

"Sherri, I can't see you later. I have to be at the police commissioner's, and I don't know how long it's going to take."

"Sounds important."

"These things are usually the opposite. He's going to tell us just how important it is that we get a quick solution to this case, that the newspapers and television stations are all over his back, that the whole country is making fun of New York City because we lost a player on the field during the game and we don't even know how or why it happened. He is going to, as they say, read us the riot act and we will look ashamed and nod politely and tell him we'll try to do better and that we have several promising leads."

"Do you?"

"Well, the player, Ellsworth, has admitted to the killing. That we have. But he doesn't know who ordered it. We have no record of a guy named McDonald. The office building Ellsworth said he was taken to in Los Angeles is owned by the Fuji Corporation, for God's sake, and the suite rented to McDonald Enterprises is paid for the full year, every year, with a check from Holiday Business, Inc., which has no individual owners or officers, as far as we can determine, and which in turn leases it to McDonald Enterprises. It's a shell corporation, impossible to trace."

"So you don't know who McDonald is?"

"No, we don't. You're probably one of only two or

three people who have ever met him, and you don't have a clue, either, do you?"

"No."

"So we have the guy who admits murdering Adam. He told us how. It fits. He said he threw the weapon in the trash in the locker room and it went out with the garbage that night, lost forever. That fits. Why did he do it? Because he was being threatened with exposure for fixing games, because they told him if he didn't do it he'd stop getting all that extra money, because he's a bad guy to start with and I hope they find him hanging in his cell someday after he's convicted. But who ordered it? Why? How the scheme was implemented? We don't know shit."

"You'll find it, Gerry. I know you will."

"Yeah. I hope so. Listen; I'll talk to you as soon as I get finished."

"I'll be here." She paused, and it seemed like a long time. "Honey," she added.

Then Keegan dialed his own apartment, accessed the answering machine, and listened to the newly married Ed Buck.

"Gerry, damn it, I need to come home. My office is on my ass about taking this sudden honeymoon vacation. I'm losing my fucking mind out here and I can't eat any more fish. Leigh is being brave, but she is going nuts, too. She hasn't called her office, like you said, but she would like to get back to work.

"I heard about Ellsworth. He admitted it, right? So it's over, right? Damn it, Gerry, get us out of here."

Keegan smiled. He called the Bucks' answering machine.

"Not yet, children," he said. "But soon. Meanwhile, enjoy."

Then he went off to the meeting that he had no choice but to attend.

He arrived with Captain Nelson at two-thirty, as ordered. Commissioner Fox was seated behind his desk when the uniformed cop, a guy Keegan knew named Halloran, ushered them in.

"Leave us, Tommy," Fox said.

Halloran disappeared.

Fox looked at them, then began speaking. "In about twenty-five minutes, an old man will be joining us," he said. "He is almost seventy-five years old and, to our knowledge, he is the most influential and important man in organized crime. His name is Anthony Assante."

"Jesus Christ," Nelson murmured, totally unaware that he had spoken. "Assante? Jesus Christ. What's he doing here? And why is he showing up? Is he under arrest? Am I losing my mind?"

Commissioner Fox managed a wan smile. "He says he has information we have wanted for a long time. He says he is ready to give it to us."

"Damned right he has information," Nelson said. "It could take weeks to get everything out of that old son of a bitch. He has his fingers on everything. Everything. We can tie a dozen murders to that cocksucker alone. Drugs, gambling, prostitution, bank fraud, money laundering . . . should I go on? He's got it all, probably in his head. What the hell has scared him this much?"

Keegan, who had remained silent, spoke one word: "McDonald."

"Who?" Both men asked it at once.

"Arthur McDonald. The man Sherri Novak said she was taken to meet once. The same guy Harlan Ellsworth said he was taken to see. Except he's not McDonald. There is no record of this guy named

McDonald. Nowhere. Not in any of our case files. None of our sources know him or anything about him. There is an office in Los Angeles called McDonald Enterprises. Doesn't exist. Rent is paid by the year, 200 grand a year, from the checkbook of a dummy corporation. For all we know, Arthur McDonald could be the president of the United States or the pope or Leonardo DiCaprio. But he sure has scared the shit out of Anthony Assante, hasn't he?"

There was a quiet rap on the door. "Come," said Fox. Tommy Halloran, pale, led a small old man into the room.

He looked at the three men present.

"Good afternoon, gentlemen," he said. "I am Anthony Assante."

He sat.

"I have come without an attorney and without a driver. I am alone. I am totally and completely in your control and under your protection. Have I made myself clear?"

"Yes, Mr. Assante," said Fox. "What is it you want to share with us?"

"Everything. Fifty years of everything I have ever been involved with, but there is a price."

"Of course there is. What did you have in mind?"

Assante smiled, and it was a sad, old man's smile. "I want complete privacy. I want an identity, all the money I can free up without a single question being asked. I want to leave the country, and I do not intend to tell anyone where I am going. I will ask that you arrange my departure and that, when this is all finished, all the records and transcriptions and tapes are erased or destroyed. I will give you everything."

"We accept," the commissioner said. "Where would you like to start?"

A pause. Assante took a deep breath and stared at the three men, each in turn, hard, cold eyes reading their thoughts.

"I will start with a man named Arthur McDonald," he said. "His real name is Giovanni Impelliteri, and he is one thousand times more important in this world of organized crime than anyone else."

THIRTY NINE

ED put the phone down, looked at Leigh, and shook his head. "Not yet," he said. "It sounds like it's getting closer, but not yet. I don't know how much more I can take, babe. What about you?"

"I think we should do what Gerry says," she said, tan because of their almost-constant walks along the deserted beaches despite the fact that it was November, albeit a mild, warm November. "I'm afraid of these people. Eddie, and I don't want to risk what we have. Not now. Not ever."

"Yeah, I know. But, Leigh, what do I do about my job? I can't be on a honeymoon forever, especially since it was such an unexpected thing to do. I have responsibilities. I have to do something."

"Tomorrow. Let's talk tomorrow. Not tonight. Let's go to that Italian place for dinner tonight, OK? Down the road, on the corner. What's it called? Raymond's? Let's, Ed. It might be our last night here. I know you want to go back, and I don't think there's going to be a way I can stop you."

He smiled. Relaxed. Reached for her.

"Let's don't get dressed just yet," he said as they tumbled on the bed in the suite of the St. Rita. "There are a few things I haven't shown you yet."

She smiled. "And just imagine how many things

there are I still have to show you, darling."

He feigned anger but couldn't hold it and broke into laughter instead. "Yeah, right. Well, here's your chance."

There was very little speaking for a long time after that, just the whispers and murmured words that two people dramatically in love share with each other and no one else, never anyone else. And then they were in each other's arms, nearly asleep, just drowsing in that warm, insulated feeling that comes only sometimes, even with people so in love.

"Pretty good," he said. "I think you have a lot of potential."

"Mmmmmm, and I'm glad of it, you know?"

They dressed and walked the six blocks or so in the fading daylight, the weather chilly but not cold, to the little restaurant they had grown to like a lot more than the all-seafood joint with the plastic plates and the greasy fries.

They had stopped at the liquor store a block before the restaurant. Raymond's was a BYOB place, and for less than ten bucks they got bottle of a superb Pinot Noir. It was a special night, a special meal, and they both knew it was their last one on this island, in this comfortable place that had served as a honeymoon and a retreat and, more than they knew, a safe haven.

Dinner was concluded before nine, and a casual stroll back to the St. Rita put a perfect punctuation point on the night.

"Leigh, we have to go tomorrow; we have to. I'm going to go back to work. I'm not going to listen to Gerry. Adam was murdered, and they found out who did it. I'll let the guys who know how to do it find out who ordered it, why it was done, all that. But we're going home."

She nodded her head, though in the dark he couldn't see it. "I understand and I guess I agree," she said. "We're married, and we have to do this together. We can't hide and run scared. I won't go back to work for Drexler. He's dirty. He's weak. I couldn't possibly trust him again, and I think Gerry has already contacted him. So yes, we'll go back tomorrow."

They went upstairs, to their second-floor nest and decided to throw things into the suitcases, everything except what they'd need for the morning. That didn't take long. Ed carried the two suitcases downstairs to the rented car, unlocked the trunk, and deposited them. They'd leave early. Get to Manhattan by ten, unpack, sort things out, and be ready for work the next day.

It was only when he was returning to the entrance of the St. Rita that he saw, from the corner of his eye, a white piece of paper, torn from a spiral notebook, under the windshield wiper of the rented car.

He took it. Scrawled in crayoned block letters were the words:

DON'T START THE CAR. CALL THE POLICE.

FORTY

ED carried the piece of paper into the room and held it out for Leigh to see. Then he called the Ship Bottom police, asked for Sgt. Andrew Rollo.

"This is Rollo."

"This is Ed Buck, Sergeant. You stood up for us at our wedding the other day?"

"Oh, yes. How are you, Mr. Buck? Surprised you're still here."

"Sergeant, I need to see someone. Right now. I'm at the St. Rita."

The policeman noted the urgency, something just short of panic, in Ed's voice. "I'll be right there."

"We'll be waiting outside, next to a gray Buick, with New York tags."

"Fine. Three minutes."

And it was probably three minutes exactly when a cruiser pulled up, lights flashing but no siren waking the neighborhood. Rollo stepped out and approached them.

"What's the problem?"

"This is." Ed handed him the paper. "It was on the windshield. It wasn't there at six when we went to dinner. It was there at ten, when we came back."

Rollo paled. Then he walked back to his car, picked up the radiophone, and called the station. "This is

Rollo," he said. "I need the bomb squad here. Now. St. Rita Hotel. Gray Buick."

He returned to Ed and Leigh, huddled against the oncoming chill of the night, a biting wind slicing in off the ocean. "Somebody will be right here," he said. "Let's go sit in my car. It's warm," he offered, glancing at Leigh, who was trembling, though he wasn't sure whether it was from fear or the cold. "Is there somebody you want me to call?"

"Yes," Ed said. "Detective Sergeant Joseph Keegan, New York City, Seventeenth Precinct. Just tell him it's me. He knows we're here. And if he isn't in, tell the switchboard operator to find him. Tell him it has to do with the case he's working on."

Keegan was in. He told Rollo not to touch anything, not to allow the Ship Bottom police to tinker with whatever explosive device was found in the car. That brought a mild protest, quickly squashed when Keegan said it was part of a murder investigation and anyone who touched the car would be guilty of compromising possible evidence. Even Rollo's boss, Chief Bill Hudson, who had already shown up at the scene, agreed. "We'll leave it the way it is, Detective," he said. "But get somebody down here fast. I don't like the idea of a bomb in a car parked next to one of our hotels."

"Already on their way, Chief, and thanks," said Keegan.

And about an hour later, a bomb unit truck and an unmarked New York police car were screeching to a halt next to the small crowd gathered at the St. Rita. Keegan was in the unmarked car, and first he went to Ed and Leigh.

"You guys all right?"

"Yeah, just scared to death," Leigh said. Ed just nodded.

"Not to worry. Whatever there is, we'll find it. You've got a ride home. Now. Not tomorrow. Go upstairs and get the rest of your stuff."

When they emerged again, the car's hood was up. Two men were on sliders underneath the chassis, bright floodlights illuminating their efforts. Two more had their heads in the engine. A fifth was kneeling next to an open door, slowly checking the seats, the steering column, anywhere and everywhere a small amount of explosive could be secreted, because combined with the explosion of the gasoline in the car's tank not much was needed to incinerate those in the auto.

The skilled team went through everything, from the starter to the fuel pump, from the cables leading to the battery to the wiring needed to activate the radio, the cassette deck, and the CD player. The seat cushions were pulled out, eliminating the possibility of pressure-sensitive detonators. The underchassis search proved equally empty. The driveshaft was clean.

But not the brake pads. Once the car got up to fifty miles an hour, the Bucks would have been gone—instantly, blindingly, unavoidably.

The bomb unit's leader, Boomer Reilly, nodded. "If you ask me, these people have really pissed off somebody important."

"Yeah. But with the note being found, somebody was telling them to be careful, to be aware that they had been found. Whoever wrote the note wasn't an enemy, yet I don't think he was a friend."

The device was disconnected, five ounces of plastic explosive that would have triggered the gas tank like a Fourth of July firecracker. The police would tow the car back to New York, check it over, dust for fingerprints that no one expected to find, and then call the rental company to take possession.

The Bucks drove home with Keegan. "I didn't want you coming back yet," he said, "but somebody obviously knows where you are, so it doesn't make much difference. I'll have people with you around-the-clock."

"Gerry, what's going on? Ellsworth confessed, right? He did it, right? You've got him. It's over. Why would somebody want to kill us now?"

"I don't know for sure, but no, it's not over," Keegan said, shaking his head, watching as the Garden State Parkway came closer to turning into the New Jersey Turnpike. "We got the mechanic, we don't have the guy who ordered it, and we don't know exactly why, except that Benson wanted out, and now we have at least a dozen guys in the National Football League who are doing the same thing. Ellsworth'll turn them in. He's looking for some kind of break, and he'll probably get something.

"But we need to know who, and why, and how. And you two are right in the middle of it, I'm afraid. You are the ones who blew the first whistle. This is very big. This afternoon a man named Anthony Assante, a man so important he called the private telephone number of Commissioner Fox, dialed it and just told him he wanted a meeting. I can't tell you everything, but he turned on a man we only suspected even existed, maybe the biggest catch in the history of organized crime."

"The McDonald guy?" Ed asked.

"Yeah, but it isn't McDonald. That's a cover. The guy's whole life has been a cover. We aren't even sure who he started out being, but the McDonald story covers a guy named Giovanni Impelliteri, once known as Johnny Imp, except our records say that he has been dead a long time now. Assante is giving him to us because he's afraid for his life. He says there are about five people in the world who know McDonald's real name, who know the whole thing. He owns half the fucking United States, and it's getting more and more fuzzy every day.

"There's a son, a son who doesn't know he's the guy's son, and he works for him, for God's sake. He was taken away as an infant and brought up by one of Impelliteri's oldest friends. Nobody knows why, exactly, but he keeps going. He doesn't need money, he doesn't have many, if any, friends, and the closest to that was this guy Assante, and they worked together for damned near fifty years before this suddenly fell apart.

"Why? Because Assante was in charge of the pro football deal, because he assigned Impelliteri's 'secret son,' some goon named Rico Scalzi, to off the little worm DeSalvo and now Impelliteri thinks it has put him in a compromising position. So he has ordered a hit on his son and Assante figures he isn't far behind. He's right, of course, which is why he came in."

Ed thought. "God, what a great story," he finally said. "It's mine, isn't it?"

Keegan smiled. "Yeah, it's yours. Tell me something; aren't you even a little bit scared?"

"Shit, yes. I'm scared to death. But the best way to get past being afraid is to go right at the fear. It's an old football thing, maybe. Like you go right at the other team's best defensive lineman to get your running game working. If you defeat him, the rest of them give up. It works."

Leigh fell asleep on Ed's shoulder as they cut through the darkness, stirring when the car passed the vile stench generated by the chemical and gasoline refineries at Exit 13 of the Turnpike. "I have a friend who lives in one of the nicest parts of the country, right here in New Jersey," Keegan said. "Right on the ocean, quiet little town, nothing but money, and he says that he loves it when people think the state is made up of the Turnpike, a connection between New York City and Philly, and this exit. Keeps away the riffraff, so to speak."

FORTY ONE

IMPELLITERI knew that Assante had turned. He had expected it, because Anthony was smart enough to know that a hit on Rico was a hit on himself as well. Impelliteri knew that a first meeting had already been held, and he was as sure as anything in the world that he had been named, had been delivered to the police. He knew that Nick Conti had been paid and the hit had been put in motion. He knew that the Novak girl had been spirited away from the safe house near Gracie Mansion and he was in the process of locating her again. He knew that Buck and the woman had left New York, because he knew they had rented a car. He assumed from that they planned a somewhat local destination; one does not rent a car to drive to an airport.

Impelliteri knew all these things and more. He knew that the black, the football player, had been arrested and brought to New York and formally charged with the murder of the other football player. Everyone knew that. It was impossible not to hear that story, told and retold and on and on and on. He knew, further, that Ellsworth knew nothing more than what he had been told and all that added up to nothing. He knew that the detective had discovered the method of murder, although, of course, not the weapon. He knew the professional football thing was over, absolutely and positively.

But Assante had turned. He had walked into the arms of the police and made his deal. He had given them everything, most especially the name.

He knew all this and he knew one thing more. For the last time in his life, he would have to disappear. Arthur McDonald, now unmasked, was going to have to be found dead. He had enough money secreted around the world to live out his years in great comfort, and because of the wealth he would find people to protect him, to hide him. They all wanted a piece of the fortune. It had always been easy to deal with people, because if you had money, you had what they wanted.

He would rescind the contract, if he could. He would let Rico live without ever knowing the truth. But he could not. Conti was never reachable when he was on an assignment. To be able to be contacted would compromise his anonymity, and Nick Conti was the consummate professional. Of all the things Impelliteri had done with no thought or conscience, issuing the contract on his son was the only one that hurt him. He was logical enough to see the wisdom in it. There were few men who would understand the need. But logic, which had always ruled his life, along with a ruthless determination to succeed, was suddenly being tweaked by passion.

It surprised him, somewhat, to know he still had the ability to feel. He thought of Maria and what she would say when they were together again. He thought of Rico, who would also be there, waiting, accusing. Giovanni had always thought that the next life, or the afterlife, would be one of joy. This would not accomplish that.

He reached for the telephone and dialed Rico's number. There was no answer, nor was there an answering machine. He dialed again, to be sure he had not erred, but there was no answer again after ten rings.

So he dialed another number. A man at an airport in Newark he had bought a long, long time ago, a man whose job was important, a man who was influential and able to override all the petty airport/airline rules and regulations.

The man answered on the first ring.

"This is your friend from New York, I need a favor."

"Name it."

"I want to find a traveler. He probably left last night, or early today. There are three possible names. Rico Scalzi. Rick Stone. Michael Prince. It is very important."

"Hold on."

A pause.

He heard the faint sound of fingers hitting keyboard strokes, a short beeping sound, then another. Then a repeat of the combination.

"Sir, I have Rico Scalzi. He left New York last night, from La Guardia. He went to Fort Lauderdale."

He had been warned, probably by Assante. Good. It was something his father should have done.

"Thank you. I am in your debt."

Another call.

"Yes?"

"I would like to speak to Angelo."

"This is Angelo. Who is this?"

"Your friend from New York."

Silence. Then, "It is my honor that you have called. How may I help you?"

"Rico arrived last night in Fort Lauderdale. Track him. Find him, but do not let him know. Then guard him."

"Yes."

"This is of the greatest importance. If anything happens to him, it will be on your head."

"I understand."

"Nicholas Conti is looking for him."

"Sweet Jesus. I understand."

Giovanni placed the phone back in its cradle. Angelo Bartoli would find Rico and would put enough people between him and the assassin. He would save Giovanni's son. He was very good at things like this, which was why he was given the South Florida area as his own. Rico was probably headed to the Keys, not to Miami Beach, where his mother lived. He would not do that. He would not bring anything on his mother. Giovanni knew that Rico had purchased a house a long time ago well down the road to Key West, on Little Duck Key, quiet, protected, with limited access. It would be difficult for Conti to reach him; conversely, it would be difficult for Rico to get off the key if Conti did get through.

But Bartoli's men would almost certainly stop Conti. And if he had to be killed, it was long overdue anyway.

FORTY
TWO

RICO never left New York. He knew, felt, that something was wrong. So he did what he had been taught and what he probably never had been taught as well, which was to act defensively, turn on the trouble and surprise it.

He bought the ticket for Fort Lauderdale and gave it to a friend. It was the first thing they would look for and, having found a record, the single greatest subterfuge possible, one that would convince them he had acted just as Assante had suggested, that he had done just what they wanted him to do.

Instead, having rented a car the morning after the flight, he drove upstate New York, to a town named Corning-on-Hudson, where he owned a small cabin no one knew about. No one. He spent two days there, waiting. Then he drove back, timing his return so that he would arrive just after midnight in Pound Ridge—at the home of Giovanni Impelliteri.

There was no problem gaining access. The guards knew him. He was one of the two or three most important people in the organization. No one would question his sudden appearance, even at such an unusual time. When the leader of the bodyguard team offered to notify Mr. McDonald that Rico had arrived, there was no disagreement.

"Yeah, good idea," he said. "We don't want to surprise him in his sleep."

The man looked at him. "Rico, house rules. I have to search you."

Scalzi smiled. "Of course you do. I would have turned you in if you didn't." He calmly lifted his hands over his head, spread his legs, and allowed himself to be frisked. There would be nothing found. He had learned a long time ago that he needed nothing more than his two hands, if murder was on his mind.

"He says to wait upstairs for him, in the sitting room," the man said, returning the in-house telephone handset to its hook on the wall. "I'll show you."

"I know the way," Rico replied, still smiling. "I've been here before."

"No, I'll show you."

Another smile. "Sure, Frankie. I understand. It's your job."

He was led to the sitting room. Frankie indicated he would wait with him until McDonald arrived. Once again, Rico had no problem. He sat on a large overstuffed armchair, crossed his legs, and tried to make small talk.

"Tough job, being on the road at this hour of the night." He smiled. "But you know how it is. You do what you're told to do."

Frankie nodded. "Yeah, all the time. No choice."

They heard the old man enter, and he looked as if he had just walked in from a night on the town, aside from the fact that he was wearing a bathrobe and leather slippers. His hair was tightly combed. His eyes were alive, his moves belying the truth his age told.

"Rico, Rico, what a pleasure," he said.

Rico rose, approached the old man, dropped to one knee, and lightly touched the hand offered by Mc-

Donald, who turned to the guard. "Frankie, leave us," he said, and took a seat facing Rico, who had returned to the upholstered armchair. Impelliteri's sense of poise and grace impeccable, he smiled benignly. "What brought you here, Rico? What can I do for you?"

"Why did you put a contract out on me, Giovanni?"

That startled the old man. In one sentence, Rico Scalzi had told him two things he wasn't supposed to know, Impelliteri's real name and that he knew about the Conti contract.

"What are you talking about?" Impelliteri asked, allowing his voice to remain calm.

"Don't treat me like a fool, I'm your son. Assante told me to leave, but he didn't tell me why. He didn't have to tell me. I knew when I got the call. Why?"

Reacting as if he had just taken a blow to the stomach, Impelliteri began to crumble, to lose his composure. "My son? Contract? Rico, Rico, what has happened to you?"

"My mother . . . my real mother . . . found out what happened, what you had done. She knew. For the last fifteen years of her life, she knew. And she never told you. But she told me. I knew. I loved Maria Scalzi as if she had been my mother, but I loved my mother as well, my real mother. Your wife. I didn't see her much, because you would have known. I wanted to tell you I knew, a hundred times, but I didn't. I knew you had reasons, had to have reasons. It was my life, my place in the family. I was grateful for what I had."

He didn't think there were actual tears in his eyes, but he did feel an unaccustomed dampness.

"But you put out a contract on me. With Nick Conti. To have your own son killed, that is something I cannot understand. You tell me why."

It was really at an end, all the lying and the pretense. What to say? What to do?

"It was business, Rico, foolish business. When Assante had you execute that piece of shit, that DeSalvo, he involved you more than he should have, more than was safe. The football player was a mistake; the project was a mistake. We made a lot of money, yes, but it was a mistake nevertheless. You don't know the size of the organization, the amount of money, the responsibilities and the obligations, and the impossible need to act coldly, ruthlessly. It was the most efficient way. I am sorry, truly, truly sorry, for having made that decision. I will call it off. I have already tried to do that."

"You can't stop Conti," Rico said.

"But he can be killed," Impelliteri replied. "I have spoken to our man in Florida. He has people surrounding your home on Little Duck Key. Yes. I know. I have made sure to keep up with everything you have done, all your life. And I am proud of you, Rico. I don't think you can believe that, and I know you can never love me as your father, because no father would ever have done what I did. But I am proud of you, and now I am in your hands, at your mercy. What will you do?"

Rico thought about that. He got up, walked to the bar against the wall behind his father, and poured scotch, straight, no ice, no water, into a tumbler. He walked back to his chair, swirling the drink, staring at the amber liquid as if searching for an answer.

Finally he spoke, looking up, staring straight at Impelliteri.

"Nothing."

"Nothing. What do you mean, nothing?"

"I plan to do nothing, Father. I am going to leave. I am going to disappear. No one will ever find me, not even you. I have prepared many identities, homes, ready cash. I will never be found. Rico Scalzi will no longer exist. Or Arthur McDonald. I have no mother now. I have no father. I have no identity."

The overwhelming sadness penetrated Impelliteri's normally stone-cold shell. "You are my son. I would like to know there is still something we can have together."

"No, there is not," Rico said solemnly. "It is much too late for anything like that. We have never been father and son, although I wanted it from the moment I learned the truth. I waited for you to tell me, to open your heart. You chose not to include me in any part of your life, not even to acknowledge that I was your son. I accepted that. But it hardened me, Father. I cannot go back. I cannot go where I have never been."

He rose to leave.

"Is there nothing I can do, then?" Giovanni asked. "Is there no way to save any of this? It was all my fault, my mistake. Is there anything I can do now?"

Rico, towering above his aging father, nodded his head. "There is one thing," he said.

"What is it?" the old man asked, grasping at this proffered straw.

"You can die for me," Rico Scalzi said, withdrawing a small pistol successfully hidden from the cursory pat-down administered by those who knew and feared him. "You can die for all the pain and suffering you brought to my mother, not for anything else. Just for her."

Then, calmly, he shot Giovanni Impelliteri in the forehead. One bullet, penetrating the brain. The most powerful man in organized crime was dead before he could blink, dead well before his crumpled body softly struck the carpeted floor.

Rico closed the door behind him quietly, not once

looking back, and walked down the staircase. He nodded at the chief of the bodyguard unit.

"The old man went back to sleep," Rico said. "I would leave him alone. He looked very tired. Even I hated to bother him, but it was important."

Frankie nodded, aghast at the thought of bothering this powerful old man. "No problem," he said. "The morning crew will wake him at the usual time. He usually sleeps until ten these days."

Rico nodded. "Thanks, Frankie. See you around. Oh, Frankie, you missed something before."

"What?"

"This," he said, taking the small pistol from his jacket pocket and shooting the guard, just once. Once was enough, and Rico wanted the noise to bring the other two men running. It did. They were dead two shots later. The morning staff would find the three dead men downstairs and the most important dead man they will have ever found upstairs in the sitting room of one of the most expensive safe houses in all of Westchester County. As things turned out, however, it wasn't quite as safe as advertised. The son of the most powerful man in organized crime had had no trouble penetrating all the protective devices and ending the reign of the man who lived there surrounded by secrets.

FORTY
THREE

NICK Conti arrived at Miami International Airport early in the morning. He rented a car, using one of the dozens of credit cards in his possession, along with one of the dozens of driver's licenses, this one identifying him as Mark Pearl of Des Moines, Iowa.

He knew the way, leaving the rental lot, turning left on Biscayne Boulevard, then left again, then right on 836. Soon after that he found himself on the Florida Turnpike, and that flowed into southbound Route 1, the only road access in and out of that special area of the state of Florida called the Keys.

They sped by, Key Largo turning into Marathon Key, to Tavernier Key, to Islamorada, and finally to one of the smaller ones, Little Duck Key, a high-income, low-profile spit of land surrounded by water. It was one of the most expensive sites in the United States as well as one of the most secure and relatively unknown. Men from New York and New Jersey, from Philadelphia and Atlanta, from as far west as Chicago and Kansas City and Dallas, had acquired property on Little Duck Key years ago. It was a haven. It was possible to register ownership under corporate names or false names. The homes were Caribbean-style—meaning tropical elegance. Open verandas led to giant heated pools, to boat slips and second-floor master bedrooms under a canopy of retractable glass. Tiled kitchens, from floor to walls to counters. Living rooms and dens that stared out into the Atlantic.

Rico's home, bought with cash and owned by Americo Impelliteri Enterprises, sat at the end of the key, with nothing around it but water on three sides. This morning the water was particularly blue, azure blue, reflecting white-fluffed clouds chasing each other across eternal skies. There was a staff, full-time and well paid, composed of those who knew nothing about the home's owner and those who knew almost everything. The latter group, of course, was in charge. His privacy was their first priority. They kept secrets the old-fashioned way: they would die before relinquishing any information to anyone.

It was the biggest estate on the key, located at 1 Tarpon Run, stupendous in white stucco and white brick. A magnificent property, valued together with the land and the home on it at more than $10 million.

This morning, while its owner was still in New York, a visitor arrived. The man in the gatehouse at the entrance to the residential portion of Little Duck Key politely asked for identification, and Mr. Mark Pearl of Des Moines, Iowa, eagerly presented his driver's license.

"Sure is pretty here," he said.

"Where are you going?" asked the guard.

"To see my friend Rico. He lives here."

"Rico who?"

"Rico Scalzi," said Nick Conti.

The man shook his head. "No Scalzi here. Maybe you have the wrong key."

"This is Little Duck Key?"

"Yep, but no Scalzi. Here, see for yourself." He held out a two-page list of names of those who owned the homes on Little Duck Key. Conti, confused, scanned them, and one popped up as if it had suddenly become alive.

And lethal.

"Rico Impelliteri?" he asked out loud, but to himself. "Impelliteri? Who the hell is Impelliteri?"

The guard smiled, although not benignly. "Maybe it was the gentleman who called last night from Fort Lauderdale and told us you might be coming our way, Nicholas Conti. Maybe it was that man."

Before Nick could reach for the Walther-PPK in his shoulder holster, the passenger side door was pulled open and hands grabbed his arm. Big, strong, hairy hands.

"You'd better come with us, sir," said the man, who might have been banned from the NFL for being too big or for having too many muscles. "And I think that maybe you'd better do it quietly."

Conti relaxed every muscle. This was not the time for bravery. He nodded and stepped out of the car, and the guard held a gun on him, the muzzle pointed at his face and only a foot away. The biggest man Nick Conti ever saw slid across and drove the car up one of the winding roads on Little Duck Key. Conti was left standing just outside the gatehouse, the guard still inside, the gun pointed directly at his face.

"Many of us have respected you for years, admired you, and tried to be like you. I am glad to have the chance to meet you, Nick Conti," the guard said.

"Thank you. Is there anything I can do to change your mind? Is there enough money to let me get back in my car and drive out of here? Or just walk out of here and hitch a ride?"

The man didn't respond. He looked as if he was deep in thought. Finally, sadly, he shook his head.

"There probably is enough money, Nick," he said, "but there would be no way I'd have a chance to spend it. All the big guys want you. They are all looking for you."

"All of them?"

"Yes. Assante pulled the contract. You know what that means."

Nick nodded.

He offered no resistance as the man led him to the rear of the gatehouse, nor did he have any regrets when the bullet from the .38 special, its sound nearly inaudible, tore through the side of his head.

The contract on Rico Scalzi had been canceled.

FORTY
FOUR

ANTHONY Assante was shaken, ashen.

"Impelliteri is dead? How?"

Police Commissioner James Fox nodded. "He was shot. Once through the forehead. He was found this morning by a man we are holding for his own protection. Three men downstairs were found dead, too. Each shot once. There were no witnesses; we found no fingerprints, nothing. Someone came in and did it, then left and didn't leave a clue."

They were together in Fox's office on Varick Street, not the normal public display office up near Gracie Mansion but the place where Fox did most of his work, away from prying eyes and media attention. It was sparsely furnished, mostly in government-issue metal-and-wood desks and chairs, gray filing cabinets, standard-issue telephones. A working office, stripped of the trappings of a man of his importance and stature.

"Rico Scalzi," said Assante, quietly, while feeling his immunity slipping away. If there was no Impelliteri-McDonald, then he would not be needed as much. Oh, sure, there were mysteries to unravel, crimes to be solved by putting a name to the deed, but without McDonald, without Assante's willingness to testify, there were significantly fewer reasons for the police and the Feds to need him.

"Who?" Fox asked.

"Scalzi. Rico Scalzi. He killed DeSalvo. I told you that. He was always close to the top. He was my lieutenant. Giovanni liked him, liked him a lot. His father was one of the best plate men in the world. You know, plates? Money? Stocks? Counterfeit stuff, you know?"

"Yes."

"Rico had two brothers. Both of them were killed working for me. When his father died, I sent his mother to Florida, set her up big. But it was McDonald's idea, McDonald's money. He just didn't want anybody to know, and that wasn't unusual, because he never wanted anybody to know anything about what he did. He bought that old woman a $4 million house in South Florida. I couldn't figure out why. He was never that generous, even to people who did great favors, who gave their lives."

Fox nodded. "But why do you say Rico Scalzi is responsible for this killing?"

"Because he would have been the only one, besides myself, who could get past the guards in that house without too much suspicion. It was him. There could not have been anyone else."

"Why would he do it?"

"Because two days ago, right before I called you and gave myself up, I was ordered to put a contract out on Rico. Only Giovanni could have issued that big a contract. I was really surprised, but he was running scared. Once Rico murdered DeSalvo, which was my decision, he was afraid there would be too much attention focused on the business, on all the other parts of it. And I was shocked, because I thought he really liked Rico."

"Who did you give the contract to?"

"Nick. Nick Conti. Best one I know, aside from Rico himself."

"Where is Scalzi?"

"Now I don't know. I thought he was going to Florida. He has a house down there, hidden in the Keys. I checked the airlines. He took a Continental flight the other night. So I gave Conti the contract, but then I changed my mind. Once I decided I was coming in, I put a cancel on the contract. I owed Rico that much."

"How do you cancel a contract, Anthony?"

"You kill the assassin. I called somebody in Fort Lauderdale who works for us, who knows everybody and can do anything down there, and told him there was a contract that had to be canceled. I gave him all the information."

Fox thought about that. "But Rico never got there, not if you say only he could have walked into McDonald's home and done the killings. So Conti went on a wild goose chase anyway, didn't he?"

Assante nodded. "I guess so, yes. But it doesn't matter."

"Why?"

"Because Conti is dead by now. He would have had no chance, once the area was alerted, once all those people were looking for him. I told them where he would go. I know he's dead."

Fox thought that was a bonus, not a disaster, except for the fact that Conti might have provided crucial information about his involvement in other killings that had never been solved.

Now it was Assante who looked at Fox, not nearly as authoritative as he had been moments ago, not as arrogant, not as sure of himself.

"What about our deal, Commissioner?"

"I think we still have a deal, Anthony. It will take a long time for us to find out everything you know. Until then, you'll be safe and comfortable. No one will get to you; no one will know where you are."

"And then?"

"Then? What the hell, Anthony, without McDonald around we can't pin anything on you. Once we're finished, you will be free to leave. We'll take all the information you give us, and, in return, we won't press any charges. You'll be a free man."

It was a death sentence, and Anthony Assante almost admired the sophistication, the irony, and the finality of it all. In fact, it brought a tight, hard smile to his face when he looked at Fox, the hard edge back in his voice, the cold stare back in his eyes. "I think I'd like to stick around, Commissioner," he said. "When you're finished with me, find a place to keep me. But if you decide not to do that, I will ask for transportation out of the country. There are a few places I can go and be able to live with some comfort, with a minimum of time spent looking over my shoulder and in darkened doorways. I will not cooperate on any level until you assure me of at least that much."

Fox nodded. "I don't think there'll be a problem with that, Anthony. And I think it is a wise decision."

FORTY
FIVE

DESPITE all Keegan's misgivings and warnings, Ed went back to work. The sports department held a quick little surprise party for him, a sort of postmarriage bachelor party, and that surprised him, because usually there wasn't much closeness in that office, just guys doing their jobs and paying their bills. The management and ownership of the newspaper purposely created that attitude and made it flourish. Too much fraternization, they felt, led to less than total efficiency. The older employees, both desk guys and reporters, were periodically offered a buyout or convinced to take early retirement, whether they wanted to or not. Refusing meant, in most cases, a warning that there would never be another raise and that those who were assigned regular beats would be taken off and assigned to the most menial jobs, covering local high school sports or harness racing or bowling.

People got the message. And the company earned its reputation on merit.

But for now, Ed had no concern about being told it was time to leave. He had, in fact, planned on staying only another few years and then beating them to the punch by resigning, taking a job with another newspaper or settling in to write the books and freelance magazine articles he had never been able to pursue before.

So he went back to work. The Giants were scheduled to play Philadelphia the next weekend, down there in Veterans Stadium, and he told his bosses that he was going to go. No problem. He did the best job of anybody on the staff, and his return was welcomed. He was told not to touch on the Adam Benson death, since it was a news section story now and Ed's closeness to the victim was viewed by the often-skewed management as a liability, a distraction from unbiased journalism.

Leigh had resigned from DD Ads by phone, but having learned that David Drexler was under investigation by the police and was about to be indicted for his involvement in gambling and conspiracy, she agreed to have lunch with the firm's vice president, now its president, a good guy named Jack Sutton. He pleaded with her to stay, at a better position and more salary and the choice of managing whichever accounts suited her fancy.

She accepted. Despite her misgivings and the bad experience at DD Ads, the money was too much to pass up and her new and broader authority was satisfying in that it propelled her right up and through that glass ceiling that still existed, in spades, up and down Madison Avenue.

She talked it over with Ed late one night, and he agreed that it was too much to pass up, on various levels and for several reasons. So she went back to work, Sutton moving into Drexler's office and she taking over Sutton's, which was right next to it and attached by a connecting door. One of her most satisfying early decisions was to respond to a call from Gene Medici of the Skeezixs Candy Company, who wanted DD Ads to take over his billing again.

Sutton gave her the choice. She told Medici to go fuck himself.

"Jack, I just threw away millions of dollars in billing," she said when that conversation ended abruptly.

Sutton smiled. "I bet myself that's what you'd do. I won dinner for you and Ed and me and my wife at an expensive restaurant of my choice."

Leigh accepted with a laugh.

Harlan Ellsworth's trial was scheduled to begin in a month's time. He planned to plead guilty, to tell everything he knew and perhaps make some kind of deal for himself. But the murder was done by him, clearly. It was premeditated, carefully planned and executed. At best, he would spend the rest of his life in jail.

Some of O.J. Simpson's Dream Team defense staff, including its chief, Johnny Cochrane, offered to take on the Ellsworth case pro bono, seeing the chance to fight organized crime, its infiltration into legitimate businesses, the high-profile nature of the NFL's involvement, and, by the way, the fact that Ellsworth had been coerced by the "white criminal establishment" to commit the murder in the first place. As things turned out, the Dream Team's contribution to the Ellsworth case was to provide the best laugh line heard in years.

Ellsworth was found guilty. Quickly, definitively. He was sentenced to life without parole in Dannamora. Three years later he would be killed in a fight with three other inmates, late at night in the laundry room. He was stabbed to death, ironically, by an ice pick in his jugular vein.

Assante was under wraps and would be for months. No one besides Gerry Keegan, Commissioner Fox, and a half-dozen handpicked members of the NYPD and the FBI knew where he was. Keegan was in charge of the Assante debriefing, somewhere deep in a remote area of Delaware. It was time spent away from his office, his job, his friends, and Sherri Novak, maybe especially Sherri Novak, who had been moved out of Keegan's mother's house and put into a true safe house, a federal location for those being prepped to begin new lives in the Witness Protection Program.

McDonald's death had been headline news for a week, especially when it was discovered (with a little help from the commissioner's office) that the man was really Giovanni Impelliteri, thought to have been killed in World War II. Information provided by Assante resulted in the arrest of more than twenty organized crime heads, many of whom had been suspected of various indiscretions for years but had never allowed themselves to be touched. It would take years to find all the money, all the holdings, all the hooks he had placed into all the various legitimate enterprises in the country, but early information had already projected his net worth at more than $2 billion.

The FBI, sharing information provided by Ellsworth and confirmed by Assante, arrested eight professional football players, charged each with racketeering and gambling. They were promptly suspended for life by league commissioner A. Scott Small, and a study was soon under way to determine whether all the games they had allegedly fixed could be identified. The Dallas Cowboys lost a star wide receiver and an offensive tackle; the New York Jets lost their starting quarterback. Also indicted were a Miami running back and an Oakland quarterback. It would take a long time for the NFL to recover.

It was a Friday night. Ed was going to the Giants' game in Philadelphia the next morning, taking the train from Penn Station. Leigh was going to spend the weekend home, catching up on her work files, planning her week.

Just after eleven o'clock, the telephone rang.

Ed answered.

"Ed Buck?"

"Yes."

"My name is Rico Scalzi. We need to talk."

"Talk about what?"

Leigh, just half-listening, suddenly snapped to attention when she heard the strange edge in her husband's voice.

"About Sherri Novak. About your friend Adam Benson. About how easily I found you and your new wife in Long Beach Island and how easily I will always be able to find you and your new wife, wherever you go, wherever you are."

"Who the fuck do you think you are?" Ed barked, and surprised himself when he did. Why wasn't he afraid? Why wasn't he trembling? Why wasn't the tightness in the pit of his stomach reflecting in a wavering, quavering voice? "You're a fucking hoodlum, you ran off when it got hot, and now you're probably sitting in some fleabag hotel room jerking off, playing these games on the phone. What's next, you call some massage parlor or escort service and come all over the wall when you hear the girl answer the phone?"

It was Scalzi who was taken aback. "You don't understand, Buck. Before you get yourself in real trouble, shut your fucking mouth and just listen to me. Who do you think it was who arranged to leave that note on the car windshield in Long Beach Island that night? Assante had ordered it to be wired. You and the woman were supposed to become millions of pieces of fish bait when you pushed it up to fifty miles an hour. I didn't want more deaths on my conscience. I wasn't there. But I have friends all over. It was not difficult to find and to plant the sheet of paper—it was lined notebook paper, torn from a spiral binding, in case you aren't sure we're talking about the same thing—so that you'd call the police and they'd decide to wait for your friend Keegan and the New York bomb squad clowns to show up."

Calmer now, but still tight, Ed responded, "Thank you. So what do you want?"

"I want you to call Keegan. I want to meet with him, alone. I am going to leave the country and I want to clean up a few things. Get in touch with him. I'll call later tonight. And if it works, I promise that will be the last time you ever hear from me, and the last time you ever have to worry about this thing again."

The line went dead.

Ed quickly pressed *69, which was supposed to provide the number of the last call received. But all the electronic voice said was: "The last call placed to this telephone number is not within the allowable callback distance."

Leigh, her face white, her hands cold, clearly and obviously frightened, asked, "Who was that?"

"Rico Scalzi," Ed said. "He wants to meet with Gerry."

"God, isn't this thing ever going to be over? He's the one who killed DeSalvo. He's the one who killed McDonald. All those bodyguards. He helped to fuck up poor Sherri. What would that animal want from Gerry?"

"I don't know, baby, but I have to tell him."

Finding Gerry Keegan was more difficult than Ed thought it would be. He wasn't home. He wasn't at the police station. A call to the special number from which he could always retrieve messages, especially urgent ones, took two hours for him to return. It wasn't until two in the morning that Ed's phone rang.

"Ed? What's going on?"

"We got a call from Rico Scalzi, Gerry. He wants to see you. He says he's leaving the country and he wants to talk to you. Tomorrow sometime. He said something about cleaning up a few things."

"What's supposed to happen?"

"He'll call me back. You're supposed to tell me when and where you can meet him. Gerry, I didn't know what else to do."

"You did the right thing. When he calls, tell him tomorrow morning. Six o'clock. There's an all-night diner on Hudson Street, down near the Holland Tunnel. Cabbies and truck drivers go there. Cops. Bums. Limo drivers. It's called Metro. Just Metro. Tell him to be there."

"Gerry, he said you alone. Just you."

Keegan paused. "Yeah, right. So tell him I'll be alone."

"Where are you? Why was it so hard to find you?"

"I'm with Assante. You don't need to know where. But I'll be at the Metro in the morning. And don't you dare show up; don't you be anywhere near there."

FORTY
SIX

KEEGAN turned to his FBI counterpart, Alex Henley. "It was my friend the sportswriter," he said. "Scalzi just called him. He wants to talk to me. In the morning. Says he's got some stuff to spill before he vanishes."

Assante was within hearing range. He smiled. Giovanni's son was coming in, too. And at this moment, only he and Rico knew he was the son of the terrible man. "You'll never get him," Assante murmured, but Keegan heard him. So did Henley.

"We will, Anthony. Why is he so fucking special?"

Assante fixed Henley with a cold stare. "He was DeSalvo's lieutenant, big guy, did some killings for me. Not too bright, but loyal. Very loyal. I took care of his parents. His father worked for us. When he died, you know we sent his mother to Florida. His brothers, two of them, died working for me. Got caught in that situation at the piers fifteen years ago. I always took care of Rico; he was always loyal."

"So how would he know it was Impelliteri who put out the hit?"

Assante sneered. "He isn't stupid, just slow. He knew I was second in charge of everything. He knew I would not have done that to him. Couldn't, without permission, even if I had wanted to. So he figured it was Impelliteri, since he had to assume I never would have ordered it. After that, he was just acting on instinct, looking for revenge and trying to guarantee his future safety. He had to kill Giovanni. It was automatic."

"So now, why would he want to see me? What could he offer me that you can't? He must know we have you."

Assante shook his head. "That the part I don't know," he said. "I really, honestly don't know. He has some information. Not big stuff. Not important stuff. He was never involved in the business end. Just the mechanics of it. I don't know. Maybe he's looking for a deal."

"I'll see him," Keegan said. "Should I send your regards?"

"Yeah, my regards. Tell him it was nothing personal, never anything personal. Tell him it was me who put out the contract because Impelliteri ordered it, but tell him it was me who canceled it. On my own."

"Right."

Keegan got up from the chair. "Get me a ride up to New York," he said to Henley, who nodded in agreement. "But you aren't going alone, Gerry. Nobody is that stupid."

"I know. But I don't want him to know. Please, dress up some bums or something. It's an easy place to be anonymous in; that's why I picked it. A guy in a limo driver's suit, maybe a guy looks like a cabbie. Just place 'em around the area; there's lots of small tables. Single tables. Most people in there that early are singles."

"OK, I'll take care of it. I'll get Johnson to drive you up. From here, what, about three hours? You'll have time for a shower."

Keegan chuckled. "Yeah, but I wish I had time to sleep. I guess that'll come later, when this is all done. I don't think I can be wired, but I'll use one of those little coin recorder/transmitters you guys invented."

Henley smiled. "You have them? They aren't police-issue yet."

Keegan smiled in return. "The police didn't issue them," he said. "But I have them. It's what I used on Leigh when she met with that piece of shit Drexler."

He got up and went to the small dormitory-style room down the hall, where he had been staying during this debriefing vigil, splashed water on his face, threw some things into a small duffel bag, and changed into clean clothes. "I guess I'm ready," he said to himself. "Just me and my toothbrush and clean underwear."

FORTY
SEVEN

THE drive north was uneventful. It was dark, with a tinge of the light that would come in another hour or so. The driver knew not to talk, figuring maybe Keegan would catch a few hours of sleep, and he made sure it looked that way, closing his eyes, hunkering down with his head against the door, but he didn't sleep. He was thinking about Rico Scalzi, about what would transpire, what would come out of the mouth of this man when he sat face-to-face with him.

He was thinking, too, about Sherri. He had decided, and he hoped she had, that there was something there worth going for, some connection they both recognized but were afraid to verbalize.

Yet.

He had decided to tell her when this was over, when whatever her involvement in this thing had been was fleshed out and flushed away, when she had been cleared—which he knew she would be—and when there was a chance that they might try for a normal life. He recognized the Sherri behind the Sherri, and maybe nobody else ever had, as an intelligent, warm, tough woman with a wide streak of survivor mentality and an acceptance of reality enough so that she could deal with whatever came along in order to keep herself going forward.

They arrived at the mouth of the Holland Tunnel, on the Jersey side, at five-thirty. They'd be there before six. Johnson was to drop him off and just leave. The two men put in place were already there, or should be. Not even someone as street-smart as Scalzi would be able to pick them out, even if they were the only other guys in the place. He was sure of that.

The coin recorder/transmitter was hanging from a chain around his neck, under his shirt, which was buttoned at the collar because he was wearing a tie. It was typical plainclothes apparel—wrinkled, nondescript blue blazer, white shirt, solid blue tie, dark gray slacks, black shoes with shoelaces. You could buy the whole outfit for under a hundred dollars: In fact, he had. Clothes were way down on Keegan's list of priorities, although maybe that would change soon.

Johnson dropped him off a block before they reached the Metro. No exchange of words, no final message to be carried back. Keegan just opened the door at a traffic light and got out, nodding. Johnson nodded back and continued driving, going to a designated uptown office building where he would wait until summoned.

Keegan walked the block quickly, observing the not-only-homeless-but-drunk sleeping in the doorways. Home sweet home.

The Metro had glass windows from floor to ceiling, maybe fifteen feet high. It was a big, bare, cold room, cafeteria-style counters in the rear, waitresses if you wanted them lounging against the far wall, small, cheap tables, with one or two chairs, scattered in an obvious random placement, maybe forty of them.

Six of the tables were occupied by single men. Two others had been taken by couples, the stay-out-late residue of a Friday night. There were four kids at another table, in jeans and sweats, loud and still halfway drunk, laughing and drinking coffee and each of them determined not to say how tired he was.

At one of the six single tables, the farthest away from anyone else, was a big man, had to be six-six, had to weigh 250, 260. He was "dressed down," but that was obvious to a trained detective. He was wearing jeans and a pullover gray sweater. Boots, black and simple, untooled. He looked up and nodded.

Keegan nodded back and walked over. "I'm Keegan," he said.

"Scalzi." It was a deep voice, and its timbre and resonance belied Assante's description of the man's lack of mental acuity. There was intelligence there, Keegan felt it, and a cold, hard edge that he suspected was always there and not just affected for this meeting.

"What did you want to tell me?" Keegan asked. Clearly, there was no basis nor reason for small talk.

"I want complete immunity," Scalzi said. "I want to be allowed to leave the country. I want to visit a few banks first, make a few wire transfers, and then I will be gone."

"Yeah, right. And what do I get in return?"

"All of it. Every place where Giovanni Impelliteri had money. Every company that he had a hook into. Every person who ever cooperated with him. Every fix and every stock market swindle and all of it. Every fucking detail of the man's life and holdings."

"And how would you know all this? All of our information puts you as just another soldier in the organization's army."

Rico smiled mirthlessly. "No, I'm not just another soldier. I am Giovanni Impelliteri's only son."

The words *holy shit* came instantly to mind, though of course they were not verbalized. Instead, Keegan sat still, staring at Scalzi, formulating a response.

"We have no record of Giovanni Impelliteri having had a child," Keegan said, finally. "How do I know you're telling me the truth?"

Scalzi smiled, his huge hands wrapped around a coffee cup. "First, why would I claim to be the son of a monster unless it was true?"

"For the money," Keegan shot back.

"No, not that. I don't care about his money. I have money. I learned my history fifteen years ago, and I've been preparing ever since. I want to trade this information to guarantee my privacy. I'll make three promises. First, I will leave the country. Second, I will provide you with everything I know about my father's dealings. Third, I will never return to the United States."

"And we have to do what, exactly?"

"Actually, not much. I won't allow you to question me, like you're doing with poor old Assante right now. And I won't be locked up, not even temporarily. I've spent the last five years recording everything I know, everything I ever heard. Names and addresses, telephone numbers, and bank account numbers. The entire network, all of it, from the drugs, to the gambling, to the stock market, to the banks that cleaned his money, to all the cops in about twenty-five cities who were on his payroll. There are some incredibly important and well-known politicians on the list, with enough documentation to burn them. It is the biggest, most important collection of information ever put together. I guarantee the accuracy of it. And it's worth my freedom."

He paused, and a small smile visited his mouth, one best and perhaps only capable of being described as ironic.

"The pro football thing was peanuts, didn't matter,"

he said. "My father and Anthony allowed that stupid little man, DeSalvo, to sell them on it. They didn't make more than nine, ten million on the whole thing. Shit, they made that much in a week with the drugs and ten times that much in the stock market, with construction contracts, rigged bids, government jobs. Shit, it was stupid. I tried to tell Assante, but he wouldn't listen. It was pro football that brought down the biggest and most profitable organization in the country."

Keegan spoke quietly. "I have to talk to my bosses," he said, "tell them the offer. I feel pretty strong that they'll accept it. How can I reach you?"

Rico Scalzi/Impelliteri shook his head.

"No, the answer comes now. I know you have two men here. The guy who looks like a cabbie at the table off to my left. The other one, older guy with a belly, dressed like a limo driver, behind us, middle of the room. What you don't know is that I have people here, too. One guy has a gun trained on your cabbie; another is locked into the limo driver. And those four young guys? They're mine. They are freaky, but they do wonderful things with explosives. Make a decision. Do it now. I'll tell you where the tapes are. There are more than one hundred of them in all, and you have my word that everything on them is true and, even better, can be proved."

This was not a decision Keegan could make on his own. He was being asked to set free potentially the most important witness ever reined in by any law enforcement agency in history. He was being asked to let someone who had killed repeatedly, who had done the dirtiest of dirty work for organized crime, waltz off untouched, leave the country with enough money to live like a king for the rest of his life.

Sitting in a dingy diner, early on a Saturday morning,

gray and dreary, chill and cold, he was being asked to reach well beyond his authority, well past his parameters, and he had to do it now.

Rico sat, motionless, staring directly at him with dark, fiery eyes. Was he really willing to give a signal, which might be as simple as a finger crooking or a leg being crossed, and cause the deaths of everyone in the diner, including his own? Was he that cold?

Yes, he thought.

"Yes," he said. "Where are the tapes?"

Scalzi smiled. He reached into his shirt pocket—and Keegan knew that at least eight pairs of eyes were watching intently, that eight men were tensed, focusing on what would happen and what their next move would be—and extracted a folded slip of white paper.

"It's a safe-deposit box," Rico said. "Salvation National Bank, Madison and 18th. You go to an assistant manager named Richard Brightley. You tell him that you are the man Rico Scalzi sent to pick up the material. That is all you have to do. He will take you to the boxes, unlock it, and hand you a large metal box that is locked inside the safe-deposit box. You will find all the tapes and notebooks filled with more information. Good hunting. I'm leaving now. When I get up now, I will smile and shake your hand. That will be the release for the men I have here. Then we all leave. You won't try to follow me or have me followed. You will never hear from me again. I have given you my word. Tell Assante I said thank you for pulling back the contract. Tell your friend Buck I didn't mean to frighten him. I was the one who arranged that note to be left on his windshield. I didn't know for sure whether my father had ordered him hit, and he didn't deserve that."

He paused, prepared to rise.

"And tell Sherri Novak, wherever she is being held,

that you are a good man and that nothing was ever personal."

He smiled then, stood, extended his hand, and shook Keegan's. And when he left the dingy diner, the two singles casually exited, and the four young guys, still laughing and making noise, started arguing about who was going to pay the bill.

It was over.

Keegan went back to his apartment for a shower and breakfast. He could not call Sherri yet, nor did he want to speak to his immediate superiors yet, either. At nine o'clock, he was at the Salvation National Bank as the doors were opened for the normal half-day Saturday business.

He walked in, found a tall, gangly man at the desk with the nameplate Richard Brightley, identified himself, and was ushered to the safe-deposit box vault.

"Mr. Scalzi said you were his brother-in-law, and even so this is very irregular," Brightley said. "But he has been such a good customer for so long that, well, I'm doing him the favor. I have his key here"—he reached into his pocket—"and I am to keep it when you leave. It is bank property, you know."

"I certainly appreciate all you have done, Mr. Brightley," Keegan replied, playing out the role. "This is very old and sentimental stuff. You've done us a big favor."

Richard Brightley saw no reason to mention the $5,000 in cash that Rico Scalzi had handed him, in a plain white envelope, when he agreed to do him this favor. Nobody would know; nobody would care—it was just a favor to a good and loyal bank customer.

Keegan took the metal strongbox Brightley extended, having extracted it from a large safe-deposit box. "Oh,

Mr. Keegan, Mr. Scalzi said to tell you the key for the box is taped underneath."

So common, so ordinary, so harmless.

"Thank you, Mr. Brightley. I'll be going now."

And Gerry Keegan walked out of the bank, onto Madison Avenue, with enough information to bring down corrupt policemen, politicians, and corporations, not to mention bringing a hopefully fatal blow to the world of organized crime.

He was reasonably sure his bosses, and especially Police Commissioner Fox, would agree with his decision.

He stopped another taxi and went back to his apartment, from where he called the private home telephone of Police Commissioner James Fox, who lived in a brownstone in the Bay Ridge section of Brooklyn.

"Yes?"

"Detective Keegan, Commissioner. I have to see you right now."

"Now? Where the hell are you, Detective?"

"At home. In Manhattan. I have something you won't believe, and I have a story to tell that I hope you'll believe."

"I'm sending a car, I know the address. And, Keegan? This better be good."

Keegan smiled to himself. "Commissioner, I think it's very good. I'll be there as soon as your car arrives."

"It's already on the way," the commissioner said, hanging up.

Then Keegan called Ed's apartment.

"It's me, Gerry. It's all over."

"What? Tell me? Did you see him? What's happening?"

"Tonight, Eddie. Don't go to Philly. Fuck the game.

I just made you a Pulitzer Prize–winning crime reporter."

Finally, he called the number where Sherri was being held.

"This is New York City Detective First Class Joseph Gerard Keegan," he said, "and I must speak with Miss Sherri Novak. Immediately. It is police business."

"Yes, Detective," said the male receptionist at this intensely private facility.

A long pause ensued, and Keegan knew that the beeps and whirring noises were designed to prevent eavesdropping and recording. Finally, he heard Sherri's voice.

"Gerry? What's wrong?"

"Something very serious, Sherri."

"Oh, God. What is it?"

"I'm in love with you."

There was stone silence, and it dragged on for more than sixty seconds. Finally, the noise he heard sounded remarkably like someone softly weeping.

"Detective, I think I know how to remedy the problem," she stammered. "Yes, I will marry you."

FORTY
EIGHT

FOX was furious that Keegan had allowed Scalzi to walk. His face turned red. His voice rose well above acceptable decibels. Small droplets of spittle gathered on his lips.

"How the fuck could you have done that?" he bellowed. "It was well beyond your authority. I am going to put you on suspension, and there will be an investigation, and I wouldn't be a bit surprised if you lose your badge and face criminal charges."

"Commissioner, here, take this strongbox," Keegan said, surprisingly calm.

"What's this?"

"Oh, thirty years or so of answers. Numbers, names, dates. Everything on the empire Impelliteri built. Tapes. Notebooks. Proof of everything. It was the deal I made with Scalzi."

Fox was dumbstruck. "Where did you get this?"

"From Giovanni's son."

"He had no son."

"He did. Rico Scalzi."

Commissioner Fox had nothing to say.

Later that night, Keegan was sitting in the Bucks' living room. Ketel One was pouring freely, and a few contraband Cuban cigars were fouling the air. He told the whole story, gave all the information to his friend